Praise for *Comanche Moon* by Larry McMurtry

"McMurtry's revisionist vision of frontier life is always compelling."
—Jay Freeman, *Booklist*

"The [frontier] myth is intact, if a tad tattered by McMurtry's darkly comedic touch and sly debunking of chivalric conventions. But at its core are McMurtry's respect and gift for exaggerated and fanciful pageantry and heroic form."
—Bill Bell, *New York Daily News*

"A sprawling, picaresque novel."
—Andy Solomon, *The New York Times Book Review*

"[A] fine tableau of western life, full of imaginative exploits, convincing historical background, and characters who are alive."
—*Kirkus Reviews*

"A monumental work that has few equals in current literature."
—Thomas L. Kilkpatrick, *Library Journal*

"*Comanche Moon* has its considerable pleasures . . . a singular treat."
—Michael Berry, *San Francisco Examiner & Chronicle Book Review*

"McMurtry is one of our finest storytellers, and he's at his best here."
—Kyle Smith, *People*

"Consistently entertaining."
—Gene Lyons, *Entertainment Weekly*

"Almost impossible to put down . . . McMurtry knows how to deploy his most suspenseful episodes for maximum effect. He treats his large cast of characters with humor and respect."
—Judith Wynn, *Boston Herald*

D0050230

Comanche Moon

A novel by
Larry McMurtry

Simon & Schuster Paperbacks

NEW YORK LONDON TORONTO SYDNEY

Simon & Schuster Paperbacks
Rockefeller Center
1230 Avenue of the Americas
New York, NY 10020

First Simon & Schuster paperback edition 2003

SIMON & SCHUSTER PAPERBACKS and colophon are trademarks of
Simon & Schuster, Inc.

For information regarding special discounts for bulk purchases,
please contact Simon & Schuster Special Sales at
1-800-456-6798 or business@simonandschuster.com.

Designed by Colin Joh

Manufactured in the United States of America

10

The Library of Congress has cataloged the
hardcover edition as follows:
McMurtry, Larry.
Comanche moon: a novel/Larry McMurtry.
p.   cm.
1. Comanche Indians—Fiction. I. Title.
PS3563.A319C66 1997   813'.54—dc21   97-29609

ISBN-13: 978-0-684-80754-6
ISBN-10:   0-684-80754-8
ISBN-13: 978-0-684-85755-8 (Pbk)
ISBN-10:   0-684-85755-3 (Pbk)

FOR SUSAN SONTAG
She's rangered long . . .
She's rangered far . . .

Book I

1.

CAPTAIN INISH SCULL liked to boast that he had never been thwarted in pursuit—as he liked to put it—of a felonious foe, whether Spanish, savage, or white.

"Nor do I expect to have to make an exception in the present instance," he told his twelve rangers. "If you've got any sacking with you, tie it around your horses' heads. I've known cold sleet like this to freeze a horse's eyelids, and that's not good. These horses will need smooth use of their eyelids tomorrow, when the sun comes out and we run these thieving Comanches to ground."

Captain Scull was a short man, but forceful. Some of the men called him Old Nails, due to his habit of casually picking his teeth with a horseshoe nail—sometimes, if his ire rose suddenly he would actually spit the nail at whoever he was talking to.

"This'll be good," Augustus said, to his friend Woodrow Call. The cold was intense and the sleet constant, cutting their faces as they drove on north. All the rangers' beards were iced hard; some complained that they were without sensation, either in hands or feet or both. But, on the llano, it wasn't yet full dark; in the night it would undoubtedly get colder, with what consequences for men and morale no one could say. A normal commander would have made camp and ordered up a roaring campfire, but Inish Scull was not a normal commander. "I'm a Texas Ranger and by God I range," he said often. "I despise a red thief like the devil despises virtue. If I have to range night and day to check their thieving iniquity, then I'll range night and day.

"Bible and sword," he usually added. "Bible and sword."

At the moment no red thieves were in sight; nothing was in sight except the sleet that sliced across the formless plain. Woodrow Call, Augustus McCrae, and the troop of cold, tired, dejected rangers were uncomfortably aware, though, that they were only a few yards from the western edge of the Palo Duro Canyon. It was Call's belief that Kicking Wolf, the Comanche horsethief they were pursuing, had most likely slipped down into the canyon on some old trail. Inish Scull might be pursuing Indians that were below and behind him, in which case the rangers might ride all night into the freezing sleet for nothing.

"What'll be good, Gus?" Woodrow Call inquired of his friend Augustus. The two rode close together as they had through their years as rangers.

Augustus McCrae didn't fear the cold night ahead, but he did dread it, as any man with a liking for normal comforts would. The cold wind had been searing their faces for two days, singing down at them from the northern prairies. Gus would have liked a little rest, but he knew Captain Scull too well to expect to get any while their felonious foe was still ahead of them.

"What'll be good?" Call asked again. Gus McCrae was always making puzzling comments and then forgetting to provide any explanation.

"Kicking Wolf's never been caught, and the Captain's never been run off from," Gus said. "That's going to change, for one of them. Who would you bet on, Woodrow, if we were to wager—Old Nails, or Kicking Wolf?"

"I wouldn't bet against the Captain, even if I thought he was wrong," Call said. "He's the Captain."

"I know, but the man's got no sense about weather," Augustus remarked. "Look at him. His damn beard's nothing but a sheet of brown ice, but the fool keeps spitting tobacco juice right into this wind."

Woodrow Call made no response to the remark. Gus was overtalkative, and always had been. Unless in violent combat, he was rarely silent for more than two minutes at a stretch, besides which, he felt free to criticize everything from the Captain's way with tobacco to Call's haircuts.

It was true, though, that Captain Scull was in the habit of spitting his tobacco juice directly in front of him, regardless of wind speed or direction, the result being that his garments were often stained with tobacco juice to an extent that shocked most ladies and even offended some men. In fact, the wife of Governor E. M. Pease had recently caused something of a scandal by turning Captain Scull back at her door, just before a banquet, on account of his poor appearance.

"Inish, you'll drip on my lace tablecloth. Go clean yourself up," Mrs. Pease told the Captain—it was considered a bold thing to say to the man who was generally regarded as the most competent Texas Ranger ever to take the field.

"Ma'am, I'm a poor ruffian, I fear I'm a stranger to lacy gear," Inish Scull had replied, an untruth certainly, for it was well known that he had left a life of wealth and ease in Boston to ranger on the Western frontier. It was even said that he was a graduate of Harvard College; Woodrow Call, for one, believed it, for the Captain was very particular in his speech and invariably read books around the campfire, on the nights when he was disposed to allow a campfire. His wife, Inez, a Birmingham belle, was so beautiful at forty that no man in the troop, or, for that matter, in Austin, could resist stealing glances at her.

It was now full dusk. Call could barely see Augustus, and Augustus was only a yard or two away. He could not see Captain Scull at all, though he had been attempting to follow directly behind him. Fortunately, though, he could hear Captain Scull's great warhorse, Hector, an animal that stood a full eighteen hands high and weighed more than any two of the other horses in the troop. Hector was just ahead, crunching steadily through the sleet. In the winter Hector's coat grew so long and shaggy that the Indians called him the Buffalo Horse, both because of his shagginess and because of his great strength. So far as Call knew, Hector was the most powerful animal in Texas, a match in strength for bull, bear, or buffalo. Weather meant nothing to him: often on freezing mornings they would see Captain Scull rubbing his hands together in front of Hector's nose, warming them on his hot breath. Hector was slow and heavy, of course—many a horse could run off and leave him. Even mules could outrun him—but then, sooner or later, the mule or the pony would tire and Hector would keep coming, his big feet crunching grass, or splashing through mud, or churning up clouds of snow. On some long pursuits the men would change mounts two or three times, but Hector was the Captain's only horse. Twice he had been hit by arrows and once shot in the flank by Ahumado, a felonious foe more hated by Captain Scull than either Kicking Wolf or Buffalo Hump. Ahumado, known as the Black Vaquero, was a master of ambush; he had shot down at the Captain from a tiny pocket of a cave, in a sheer cliff in Mexico. Though Ahumado had hit the Captain in the shoulder, causing him to bleed profusely, Captain Scull had insisted that Hector be looked at first. Once recovered, Inish Scull's ire was such that he had tried to persuade Governor Pease to redeclare war on Mexico; or, failing that, to let him drag a brace of cannon over a thousand miles of desert to blast Ahumado out of his stronghold in the Yellow Cliffs.

"Cannons—you want to take cannons across half of Mexico?" the astonished governor asked. "After one bandit? Why, that would be a damnable expense. The legislature would never stand for it, sir."

"Then I resign, and damn the goddamn legislature!" Inish Scull had said. "I won't be denied my vengeance on the black villain who shot my horse!"

The Governor stood firm, however. After a week of heavy tippling, the Captain—to everyone's relief—had quietly resumed his command. It was the opinion of everyone in Texas that the whole frontier would have been lost had Captain Inish Scull chosen to stay resigned.

Now Call could just see, as the sleet thinned a little, the white clouds of Hector's breath.

"Crowd close now," he said, turning to the weary rangers. "Gus and me will keep up with Hector, but you'll have to keep up with us. Don't veer to the right, whatever you do. The canyon's to the right, and the drop is sheer."

"Sheer—that means straight down to doom," Augustus said to

the men. He remembered the first time he and Woodrow had skirted the Palo Duro, after foolishly signing up for an ill-planned expedition whose aim had been to capture Santa Fe and annex Nuevo Mexico. That time the whole troop, more than one hundred men, had to scramble over the edge of the canyon to escape a blazing ring of grass, set afire by Buffalo Hump's Comanches. Many of the men and most of the horses had fallen to their deaths. But, on that occasion at least, they had made their scramble in daylight and had run for the cliffs over firm prairie. Now it was dusk on a winter's night, with no cover, poor visibility, and ground so slick that it was hard even to travel at a steady clip. A slip on the edge of the canyon would send a man straight into space.

"You didn't loan me that sacking— don't you have any?" Augustus asked.

"I have mine—where's yours?" Call asked. "I don't know if mine will stretch for two horses."

Augustus did not reply. In fact, he had been in a whore's tent near Fort Belknap when the news came that Kicking Wolf had run off twenty horses from a ranch near Albany. Gus had barely had time to pull his pants on before the rangers were in the saddle and on the move. It had been a warmish day, and he was sweaty from his exertions with the whore—the notion that four days later he would be in a sleet storm at dusk on the Palo Duro, a storm so bad that his horse's eyelids were in danger of freezing, had never crossed his mind. Most pursuits of Comanche or Kiowa lasted a day or two at most—usually the Indians would stop to feast on stolen horseflesh, laying themselves open to attack.

Kicking Wolf, of course, had always been superior when it came to making off with Texas horses. On the errant Santa Fe expedition, when Call and Augustus had been green rangers, not yet twenty years old, Kicking Wolf had stolen a sizable number of horses from them, just before the Comanches set the grass fire that had trapped the whole troop and forced them into the very canyon they were skirting now.

"I plumb forgot my sacking," Gus admitted—he didn't mention the whore.

"You can have my sacking," Call said. "I don't intend to ride a blind horse, sleet or no sleet." Horses were apt to slip or step in holes even when they could see where they were going. To be riding a blind horse over slippery footing on the edge of a canyon seemed to him to be asking for worse trouble than frozen eyelids.

While Augustus was adjusting Call's piece of rough sacking over his horse's eyes, Long Bill Coleman came trotting up beside them. Long Bill had been with them on the Santa Fe expedition, after which, due to the rigors he had endured on their march as captives across the Jornada del Muerto, he had given up rangering in favor of carpentry, a change of profession that only lasted a few months, thanks to Bill Coleman's inability to drive a nail straight or saw a plank evenly. After six months of bent nails and crookedly sawn planks, Long Bill gave up on town trades forever and rejoined the ranger troop.

"It's night, ain't we stopping, Gus?" Long Bill asked.

"Do we look like we're stopped?" Gus replied, a little testily. Long Bill had the boresome habit of asking questions to which the answers were obvious.

"If we were stopping there'd be a campfire," Gus added, growing more and more annoyed with Long Bill for his thoughtless habits. "Do you see a campfire, sir?"

"No, and don't you be sirring me, you dern yapper," Long Bill said. "All I was asking is how long it will be before we have a chance to get warm."

"Shush," Call said. "You two can argue some other time. I hear something."

He drew rein, as did Gus. The rangers behind crowded close. Soon they all heard what Call heard: a wild, echoing war cry from somewhere in the dark, sleety canyon below. The war cry was repeated, and then repeated again. There was one voice at first, but then other voices joined in—Call, who liked to be precise in such

16

matters, thought he counted at least seven voices echoing up from the canyon. He could not be sure, though—the canyon ran with echoes, and the gusts of north wind snatched the war cries, muffling some and bringing others closer.

"They're mocking us," Call said. "They know we can't chase 'em down a cliff in the dark—not in this weather. They're mocking us, boys."

"It's nothing but extremes around this damn Palo Duro Canyon," Long Bill remarked. "Last time we was here we nearly got cooked, and this time we're half froze."

"I guess your mouth ain't froze, you're still asking them dumb questions," Gus observed.

"I wonder if the Captain heard that?" Call said. "The Captain's a little deaf."

"Not that deaf, he ain't," Gus said. "When he wants to hear something, he hears it. When he don't want to hear it, you might as well save your breath."

"What'd you ever say to the Captain that he didn't want to hear?" Call asked, dismounting. He intended to make careful approach to the canyon edge and see if he could spot any campfires down below them. If there was evidence of a sizable camp of Comanches, perhaps Captain Scull could be persuaded to make camp and wait for a chance to attack.

"I asked him for a five-dollar advance on my wages, one time," Augustus said. "He could have said no, but he didn't say anything. He just acted as if I wasn't there."

"You shouldn't have asked in the first place," Call said. "Wages are supposed to last till payday."

"I had expenses," Gus said, knowing well that it was pointless to discuss financial problems with his frugal friend. Woodrow Call rarely even spent up his wages in the course of a month, whereas Gus never failed to spend his to the last penny, or perhaps even a few dollars beyond the last penny. Something always tempted him: if it wasn't just a pretty whore it might be a new six-shooter, a fine vest, or even just a better grade of whiskey, which, in most of the places he bought whiskey, just meant a liquor mild enough that it wouldn't immediately take the hide off a skunk.

Before they could discuss the matter further, they heard sleet crunching just ahead, and suddenly the great horse Hector, his shaggy coat steaming, loomed over them. Captain Inish Scull hadn't stopped, but at least he had turned.

"Why are we halted, Mr. Call?" he asked. "I didn't request a halt."

"No sir, but we heard a passel of whooping, down in the canyon," Call said. "I thought I'd look and see if I could spot the Comanche camp."

"Of course there's a camp, Mr. Call, but they're the wrong Comanches," Captain Scull said. "That's Buffalo Hump down there—we're after Kicking Wolf, if you'll remember. He's our horse-thief."

As usual, Captain Scull spoke with complete assurance. They had only been on the edge of the Palo Duro a few minutes, and it was too dark to see much, even if the sleet would have let them. Buffalo Hump and Kicking Wolf, though rivals, often raided together: how did the Captain know that one was camped in the canyon and the other ranging somewhere ahead?

They had a gifted scout, to be sure, a Kickapoo named Famous Shoes, but Famous Shoes had been gone for two days and had made no report.

"That's Buffalo Hump's main camp down there, Mr. Call," Inish Scull said. "We're no match for him—we're only thirteen men, and anyway it's Kicking Wolf I want. I expect to overtake him on the Canadian River about sunup day after tomorrow, if there *is* a sunup day after tomorrow."

"Why, sir, there's always sunup," Long Bill Coleman said—he was a little jolted by the Captain's remark, and the reason he was jolted was that his large wife, Pearl—the one town trade he hadn't abandoned—was convinced on religious grounds that the world would end in the near future. Pearl's view was that the Almighty would soon pour hot lava over the world, as a response to human wickedness. Now they were beside the Palo Duro Canyon, a big, mysterious hole in the ground—what if it suddenly filled up with hot lava and overflowed onto the world? Cold as he was, the prospect of the world ending in a flood of hot lava did not appeal to Long Bill at all. The fact that Captain Scull had questioned whether there would be a sunup had the effect of making him nervous. He had never met a man as learned as Captain Scull—if the Captain had some reason to doubt the likelihood of future sunrises, then there might be something to Pearl's apprehension, after all.

"Oh, I'm confident the sun will do its duty, and the planets as well," Captain Scull said. "The sun will be there, where it should be. Whether we will see it is another matter, Mr. Coleman."

Gus McCrae found the remark curious. If the sun was where it should be, of course they would see it.

"Captain, if the sun's there, why wouldn't we see it?" he asked.

"Well, it could be cloudy weather—I expect it will be," Captain Scull said. "That's one reason we might not see sunup. Another reason is that we all might be dead. Beware the pale horse, the Bible says."

Inish Scull let that remark soak in—it amused him to say such things to his untutored and uncomprehending men. Then he turned his horse.

"Don't be peeking into canyons unless I tell you to, Mr. Call," he said. "It's icy footing, and too dark for accurate observation anyway."

Call was irked by the Captain's tone. Of course he knew it was icy footing. But he said nothing—by then Inish Scull had turned his great horse and gone clomping away, into the night. There was no one to say anything to, except Augustus and Long Bill. After one more glance into the darkening canyon, he got back on his horse and followed his captain north.

2.

"GUN-IN-THE-WATER is with them," Blue Duck said. "Gun-in-the-Water and the other one—Silver Hair McCrae."

Buffalo Hump sat on a deerskin near his campfire. He was under an overhanging rock, which held the heat of the campfire while protecting him from the driving sleet. He was splitting the leg bone of a buffalo. When splitting a bone he was particular and careful—he did not want to lose any of the buttery marrow. Most men were impatient, young men especially. When they attempted the old tasks, they took little care. Blue Duck, his son, rarely split a bone, and when he did, he lost half the marrow. Buffalo Hump had fathered the boy on a Mexican captive named Rosa, a beautiful but troublesome woman who persisted in trying to escape. Buffalo Hump caught her three times and beat her; then his wives beat her even more harshly, but Rosa was stubborn and kept escaping. The winter after the boy was born she escaped again, taking the young baby with her. Buffalo Hump was gone on a raid at the time—when he got back he went after Rosa himself, but a great wind came, blowing snow over the prairie in clouds so thick that even the buffalo turned their backs to it. When he finally found Rosa, under a cutbank on the Washita, she was frozen, but the boy, Blue Duck, was alive, still pulling on her cold teat.

It was a good sign, Buffalo Hump thought then, that the boy was strong enough to survive such cold; but the boy grew up to be even more troublesome than his mother. Blue Duck stole, killed, and fought bravely, but all without judgment. He had no interest in the old weapons; he coveted only the white man's guns. His temper was terrible—he had no friends. He would kill a Comanche or a friendly Kiowa as quickly as he would kill a Texan. The elders of the tribe finally came and talked to Buffalo Hump about the boy. They reminded him that the boy was half Mexican. They thought maybe the Mexicans had put a witch inside Blue Duck when his mother died. After all, the boy had suckled a dead woman's teat; death might have come into him then. The old men wanted to kill Blue Duck, or else expel him from the tribe.

"I will kill him, when he needs to be killed," Buffalo Hump told them. He didn't like Blue Duck much, but he didn't kill him, or send him away. He delayed, hoping the boy would change with age. Two of his wives were barren and his only other son had been killed years before on the Brazos, by the white ranger Call, whom the Comanche called Gun-in-the-Water." Blue Duck had no good in him, that he could see, but he had no other living son and did not want to kill him if he could avoid it. Perhaps Blue Duck did have evil in him, an evil that prompted his sudden killings; but the evil might be there for a purpose. Blue Duck might be so bad that he would be the leader who drove back the whites, who were squirming like maggots up the rivers and onto the *comanchería*. Buffalo Hump was undecided. He knew he might have to kill Blue Duck to keep harmony in the tribe. But, for the moment, he waited.

He did not look up at his tall son until he had split the heavy bone expertly, exposing the rich marrow, which he sucked until the last drop was gone. As Buffalo Hump grew older, his appetites had changed. When they took buffalo now, he only ate the liver and, sometimes, the hump. But he insisted on first pick of the bones, so he could find the marrow. He knocked down prairie chickens whenever he could, and had developed a taste for possums, ground squirrels, prairie dogs, and armadillo. When one of his wives wanted to please him she would catch him a plump prairie hen or perhaps a young possum. The elders of the tribe thought it odd that their great chief no longer hungered for horsemeat or buffalo. Buffalo Hump didn't care what the elders thought, not in this instance. He had heard much prophecy, from many elders, and little of it had come true; worse, the only prophecies that *had* come true were the bad ones. The whites were more numerous than ever, and better armed. Even a simple raid on a small farm—just a couple and their children—could seldom be accomplished without a warrior or two falling to the white man's guns. Even the Mexicans in poor villages were better armed now. Once, the mere appearance of a single Comanche warrior could cause such panic in the villages of Mexico that the men could ride in and take captives almost at will; but now even the smallest, poorest villages were apt to put up stiff resistance.

Also, now, the Texans came with bluecoat soldiers, and with agents who talked to the elders of the People about the advantages of reservation life. Some of the chiefs and elders, tired of running and fighting, had begun to listen to these agents of the Texans. So far the Comanches were still a free people, but Buffalo Hump knew, and the elders knew as well, that they could not simply scare the whites away by tortures and killings, or by taking a few captives now and then. There were too many Texans—too many. The very thought of them made him weary and sad.

Finally, when he had finished with his marrow bone, he tossed it aside and looked up at Blue Duck. The boy was tall and strong, but also rude, impatient, disrespectful.

"If you saw Gun-in-the-Water, why didn't you kill him for me?" he asked his son. "You should have brought me his hair."

Blue Duck was annoyed—he had brought his father a report on the Texans and had not expected criticism.

"He was with Big Horse Scull," he said. "He had men with him."

He stopped, uncertain. Surely his father did not expect him to kill a whole troop of rangers, on a day when the sleet was so bad a horse could not run without slipping.

Buffalo Hump merely looked at Blue Duck. He was gaunt now; his great hump was a weight he had grown tired of carrying. Once it had scarcely slowed him, but now he had to manage carefully if he was to avoid embarrassment.

"You can kill him. I give him to you," he said to Blue Duck. "Do you think you can kill him tomorrow?"

"I told you he was with Big Horse," Blue Duck said. The old man annoyed him. He knew that his father had been the greatest Comanche leader ever to ride the plains—from the age of ten, Blue

Duck had been allowed to ride with him on raids and had seen how terrible his anger was against the Mexicans and the whites. No one in the tribe could throw a lance as far and as accurately as Buffalo Hump—and only Kicking Wolf was as quick and deadly with the bow. Though nowadays his father raided less, he was still a man to be feared. But he was older; he no longer had the strength of the bear, and the ugly hump, though it might scare the Texans, was just an ugly mound of gristle on the old man's back. It had white hairs sticking out of it. Soon his father would just be an old chief, worn out, no longer able to raid; the young warriors would soon cease to follow him. He would just be an old man, sitting on his deer hides sucking at greasy bones.

"If you can't kill Gun-in-the-Water, kill the other one—kill McCrae," Buffalo Hump suggested. "Or if you are too lazy to kill a strong fighting man, then kill the Buffalo Horse."

"Kill the Buffalo Horse?" Blue Duck asked. He knew he was being insulted, but he tried to hold his temper. Buffalo Hump had his lance at his side, and he was still quick with it. The ranger they called "Big Horse"—Scull, the great captain—rode the Buffalo Horse. Why ask him to kill the horse—why not ask him to kill Scull?

"I will kill Scull," Blue Duck said. "Later we can kill the Buffalo Horse—he is so big it will take all winter to eat him."

Buffalo Hump regretted that his son was boastful. Blue Duck thought he could kill anybody. He hadn't learned that some men were harder to kill than even the great grizzly bears. Once the great bears had lived in the Palo Duro, and along the broken ledge that the whites called the caprock. In his youth, Buffalo Hump had killed three of the great bears. It had not been easy. One of his legs bore a scar from the claws of the last of these bears—when he went into battle he wore a necklace made from that bear's teeth and claws.

Now there were none of the great bears in the Palo Duro or along the caprock. They had all gone north, to the high mountains, to escape the guns of the Texans. Now his boastful son stood before him, a boy with none of the wisdom of the great bears. Blue Duck thought he could kill Scull, but Buffalo Hump knew better. Big Horse Scull was a short man, but a great fighter—even without a weapon he would win against Blue Duck. He would tear open Blue Duck's throat with his teeth, if he had to. Scull might suffer injuries, but he would win.

"You can't kill Big Horse," Buffalo Hump told the boy, bluntly. Blue Duck was tall and strong, but he was awkward. He had not yet learned how to run smoothly. He was too lazy to learn to use the old weapons—he could not throw a lance accurately, or hit an animal with an arrow. He wore a great knife that he had taken off a dead soldier, but he did not know how to fight with a knife. Without his gun he was helpless, and he was too foolish even to realize that he might lose his gun, or that it might misfire. Buffalo Hump liked weapons that he had made himself, and could depend on. He chose the wood for his own arrows; he scraped and honed the shafts and set the points himself. He chose the wood for his bow and saw that the bowstrings were of tough sinew. Every night, before turning to his women, he looked at his weapons, felt them, tested them; he made sure his lance head was securely set. If he had to fight in the night, he wanted to be ready. He did not want to jump into a fight and discover that he had mislaid his weapons or that they were not in good working order.

All Blue Duck knew of weapons was how to push bullets into a pistol or a rifle. He was a boy, too ill prepared to give battle to a warrior as fierce as Big Horse Scull. Unless he was lucky he would not even be able to kill Gun-in-the-Water, who had been too quick for his other, better son, in the encounter on the Brazos years before.

"I did not give you Big Horse, I gave you Gun-in-the-Water," Buffalo Hump said. "Go take him if you can."

"There are only twelve Texans, and Big Horse," Blue Duck said. "We have many warriors. We could kill them all."

"Why have they come?" Buffalo Hump asked. "I have done no raiding. I have been killing buffalo."

"They are chasing Kicking Wolf," Blue Duck said. "He stole many horses."

Buffalo Hump was annoyed—Kicking Wolf had gone raiding without even asking him if he cared to go, too. Besides, he did not feel well. In bitter weather an ache made his bones hurt—the ache seemed to start in his hump. It made his bones throb as if someone were pounding them with a club. The cold and sleet were of little moment—he had lived with plains weather all his life. But in recent years the ache in his bones had come, forcing him to pay more attention to the cold weather. He had to be sure, now, that his lodges were warm.

"Why are you talking to me about killing these Texans?" he asked Blue Duck. "If it is Kicking Wolf who has brought them, let him kill them."

Blue Duck was disgusted with the old man's attitude. The whites were only a few miles away. With only half the warriors in their camp they could kill the whites easily. Maybe they could even capture Gun-in-the-Water and torture him. It was easy to cripple a man when the footing was so bad. His father would at last have his vengeance and they could all boast that they had finished Big Horse Scull, a ranger who had been killing Comanches almost as long as Buffalo Hump, his father, had been killing whites.

Yet Buffalo Hump just sat there, tilted sideways a little from the weight of the ugly hump, sucking marrow from buffalo bones. Blue Duck knew his father didn't like Kicking Wolf. The two had quarreled often: over women, over horses, over the best routes into Mexico, over what villages to raid, over captives. Why let Kicking Wolf have the glory of killing Big Horse and his rangers?

It was on Blue Duck's tongue to call the old man a coward, to tell him it was time he stayed with the old men, time he let the young warriors decide when to fight and who to attack.

But, just as Blue Duck was about to speak, Buffalo Hump looked up at him. The older man had been fiddling with the knife he used to split the buffalo leg bone—suddenly his eyes were as cold as the snake's. Blue Duck could never avoid a moment of fear, when his father's eyes became the eyes of a snake. He choked off his insult— he knew that if he spoke, he might, in an instant, find himself fighting Buffalo Hump. He had seen it happen before, with other warriors. Someone would say one word too many, would fail to see the snake in his father's eyes, and the next moment Buffalo Hump would be pulling his long bloody knife from between the other warrior's ribs.

Blue Duck waited. He knew that it was not a day to fight his father.

"Why are you standing there?" Buffalo Hump asked. "I want to think. I gave you Gun-in-the-Water. If you want to fight in the sleet, go fight."

"Can I take some warriors?" Blue Duck asked. "Maybe we could take him and bring him back alive."

"No," Buffalo Hump said. "Kill him if you are able, but I won't give you the warriors."

Angered, Blue Duck turned. He thought the old man was trying to provoke him—perhaps his father was seeking a fight. But Buffalo Hump was not even looking at him, and had just put his knife back in its sheath.

"Wait," Buffalo Hump said, as Blue Duck was about to walk away. "You may see Kicking Wolf while you are traveling."

"I may," Blue Duck said.

"He owes me six horses," Buffalo Hump said. "If he has stolen a lot of horses from the Texans, it is time he gave me my six. Tell him to bring them soon."

"He won't bring them—he is too greedy for horses," Blue Duck said.

Buffalo Hump didn't answer. A gust of wind blew shards of sleet into the little warm place under the rock. Buffalo Hump knocked the sleet off his blanket and looked into the fire.

3.

BY MORNING Augustus McCrae was so tired that he had lost the ability to tell up from down. The dawn was sleet gray, the plain sleet gray as well. There was not a feature to stop the eye on the long plain: no tree, ridge, rise, hill, dip, animal, or bird. Augustus could see nothing at all, and he was well known to have the best vision in the troop. The plain was so wide it seemed you could see to the rim of forever, and yet, in all that distance, there was nothing. Augustus, like the other rangers, had been in the saddle thirty-six hours. Before the chase started he had been up all night, whoring and drinking; now he was so tired he thought he might be losing his mind. There were those among his comrades who thought that it was excessive whoring and drinking that had caused Gus's hair to turn white, almost overnight; but his own view was that too many long patrols had fatigued his hair so that it had lost its color.

Now, when he looked up, the horizon seemed to roll. It was as if the plain was turning over, like a plate. Augustus's stomach, which had little in it, began to turn, too. For a moment, he had the sensation that the sky was below him, the earth above. He needed to see something definite—an antelope, a tree, anything—to rid himself of the queasy sensation he got when the land seemed to tip. It grew so bad, the rolling, that at one point he felt his own horse was above him, its feet attached to the sky.

The more Gus thought about it, the angrier he became at Captain Scull.

"If he don't stop for breakfast I'm just going to dismount right here and die," Gus said. "I'm so tired I'm confusing up with down."

"I guess he'll stop when he hits the Canadian," Call said. "I doubt it's much further."

"No, and I doubt the North Pole is much further, either," Gus said. "Why has he brought us here? There's nothing here."

Call was weary, too. All the men were weary. Some slept in their saddles, despite the cold. Under the circumstances, Call just wanted to concentrate on seeing that no one fell behind, or straggled off and got lost. Though the plain looked entirely flat, it wasn't. There were dips so shallow they didn't look like dips, and rises so gradual they didn't seem to be rises. A ranger might ride off a little distance from the troop, to answer a call of nature, only to find, once the call was answered, that he had traversed a dip or crossed a rise and become completely lost. The troop would have vanished, in only a few minutes. A man lost on the llano would wander until he starved—or until the Comanches got him.

Call wanted to devote what energies he had to seeing that no one got lost. It was vexing to have to turn his attention from that important task to answer Gus's questions—particularly since they were questions that Gus himself ought to know the answer to.

"He brought us here to catch Kicking Wolf and get those horses back," Call said. "Did you think he was leading us all this way just to exercise our horses?"

Ahead they could see Inish Scull, his coat white with sleet, moving at the same steady pace he had maintained the whole way. Hector's shaggy coat steamed from melting sleet. It crossed Call's mind to wonder just how far Hector could travel without rest. Would it be one hundred miles, or two hundred? The Captain was well ahead of the troop. Seen from a distance he seemed very small, in relation to his huge mount. Seen up close, though, that changed. No one thought of Inish Scull as small when his eyes were boring into them, as he delivered commands or criticisms. Then all anyone remembered was that he was a captain in the Texas Rangers—size didn't enter into it.

Augustus's head was still swimming. The horizon still rocked, but talking to Woodrow helped a little. Woodrow Call was too hard-headed to grow confused about up and down; he was never likely to get sky and land mixed up.

"He's not going to catch Kicking Wolf," Gus said. "I expect the reason he's rarely run off from is because he's careful who he chases. If you ask me, he usually just chases the ones he knows he can catch."

Call had been thinking the same thing, though he had no intention of saying it in front of the men. He didn't like to be doubting his captain, but it did seem to him that Captain Scull had met his match in the game of chase and pursuit. Kicking Wolf had had nearly a day's start, and the shifting weather made tracking difficult. Inish Scull didn't like to turn his troop, any more than he liked to turn his own head when spitting tobacco juice. He seemed to think he could keep an enemy ahead of him by sheer force of will, until he wore him down. But Kicking Wolf had lured the Captain onto the llano, which was his place. He wasn't subject to anybody's will—not even Buffalo Hump's, if reports were true.

Then Augustus spotted something moving in the sky, the first sign he had seen that there was life anywhere around.

"Look, Woodrow—I think that's a goose," Gus said, pointing at the dark in the gray sky. "If it comes in range I mean to try and shoot it. A fat goose would make a fine breakfast."

"Geese fly in flocks," Call reminded him. "Why would one goose be flying around out here?"

"Well, maybe it got lost," Gus suggested.

"No, birds don't get lost," Call said.

"A bird dumb enough to fly over this place could well get lost," Gus said. "This place is so empty an elephant could get lost in it."

The bird, when it came in sight, proved to be a great blue heron. It flew right over the troop; several of the men looked up at it and felt some relief. All of them were oppressed by the gray emptiness they were traveling in. The sight of a living thing, even a bird, stirred their hopes a little.

"I see something else," Gus said, pointing to the west. He saw a moving spot, very faint, but moving in their direction, he felt sure.

Call looked and could see nothing, which vexed him. Time and again he had to accept the fact that Augustus McCrae had him beaten, when it came to vision. Gus's sight just reached out farther than Call's—that was the plain fact.

"I expect it's Famous Shoes," Gus said. "It's about time that rascal got back."

29

"He ain't a rascal, he's our scout," Call said. "What's rascally about him?"

"Well, he's independent," Augustus commented. "What's the use of a scout who goes off and don't bring back a report but every two or three days? And besides that, he beat me at cards."

"An Indian who can beat a white man at cards is a rascal for sure," Long Bill volunteered.

"I expect it just took him this long to find Kicking Wolf's track," Call said.

A few minutes later they sighted the Canadian River, a narrow watercourse cutting through a shallow valley. There was not a tree along it.

"Now, that's a disappointment," Augustus said. "Here we are at the river, and there's not any dern wood. We'll have to burn our stirrups if we want to make a fire."

Then Call saw Famous Shoes—Inish Scull had stopped to receive his report. What amazed Call was that Famous Shoes had arrived so swiftly. Only moments before, it seemed, the scout had been so far away that Call hadn't even been able to see him; but now he was there.

"I'm about to quit rangering, if it means coming to a place where I can't tell up from down," Augustus said, annoyed that there seemed no likelihood of a good roaring fire beside the Canadian.

Call had heard that threat from Augustus before—had heard it, in fact, whenever Gus was vexed—and he didn't take it seriously.

"You don't know how to do anything besides ride horses and shoot guns," Call told him. "If you was to quit rangering you'd starve."

"No, the fact is I know how to gather up women," Augustus said. "I'll find me a rich fat woman and I'll marry her and live in ease for the rest of my days."

"Now you're talking bosh," Call said. "If you're so good at marrying, why ain't you married Clara?"

"It's far too cold to be talking about such as that," Augustus said, vexed that his friend would bring up Clara Forsythe, a woman far too independent for her own good, or anybody else's good either—his in particular. He had proposed to Clara the day he met her, in her father's store in Austin, years before, but she had hesitated then and was still hesitating, despite the fact that he had courted her fast and furiously, all that time. Clara would admit that she loved him—she was not the standoffish sort—but she would not agree to marry him, a fact that pained him deeply; despite all he had done, and all he could do, Clara still considered herself free to entertain other suitors. What if she married one? What could he do then but be broken-hearted all his life?

It was not a circumstance he wanted to be reminded of, on a morning so cold that he couldn't tell up from down—and he particularly resented being reminded of it by Woodrow Call, a man inept with women to such a degree that he had entangled himself with a whore. Maggie Tilton, the whore in question, was plenty pretty enough to marry, though so far, Woodrow had shown no sign of a willingness to marry her.

"You're no man to talk, shut up before I give you a licking," Gus said. It was an intolerable impertinence on the part of Woodrow Call to even mention Clara's name, especially at a time when they were having to struggle hard just to avoid freezing.

Call ignored the threat. Any mention of Clara Forsythe would provoke Augustus into a display of fisticuffs; it always had. Call himself avoided Clara when possible. He only went into the Forsythe store when he needed to buy cartridges or some other necessity. Though certainly pretty well beyond the norm, Clara Forsythe was so forward in speech that a man of good sense would plan his day with a view to avoiding her. Even when she was only selling Call a box of cartridges or a tool of some sort, Clara would always find a way to direct a few words to him, though—in his view—no words were called for, other than a thank you. Instead of just handing him his change and wrapping up his purchase, Clara would always come out with some statement, seemingly mild, that would nonetheless manage to leave him with the impression that there was something not quite right about his behavior. He could never figure out quite what he did to annoy Clara, but her tone with him always carried a hint of annoyance; a strong enough hint, in fact, that he tried to time his visits to the afternoons, when her father usually tended the store.

Maggie Tilton, the whore he liked to see, never gave him the sense that there was anything wrong with his behavior—if anything, Maggie swung too far in the other direction. She could see no wrong in him at all, which made him feel almost as uncomfortable as Clara's needlegrass criticisms. Maybe the fact that one was a whore and the other respectable had something to do with it—in any case Augustus McCrae was the last person whose opinion he felt he needed to listen to. Gus's mood bobbed up and down like a cork, depending on whether Clara had been sweet to him or sour, soft or sharp, friendly or aloof. In Call's view no man, and particularly not a Texas Ranger, ought to allow himself to be blown back and forth by a woman's opinion. It wasn't right, and that was that.

Long Bill was close enough to hear Gus threaten to give Call a licking, a threat he had heard uttered before.

"What's got *him* riled?" Long Bill inquired.

"None of your business. Get gone, you fool!" Gus said.

"You must have swallowed a badger, Gus—I swear you're surly," Long Bill said. "I wonder if Famous Shoes has seen any wood we could make into a nice fire, while we're wandering."

Before anyone could answer, Inish Scull, their captain, gave a loud yell of rage, wheeled Hector, and spurred him into a great lumbering run toward the west. The sleet spumed up in clouds behind him. Inish Scull didn't wave for the troop to follow him, or give any indication that he cared whether the twelve rangers came with him or not. He just charged away, leaving Famous Shoes standing alone by a large, steaming pile of horse turds which Hector had just deposited on the prairie.

"Well, there goes Captain Scull—I expect he's sighted his prey," Long Bill said, pulling his rifle from its scabbard. "We best whip up or we'll lose him."

The troop, with Gus at its head, immediately clattered off after

Captain Scull, but Call didn't follow, not at once. He didn't fear losing contact with the Captain while he was riding Hector—an elephant could not leave a much plainer track. He wanted to know what Famous Shoes had said to provoke the charge.

"Is it Kicking Wolf?" he asked the Kickapoo. "Is it going to be a fight?"

Famous Shoes was a slight man with a deceptive gait. He never seemed to hurry, yet he had no trouble keeping up with a troop of horsemen. Even if the horsemen charged off, as Inish Scull and the whole troop had just done, Famous Shoes would usually manage to catch up with them by the time a campfire was made and coffee boiling. He moved fast, and yet no one ever saw him moving fast, a thing Call marveled at. Sometimes he responded to questions and sometimes he didn't—but even if he chose to answer a given question, the answer would usually lay a little sideways to the question as it had been phrased.

At the moment he was looking closely at the smoky green pile of Hector's droppings.

"The Buffalo Horse has been eating prickly pear," he said. "I guess he don't like this icy grass."

"Kicking Wolf," Call repeated. "Is it Kicking Wolf they went off after?"

Famous Shoes looked at Call with mild surprise, his usual look when responding to direct questions. The look left Call with the feeling that he had missed something—what, he didn't know.

"No, Kicking Wolf is over by the Rio Pecos," Famous Shoes said. "The Captain will have to ride a faster horse if he wants to catch Kicking Wolf. The Buffalo Horse is too slow."

That was Call's opinion too, but he didn't say it.

Then Famous Shoes turned away from the dung pile and gestured toward the west.

"Kicking Wolf didn't really want those horses—not the geldings," he said. "He only wanted the three studhorses, to breed to his young mares. Those are good young studhorses. They will make him some fine colts."

"If he only kept three, what'd he do with the others?" Call asked.

"He butchered them," Famous Shoes said. "His tribe took the meat, but the women didn't do a very good job of butchering all those horses. There is plenty of meat left. We can take it if we want to."

"If we ain't going to catch Kicking Wolf today, maybe the Captain will let Deets cook up some of the meat," Call said. "We're all hungry."

Deets was a young black man, making his second trip with the troop. He had been found sleeping in the stables one morning, covered with dust and hay. He had escaped from a large group of stolen slaves who were being driven into Mexico by the famous chief Wildcat, a Lipan who had perfected the practice of selling stolen slaves to rich Mexican ranchers. Call had been about to chase the boy off, for trespassing on ranger property, but Inish Scull liked Deets's looks and kept him to do the stable work. He was made a cook one day when the Captain happened to taste a stew he had cooked up for some black families who were at work building homes for the legislators.

Famous Shoes didn't reply, when Call mentioned eating. He seemed to live on coffee, rarely taking food with the rangers, though he *was* known to have a fondness for potatoes. Often he would slip two or three raw spuds in his pouch, before setting off on a scout. Raw potatoes and a little jerky seemed to be what he lived on.

Call knew that he ought to be hurrying after the troop, but he could not resist lingering for a moment with Famous Shoes, in hopes of learning a little bit about tracking and scouting. Famous Shoes didn't look smart, yet he made his way across the llano as easily as Call would cross a street. Captain Scull was particular about scouts, as he was about everything. He didn't trust anybody—not even his wife, by some reports—yet he allowed Famous Shoes to wander for days at a stretch, even when they were in hostile territory. Call himself knew little about the Kickapoo tribe—they were supposed to be enemies of the Comanches, but what if they weren't? What if, instead of helping them find the Indians, Famous Shoes was really helping the Indians find them?

Call thought he would try one more query, just to see if Famous Shoes could be persuaded to answer the question he was asked.

"I thought there was plentiful antelope, up here on the plains," he said. "I've et antelope and it's a sight tastier than horsemeat. But we ain't seen an antelope this whole trip. Where'd they all go?"

"You had better just fill your belly with that fresh horsemeat," Famous Shoes said, with an amused look. "The antelope are over by the Purgatory River right now. There is good sweet grass along the Purgatory River this year."

"I don't know why this grass wouldn't be sweet enough for them," Call said. "I know it's icy right now, but this ice will melt in a day or two."

Famous Shoes was amused by the young ranger's insistence. It was not the young man's place to question the antelope. Antelope were free to seek the grass they preferred—they did not have to live by the Palo Duro, where the grass was known to be bitter, just because some Texans liked antelope meat better than horsemeat. It was typical of the whites, though. Seventeen horses were dead and there was plenty of tasty meat left on their carcasses. Those horses would never eat grass again, sweet or bitter; only the three stallions Kicking Wolf had kept would know the flavor of grass again. Yet, here was this young man, Call, expecting to find antelope standing around waiting to be shot. Only buffalo were peculiar enough to stand around waiting to be shot by the white men, which was why the numbers of buffalo were declining. There were plenty of ante-lope, though—they lived wherever the grass was sweetest, along the Purgatory or the Canadian or the Washita or the Rio Pecos.

"I don't think we will see any antelope today," Famous Shoes said—and then he left. The rangers had galloped away to the west, but Famous Shoes turned north. It vexed Call a little. The man was their scout, yet he never seemed to travel in the same direction as the troop.

"I'd be curious to know where you're heading," he asked, trotting after the scout, in a polite tone. After all, the man hadn't really done anything wrong—he just did things that seemed peculiar.

Famous Shoes had been moving in a light trot when Call followed him and asked him the question. He looked up at Call, but he didn't slow his motion.

"I'm going to see my grandmother," he said. "She lives up on the Washita with one of my sisters. I guess they are still there, if they haven't moved."

"I see," Call said. He felt foolish for having asked.

"My grandmother is old," Famous Shoes said. "She may want to tell me a few more stories before she dies."

"Well, then, that's fine," Call said, but Famous Shoes didn't hear him. He had begun to sing a little song, as he trotted north. Famous Shoes' voice was soft, and the wind still keened. Call heard only a snatch or two of the song, before Famous Shoes was so far away that the song was lost in the wind.

A little perplexed, feeling that he might somehow have been out of order, Call turned his horse and began to lope west, after the troop. The tracks of Hector, the Buffalo Horse, were as easy to follow as a road. He wondered, as he loped over the cold plains, what made Indians so much like women. The way Famous Shoes made him feel, when he asked a question, was not unlike how Clara Forsythe made him feel, when he ventured into her store. With both the Indian and the women he was always left with the feeling that, without meaning to, he had made some kind of mistake.

Before he could worry the matter much more he saw a horseman approaching, back along the trail Hector had made. For a moment, he was fearful enough to heft his rifle—out on the plains, a Comanche could pop out at you at any time. Maybe one had got between him and the troop and was planning to cut him off.

Then, a moment later, he saw that it was only Gus, coming hell for leather back along the sleety trail.

"Why'd you lag, Woodrow? We thought you'd been ambushed," Gus said, a little out of breath from his rapid ride.

"Why no, I was just talking to Famous Shoes," Call said. "You didn't need to lather your horse."

"We heard that whooping last night—you *could* have been ambushed," Augustus reminded him.

"I ain't ambushed, let's go," Call said. "The boys will eat all the breakfast if we don't hurry."

Augustus was annoyed. His friend could at least have thanked him—after all, he had put his own life at risk, coming back alone to look for him.

But then, the fact was, Woodrow Call just wasn't the thanking kind.

4.

THE MORNING Inez Scull first called Jake Spoon into her bedroom, she was sitting on a blue velvet stool. The bedroom was in the Sculls' fine brick mansion on Shoal Creek, the first brick house in Austin, the rangers had been told. Jake had only been with the rangers three months at the time, working mainly as a kind of orderly for Captain Scull. His chief task was to groom Hector, and get him saddled when the Captain required him. Now and again Captain Scull would dispatch Jake to run an errand for Madame Scull—"Madame Scull" was how she preferred to be addressed. Usually the errand would consist of picking up packages for her at one of the more prominent stores. Jake had come to Texas with a group of ragged settlers from Kansas; he had never seen such buying as the Sculls routinely indulged in. The Captain was always ordering new guns, or saddlery, or hats or gloves or spyglasses. The big dining room table in the Scull mansion was always littered with catalogues of all descriptions—catalogues of combs or dresses or other frippery for Madame Scull, or knives or fine shotguns or microscopes or other gadgets for the Captain. The house even boasted a barometer, a thing Jake had never heard of, and also a brass ship's clock at the head of the stairs, a clock that sounded bells every hour and half hour.

Jake had never been, or expected to be, in a fine lady's bedroom when the kitchen girl, Felice, a young high yellow girl he had taken a bit of a fancy to, came outside and told him that the lady of the house wanted to see him upstairs. Jake was a little nervous, as he went up the stairs. Madame Scull and the Captain were often out of temper with one another, and were not quiet in their expressions of rage or discontent. More than once, according to Felice, the Captain had taken a bullwhip to his lady, and, more than once, she had taken the same bullwhip to him—not to mention quirts, buggy whips, or anything else that lay to hand. At other times, they screamed wild curses at one another and fought with their fists, like two men. Some of the Mexican servants were so alarmed by the goings-on that they thought the devil lived in the house—a few of them fled in the night and didn't stop until they were across the Rio Grande, more than two hundred and fifty miles away.

Still, both the Captain and Madame Scull had been very nice to Jake. Madame Scull had even, one day, complimented him on his curly hair.

"Why, Jake, those curls will soon be winning you many female hearts," she said to him one morning, when he was carrying out a package she wanted sent off.

The men, Augustus McCrae particularly, scoffed at Jake for accepting soft work at the Captain's house, when he should have been out riding on Indian patrols. But Jake had no fondness for horses, and, besides, had a mighty fear of scalping. He was but seventeen, and considered that he had time enough to learn about Indian fighting. If, as some predicted, the Indians were whipped forever, before he got to fight them, it would not be a loss that grieved him much. There would always be Mexican bandits to engage the rangers—Jake supposed he could get all the fighting he wanted along the border, and soon enough.

When Madame Scull called him upstairs he supposed it was just to carry out another package; the worst it was likely to entail was hanging a drape—Madame Scull was always getting rid of drapes and replacing them with other drapes. She was always shifting the furniture too, much to Captain Scull's vexation. Once he had come home from a dusty scout and started to plop down in his favorite chair, with one of the scientific books he loved to pore over, only to discover that his favorite chair was no longer in its spot.

"Goddamnit, Inez, where's my armchair?" he asked. Jake, flirting with Felice, had happened to be in earshot when the outburst came.

"That smelly thing, I gave it to the nigras," Mrs. Scull remarked coolly.

"Why, you hairy slut, go get it back right now!" the Captain yelled—the comment startled Jake considerably and put Felice in such a fright that she lost all interest in courting.

"I've never liked that chair, and I'll decide what furniture stays in my house, I reckon," Madame Scull said. "If you like that chair so much, go live with the nigras—I, for one, shan't miss your damn tobacco stains."

"I want my chair and I'll have it!" the Captain declaimed; but at that point Jake ran out of the kitchen and hunted up a task to do in the stables. He had never expected to hear a captain in the Texas Rangers call his wife a slut, much less a hairy slut. Behind him, as he hurried off the porch, he heard the argument raging, and a crash of china. He feared the Sculls might be approaching the bullwhip stage, and didn't want to be anywhere around.

The morning he got called into the bedroom he had to make the same dash again, only faster. When he came into the bedroom, Mrs. Scull beckoned him over to the blue velvet stool where she sat. She was red in the face.

"Ma'am, is it the drapes again?" Jake asked, thinking she might have got a little too much sun through the long windows beside her bed.

"It ain't the drapes, thank you, Jake," Inez Scull said.

"My sweet boy," she added. "I do so fancy dimpled boys with curly hair."

"Mine's always been curly, I guess," Jake said, at a loss how to respond to the remark. Madame Scull still had the same, sun-flushed look on her face.

"Stand a little bit closer, so I can see your dimples better," Inez Scull said.

Jake obediently placed himself within arm's length of the stool, only to get, in the next moment, the shock of his life, when Madame Scull confidently reached out and began to unbutton his pants.

"Let's see your young pizzle, Jakie," she said.

"What, ma'am?" Jake said, too startled to move.

"Your pizzle—let's have a look," Madame Scull repeated. "I expect it's a fine one."

"What, ma'am?" Jake said again. Then a sense of peril came over him, and he turned and dashed out of the room. He didn't quit dashing until he had reached the ranger stables. Once there, he squeezed into a horse stall and got his pants rebuttoned properly.

He spent the rest of the day and most of the next few days as far from the Scull mansion as he could get and still do his work. Jake didn't know what to think about the incident—at times, he tried to persuade himself that he dreamed it. He desperately wanted to find someone to confide in, but the only person in the troop that he could trust with such dangerous information was Pea Eye Parker, a gangly, half-starved youth from the Arkansas flats who was not much older than himself. Pea Eye had come to Texas with his father to farm, only to have his father, a brother, and three sisters die within a year. Woodrow Call had happened to notice Pea Eye in an abandoned cornfield one day—the farmer had been burned out and his wife killed by Comanches. Pea Eye was sitting by a fence, eating the dried-out corn right off the cob.

"Ain't that corn too dry to chew?" Call asked him. The young fellow looked to be seventeen or eighteen—he didn't even have drinking water to wash the dry kernels down with.

"Mister, I'm too hungry to be picky," Pea Eye said. He looked hollow in the eyes, from starvation and fatigue. Woodrow Call had seen something in the boy that he liked—he had let Pea Eye ride behind him, into Austin. Pea Eye soon proved to be adept at horse-shoeing, a task most rangers shunned. Augustus McCrae particularly shunned it, as he would shun cholera or indigestion. Pea Eye had wanted to ride out with the troop, of course, but Captain Scull had left him in town at first, considering him a little too green for the field. But when the time came to visit Fort Belknap, the Captain decided to leave Jake and take Pea Eye. It was the day before they were to leave that Madame Scull put her hand in Jake's pants. Jake could not, with the troop's departure at hand, bring himself to say anything about the incident to Pea Eye, fearing that, in his excitement, he might blab.

On the morning the troop was to leave, Jake half expected Captain Scull to walk up and kill him, but the Captain was as pleasant to him as ever. As the troop was preparing to mount, the Captain turned to him and informed him calmly that Madame Scull wanted him to be her equerry, while the troop was gone.

"Her what?" Jake asked—he had not heard the term before.

"Equerry, *equus*, equestrian, equestrienne," Captain Scull said. "In other words, Inez wants you to be her horse."

"What, sir?" Jake asked. Since he began to deal with the Sculls, he had come to question both his eyesight and his hearing: for the Sculls frequently said and did things he couldn't understand or believe, even though he heard them said and saw them happen. In his old home in Kansas, nobody said or did such things—of that, Jake was sure.

"She'll have her way, too, boy!" the Captain said, his temper mounting at the thought of his wife's behavior. "She'll ride you to a lather before I'm halfway to the Brazos, the wild hussy!"

"What, sir?" Jake asked, for the third time. He had no idea what the Captain was talking about, or why he supposed that Mrs. Scull wanted to ride him.

"Boy, are you a stutterer, or have you just got a brick for a brain?" the Captain asked, coming close and giving Jake a hard look.

"Inez wants to mount you, boy—ain't that clear to you yet?" he

41

went on. "Her father's the richest man in the South. They've three hundred thousand acres of prime plantation land in Alabama, and a hundred thousand more in Cuba. 'Inez' ain't her name, either—she just took that name because it matches mine. In Birmingham she's just plain Dolly, but she was raised in Cuba and thinks she has a right to the passions of the tropics."

He paused, and glared at the big brick house on the slope above the creek. Around him, the men were mounting their horses for the long ride to Fort Belknap. Inish Scull glared at his mansion, as if the house itself were responsible for the fact that his wife would not desist from unseemly passions.

"Lust is the doom of man—I've often forsworn it myself, but my resolve won't hold," the Captain said, stepping close to Jake. "You're a young man, take my advice. Beware the hairy prospect. Do that and improve your vocabulary and you'll yet make a fine citizen. Old Tom Rowlandson, now there was a man who understood lust. He knew about the hairy prospect, Tom Rowlandson did. I've a book of his pictures right up in my house. Take a peek in it, boy. It might help you escape Inez. Once you start tupping with slavering sluts like her, there's no recovery: just look at me! I ought to be secretary of war, if not president, but I'm doing nothing better than chasing heathen red men on this goddamn dusty frontier, and all because of a lustful rich slut from Birmingham! Bible and sword!"

A few minutes later the troop rode away, planning to be gone for a month, at least. Jake felt regretful for a few hours—if he had tried harder to persuade the Captain to take him along, the Captain might have relented. After all, he had taken Pea Eye. If there was a fight, it might have meant a chance for glory. But he hadn't pressed to go, and the Captain had left him with the problem of Madame Scull. With the Captain gone and the threat of immediate execution removed, Jake found that his mind came to dwell more and more on what Madame Scull had done. There was no denying that she was a beautiful woman: tall, heavy bosomed, with a quick stride and lustrous black hair.

It seemed to Jake that the Captain, for whatever reason, had simply handed him over to Madame Scull. He was supposed to be her equerry—that was now his job. If he didn't do his equerrying well, the Captain might even dismiss him from the rangers when the troop returned.

By the time the troop had been gone half a day, Jake Spoon had persuaded himself that it was his duty to present himself at the Scull mansion. He had taken to going to the mansion regularly in order to intercept Felice at the well, where she was frequently sent. Madame Scull was reckless in her use of water—trips to fetch it took Felice back and forth to the well for much of the day.

This time, though, when Felice came out the back door with her bucket, she was limping. Felice was a quick girl, who normally walked with a springy step. Jake hurried over, anxious to see why she was lame, and was surprised to see that she had a black eye and a big bruise on one cheek.

"Why, what done that? Did the Captain strike you?" Jake asked.

"No, not the Captain . . . the Missus," Felice said. "She beat me with the handle of that black bullwhip. I got marks all over, from where that woman beat me."

"Well, but why?" he asked. "Did you sass her, or drop a plate?"

Felice shook her head. "Didn't sass her and didn't drop no plate," she said.

"But you must have done something to bring on a licking," Jake said. Felice's dress had slipped off one shoulder as she struggled with the heavy water bucket—Jake saw a swollen black bruise there, too.

Felice shook her head. Jake didn't understand. She had come from Cuba with Madame Scull, had been a servant to her since she was a girl of six. When she was younger the Missus might slap her once in a while, for some slip, but it was only later, once Felice had begun to fill out as a woman, that the Missus had begun to beat her hard. Lately, the beatings had become more and more frequent. If Captain Scull even glanced at Felice as she was serving breakfast, or requested a biscuit or a second cup of coffee, the Missus would often corner her later in the day and quirt her severely. Sometimes she punched her, or grabbed Felice's hair and tried to yank it out.

There was no knowing when the Missus might beat her, but yesterday had been the worst. The Missus caught her in the hall and beat her with the handle of the bullwhip—beat her till her arm got tired of beating. One of Felice's teeth was loose—the Missus had even hit her in the mouth.

Jake understood that Felice was a slave, and that the Sculls could do whatever they wanted to with her; still, he was shocked at the bruises on Felice's face. In Kansas, few people still owned slaves; his own family had been much too poor to afford one.

Jake offered to carry the water bucket, which was heavy. As they were nearing the house he happened to glance up and see Madame Scull, watching them from a little balcony off her bedroom. Jake immediately lowered his eyes, because Madame Scull had no clothes on. She just stood on the balcony, her heavy bosom exposed, brushing her long, black hair.

Jake glanced over at Felice and was surprised to see tears in her eyes.

"Why, Felice, what is it?" he asked. "Are you hurt that bad?"

Felice didn't answer. She didn't want to try and put words to her sorrow. She had come to like Jake. He was polite and let her know that he liked *her*; besides, he was young and his breath was sweet when he tried to kiss her—not foul with tobacco smells like the Captain, who lost no opportunity to be familiar with her. Felice had been thinking of meeting Jake behind the smokehouse, one night—he had been pleading with her to do just that. Felice wanted to slip out with Jake—but she knew now that she couldn't, not unless she wanted to be beaten within an inch of her life. The Missus wanted Jake, that was plain. There she stood on the balcony, showing Jake her titties. The Missus would take him, too. Felice knew that she would have to give up on him and do it immediately, or else risk bad trouble. The Captain was gone—despite his stinking breath the Captain would sometimes take up for Felice, just to be contrary. But she belonged to the Missus, not the Captain. If the Missus got too jealous, she might even sell her. Several old ugly men had cast glances at her when they came to visit the Sculls. They looked like rich men, too—one of them might buy her and use her harder than the Missus did. In Cuba, she had seen bad things happen to slaves: brandings and horsewhippings and even hangings. The Missus had never done anything that bad to her, but if she got sold to some old ugly man, he might chain her and hurt her bad. Jake wasn't worth such a risk—nothing was worth such a risk. But it still made her fill with sorrow, that the Missus would take the one person who was sweet to her.

Once they got inside the house Jake didn't know what to do, other than set the water bucket on the stove. Felice had gone silent; she wouldn't speak at all. She wiped away her tears on her apron and went about her tasks, looking down. She wouldn't turn to him again—not a word, and not a look. It was a big disappointment. He thought he had about persuaded her to slip out some night and meet him behind the smokehouse—then they could kiss all they wanted.

But that plan seemed to be spoiled, and he didn't know why.

He was about to leave in dejection and go back to the ranger stables, when old Ben Mickelson, the skinny, splotchy butler, came in, shaking from drink. Ben wore a shiny old black coat and took snuff, sniffing so loudly that it caused Jake to flinch if he happened to be nearby.

"Madame would like to see you upstairs," old Ben told him, in his dry voice. "You're late as it is—I wouldn't be later."

Old Ben had an ugly way of pushing out his lips, when he was spoken to by anyone but the Master or the Mistress. He pushed them out at Jake until Jake wanted to give him a hard punch.

"What am I late for? I ain't been told," he said. The thought of going upstairs made him more and more nervous.

"I ain't the Madame—if she says you're late, I guess you are," old Ben said.

In fact, Ben Mickelson hated young men indiscriminately, for no better reason than that they were young and he wasn't. Sometimes he hated young men so hard that he got violent notions about them, notions that affected him like a fever. Right at the moment, he was having a violent imagining in which young Jake was being chewed on by seven or eight thin hungry pigs. There were plenty of thin hungry pigs running loose within the town of Austin, too. It was against the ordinances, but the skinny half-wild pigs didn't know there was an ordinance against them. They kept running loose, a menace to the populace. If six or seven of the wild pigs cornered Jake, they would soon whittle him down to size. Then the Madame wouldn't be so anxious to get him between her legs, not if he was well chewed by some hungry pigs.

Old Ben was violently jealous of the Madame and her lusts. Once, years before, in a moment of anxious weakness, Inez Scull had pulled Ben's pants down in a closet and coupled with him then and there. "You're an ugly old thing, Ben," she told him, after the brief act was over. "I don't fancy men with liver spots, and you've got 'em." Ben Mickelson was a little crestfallen. Their embrace, though brief, had been passionate enough to dislodge almost every garment hanging in the closet. He thought he might expect a compliment, but all he got was a comment about his liver spots.

"I expect it's the climate, Madame," he said, as Inez Scull was fastening her bodice. "I never got spots when we lived in Boston."

"It's not the climate, it's all that whiskey you drink," Madame Scull said, whereupon she left and never touched Ben Mickelson again. For days and weeks he lingered by the closet, hoping Madame Scull would come by in a lustful state again—so lustful that she would be inclined to overlook liver spots. But what had occurred in that closet, amid ladies' shoes and fallen dresses, was never repeated. Years passed, and Ben Mickelson got bitter. Jake Spoon, not yet eighteen, with his dimples and curls, baby fat still in his cheeks, would not likely be liver-spotted, and that fact alone was enough to make Ben Mickelson hate him.

Jake looked at Felice, as he stood at the foot of the stairs, but

Felice would not meet his eye. He thought he saw tears on her cheeks, though—he supposed she still ached from the beating.

Felice turned and took up her broom, so old Ben wouldn't see her tears. Old Ben had to be watched and avoided. He was always poking at her with his skinny fingers. But the threat of his fingers didn't cause her tears. She cried because she knew she would have to hold herself in, not let herself start feeling warm about any of the boys that came to the house. The Missus wanted all the boys for herself. Jake had been kind to her, helping her carry water and doing little errands for her when he could. She had begun to want to see him behind the smokehouse—but that was lost. When Jake came back down the stairs, he would be different. He would have the Missus's smell on him. He wouldn't be sweet to her anymore, or help her carry water or feed the chickens.

As Felice swept she felt old Ben following her, getting closer, hoping for a pinch or a grab. It filled her with fury, suddenly; she wasn't going to have it, not this morning, when her new feeling for Jake had just been crushed.

"You scat, you old possum!" Felice said, whirling on the butler. The anger in her face startled old Ben so that he turned on his heel and went to polish the doorknobs. It was a hard life, he felt, when a butler wasn't even allowed to touch a saucy yellow girl.

When Jake approached Madame Scull's bedroom he felt a deep apprehension, a fear so deep that it made his legs shaky. At the same time he felt a high excitement, higher than what he felt when he managed to snatch a kiss from Felice. It was a little like what he felt when he visited one of the whore tents down by the river with Gus McCrae, a treat he had only been allowed twice.

But this excitement was higher. Madame Scull wasn't a whore, she was a great lady. The Scull mansion was finer by far than the Governor's house. Jake was conscious that his pants were ragged, and his shirt frayed. To his horror he saw, looking down, that he had forgotten to wipe his feet: he had muddied the carpet at the head of the stairs. Now there was mud on Madame Scull's fine carpet.

Then he noticed Inez Scull, watching him from the bedroom door. She had the same sun-flushed look on her face that she had had when she put her hand in his pants.

"Ma'am, I'm sorry, I tracked in mud," he said. "I'll get the broom and clean it up for you."

"No, hang the mud—don't you be running off from me again," Madame Scull said.

Then she smiled at him. She had put on a gown of some kind, but it had slipped off one shoulder.

" 'Come to my parlor,' said the spider to the fly," Inez said, thinking how glad she was that Inish had had to leave to chase red Indians. The Comanche might be an inconvenience to the ragged settlers, but they were a boon to her, the fact being that her husband's embraces had long since grown stale. Austin was a dull, dusty town, with no society and little entertainment, but there was no denying that Texas produced an abundance of fine, sturdy young men. They were hardly refined, these boys of the frontier, but then she wasn't seeking refinement. What she wanted was fine sturdy boys, with curls and stout calves, like the one who stood before her at the moment. She walked over to Jake—he *had* tracked rather a lot of mud up her stairs—and took up where she had left off, quickly opening his pants, confident that in a week or less she could cure him of embarrassment where fleshly matters were concerned.

"Let's see that little pricklen again," she said. "You scarcely let me touch it the other day."

Jake was so shocked he could not find a word to say.

" 'Pricklen,' that's what my good German boy called it," Inez said. "My Jurgen was proud of his pricklen, and yours is nothing to be ashamed of, Jakie."

She began to lead Jake down the long hall, looking with interest at what had popped out of his pants. His pants had slipped down around his legs, which meant that he couldn't take very long steps. Madame Scull led him by the hand.

"I expect I'd have my Jurgen and his pricklen yet if Inish hadn't hanged him," Madame Scull said casually.

At that point, hoping he hadn't heard right, Jake stopped. All he could see was the hang noose, and himself on the gallows, with the boys standing far below, to watch him swing.

"Oh dear, I've given you a fright," Inez said, with a quick laugh. "Inish didn't hang my Jurgen for *this*! He wouldn't hang a fine German boy just because he and I had enjoyed a little sport."

"What'd he hang him for, then?" Jake asked, unconvinced.

"Why, the foolish boy stole a horse," Madame Scull said. "I don't know what he needed with a horse—he *was* rather a horse, in some respects. I was quite crushed at the time. It seemed my Jurgen would rather have a horse than me. But of course Inish caught him, and took him straight to the nearest tree and hung him."

Jake didn't want to hang, but he didn't want to leave Madame Scull, either. Anyway, with his pants around his ankles, he could hardly walk, much less run.

They were near a big hall closet, where coats and boots were kept. Jake noticed that Madame Scull was freckled on her shoulders and her bosom, but he didn't have time to notice much more, because she suddenly yanked him into the closet. Her move was so sudden that he lost his balance and fell, in the deep closet. He was on his back, amid shoes and boots, with the bottoms of coats hanging just above him. Jake thought he must be crazy, to be in such a situation. Madame Scull was breathing in loud snorts, like a winded horse. She squatted right over him, but Jake couldn't see her clearly, because her head was amid the hanging coats. There was the smell of mothballs in the closet, and the smell of saddle soap, but, even stronger, there was the smell of Inez Scull, who was not cautious in her behavior with him—not cautious at all. She flung coats off their hangers and kicked shoes and boots out into the hall, in order to situate herself above him, exactly where she wanted to be.

To Jake's amazement, Madame Scull began to do exactly what the Captain had told him she would do: make him her horse. She sank down astride him and rode him, hot and hard, rode him until he was lathered, just as the Captain had said she would, though the Captain himself was probably not even halfway to the Brazos River yet. He wondered, as she rode him, what the servants would think if one of them happened to come upstairs and notice all the shoes Madame Scull had kicked out into the hall.

5.

KICKING WOLF had killed the seventeen geldings in a barren gully. The butchering had been hasty; though the best meat had been taken, much was left. The rocks in the gully were pink with frozen blood. The carcasses all had ice on their hides—Augustus saw one horse who had ice covering its eyes, a sight that made his stomach rise. Guts had been pulled out and chopped up; those left had frozen into icy coils. Buzzards wheeled in the cold sky.

"I thought I was hungry a minute ago," Augustus said. "But now that I've seen this I couldn't eat for a dollar."

Many of the men were dead asleep, slumped wherever they had stopped. Captain Scull sat on a hummock of dirt, staring toward the west. Now and then, he spat tobacco juice on the sleety ground.

"I can eat," Call said. "It won't cost nobody a dollar, either. I've seen the day when you didn't turn up your nose at horsemeat, I recall."

"That was a warmer day," Gus commented. "It's too early to be looking at this many butchered horses."

"Be glad it ain't butchered men," Call said.

Deets, the black cook, seemed to be the only man in the outfit who could muster a cheerful look. He had a stew pot bubbling already, and was slicing potatoes into it when they rode up.

"If Deets can make that horsemeat tasty, I might sample a little," Augustus said. At the sight of the bubbling pot, he felt his appetite returning.

Long Bill Coleman had his feet practically in the fire, his favorite posture when camped on a cold patrol. He had fallen asleep and was snoring loudly, oblivious to the fact that the soles of his boots were beginning to smoke.

"Pull him back, Deets, his feet are about to catch fire," Augustus said. "The fool *will* sleep with his feet amid the coals."

Deets pulled Long Bill a yard or two back from the fire, then offered them coffee, which they took gratefully.

"Why'd you let all these boys nod off, Deets?" Gus said. "Old Buffalo Hump might come down on us at any minute—they best be watching their hair."

"Let 'em nap—they ridden for two days," Call said. "They'll wake up quick enough if there's fighting."

Deets took a big tin cup full of coffee over to Captain Scull, who accepted it without looking around. The Captain's mouth was moving, but whatever he was saying got lost on the wind.

"Old Nails is talking to himself again," Augustus observed. "Probably cussing that feisty wife of his for spending money. They say she spends twenty-five dollars ever day of the week."

Call didn't think the Captain was cussing his wife, not on a bald knob of the prairie, icy with sleet. If he was cussing anybody, it was probably Kicking Wolf, who had escaped to the Rio Pecos with three fine stallions.

"What was he saying, Deets?" he asked, when the black man came back and began to stir the stew.

Deets did not much like reporting on the Captain. He might get the talk wrong, and cause trouble. But Mr. Call had been good to him, giving him an old ragged quilt, which was all he had to cover with on the cold journey. Mr. Call didn't grab food, like some of the others, or cuss him if the biscuits didn't rise quick enough to suit him.

"He's talking about that one who shot him—down Mexico," Deets said.

"What? He's talking about Ahumado?" Call asked, surprised.

"Talking about him some," Deets admitted.

"I consider that peculiar information," Augustus said. "We're half a way to Canada, chasing Comanches. What's Ahumado got to do with it?"

"He don't like it that Ahumado shot his horse," Call said, noting that some of the men around the campfire were so sound asleep they looked as if they were dead. Most of them were sprawled out with their mouths open, oblivious to the wind and the icy ground. They didn't look as if they would be capable of putting up much resistance, but Call knew they would fight hard if attacked.

The only man he was anxious about on that score was young Pea Eye Parker, a gangly boy who had only been allotted an old musket. Call didn't trust the gun and hoped to see that the boy got a repeating rifle before their next expedition. Pea Eye sat so far back from the campfire that he got little succor from it. He was poorly dressed and shivering, yet he had kept up through the long night, and had not complained.

"If you pulled in a little closer to the campfire you'd be warmer," Call suggested.

"It's my first trip—I don't guess I ought to take up too much of the fire," Pea Eye said.

Then he swiveled his long neck around and surveyed their prospects.

"I was raised amid trees and brush," he said. "I never expected to be no place where it was this empty."

"It ain't empty—there's plenty of Comanches down in that big canyon," Augustus informed him. "Buffalo Hump's down there— once we finally whip him, there won't be nothing but a few chigger Indians to fight."

"How do you know we'll whip him?" Call said. "It's bad luck to talk like that. We've been fighting him for years and we ain't come close to licking him yet."

Before Augustus could respond, Captain Scull abruptly left the hummock where he had been sitting and stomped back into camp.

"Is that stew ready? This is a damn long halt," he said. Then he glanced at Call, and got a surprised look on his face.

"I thought Famous Shoes was with you, Mr. Call," Scull said. "I had no reason to suspect that he wasn't with you, but I'll be damned if I can spot him. It might be the glare off the sleet."

"No sir, he's not with me," Call said.

"Damn it why not?" Captain Scull asked. "If he's not with you, you'll just have to go fetch him. We'll save you some of the stew."

"Sir, I don't know if I *can* fetch him," Call said. "He went to visit his grandmother. I believe she lives on the Washita, but he didn't say where, exactly."

"Of course you can fetch him—why shouldn't you?" Scull asked, with an annoyed look on his face. "You're mounted and he's afoot."

"Yes, but he's a swift walker and I'm a poor tracker," Call admitted. "I might be able to track him, but it would be chancy."

"What a damned nuisance—the man's gone off just when we need him most," Inish Scull said. He tugged at his peppery gray beard in a vexed fashion. When a fit of anger took him he grew red above his whiskers; and, as all of the men knew, he was apt to grow angry if offered the slightest delay.

Call didn't say it, but he found the Captain's comment peculiar. After all, Famous Shoes had *been* off, ever since they crossed the Prairie Dog Fork of the Brazos. The scout wandered at will, returning only occasionally to parley a bit with the Captain, as he just had that morning. Based on past behavior, Captain Scull had no reason to expect to hear from Famous Shoes for a day or two more, by which time the scout could have visited his grandmother and returned.

It was impatient and unreasonable behavior, in Call's view: but then, that seemed to be the way of captains, at least the ones he had served. They were impatient to a fault—if they didn't get a fight one place, they would turn and seek a fight somewhere else, no matter what the men felt about it, or what condition they were in. They had missed Kicking Wolf, so now, if Deets was right, the Captain's thoughts had fixed on Ahumado, a Mexican bandit hundreds of miles to the south, and a marauder every bit as capable as Kicking Wolf or Buffalo Hump.

Still, Call had never disobeyed an order, or complained about one, either—it was Gus McCrae who grumbled about orders, though usually he was circumspect about who he grumbled to. Call knew that if the Captain really wanted him to go after Famous Shoes, he would at least have to try. Call felt lank—he thought he had better quickly gulp down a plate of stew before he went off on a pursuit that might take days.

Captain Scull, though, did not immediately press the order. He stood with his back to the fire, swishing the remains of his coffee around in his cup. He looked at the sky, he looked at the horses, he looked south. Call held his peace—the muttering about Ahumado might only have been a momentary fancy that the Captain, once he had assessed the situation, would reject.

The Captain sighed, gulped down the rest of his coffee, held out the cup for Deets to refill, and looked at Call again.

"I got short shrift from my grandmothers," he remarked. "One of them had ten children and the other accounted for fourteen—they were tired of brats by the time I came along. How long do you think Famous Shoes planned to visit?"

"Sir, I have no idea," Call admitted. "He wasn't even sure his grandmother still lived on the Washita. If he don't locate her I expect he'll be back tomorrow."

"Unless he thinks of somebody else to visit," Augustus said.

Call hastily got himself a plate of stew. He felt he had been a little derelict in hesitating to set off immediately in pursuit of Famous Shoes. After all, the man could scarcely be more than five miles away. With reasonable luck, he ought to be able to overtake him. It was only the featurelessness of the plains that worried him: he might ride within a mile of Famous Shoes and still miss him, because of the dips and slantings of the prairie.

Now he felt like he ought to be ready to leave, if that was what the Captain wanted.

"Taters ain't cooked yet," Deets informed him, as he dished up the stew. "That meat mostly raw, too."

"I don't care, it'll fill me," Call said. "If you'd like me to go look for him, Captain, I will."

Inish Scull didn't respond—indeed, he gave no indication that he had even heard Woodrow Call. Captain Scull was often casual, if not indifferent in that way, a fact which vexed Augustus McCrae terribly. Here Woodrow, who was as cold and hungry as the rest of them, was offering to go off and run the risk of getting scalped, and the Captain didn't even have the good manners to answer him! It made Gus burn with indignation, though it also annoyed him that Call would be so quick to offer himself for what was clearly a foolish duty. Famous Shoes would turn up in a day or two, whether anybody looked for him or not.

"I was thinking of Mexico, Mr. Call," Captain Scull said finally. "I see no point in pursuing Kicking Wolf for the sake of three horses. We'll corner the man sooner or later, or if we don't get him the smallpox will."

"What? The smallpox?" Augustus said; he had a big nervousness about diseases, the various poxes particularly.

"Yes, it's traveling this way," Inish Scull said impatiently, his mind being now on Mexico.

"The theory is that the Forty-niners spread it among the red men, as they were running out to California to look for gold," he added. "Very damn few of them will find any of the precious ore. But they've brought the pox to the prairies, I guess. The Indians along the Santa Fe Trail have it bad, and I hear that those along the Oregon Trail are dying by the hundreds. It'll be among the Comanches soon, if it ain't already. Once the pox gets among them they'll die off so quick we'll probably have to disband the rangers. There'll be no healthy Indians left to fight."

Captain Scull finished his speech and lifted his coffee cup, but before he could sip, a peppering of gunfire swept the camp.

"It's Buffalo Hump, I knowed it!" Augustus said.

Call had only gulped down a few bites of stew when the shooting started. He ran back to his horse and pulled out his rifle, expecting the Indians to be upon them, but when he turned the prairie looked empty. Most of the rangers had taken cover behind their horses, there being no other cover to take.

Captain Scull had drawn his big pistol, but had not moved from his spot by the coffeepot. He had his head tilted slightly to one side, watchful and curious.

"We just lost Watson," he said, examining the camp. "Either that, or he's enjoying a mighty heavy nap."

Augustus ran over and knelt by Jimmy Watson, a man a year or two older than himself and Call. At first he saw no wound and thought the Captain might be right about the heavy nap, but when he turned Jimmy Watson slightly he saw that a bullet had got him right under his armpit. He must have been lifting his gun and the bullet passed just beneath it and killed him.

"Nope, Jim's dead," Gus said. "I wish the damn Comanches would stand up, so we could see them."

"Wish for Christmas and roast pig, while you're wishing," Call said. "They ain't going to stand up."

Then, a moment later, five young warriors appeared on horseback, a considerable distance from the camp. They were yelling and whooping, but they weren't attacking. The lead horseman was a tall youth whose hair streamed out behind him as he raced his pony.

Several of the rangers lifted their rifles, but no one fired a shot. The Comanches had gauged the distance nicely—they were already just out of rifle range.

Call watched Captain Scull, waiting for him to give the order to mount and pursue—the Captain had taken out his binoculars and was studying the racing horsemen.

"I was looking for brands on the horses," he said. "I was hoping our Abilene ponies might be there. But no luck—they're just Comanche ponies."

All the rangers stood by their horses, waiting for the order to pursue the Comanches, but Captain Scull merely stood watching the five young warriors race away, as casual as if he had been watching a Sunday horse race.

"Captain, ain't we gonna chase 'em? They kilt Jimmy Watson," Augustus asked, puzzled by the Captain's casual attitude.

"No, we'll not chase them—not on tired horses," the Captain said. "Those are just the pups. The old he-wolf is down there some-where, waiting. I doubt those youngsters expected to hit anybody, when they shot—they were just trying to lure us down into some box canyon, where the he-wolf can cut us off and tear out our throats."

He turned and put his binoculars back in their leather case.

"I'd prefer to wait for that stew to mature and then take break-fast," he said. "If the old he-wolf wants us bad enough, let him come. We'll oblige him with a damn good scrap, and when it's over I'll take his hide back to Austin and nail it to the Governor's door."

"Sir, what'll we do with Jimmy?" Long Bill asked. "This ground's froze hard. It'll take a good strong pick to hack out a grave in ground like this, and we ain't got a pick."

Captain Scull came over and looked at the dead man—he knelt, rolled the man over, and inspected the fatal wound.

"There's no remedy for bad luck, is there?" he said, addressing the question to no one in particular. "If Watson hadn't raised his arm just when he did, the worst he would have gotten out of this episode would have been a broken arm. But he lifted his gun and the bullet had a clear path to his vitals. I'll miss the man. He was someone to talk wives with."

"What, sir?" Augustus asked. The remark startled him.

"Wives, Mr. McCrae," Inish Scull said. "You're a bachelor. I doubt you can appreciate the fascination of the subject—but James Watson appreciated it. He was on his third wife when he had the misfortune to catch his dying. He and I could talk wives for hours."

"Well, but what happened to his wives?" Long Bill inquired. "I'm a married man. I'd like to know."

"One died, one survives him, and the one in the middle ran off with an acrobat," the Captain said. "That's about average for wives, I expect. You'll find that out soon enough, Mr. McCrae, if you take it into your head to marry."

Augustus was thoroughly sorry that the subject of marriage had come up. It seemed to him that he had been trying to get married for half his life—he had just happened, unluckily, to fall in love with the one woman who wouldn't have him.

"Sir, even if one of his wives did run off with an acrobat, we've still got to bury him, someway," Long Bill said. Once Long Bill got his mind on something he rarely allowed it to be deflected until the question at hand was closed. Now the question at hand was how to bury a man when the ground was too frozen to yield them a grave. When Jimmy Watson had been alive he needed wives, apparently, and it was a need Long Bill understood and sympathized with. But now he was dead: what he needed was a grave.

"Well, I suppose we do need to bury James Watson—that's the Christian way," the Captain said. "It was not the way taken by my cousin Willy, though. Cousin Willy was a biologist. He studied with Professor Agassiz, at Harvard. Willy was particularly fond of bee-tles—excessively fond, some might say. He fancied tropical beetles, in particular. Professor Agassiz took him to Brazil, where there are some wonderful beetles—more beetles than any place in the world except Madagascar, Willy claimed. They've even got an undertaker beetle, down there in Brazil."

"What kind?" Augustus asked. He had vaguely heard of Brazil, but he had never heard of an undertaker beetle.

"An undertaker beetle, sir," Captain Scull went on. "Willy wanted to go back into the food chain the fastest way possible, and the fastest way to have himself laid out naked in a tidy spot where these undertaker beetles were plentiful.

"So that's what they did with Will," the Captain continued. "They had no choice—Willy had fixed it all in his will. They laid him out naked in a pretty spot and the beetles immediately got to work. Pretty soon Willy was buried, and by the next day he was part of the food chain again, just as he wished. If we left James Watson to the coyotes and the buzzards, we'd be accomplishing the same thing."

Long Bill Coleman was horrified by such talk. He was unfamiliar with Brazil, and the thought of being buried by beetles gave him the shudders. Not only was the Captain forgetting about Jimmy Watson's widow, whose feelings about the burial had to be considered, he was even forgetting about heaven.

"Now then, that's strange talk," he said. "How would a man get up to heaven, with no one to say any scriptures over him, and with just a dern bunch of beetles for undertakers? Of course, out here in the baldies we can't expect undertakers, but I guess I'll try to bury my pards myself—I wouldn't trust the job to a bunch of dern bugs."

"My cousin Willy was of an agnostical bent, Mr. Coleman," the Captain said. "I don't think he believed in heaven, but he did believe in bugs. They're not to be underrated, sir—not according to my cousin Willy. There are more than a million species of insects, Mr. Coleman, and they're a sight more adaptable than us. I expect there will be bugs aplenty when we humans are all gone."

Young Pea Eye Parker was so hungry, he found it hard to pay attention to the conversation. For one thing, he couldn't figure out what a food chain could be, unless the Captain was talking about link sausage. How a beetle in a country he had never heard of could turn a dead man into link sausage was beyond his ken. Deets's stew pot was bubbling furiously; now and then, a good odor drifted his way. His only opinion was that he himself did not intend to be buried naked. It would be a hard shock to his ma if he came walking into heaven without a stitch.

Deets, stirring the stew, did not like to be discussing dead folks so boldly—for all they knew, the dead could still hear. Just because the lungs stopped working didn't mean the hearing stopped, too. The dead person could still be in there, listening, and if a dead person was to hear bad things said about him, he might witch you. Deets had no desire to be witched—when it became necessary to make some comment about a dead person, he made sure his comment was respectful.

Call was vexed. He was prepared to go fight the Comanches who had just killed Jimmy Watson—if the rangers had pressed the pursuit at once, they might have got close enough to bring down a

Comanche or two. He didn't think Buffalo Hump was waiting to ambush them; to him it just looked like a party of five young braves, hoping to count coup on the white men—and they *had* counted coup. How could the Captain stand around talking about beetles when one of their men had been killed?

Augustus knew what his friend was feeling—he himself felt exactly the same thing. The Comanches had killed a Texas Ranger and got away clean. Behavior such as that would soon make the rangers the laughingstock of the prairies. And yet Captain Scull's reputation as a deadly and determined fighter was well earned. He and Call had often seen the Captain deal out slaughter. What was wrong with him this morning?

Captain Scull suddenly looked at the two young rangers, a trace of a smile on his lips—his look, as was often the case, made both men feel that he could read their minds.

"Why, do I smell discontent? I believe I catch a whiff of it," the Captain said. "What's the matter, Mr. Call? Afraid I've lost my vinegar?"

"Why, no sir," Call said, truthfully. Despite his pique, he had not supposed that Captain Scull had lost his fight. What he felt was that the Captain, as a commander, was changeable in ways he didn't understand.

"I would have liked to punish those braves, while we still had a chance to catch them," Call added.

"That was my thought, too," Augustus said. "They killed Jimmy Watson, and he was a mighty fine fellow."

"That he was, Mr. McCrae—that he was," Captain Scull said. "Normally I would have given chase myself, but this morning I'm not in the mood for it—not right this minute, at least."

Inish Scull went to his saddlebags and took out the huge brown plug of tobacco he cut his chaws from. He had a special little knife with a mother-of-pearl handle, just for cutting his tobacco. He was so fearful of losing his little knife that he kept it attached to his belt by a thin silver chain, such as he might use on a pocket watch.

The Captain took out his knife, found a place not far from the fire, and began to cut himself a day's worth of chaws, working carefully—he liked to make each chaw as close to square as possible. Often, once the Captain had cut off a chaw, he would hold it up for inspection, and trim it a little more, removing a sliver here and a sliver there, to make it a little closer to square.

"I believe our stew's about ready, Deets," he said, once he had restored the big brownish plug to his saddlebag. "Let's eat. I might recover my chasing mood once I've sampled the grub.

"Ever work in an office, Mr. Call?" he then inquired, as the men lined up with their tin plates to get their stew. Call was startled. Why would the Captain suppose he had ever worked in an office, when the records plainly showed that he had been employed as a Texas Ranger from the age of nineteen?

"No sir, I've worked outside my whole life," Call said.

"Well, I *have* worked in an office, sir," the Captain said. "It was the Customs House in Brooklyn, and I was sent to work there by my pa, in the hope of breaking me of certain bad habits. I worked there for a year and did the same thing, in the same way, every day. I arrived at the same time, left at the same time, took my sip of wine and bite of bread at the same time. I even pissed and shat at the same time—I was a regular automaton while I held that office job, and I was bored, sir—bored! Intolerably bored!"

Inish Scull's face reddened suddenly, at the memory of his own boredom in the office in Brooklyn. He neatly stacked up his ten squares of cut tobacco and looked at Call.

"The tragedy of man is not death or epidemic or lust or rage or fitful jealousy," he said loudly—his voice tended to rise while declaiming unpleasant facts.

"No sir, the tragedy of man is boredom, sir—boredom!" the Captain said. "A man can only do a given thing so many times with freshness and spirit—then, no matter what it is, it becomes like an office task. I enjoy cards and whoring, but even cards and whoring can grow boresome. You tup your wife a thousand times and that becomes an office task, too."

Scull paused, to see if the hard truths he was expounding were

61

having any effect on his listeners, and found that they were. All the men were listening, with the exception of an old fellow named Ikey Ripple, who had gulped a little stew and fallen back to sleep.

"You see?" the Captain said. "Mr. Ike Ripple is bored even now, even though Buffalo Hump could show up any minute and lift his hair.

"Now . . . *that's* my point, sir!" he said, looking directly at Call. "I will break the resistance of the goddamn red Comanches on these plains, given the time and the resources, but I'll be damned if I'll jump up and chase every Indian brat that fires a gun off at me. Do that and it becomes office work—do you get my point, Mr. Call?"

Call thought he got the point, but he wasn't sure he agreed with it. Fighting Indians meant risking your life—how many men in offices had to risk their lives?

"Why, yes, Captain, I believe I do," Call said mildly. After all, the Captain was older—he had survived more Indian fights than any man on the frontier. Perhaps they had grown boresome to him.

"Uh, Captain, you never said how your cousin died—that one that got buried by the beetles," Long Bill remarked. The details of the unorthodox burial had been preying on his mind; he was curious as to what sort of death had led up to it.

"Oh, cousin Willy—why, snakebite," the Captain said. "Willy was bitten by a fer-de-lance, one of the deadliest snakes in the world."

He had begun to stuff the square-cut plugs of tobacco into his coat pocket, for use during the day.

"He was a scientist to the end, our William," he went on. "He timed his own death, you know—timed it with a stopwatch."

"Timed it? But why, sir?" Gus asked. "If I was dying of snakebite I doubt I'd get out my watch."

"Oh—then what would you do, Mr. McCrae?" the Captain asked, in a pleasant tone.

Augustus thought of Clara Forsythe, so fetching with her curls and her frank smile.

"I believe I'd just scrawl off a letter to my girl," Gus said. "I'd be wanting to bid her goodbye, I expect."

"Why, that's fine—that's the human instinct," Captain Scull said. "You're a romantic fellow, I see. So was our Willy, in his way—only he was romantic about science. Professor Agassiz taught him to never waste an experience, and he didn't. The average time of death from the bite of a fer-de-lance is twenty minutes. I expect Willy hoped to improve on the average, but he didn't. He died in seventeen minutes, thirty-four seconds, give or take a second or two."

Captain Scull stood up and looked across the gray plain.

"Willy was alone when he was bitten," the Captain said. "His stopwatch was in his hand when they found him. Seventeen minutes and thirty-four seconds, he lived. Now that's bravery, I'd say."

"I'd say so too, Captain," Call said, thinking about it.

6.

"DO YOU BELIEVE that tale about the beetles and the stopwatch?" Augustus asked. Call sat with his back to a large rock, looking off the edge of the canyon; the wind had died, the sleet had stopped blowing, but it was still bitter cold. In the clear night they could see Comanche campfires, far below them and halfway across the Palo Duro Canyon.

"There's forty campfires down there," Call commented. "There's enough Indians in this canyon to wipe us out six times."

"Well, but maybe they ain't interested—the Captain wasn't," Gus replied. "Why don't you just answer the question I asked you?"

"I'm on guard duty, that's why," Call said. "We need to be listening, not talking."

Augustus found the remark insulting, but he tried not to get riled. Woodrow was so practical minded that he was often rude without intending rudeness.

"I'm your oldest friend, I guess I can at least ask you a question,"

Augustus said. "If I can't, then I've a notion just to roll you off this bluff."

"Well, I do believe the Captain's story—why wouldn't I?" Call said.

"Myself, I think it was just a tale," Gus said. "He wasn't in the mood for an Indian fight, so he told us a tale. You're so gullible you'd believe anything, Woodrow. I've never met anybody who behaves like the people the Captain talks about."

"You don't know educated people, that's why," Call said. "Besides, his cousin was in Brazil. You've never been to Brazil—you don't know how people behave down there."

"No, and if they've got snakes that can kill you in seventeen minutes, I ain't never going, either," Augustus said.

Call watched the wink of campfires in the darkness far below.

"Oh Lord, I hope the Captain don't drag us off to Mexico," Gus said. "I'd like to see my Clara before the month's out."

Call was silent—if he didn't respond, maybe the subject of Clara Forsythe would die away. Usually it didn't die quickly, though. For ten years, at guard posts all over the Texas frontier, he had listened to Augustus talk about Clara Forsythe. It wasn't even that the subject was boresome, particularly—it was just that it was pointless. Clara had set her mind against marrying Gus, and that was that.

"Buffalo Hump's down there," he remarked, hoping Gus would accept a change of subject. Under the circumstances it would be a prudent change. Buffalo Hump might be older now, but he was still the most feared war chief on the southern plains. If he woke up in the mood to do battle, Gus would have more to worry about than Clara's refusal.

"I miss Clara," Augustus said, ignoring his friend's feint. "It helps to talk about her, Woodrow. Don't be so stingy with me."

Of course, Augustus knew that Woodrow Call hated talking about romance, or marriage, or anything having to do with women. He wouldn't even discuss poking, one of Augustus's favorite topics of discussion, as well as being a highly favored activity. Many a night he had sat with Woodrow Call on guard duty and engaged in the same tussle, when it came to conversation. Call always wanted to talk about guns, or saddles, or military matters, and Gus himself would try to steer the conversation onto love or marriage or women or whores—something more interesting than the same old boots-and-saddles stuff.

"I expect you're a lucky man, Woodrow," he said. "You'll probably be married long before I am."

"That wouldn't be hard," Call admitted. "You'll never be married, unless you give up on Clara. She don't mean to marry you and that's that."

"Hush that talk," Gus said. "If you knew anything about women you'd know that women change their minds every day. The only reason you don't want to hear no talk of marriage is because you know you ought to marry Maggie, but you don't want to. You'd have made a good Indian, Woodrow. You've got no use for the settled life."

Call didn't argue; what Augustus said was true, in the main. Maggie Tilton was a kind woman who would undoubtedly make some man a good wife—but he would not be that man. The truth was he'd rather be right where he was, sitting on a canyon's rim, looking down on the campfires of the last wild, dangerous Indians in Texas, eating horsemeat stew and breasting weather that would freeze you one night and burn your skin off the next day, than to live in a town, be married, and buy vittles out of a store. Maggie was pretty and sweet; she might yet find a man who would protect her. He himself had no time to protect anybody, except himself and his comrades. That was the way it was, and that was the way it would stay, at least until the Indians camped below them had been whipped and scattered, so that they could no longer raid, burn farms, take white children captive, and scare back settlement on the southern edge of the plains.

Augustus was bored, and when he was bored he liked to devil his friend as much as possible. It annoyed Call that he wouldn't just shut up. It was a fine, still night. Now and then he could hear the Comanches' horses nickering, from the floor of the canyon.

"I know one thing," he said. "If I was a Comanche I would have had your scalp long before this. You're so dern careless it's lucky you've even survived."

"Now that's brash talk," Augustus said. "You could spend a lifetime trying to take my scalp, and not disturb a hair."

"That's bragging," Call replied. "You've always had a troop of rangers with you—that's why you have your hair."

"If I'm going to take risks I prefer to take them with women," Gus said. "Any fool can wander off and get scalped."

"Go back to camp—it ain't your turn to stand guard anyway," Call told him. "I'd rather listen to owl hoots than to listen to you yap."

Augustus was mildly insulted, but he made no move to leave.

"I wonder what Jimmy Watson and the Captain had to say to one another about wives," he said. "I would have liked to listen in on a few of those conversations."

"Why, it would be none of your business," Call told him.

"That wife of the Captain's is fancy," Augustus said. "A woman who can spend twenty-five dollars every day of the week is too dern expensive for me."

"He's rich and so is she—I don't suppose it matters," Call said.

Augustus gave up on getting his friend to talk about women—he scooted a little closer to the edge of the deep canyon.

"Look down there, Woodrow," he said. "That's probably all that's left of the fighting Comanche."

"No it ain't," Call said. "There's several bands off to the west— they call them the Antelopes. However many there are, it's enough to scare most of the white people out of the country north of the Brazos. They just picked off one of us, this very day."

"Woodrow, you're the most arguesome person I've ever met," Augustus said. "Here I've been trying to talk sense to you all night and you ain't agreed with a single thing I've said. Why am I even talking to you?"

"I don't know, but if you'll stop we can stand guard in peace," Call said.

Augustus made no answer. He scooted a little closer to where Call sat and pulled his long coat up around his ears, as protection from the deep cold of the night.

7.

BUFFALO HUMP had taught Blue Duck that the safest time to attack a white man, and a Texas Ranger particularly, was while the man was squatting to do his morning business. The whites were foolish in their choice of clothes; they wore tight trousers that slowed their movements when they squatted to shit. Blue Duck, like most braves, only wore leggins—even those he discarded unless it was bitter cold. The leggins didn't interfere with his movements, if he had to rise quickly. But a squatting white man was like a hobbled horse: you could put an arrow in him or even jump on him and cut his throat before he could get his pants up and run.

Blue Duck knew they had killed a ranger the morning before. He had seen the other men hacking out a shallow grave with their bowie knives. They even spent a long time gathering rocks and piling them on the grave, to protect the corpse; a foolish labor. Then they sang a death song of some kind over the rocks, and rode off.

As soon as the rangers were out of sight Blue Duck quickly scattered the rocks and pulled out the corpse—of course it was stiff as wood. He tied the corpse on his pony and followed the whites all day. He was alone. The other braves had spotted three antelope and had gone off to run them down. He doubted that they would catch up with the antelope, but he didn't try to stop them from leaving. There was more bravery in following the Texans alone. Perhaps he would be able to kill Gun-in-the-Water, or even Big Horse Scull. After all, even Big Horse would have to shit sometime. Perhaps he could get him with an arrow, while he squatted.

That night, when the rangers camped, Blue Duck made a big circle around them, carrying the corpse. He wanted to put the dead ranger where the others would find him in the morning. First, though, he untied the corpse and began to hack it up. He scraped the icy scalp away from the skull. Then he cut off the man's privates and sliced open his body cavity. He pulled out the frozen organs and smashed the man's ribs with a big rock. He had with him a little axe that he had found in a burned-out farmhouse near the Brazos. With the little axe he cut the man's feet off and threw them into the canyon, to assure that the ranger would be a cripple in the spirit world. Finally, with a single blow of the axe, he split open the man's skull. Then he shot three arrows into the man's legs—his arrows. He wanted the whites to know that he was Blue Duck, a warrior equal to his father, Buffalo Hump.

In the darkness he brought the hacked-up corpse as close to the ranger camp as he dared come. He didn't want them to ride away and miss it, so he put it near the horses. It was only an hour before dawn. Soon the rangers would be stumbling off to do their shitting. He would wait, a little distance away. Perhaps Big Horse would walk out, hoping to shit in private. If he came Blue Duck meant to wait until his pants were tight against his legs, before trying to kill him.

While it was still dark he walked over toward the canyon, to make sure his horse was still there. Once while sneaking up on some Kiowa he had failed to secure his horse, a skittish pony. The horse ran off, causing him to miss the battle. He had to walk all the way back to the Comanche camp, a humiliation he had not forgotten.

It was while returning to his horse that he saw Gun-in-the-Water. The other one, Silver Hair McCrae, was walking back toward the camp, his shoulders hunched. It was cold and misty; the clouds of McCrae's breath were whiter than the mist. Blue Duck thought McCrae would surely see him, but McCrae was taken by a fit of coughing as he stumbled on toward the camp.

He was almost to his horse when he saw Gun-in-the-Water walking along, a pretty rifle in his hands. Blue Duck immediately decided to kill him. Gun-in-the-Water went into a little shallow gully near the edge of the camp and began to take down his pants.

It was then that Blue Duck made his mistake. He had a gun and a bow as well—he preferred the gun and was out of practice with the bow; it was a failing his father had often chided him about. His father still practiced every day, shooting arrows at prickly pear, or jackrabbits, or anything he thought might sharpen his aim.

Blue Duck knew that he could easily kill Gun-in-the-Water with his gun; but he had not yet checked on his horse. If he fired a gun and his horse was not still there, the rangers could run him down and kill him. He thought he had better attempt to kill Gun-in-the-Water with an arrow, which meant creeping a little closer. He crept a little closer and was just raising up to draw the bow when Gun-in-the-Water, still squatting, brought up his rifle and shot him. Blue Duck shot his arrow just as the bullet struck him; the arrow missed completely, sailing over Gun-in-the-Water's head.

The bullet had gone into his side, spilling blood down his leg, but Blue Duck could not pause to think about how badly he might be hurt. He had to run for his life. Gun-in-the-Water fired again and hit him again, this time only in the arm. Blue Duck ran as fast as he could. He could hear the rangers yelling. Soon the great Buffalo Horse would be thundering after him. His horse was still there, and in a moment he was on him, clutching his rifle and his bow. He flailed at the horse and the horse ran well, but before he had gone many yards there was a shot and his horse fell. Blue Duck was up at once—he saw that it was McCrae who had shot his horse. McCrae, mounted, was already in pursuit, and, just behind him, Blue Duck saw Scull, on his great steed. Big Horse Scull was waving a big sword—it was known that he liked to kill with the sword, when circumstances allowed it.

Blue Duck ran for his life, embarrassed by his own carelessness. He knew that the whites would tell that his arrow had flown over Gun-in-the-Water's head; Buffalo Hump would be dark in his displeasure. He raced along the edge of the canyon, looking for a place that he could go down but that a horse could not. The Buffalo Horse had already outrun McCrae, whose mount had come up lame. It was Big Horse Scull and the Buffalo Horse who were pounding down upon him.

Then, desperate, Blue Duck jumped—he had come to a place where the drop was not sheer. He jumped fifteen feet and rolled and rolled—the slope was slick with frost. He could not stop rolling but he held on to his weapons. Bullets were hitting all around him, zinging off the frozen ground. But the depths of the canyon were still in darkness—the farther he rolled, the more the night protected him. A hard little rock gouged his ribs and then he slammed into a large boulder, stopping his roll. The shots had stopped. The rangers could no longer see him and had decided not to waste any more bullets. Blue Duck crawled behind the boulder, panting. He knew that Big Horse Scull had almost caught him. He wasn't scared—he knew that even the Buffalo Horse could not follow him down the steep sides of the canyon—but he was out of breath and confused. When he could breathe a little better he stood up and satisfied himself that his wounds would not kill him. He heard the beat of wings and looked up to see a red hawk, flapping just above him, climbing into the air, higher and higher, toward the rim of the canyon. He wished he could become a hawk—then he could glide down into the canyon on hawk wings and drop right into the camp.

But he was not a hawk. The slope was icy and the drop steep but Blue Duck limped along. He knew it was not wise to wait. Gun-in-the-Water and McCrae might be bold enough to climb down into the canyon after him. As he made his way down, slipping now and then on patches of ice, he took care to keep his weapons tight in his hands. His father might approve of his bold attack on the rangers, but only if he came back with his weapons in good order. Buffalo Hump was always scornful of warriors who lost weapons in battle. A bow to him was a special thing—it should always be in the hands of the warrior it belonged to, not in the hands of his enemy. If the enemy had his bow, a witch doctor might be able to witch it in such a way that it would never shoot arrows accurately again. Rifles, to Buffalo Hump, were of lesser importance; they came from the whites and were not made with skills the Comanche had learned. The gun Buffalo Hump allowed Blue Duck to have was old and not very reliable, but it was a gun, and it would be foolish to let any gun fall into the hands of an enemy.

When Blue Duck stopped a minute he listened for the sound of horses. Surely the shooting had been heard in camp. Some warriors ought to be on their way to investigate. Now, to the east, the canyon rim was orange with light. If the rangers were following him they would soon be able to shoot at him from a long distance. He hurried as much as he could, trying to get well down into the canyon before light came, but he had to be careful. He did not want to lose his footing on a patch of ice and start rolling again.

Perhaps his father would come, Blue Duck hoped. Sometimes Buffalo Hump rode out just before dawn, on a short hunt. He was better than anyone in camp at surprising young deer at their morning feeding. Often he would arrive back in camp with a doe or a big yearling fawn slung over his horse. Buffalo Hump's young wife, Lark, was good at working deerskins. She had made a soft cloak that Buffalo Hump could throw over his great hump. Lark was comely and plump—Blue Duck thought that Lark was one of the reasons his father had little interest in fighting. He preferred to stay with Lark, letting her feed him, and enjoying the warmth of her young body. Lark had come from the band led by old Slow Tree, who was so afraid of Buffalo Hump that he had let him take the girl for only a few horses, a thing that made Kicking Wolf angry. He himself had bought two wives from old Slow Tree and had even tried to buy Lark before Buffalo Hump saw her. But Slow Tree had never given Kicking Wolf any bargains, when it came to purchasing wives; the contrary old chief had refused absolutely to let Kicking Wolf buy Lark only a month before he let her become the wife of Buffalo Hump.

Blue Duck limped on down and finally reached the floor of the canyon. When he looked up he saw to his astonishment that the Buffalo Horse was still at the canyon rim, high above him. Big Horse Scull was not on him—the horse was just standing there. It was a worrisome thing: the Buffalo Horse might be some kind of witch animal that would cause his death if he were not careful.

Blue Duck hurried as fast as he could, worried about the witch horse high above him. Probably it was the witch horse that had alerted Gun-in-the-Water, enabling him to put a bullet into Blue

Duck without even aiming his gun. The more Blue Duck thought about it, the angrier it made him—the next time he had an opportunity to kill Gun-in-the-Water he meant to come on him while he slept and cut his throat—he vowed never again to embarrass himself by sending an arrow over an enemy's head. There was no question of missing when you drew a knife across a man's throat.

Blue Duck knew he had better get home and explain that a witch had been involved, before his father heard the story from someone else. Buffalo Hump had a way of knowing what had happened to one of his people before anyone else in the tribe. Old women told him things that they had heard from crows or hawks— things that had happened far from camp, so far that no warrior would have time to return and report. Some old woman might already have heard about the wild arrow from a bird, and told his father, which would not be a good thing, particularly not on a day when he had lost a horse—it was a loss his father would be sure to resent. The whites had a lot of horsemeat already; perhaps they would not even bother to butcher his horse, in which case he could go back later and get the meat and bring it to Lark, who was the only one who could cook for his father now. His other two wives were angry because of Lark and rarely lifted a hand to cook for Buffalo Hump now. Since he liked the plump young woman so much his older wives saw to it that she did all the work. One of the wives, old Heavy Leg, even made Lark go around the outside of the camp and collect the turds that people dropped in their shitting. Heavy Leg told Lark that they might need the turds for fuel, but that was absurd. The Comanches did not burn human turds for fuel, not in a wooded canyon where there were many buffalo chips to be gathered. When Lark protested, the two old wives, Heavy Leg and Hair-on-the-Lip, beat her with an axe handle they had found in a white man's wagon. Hair-on-the-Lip got her name because she had a mustache, like a white man. Even so, Hair-on-the-Lip had been Buffalo Hump's favorite wife for many years. Even now he sometimes made Lark leave the lodge so he could joke around with Hair-on-the-Lip.

Blue Duck walked halfway across the canyon—he was angry that no one had responded to the shooting and come to see if he was in trouble. Then he saw Slipping Weasel and Last Horse riding toward him. They were just trotting their horses, not in any hurry; even after they came close enough to see that he was limping they only put their horses into an easy lope. Buffalo Hump was not with them, nor were any of the other warriors. Though he was now in sight of the camp, no one was paying much attention. The sun had touched the bottom of the canyon now—people were just standing around looking at it, enjoying the warmth after so many cold days.

"You have a lot of blood on your leg," Slipping Weasel said, when Blue Duck came limping up to them.

"Where did you get all that blood?" Last Horse inquired.

"Are you stupid? It's my blood," Blue Duck told them. "It's my blood and it came from inside me."

He regarded Slipping Weasel as one of the most ignorant members of the band. Why was it necessary to ask where he got the blood on him when it was obvious that he was wounded? Slipping Weasel was so dumb that Blue Duck tried to avoid going on raids with him. He made too many mistakes, and was forgetful as well. Once he had even forgotten a captive and the captive had drowned in a flooded creek, trying to run away.

"You have many wounds today—you have been busy," Last Horse said, as if being wounded was a pleasant thing.

The two warriors were not trying to help him, particularly; they had just ridden over out of curiosity, to see what might have occurred. Even when they realized he was wounded they did not become any more helpful. Neither of them offered him a horse to ride to camp, a discourtesy that made him want to pull out his knife and stick it in both of them.

He wanted to, but he held back, afraid of what would happen if he killed them both. Slipping Weasel had already told him that the old men had talked to Buffalo Hump about sending him out of the tribe. It was because of his Mexican blood, Blue Duck felt sure. Several young men in the tribe had been born of white captives, or brown captives, and the old men didn't like it. The half-breeds were sometimes driven out. The old men might tell his father that it was because of his behavior, his fighting, that he should be sent away, but Blue Duck didn't believe it. They wanted to be rid of him because he carried his mother's blood. He often thought of leaving the tribe himself, but hadn't, because he was not ready and not equipped. He had only a poor gun, and now he had no horse. When he was ready he meant to leave of his own accord—one morning his father would just discover that he was gone. He would shame the old ones, though, by killing more whites than any of the young men who were pure blood, of the tribe.

"Get off your horse, I need it," Blue Duck said, walking over to Slipping Weasel.

Slipping Weasel was shocked that Blue Duck would be so rude. There was a polite way to inquire about borrowing horses, but Blue Duck had not bothered about the polite way—more and more he did not bother with the polite way, which is why many of the younger warriors did not want to go with him when he wanted to hunt or raid. He was not a great chief, like his father. He could not simply order people to give him horses. It was true that he was wounded and would probably like to ride a horse to camp, but the camp was not far away. Why would he need a horse now, when he had to walk only a little distance farther?

Besides, Slipping Weasel and Last Horse had been thinking of going on a deer hunt. If Blue Duck had been badly hurt they would have helped him without question—but he wasn't badly hurt. There was no reason they should waste time when the deer were farther down the canyon, waiting to be killed. Last Horse had seen them just at dusk—they would not have grazed far in one night, especially since they would have to paw at the sleety grass with their hooves before they could eat it.

"I see the Buffalo Horse up there," Last Horse remarked. The whole rim of the canyon was bright now, with the sunny dawn.

"If he had stepped on you, you would not need to borrow anybody's horse, because you would be dead," he added. "That horse has big feet."

"I see him standing up there," Slipping Weasel said, looking up at the Buffalo Horse. He would have liked a closer look at the great horse—all the Comanches would have liked a closer look. But there was no way to get one without having to fight Big Horse Scull.

"I have heard that the Buffalo Horse can fly," Last Horse said. "They say his wings are larger than the wings of many buzzards put together. If he flies down here while we are talking I am going to run away."

"If he flies down here I will shoot him," Slipping Weasel said. He too had heard the rumor that the Buffalo Horse could fly. He watched the horse closely; he too meant to run if the Buffalo Horse suddenly spread his wings and flew down at them.

Blue Duck didn't bother replying to such foolishness. If the Buffalo Horse could fly, Scull would long ago have flown above the Comanche people and killed them all. His father had once told him that there were vision women who could teach a man to fly, but no one had introduced him to such a vision woman. Buffalo Hump admitted that he himself might not be able to fly, because of the weight of his hump, but he thought that other men might be able to, if they could find the right old woman to teach them.

Blue Duck walked on away from the two men—he decided not to bother with their horses. The two vexed him so, that he might forget and kill them if he stayed around them; then he would be driven from the camp before he was ready to go.

When Blue Duck walked away, Slipping Weasel saw that most of his back was covered with fresh blood. The sight made him feel a little guilty. Blue Duck might have a worse wound than he and Last Horse supposed. What if he were to die before he reached camp? Men could die very suddenly, once they lost too much blood. One minute they might be walking and the next minute they might be dead.

Part Mexican or not, Blue Duck *was* the son of Buffalo Hump, and Buffalo Hump was their great chief. Though he didn't seem to be particularly fond of Blue Duck, there was no telling what Buffalo Hump might do if his own son dropped dead from a wound received fighting the white men. It would come out, of course, that he and Last Horse had failed to lend him a horse, although he was bleeding a lot. It would not please Buffalo Hump; there was no telling what he might do.

With that in mind Slipping Weasel trotted after Blue Duck—the deer down the valley could wait a few minutes, before they were killed.

"You had better take my horse," he said. "You have too much blood coming out of you—I don't think you should be walking."

Blue Duck ignored him. He was close to the camp now. Why should he take a horse when he had already done the walking?

Besides, now that he was close to camp and no longer had to fear that Gun-in-the-Water or Silver Hair McCrae would slide down the canyon wall and ambush him, he was in no great hurry to get home. He would soon have to admit to his father that he had lost a horse, and his father would not be pleased.

8.

"YOUR MONGOL HUN cooked his meat by horse heat," Inish Scull observed. He was comfortably seated on a large rock at the edge of the Palo Duro, studying the distant Comanche camp through his binoculars. Gus and Call had both wanted to scamper down the slope after the fleeing warrior, but Inish Scull waved them back.

"Nope, it's too shadowy yet," he said. "We'll not be skating down a cliff this morning after one red killer. He might have a few friends, scattered among those rocks."

"I don't think so, Captain," Call said. "He was alone when he came at me."

"That doesn't contradict my point," the Captain said, a little sharply. Woodrow Call, though a more than competent fighting man, had a disputatious nature—not a welcome thing, in Inish Scull's command.

"If his friends were hiding in the rocks, then they couldn't have been with him when he shot the arrow at you, now could they?" Scull said. "Human beings are rarely in two places at once, Mr. Call."

Call didn't reply. Of course human beings couldn't be in two places at once; but the fleeing boy was well past the rocks in question, and no one had appeared to join him.

Augustus was puzzled by the remark about horse heat, a form of heat he had never heard of; nor was he exactly clear about the Mongol Huns. The Captain was always talking about faraway places and peoples he had never heard of, Gurkhas and Zulus and Zouaves and the like, frequently launching into a lecture just as Augustus was possessed of a powerful urge to sleep. What he wanted to do at the moment was stretch out on a big rock and let the warm sun bake the chill out of him.

It was Woodrow Call who liked to hear the Captain discourse on the wars of history, or weaponry, or fighting tactics of any kind. The Captain had even given Call a ragged old book about Napoleon; though the book had one cover off, Call carried it in his saddlebags and read in it a page or two at a time, at night by the campfire.

"What is horse heat, Captain?" Augustus asked—he did not want to seem indifferent to Inish Scull's instruction. Indifference might result in Woodrow getting promoted over him, a thing he would find intolerable.

"Horse heat?" Inish said. "Why, your Mongol would slice off his steak in the morning and stick it under his saddle blanket. Then he'd gallop along all day, with the steak between him and the horse. Your Mongol might ride for fourteen hours at a stretch. By the time he made camp the steak would be cooked enough to suit him—a little horse heat and a lot of friction would do the job."

"Fourteen hours under a saddle blanket?" Augustus said. "Why, it would just be horsehairs mostly, by then. I doubt I could stomach horsemeat if it had been under a saddle blanket all day."

The Captain raised his binoculars—he had been looking down the canyon, where the sizable Comanche horse herd grazed.

"Buffalo Hump and his boys are hardly shy of horseflesh, at the moment," he said. "There must be nearly a thousand horses in that herd. I wonder what would happen if we tried to spook his ponies."

"We'd need to find a good trail down off this rim," Call said, but Captain Scull seemed hardly to hear him. He was imagining a grand charge.

"These red men are in their winter camp," he said. "I expect they're lazy and well fed. There's buffalo meat drying everywhere. We could come down like the wolf on the fold. It would be a chase you'd never forget."

Augustus was annoyed. Just when he wanted to stretch out and enjoy the sunlight, the Captain wanted to run off the Comanche horse herd, a mission that was sure to be perilous.

"I expect they'd stop feeling lazy pretty quick, if we was to run off their horses," he said.

Inish Scull, binoculars to his eyes, suddenly stiffened. He had his glasses fixed on a certain lodge in the Comanche camp.

"That's him, gentlemen—I told you. That's Buffalo Hump. Bible and sword," the Captain said in an excited tone.

Call strained his eyes, but could barely see the lodges, across the canyon. Augustus, whose vision was the talk of the rangers, saw people, but they were the size of ants. He had once owned a good brass spyglass, but had lost it in a card game several months before. He had meant to get another, but so far had been prevented by poverty from acquiring that useful tool.

Inish Scull had not moved—his binoculars were still trained on the same spot.

"That young brave you chased is talking to Buffalo Hump—I expect it's his son. The young wolf's bold, like the old wolf. We put some bullets in him, though. He's leaking considerable blood."

"Not enough bullets, I guess," Call said. "He made it back to camp."

"Yes, and the rascal had a good look at the troop," Scull said. "He knows our numbers—in fact, he reduced our numbers, the damned scamp. He has a Mexican look—the son of a captive, I expect. Here, gentlemen, I'll share my glass. It's not every day you get to watch Buffalo Hump at breakfast."

It's not every day I'd want to, Call thought, but he eagerly took the binoculars. It took him a moment to focus them, but when he did he saw the great hump man, Buffalo Hump, a figure of nightmare across the southern plains for longer than he and Augustus had been rangers. Call's last good look at the man had come twelve years earlier, during an encounter in the trans-Pecos. Now, there he stood. A young wife had spread a buffalo robe for him, but Buffalo Hump declined to sit. He was looking around, scanning the rims of the canyon. As Call watched, Buffalo Hump looked right at him—or at least at the large rock where they all sat.

"He's looking for us, Captain," Call said. "He just looked right at me."

"Let me look," Augustus said. "He almost got me once, the devil. Let me look."

Call handed Gus the binoculars—when Augustus trained them on Buffalo Hump, the man was still standing, his head raised, looking in their direction.

"He's older, but he ain't dead, Woodrow," Gus said.

When he handed the binoculars back to Captain Scull he felt his stomach quivering—an old fear unsteadied his mind, and even his hand. His first glimpse of Buffalo Hump, which had occurred in a lightning flash many years before, was the most frightening moment in all his time as a fighting man on the Texas frontier. He had only escaped the hump man that night because of darkness, and because he had run as he had never run, before or since, in his life. Even so, he bore a long scar on one hip, from where Buffalo Hump's lance had struck him.

"Did you see, Woodrow?" he said. "He still carries a big lance, like the one he stuck in me."

"Why, you're right, sir," Inish Scull said, studying Buffalo Hump through his binoculars again. "He does have a lance in his hand. He's devoted to the old weapons, I suppose."

"Why not?" Call said. "He come near to wiping out our whole troop the first time we fought him, and he didn't have nothing but a bow and a knife and that lance."

"It's practice, you see," Scull said. "The man's probably practiced with those weapons every day of his life since the age of four."

Call had fought the Comanches as hard as any ranger, and yet, when he had looked down at them through Captain Scull's glass, saw the women scraping hides and the young men racing their ponies, he felt the same contradictory itch of admiration he had felt the first time he fought against Buffalo Hump. They were deadly, merciless killers, but they were also the last free Indians on the southern plains. When the last of them had been killed, or their freedom taken from them, their power broken, the plains around him would be a different place. It would be a safer place, of course, but a flavor would have been taken out of it—the flavor of wildness. Of course, it would be a blessing for the settlers, but the settlers weren't the whole story—not quite.

Inish Scull had lowered his binoculars—he had stopped watching the Indians and was staring into space.

"It's the quality of the opponent that makes soldiering a thing worth doing," he said. "It ain't the cause you fight for—the cause is only a cause. Those torturing fiends down there are the best opponents I've ever faced. I mean to kill them to the last man, if I can—but once it's done I'll miss 'em."

He sighed, and stood up.

"When we finish this fight I expect it will be time to go whip the damn Southern renegades—there'll be some mettle tested in that conflict, let me assure you."

"Renegades, sir," Call said, a good deal puzzled by the remark. "I thought the Comanches were about the last renegades."

Inish Scull smiled and waved a hand.

"I don't mean these poor savages," he said. "I mean the Southern fops who are even now threatening to secede from the Union. There'll be blood spilled from Baltimore to Galveston before that conflict's settled, I'll wager. It's the Southern boys I called 'renegades'—and they *are* renegades, by God. I'd like to ride south on my good horse, Hector, and kill every rebel fop between Charleston and Mobile."

Captain Scull cased his binoculars and looked at the two of them with a mean grin. "Of course, all rebels ain't fops, gentlemen. There's mettle on both sides, plenty of it. That's why it will be a terrible war, when it comes."

"Maybe it won't come, Captain," Augustus said, with a glance at Call. He was uneasily aware that the Captain was a Yankee, whereas he and Call were Southern. If such a war did come, the Captain and the two of them might find themselves on different sides.

"It will come within five years," Inish Scull said confidently. He stood up, walked to the very edge of the cliff, and spat a great arc of tobacco juice into the canyon.

"It'll be brother against brother, and father against son, when that war comes, gentlemen," he said. He turned and was about to walk to his horse when Augustus saw a movement, at the far south end of the canyon. It was just some moving dots, but there had been no dots there a few minutes earlier, when they had been looking at the Comanche horse herd.

"Captain, look," he said. "I think there's more Indians coming."

Inish Scull took out his binoculars and scanned the southern distance with some impatience.

"Damn it, every time I make a sensible plan, something happens to thwart me," he said. "There *are* more Indians coming. If we tried to spook the horse herd now, we'd be heading right into them."

Call looked where the others were looking but could only see a faint, wavy motion.

"Mr. Call, go rouse the men—we better skedaddle," Scull said. "It's old Slow Tree and he's got his whole band with him. We're but twelve men, and Buffalo Hump knows it. Even if he's not in much of a fighting mood, some of the young men are bound to be excited by an advantage like that."

Call knew that was true. It was well enough to look forward to the day when the Comanche would be a broken people, no longer dangerous—but that day was not in sight, and speculation along those lines was premature, in his view. There were now four or five hundred Comanche warriors right below them, a force strong enough to overrun any army the U.S. government could put in the field. Call could now see a line of Indians, moving up from the south. They were still the size of ants, but he knew they would sting a lot worse than ants, if it came to a fight.

"Go, Mr. Call—go," Captain Scull said. "Wake up the nappers and get everyone mounted. We're a tempting morsel, sitting up here on the top of this hole. At least we better make ourselves a morsel in motion."

When Augustus looked to the south again he saw that the lead warriors had scared up a little pocket of buffalo that had been grazing in a small side canyon. There were only four buffalo, running for their lives, with a wave of warriors in pursuit.

"Those buffalo would have done better to stay hid," he remarked. "They'll soon be harvested now."

Inish Scull seemed uninterested in the buffalo.

"I met old Slow Tree once, at a big parley on the Trinity," he said, his binoculars still pointed south. "Quite the diplomat, he is. He'll talk and promise peace, but it's just diplomacy, Mr. McCrae. It won't help the next settler he encounters, out on the baldies somewhere."

He paused and spat.

"I'll take Buffalo Hump over your diplomatic Indians," he said. "Buffalo Hump don't parley—don't believe in it. He knows the white man's promises are worth no more than Slow Tree's. They're worth nothing, and he knows it. He scorns our parleying and peace-piping and the lot. I admire him for it, though I'd kill him in a second if I could get him in range."

Augustus was watching the buffalo chase. Only once, long ago, had he had the opportunity to watch Indians run buffalo. That time it had been two tired Indians and one tired buffalo—in their desperation to bring down the meat they had chased the buffalo right through a ranger encampment, to the astonishment of the rangers, who roused themselves from cards and singsongs just in time to shoot the animal. The tired Comanches, badly disappointed, made it into the brush before the disorganized rangers could think to shoot them.

This time there were four buffalo and at least twenty young Indians in pursuit. Soon the buffalo fanned out, each with four or five Comanches at tail and side. None of the Comanches had guns. Augustus saw one buffalo absorb six arrows without slackening its pace. Another was lanced and almost managed to turn under the horse of the young brave who lanced it, but the brave avoided the charge and returned to strike the buffalo twice more.

Soon, prickling with arrows, the buffalo began to stumble. Two fell, but two ran on.

Inish Scull, by now, was as absorbed in the chase as Augustus.

"What grand sport!" Inish Scull exclaimed. "I wish Hector and I were down there. Big Horse Scull and the Buffalo Horse could show them what for, I reckon!"

Augustus didn't say anything, but he agreed. He and Woodrow had run buffalo a few times; even Woodrow got caught up in the sport of it. Even though they might need the meat, there was always a letdown when the buffalo fell and the skinning and butchering had to begin.

The third buffalo, prickly with arrows, finally fell, but the fourth ran on, although the whole force of Comanches was now after it, the braves crowding one another in order to aim their arrows.

"Look at it—why, you'd think the beast was immortal," Inish Scull said. "There must be thirty arrows in it."

The buffalo, though, was not immortal. Finally it stopped, swung its head at its pursuers, and dropped to its knees. It bellowed a frothy bellow that echoed off the canyon walls. Then it rolled on its side and lay still—the young Comanches milled around it, excited from the chase.

Augustus watched for a moment. The Indian women were already skinning the first of the buffalo to fall.

"That's that—let's be off, sir—else they'll be skinning us next," Captain Scull said.

Augustus mounted, but turned his horse to watch the scene for another moment. He hadn't done the chasing or made the kill, but, for some reason, he felt the same letdown as if he had. The Comanche braves had stopped milling. They simply sat on their horses, looking down at the fallen beast. Though he could barely see the fallen animal—it was just a dot on the canyon floor—in his mind's eye he saw it clearly. He was reminded of an old bull buffalo he and Call and Bigfoot Wallace, the famous scout, had struggled to kill years before on the Mexican plain. They had shot the beast more than twenty times, chased it until one of their horses died, and had finally had to dispatch it with their bowie knives, a process that bloodied Augustus from shoulder to calf.

The Comanche boy who had dealt the fourth buffalo the final lance hit was probably just as bloody—that buffalo, too, must have poured blood from a number of wounds before it rolled its eyes up in death.

Looking down on the scene from high above, Augustus, though he couldn't say why, felt a mood of sadness take him. He knew he ought to be going, but he could not stop looking at the scene far below. A line of Indian women were moving out from the camp, ready to help cut up the meat.

Inish Scull paused a moment. He saw that his young ranger had been affected by the chase they had just observed, and its inevitable ending.

"*Post coitum omne animal triste*," he said, leaning over to put a hand, for a moment, on the young man's shoulder. "That's Aristotle."

"What, sir?" Augustus asked. "I expect that's Latin, but what does it mean?"

" 'After copulation every animal is sad,' " the Captain said. "It's true, too—though who can say why? The seed flies, and the seeder feels blue."

"Why is it?" Augustus asked. He knew, from his own memories, that the Captain had stated a truth. Much as he liked poking, there was that moment, afterward, when something made his spirits dip, for a time.

"I don't know why and I guess Aristotle didn't either, because he didn't say," Scull observed. "But it's not only rutting that can bring on that little gloom. Killing can do it too—especially if you're killing something sizable, like a buffalo, or a man. Something that has a solid claim to life."

He was silent for a moment, a little square cut chaw of tobacco in his hand.

"I grant that it's a curious thing," he said. "The acts ain't much alike, and yet the gloom's alike. First excitement, then sadness. Those red boys killed their game, and they needed to kill it, too. A buffalo is to them what a store would be to us. They have to kill the buffalo to live. And they have killed it. But now they're sad, and they don't know why."

Well, I don't know why neither, Augustus thought. I wish that old man who talked about it to begin with had said why.

In a moment they turned back toward camp. Augustus fell in behind the big horse. When they came over the first little rise they saw the camp boys, rushing around like ants, packing up.

9.

"WHERE IS HIS SCALP? I don't see it," Buffalo Hump said, when Blue Duck walked up to him, dripping blood. "I thought you were going to bring me the scalp of Gun-in-the-Water?"

"He is quick," Blue Duck admitted. "He shot me while he was

shitting. I didn't know anyone could shoot straight while they were shitting."

Buffalo Hump looked the boy over. He saw no wounds that looked serious.

"I had another son once," Buffalo Hump said. "Gun-in-the-Water shot him too—shot him dead. He was almost drowned in the Brazos River but he was still quick enough to kill my son. You're lucky he didn't kill you too. Where is your horse?"

The boy stood before him wearing a sullen look. No doubt he had run across the canyon, hoping to be praised because he had gone alone against the whites and been wounded. It was a brave thing: Buffalo Hump didn't doubt the boy's courage. Blue Duck always led the charge, and could not sleep for days, from excitement, when a raid was planned.

Bravery was important in war, of course, but that did not mean that a warrior could afford to neglect the practicalities of war. The boy seemed to have rolled much of the way down the canyon and kept his weapons undamaged, which was good. On the other hand, he had lost a horse, which was not good. Also, he had attacked a proven warrior, Gun-in-the-Water, without being sure of his kill. Courage would not keep a warrior alive for long if courage was not backed up by judgment.

"My horse is dead," Blue Duck admitted. "Silver Hair McCrae shot him—I was running for my life. Big Horse Scull almost cut me with the long knife."

Buffalo Hump motioned to Hair-on-the-Lip, indicating that she was to tend to the boy's wounds. Slow Tree was approaching, at the head of his band, and would have to be greeted with the proper ceremony. Though Buffalo Hump would have liked to lecture the boy some more, he could not do it with Slow Tree and his warriors only half a mile from camp. He looked sternly at his young wife, Lark—he did not want her tending Blue Duck's wounds. The women made much of Blue Duck, old women and young women too. He did not want Lark to be doctoring his handsome son. He had seen many unfortunate things happen, in his years as a chief. Sometimes young women, married to old men, could not resist coupling with the old men's sons, a thing that made bitter blood. If Lark was reckless with Blue Duck he would beat her so that she could not move for three days, and then he would drive Blue Duck out of camp, or else kill him.

"Why is Slow Tree coming?" Blue Duck asked, as Hair-on-the-Lip began to poke at the wound in his side.

Buffalo Hump walked away without answering. It was none of Blue Duck's business why Slow Tree had chosen to visit. Slow Tree could come and go as he pleased, as did all the Comanche. He himself was not particularly pleased to see the old man coming, though. Slow Tree was very pompous; he insisted on making long speeches that were boring to listen to. Buffalo Hump had long since heard all that Slow Tree had to say, and did not look forward to listening to him anymore. Because he was old and lazy, Slow Tree had even begun to argue that the Comanche should live in peace with the Texans. He thought they ought to go onto reservations and learn to grow corn. He pointed out that the buffalo were no longer plentiful; soon the Comanche would have to find something else to eat. There were not enough deer and antelope to feed the tribe, nor enough wild roots and berries. The People would starve unless they made peace with the whites and learned their agriculture.

Buffalo Hump knew that on some points Slow Tree was right. He himself had ridden all the way north to the Republican River to find enough buffalo, in the fall just passed. The whites were killing more and more buffalo each year, and the People would, someday, have to find something else to eat. Such facts were plain; he did not need a long speech from Slow Tree to explain what was obvious.

What Buffalo Hump disagreed with was Slow Tree's solution. He himself did not like corn, and did not plan to grow it. Instead, since the white men were there in his land, his country, he meant to live off *their* animals: their horses, their pigs, and particularly their cattle. The land along the Nueces boiled with cattle. They were as plentiful as buffalo had once been. He himself preferred horsemeat to the meat of the cow, but the meat of the cow would suffice, if it proved impossible to kill enough buffalo or steal enough horses to get the band through the winter.

Some of the cattle were as wild as any buffalo, but because they were small animals the Texans seemed to think they owned them. The cattle were so numerous that the Comanches, once they practiced a little, could easily steal or kill enough of them to survive.

Buffalo Hump considered himself as wild as the buffalo or the antelope or the bear; he would not be owned by the whites and he would not tear up the grass and grow corn. But Slow Tree, evidently, was no longer too wild to be owned, so now he talked of peace with the whites, though that was not the reason for his visit. The old man knew that Buffalo Hump's band had buffalo—what he had come for was to eat.

Slow Tree was a great Comanche chief, and Buffalo Hump meant to welcome him with proper ceremony. But that did not mean that he trusted the old man. Slow Tree had been a great killer, when he was younger, and an unscrupulous killer too. Slow Tree was old; he had heard things from the old women of the tribe that the younger Comanches did not know. Long ago Buffalo Hump had been told by his grandmother that he could only die if his great hump was pierced. Old Slow Tree knew of this prophecy. Several times, over the years, in camp here and there, usually after feasting and dancing, Buffalo Hump would get an uneasy feeling. Three times he had turned and found that Slow Tree was behind him. Once Slow Tree had had a lance in his hand; another time he held a rifle, and he had had a cold look in his eye—the look of the killer. Slow Tree had long been jealous of Buffalo Hump's prowess as a raider. Once, on a raid all the way to the Great Water, Buffalo Hump had run off three thousand horses—it was a raid all the young warriors sang about and dreamed of equaling. Slow Tree, though fierce in battle, had never made such a raid. He didn't like it when the young men sang of Buffalo Hump.

But, always, because of the uneasy feeling he got, Buffalo Hump had turned before Slow Tree could strike with the lance or fire the gun. He had saved himself, but he had never trusted Slow Tree and still didn't. The fact that the man was old did not mean he was harmless.

Buffalo Hump turned to look at his young wife, Lark; her eyes were cast down in modesty. Heavy Leg and Hair-on-the-Lip, his other wives, had stripped the boy, Blue Duck, in order to tend his wounds. He stood naked not far from Lark, but Lark kept her eyes cast down. She was the wife of Buffalo Hump—she looked at her husband, when she wanted to look at a man.

Blue Duck became impatient with the women, who were smearing grease on his wounds.

"There are only a few whites up there," he said to his father—he pointed toward the top of the canyon. "I killed one of them last night—there are only a few left. We could kill them all if we hurry."

"I imagine you scared them so badly that they are running away by now," Buffalo Hump said casually. "We would have to chase them to the Brazos to kill them, and I don't want to chase them. I have to wait for Slow Tree and listen to him tell me I should be growing corn."

Blue Duck was sorry he had spoken. His father had only mocked him, when he said the whites were afraid of him. Big Horse Scull was not afraid of him, nor Gun-in-the-Water, nor McCrae. He wanted to go back and kill the Texans, but Buffalo Hump had already turned and was walking away. Slow Tree had entered the camp and had to be shown the proper respect. Blue Duck wasn't interested in the old chief himself, but he had heard that Slow Tree had several pretty wives. He was impatient with the women who were dressing his wounds—he wanted to go over and have a look at Slow Tree's wives.

"Hurry up," he said, to Hair-on-the-Lip. "I have to go stand with my father. Slow Tree is here."

Hair-on-the-Lip didn't like the rude boy, whelp of a Mexican woman. Rosa, the boy's mother, had once been Buffalo Hump's favorite, but she had run away and frozen to death on the Washita River. Now Lark was his favorite—Lark was young and plump—but he still kept Hair-on-the-Lip with him many nights, because she had the gift of stories. She told him many stories about the animal people, but not just the animal people. She knew some old Comanche women who were lustful and full of wickedness. The old women hid in the bushes, looking for young men. Buffalo Hump had had only a few wives, unlike Slow Tree and some of the other chiefs. He told Hair-on-the-Lip that it would be too much trouble to have more wives. He wanted to save his strength for hunting, and for fighting the whites. He liked to hear about women, though, particularly the old lustful women who were always in the bushes, trying to get young boys to couple with them. Many nights Hair-on-the-Lip had lain with Buffalo Hump, while the cold wind blew around the lodges. Hair-on-the-Lip was not pretty and she was not young—the young women of the tribe wondered why such a great chief would stay with her, when he could have the youngest and prettiest wives.

Those younger women didn't know how much he liked the stories.

10.

CLARA WAS UNPACKING some new crockery for the store when she happened to glance up and see Maggie Tilton crossing the street—Maggie, too anxious to stop herself, was coming to inquire about Woodrow Call. Every few days Maggie came on the same errand, thinking Clara might have some news of the rangers. Clara didn't—but she could well understand Maggie's anxiety—she herself grew worried when several weeks passed without news of Gus McCrae. Except for the anxiety, though, their positions in regard to the men in question were opposite: Maggie's one hope was that Woodrow Call would someday unbend enough to marry her, while Clara was doing everything she could to check her foolish passion for Gus McCrae. Clara was doing her best *not* to marry Gus, while Maggie pinned all her hopes on finally marrying Woodrow. Maggie and Clara talked little—their respective stations didn't permit it. What little conversation they had was usually just about the small purchases Maggie made. Yet they had become, if not friends, at least women who were sympathetic to one another because of their common problem: what to do about the menfolk.

The dishes and cups Clara was unwrapping and setting on the counter were nice, serviceable brown stoneware from Pennsylvania. Only the day before she had had a bit of a tiff with her father, over the stoneware. Usually George Forsythe let Clara have her way, when it came to ordering dishware, but, in this case, he happened to look at the bill and had what for him was a fit. He took off his coat, put it back on, told Clara she was bankrupting him with her impulsive ordering, and walked out of the store, not to return for three hours. Clara was more amused than offended by her father's little fit. George Forsythe considered that he and he alone knew what was best for the solid frontier citizens who frequented their store. Whenever Clara ordered something that appealed to her, even if it was as simple as a pewter pitcher, her father invariably concluded that it was too fancy; soon the store would fill up with things Clara liked that the customers either didn't want or couldn't afford; and ruin would follow.

"I've had a store on this street since it started being a street," he informed his daughter—sometimes, when he was particularly exercised, he even wagged his finger at her—"and I know one thing: the people of Austin won't shell out for your fancy Eastern goods."

"Now, that's not true, Pa," Clara protested. "Mrs. Scull shells out for them. Besides, nearly all our goods are Eastern goods. That's about the only place they make *goods*, seems like."

"As for that woman, I consider her little better than a harlot," her father said. Most of the citizens of Austin looked up to George Forsythe; they had voted him mayor twice; but Inez Scull looked *down* on him, as she would on any tradesman, and she was quick to let him know it.

"Just hold off on the Philadelphia plates," her father told her, at the height of his fit, just before he walked out. "Plain plates and plain cutlery will serve around here just fine."

The point of the brown stoneware, as Clara meant to tell him once he cooled down, was that it *was* plain; and yet it was satisfying to look at and solid besides. Clara loved the look and feel of it; she believed her father to be wrong, in this instance. After all, she had been working with him in the store for a decade; she felt she ought to have a right to order a little nice crockery now and then, if she took the notion. If Inez Scull happened to like it she would buy all of it anyway; Inez Scull always bought all of anything she liked, whether it was a swatch of pretty cloth or two new sidesaddles that happened to appeal to her. George Forsythe, seeing her shaky old butler loaded down with two new sidesaddles, could not resist asking why she needed two.

"Why, one for Sunday, of course," Inez said, with a flounce. "I can't be seen in the same old saddle seven days a week."

"But those two are just alike," George pointed out.

"Nonetheless, one is for Sunday—I doubt you'd understand, sir," Inez said, as she swept out of the store.

Clara loved the look and feel of the new stoneware and felt sure her father was wrong in assuming that it wouldn't appeal to local tastes. After all, Austin was no longer just a frontier outpost, as it had been when her father and mother opened the store. There were respectable women in Austin now, even educated women, and they weren't all as high-handed as Inez Scull. Clara herself didn't care for either Scull—the famous Captain had twice taken advantage of her father's absence to attempt to be familiar with her, once even trying to look down her bodice on a hot day when she had worn a loose dress. On that occasion Clara slapped him smartly—she considered that she had tolerated quite enough, famous man or not—but the Captain had merely bowed to her and bought himself a speckled cravat. But, like it or not, the Sculls were too wealthy to throw out entirely—had it not been for their profligate spending, her father might, at times when drought dried up the farms and sapped the resources of the local livestock men, have had to worry seriously about the bankruptcy he accused Clara of bringing upon him.

His fits, though, Clara knew, weren't really about the store, or the ordering, or the Eastern crockery; they were about the fact that she was unmarried, and getting no younger. Suitor after suitor had failed to measure up; her twenties were flying past, and yet, there she was, still on her father's hands. She ought, in his view, to have long since become a well-established wife, with a hardworking husband to support her.

Many hardworking men, solid citizens, well able to support a wife, had sat in the Forsythe parlor and made their proposals. All were refused. Some licked their wounds for a few years and came back with new proposals, only to have those rejected too. After two tries and two failures most of the local men gave up and took wives who were less exacting; only Augustus McCrae, and a man named Bob Allen, a rancher who wished to venture up to Nebraska and trade in horses, persisted year after year. In his own mind and everyone else's, Gus McCrae, the proud Texas Ranger, seemed to have the inside track; yet in Clara's mind, though she dearly loved Gus McCrae, the issues were not so clear, nor the resolution so simple.

Still, her father could not be blamed too much for worrying that she might never find—or at least might never accept—a decent mate. Her mother, so sickly that she rarely ventured downstairs, worried too, but said little. The thing they all knew was that there was hardly another respectable young woman in Austin who, at Clara's age, was still unmarried.

In fact, one of the few women Clara's age who *was* still single was Maggie Tilton, the young woman who was walking slowly and a little forlornly across the dusty street toward the store. Maggie, though, could not be included in the Forsythes' reckoning, because she was not one of the respectable young women of Austin. Inez Scull might behave like a harlot, while enjoying the prestige and position of being the Captain's wife, but Maggie Tilton *was* a harlot. She had survived some rough years in the tents and shacks of Austin, moved to San Antonio for a bit, and then came back to Austin. She had tried to rise but failed and had come back to be where Woodrow Call was—or at least where he was quartered when the rangers were not in the field.

Clara watched, with interest, as Maggie came up the steps and hesitated a moment, as she looked at herself in the glass window; it was as if she had to reassure herself that she looked respectable enough to enter a regular store—Maggie always stopped and looked at herself before she would venture in to buy a ribbon, or a powder for headaches, or any little article of adornment.

In Clara's view Maggie looked plenty respectable. Her clothes were simple but clean, and she was always neat to a fault, as well as being modestly dressed. Madame Scull, for one, could scarcely be bothered to conceal her ample bosom—even Clara's own father, George Forsythe, the former mayor, had trouble keeping his eyes off Inez Scull's bosom, when it was rolling like the tide practically under his nose.

Maggie, though, was always proper to a fault; there was nothing flashy about her appearance. And yet she did what she did with men, with only the sadness in her eyes to tell of it, though that sadness told of it eloquently, at least to Clara. Sometimes Clara wished she *could* talk to Maggie—she longed to shake her good and tell her to forget about that hardheaded Woodrow Call. In her view Maggie ought to marry some decent farmer, many of whom would have been only too pleased to have her, despite her past.

Sometimes, lying alone at night in her room above the hardware store, a room that had been hers since birth, to which, so far, she had been reluctant to admit any man—though Gus McCrae had impulsively crowded into it once or twice—Clara thought of Maggie Tilton, in her poor room down the hill. She tried, once or twice, in her restlessness, to imagine that she and Maggie had traded places; that she was what Maggie was, a whore, available to any man who paid the money. But Clara would never make the imagining work, not quite. She could picture herself down the hill, in a shack or a tent, but when it came to the business with men she was not able to picture it, not really. Though fervent in her kissing with Gus McCrae—fervent and even bold, riding alone with him into the country, to swim at a particular spring—she still stopped short, well short, of what Maggie Tilton did regularly, for money, in order to survive.

Clara stopped far shorter with Bob Allen, the large, silent horse trader; despite two years of courtship, Mr. Allen had not yet touched her hand. Augustus, who considered Mr. Allen an ignorant fool, would never have put up with such restraints. Gus had to touch her and kiss her, to dance with her and swim with her, and was sulky and sometimes rude when she refused him more. "It's your fault I'm a drunkard and a whorer," Gus told her, more than once. "If you'd just marry me I'd be sober forever, and I'd stay home besides."

Clara didn't believe the part about staying home; Gus McCrae was by nature much too restless for her taste. The rangering was just an excuse, she felt. If there were no Indians to chase, and no bandits, Gus would still find reasons to roam. He was not a settled man, nor did she feel she could settle him. He would always be off with Woodrow Call, beyond the settlements somewhere, adventuring.

Still, she felt a little guilty, where Gus was concerned—she knew there was some justice in his complaint. Though she suffered when he was in the whore tents, somehow she could not resign herself, or commit herself, to begin the great business of married life with him. Though Gus moved her in ways no other man ever had or, she feared, ever would, something in her still refused.

Clara tried to look at life honestly, though, and when she thought closely about herself and Gus, and Maggie and Call, she could not feel that her refusals gained her any honor or moral credit. Was she any better than Maggie Tilton, who at least gave an honest service for money paid, and met an honest need?

Clara didn't think she was better, and she knew she was as hard on Gus McCrae—whom she dearly loved—as Woodrow Call was on Maggie Tilton.

Clara didn't like—indeed, couldn't abide—Woodrow Call. His appearance, even on the mildest errand, brought out a streak of malice in her which she could not restrain. She seldom let him leave her company without cutting him with some small criticisms. Yet Woodrow Call was a much respected ranger, courageous and even in judgment, the last being a quality that Augustus McCrae could not yet lay claim to, though he was as courageous as any man. Perhaps

Call even loved Maggie, in his way; he sometimes bought her small trinkets, once even a bonnet, and had twice come to fetch medicines for her, when she was poorly. There must be good in the man, else why would Maggie pine so, when he was away? She surely didn't pine for every man who paid her money and used her body.

Still, the one thing Maggie needed most was marriage; it might be the one thing Gus McCrae needed most, as well. But Call couldn't or wouldn't give it to Maggie, and she couldn't give it to Gus. It was a linkage that irked her, but that she could neither ignore nor deny.

When Maggie stepped in the door, after giving herself a thorough inspection, Clara smiled at her, and Maggie, surprised as she always was by Clara's friendliness, shyly smiled back.

"Why, it's you. How I wish we were sisters," Clara said, surprising herself and startling Maggie so deeply that she blushed. But the store was empty; what harm could the remark do? Besides, it was what she felt—it had always chaffed Clara that she was expected to live by rules she hadn't made; all the rules were made by men, and what dull rules they were! How much pleasanter life would be if she could treat Maggie as she would treat a sister, or, at least, as she would treat a friend.

"Oh, Miss Forsythe, thank you," Maggie said. She knew she had received a great compliment, one so unexpected that it left her abashed and silenced; for years she was to remember Clara's impulsive statement and felt happiness at the memory. She also felt a little puzzlement. Clara Forsythe was the most respected and sought-after young woman in Austin. Many of her own customers, the young ones particularly, worshiped Clara; several had even proposed to her. Maggie could not imagine why a woman in Clara's position would even want her friendship, much less want her for a sister.

Clara realized she had embarrassed her customer and tried to put her at ease by directing her attention to the stoneware.

"We just got these cups and plates from Pennsylvania," she said. "My pa thinks they're too fancy, but I think they're the very thing."

Maggie agreed, but she only let her eyes linger on the nice brown crockery for a moment. She had to be cautious when shopping, so as not to start yearning for fine things she could never afford. She *did* like pretty things too much; once her fancy seized on a particular ring or dress or trinket, she could scarcely think of anything else, for days. She especially wanted to impress on Woodrow that she was a good manager. She didn't owe a cent to anyone, and had never asked Woodrow—or any man—for a cent more than she was due. She had long since stopped wanting Woodrow Call to pay her, when he came to her—but he insisted, leaving the money under a plate or a pillow if she refused to take it.

Maggie, just for a moment, wished she *could* be Clara Forsythe's friend. If they could talk freely she felt sure Clara would understand why she no longer wanted Woodrow's money. Clara's smile was frank and friendly, but before Maggie could even enjoy her little fancy an old man with a stringy beard came in and stomped right between them.

"Horseshoe nails?" he asked Clara.

"Yes sir, in the back—it's the bin on the right," Clara said.

With a customer in the store Maggie didn't feel she ought to be talking to Miss Forsythe about crockery—much less about anything else. Besides, the man was a customer of hers as well. His name was Cully Barnstone—he had visited her frequently in the last year. His presence, as he sacked up horseshoe nails, drove home a point that Maggie knew she should not, even momentarily, have forgotten. She and Clara Forsythe weren't sisters, and couldn't be friends. Clara had never been offered money for the service of love, and never would be. She might have her own difficulties with Augustus McCrae, but she would never experience the shame of being given money by the one man in the world she wanted to give herself to.

Clara was annoyed with old Cully Barnstone, for coming in just when she might have had a word of conversation with Maggie; but there was nothing she could do about it. The store was open; anyone who wanted to buy something was free to come in. When Mr.

Barnstone came to the counter to pay for his nails, Maggie turned away. She wandered listlessly around for a bit, keeping well to herself; she picked up a bonnet and a little hat but put both back without trying them on. In the end she merely bought a packet of darning needles and some red thread.

"Thank you," she said, when Clara gave her her change.

"There's no news from those wild ranger boys," Clara said. "I suppose they're still up on the plains, freezing their ears."

"Yes, it's been sharp weather—I expect they're cold," Maggie said, as she went out the door.

11.

WHEN PEA EYE set out north with the rangers on his first expedition, he was as proud as he had ever been in his life. Mr. Call, who found him in a cornfield, fed him, and persuaded Captain Scull to give him a tryout as a ranger, had emphasized to him that it was just a tryout.

"We need men and I think you'll do," Call told him, rather sternly. "But you watch close and follow orders. I told the Captain I'd vouch for you—don't you disgrace me now and make me regret speaking up for you."

"I won't, sir, I'll watch close," Pea Eye said, not entirely sure what he would have to be watching.

"If you get scalped, don't sit around yowling, either," Gus McCrae said. "People survive scalpings fine if they don't yowl."

He said it to josh the boy a little, but Pea Eye's big solemn eyes opened a little wider.

"What's the procedure, then?" he asked. Long Bill Coleman, an experienced man, had told him there were procedures for every eventuality, in rangering.

Pea Eye meant to do all he could to avoid a scalping, but in the event that one occurred he wanted to know what steps he should take—or not take.

"Just sit there calmly and bite a stick," Gus told him, doing his best to keep a straight face. "Somebody will come and sew up your head as soon as there's a lull in the killing."

"Why'd you tell him that?" Call asked later, when he and Augustus were cleaning their weapons. "Of course he'll yowl if he gets scalped."

"No he won't, because I instructed him not to," Augustus said. "But if I get scalped you'll hear some fine yowling, I bet."

On the trek north Pea Eye's job was to inspect the horses' feet every night, to see that no horses had picked up thorns or small rocks that might cause lameness. In the event of a chase a lame horse would put its rider in serious jeopardy; Pea Eye inspected every hoof at night and made sure that the horses were well secured.

Then the sleet came and he had a hard time looking close. In the worst of the storm he could barely see his horse; at night he had to deal with the horses' feet mostly by feel. His hands got so cold when he worked that he was afraid he might have missed something in one hoof or another; but none of the horses went lame.

Deets, the black man, seeing Pea Eye try to inspect the hooves in the dark, brought him a light and stayed with him while he went down the line of horses, picking up their hooves one by one. It was a kind thing, which Pea Eye never forgot. Most of the men stayed as close to the fire as they could get, but Deets left the warmth and came to help him make sure that the horses' feet were sound.

On the fourth day of cold, Pea Eye began to wish Mr. Call had just left him in the cornfield. Proud as he was to be a ranger, he didn't know if he could survive the cold. He got so cold at night and in the bitter mornings that he even forgot to be afraid of scalping Indians, or even death. All he could think of was how nice it would be to be in a cabin with a big fireplace and a roaring fire. It was so cold his teeth ached—he began to try to sneak food into his mouth in small quick bites, so the cold wouldn't get in and freeze his teeth worse than they already were.

Augustus McCrae, who seemed able to ignore the cold, noticed Pea sneaking in the tiny bites and decided a little more joshing wouldn't hurt.

"You ought to duck your chin down into your shirt, if you're going to try and eat in this breeze," he said. "If you ain't careful your tongue will freeze and snap off like you'd snap a stick."

"Snap off?" Pea Eye asked, horrified. "How could it snap off?"

"Why, from talking," Gus said, with a grin. "All you have to do is ask for a cup of coffee and your tongue's liable to fall right into the cup."

Later Pea Eye told Deets what Mr. McCrae had said and they debated the matter quietly. Pea was so cautious about opening his mouth that he could barely make himself heard.

"Your tongue's inside your head," Deets pointed out. "It's got protection. Ain't like your finger. Now a finger might snap off, I expect, or a toe."

Pea Eye's fingers were so cold he almost wished they would snap off, to relieve the pain, but they didn't snap off. He had been blowing on his fingers, blowing and blowing, hoping to get a little warmth into them, when the Indians attacked and killed Ranger Watson. Pea Eye had been about to step right past the man, in order to take cover behind some saddles, when he heard Jimmy Watson give a small grunt—just a small quick grunt, and in that instant his life departed. If Pea Eye had not moved just when he did, making for the saddles, the bullet might have hit him—it passed just behind his leg and went only another yard or more before striking Jim Watson dead.

No one in the troop was as glad to see the sun shine, the morning they finally headed south, as Pea Eye Parker.

"The dern old sun, it's finally come out again," he said, to Long Bill Coleman.

To Pea Eye's surprise, he almost cried, so happy was he to see the familiar sun. He had always despised cloudy weather, but he had never despised it as much as he had during the recent days of cold.

Fortunately Long Bill Coleman took no interest in Pea Eye's remark and didn't see him dash away a tear. Long Bill was attempting to shave, using a bowl of water so cold that it had a fine skim of ice on it; he considered the whole trip an intolerable waste of time—in that it was no different from most expeditions against the Comanches, only, in this instance, colder.

"Me, I'll take Mexico over these dern windy plains," he told Augustus McCrae, when the troop was on the move south.

"Me too, Billy—there's plenty of whores in Mexico, and pretty ones, too," Gus remarked.

"Now, Gus, I'm married, don't be reminding me of the temptations of the flesh," Long Bill admonished. "I got enough flesh right there at home—there's no shortage of flesh on Pearl."

Augustus thought the comment dull, if not foolish.

"I know you've got a fat wife, Billy," he said. "What's your point about Mexico? I thought that was what we were talking about."

"Why, the point is, it's convenient," Long Bill said. "In Mexico there's Mexicans."

The remark seemed even duller to Augustus than the one before it. Since marriage to Pearl, Long Bill had lost much of his liveliness, in Gus's opinion. He had grown dull, cautious, and even pious. His wife, Pearl, was a large woman of little attraction, a bully and a nag. Had he himself been married to Pearl he would have endeavored to spend as much time as possible in the nearest bordello.

"In Mexico there's usually someone to ask where the bandits are," Long Bill went on. "And there's trees to hang them from, once we corner them. Out here on the plains there's no one to ask directions from, and if we do see an Indian he's apt to be way down in the canyon, where you'd have to scramble to get at him."

Augustus didn't answer. The fact was, he missed Clara. No amount of easily located bandits, or hanging trees, made up for that one fact. A good two-week jaunt on the prairies always lifted his spirits, but then, inevitably, there'd come a night by the campfire or a groggy morning when he'd remember his old, sweet love and wonder if he'd been foolish to let his long courtship lapse, just for the sake of adventure. Despite her standoffish ways, Augustus felt, most of the time, that there was little likelihood that Clara would actually marry anyone but himself; at other times, though, the demon of doubt seized him and he was not so sure.

Pea Eye found Mr. McCrae puzzling—Mr. Call he was more comfortable with, because Mr. Call only spoke to him of practical matters. Mr. McCrae *sounded* convincing, when he talked, but a good deal of what he said was meant in jest, like the business about his tongue snapping off.

The hardest part of Pea Eye's job, as the company farrier, was to see that the Captain's big horse, Hector, did not get anything wrong with his feet. Pea Eye had never seen an elephant, but he doubted that even an elephant had feet as heavy and hard to work with as Hector. The Captain had to have special horseshoes forged, to fit the big horse's feet. When Pea Eye did manage to lift one of Hector's hooves the big horse would immediately let his weight sag onto Pea Eye—he could just support the weight, but it left him no strength with which to clean out the hoof. Several times Deets, seeing his plight, had come over and helped him support the big horse long enough that his feet could be properly cleaned.

"Much obliged," Pea Eye always said, when Deets helped him.

"Welcome, sir," Deets would reply.

It unnerved Pea Eye to be addressed as "sir," though he knew that was how black people normally addressed white people. He didn't know if it would be correct just to ask Deets to call him by his name; he intended to discuss the point with Mr. Call when the time was right.

Then, to his dismay, though they traveled south through a day of sunlight, the cold struck again. On the third day of their ride south the sky turned slate black and an icy wind was soon slicing at their backs and making their hands sting.

That night Hector leaned particularly heavily on Pea Eye, and Deets was too busy preparing a meal to help him. Pressing up against the big horse caused Pea Eye to break a sweat; when he finished, the sweat froze on his shirt before he could even walk back to the fire. The sun had just gone down; Pea Eye did not know how he was going to make it through the long winter night. He had only a thin coat and one blanket; few of the men had more. Deets didn't have a coat at all, just an old quilt he kept wrapped around himself as he worked.

It was Deets who showed Pea a way to survive, as the cold deepened. Deets took a little spade and dug out one side of a small hummock of dirt; he dug it so that it formed a sort of bank. Then he made a small fire up against the bank of dirt. He brought a few coals over in a small pan, and, from the coals, made a fire near enough to the bank that the bank caught the heat and reflected it back.

"Here, sit close," Deets said, to Pea Eye. "It ain't much, but it will warm us."

He was right. Pea Eye could never get close enough to the big campfire to derive more than a few moments of warmth from it. But the little fire reflected off the bank of dirt, warmed his hands and his feet. His back still froze and his ears pained him badly, but he knew he would survive. Even with the good fire it was difficult to sleep, though; he would nod for a few minutes and then an icy curl of wind would slip under his collar and chill his very backbone.

Once, in a few minutes of sleep, Pea Eye had a terrible dream. He saw himself freeze as he was walking; he stopped and became immobile on the white plain, like a tree of ice. Pea Eye tried to call out to the rangers, but his voice could not penetrate the sheath of ice. The rangers rode on and he was alone.

When he woke from the dream there was a red line on the eastern horizon; the sun glowed for a moment and then passed above the slatelike clouds, which reddened for a little while but did not allow the sunlight through.

"Much obliged for keeping this fire going," Pea Eye said—all night Deets had fed the fire little sticks.

"You welcome, sir," Deets said.

Pea Eye, cold but glad to be alive, could not contain himself about the "sir" any longer.

"You don't need to be sirring me, Deets," he said. "I ain't a sir, and I doubt I ever will be one."

Deets was startled by the remark. He had never heard such an opinion from a white man, never once in his life. In Texas a black man who didn't call a white man "sir" could get in trouble quick.

Of course Pea Eye wasn't really a grown man yet—he was just a tall boy. Deets supposed his youth might account for the remark.

"What'll I say?" he asked, with a puzzled look. "I got to call you something."

"Why, just 'Pea Eye' will do," Pea Eye said. "I'm just plain 'Pea Eye' so far."

Deets didn't think it *would* do, not in the hearing of the other rangers at least. He turned away and went to gather a few more sticks—the fire was burning well but he needed a little time in which to think about what Mr. Pea had just said.

Then, while he was pulling up a half-buried twist of sagebrush, it occurred to him that his mind had found a solution. He thought of the tall white boy as "Mr. Pea"—he would call him "Mr. Pea."

When he came back with the wood the young ranger was still holding his hands to the little fire.

"I guess I just call you 'Mr. Pea,' if it suits you," Deets said.

"Why, yes—that'll do fine," Pea Eye said. "I guess I'm a mister—I guess everybody's a mister."

No, I ain't, black people ain't, Deets thought—but he didn't say it.

12.

FAMOUS SHOES was eating a good fat mallard duck when the Comanche boys found him. He had noticed some ducks on the south Canadian and had crept down to the water and made a clever snare, during the night. His trip to the Washita had been a disappointment. He did not find his grandmother, who had gone to live on the sweet-grass hills near the Arkansas River, but he did find his Aunt Neeta, a quarrelsome old woman who was living with some mixed-blood trapping people in a filthy little camp. The trapping people mostly trapped skunks and muskrats—there were hides everywhere, some of them pretty smelly. The minute he arrived his aunt began to upbraid him about a knife she had lent him years before which he had broken accidentally. At the time he had been trying to remove a good length of chain from an old wagon that had fallen apart on the prairies. He thought the chain might come in handy, but all the chain did was break the tip off his aunt's knife. Only the tip was broken, most of the knife would still cut, but his Aunt Neeta considered that the knife was now useless and had never forgiven Famous Shoes for his carelessness. Famous Shoes only stayed on the Washita long enough to be courteous, before making his way back to the south Canadian, where he discovered the little flock of fat ducks.

Then the five Comanche boys showed up and began to talk about killing him. One of the boys wanted to kill him immediately, just because he was a Kickapoo, and another because he had scouted for Big Horse Scull. The rudest boy, though, was Blue Duck, who wanted to kill him just because he was there. Famous Shoes did not think the boys would do him much harm. In any case he was hungry—he went on eating the duck while the boys walked around him, saying ugly things. They were just boys, it was normal that they would strut around and make rude remarks. The boys had been chasing a deer when they found him, but they had lost its track. Famous Shoes had seen the deer only that morning, running east. The Comanche boys were so impatient that they had over-looked a plain track and let the deer get away. The deer had looked exhausted, too—the boys would have had it if only they had kept their minds on their business.

"That deer you were chasing got away," he told them. "There are plenty of fat ducks on this river, though."

"We want to kill Big Horse today, where is he?" Blue Duck asked. "He tried to cut me with the long knife but I was too quick. A vision woman taught me how to fly, so I flew down into the canyon and got away."

"You are lucky you found that vision woman," Famous Shoes said. He didn't believe that Blue Duck could fly, but the boy had such a bad reputation for killing people that he thought the best thing to do was be polite, keep eating his duck, and hope to get through the morning without being shot. Blue Duck had an old rifle and kept pointing it at him as he ate, a very rude thing.

"You come to our camp—my father might want to torture you," Blue Duck said. "He is angry because you brought Big Horse here."

"Big Horse is chasing Kicking Wolf," Famous Shoes informed them. "He has given up and is on his way south by now. He is not going to bother your father."

Nevertheless he was forced to humor the boys. Instead of settling down they began to threaten him with arrows. Famous Shoes decided he had better go with them—they were young boys; they might want to take a scalp just for practice. He trotted along in front of them as they made their way to the canyon. He was not worried that Buffalo Hump would torture him. Buffalo Hump owed him a debt and would never offer him violence, even though he scouted for the Texans.

The debt had come about because of Buffalo Hump's grandmother, a famous prophet woman. One winter years before, when there were few buffalo on the prairies where the Comanche hunted, the tribe had had to move north, beyond the Arkansas. The old woman's death was at hand; she was too weak to make the cold journey to the north. So, in the way of such things, she was left with a good fire and enough food to last her until her passing. Everyone said goodbye and the band went north to seek game.

But the old woman's time was slow in coming. When Famous Shoes chanced upon her, in her little dying place on the Quitaque, she was weak but still alive. Her fire was out and her food was gone but she was restless with visions and could not die. Famous Shoes had been in Mexico and had come back to seek advice from his grandfather; but, instead of finding his grandfather, he found Buffalo Hump's old grandmother, and struck up a friendship with her in her last days. He stayed with her for a week, keeping her fire going through the cold nights.

Famous Shoes knew that it was a delicate thing he was doing. What if the old woman got so healthy that she decided to stay alive? Then he would have an old Comanche woman on his hands, which would anger his grandfather, if he ever found him. His grandfather hated two things, rainy weather and Comanches. Besides, for a Kickapoo to attend a Comanche at such a time was not entirely proper—once an old one was left to die, and the farewells were said, it was their duty to go on and die. He was beginning to worry that he had gotten himself into a difficulty when the old woman closed her eyes and ceased to breathe. Famous Shoes saw to it that her remains were treated correctly, a thing that was the duty of any traveler; then he went on his way.

When Buffalo Hump found out that Famous Shoes had been helpful to his grandmother in her dying he told his warriors that the Kickapoo was to be left alone, and even made welcome at their campfires if he cared to visit. Famous Shoes was glad Buffalo Hump had given such an order; it had probably saved his life several times. Even so, he did not seek out Buffalo Hump, or visit Comanche campfires. He did not think it wise. Buffalo Hump might follow the rules of courtesy, but being near him was too much like being near a bear. It was possible to come close to a bear, even a grizzly, and talk to it; the bear might allow it. But the bear was still a bear, and might stop allowing the courteous talk at any time. If the bear changed his mind about how he felt, the person trying to exchange courtesies with him might be dead. Besides, for all Famous Shoes knew, Buffalo Hump might not have liked his grandmother very much. She might have been quarrelsome, like his Aunt Neeta. Buffalo Hump's respect might have its limits.

When Famous Shoes walked into the Comanche camp Blue Duck rode right beside him, making his horse prance and jump. The boy wanted everyone to think he had brought in an important captive. Some of the young warriors rode up to Famous Shoes a few times, to taunt him, but he ignored their taunts and went on calmly through the camp.

To his surprise he saw old Slow Tree, sitting on a robe with Buffalo Hump. Slow Tree was talking, which was no surprise—Slow Tree was always talking. Buffalo Hump looked angry—no doubt the old chief had been making boring speeches to him for a long time. Slow Tree might have been bragging to Buffalo Hump about how many times he had been with his wives; he wanted everyone to believe that he was always at his women, bringing them great pleasure. Slow Tree had always been boastful, but he had once been a terrible fighter and had to be treated respectfully, even though he was old and boring.

"What are you doing here?" Buffalo Hump asked, when Famous Shoes walked up. "Your white friends were here but now they have gone south. The Buffalo Horse was here three days ago but I don't see him today."

"Your son made me come," Famous Shoes replied. "He came with these other boys and made me come. I was on the Canadian, eating a duck. I would not have bothered you if these boys had let me alone. They said you might want to torture me awhile."

Buffalo Hump was amused. The Kickapoo was an eccentric person who was apt to turn up anywhere on the llano on some outlandish errand that no other Indian would bother about. The man would walk a thousand miles to listen to a certain bird whose call he might want to mimic. Most people thought Famous Shoes was crazy, but Buffalo Hump didn't. Though a Kickapoo, the man had respect for the old ways. He behaved like the old ones behaved; the old ones, too, would go to any lengths to learn some useful fact about the animals or the birds. They would figure that someone might need to know those facts; they themselves might not need to, but their children might, or their grandchildren might.

Very few Comanches would go to the trouble Famous Shoes went to, when it came to seeking useful information. It made Buffalo Hump annoyed with his own people, that this was so. The Kickapoos were a lowly people who had never been good at war. The Comanches wiped them out wherever they found them, and did this easily. Even young boys no more skilled than his son could easily slaughter Kickapoos wherever he found them. Yet it was Famous Shoes, a Kickapoo, who sought the knowledge that few Comanches were now even interested in.

Besides, the man was funny. He would just walk into an enemy camp and offer himself up for torture as if torture were a joke.

Then Slow Tree, who was rarely polite, pointed a pipe he was smoking at Famous Shoes and made an ugly speech.

"If you came into my camp I would hang you upside down and put a scorpion in your nose," he said. "When the scorpion stung you it would kill your brain. Then you could wander around eating weeds, for all I care. I don't like Kickapoos."

Famous Shoes ignored the old man, though he decided on the spot to avoid the country where Slow Tree hunted until the old chief was finally dead. He had never heard that a scorpion bite could kill a brain, but it might be true, especially if the scorpion stung you inside your nose. The nose was not far from the brain—the poison of the scorpion would not have far to travel.

"I was on the Washita looking for my grandmother," Famous Shoes said, thinking it would be wise to change the subject. "There are many deer in the Washita country. If you are wanting deer, that is where I would go."

Blue Duck stood nearby, strutting and playing with a hatchet he wore in his belt. He wanted the band to know that he was responsible for bringing in the Kickapoo. If his father didn't appreciate it, maybe Slow Tree would. It was clear that the great chief Slow Tree had no fondness for Kickapoos.

Buffalo Hump was engaged in the delicate task of being polite to Slow Tree, a man he neither liked nor trusted. He didn't need an irritating boy standing nearby, playing with a hatchet. Blue Duck wanted people to think he had captured someone important, but Famous Shoes wasn't important. He was just an eccentric Kickapoo.

"Why did you bring this man here?" he asked, looking at his son coldly. "You should have left him to eat his duck. If you see him again, leave him alone."

He did not want to mention the fact that Famous Shoes had helped tend his grandmother while she died. The business with his grandmother was between himself and Famous Shoes; it was not a matter he wanted to discuss with everyone.

Blue Duck was shocked that his father would speak to him so, in front of Slow Tree and the worthless Kickapoo. He turned away at once and caught his horse. Then he gathered up his weapons, and a robe to protect him from the cold, and left the camp.

Buffalo Hump made no comment. Soon they saw the angry boy winding up the trail out of the canyon.

"If he was my son I would let him hang you upside down and put the scorpion in your nose," Slow Tree said to Famous Shoes.

Famous Shoes didn't answer—why respond to such a stupid comment? Blue Duck was not Slow Tree's son. He thought he would probably go up the other side of the canyon when he left, though. It would be good to have the great Palo Duro Canyon between himself and the rude, angry boy.

There was silence, for a time. Slow Tree was annoyed because Buffalo Hump was ignoring everything he said. Buffalo Hump listened in a polite manner, but he made no move to take Slow Tree's advice. He wasn't even interested in torturing a Kickapoo, which most Comanches would do immediately, without waiting for a chief's permission.

"My wives will feed you and then you can go," Buffalo Hump said, to Famous Shoes.

"I had that fat duck, I don't need to eat," Famous Shoes said. "I had better go look for Big Horse Scull before he gets lost."

"Kicking Wolf is following him now too," Buffalo Hump remarked casually. "He wants to steal the Buffalo Horse."

"I better go," Famous Shoes said. The news he had just heard shocked him badly. Big Horse Scull had been following Kicking Wolf, but now it was the other way around. Of course Kicking Wolf was already a famous horsethief, but stealing the Buffalo Horse would be a powerful act. If Kicking Wolf could steal the Buffalo Horse his people would sing about him for many years.

Famous Shoes changed his mind about eating, though. One fat duck wouldn't last him forever, and Buffalo Hump's wives had made a stew with a good smell to it. He squatted and ate a big bowl full, while Buffalo Hump sat patiently on his robe, listening to old Slow Tree brag about how happy he made his wives.

13.

JAKE CAME IN the door, avoided Felice's eye, turned into the hall, and started up the stairs, only to find old Ben Mickelson planted squarely in his way. Jake despised old Ben, for being a disgusting, profane, purple-lipped old drunkard, but he *was* the Sculls' butler and it was necessary to be polite to him.

It was necessary but it wasn't easy: old Ben was looking at Jake with a mean gleam in his watery blue eyes.

"Not today, you don't, you damned lout!" Ben Mickelson said.

Jake thought he must have misheard. Every day for three weeks he had hurried up to the Scull living quarters and been welcomed ardently by the lady of the house. Yesterday she had been particularly ardent—Inez Scull straddled him on the chaise longue and bounced so vigorously that the chaise broke. Then she dragged Jake onto the couch and continued no less vigorously. By the time Madame Scull quieted down, every piece of furniture that had a flat surface had been made use of in their sport.

So why was old Ben Mickelson barring his access to the stairs?

"Mind your words, Ben, if you don't want a licking," Jake said— it occurred to him, for a moment, that the Captain might be back, but if the Captain was back the boys would be back too, and he hadn't seen them.

"Not today, you ain't going up, and not tomorrow and not the next day and not the next week and not the next month and not ever!" old Ben said, the words bursting out of his mouth like gobbets of bile.

"But what's wrong?" Jake asked, confused.

"Nothing's wrong—you just be gone now. We don't need to be seeing the likes of you around the big house again."

Jake wanted to grab the old man by his scrawny neck and shake him good, but he didn't quite dare. Something *was* wrong, he just didn't know what. Yesterday Madame Scull had called him "Jakie," and could hardly wait to get out his little pricklen, as she called it. But today Ben Mickelson stood on the stairs looking at him in a gloating way.

"Be gone," Ben said, again. "I'll be calling the sheriff on you if you don't. The sheriff will know what to do with a lout like you, I guess."

Jake was confused and disappointed. He knew the old butler hadn't just decided to dismiss him on his own authority, because he had no authority. He might curse the kitchen girls and pinch them under the stairs, but he was only a butler. Jake knew that if he wasn't allowed up it was because Madame Scull didn't want him up—but why? He had tried to be cooperative, no matter what wild game Inez Scull suggested; and some of her games went far beyond the bounds of anything he had ever supposed he would be doing in his life. But he had done them, and Madame Scull had yelled and kicked with pleasure. So why was the old butler now planted in his way?

"All right, Ben," Jake said, feeling deflated. He wandered back into the kitchen, where Felice was churning butter. She didn't look up, when he came in—Felice was careful never to raise her eyes to him, anymore. But now he felt lonely—he had been turned out. He would have liked a smile from Felice; he had a sense that she felt he had treated her bad, though he had only done what he had been told to do by the Captain's wife. Felice had no cause to turn her head every time he entered the room.

"Well, I guess the Missus ain't up," he said, idling for a moment. "I'd sure like a glass of buttermilk before I go to work."

Felice got up without a word and poured him a tumbler full of buttermilk from the big crock where they kept it. Captain Scull too liked buttermilk—he had been known to drink off a quart, on days when he came in with a thirst for buttermilk.

Jake thanked Felice, thinking it might melt her reserve, but Felice went back to her churning without even a nod.

Jake was sitting on the back step, drinking buttermilk and wondering what he could find to do all day, when Inez Scull strode out of the house. She had on her riding habit and was pulling on a glove. When she saw Jake sitting on the step with the tumbler of buttermilk she did not look pleased.

"Who told you to sit on my stoop and guzzle my buttermilk?" she asked, her black eyes snapping. Jake was taken aback by her look, which was icy, and her tone, which was hot. He jumped to his feet in embarrassment.

"I suppose you got the buttermilk from that yellow bitch," she said. "I'll quirt her soundly when I get back."

"Why, the crock was full, I thought I could drink one glass," Jake said, very nervous.

"That's the Captain's buttermilk, it's not for common use," Inez said. "I instructed the butler to inform you that we didn't need you around here anymore. I suppose I'll have to whack that old sot a time or two, if he forgot to tell you."

"He told me, I was just resting a minute," Jake said, confused by the coldness in Madame Scull's tone. Only yesterday she had pressed hot affections on him—today she acted as if she scarcely knew him.

"Get off my step, I told you," Inez said. "I don't want you around here—and stay away from that yellow bitch, too. I don't want you indulging in any irregularities with the servants."

Madame Scull poked him, not gently, with the toe of her riding boot. Jake jumped up and hurried down the steps. Then he remembered that he still had the tumbler in his hand.

"I thought you liked me!" he blurted out.

Madame Scull's lip curled. "Like you? A common thing such as yourself? I've stooped to many follies but I doubt I'd allow myself to like a common farm boy," she said.

Jake sat the tumbler on the step, where Felice would find it and take it in.

He was walking slowly and sadly back down the main street of Austin, trying to puzzle out why he had been welcome one day and shunned the next, when he heard a horse galloping close behind him.

Madame Scull was coming, on her fine thoroughbred, Lord Nelson. The horse was worth as much as a house, some of the rangers claimed. Two men stood guard over Lord Nelson, all night, at the Scull stables, lest Indians try to sneak in and steal him. Madame Scull raced Lord Nelson over the prairies at full speed, usually alone.

As Inez Scull came abreast of Jake she drew rein and ran her quirt lightly through his hair, which she herself had just cut, the day before, with her scissors, after their sweaty sport.

"It was the curls, Jakie," Inez said, the ice still in her voice. She flicked her quirt again through his short hair.

"The curls," she said. "I suppose I found them briefly appealing. But then I cut them off. So that's all done now, ain't it?"

Then she put the spurs to Lord Nelson and went galloping straight out of town.

14.

KICKING WOLF could move without sound. When he decided to steal the Buffalo Horse he only took Three Birds with him—except for himself, Three Birds was the quietest warrior in the band. Fast Boy and Red Badger were brave fighters, but clumsy. They could not approach a horse herd in the soundless way that was required if a tricky theft was being contemplated. Kicking Wolf prayed every night that he could keep his grace with animals—few Comanches could go into a horse herd at night without alarming the horses. Buffalo Hump could not do such delicate work, not at all. He was a great raider, Kicking Wolf acknowledged. Buffalo Hump could run off many horses, and kill whatever white men or Mexicans got in his way. But he could not go into a horse herd at night and steal a mare or a stallion—he was too impatient, and he did not bother to disguise his smell. Mainly, he was a fighter, not a thief.

Kicking Wolf, though, was very careful about his smell, and he had instructed Three Birds how to eliminate his odor before going into a horse herd. Kicking Wolf would eat little, for a day or two before a raid. He wanted his body to empty out its smells. Then he gathered herbs and rubbed them on himself, on his armpits, on his privates, on his feet. He chewed sweet roots to make his breath inoffensive. He prepared carefully, but mainly it was his grace, his ability to move without sound, that enabled him to go into a herd of strange horses at night and not alarm them. He wanted to be able to move close to the horses and stroke them—he wanted the stroking to begin before the horse was even aware that a man was there. Once he had the horse's trust he could move through the herd seeing that all the horses stayed calm. It was important to start with a horse that had calmness in him—often Kicking Wolf would study a horse herd for a few days, until he had selected the horse that he would approach first—it had to be a horse with calmness in it, a horse unlikely to panic.

Once Kicking Wolf had chosen the first horse, he would pray in the morning that his grace would not desert him; then he could move into the herd with confidence and stroke the lead horse. He liked a night that was cloudy but not entirely moonless, when he went to steal horses. He wanted to be able to see where the ground was—and so would the horses. In complete darkness a horse might brush up against a thornbush and panic if it rattled. A whole herd might break into a run in an instant, if they heard a strange sound.

Kicking Wolf was proud of being the best of the Comanche horsethieves—he had honed his skills for many years. Simply stealing many horses had never been enough for him; he only wanted to steal the best horses—the horses that would run the fastest, or make the best studs. He wanted to steal the horses that the Texans would miss most. Plow horses he never touched. Invariably, when he got back to camp with the horses he had stolen, the other warriors would be jealous. Even Buffalo Hump was a little jealous, although he pretended not to notice Kicking Wolf and his horses.

The other warriors always offered to trade Kicking Wolf for his horses—they would offer him guns, or their ugly old wives, or even, occasionally, a young pretty wife; but Kicking Wolf never traded—he kept his horses and because of them was envied by every warrior in the tribe.

From the moment Kicking Wolf first saw the Buffalo Horse he wanted to steal it. The Buffalo Horse was the most famous horse in Texas. If he could steal such an animal it would make the Texans look puny. It would shame their greatest warrior, Big Horse Scull. It would bring glory back to the Comanche people—the women and the young men would all make songs about Kicking Wolf. The medicine men could take piss from the Buffalo Horse and use it in potions that would make the young men brave and the women amorous. Buffalo Hump would sulk, for he would know that Kicking Wolf had done a great thing, a thing he himself could never have done.

When he saw that the Texans were not going to go chase him to the Rio Pecos he rested for three days in a little cave he had found. He built a warm fire and feasted on the tender meat of one of the young mares he had killed. Then he heard from Red Badger that Blue Duck had attacked the Texans with a few young warriors and killed one ranger. Red Badger was so fond of one of the young women who had come to the camp with Slow Tree that he could not stay in one place. He was in love with the young woman, who was the wife of old Skinny Hand. Though old, Skinny Hand was a violent fighter; Red Badger had to be careful, for Skinny Hand would certainly shoot him if he caught him slipping out with his young wife. Red Badger said that Buffalo Hump was bored with Slow Tree but was trying to be polite.

Kicking Wolf soon got almost as bored with Red Badger as Buffalo Hump was with Slow Tree. Red Badger was a foolish person who was so crazy about women that he could not accomplish much as a warrior. He talked about women so much that everyone who had to listen to him was bored. Fast Boy was so bored that he wanted to tie Red Badger up and cut out his tongue. Everyone was almost that bored, but of course they could not simply cut out a warrior's tongue.

The fact that it was so cold made Kicking Wolf decide that it might be a good time to steal the Buffalo Horse. The Texans did not like cold. They did not know how to shelter themselves and keep themselves warm, as he was doing in his little cave. When it was cold the Texans all huddled around fires and went to sleep. New snowflakes were falling outside his little cave—it was not going to be warm for many days. Even if the Texans went on south across the llano, the cold and sleet would follow them. With the weather so cold the Texans would not be very watchful of the horses.

At night Scull hobbled the Buffalo Horse, but did not keep it on a grazing rope. Once Kicking Wolf had called the Buffalo Horse by whistling at him—he whistled twice and the big horse came trotting right to him.

Kicking Wolf also noticed that the Buffalo Horse was very alert. If a wolf crossed the prairie, or even a coyote, the Buffalo Horse would be the first to raise its head and look. It did not whinny, though, like some of the younger horses, who might be frightened by the smell of a wolf. The Buffalo Horse had no reason to fear wolves, or anything else on the llano.

When the morning dawned, gray as sleet, Kicking Wolf walked a mile from his cave and sat on a low hill to pray. When he had prayed some hours he went back to camp and told the few warriors there that he had decided to steal the Buffalo Horse. It was a plan he had never mentioned to anyone. The warriors were so surprised that they could not think of any words to say—it was such a bold idea that everyone was a little scared, even Fast Boy. Kicking Wolf was a great horse stealer, they all knew that. But the Buffalo Horse was a special horse; he was the horse of Scull, the terrible captain with the long knife. What would Scull do if he woke up to find his great horse missing?

"We will all go with you," Red Badger said, after a few minutes' thought.

"Three Birds will go with me," Kicking Wolf said. "No one else."

Red Badger wanted to go—stealing the Buffalo Horse was a great and audacious thing; any warrior would want to help do such a great thing. But the firm way Kicking Wolf had spoken caused Red Badger to swallow his protests. Kicking Wolf had spoken in a way that did not invite disagreement.

Fast Boy had meant to say something, also, but Kicking Wolf had such a cold look in his eye that Fast Boy did not speak.

"Where will you take the Buffalo Horse when you steal him?" Red Badger asked. The more he thought about what Kicking Wolf planned, the more his breath came short. It was a big thing, to steal such an animal. Many of the Comanches thought the Buffalo Horse was a witch horse—some even thought it could fly. Some of the old women claimed they had heard the whinny of a great horse, coming from high up in the sky, on dark nights when there was no moon.

"I will take him to Mexico," Kicking Wolf said. "To the Sierra Perdida."

"Ah, the Sierra Perdida," Red Badger said. "I don't know if the Texans will follow you that far."

"If they try to follow us past the Brazos you can shoot them," Kicking Wolf added. It was a little joke. Red Badger had a repeating rifle of which he was very proud; he cleaned it and rubbed it every night. But Red Badger had weak eyesight; he couldn't hit anything with his rifle. Once he had even missed a buffalo that had been lying down. Red Badger's poor vision made the buffalo seem as if it were standing up, so he kept shooting over it. In battle he shot wildly, hitting no one. Some of the warriors were even afraid Red Badger might accidentally shoot one of them. He would not be the one to protect them from the Texans, if they followed past the Brazos.

Fast Boy was taken aback by Kicking Wolf's statement about the Sierra Perdida. Those mountains were the stronghold of Ahumado, the dark-skinned bandit whom the whites called the Black Vaquero, because he was so cruel and also because he was so good at stealing cattle from the big ranches of the Texans, down below the Nueces River. Ahumado hated the Texans and killed them in many cruel ways; but what made Kicking Wolf's statement startling was that he also hated Comanches—when he caught Comanches he killed them with tortures just as bad as those he visited on the Texans.

"The Black Vaquero lives in the Sierra Perdida," Fast Boy reminded Kicking Wolf. "He is a bad old man."

"That is where I am going—the Sierra Perdida," Kicking Wolf repeated, and then he was silent.

Fast Boy didn't say more, mainly because he knew that it was easy to put Kicking Wolf in a bad mood by questioning his decisions. He was far worse than Buffalo Hump in that regard. Buffalo Hump didn't mind questions from his warriors—he wanted the men he fought with to understand what they were supposed to do. And he gave careful orders. Problems with Buffalo Hump would come only if the orders were not carried out properly. If some warrior failed to do his part in a raid, then Buffalo Hump's anger would be terrible.

With Kicking Wolf, though, it was unwise to rush in with questions, even though what he wanted to do seemed crazy. Stealing the Buffalo Horse was a little crazy, but then Kicking Wolf was a great stealer of horses and could probably manage it; but the really crazy part of his plan was taking the horse to Ahumado's country, a thing that made no sense at all. Even Buffalo Hump was careful to avoid the Sierra Perdida when he raided into Mexico. It was not from fear—Buffalo Hump feared nothing—but from practicality. In the Sierra Perdida or the villages near it there were no captives to take, because Ahumado had already taken all the children from the villages there —if he did not keep the captives as slaves, he traded them north, to the Apaches. Some people even speculated that Ahumado himself was Apache, but Famous Shoes, the Kickapoo, who went everywhere, said no, Ahumado was not an Apache.

"Ahumado is from the south," Famous Shoes said.

When questioned about the statement Famous Shoes could not be more specific. He did not know what tribe Ahumado belonged to, only that it was from the south.

"From the south, where the jungle is," he said.

None of the Comanches knew the word, so Famous Shoes explained that the jungle was a forest, where it rained often and where Jaguar, the great cat, hunted. That was all Famous Shoes knew.

Fast Boy did not ask any more questions, but he thought he

ought to make his views clear about the foolish thing Kicking Wolf wanted to do. Fast Boy was a warrior, a veteran of many battles with the whites and with the Mexicans. He had a right to speak his mind.

"If we go into the Sierra Perdida, Ahumado will kill us all," he said.

Kicking Wolf merely looked at him coldly.

"If you are afraid of him you don't have to go," Kicking Wolf said.

"I am not afraid of him and I know I don't have to go," Fast Boy said. "I don't have to go anywhere, except to look for something to eat. I wanted you to know what I think."

Red Badger was of the same opinion as Fast Boy but he didn't want to state his views quite so plainly.

"Once I was in Mexico and a bad thorn stuck in my knee," he said. "It was a green thorn. It went in behind my knee and almost ate my leg off. That thorn was more poisonous than a snake."

He paused. No one said anything.

"Ever since then I have not liked going to Mexico," Red Badger added.

"You don't have to go, either," Kicking Wolf said. "Once Three Birds and I have the Buffalo Horse we will go alone to Mexico."

Three Birds looked at the sky. He had heard some geese and looked up to see if he could spot them. He was very fond of geese and thought that if the geese were planning to stop somewhere close by, he might go and try to snare one.

The geese were there, all right, many geese, but they would not be stopping anywhere nearby. They were very high, almost as high as the clouds. No one else had even noticed them, but Three Birds had good hearing and could always hear geese when they were passing over, even if they were high, near the clouds.

He made no comment about the business of Mexico. It seemed risky, to him, but if Kicking Wolf wanted to go, that was enough for Three Birds. When there was discussion he rarely spoke his thoughts. He liked to keep his own thoughts inside him, and not mix them up promiscuously with the thoughts of other warriors, or of women, or of anyone. His thoughts were his; he didn't want them out in the air. Because of the firm way he stuck to his preference and kept his thoughts inside himself, some Comanches thought he was a mute. They thought he was too dumb to talk and were puzzled that Kicking Wolf put so much stock in his ability.

Sometimes even Kicking Wolf himself was annoyed by Three Birds' silence, his unwillingness to give an opinion.

"What is wrong with you?" he asked Three Birds one time. "You never speak. Where are your words? Are you so ignorant that you have forgotten all your words?"

Three Birds had been a little offended by Kicking Wolf's rude speech. When Kicking Wolf asked him that question Three Birds got up and left the camp for a week. He saw no reason to stay around if Kicking Wolf was going to be rude to him. He had not forgotten his words and would speak them when he felt like it. He did not feel he had to speak idle words just because Kicking Wolf had decided that he was in a mood to hear him speak.

What Three Birds saw, when he looked in the sky, besides the geese that were not stopping, was that it was going to get even colder than it had been; it was going to stay very cold for a while yet. There would be more snow and more sleet.

"When will you steal the Buffalo Horse?" Red Badger asked. Red Badger was the opposite of Three Birds. He could not hold in his questions, or stay quiet for long. Red Badger often talked even when he had nothing to say that anyone at all would want to hear.

Kicking Wolf didn't answer the loquacious young warrior. He was thinking of the south, and of how angry Big Horse Scull would be when he woke up and discovered that his great warhorse was gone.

15.

MAGGIE COULD TELL by the footsteps that the man outside her door was drunk. The footsteps were unsteady and the man had just lurched into the wall, though it was early morning. A man so drunk at that hour of the morning that he could not walk steadily might have been drinking all night. The thought made her very apprehensive, so apprehensive that she considered not opening her door. A man that drunk might well be violent—he might beat her or tear her clothes. Maybe he would be quick and pass out—that sometimes happened with men who were very drunk—but that was about the best that she could expect, if she opened her door to a drunk. Some drunks merely wallowed on her, unable to finish; or the exertion might agitate the man's stomach—more than once men had thrown up on her or fouled her bed with vomit.

For Maggie, it had never been easy, opening her door to a man. Once the door was open she was caught; if a bad man or a cruel man was standing there, then she was in for a bad time. Sometimes, of course, the customer outside her door would just be some unhappy man whose wife had passed away. Those men, who were just looking for a little pleasure or comfort, were not a problem. The men she feared were the men who wanted to punish women— that was the chief peril of her profession; Maggie had endured many sweaty, desperate times, dealing with such men.

She always opened the door, though; not opening it could cause consequences just as grave. The man outside might grow angry enough to break down the door, in which case the landlord might throw her out. At the very least, she would have to pay for the door. Besides that, the customer might go to the sheriff and complain; he might claim that she had stolen money—that or some other accusation. The word of any man, however dishonest, was worth more with a sheriff than the word of a whore. Or the aggrieved customer might complain to his friends and stir them up; several times gangs of men had caught her, egged on by some dissatisfied customer. Those times had been bad. Much as it might frighten her to open her door, Maggie never let herself forget that she was a whore and had to live by certain rules, one being that you opened the door to the customer before the customer got mad enough to break it down.

Still, it was her room—she felt she could at least take her time buttoning her dress. It was important to her that her dress be buttoned modestly before she let a man into her room. She knew it might seem contradictory, since the man outside was coming in to pay her to *unbutton* the same dress; but Maggie still buttoned up. She felt that if she ever started opening the door with her dress unbuttoned she would lose all hope for herself. There was time enough to do what she had to do when the man had paid his money.

She opened the door cautiously and received a grim shock: the person who had just lurched down the hall was the young ranger Jake Spoon, who had only been in the troop a few weeks. He was so drunk that he had dropped to his knees and was holding his stomach—but when he saw Maggie he mastered his gut and put out a hand, so she could help him up.

"Why, Mr. Spoon," Maggie said. "Are you sickly?"

Instead of answering Jake Spoon crawled past her, into her room. Once inside he got to his feet and walked unsteadily across the room to her bed—then he sat down on the bed and began to pull off his boots and unbutton his shirt. Jake Spoon looked up at her mutely—he seemed to be puzzled by the fact that she was still standing in the doorway.

"I got money," he said. "I ain't a cheat."

Then he pulled his shirt off, dropped it on the floor, and stood up, holding on to a bedpost to steady himself. Without even looking at her again he opened his pants.

Maggie felt her heart sink. Jake was a Texas Ranger, although just come to the troop. In the years that Maggie had been seeing Woodrow Call it had become known to the rangers that she and Woodrow had an attachment. It was not yet the sort of attachment that Maggie yearned for; if it had been she would not have been renting a cheap room, and opening her door to drunken strangers.

But it was an attachment; she wanted it and Woodrow wanted it, though he might have been slow to admit it. Sensing the attachment, the other rangers who knew Woodrow well had gradually begun to leave Maggie alone. They soon realized that it was distasteful to her, to be selling herself to Woodrow's friends. Though

Call never said anything directly, the rangers could tell that he didn't like it if one of them went with Maggie. Augustus McCrae, an indiscriminate whorer, would never think of approaching Maggie, although he had long admired her looks and her deportment. Indeed, Gus had often urged Woodrow to marry Maggie, and end her chancy life as a whore, a life that so often led to sickness or death at an early age.

Woodrow had so far declined to marry her, but lately he had been more helpful, and more generous with money. Now he sometimes gave her money to buy things for her room, small conveniences that she couldn't afford. It was her deepest hope and fondest dream that Woodrow would someday forbid her to whore; maybe what they had wouldn't go as far as marriage, but at least it might remove her from the rough traffic that had been her life.

Woodrow's argument, the few times they had approached the subject, was that he was often gone for months on hazardous patrols, any one of which could result in his death. He felt Maggie ought to take care of herself and continue to earn what she could in case he was cut down in battle. Of course, Maggie knew that rangering was dangerous and that Woodrow might be killed, in which case her dream of a life with him would never be realized.

She never spoke of her life as a whore, when she was with Woodrow; in her own mind her real life was *their* life. The rest of it she tried to pretend was happening to someone else. But the pretense was only a lie she told herself to help her get through the days. In fact it *was* her who opened her door to the men, who took their money, who inspected them to see that they were not diseased, who accepted them into her body. She had been a desperate girl, with both parents dead, when she was led into whoring in San Antonio; now she was no longer a girl, but the desperation was still with her. She felt it even then, as Jake Spoon stood there in her room, drunk almost to the point of nausea, with his pants open, pointing himself at her and waiting sullenly.

Woodrow didn't know about her desperation—Maggie had never told him how much she hated what she did. He might have

124

sensed it at times, but he didn't know how hard it was, on a morning when all she wanted to do was sit quietly and sew, to have to deal with a man so drunk that he had to crawl into her room. Worse than that, he was a ranger, the same as Woodrow; he ought to have known to seek another whore.

"Why are you standing over there? I'm ready," Jake said. His pants had slipped down to his ankles; he had to bend to pull them up, so he could dig into his pocket and come out with the coins.

"But you're sickly, Mr. Spoon—you can barely stand up," Maggie said, trying to think of some stratagem that would cause him to get dressed again and go away.

"Don't need to stand up and I ain't sick," Jake said, though, to his dismay, the act of speaking almost caused his stomach to come up. He swayed for a moment but fought the nausea down. It was the whore's fault, he decided—she hadn't come over to help him with his clothes, as a whore should.

He fumbled again for the coins and finally got them out of his pocket.

Looking at the whore, who had closed the door behind her but still stood across the room, staring at him, Jake felt his anger rising. Her name was Maggie, he knew; the boys all said she was sweet on Woodrow Call, but Woodrow Call was far up the plains and the warning meant little to Jake. All whores were sweet on somebody.

"Come here—I got the money!" he demanded. In his mind, which swirled from drink, was the recent memory of the wild games he had played with Inez Scull—acts so raw that even whores might not do them. He didn't like it that the whore he had chosen was so standoffish. What of it if she was sweet on Woodrow Call?

Maggie saw there was no way out of it, without risking the sheriff, or a worse calamity. In another minute the young ranger would start yelling, or else do her violence. She didn't want the yelling or the violence, which might lead to her having to move from the room she had tried to make into a pleasant place for Woodrow to visit when he was home.

She didn't want to get thrown out, so she went across the room and accepted Jake Spoon's money. She didn't look Jake in the eye; she tried to make herself small. Maybe, if she was lucky, the boy would just do it and go.

Maggie wasn't lucky, though. The minute she took Jake's money he drew back his hand and slapped her hard in the face.

Jake slapped the whore because he was angry with her for being so standoffish and lingering so long, but he also gave her the slap because that was how Madame Scull had started things with him. The minute he walked up stairs she would come out of the bedroom and slap his face. The next thing he knew they would be on the floor, tussling fiercely. Then they would do the raw things.

He wanted, again, what he had had with Inez Scull. He didn't understand why she had cut his hair and thrown him out. Her coldness upset him so that he stole a bottle of whiskey from a shed behind the saloon and drank the whole bottle down. The whiskey burned at first, and then numbed him a little, but it didn't cool the fever he felt at the memory of his hot tusslings with Inez Scull. Only a woman could cool that fever, and the handiest woman happened to be Woodrow Call's whore.

She had very white skin, the whore—when he slapped her, her cheek became immediately red. But the slap didn't set things off, as it had when Madame Scull slapped him. Maggie, Call's whore, didn't utter a sound. She didn't slap him back, or grab him, or do anything wild or raw. She just put the money away, took off her dress, and lay back on the bed, waiting. She wouldn't even so much as look at him, although, in an effort to make her a little more lively, he pulled her hair. But neither the slap nor the hair pulling worked at all. Except for flexing herself a little when he crawled on top of her, the whore didn't move a muscle, or speak or cry out or yell or bite or even sigh. She didn't scream and kick and jerk, as Madame Scull did every time they were together.

As soon as the young ranger finished—it took considerably longer than she had hoped—Maggie got off the bed and went behind a little screen, to clean herself. She meant to stay behind the screen, hiding, until Jake Spoon left. She knew she would have a bad bruise on her cheek, from the slap. She didn't want to see the young man again, if she could help it.

Again, though, Maggie was not lucky. While she was cleaning herself she heard Jake retching and went out to find him on his hands and knees again. At least he was vomiting in a basin; he had not ruined the new carpet she had saved up to buy.

Jake Spoon heaved and heaved. Maggie saw how young he was and took a little pity. When he finished being sick she cleaned him up a little and helped him out the door.

16.

"NOW BOYS, LOOK THERE!" Inish Scull said, pointing westward at a small red butte. "See that? Pretend it's your Alps."

"Our what, Captain?" Long Bill inquired. It was breakfast time—Deets had just fried up some tasty bacon, and the breeze, though chilly, could be tolerated, particularly while he was sitting at the campfire holding a tin mug of scalding coffee that in texture was almost as thick as mud. All the rangers were hunched over their cups, letting the steam from the scalding coffee warm their cold faces. The exception was Woodrow Call, already saddled up and ready to ride—though even he had no notion of where they were headed, or why. They had traveled due south for a few days, but then the Captain suddenly bent to the west, toward a long empty space where, so far as any of the rangers knew, there was nothing to see or do.

The low, flat-topped hill was red in the morning sunlight.

"The Alps, Mr. Coleman!" the Captain repeated. "If you find yourself in Switzerland or France you have to cross them before you can get to Italy and eat the tasty noodle. That was Hannibal's challenge. He had all those elephants, but the Alpine passes were deep in snow. What was he to do?"

Captain Scull was drinking brandy, his morning drink and his evening drink, too, when he could have it. One well-padded brace of saddlebags contained nothing but brandy. A tipple or swallow or two in the morning cleared his head wonderfully, when he was campaigning, and also rarely failed to put him in a pedagogical mood. History, military history in particular, was his passion. Harvard wanted him to teach it, but he saw no reason to be teaching military history when he could go out in the field and make it, so he packed up the ardent Dolly Johnson, his Birmingham bride, and went to Texas to fight in the Mexican War, where he promptly captured three substantial towns and a number of sad villages. The air of the raw frontier so invigorated him that he gave little thought to going back to Boston, to the library and the ivied hall. Because of his long string of victories in Mexico he was soon offered the command of the disheveled but staunch band of irregulars known as the Texas Rangers.

Inish Scull was convinced, from what he knew of politics, that a great civil conflict was looming in America, but that conflict was yet some years away. When it came, Inish Scull meant to have a generalship—and what better way to capture the attention of the War Department than to whip the Comanche, the Kiowa, the Apache, the Pawnee, or any other tribe that attempted to resist the advance of Anglo-Saxon settlement?

Scull might not have broken the wild tribes yet, but he had harried them vigorously for almost ten years, while, little by little, settlement crept up the rivers and into the fertile valleys. Farms and ranches were established, burned out by the red men, and built again. Small poor townships were formed; wagon roads rutted the prairie; and the government slowly placed its line of forts along the northern and western line of settlement. All the while, Scull and his rangers ranged and ranged, hanging cattle thieves in the south and challenging the fighting Indians to the north.

Still, now and then, with a prickle of brandy in his nostrils, and a cold wind worthy of New England cooling his neck, Scull found that the professor was likely to revive in him, a little. At moments he missed the learned talk of Cambridge; at times he grew depressed when he considered the gap in knowledge between himself and the poor dull fellows he commanded—they were brave beyond reason, but, alas, untutored. Young Call, it was true, was eager to learn, and Augustus McCrae sometimes mimicked a few lines of Latin picked up in some Tennessee school. But, the truth was, the men were ignorant, which is why, from time to time, with no immediate enemy to confront, he had started giving little impromptu lectures on the great battles of history. It was true that the little butte to the west did not look much like an Alp, but it was the only hill in sight, and would have to serve.

"No, you see, Hannibal and his elephants were on the wrong side of the hills—or at least he wanted his enemies to think so," Scull said, pacing back and forth, his brandy glass in his hand. He hated to drink brandy out of anything but glass. On every patrol he carefully wrapped and packed six brandy glasses, but, despite his caution, he would usually be reduced to taking his brandy out of a tin cup before the scout was finished.

"What was he doing with elephants if he was out there in the snows?" Augustus asked. He hated it when the Captain got in one of his lecturing moods—though, since as far as he could tell they were just wandering aimlessly now, it probably didn't much matter whether they were riding or getting a history lesson. Now there the Captain was, drunk on brandy, pointing at some dull little hill and prattling on about Hannibal and elephants and snow and Alps and Romans. Gus could not remember ever having heard of Hannibal, and he did not expect to enjoy any lecture he might receive, mainly because one of his socks had wrinkled up inside his boot somehow and left him a painful blister on the bottom of his foot. He wanted to be back in Austin. If he limped into the Forsythe store looking pitiful enough Clara might tend to his blister and permit him a kiss besides. Instead, all he had in the way of comfort was a mug of coffee and a piece of sandy bacon, and even that comfort was ending. Deets had just confided in him that they only had bacon for one more day.

"Why, Hannibal was African," Scull said. "He was a man of Carthage, and not the only great commander to use war elephants, either. Alexander the Great used them in India and Hannibal took his on over the Alps, snow or no snow, and fell on the Romans when they least expected it. Brilliant fighting, I call it."

Call tried to imagine the scene the Captain was describing—the great beasts winding up and up, into the snowy passes—but he had never seen an elephant, just a few pictures of them in books. Though he knew most of the rangers found it boresome when the Captain started in lecturing, he himself enjoyed hearing about the battles Captain Scull described. His reading ability was slowly improving, enough so that he hoped, in time, to read about some of the battles himself.

Just as the Captain was warming to his subject, Famous Shoes suddenly appeared, almost at the Captain's elbow. As usual, all the boys gave a start; none of them had seen the tracker approach. Even Captain Scull found Famous Shoes' suddenly appearances a little unnerving.

"I was in the camp of Buffalo Hump, he has a new wife," Famous Shoes said. "His son took me prisoner for a while—he was the one who killed Mr. Watson. They call him 'Blue Duck.' His mother was a Mexican woman who froze to death trying to get away from Buffalo Hump."

Inish Scull smiled.

"You'd make a fine professor, sir," he said. "You've managed to tell us more about this scamp Blue Duck than I've been able to get across about Hannibal and his elephants. What else should I know? Has Kicking Wolf crossed the Alps with those stallions yet?"

His witticism was lost on Famous Shoes, who did not particularly appreciate interruptions while trying to deliver his reports.

"Slow Tree came into camp with many warriors and many women," Famous Shoes went on. "Slow Tree wanted to kill me but Buffalo Hump will not let anybody kill me."

"Whoa, that's news—why not?" Scull asked.

"I helped his grandmother die," Famous Shoes said. "I do not have to worry about Buffalo Hump."

"Is that all?" Scull asked.

"You do not have to worry about Buffalo Hump either," Famous

Shoes said. "He is still with Slow Tree. But Kicking Wolf is following you now."

"Kicking Wolf—why, the rascal!" Scull exclaimed. "A few days ago I was following *him*. Why would the man we were chasing want to follow us?"

"He probably wants to steal more horses," Call said. "Stealing horses is what he's good at."

"It could be that, or he might mean to cut our throats," Inish Scull commented. He looked at the scout, but Famous Shoes seemed to have no opinion as to Kicking Wolf's plans.

"I didn't see him," he said. "I only saw his tracks. He has Three Birds with him."

"Well, that doesn't tell me much," Scull said. "I've not had the pleasure of meeting Mr. Three Birds. What kind of fellow is he?"

"Three Birds is quiet—he does not speak his thoughts," Famous Shoes said. "The two of them are alone. The rest of the warriors are at the feast Buffalo Hump is giving for Slow Tree."

"If it's just two of them, I say let 'em come," Augustus said. "I expect we can handle two Indians, even if one of them *is* Kicking Wolf."

Call thought the opposite. Two Indians would be harder to detect than fifteen. It struck him as peculiar that Kicking Wolf chose to follow them just then; after all, he had just escaped with three fine stallions. They were probably better horses than any the ranger troop could boast—with the exception of Hector, of course.

Scull strode up and down for a while, looking across the plain as if he expected to see Kicking Wolf heave into sight at any moment. But, except for two hawks soaring, there was nothing to see in any direction but grass.

"I have known Three Birds for a long time," Famous Shoes said. "He does not hate Kickapoos. Once I helped him track a cougar he had shot. I think that cougar might have got away if I hadn't tracked it with him."

Augustus was sometimes irked by Famous Shoes' pompous way of talking.

"I expect he's forgot about that cougar by now," he said. "He might step up and cut your throat before he could call it to mind."

Famous Shoes considered the remark too absurd to reply to. Three Birds would never forget that he had helped him track the cougar, any more than Buffalo Hump would forget that he had been kind to his dying grandmother.

"Want me to see if I can surprise them, Captain?" Call asked—he was impatient with the inactivity. Talk was fine at night, but it was daytime and his horse was saddled and eager.

"You can't catch them," Famous Shoes said. "They are following you, but they are not close, and they have better horses than you do. If you chase them they will lead you so far away that you will starve before you can get back."

Call ignored the scout and looked at the Captain—he saw no reason to tolerate a hostile pursuit.

Captain Scull looked at the young man with amusement—he obviously wanted to go chase Indians, despite the scout's plain warning.

"I've been out there before and I didn't starve," Call informed him.

Scull pursed his lips but said nothing. He walked over to his saddlebags and rummaged in them until he came out with a small book. Then he walked back to the campfire, settled himself comfortably on a sack of potatoes, and held up the book, which was well used.

"Xenophon," he said. "The March of the Ten Thousand. Of course, we're only twelve men, but when I read Xenophon I can imagine that we're ten thousand."

Augustus had quietly saddled up—if there was a pursuit, he wanted to be part of it. Several other rangers began to stir themselves, pulling on their boots and looking to their guns.

"Here, stop that!" Captain Scull said suddenly, looking up from his book. "I won't send you off to chase a phantom, in country this spare. Just because Mr. Call didn't starve in it on his last visit doesn't mean he couldn't starve tomorrow—and the rest of you too.

"There's always a first time, they say," he added. "I expect it was some smart Greek said that, or else our own Papa Franklin."

Then he paused and smiled benignly at his confused and ragged men.

"Ever hear Greek read, boys?" he asked. "It's a fine old language—the language of Homer and Thucydides, not to mention Xenophon, who's our author today. I've a fair amount of Greek still in my head. I'll read to you, if you like, about the ten thousand men who marched home in defeat."

Nobody said yes, and nobody said no. The men just stood where they were, or sat if they had not yet risen. Deets put a few more sticks on the fire.

"That's fine, the ayes have it," Captain Scull said.

He looked around with a grin, and then, sitting on the sack of potatoes, and squinting in order to see the small print of his pocket Xenophon, he read to the troop in Greek.

"That was worse than listening to a bunch of Comanches gobble at one another," Long Bill said, once the reading was over and the troop once again on the move.

"I'd rather listen to pigs squeal than to hear goings-on like that," Ikey Ripple added.

Augustus had disliked the reading as much as anyone, but the fact that Long Bill had spoken out against it rubbed him the wrong way.

"That was Greek," he reminded them haughtily. "Everybody ought to hear Greek now and then, and Latin too. I could listen all day to someone read Latin."

Call knew that Augustus claimed some knowledge of Latin, but he had never been convinced by the claim.

"I doubt you know a word of either language," Call said. "You didn't understand that reading and neither did anybody else."

Unlike the rangers, Famous Shoes had been mightily impressed by the Captain's reading. He himself could speak several dialects and follow the track of any living animal; but Captain Scull had followed an even harder and more elusive track: the tiny, intricate track that ran across the pages of the book. That Big Horse Scull could follow a little track through page after page of a book and turn what he saw into sound was a feat that never ceased to amaze the Kickapoo.

"That might be the way a god talks," he commented.

"Nope, it was just some old Greek fellow who lost a war and had to tramp back home with his ten thousand men," Augustus said.

"That's a lot of men," Call said. "I wonder how many fought on the side that won."

"Why would you care, Woodrow? You didn't even like hearing Greek," Augustus pointed out.

"No," Call said, "but I can still wonder about that war."

17.

KICKING WOLF was amused by the carelessness of Big Horse Scull, who put three men at a time to guard the rangers' horses and the two pack mules, but did not bother with guards for the Buffalo Horse. The men on guard were rotated at short intervals, too—yet Scull did not seem to think the Buffalo Horse needed watching.

"He does not think anyone would try to steal the Buffalo Horse," Kicking Wolf told Three Birds, after they had watched the rangers and their horses for three nights.

"Scull is careless," he added.

Three Birds, for once, had a thought he didn't want to keep inside himself.

"Big Horse is right," Three Birds said. He pointed upward to the heavens, which were filled with bright stars.

"There are as many men as there are stars," Three Birds said. "They are not all here, but somewhere in the world there are that many men."

"What are you talking about?" Kicking Wolf said.

Three Birds pointed to the North Star, a star much brighter than the little sprinkle of stars around it.

"Only one star shines to show where the north is," Three Birds said. "Only one star, of all the stars, shines for the north."

Kicking Wolf was thinking it was pleasanter when Three Birds didn't try to speak his thoughts, but he tried to listen politely to Three Birds' harmless words about the stars.

"You are like the North Star," Three Birds said. "Only you of all the men in the world could steal the Buffalo Horse. That horse might be a witch—some say that it can fly. It might turn and eat you, when you go up to it. Yet you are such a thief that you are going to steal it anyway.

"Big Horse doesn't know that the North Star has come to take his horse," he added. "If he knew, he would be more careful."

On the fourth night, after studying the situation well, Kicking Wolf decided it was time to approach the Buffalo Horse. The weather conditions were good: there was a three-quarter moon, and the brightness of the stars was dimmed just enough by scudding, fast-moving clouds. Kicking Wolf could see all he needed to see. He had carefully prepared himself by fasting, his bowels were empty, and he had rubbed sage all over his body. Scull even left a halter on the Buffalo Horse. Once Kicking Wolf had reassured the big horse with his touch and his stroking, all he would have to do would be to take the halter and quietly lead the Buffalo Horse away.

As he was easing along the ground on his belly, so that the lazy guards wouldn't see him, Kicking Wolf got a big shock: suddenly the Buffalo Horse raised its ear, turned its head, and looked right at him. Kicking Wolf was close enough then that he could see the horse's breath making little white clouds in the cold night.

When he realized that the Buffalo Horse knew he was there, Kicking Wolf remembered Three Birds' warning that the horse might be a witch. For an instant, Kicking Wolf felt fear—big fear. In a second or two the big horse could be on him, trampling him or biting him before he could crawl away.

Immediately Kicking Wolf rose to a crouch, and got out of sight of the Buffalo Horse as fast as he could. He was very frightened, and he had not been frightened during the theft of a horse in many years. The Buffalo Horse had smelled him even though he had no smell, and heard him even though he made no sound.

"I think he heard my breath," he said, when he was safely back with Three Birds. "A man cannot stop his breath."

"The other horses didn't know you were there," Three Birds told him. "Only the Buffalo Horse noticed you."

Though he was not ready to admit it, Kicking Wolf had begun to believe that Three Birds might be right. The Buffalo Horse might be a witch horse, a horse that could not be stolen.

"We could shoot it and see if it dies," Three Birds suggested. "If it dies it is not a witch horse."

"Be quiet," Kicking Wolf said. "I don't want to shoot it. I want to steal it."

"Why?" Three Birds asked. He could not quite fathom why Kicking Wolf had taken it into his head to steal the Buffalo Horse. Certainly it was a big stout horse whose theft would embarrass the Texans. But Three Birds took a practical view. If it was a witch horse, as he believed, then it could not be stolen, and if it wasn't a witch horse, then it was only another animal—an animal that would die someday, like all animals. He did not understand why Kicking Wolf wanted it so badly.

"It is the great horse of the Texans—it is the best horse in the world," Kicking Wolf said, when he saw Three Birds looking at him quizzically.

Once he calmed down he decided he had been too hasty in his judgment. Probably the Buffalo Horse wasn't a witch horse at all—probably it just had an exceptionally keen nose. He decided to follow the rangers another day or two, so he could watch the horse a little more closely.

It was aggravating to him that Famous Shoes, the Kickapoo tracker, was with the Texans. Famous Shoes was bad luck, Kicking Wolf thought. He was a cranky man who was apt to turn up anywhere, usually just when you didn't want to see him. He enjoyed the protection of Buffalo Hump, though: otherwise some Comanche would have killed him long ago.

The old men said that Famous Shoes could talk to animals—they believed that there had been a time when all people had been able to talk freely with animals, to exchange bits of information that might be helpful, one to another. There were even a few people who supposed that Kicking Wolf himself could talk to horses—otherwise how could he persuade them to follow him quietly out of herds that were well guarded by the whites?

Kicking Wolf knew that was silly. He could not talk to horses, and he wasn't sure that anyone could talk to animals, anymore. But the old people insisted that some few humans still retained the power to talk with birds and beasts, and they thought Famous Shoes might be such a person.

Kicking Wolf doubted it, but then some of the old ones were very wise; they might know more about the matter than he did. If the Kickapoo tracker could really talk to animals, then he might have spoken to the Buffalo Horse and told him Kicking Wolf meant to steal him. Whether he could talk to animals or not, Famous Shoes was an exceptional tracker. He would certainly be aware that he and Three Birds were following the Texans. But he was a curious man. He might not have taken the trouble to mention this fact to the Texans—he might only have told the Buffalo Horse, feeling that was all that was necessary.

It was while watching the Buffalo Horse make water one evening that Kicking Wolf remembered old Queta, the grandfather of Heavy Leg, Buffalo Hump's oldest wife. Queta, too, had been a great horsethief; he was not very free with his secrets, but once, while drunk, he had mentioned to Kicking Wolf that the way to steal difficult horses was to approach them while they were pissing. When a horse made water it had to stretch out—it could not move quickly, once its flow started. Kicking Wolf had already noticed that the Buffalo Horse made water for an exceptionally long time. The big horse would stretch out, his legs spread and his belly close to the ground, and would pour out a hot yellow stream for several minutes. If Big Horse Scull was mounted when this happened he sometimes took a book out of his saddlebags and read it. On one occasion, while the Buffalo Horse was pissing, Scull did something very strange, something that went with the view that the Buffalo Horse was a witch horse. Scull slipped backward onto the big horse's rump, put his head on the saddle, and raised his legs. He stood on his head in the saddle while the Buffalo Horse pissed. Of course it was not unusual for men who were good riders to do feats of horsemanship—Comanche riders, particularly young riders, did them all the time. But neither Kicking Wolf nor Three Birds had ever seen a rider stand on his head while a horse was pissing.

"I think Big Horse is crazy," Three Birds said, when he saw that. Those were his last words on the subject and his only words on any subject for several days. Three Birds decided he had been talking too much; he went back to his old habit of keeping his thoughts inside himself.

Kicking Wolf decided he should wait until the Buffalo Horse was pissing before he approached him again. It would require patience, because horses did not always make water at night; they were more apt to wait and relieve themselves in the early morning.

When he mentioned his intention to Three Birds, Three Birds merely made a gesture indicating that he was not in the mood to speak.

Then, that very night, opportunity came. The men who were around the campfire were all singing; the Texans sang almost every night, even if it was cold. Kicking Wolf was not far from the Buffalo Horse when the big horse began to stretch out. As soon as the stream of piss was flowing from the horse's belly, Kicking Wolf moved, and this time the big horse did not look around. In a minute, Kicking Wolf was close to him and grasped the halter—the Buffalo Horse gave a little snort of surprise, but that was all. All the time the Buffalo Horse was pissing Kicking Wolf stroked him, as he had stroked the many horses he had stolen. When the yellow water ceased to flow Kicking Wolf pulled on the halter, and, to his relief, the big horse followed him. The great horse moved as quietly as he did, a fact that, for a moment, frightened Kicking Wolf. Maybe he was not the one playing the trick—maybe the Buffalo Horse *was* a witch horse, in which case the horse might be following so quietly only in order to get him off somewhere and eat him.

Soon, though, they were almost a mile from the ranger camp, and the Buffalo Horse had not eaten him or given him any trouble at all. It was following as meekly as a donkey—or more meekly; few donkeys were meek—then Kicking Wolf felt a great surge of pride. He had done what no other Comanche warrior could have done: he had stolen the Buffalo Horse, the greatest horse that he had ever taken, the greatest horse the Texans owned.

He walked another mile, and then mounted the Buffalo Horse and rode slowly to where he had left Three Birds. He did not want to gallop, not yet. None of the rangers were alert enough to pick up a horse's gallop at that distance, but Famous Shoes was there, and he might put his ear to the ground and hear the gallop.

Three Birds was in some kind of trance when Kicking Wolf rode up to him. Three Birds had their horses ready, but he himself was sitting on a blanket, praying. The man often prayed at inconvenient times. When he looked up from his prayer and saw Kicking Wolf coming on the Buffalo Horse all he said was, "Ho!"

"I have stolen the Buffalo Horse," Kicking Wolf said. "You shouldn't be sitting on that dirty blanket praying. You should be making a good song about what I have done tonight. I went to the Buffalo Horse while he was making water, and I stole him. When Big Horse Scull gets up in the morning he will be so angry he will want to make a great war on us."

Three Birds thought that what Kicking Wolf said was probably true. Scull would make a great war, because his horse had been stolen. He immediately stopped praying and caught his horse.

"Let's go a long way now," he said. "All those Texans will be chasing us, when it gets light."

"We will go a long way, but don't forget to make the song," Kicking Wolf said.

18.

"Genius! It's absolute genius!" Inish Scull said, when told that his great warhorse, Hector, had been stolen. "The man took Hector right out from under my nose. The other horses, now that took skill. But stealing Hector? That's genius!"

It was hardly the reaction the rangers had expected. The four men on guard at the time—Long Bill Coleman, Pea Eye Parker, Neely Dickens, and Finch Seeger—were lined up with hangdog looks on their faces. All of them expected the firing squad; after all, they had let the most important horse in Texas get stolen.

None of them had seen or heard a thing, either. The big horse had been grazing peacefully the last time they had looked. They had been expecting Kicking Wolf to try for the other horses. It hadn't occurred to any of them that he might steal the big horse.

"You should have expected it!" Call told them sternly, when the theft was discovered. "He might be big, but he was still a horse, and horses are what Kicking Wolf steals."

Augustus McCrae, like Captain Scull, could not suppress a sneaking admiration for Kicking Wolf's daring. It was a feat so bold it had to be credited, and he told Woodrow as much.

"I don't credit it," Call said. "It's still just a thief stealing a horse. We ought to be chasing him, instead of standing around talking about it."

"We've been chasing him off and on for ten years and we ain't caught him," Gus pointed out. "The man's too fleet for us. I'd like to see you go into Buffalo Hump's camp and steal one of his horses sometime."

"I don't claim to be a horsethief," Call said. "The reason we don't catch him is because we stop to sleep and he don't."

Call felt a deep irritation at what had happened. The irritation was familiar; he had felt it almost every time they had gone after the Comanches. In a direct conflict they might win, if the conflict went on long enough for their superior weaponry to prevail. But few engagements with the Comanche involved direct conflict. It was chase and wait, thrust and parry—and, always, the Comanches concentrated on what they were doing while the rangers usually piddled. Their own preparations were seldom thorough, or their tactics precise—the Comanches were supposed to be primitive, yet they fought with more intelligence than the rangers were usually able to muster. It irked Call, and had always irked him. He resolved that if he ever got to be a captain he would plan better and press the enemy harder, once a battle was joined.

Of course the force they had to deploy was not large. Captain Scull, like Buffalo Hump, preferred to mount a small, quick, mobile troop. Yet in Call's view there was always something ragtag about the ranger forces he went out with. Some of the men would always be drunk, or in love with a whore, or deep into a gambling frenzy when the time came to leave; they would be left behind while men who were barely skilled enough to manage town life would join up, wanting a grand adventure. Also, the state of Texas allotted little money for the ranger force—now that the Comanches had stopped snatching children from the outskirts of Austin and San Antonio, the legislature saw no need to be generous with the rangers.

"They don't need us anymore, the damn politicians," Augustus said. He had become increasingly resentful of all forms of law and restraint. The result of the legislature's parsimonious attitude toward frontier defense meant that the rangers often had to set out on a pursuit indifferently mounted and poorly provisioned. Often, like the Indians they were pursuing, they had to depend on hunting—or even fishing—in order to survive until they could get back.

Now, though, Kicking Wolf had stolen the big horse, and all Captain Scull could think of to do was call him a genius.

"What is a genius, anyway?" Augustus asked, addressing the question to the company at large.

"I guess the Captain's a genius, you ought to ask him," Call said.

The Captain, at the moment, was walking around with Famous Shoes, attempting to discover how the theft had been accomplished.

"A genius is somebody with six toes or more on one foot," Long Bill declared. "That's what I was told at home."

Neely Dickens, a small, reedy man prone to quick darting motions that reminded Gus of minnows, took a different view.

"Geniuses don't have no warts," he claimed.

"In that case I'm a genius because I am rarely troubled with warts," Augustus said.

"I've heard that geniuses are desperate smart," Teddy Beatty said. "I met one once up in St. Louis and he could spell words backwards and even say numbers backwards too."

"Now, what would be the point of spelling backwards?" Augustus asked. "If you spell backwards you wouldn't have much of a word. I expect you was drunk when you met that fellow."

Finch Seeger, the largest and slowest man in the company when it came to movement, was also the slowest when it came to thinking. Often Finch would devote a whole day to one thought—the thought that he wanted to go to a whorehouse, for example. He did not take much interest in the question of geniuses, but he had no trouble keeping an interest in food. Deets had informed the company that there was only a little bacon left, and yet they were a long way from home. The prospect of baconless travel bored into Finch's mind like a screwworm, so painfully that he was moved to make a comment.

"Pig," he said, to everyone's surprise. "I wish we had us a good fat pig."

"Now Finch, keep quiet," Augustus said, though the comment was the only word Finch Seeger had uttered in several days.

"No one was discussing swine," Gus added.

"No one was discussing anything," Call remarked. "Finch has as much right to talk as you have."

Finch ignored the controversy his remark had ignited. He looked across the empty prairie and his mind made a picture of a fat pig. The pig was nosing around behind a chaparral bush, trying to root out a mouse, or perhaps a snake. He meant to be watchful during the day, so that if they came upon the pig he saw in his mind they could kill it promptly and replenish their bacon supply.

"Well, that's one less horse," Long Bill commented. "I guess one of us will have to ride a pack mule, unless the Captain intends to walk."

"I doubt he intends to walk, we're a far piece out," Call said, only to be confounded a few minutes later by the Captain's announcement that he intended to do just that.

"Kicking Wolf stole Hector while Hector was pissing—it was the only time he could have approached him," Scull announced to the men. "Famous Shoes figured it out. Took him while he was pissing. Famous Shoes thinks he might have whispered a spell into his ear, but I doubt that."

While the rangers watched he began to rake around in his saddlebags, from which he extracted his big plug of tobacco, a small book, and a box of matches wrapped in oilskin. He had a great gray coat rolled up behind his saddle, but, after a moment's thought, he left it rolled up.

"Too heavy," he said. "I'll be needing to travel light. I'll just dig a hole at night, bury a few coals in it, and sleep on them if it gets nippy."

Scull stuffed a coat pocket full of bullets, pulled his rifle out of its scabbard, and scanned the plain with a cheerful, excited look on his face, actions which puzzled Call and Gus in the extreme. Captain Scull seemed to be making preparations to strike out on foot, although they were far out on the llano and in the winter too. The Comanches knew where they were, Buffalo Hump and Slow Tree as well. What would induce the Captain to be making preparations for foot travel?

And what was the troop to do, while he walked?

But Scull had a cheerful grin on his bearded face.

"Opportunity, men—it knocks but once," he said. "I think it was Papa Franklin who said that—it's in *Poor Richard,* I believe. Now, adversity and opportunity are kissing cousins, I say. My horse is missing but he's no dainty animal. He leaves a big track. I've always meant to study tracking—it's a skill I lack. Famous Shoes here is a great authority. He claims he can even track bugs. So we'll be leaving you now, gentlemen. Famous Shoes is going to teach me track-ing, while he follows my horse."

"But Captain, what about us?" Long Bill asked, unable to sup-press the question.

"Why, go home, boys, just go home," Captain Scull said. "Just go home—no need for you to trail along while I'm having my instruc-tion. Mr. Call and Mr. McCrae, I'll make you co-commanders. Take these fine men back to Austin and see that they are paid when you get there."

The rangers looked at one another, mightily taken aback by this development. Famous Shoes had not returned to camp. He was waiting on the plain, near where the big horse had been taken. Captain Scull rummaged a little more in his saddlebags but found nothing more that he needed.

"I've got to pare down to essentials, men," he said, still with his excited grin. "A knife, some tobacco, my firearms, matches—a man ought to be able to walk from Cape Cod to California with no more than that. And if he can't he deserves to die where he drops, I say."

Call thought the man was mad. He was so impatient to be strik-ing out alone, into the middle of nowhere, that he didn't even want to stop and give proper orders—he just wanted to leave.

So—suddenly and unexpectedly—he and Augustus had been thrown into a situation they had often discussed. They were in charge of a troop of rangers, if only for the course of a homeward journey. It was what they had long desired, and yet it had arrived too suddenly. It didn't seem right.

"So, we are just to go home?" Call said, to be sure he had it right.

"Yes, home," Captain Scull said. "If you encounter any rank ban-dits along the way, hang them. Otherwise, get on home and wait until you hear from me."

We won't hear from you, you fool, Augustus thought. But he didn't say it.

"What will we tell Mrs. Scull?" he inquired.

"Why, nothing," Scull said. "Inez ain't your concern, she's mine. If I were you I'd just try to avoid her."

"Sir, she may be worried," Call said.

The Captain stopped rummaging in his saddlebags for a moment and turned his head, as if the notion that his wife might be worried about him was a novelty he had never before considered.

"Why, no, Mr. Call," he said. "Inez won't be worried. She'll just be angry."

He grinned once more at the troop, waved his hand, picked up his rifle, and strode off toward Famous Shoes, who fell in with him without a word. The two men, both short, walked away into the empty distance.

"Well, there they go, Woodrow," Gus said. "We're captains now, I reckon."

"I reckon," Call said.

19.

THE DEPARTURE of their captain was so sudden, so unexpected, and so incomprehensible to the rangers, one and all, that for a time they all stood where they were, staring at the two departing figures, who were very soon swallowed up by a dip in the prairies.

"If I wasn't awake I'd think I was asleep," Long Bill said. "I'd think I was having a dream."

"Don't you be bossing me yet, Gus," he added, a moment later. "This might just be a dream."

"No, it's no dream," Call said. "The Captain left, and he left on foot."

"Well, the fool ought to have taken a horse, or a mule, at least," Augustus said. His thoughts were confused, from the suddenness of it. Captain Scull was gone and now he was a captain himself, or half of one, at least.

"That's my view," Neely Dickens said. "If he didn't like none of the spare horses he could have taken the mule, at least. Then he'd have something to eat if there wasn't no game to be found."

"He's with Famous Shoes," Call reminded them. "Famous Shoes travels all over this country and he don't starve."

"He might find that pig before we do," Finch Seeger remarked apprehensively. The pig he had seen in his mind, rooting behind a chaparral bush, had quickly become a reality to him. He was annoyed by the thought that Captain Scull might beat him to the pig—in his mind the pig belonged to the troop—Deets could cook it up in a tasty way.

The country did not look like pig country, to Deets. "I be happy with a few prairie dogs," he whispered to Pea Eye.

Pea Eye was wishing ever more powerfully that he had not chosen to become a Texas Ranger so early in his life. His understanding of the business was that captains always stayed with their troops, yet their captain had just walked off. It was confusing behavior; and it was still windy, too. He thought he might like rangering a little better if the wind would just die.

It did not take Augustus McCrae more than three minutes to adjust to his promotion to captain. He had been feeling rather gloomy, thanks to low grub and uncertain prospects, and now all of a sudden he was a captain, a thing that made him feel better almost immediately. He decided that his first act as captain would be to press for a quick return to Austin, so he could tell the news to Clara. Now that he was a captain she would have no excuse to refuse him. He meant to point that out to her plainly, as soon as they arrived.

"Now, don't you be bossing me too hard today, Gus," Long Bill said. "I've got to have a day or two to adjust to this notion that you're a captain."

"That's twice you've said that. I order you to shut up about it," Gus said. "You oughtn't to be picking on me anyway. Woodrow's a captain too and he'll be a harder boss than me once he gets the hang of the job."

"Hang of it? Surviving's the hang of it," Call said. "I scarcely even know where we are, and I doubt you do either."

"Well, we're west, I know that," Augustus said. "Dern the Captain, why'd he take our scout?"

"Scout up my fat pig, if you don't mind," Finch Seeger said. "He's behind a bush, rooting up a snake, I expect."

All the rangers felt a little embarrassed by Finch's fixation on an imaginary pig. Finch Seeger was a ranger mainly because of his strength. If a log was in the way of a wagon, Finch could dismount and remove it without assistance; but of course that skill was useless on the llano, where there were few obstructions to free travel. With no logs to clear away, Finch's usefulness as a ranger was much diminished. The fact was, Finch was not entirely right in the head. Once he formed a notion that pleased him, he wrapped his mind around it like a chain.

"Now hush about that hog, Finch," Neely Dickens said. He was a little embarrassed for his friend. Anybody could see they weren't likely to encounter a pig.

"We're in dry country," Call said. "We better decide which river to make for."

"I vote for the good old Brazos," Long Bill said. "The Brazos ain't far from my home and my Pearl."

Call walked off a little distance, hoping Augustus would follow. He considered Captain Scull derelict, for simply walking off from his command. The fact that he had split the command between himself and Augustus didn't seem very sensible, either. Though he and Augustus were good friends, they had a way of disagreeing about almost everything. As soon as he said they ought to make for the Brazos, Gus would argue that they were closer to the Pecos. Fear of disagreement had prompted him to walk off. He didn't want to start off his captaincy by quarreling in front of the boys.

Augustus, though, once he came and joined Call, proved hesitant. Though he was pleased for a few minutes to be a captain, the responsibility of it quickly came to seem overwhelming. What if he gave an order and it proved to be the wrong order? All the men might die. Woodrow's first remark had been correct: surviving was what they had to think of. They had only one day's food, and little water. The very emptiness of the plain was daunting. One direction might be no better than another.

"Which way do you think we ought to go?" Woodrow asked— Augustus opened his mouth to answer and then realized he didn't know what to say. The weight of command had suddenly become very heavy. He had no idea which way they ought to go.

"Aren't you going to say something?" Woodrow asked. "You've been talking ever since I've known you, why'd you suddenly dry up?"

"Because I don't know how to be a captain—at least I'm man enough to admit it," Augustus said. "What do you think we ought to do, if you know so much?"

"I *don't* know so much," Call said. "I've taken orders the whole time I've been a ranger. Why would I know any more than you do?"

"Because you're a studier, Woodrow," Augustus said. "You've been reading in that book about Napoleon for years. Me, I'm mainly just a whorer."

He took one more look at the landscape, and then turned to his friend.

"All right," he said. "I'll try to captain if you'll help. I favor trying to strike the Red River. I expect the Pecos is closer but there's little game on the Pecos. If we go that way we'd probably have to eat the horses. We've got those extra mules. I say we eat the mules, if we have to, and make for the Red. There's plentiful deer along the Red."

To Gus's relief, Woodrow Call smiled, a rare thing in general, Woodrow being mainly solemn, but especially rare considering the hard circumstances they faced.

"The Red was my thinking too," Call said.

"Is it?" Augustus said, relieved. Usually Woodrow took the opposite view, just because it was opposite, as far as he could tell.

Both of them turned for a moment and looked at the camp, fifty yards away. All the rangers were looking at them, waiting to see if they would quarrel.

"The boys depend on us now," Call said. "It's up to us to get them home."

"I just hope we don't run into a big bunch of Comanches," Augustus said. "A big bunch of Comanches could probably finish us."

"One of us will have to scout, and the other stay with the troop," Call said.

"I agree," Gus said.

"It's a big thing we're taking on," Call said. "We need to keep our heads and do it right."

"We'll get these boys home," Augustus said, proud but a little nervous. He looked once more at Woodrow, to be sure they were still agreed on the directions.

"So the Red River it is?" he said.

"Yes, and let's get started," Call said. "The Red River it is."

20.

FAMOUS SHOES was surprised to see that Big Horse Scull could walk so well. Usually he could easily walk off and leave any white man, but he did not walk off and leave Scull. When they camped the first night the man did not seem tired, nor did he insist on the large wasteful fires that the whites usually made when the nights were cold. Their fire was only a few sticks, with just enough flame to singe the prairie chicken Scull had hit with a rock. The clouds blew away and the stars above them were very clear, as they divided the skinny bird, which was old and tough.

Famous Shoes had begun to realize that Scull was a very unusual man. They had walked all day at a fast clip, yet Scull did not seem tired and did not appear to want sleep. Famous Shoes yawned and grew sleepy but Scull merely kept chewing his tobacco and spitting out the juice. Famous Shoes thought Scull might be some form of witch or possessed person. He was not a comfortable man to be with. There was something in him like the lightning, a small lightning but still apt to flash at any moment. Famous Shoes did not enjoy being with a man who flashed like lightning, causing unquiet feelings, but there was not much he could do about it.

"Do you know this Ahumado?" Scull asked.

"No," Famous Shoes said, very startled by the question. They were pursuing Kicking Wolf, not Ahumado.

"No one knows Ahumado," he added. "I only know where he lives."

"Somebody must know him," Scull said. He had begun to think of walking to Mexico, to kill Ahumado, the man who had shot him and also Hector. The thought of a lone strike had only occurred to him that day. Once he had wanted to take cannons to Mexico, to blast Ahumado out of the Yellow Cliffs. But now that he was alone on the prairie, with only the tracker for company, Inish Scull felt that it was time for a turning. Commanding men was a tiresome chore, one he had done long enough. He might do it again, once the great civil conflict came, but now he had the desire to cast off all that had gone before and go into Mexico alone. The remote parts of the world haunted him: Africa, the Arctic, the great peaks of Asia. He didn't want merely to go back to Austin, to Inez, to the rangers. He wanted an adventure, and one he could pursue alone.

"A military unit is a fine thing when it works," he said. "But it usually don't work. A solitary feat of arms is better, if the foe is worthy. This Kicking Wolf ain't much of a foe, though I grant that he's a brilliant thief. But I doubt that he's much of a killer—the two skills don't go together."

Famous Shoes didn't know what to make of that comment. There were plenty of dead Texans and Mexicans and Indians who were dead because of Kicking Wolf—their families considered him killer enough. If Scull wanted to fight someone who killed better than Kicking Wolf, he should not have passed up Buffalo Hump, a man who could kill plenty well.

He didn't comment. It was night, a good time for napping. If they wanted to catch Kicking Wolf and get the Buffalo Horse back, they would need to be up walking plenty early.

"This fellow Ahumado's been a notable bandit for a long time," Scull said. "Somebody must have some information about him."

Famous Shoes kept quiet. Ahumado was a bad, cruel man; even to talk of him was bad luck. Ahumado worked very bad tortures on the people he caught. In Famous Shoes' view it was unwise even to think of a man that bad. The old people of Mexico thought Ahumado could pick up thoughts out of the air. If Scull kept talking about him, or even thinking about him, Ahumado might pick the thoughts out of the air and come north looking for them.

Scull fell silent for a while. Famous Shoes was hoping he would nod, and sleep. It was better to sleep a little and then apply themselves to the pursuit of Kicking Wolf than to be talking around a campfire about Ahumado. The smoke of the fire might drift south into Mexico, carrying their thoughts with it. Perhaps Ahumado was so wise that he could find out what people were saying about him just from little whiffs of drifting smoke. It was a new thought—Famous Shoes didn't know if it was true. But it *might* be true, which was a good reason to stop talking about Ahumado.

"He might be a man to match me," Scull said. "Very damn few can match me. I have to seek them out, otherwise the salt might lose its savor."

"We have to track Kicking Wolf first, and that will take a lot of time," Famous Shoes said.

Scull had taken his little book out of his pocket, but he didn't look into it. He merely held it in his hand, as he stared into the fire.

On the plain to the south, two wolves began to howl. One howled and then another answered, which was very disturbing to Famous Shoes. Many coyotes often spoke to one another, but it was rare for two wolves to howl. Famous Shoes didn't know what it meant, but he didn't like it. The two wolves should not be speaking to one another, not so early in the night. When he got home he meant to ask the old ones what it meant when two wolves howled early. He would have to seek the old ones—they would surely know.

21.

WHEN CALL FOUND THE DEAD BOY, and the tracks of twenty horses going north, he knew there would not be a simple trek back to Austin. The Indians were not far—piles of horse turds were still warm, and the blood from the boy's crushed skull had only just coagulated. Call was less than a mile ahead of the troop, scouting. The boy was no more than six years old, skinny and pale, and the raiders who killed him had only just passed. Probably he had been too sickly to travel; they had hit him in the head with a rifle butt and left him, dead or dying.

Call pulled his rifle out of its scabbard and got down to examine the tracks. It was annoying that Scull had taken Famous Shoes—the Kickapoo could have read the tracks easily, told them what band the raiders belonged to, and, probably, how many captives they were carrying into captivity. Call was not so skilled, nor was anyone else in the troop.

He knelt by the dead boy and felt again the weariness that the sight of such quick, casual death raised in him. The boy was barefoot, and so skinny that it seemed he had never had a filling meal in his life; probably he hadn't. The likelihood was that he had been snatched off some poor farm off one of the several branches of the Brazos, the river that tempted settlement most, due to the fertility of its long, lightly wooded valleys.

When the troop came in sight and saw that Call was dismounted, the rangers spurred up and sped to him, only to stop and stare in silence at the dead boy, the thin line of blood from his broken skull streaking the gray grass.

"Lord, he was just a young 'un," Long Bill said.

"I just missed the raiding party," Call said. "I doubt they're five miles ahead."

Augustus, whose keen vision was his pride, looked far north and saw the raiding party—they were so far away that they were dots—too far away for him to make a count.

"I expect it was a hundred Indians at least, from all these tracks," Neely Dickens said, unnerved by the thought that there might be a massive army of Indians nearby.

"I can see them, you fool—there's not more than twenty," Augustus said. "And some of them are probably captives."

"I ain't a fool and don't you be cussing me just because you got made a captain," Neely replied. His pride was easily wounded; when insulted he was apt to respond with a flurry of fisticuffs.

To Augustus's annoyance Neely looked as if he might be about to flare into the fistfight mode, even though they were in a chancy situation, with major decisions to be made.

"Well, you gave a high count, I'm sorry I bruised your feelings," Gus said. He realized that he had to watch his comments, now that he had risen in rank. In the old days a man who didn't appreciate his remarks could take a swing at him—several had—but now that he was a captain, a man who tried to give him a licking might have to be court-martialed, or even hung. Though Neely's fistfights were ridiculous—Neely was small and had never whipped anybody— Augustus thought it behooved him to be tolerant in the present situation; there were larger issues to be decided than whether Neely Dickens was a fool.

Call was glad Gus had made amends to Neely—it wouldn't do to have a big silly dispute, with Indians in sight.

"What do we do, Woodrow?" Long Bill asked. "Do we chase the rascals or do we let 'em go?"

The minute he spoke Long Bill wondered if he had done wrong to call Woodrow by his first name. He had known Call for years and always called him merely by his name, but now Woodrow was a captain and Gus too. Was he expected to address both of them as "Captain"? He felt so uncertain that merely speaking to either one of them made him nervous.

"I doubt this boy was the only captive," Call said. "It's a large party. They might have his sisters and brothers, if he had any, or even his mother."

"They probably stole a few horses, too," Augustus said. "I say we go after them."

Call saw that Deets already had the dead boy's grave half dug. Deets had been given a sidearm, but no rifle, when they left Austin. An old pistol with a chipped sight was all he had to defend himself with—it was something Call meant to remedy, once they got home.

"Should we take all the boys, or just the best fighters?" he asked Augustus. That was the most worrisome question, in his view.

"I guess take 'em all," Gus said. He was well aware that the men's fighting abilities varied greatly; still, it was a large party of Indians: the rangers ought to attack with a respectable force.

Call wasn't so sure. Half the men, at least, would just be in the way, in a running battle. But the complexities of being a captain had begun to present themselves to him forcefully. If they just took the good fighters, who would take care of those who were left? As a group the less able men would be lucky to stay alive, even without Indians. They'd get lost, or hunt badly; they might starve. But if he took them and they got killed or captured, their lives would be on his conscience, and Augustus's.

Another practical side of captaining was just beginning to worry him, and that was horses. It had been poor grazing lately, and they had had many hard days. None of the horses were in good flesh. The skinniest had suffered as much as the men from the cold, sleety weather. Famous Shoes could have looked at the tracks and told them exactly what kind of condition the Indian horses were in, but he couldn't do that. However well or poorly the men fought, it would be the quality of their horseflesh that determined the outcome, if there was a long chase. It might be that their horses weren't a match for the Indian horses, in which case a chase would prove futile.

"What if we can't catch them? Our horses might be too poorly," Call asked.

"I don't know—but we've got to try," Augustus said. "That's a dead boy we're burying. We can't just go home and tell them we found a dead boy and didn't try to punish the killers, especially since they're in sight."

"In *your* sight—I can't see them," Call said, but of course he agreed with the point. The boy was dead. It was the second time in his career that he had stumbled on a dead body, on the prairie—the first, long ago, had been a prospector of some kind. The chance of his finding the two bodies, on the wide plain, struck him—if his route had varied by even fifty yards he might never have seen either body.

The boy, particularly, would have been hard to see, curled up like a young goat in some low grass. Yet Call had found him. It was curious—but there it was.

Neely Dickens, besides being quick to flare up, was also prone to attacks of severe pessimism if an undertaking of a dangerous nature was anticipated. When it became clear that they would all be required to go in pursuit of the raiding party, Neely immediately fell prey to dark forebodings.

"North—I thought we was through going north," he said. "I despise having to travel back toward the dern north, where it's so windy."

"Then why'd you get in the rangers, anyway?" Teddy Beatty asked. "Rangers just go whichever direction they need to. You're in the wrong profession if you're picky about directions."

"Couldn't get no other job," Neely admitted. "If I'd known I was going to have to go north I'd have tried to make it to Galveston instead."

Augustus found the remark puzzling. Why would a fear of the north convince anybody that they ought to go to Galveston?

"Why Galveston, then, Neely?" he asked. The boy's grave had been hastily covered and the troop was ready to move in the direction Neely despised.

"Ships," Neely said. "If I was in Galveston I might could hide in a ship."

"That don't make no sense," Long Bill observed. "Ships go north too."

Neely Dickens was sorry he had ever brought the matter up. All the rangers were looking at him as if he were daft, which he wasn't. All his life he had heard stories about Comanche tortures. Several of the older rangers had described the practices to him. Comanches slit people open and poured hot coals into them while they were still alive.

"I won't have no Comanche cutting a hole in my belly and pouring in hot coals," he said, by way of explanation of his dislike of the northerly direction.

"Shut up that talk—let's go," Call said. The men had been blue and apprehensive since Captain Scull left anyway—dwelling on the prospect of torture would only make matters worse. He knew from experience that when morale began to slip among a group of tired, ill-fed, nervous men, a whole troop could soon be put at risk, and he didn't intend to let that happen, not on his first try at being a captain. He turned his horse and stopped the troop for a moment.

"You need to think about your horses first and foremost," he said. "Be sure their feet are sound. A lame horse will get you scalped quicker than anything in this country."

"And be sure to sight your rifles every morning, too," Augustus added. "Bouncing around all day in a saddle scabbard can throw a gun off sight. If a red warrior forty feet away is about to put an arrow in you, you don't want to have to stop and fix your sight."

Teddy Beatty resented such instruction, particularly since the two captains were both younger than he was.

"I can't think about horses and guns all the time," he said, in a tone of complaint. "There's too much time for thinking out here on the plains."

"Think about whores, then," Augustus said. "Pretend you won enough money in a card game to buy fifty whores."

"Buy fifty whores and do what with them?" Long Bill asked. "That's too many whores to worry with even if I wasn't a married man—and I *am* a married man."

"It's just something to think about that's more cheerful than torture," Augustus explained.

"Survival's more cheerful than torture," Call said. "Watch your weapons and your horses and stay close to the group. That way you won't suffer nothing worse than hearing Gus McCrae talk about whores seven days out of the week."

Neely Dickens heard the words, but the words didn't change his opinion. In his view it was hot coals in the belly for sure, if a man lingered too long in the north, in which direction, led by their young captains, they were even then tending. Neely still thought the best plan would be to make for Galveston and hide out in a ship.

22.

MAUDY CLARK only wanted to die—die and have no more freezing, no more outrage, no more having to worry about what Tana, the cruelest of her captors, would do to her at night, when they camped. Tana led the horse she was tied to himself; sometimes, even as they rode, he would drop back to pull her hair or beat her with a mesquite switch. Those torments were minor compared to what Tana and the other three Comanches did to her in camp. She had never expected to have to bear such abuse from men, and yet she still had two living children, Bessie and Dan, and could not allow herself to think too much about the luxury of death.

William, her husband, had been away, driving some stock to Victoria, when the four Comanches burst into her cabin and took her. The babe at her breast, little Sal, they had killed immediately by dashing her head against a log. Eddie, her oldest boy, hurt his leg in the first scuffle—the pain was such that he couldn't stop whimpering at night. Maudy would hear him crying even as she endured her torments. On the sixth day the Comanches lost patience with his crying and smashed his head in with a gun butt. Eddie was still breathing when they rode on—Maudy prayed someone would find Eddie and save him, but she knew it was an empty prayer. Eddie's head had been broken; no one could save him even if they found him, and who would find a small dying boy in such emptiness?

But Bessie and Dan, three and five, were still alive. They were hungry and cold, but they had not been hurt, apart from scratches received as the horses crashed through the south Texas brush. Several times, during periods of outrage, Maudy had thought of grabbing a knife and slashing her own throat, but she could not surrender her life while her children needed her. Bessie and Dan had stopped watching what the men did to their mother. They sat with their eyes down, silent, trying to get a little warmth from the campfire. When the men let her tend them, Maudy fed them a few scraps of the deer meat she was allowed. She meant to keep them alive, if she could, until rescue came.

"Pa will be coming—he'll take us home," she told them, over and over.

Maudy knew that part was a lie. William wouldn't be the one to find them, if they were found and saved. William barely had the competence to raise a small crop and gather a few livestock; he would never be able to follow their trail from the brush country to the empty plains. Besides, he had left home to be gone two weeks or more; he might not yet even realize that his cabin was burned, his baby dead, his pigs scattered, and his family stolen. Once he did discover it, there would be little he could do.

Yet Maudy held on to hope, for Bessie and Dan if not herself. She didn't know why the young Comanche Tana hated her so, but in his eyes she saw her death. She had seen children brought back from Comanche captivity before, and most recovered. Bessie and Dan were sturdy children; they would recover too. But for herself she had no hope. She and William had discussed the prospect of capture many times; everyone who farmed on the frontier knew women who had been taken. In those discussions William had always firmly instructed Maudy to kill herself rather than submit to savage outrage. There was always a loaded pistol in the cabin, just for that purpose. William hated Indians. His parents and both his brothers had been killed in Indian raids on the Sabine River. More important to William even than the lives of his children was the knowledge that his wife, Maudy, would not be sullied by the embraces of red Comanches.

Maudy knew William was not alone in that feeling. Many men on the frontier made clear to their wives that they would not be accepted back, if they were taken and allowed themselves to survive. Of course, some men wavered and took their wives back anyway; but William Clark had nothing but scorn for such men. A woman who had lain with a Comanche, or any Indian, could not again hope to be a respectable wife.

So Maudy knew she was lost—she had been nursing little Sal when the braves burst in. It was a moment of deep peace, her last. She was caught before she could reach the pistol. That night, when Tana began his outraging, Maudy knew that her life with William Clark was lost and gone. William would not think her worth recovery. Even the children, if they were not brought back quickly, he might disown. But Maudy couldn't think about that; she had to concentrate on keeping her children alive. She had to see that they got warmth, and food, and that they did not provoke their captors by lagging or crying.

At first, as they rose onto the plains and the weather grew sharp, clothes were the first worry. Their farm was in the south; the three of them were lightly clad. All that remained of the cotton dress she had been wearing was a few scraps tied around her loins. When the cold deepened, the Indians let her cover the children with a bit of old blanket at night. She herself had nothing. She had not yet recovered from the birth of little Sal, a fact lost on her captors. She awoke in the morning from her few minutes of restless sleep with blood frozen on her legs. She feared, for a time, that she might bleed to death, but she didn't, though at times she was so weak that her vision swam.

Fortunately an older man, whose name was Quick Antelope, was not so cruel as Tana. He joined in her torment, but without enthusiasm, and was kindly toward the children. When she could not interest them in taking food, Quick Antelope made a soup which tempted them. Once when Tana began to beat her with a heavy stick, murder in his eyes, Quick Antelope took the stick from him and made him calm down.

It was not until later that she learned the older warrior's name. At first the only name she knew was Tana, the young man with the deep burn of hatred in his eyes, the man who beat her hardest and devised the most intricate torments for her. It was Tana who hit her with hot sticks from the fire, who outraged her longest, and spat on her if she tried to resist.

The night after they left Eddie, Maudy began to sob and could not stop. She thought of her boy, lying in the thin grass with his broken head, dying alone, and the wall around her feelings broke. She began to sob so loudly that all the warriors grew angry. Bessie and Dan were fearful; they tried to shush her, but Maudy could not be shushed. Eddie was dead, little Sal was dead; tears flooded out and she could not stop them, even though Tana dragged her through the fire by one ankle and hit her so hard he knocked out one of her front teeth. But, in her bereavement, Maudy scarcely felt the beating or the burns. She cried until she had no strength left to cry. The Comanches, disgusted and fearful, finally left her alone. Snow began to fall, drifting out of the cold sky onto the dark plains.

Finally Maudy got up and pulled the scrap of blanket over Bessie and Dan; they watched the big snowflakes flutter into the campfire, causing it to make a spitting sound. Across the campfire Tana was still looking at her, but Maudy sat close to her children and avoided his eyes.

23.

TANA WANTED QUICK ANTELOPE, Satay, and Big Neck to go on to the main camp with the captive white children and the fourteen horses they had stolen. The horses were not the skinny horses Kicking Wolf was always stealing from the poor farmers along the Brazos. These horses were used to eating good grass. They were strong fat horses, of the sort Buffalo Hump liked. Tana thought Buffalo Hump would be impressed with the horses—he wanted the other warriors to hurry and take the horses and the two children to Buffalo Hump's camp. The two children were sturdy; they had borne the trip well and could be traded, or else put to work in the camp.

What Tana wanted was to stay behind with the white woman and torture her to death, as vengeance against the whites who had killed his father. Long before, when Tana had been younger than the captive children, his father, Black Hand, had gone with many other chiefs to a big parley with the whites in a place of council.

The whites had promised the chiefs safe passage—when they went into the tent to parley, the white chief had asked all the Comanche and Kiowa leaders to leave their weapons outside. Many of the chiefs, including Black Hand, had been reluctant to do this, but the whites made them strong promises and some chiefs agreed, though they were wary. They had no reason to trust the whites, and they didn't trust them. Some of the chiefs concealed at least a knife, when they went into the tent.

They were right to be wary, for the whites immediately tried to place all the chiefs under arrest, claiming that the chiefs had not returned all the white captives they were supposed to return. Tana's father, Black Hand, protested that he had never agreed to return any captives, but the whites were arrogant and told the chiefs they would all be put in chains. The chiefs with knives immediately drew them and stabbed a few of the whites. Then they cut their way out of the tent, but the tent had been surrounded by riflemen and all but four of the chiefs were immediately cut down, or captured. Black Hand was shot in the hip and taken prisoner. That night the white soldiers tormented him with hot bayonets and in the morning they hung him, not with a rope but with a fine chain, so that he was a long time dying. Then, because Black Hand had been the most important chief to attend the parley, the whites cut off his head and kept it in a sack. They said they would return the head only when all the remaining white captives had been returned to Austin.

But it was too late to return any captives. The four chiefs who escaped told all the tribes about the dishonesty and treachery of the whites. The few captives held by the tribes at that time were immediately tortured to death.

Tana's own mother went to Austin to beg for the head of her husband. She wanted to put it with his body, so his spirit would be at rest. But the whites merely laughed at her and chased her out of town. One white man cut her legs with a whip—cut them so deeply that she still bore the scars.

Tana was young, but he had waited all his life to capture a white person, someone he could torture to avenge his father, whose head the whites had never returned. They had even lost the sack it was kept in; no one knew where the head of Black Hand was.

Though he had abused and beaten the white woman, what he had done was nothing compared to what he intended to do, once Quick Antelope and the others took the horses and left. Because of the whites and their treachery he had had no father to instruct him as he was growing up. He had yearned bitterly for his father; the torture of the skinny white woman would not make up for his loss, but it would help.

Quick Antelope, though, would not agree to go.

"We have to take all the captives to Buffalo Hump," he insisted. "Then if he says you can have the woman, you can have her. The women will help you with what you want to do."

"I do not need any women to help me," Tana said. "I want to do it here and I want to do it now. Take the horses and go."

Big Neck, though he had known Black Hand and understood the reasons why Tana wanted to torture the woman himself, agreed with Quick Antelope. Tana was only one raider, and a young one. The woman did not belong to him alone.

Satay did not take part in the argument with Tana. He made it his business to see that the stolen horses did not stray. Satay thought the white woman would die anyway, soon. Her breasts were swollen with the milk she had been feeding the infant they killed. Her breasts dripped milk all day and her legs were bloody. She had made a big fuss in the night, crying for dead children, who could not come back. Though Quick Antelope and Big Neck were right to point out to Tana that the woman did not belong to him alone, Satay would have let him have her. She would only last a few hours at most. Even if she did survive until they reached the big camp, the women would make short work of her. They made short work of white women stronger than this one.

Satay thought it was foolish to argue so much about one woman. The sun had been up for some time. They needed to be on the move. But Tana was a stubborn young warrior; he would not stop arguing. Quick Antelope and Big Neck were firm with him, though. He could prance up and down and make threats, but they were not going to let him have the woman.

Tana was very angry at the two men who opposed him. He felt like fighting them both. Quick Antelope had never been much of a fighter, but Big Neck was different. Though he looked old he moved quickly and was almost as strong as Buffalo Hump. The only way to beat him would be to kill him with an arrow, or shoot him, and Tana, though very angry, knew he would not be welcomed in the tribe if he killed Big Neck over a white woman.

"Put her on the horse," Quick Antelope said. "You can beat her some more tonight."

But Tana's rage was too great. He would not do as he was told. If he could not be left to torture the woman, at least he could kill her. It was what his father would want. He watched her, as she cowered under the little blanket with her children—he wanted her death and he wanted her to know it was coming.

"You can put the children on the horse," he told Big Neck. "I am going to kill the woman."

Tana took out his knife and began to sing a death cry. He looked at the woman and waved the knife at her. He wanted her to know he would step across the fire soon, and cut her throat.

Satay began to feel uneasy, and it was not because Tana was so determined to kill the woman. He looked around. Big Neck and Quick Antelope felt the uneasiness too. They picked up their weapons and looked around. Though no one could see any danger, they all felt that something was not right—all except Tana, who was advancing on the terrified white woman, waving his knife and singing a loud death cry.

Tana jumped across the campfire and grabbed the white woman by her long hair. He pulled her up, away from her children, so she would know a lot of fear before he put the knife to her throat. He dragged her though the fire again and lifted her up so that he could cut her throat, but Quick Antelope suddenly ran past him, bumping him a little.

The bullet hit Tana and knocked him clear of the woman before he saw the horsemen, racing toward them. He rolled over and saw that Quick Antelope had fallen too. Several horsemen were coming and coming fast. Big Neck was among the horses. Tana wanted to reach his gun, but his gun was several yards away. The horsemen were racing down a little slope toward the camp. Tana saw Big Neck leap on a horse and turn to flee, but before he was even out of camp a bullet knocked him off his horse. Tana was almost to his gun when another bullet hit him. It caused him to roll over. The ground where he fell was sandy—he wanted to reach for his gun, but he could not see. It was as if the sand was pouring over his eyelids, so heavy that he could not open his eyes. He heard the horsemen, racing closer, but the sand was so heavy on his eyes that he let it bury him—he had ceased to worry about the horsemen, he only wanted to sleep.

24.

THE PLAN, hastily established, was for eight rangers to charge the four Comanche braves, mainly to distract them. Deets was to watch the spare horses. Call and Augustus dismounted and crawled to within one hundred yards of the camp while the Comanches argued about the woman. When the young brave raised his knife to the woman, Augustus shot him; when the boy got up, he shot him a second time. Call shot the two braves standing by the weapons; one he had to shoot three times. By this time the racing rangers were almost in the camp, led by Teddy Beatty. Several of them shot at the large warrior who mounted and was about to escape, but it was a snap shot from Gus McCrae that killed him.

Call hurried down into the camp and made sure that all four Comanches were dead. Most of the men, Augustus included, were stunned to find that the battle was over so quickly.

"They're dead, Woodrow—they're dead," Augustus assured him.

All of them were surprised that the victory had been so easy.

"I guess we'll be promoted when we get home," Gus said, reloading his rifle.

"There ain't nothing to promote us to, we're already captains," Call reminded him. "If that ain't high enough for you, then I guess you'll just have to run for governor."

"He'd never get elected, he's done too much whoring," Long Bill said.

Gus knelt by the young Indian boy, to see where he had hit him. Deets came up, leading the extra horses, and went to help the two children. Call pulled a slicker off his saddle and gave it to the woman, who was almost naked. She took the slicker but didn't say thank you and didn't look at them. She was staring away.

Of course, he realized, she had been only a moment from death—perhaps she couldn't yet comprehend that she was saved. Perhaps in her blind stare she still saw the knife poised above her.

"You're saved, ma'am—we got here just in time," Call said, before backing away. He didn't think it wise to say more, or to try and rush the woman back from the place she had gone in her mind. It was a place she had had to go to survive, as much as she *had* survived, he felt sure. If she was let alone she might come back, although he realized there was a chance she wouldn't come back. What was sure was that the men who would have killed her were dead.

"You made a fine shot to keep that young one from killing her—he was ready," Call said to Gus. "They're all four dead and we got the woman and the children back, and some horses besides. We've been fair captains, so far."

Augustus was thinking how quick it had been—a few seconds of action and four men dead. Deets was talking to the two children, while the other rangers milled. Neely Dickens was becoming more and more exhilarated by the knowledge that he was alive. Long Bill busied himself counting the horses they had recovered, fourteen in all.

"I guess we won't starve now, boys, even if we get plumb lost," he said. "We got horsemeat now—horsemeat on the hoof."

Pea Eye had charged down on the Indians with the rest of the men, but had not fired his gun—he thought he would be unlikely to hit anybody, while running at such a speed. Pea Eye had heard so many tales about how devilishly accurate Indians were with tomahawks and clubs that he had kept as low on his horse's neck as possible, as he raced, hoping to avoid the tomahawks and maybe the arrows too. But then it turned out they were charging only four men, all of whom were dead by the time he reached the camp. Only one of the men had a tomahawk, and the rifles they were equipped with looked older and less reliable even than his own. Pea Eye went over to hold the horses, while Deets tended to the frightened children. He felt weak, so weak that he thought he might have to sit down. Even so he did better than Neely Dickens, who passed through his phase of exhilaration, grew weak suddenly, and fainted. Neely flopped down as if dead, but, since none of the Comanches had so much as fired a gun, no one supposed Neely to be dead. Teddy Beatty fanned him with a hat a few times and then paid him no more attention.

"He ain't hurt, the little rascal," Teddy said. "Let him nap, I say."

Call noticed that the woman had a lot of blood on her legs—the traveling must have been rough.

"We need to go," he said to Augustus. "These four are dead, but there could be forty more not far away."

"Or four hundred more—how would that be?" Augustus said. The fight had left him feeling a little distanced from himself; all the men seemed to feel that way, even Call. But it wasn't a condition they could afford to indulge, not with Buffalo Hump's camp just to the north.

"Do we bury them, Woodrow?" he asked, nodding toward the dead warriors.

It was a question Call had not had to consider before. There were four dead Comanches. Did they bury them, or leave them as they had fallen?

"I'm told the Comanches bury their own," he said, uncertain as to what was right in a such a case.

166

"I expect they would if they were here," Gus said. "But these men are dead—they can't bury themselves, and I expect they'll be bad torn up by the time a Comanche finds them."

"I'm worried about that woman," Call said. "I think she's about lost her mind."

Deets boiled a little coffee over the Comanche campfire and fed the children a little bacon; the woman would take none. The men dug a grave and put the four dead warriors in it. While they were filling it in the woman began to shriek.

"He won't want me! I can't go home!" she shrieked. Then she ran away, out onto the prairie, shrieking as she ran.

"I was afraid of this," Call said. The children were crying, though Deets tried to shush them. The men all stood, numb and confused, listening to the woman scream. Augustus mounted his horse.

"I'll get her," he said. He touched his horse with the spur and went loping after the woman.

"I was afraid of this," Call said again, looking at the stunned men.

25.

MAUDY CLARK ran away several times a day, every day, of the two weeks it took the rangers to reach Austin. Another sleet storm delayed them, and then heavy rains, which made the rivers high and treacherous. Three horses bogged in the swollen Red River and drowned.

Still, whatever the weather, Maudy Clark ran away. Once caught, she was docile—she seemed to mind Deets less than the other men, so Deets was assigned the task of seeing that she didn't escape or hurt herself. It was Deets, too, who cared for her children; she seemed not to recognize them as her children now.

"Something's broke in her, Woodrow," Gus said. "She won't even help her own young 'uns, anymore."

All the men were careful not to let Mrs. Clark snatch a knife or a gun; Call instructed them to be especially watchful. He did not want the woman to grab a weapon and kill herself.

"Bodies can heal—I expect minds can too," he said.

At night they had taken to tying Maudy's ankles with a soft cotton rope, hobbling her like a horse.

"If I were to break my whiskey jug I expect I could glue it so it would look like a fine jug," Augustus replied. "But it would still be leaky and let the whiskey run out. That's the way it is with her, Woodrow. They might get her back in church and sing hymns at her till she stops screaming them screams. But she'll always be leaky. She won't never be right."

"I can't judge it," Call said. "It's our job to bring her home. Then the doctors can judge it."

Finally they breasted all the rivers and came to the limestone country west of Austin.

"We're coming back with a passel of extra horses," Long Bill pointed out. "I expect we'll be heroes to the crowd."

Just then, Maudy Clark started screaming. She ran right through the campfire. Neely Dickens made a grab for her, but missed. Deets, who had been cooking, got up without a word and followed her into the darkness.

"Hurry up, Deets, there's bluffs out here she might fall off of," Augustus said.

"I don't know how anybody could feel like a hero with that poor woman running around out of her mind," Call said.

"Well, but she might have been dead," Long Bill said. "That brave had a knife at her throat."

"She might prefer to be dead," Call replied. "I expect she would prefer it."

Just then Deets came back, leading Maudy, talking to her softly; all the men became silent. The woman's despair dampened all their moods. They had not even had a lively card game on the trip south.

"I'm longing to see my Clara," Augustus said—they were in country that was familiar, where they had patrolled often; the familiar hills and streams made him think of his many picnics with Clara, the laughter and the kissing he had enjoyed throughout his long courtship. Surely, now that he had been promoted to captain,

Clara wouldn't make him wait any longer. Surely she would marry him now.

"I hope we can find this woman's husband," Call said.

"You better hope he'll take her back, while you're hoping," Gus said.

"That's right, Woodrow," Long Bill said. "Some men won't have their wives back, once they've been with the Comanches."

"That's wrong," Call said. "It wasn't her fault she got taken. He oughtn't to have gone off and left her unguarded."

"Sing to us, Deets," Augustus said. "It's too boresome at night, without no singing."

Deets had been singing to the two little children at night, to quiet them and put them to sleep. Without his singing they grew restless and fearful; their mother rarely came near them now. Deets had a low soothing voice, and knew many melodies, hymns mostly, and a few songs of the field; it was not only the children that were soothed by his singing. Long Bill was able to accompany Deets on his harmonica, most of the time.

Though the men were calmed by the singing, Call wasn't. Usually, after listening a few minutes, he took his rifle and went off to stand guard. What rested *him*, after a day of contending with the circumstances of travel—the girth on the pack mule might break, or they might strike a creek that looked dangerous to cross—was to be by himself, a hundred yards or so from camp. Whereas guard duty seemed to make most of the rangers sleepy—there being nothing to do but sit and stare—it made Call feel at his most alert. He had a keen ear for night sounds—the rustling of varmints, the cries of owls and bullbats, deer nibbling leaves, the death squeak of a rabbit when a coyote or bobcat caught it. He listened for variations in the regular sounds, variations that could mean Indians were near; or, if not Indians, then some rarely encountered animal, like a bear. Often he would sit all night at his guard post, refusing to change guards even when it was time.

From time to time in the night, Maudy Clark shrieked—just two or three shrieks, sounds that seemed to be jerked out of her. Call wondered if it might be dreams that called up the shrieks. He doubted the poor woman would live long enough for the violent memories to fade.

When he came back to camp, a little before dawn, only Deets and Maudy were awake. The woman was fiddling with the buttons of an old shirt Long Bill had given her. She looked wild in her eyes, as if she might be getting ready to make one of her dashes out of camp. There was gray mist rising, making it hard to see more than a few feet. If the woman got away, with it so foggy, there might be a long delay while they located her.

Deets anticipated the very thing that Call feared.

"Don't you be running now, ma'am," he said. "You'll get thorns in your feet if you do. Prickly pear all over the ground. You'll be picking them little fine stickers out all day, if you go running off now."

She had untied the cotton rope that he bound her ankles with. Gently, Deets retied it, and Maudy Clark made no protest.

"Just till breakfast," Deets assured her. "Then I'll let you go."

26.

THEY BROUGHT THE HORSES and the rescued captives into Austin on a fine sunny morning. Nothing prompted a crowd like the rangers' return, whether they had been patrolling north or south. Folks that had been dawdling in stores came into the street to ask questions. The blacksmith neglected his tasks until he heard the report. The barber left customers half shaven. The dentist ceased pulling teeth. Somebody ran to alert the Governor and the legislators, though most of the latter were drunk or in bordellos and thus not easily rounded up.

The first thing everybody noticed was that no short man on a big horse was leading the troop back home: where was the great Captain Scull?

"Tracking a horsethief, that's where," Augustus said, a little annoyed that most of the questions were about the captain who had cavalierly deserted them while they were doing brave work. Gus saw Jake Spoon lurking over by the blacksmith's and waved at him to come help with the horses. He was anxious to get on to a barroom and sample some whiskey, quick.

"Don't get too drunk," Call said, when he saw where Gus was heading. "The Governor will be wanting a report."

"Well, you report," Augustus said. "If the both of us go we'll just confuse the old fool."

"We're both captains, we both should go," Call insisted.

"I despise governors, and besides, I need to see my girl before I get into business like that," Gus said. One of the reasons he was feeling a little grim was that there was, as yet, no sign of Clara. Usually, when he rode in with the boys, she came running out of the store to give him a big kiss—it was something he would begin to look forward to while still fifty miles away.

But today, though the street was thronged, there was no Clara.

Call spotted Maggie, watching their return from a discreet spot in the shade of a building; he nodded and tipped his hat to her, an act that didn't escape the attention of Augustus McCrae. The other rangers had just penned the horses; Long Bill Coleman immediately headed for a saloon, to fortify himself a little before heading home to Pearl, his large, enthusiastic wife.

"This is a damn disgrace," Augustus muttered. "Your girl's here to smile at you and Billy has Pearl to go home to, but Clara's lagging, if she's home."

"I expect she's just running errands," Call said. "It's a passel of work, running a store that size."

Augustus, though, was growing steadily more annoyed, and also more agitated. In his mind Clara's absence could mean only one of two things: she had died, or else she'd married. What if the big horse trader Bob Allen had showed up while he was away; what if Clara had lost her head and married the man? The thought disturbed him so that he turned his horse and went full tilt back up the street toward the Forsythe store, almost colliding with a buggy as he raced. He jumped off his horse, not even bothering to hitch him, and plunged into the store, only to see old Mr. Forsythe, Clara's father, unpacking a box of women's shoes.

"Hello, Clara ain't sick, is she?" he asked at once.

Mr. Forsythe was startled by Augustus's sudden appearance.

"Who, Clara?—I'm trying to count these shoes and see that they're properly paired up," the old man said, a little nervously, it seemed to Gus. Normally George Forsythe was loquacious to a fault; he would pat Gus's shoulder and talk his arm off about any number of topics that held no interest for him, but this morning he seemed annoyed by Gus's question.

"Sorry to disturb you, I just wondered if Clara was sick—I had the fear that she might have taken ill while we were gone," Gus said.

"Oh no, Clara's healthy as a horse," Mr. Forsythe said. "Clara's never been sick a day in her life."

Where is she, then, you old fool? Gus thought, but he held his tongue.

"Is she out? I'd like to greet her," he said. "We traveled nearly to the North Pole and back since I was here."

"No, she's not here," Mr. Forsythe said, glancing at the back of the store, as if he feared Clara might pop out from behind a pile of dry goods. Then he went back to counting shoes.

Augustus was taken aback—Mr. Forsythe had always been friendly to him, and had seemed to encourage his suit. Why was he so standoffish suddenly?

"I expect she's just making deliveries," Gus said. "I hope you'll tell her I stopped in."

"Yes sir, I'll tell her," Mr. Forsythe said.

Augustus turned toward the door, feeling close to panic. What could have happened to make George Forsythe so closemouthed with him?

Then, just as Gus was about to go out the door, Mr. Forsythe put down a pair of shoes and turned to him with a question.

"Lose any men, this trip?" he asked.

"Just Jimmy Watson," Gus said. "Jimmy had fatal bad luck. We brought back three captives, though. One of them's a woman who's out of her mind."

Jake Spoon was waiting in the street, eager to tag along with him like a puppy dog, but Augustus was in no mood to be tagged—not then.

"Hello, Mr. McCrae, did you kill any Indians?" Jake asked, an eager look on his young face.

"Two. Now don't tag me, Jake, I have to report to the Governor," Gus said. "Neely will tell you all about the Indian fighting."

"Oh," Jake said, his face falling. Mr. McCrae had always been friendly with him; never before had he been so brusque.

Augustus felt guilty for being short with young Jake, but the fact was he could think of nothing but Clara—not at the moment. They had been gone for weeks: perhaps she had married. The thought stirred his mind to such a frenzy that the last thing he needed was to have to be gabbing about rangering with a green boy.

"Woodrow Call and me got made captains," he said, trying to soothe the boy's feelings a little. "Being a captain is just one duty after another, which is why I have to go see the Governor right now. He wants a report."

"Yes, we all want one," Jake said.

"You may want it, but he's the Governor and you ain't," Gus said, as he prepared to mount. His mind was in such an agitated state that—as young Jake watched in astonishment—he put the wrong foot in the stirrup and mounted the horse facing backward.

It was only when Gus leaned forward to pick up his bridle reins and saw that in fact he was looking at his horse's rump that he realized what he had done. To make matters worse, most of the rangers, having stabled their horses, were walking toward the saloon, to join Long Bill, and saw him do it. They immediately started laughing and pointing, assuming Gus was so happy to be home that he had decided to ride his horse backward, as some sort of prank.

Augustus was so stunned by what he had done that for a moment he was paralyzed. "Well, I swear," he said, unable to believe that he had accidentally done such an absurd thing. He was about to swing down and try to pretend it only *had* been a prank when he happened to look up the road that led into Austin, down a long slope.

There was a buggy coming, a buggy with two people in it—it seemed to him that the two people were holding hands, though he couldn't be sure. The woman in the buggy was Clara Forsythe, and the man looked from a distance like Bob Allen, the Nebraska horse trader.

One look was all it took to propel Gus off the horse. He didn't intend to be sitting in front of the Forsythe store, looking backward off a horse, when Clara arrived with big dumb Bob.

He swung to the ground so quickly that he almost kicked young Jake Spoon in the face with his boot.

"Go put this horse in the stable," he said, handing Jake the reins. "If Captain Call needs me, tell him I'll be in the saloon. And if he wants me to visit that Governor, he better come quick."

"Why, are you leaving again?" Jake asked, surprised.

"That's right, leaving—I'll be departing from my right mind," Augustus told him. Then he hurried across the street and strode into the saloon so fast that he almost knocked over a customer who stood a little too close to the swinging door.

"Why, hello, Captain," Long Bill said, when Gus burst in and strode to the bar. Without a word to anyone, including the bartender, Augustus reached for a full bottle of whiskey and immediately yanked out the cork. Then he threw his hat at the hat rack, but missed. His hat landed behind the bar.

"Don't call me 'Captain,' I'm plain Gus McCrae," he said. He raised the whiskey bottle to his mouth and—to the astonishment of the patrons—drank nearly a third of it straight off.

Long Bill, perceiving that his old *compañero*, now his captain, was a little disturbed, said nothing. In times of disturbance, silence seemed to him the best policy. The other rangers began to file into the saloon just then, all of them eager to wet their whistles.

"You better grab your liquor if you want any, boys," Long Bill said. "Gus means to drink the place dry and he's off to a fine start."

Augustus ignored the tedious palaver that ensued. All he could think about was Clara—he had by then convinced himself that she *had* unquestionably been holding hands with dull Bob. Instead of getting the homecoming kiss he had yearned for for several days, what did he see but the love of his life holding hands with another man! No disappointment had ever been as keen. It was worse than disappointment, it was agony, and all he could do was dull it a little with the whiskey. He took another long draw, scarcely feeling the fire of the liquor in his belly.

Quietly the rangers took their seats; quietly they ordered their own drinks.

"Gus, why did you get on your horse backward?" Neely Dickens asked. "Did you just happen to put your off foot in the stirrup, or what?"

Augustus ignored the question. He decided to refuse all discussion, of the horse incident or anything. The boys, Neely especially, would have to make of it what they could.

"It's bad table manners to drink out of the bottle," Neely observed. "The polite thing is to drink out of a glass."

Long Bill could scarcely believe his ears. Why would Neely Dickens care what Gus drank out of, and, even if he did care, why bring it up when Gus was clearly more than drunk?

"Now, Neely, I've seen men drink liquor out of saucers—there ain't just one right way," he said, nervous about what Augustus might do.

"I would not be caught dead drinking no whiskey out of a saucer," Neely said firmly. "Coffee I might drink out of a saucer, if it was too hot to sip from a cup."

Augustus got up, went behind the bar, took the largest glass he could find back to his table, filled the glass, and drank it.

"Does that suit you?" he asked, looking at Neely.

"Yes, but you never told me why you got on your horse backward," Neely said. "I don't sleep good when people won't answer my questions."

Just then Call stepped into the saloon. He saw that the whiskey bottle in front of him was half empty.

"Let's go before you get any drunker," he said. "The Governor sent his buggy for us."

"I see," Augustus said. "Did the buggy just come by itself, or is somebody driving it?"

"His man Bingham is driving it," Call said. "Bingham always drives it. Hurry up."

"I wish you'd just let me be, Woodrow," Augustus said. "I ain't in the mood for a governor today, even if he did send Bingham to fetch us."

Bingham was a very large black man who rarely spoke—he saw to it that the Governor came to no bodily harm.

"Your mood don't matter," Call said. "We're captains now, and we're due at the Governor's."

"Captaining's the wrong business for me, I expect," Augustus said. "I think I'll resign right now."

"What?" Call said. "You've been talking about being a captain for years. Why would you resign now?"

Without a word Augustus corked the whiskey bottle, retrieved his hat, and went outside.

"I may resign and I may not," he said. The buggy he had seen Clara riding in was parked by the Forsythe store, with no one in it, and the Governor's buggy, with Bingham in it, stood beside it.

"Dern, Bingham, you're nearly as wide as this buggy," Augustus observed. "The man who rides behind you won't have much of a view."

"No sir," Bingham said. "Mostly get a view of me."

"I'm surprised you'd drink like that before you say hello to Clara," Call said.

"Why would I say hello to her?" Gus asked. "I saw her taking a buggy ride with that dumb horse trader."

"No she wasn't, that was her uncle," Call told him. "Her ma's poorly and he's come for a visit."

Augustus, who had just climbed in the buggy, was so startled he nearly fell out. It had not occurred to him that Clara could be with a relative, when he saw her come down the hill.

"Oh Lord—you mean she's in the store?" he asked.

"Why, yes, I suppose so," Call said. "Were you so drunk you got on your horse backward? That's what the boys are saying."

Augustus ignored the inquiry.

"Hold this buggy, Bingham!" he demanded. "I've got to pay a short visit—then I'll report to the Governor until he's sick of listening."

"But the Governor's waiting," Call protested.

"It don't take long to kiss a girl," Gus said, jumping out of the buggy and running into the store.

Clara had her back to him when he rushed in—he had her in his arms before she even got a good look at him. But the color came up in her cheeks and the happy light into her eyes.

"Why, it's my ranger," she said, and gave him the kiss he had been yearning for.

"Yep, I'm a captain now, Clara—Woodrow's one too. We're off to see the Governor on urgent business."

"The Governor? My goodness," Clara said.

"Yes, and I'll have to hurry or Bingham might lose his job," Gus said. "The Governor expects us to report."

Clara didn't try to stop him but she followed him out the door and watched him as he vaulted into the Governor's buggy and straightened his hat.

Clara felt an old confusion, the feelings that had so often filled her when Gus came: relief that he was safe, excitement when he kissed her, joy that he still rushed in to see her first, disappointment that he left before she could even take a good look at him.

Just a kiss and then he's gone—that's my ranger, she thought. Just a kiss and then he's gone.

27.

GOVERNOR E. M. PEASE, whose campaign slogan had been "Pease and Prosperity," did not like surprises. With surprises came disorder, and he hated disorder. His firm belief was that good administration, like human happiness itself, depended on planning that was careful, intelligent, and firm. Of course, as an experienced man, he had long since been forced to recognize that life, like the state of Texas, was never going to be perfectly manageable, despite the most thorough planning. People dropped dead, fires broke out, storms flooded the land, foolish marriages were made, and the criminal element would never be entirely subdued or eliminated. Nonetheless the duty of honest men and competent state officials was to plan and plan seriously, so as to keep the element of surprise to a workable minimum.

Now two dusty young rangers stood in his office with news that he found to be nearly incredible: Inish Scull, the brilliant hero of the Mexican War, the most experienced military man in the state, had left his command and walked away on foot, merely to reclaim a stolen horse.

The Governor had a map of the western regions spread out on his desk and was attempting to get the young rangers to pinpoint the area where Captain Scull had left the troop, but it was fast becoming apparent to him that they couldn't.

"We were east of the Pecos and some ways north of the Red River," Call said.

"Way north of the Red," Augustus said. "We were several days getting down to the Red."

The Governor, whose spectacles had been unaccountably mislaid, had to squint to make out many details; but when he did squint he discovered what he already suspected, which was that there was no way of deducing where Inish Scull might be.

"Why, there's nothing there, not even a creek," the Governor said. "Inish has lost himself, and over a goddamn horse."

"Well, it was his warhorse, Governor," Gus remarked. "He held that horse in high regard."

"Yes, and what about his duty to the state of Texas?" Governor Pease said. "Did he hold that in high regard, sir?"

Call and Gus had no idea what to say. They had never met a governor before. Call thought they ought to talk as little as possible, but Augustus, as usual, found it hard to keep quiet.

"He made us both captains, before he went," he said. "I guess he thought we could get the boys home safe, and we done it, and recovered those captives too."

"Yes, though I doubt the woman will recover—they rarely do," the Governor said. "I'll endorse your promotions—the state can use a pair of competent young captains like yourselves. What stumps me is Inish. How did he expect to catch up with Kicking Wolf on foot when he had already failed to catch him horseback?"

The Governor went to the window and looked out. Far to the west huge white thunderheads floated like warships across a blue sky.

"Inish Scull is a rich man," he said. "He's always been a rich man. He could buy and sell me ten times over, and I'm no pauper. He don't need the job. He was only rangering because it interested him, and now it's stopped interesting him, I guess.

"So away he went," he added, turning back to the young men. "Away he went. He might be off to California to prospect for gold, for all we know. Meanwhile we've still got several thousand hostile Indians to contend with, and a whole nation to the south that don't like us one bit. It's a poor performance, I say."

"At least he was with Famous Shoes," Gus pointed out. "I expect Famous Shoes will guide him home."

Governor Pease was staring out the window at the Scull mansion, its strange turrets just visible above the trees along Shoal Creek.

"I'm the governor, but the rich Yankee son-of-a-bitch has never answered to me, that I recall," the Governor said. "Every time I call him in for a report, that Yankee nose of his goes up—but that ain't the worst of it. The worst is that he's left us Inez. I expect we can hold our own with the Comanches and I believe we can whip back the Mexicans, but the heavens are going to ring when Inez Scull finds out that her husband didn't care to come home."

Neither Call nor Augustus knew what to say about that.

"She's richer than Inish, you know," Governor Pease said. "They're quite a couple, the Sculls. A Yankee snob and a Southern slut. They're hell to manage, both of them."

The Governor stared glumly out the window for a while. The fact that the two young rangers were still in his office seemed to slip his mind. Below him he could see Bingham sitting in the buggy, waiting to take someone somewhere; but it was not until his reverie ended and he saw the two dusty young rangers standing by his desk that he realized Bingham was waiting for *them*.

"Why, gentlemen, excuse me—you'll think I'm daft," Governor Pease said. "Inish Scull used good judgment in making you captains, and I'll second it. You've both got a bright future, if you can keep your hair."

He had given the young rangers a careful looking over. They were polite in deportment, unlike their commander, the wild millionaire soldier who had just marched off into the wilderness for reasons of his own. Governor Pease was suddenly moved to emotion, at the sight of such sturdy, upright young fellows.

"You're the future of Texas, fine young men like yourselves," he said. "Why, either of you could wind up governor, before you're done, if you apply yourselves diligently and keep to the straight and narrow."

He patted them both on the shoulder and gave them a warm handshake before sending them away—Augustus claimed the man had even had tears in his eyes.

"I didn't see any tears," Call said, when they were in the buggy again, heading back down the hill toward the ranger corrals. "Why would he cry if he likes us so much?"

"I don't know and it don't matter—we're captains now, Woodrow," Augustus said. "You heard the Governor. He said we're the future of Texas."

"I heard him," Call said. "I just don't know what he meant."

"Why, it means we're fine fellows," Augustus said.

"How would he know that?" Call asked. "He's never even seen us before today."

"Now, Woodrow—don't be contrary," Gus said. "He's the governor, and a governor can figure things out quicker than other folks. If he says we're the future of Texas, then I expect it's so."

"I ain't being contrary," Call said. "But I still don't know what he meant."

28.

WHEN SLIPPING WEASEL came racing into camp with the news that Kicking Wolf had stolen the Buffalo Horse, there was an uproar at what a big joke it was on the Texans. Old Slow Tree was still there, talking to anyone who would listen about how the time for war with the Texans was over, how it was time for the People to grow corn, how the buffalo would soon disappear, so that the People would starve if they did not soon learn the ways of the whites and plant and reap.

Buffalo Hump had started avoiding the old chief whenever he could do so without giving offense. When Slipping Weasel came into camp Buffalo Hump was boiling a buffalo skull in a big pot he had taken from a white farm on the Trinity River.

Boiling the skull was taking a long time—Buffalo Hump had to send Lark off several times to gather more firewood. He was boiling the skull because he wanted to make himself a new shield and he needed the thickest part of the bone for the center of his shield. Very few warriors bothered to make bone shields anymore; it was slow work. And yet only the thickest part of the buffalo skull would turn back a rifle bullet. He had been fortunate enough to kill a bull buffalo with an exceptionally large head. The buffalo had been watering in the Blue River when Buffalo Hump saw him. He had driven the bull into deep water and killed him with an arrow; then he took the head and carried it all the way back to Texas, despite the flies and the smell, so he could boil it properly and make his shield. The skull was the thickest Buffalo Hump had seen in a long life of hunting—it was so thick that it would turn away any bullet, even one fired at point-blank range. It was important to him that he make the shield correctly. It would not be a very large shield, but it would protect him during the years he had left to raid.

All over camp the warriors were whooping and dancing because of the news Slipping Weasel had brought. It had been poor hunting lately, mainly because old Slow Tree was too lazy to go back to his own hunting ground—the game in the big canyon was exhausted. Naturally the news about Kicking Wolf's audacious theft cheered the young men up. Many of them wondered why it had not occurred to *them* to steal the Buffalo Horse. If they ate him they would not have to hunt so hard for a while.

Buffalo Hump thought it was a good joke too, but he did not allow the news to distract him from the task at hand, which was to fashion the best possible shield from the great head he had taken on the Blue River; far north of his usual hunting range.

When Slipping Weasel came over to sit with Buffalo Hump for a while Buffalo Hump was skimming the broth from the boiling pot and drinking it. In the broth as in the shield was the strength of the buffalo people. He gave Slipping Weasel a cup of the broth, but Slipping Weasel, a poor hunter and indifferent fighter, did not like it much.

"It has too many hairs in it," he told Buffalo Hump, who thought the comment ridiculous. It was the skull of a buffalo; of course the broth had hairs in it.

"Where is he taking the Buffalo Horse?" Buffalo Hump asked. "Why didn't he bring him here, so we could eat him?"

Slipping Weasel was silent for a while, mainly because he didn't know what to answer. He had met a Kiowa medicine man on his ride back, and the Kiowa told him that the news was that Kicking Wolf meant to take the big horse to Mexico and sell him to the Black Vaquero. Slipping Weasel did not really believe such a tale, since the Black Vaquero hated all Indians, as Kicking Wolf well knew. Buffalo Hump might not believe the story either, but it was the only explanation Slipping Weasel had to offer.

"They say he is taking the horse to Mexico—he wants to sell him to the Black Vaquero," he said finally.

Buffalo Hump didn't take that information very seriously.

"If he gets there Ahumado will boil him like I am boiling this skull," he said.

Then Slipping Weasel remembered an even more surprising thing he had heard from Straight Elbow, the old Kiowa. Straight Elbow got his name because he had never been able to bend his right arm, as a consequence of which he could not hunt well. Straight Elbow had to live on roots and acorns, like a squirrel—he searched constantly for herbs or medicines that might allow him to straighten his arm, but he never found the right medicine.

"Old Straight Elbow told me something else," Slipping Weasel admitted. "He said Big Horse Scull is following Kicking Wolf. Famous Shoes is with him, and they are both walking."

Buffalo Hump agreed that that was out of the ordinary. Once there had been whites who walked everywhere, but most of the old walking whites were dead. Now the soldiers and rangers were always mounted. He went on boiling his skull. What he heard seemed like a crazy business—Kicking Wolf and Scull were both doing crazy things. Of course, old Straight Elbow was crazy himself; there might be no truth in what he said.

Buffalo Hump, though, made no comment. He had reached the age where time was beginning to seem short. He wanted to devote all his thought to his own plans, and plans he thought he should make for his people. A few years before, when the shitting sickness struck the People—the cholera—the Comanches had died so fast that he thought the end of the People had come. Then the smallpox came and killed more people, sometimes half the people in a given band. These plagues came from the air; none of the medicine men were wise enough to cure them. He himself had gone on several vigils, but his vigils had had no effect on the plague.

Still, though many died, some lived. The Comanches were not as powerful a tribe as they had been, but there was still no one on the plains who could oppose them. They could still beat the whites back, slipping between the forts to attack farms and ranches. The white soldiers were not yet bold enough to attack them on the llano, where they lived.

Slow Tree, though boring, was not foolish; he saw what any man of sense could see: that it was the whites, not the People, who were growing more numerous. It would take many years for the young women to bear enough babies to bring the strength of the People back to what it had been before the coming of the plagues.

But the whites had not suffered much from the plagues. For every white that died, three arrived to take his place. The whites came from far places, from lands no Comanche had ever seen. Like ants they worked their way up the rivers, into the Comanche lands. Soon there would be so many that no chief could hope to kill them all in war, or drive them away.

Slow Tree was right about the buffalo, too. Every year there were fewer of them. Each fall the hunters had to range farther, and, even so, they came back with less.

Now there were signs that the bluecoat soldiers meant to come into the field against them. Soon an army might come, not just the few rangers who followed them and tried to take back captives or stolen horses. The rangers were too few to attack them in their camps; but the soldiers were not too few. For now the soldiers were only parading, but someday they would come.

Buffalo Hump saw what Slow Tree saw, but he did not intend to let the whites control him. He had never broken the earth to raise anything, and he did not intend to. It was fine for Kicking Wolf to steal the Buffalo Horse, but that was only a joke, though a bold joke.

What Buffalo Hump wanted was a great raid—a great raid, such as there had been in the past, when warriors went into even the largest towns and stole captives, or burned buildings, or ran off all the horses and livestock that they wanted. Once he himself had raided all the way to the Great Water, coming back with so many horses that they filled the plains like buffalo.

The great raids had scared the Texans so badly that they were eager for councils and treaties—they made the Comanches many promises and gave them small gifts, in hopes that they would not raid all the towns and scare the new white people away.

Buffalo Hump wanted to launch a great raid again; a raid with hundreds of warriors, into Austin and San Antonio. They would kill many Texans, take many captives, and take what booty they wanted. Such a raid would show the Texans that the Comanches were still a people to be feared. Again, they would call for councils and treaties. He himself did not believe in councils or treaties, but old Slow Tree could go. He loved to parley with the whites; he would sit under a tent for weeks, boring the whites with his long speeches.

Meanwhile, on the plains, the young women would be having babies, bringing a new generation of warriors, to replace the ones lost to the plagues.

A great raid would remind the Texans that the Comanches were a people still; they could not be turned into farmers just because the whites wanted their land.

Buffalo Hump wanted to launch such a great raid, and he wanted to do it soon, with all the warriors he could persuade to accompany him, from his band and Slow Tree's and the others. He wanted to make the raid soon, while the north wind was still sharp as a knife—while the snows fell and the sleet cut down. Never before had the Comanches made a raid in the coldest month of the winter. Whites and Mexicans both—but particularly Mexicans—had come to fear the fall, when the great yellow harvest moon shone. Along the old war trail the moon of the fall was called the "Comanche moon"; for longer than anyone could remember it had been under the generous light of the fall moon that the Comanches had struck deep into Mexico, to kill and loot and bring back captives.

For most of his life Buffalo Hump had kept to the traditional ways—like his father and grandfather before him he had followed the great Comanche war trail into Mexico in the fall. When he first raided to the Great Water his ferocity had driven whole villages to throw themselves into the sea—those who could not drown themselves were pulled out like fishes for rape or torture. The captives he had taken would fill a town, and, for every captive taken, two or three Mexicans lay dead in their villages or fields.

But, since the plagues struck, Buffalo Hump had not raided much. With the game so thin it was hard work just to keep food in the cook pots. He had not had time to follow the great yellow moon into Mexico.

Now the Mexicans were better armed than they had ever been; often they fought back, and it was pointless to go into the territory of Ahumado; he was *indio* too and could not be cowed. Besides, he had drained the villages of their wealth and himself had taken all the captives worth having.

Often now at night Buffalo Hump climbed up high, onto a spur of rock near the edge of the great canyon, to sing and pray and seek instruction from the spirits. With his heavy hump it was hard to climb the spur, but Buffalo Hump did it, night after night, for the matters he prayed about were serious. He felt it was time to raid. The high cold moon that sailed over the canyon in February was as much a Comanche moon as the fat moon of the fall. He knew that most warriors, and many chiefs too, would want to wait until fall to start the great raid, but Buffalo Hump felt strongly that the raid ought to be pressed now, as soon as stores could be got ready. South of them, in the forts along the rivers, bluecoat soldiers were training. There were many of them near the Phantom Hill. In the spring the soldiers might do what they had not yet done: come north and attack them in their camps. If the soldiers fought well and killed too many warriors, the Comanches' pride might be broken forever. Instead of following the way of free Comanches, the way of the arrow and the lance, they might begin to accept the counsel of Slow Tree, which was the counsel of defeat.

Buffalo Hump wanted to strike before any of that happened—he did not want to wait, in the hope that the white soldiers would leave them alone for another season. The People had never waited to be led into war by the whites—always they had taken war to the whites, and they would do so again.

So, night after night, Buffalo Hump climbed to the high rock and prayed for instruction. He was not a fool. He knew that the whites were stronger now; they were more numerous than the Comanche, and better armed. That was why he wanted to strike in winter. The soldiers were inside their forts, trying to keep warm. So were the farmers, and the people of the towns. They would not expect hundreds of warriors to slash down on them like sleet.

Yet he knew that, even so, the whites might win. Every time he went into the Brazos country he was shocked to see the whites filling it in such numbers. Always, too, their guns improved. They had rifles now that could spit many bullets and strike warriors fatally at ranges well beyond that of any arrow. Armed with their new guns, the whites might win; he and all the chiefs might fall in battle, in which case the day of the Comanche people would be over. If the great raid failed and the strongest chiefs were killed, then there would be no recovery for the People, and the wisdom of Slow Tree would be the wisdom that would have to prevail.

Sitting on the rock every night, in wind or sleet or snow, Buffalo Hump did not see defeat in his visions. Instead he saw the houses of the white men burning, their women killed, their children taken from them. He saw himself as he had been when young, leading his warriors into towns and villages, bursting into farmhouses and killing the whites where they stood. He saw his warriors coming back north with a great herd of livestock, enough to cover the plains where the buffalo had been.

He had not yet called a council of the braves, because, every night, his vision grew stronger. In his vision he saw a thousand warriors riding together, in war paint, wearing all the finery they could assemble, sweeping down on the white towns, singing their war songs, killing whites, and burning settlements all the way to the Great Water.

Slipping Weasel was disappointed by Buffalo Hump's casual response to his news. The whole camp was excited about it, but

Buffalo Hump was barely moved to comment. Of course, Buffalo Hump and Kicking Wolf were old rivals, and often quarreled. Maybe Buffalo Hump was glad that Kicking Wolf had left.

"You could go catch Scull," Slipping Weasel suggested. "He is walking not far from the Pecos. You could catch him in a few days."

"Am I a rabbit hunter?" Buffalo Hump said. "Scull is just a rabbit. Let him hop down to Mexico. The Black Vaquero will catch him and make a tree grow through him."

He was referring to a strange torture that the Black Vaquero sometimes inflicted on his enemies, if he caught them alive. He would trim the leaves and limbs off a small, slim tree and then sharpen the boll to a fine point. Then he would strip his enemy and lift him up and lower him onto the sharp point of the skinned tree. The man's weight would carry him downward, so that the tree went higher and higher into his body. Ahumado was an expert at the torture. He would spend an hour or more sitting a man on the sharp tree, so that as the tree passed through his body it would not pierce any vital organs and allow the man to die too easily. Sometimes the slim trees would pass all the way through the captive's body and poke out behind his body, and yet he would still be living and suffering. Once Slipping Weasel and Buffalo Hump and a few warriors had come upon a little forest of such trees, with men stuck on them like rotting fruit. There were more than ten in all, and two of the men were still alive, panting hoarsely and crying for water. It had been a startling sight, the little forest of trees with men hanging on them like fruit. The Comanches had lingered by the forest of tree-stuck men for half a day, studying the dead men and the living. The living men were in such agony that even the slightest touch made them scream with pain. Buffalo Hump and the other Comanches were surprised by the sight. They did not often see tortures that were worse than their own—all the way back to the plains they talked about the torture of the little trees. On the way home they surprised a few Texans driving a horse herd west. They wanted to catch one of the Texans and stick him on a little tree, to learn the technique, but the Texans fought so fiercely that they had to kill them all and did not get to practice the little-tree torture. Those who had seen the forest of dead and dying men did not forget it, though—none of them, after that, were eager to go into Ahumado's country.

Slipping Weasel finally got up and left Buffalo Hump alone, since the chief seemed to be in a bad mood and had little to say. More and more Buffalo Hump spent his days with his young wife, Lark. Once when they were engaged with one another they forgot themselves to such an extent that they rolled out from under their tent and coupled for a brief time in full view of some old women who were scraping a buffalo hide, the old women were agitated by the sight; they tittered about it for days. Buffalo Hump's other wives did not appreciate the tittering. A day or two later they found an excuse to beat Lark, and they beat her soundly.

Slipping Weasel thought he could find a few warriors who would want to go catch Big Horse Scull; but when he tried to talk some warriors into going they all made excuses and put him off. The reason was Buffalo Hump. Everyone knew that the chief was planning something. They saw him leave the camp night after night, to climb a rock far up the canyon, where he prayed and sang. Except for Lark he paid little attention to anyone—he only wanted to copulate with Lark or sit on his rock praying—everyone knew that he was seeking visions. Old Slow Tree had finally left the camp in annoyance because Buffalo Hump was so uninterested in his notions of how to get along with the whites.

What the warriors thought was that Buffalo Hump would soon find his vision and call them all to war. Earlier, they would have been glad to track down Big Horse Scull and take revenge on him, but now they were afraid to leave, for fear that they would not be there when Buffalo Hump called them to the war trail. Old Slow Tree's warriors did not much want to go away with him; they didn't share his peaceful views and were eager to fight the whites again.

Though it annoyed him, Slipping Weasel had to abandon his plan for catching Big Horse Scull. He waited, as the others waited, doing a little hunting, but mainly looking to his weapons. He and the other warriors spent many days making arrows, sharpening their points, smoothing their stems. They rewrapped the heads of their lances and made sure their buffalo-skin shields were taut.

Then one day Buffalo Hump finished boiling the great skull he had brought back from the Blue River. All day he worked to make the hard part into a small heavy shield, much heavier than the skin shields the other warriors carried. At dusk, when he finished the shield, he went out to the horse herd and brought back the strong white gelding he rode when he went raiding. That night he kept the horse tethered behind his tent. It was late in the night when he came out of his tent and walked back up the canyon to the high rock. He wore nothing that night but a loincloth, and he carried his bow and his new shield.

All night they heard Buffalo Hump praying. Once the sun edged into the sky, and light came to the canyon, Buffalo Hump was still sitting on the high rock, with his bow and his thick shield. When he walked back into camp, with the sun well up, there was a hush in the camp. The women didn't talk of copulating as they worked at the cooking pots, as was common in the morning. The hush silenced the children; they didn't run and play. The dogs ceased barking. Everyone knew that Buffalo Hump had found his vision. When he sat down in front of his tent and began to paint himself for war there was joy throughout the camp. Within a few minutes he sent runners to call the warriors from the other bands. Solemnly but gladly all the warriors began to do as their chief was doing. They began to put on war paint. No one asked Buffalo Hump what he was planning; no one needed to. There would be a great raid on the whites—Comanche warriors would be proud men again. The endless talk about whether to grow corn was over. Their greatest chief had found a vision, and it was not a vision of peace.

By afternoon, warriors from the nearby bands began to ride in, painted and ready. There was much selecting of horses and packing of stores. The women worked hard, but their voices were hushed. They did not want to be joking when their men were going on a raid that might mean glory or might mean death.

Finally one old warrior, old Crooked Hock, known for his great curiosity but not for his good judgment, had the temerity to ask Buffalo Hump how far he planned to raid.

Buffalo Hump did not look at the old man. He wanted to concentrate on his vision of burning houses. Anyway, he did not know how far he planned to raid—he would raid until it was time to quit. But, as he was about to answer the old man brusquely, he saw in his mind another vision, this one of the sea. The Great Water rolled toward the land and spat from its depths the bodies of whites. The vision of the sea with the white bodies bobbing in it was so powerful that Buffalo Hump realized he ought to be grateful to Crooked Hock for asking the question that had enabled him to see the final part of his vision—the vision of rolling waves spitting white bodies onto beaches of sand. The vision was so strong that Buffalo Hump stood up and yelled at the warriors loudly, his voice echoing off the canyon.

"The Great Water!" he yelled. "We are going to the Great Water, and we are going now!"

Six hundred braves rode out of the canyon behind him, the sun glinting on their lances. When sound came back to the camp it was the sound women make, talking to one another as they cooked and did chores. A few babies cried, a few dogs barked, the old men smoked. By the time the moon rose Buffalo Hump and his warriors were already miles to the south.

29.

"HECTOR LEAVES a damn large track," Scull said to Famous Shoes, after they had been walking for four days. "If we had some form of torch I believe I could track him at night."

"We don't have a torch," Famous Shoes pointed out. They were in country where there was little wood. When they made little fires to cook the game they killed, jackrabbits mostly, they had to use the branches of creosote bushes or chaparral.

"Hector will probably be slimmed down a little when I catch him," Scull said. "There's not much fodder out here."

"They may have to eat him soon," Famous Shoes warned.

"I doubt that," Scull said. "I don't think Kicking Wolf stole him to eat. I expect he stole him mainly to embarrass me. I'm for walking all night if you think we can stay with the track."

Famous Shoes thought Scull was crazy. The man wanted to walk forever, without sleep. Kicking Wolf, the man they were following, was crazy too. He was taking the horse straight to Mexico, which made no sense—Kicking Wolf's people did not live in Mexico. They lived in the other direction.

He himself was growing tired of being a scout for the whites. One crazy man was chasing another crazy man, with his help. Famous Shoes decided it must be the tobacco Scull chewed all day that made him able to walk so far. He did not want to sleep long at night, and grew restless when there were clouds over the moon, so Famous Shoes could not track. On those nights Scull sat by the fire and talked for hours. He said there were forests to the south so thick that little beasts called monkeys could live their whole lives in the trees, never touching the ground. Famous Shoes didn't believe the story—he had never seen trees that thick. He had begun to think of walking away some night, leaving Scull while he napped. After all, he had not yet got to visit his grandmother in her new home on the Arkansas. He could understand Scull's anger at Kicking Wolf for stealing his horse, but the decision to follow on foot was more evidence of Scull's insanity. Kicking Wolf traveled hard. They were not going to catch him on foot, not unless he got sick and had to stop for a few days. The evidence of the tracks was plain. Kicking Wolf and Three Birds would soon be in Mexico. Though he and Scull were walking exceptionally fast, they only had two legs, whereas the horses they were following had four.

Famous Shoes told Scull as much, but Scull would not give up, not even when they reached the desolate country where the Pecos angled toward the Rio Grande. In that country the water was so bitter from the white soil that one's turds came out white—a very bad thing. White turds meant that they were in the wrong place, that was how Famous Shoes felt. He was thinking more about walking off, but Scull had quickly mastered tracking and might follow him and shoot him if he left. He did not want to get shot by Scull's big rifle. He had begun to hope they would run into some bandits or some Indians, anything that might distract Scull long enough that he could slip away. But even if there was a fight, escape would still be risky. Who knew what a crazy man such as Big Horse Scull might do?

When they were only a day away from the Rio Grande, Famous Shoes noticed a curious thing about the tracks they were following. He did not mention it at first, but he might as well have mentioned it because Scull was such a good tracker now that he noticed it too. Scull stopped and squatted down, so as to study the tracks better. When he spat tobacco juice he spat it carefully to the side, so as not to blur the message of the tracks.

"By God, he knows we're following him," Scull said. "He's sent Mr. Three Birds back, to spy on us—now Three Birds has marked us and gone back to report. Am I right, Professor?"

That was exactly correct, so correct that Famous Shoes did not feel the need to reply. Three Birds had come back and spied on them.

"He marked us and he's gone," Scull said. "I expect he's reported to his boss by now."

"Kicking Wolf is not his boss," Famous Shoes corrected. "Three Birds travels where he pleases."

Scull got up and walked around for a few minutes, thinking.

"I wonder if there's a big camp of Indians down there somewhere that he's taking my horse to," he said.

"No, there is no camp," Famous Shoes assured him. "Comanches won't camp where their shit is white."

"I don't care for this country much myself," Scull said. "Let's get out of it."

The next day, at a winter sunset, they came to the Rio Grande. Scull stopped for a minute, to look north toward a long curve of the river. The water was gold with the thin sunset. There was no sign of

Hector or the two Indians, but to his surprise he saw an old man, walking slowly along the riverbank, going south. A large dog walked beside him.

"Now there's somebody—who would it be, walking this river alone this time of year?" he asked.

When Famous Shoes saw the old man coming he gave a start; though he had never seen the old man before he knew who he was.

"He is the Old-One-Who-Walks-by-the-River," Famous Shoes said. "He lives in a cave where the river is born. The river is his child. Every year he walks with it down to its home in the Great Water. Then he goes back to his cave, where the river is born, high in the Sierra. His wolf walks with him and kills his food."

"His wolf?" Scull said, looking more closely. "I took it for a dog."

"He has been here forever," Famous Shoes said. "The Apaches believe that if you see him you will die."

"Well, I've seen him and I ain't dead," Scull commented. "I just hope that wolf don't bite."

"If I had known I would see the Old One I would not have come with you," Famous Shoes said. "I need to see my grandmother, but now I don't know if I will be living long enough to find her."

Scull had to admit that the sight of the lone figure coming along the river at dusk was a little eerie. Certainly it was not an ordinary thing.

They went on to the river and waited for the old man to come. When he appeared the wolf had vanished. The old man came slowly. His white hair hung to his waist and he wore buckskin clothing.

"I think he has stopped speaking because he is so old," Famous Shoes said.

"I'll try him with a little Yankee English—he might want to stop and sup with us," Scull said. Earlier in the day he had shot a small owl—his plan for dinner was to have owl soup.

"Hello, sir, this is a welcome surprise," Inish said, when the old man came to where they waited. "My name is Inish Scull—I'm a

Bostoner—and this is Famous Shoes, the great professor of tracking. If you'd care to join us in a meal, we're having owl soup."

The old man fixed Scull with a lively blue eye.

"You've spit tobaccy juice up and down the front of yourself," the old man said, in a voice far from weak. "I'll have a chaw of tobaccy if you've any left after all your wasteful spitting."

Scull reached in his pocket and pulled out his plug, by then so diminished that he simply handed it to the old man, who had spoken as matter-of-factly as if they had met on Boston Common.

"It's true I'm reckless with my spittles," Scull said. "You're welcome to this tobacco—how about the owl soup?"

"I'll pass—can't digest owls," the old man said. He carried a long rifle, the stock of which he set against the ground; then he leaned comfortably on his own weapon.

"I fear it's a weak offering but we have nothing else," Scull admitted.

"Don't need it—my wolf will bring me a varmint," the old man said. He lifted one leg and rested it against the other thigh.

"I'm Inish Scull and I'm in pursuit of a horsethief," Scull said. "It's my warhorse that was taken, and I want him back. Who might you be, if I may ask?"

"I'm Ephaniah, the Lord of the Last Day," the old man said. From down the river there was the howl of a wolf.

"Excuse me, you're what?" Scull asked.

"I'm the Lord of the Last Day," the old man said. "That's my wolf, howling to let me know he's caught a tasty varmint."

He put down his other foot and without another word or gesture began moving on down the river.

Famous Shoes gestured—on a rise still lit by the last of the afterglow, the wolf waited. The old man was soon lost in the deepening dusk.

"Now that's curious," Scull said. "I'm out my tobacco, and I don't know a thing more than I did. Why would he call himself the 'Lord of the Last Day'? What does it mean?"

"The Apaches may be right," Famous Shoes said. "When you see the Old One your last day may be close."

"If mine's close I'd like to have a good feed first," Scull commented. "But I won't, not unless the hunting improves."

"We don't have to eat the owl—I hear ducks," Famous Shoes said.

Scull heard them too and looked around in time to see a large flock of teal curve over the river and come back to settle on the water.

"When it's dark I will go down and catch some," Famous Shoes said.

"Help yourself, but I plan to scorch this owl anyway," Scull said. "I won't have provender going to waste."

30.

WHEN THREE BIRDS caught up with Kicking Wolf he was walking out of a gully dragging a small antelope he had just killed. The antelope was only a fawn but Three Birds was excited anyway. They had had little meat since stealing the Buffalo Horse. The sight of the dead fawn made Three Birds so hungry he forgot his news.

"Let's cook it now," he said. "Why didn't you shoot its mother?"

"Why didn't *you* kill her?" Kicking Wolf asked. "Where have you been?"

"I had to go a long way to find Scull," Three Birds said. "He is following us but he is walking."

At first Kicking Wolf did not believe it. Three Birds often lived in his own dream time for days at a stretch. Often he would ride around so long, dreaming, that he would forget what errand he had been sent on. When someone reminded him that he had been supposed to secure a particular piece of information he would often just make up whatever came into his head, which is what he was probably doing when he claimed that Scull was following them on foot. Kicking Wolf had expected pursuit and kept up a fast pace to elude it. How could Scull expect to catch him if he was on foot? He sent Three Birds back to investigate, thinking that perhaps Buffalo Hump or some other warriors had fallen on Scull and killed him.

Now, though, Three Birds had come back with a far-fetched tale that no sensible person could believe. Three Birds was just trying to explain why he had been gone four days. Now all he could think about was eating the little antelope.

"I don't believe you—Scull had several horses," Kicking Wolf said. "Why would he follow us on foot?"

Three Birds was offended. He had ridden for days, with little food, into the country of the enemy, to find out what Kicking Wolf wanted to know. He had found it out, and now Kicking Wolf didn't believe him.

"He is following us on foot and the Kickapoo is with him," he said. "Scull is four days behind but he walks fast and does not sleep much. If we wait we can kill him, and the Kickapoo too."

Kicking Wolf gave the matter a little more thought, as he skinned the young antelope. Three Birds usually abandoned his lies if questioned closely, but he was not abandoning this lie, which might mean that it wasn't a lie. Big Horse Scull was known to do strange things. Often he would skin little birds that were much too small to eat; then he would throw the birds away and pack their skins with salt. When he traveled he would sometimes pick up beetles and other bugs and put them in small jars. Once he even sacked up some bats that flew out of a cave—what such activities added up to was some kind of witchery, that was plain. That he had chosen to follow them on foot was just more evidence that he was some kind of a witch man. Lots of Indians were out on the plains hunting—if they had seen Scull they would have killed him, yet he was still alive, which suggested more witchery.

"Famous Shoes would like to sleep but Scull wakes him up and makes him walk," Three Birds said. "When there is no moon they burn sticks to help them find the tracks."

Kicking Wolf decided Three Birds was being truthful. He gave him the best parts of the fawn, for traveling fast to bring him the information.

"We will soon be in the Sierra," Kicking Wolf said. "Ahumado will find us. I don't know what he will do. I think he will like the Buffalo Horse, but I don't know. Maybe he won't like it that we have come."

Three Birds was eating so fast that he could not figure out what Kicking Wolf was getting at. Of course no one knew what Ahumado would like, or what he would do. He was the Black Vaquero. He had killed so many people that everyone had lost count. Sometimes he killed whole villages, throwing all the people in a well and letting them drown—or he might make the villagers dig a pit and then bury them alive. He had an old man who was skilled at flaying; sometimes he would have the old man take all the skin off a man or a woman who had done something he disliked. He stuck people on sharpened trees and let the tree poke up through them. It was pointless to talk about what such a man might like or not like.

"If he doesn't like us he might stick us on a tree," Kicking Wolf said.

Three Birds grew more puzzled. Why was Kicking Wolf telling him all these things that he already knew? Ahumado only did bad things. Sometimes he hung people in cages and let them starve—or he might throw them into a pit full of scorpions and snakes. But all this was common knowledge among the Comanches, many of whom had died at the hands of the Black Vaquero. Did Kicking Wolf think such talk would scare him? Was he trying to suggest that he run away, like a coward?

"I don't know why you are taking the Buffalo Horse to this man, but if that is what you want to do, then I am going too," Three Birds said.

"It is your choice," Kicking Wolf said. He was a little ashamed of himself, for trying to scare Three Birds away. Three Birds was a brave warrior, even though he didn't fight very well and was often wandering in the dream time when he should be paying more attention to things.

When he stole the Buffalo Horse he thought he would take him to Ahumado alone. There would be much power flow from such an act. He would take a great horse from the most powerful Texan and sell him to the terrible bandit of the south. No one else had done such a thing. It was a thing that would be sung forever. Even if Ahumado killed him his feat would live in the songs.

He had not meant to share it with anybody. He had thought when they reached the river he would send Three Birds back and go into the Sierra Perdida alone, riding the Buffalo Horse. He would go to the stronghold of the Black Vaquero and offer him the great horse, in exchange for women. If he took the horse in and lived he would have the power of a great chief. Buffalo Hump and Slow Tree would have to include him in their councils. There would be great singing, because of what he had done.

But Three Birds had come with him and he could not insult him because he was a little prone to wandering in the dream time. Going to the stronghold of Ahumado would be a great test. He could not tell his friend not to come.

"I thought you might want to go home and see your family," Kicking Wolf said. "But if you don't then we had better eat this little antelope and ride through the night."

"I don't need to see anyone at home," Three Birds said simply. "I want to go with you. If we ride all night Scull will not catch up."

"That's right," Kicking Wolf said, as he cracked off a couple of the little antelope's ribs. "Big Horse Scull will not catch up."

31.

AUGUSTUS FELT STUNNED—for a moment he was unable to speak. Once, while he was reluctantly trying his hand at blacksmithing, a horse that he was shoeing caught him with a powerful kick that struck him full in the diaphragm. For ten minutes he could only gasp for breath; he could not have spoken a word had his life depended on it.

That was how he felt now, standing in the sunny Austin street with Clara Forsythe, the girl he had raced in to kiss only an hour before, holding his hand. The words Clara had just spoken were the words he had long feared to hear, and their effect on him was as paralyzing as the kick of the horse.

"I know it's hard news," Clara said. "But I've made up my mind and it's not fair to hold it back."

After leaving Governor Pease, Augustus had gone straight to a barber, meaning to get shaved and barbered properly before hurrying back to Clara to collect more kisses. She had consented to one more, but then had led him out the back door of the store, so that neither her father nor a casual customer would interrupt them while she was telling Gus the truth she owed him, which was that she had decided to marry Robert F. Allen, the horse trader from Nebraska.

Augustus went white with the news; he was still white. Clara stood close to him and held his hand, letting him take his time, while he absorbed the blow. She knew it was a terrible blow, too. Augustus had courted her ardently from the day he met her, when she had been barely sixteen. She knew that, though much given to whoring, he loved only her and would marry her in an instant if she would consent. Several times she had been tempted to give in, allow him what he wanted, and attempt to make a marriage with him. Yet some cool part of her, some tendency to think and consider when she was most tempted just to stop thinking and open her arms, had kept her from saying yes. What stopped her was the feeling that had come over her when he rushed off to see Governor Pease: one kiss and then you're gone. Augustus was a Texas Ranger: at the end of the kissing or what followed it, there'd be an hour when he would be gone; she would have to carry, for days or weeks, a heavy sense of his absence; she would have to cope with all the sad feelings that assailed her when Gus was away. Clara was active: she wanted to live the full life of her emotions every day—she didn't like the feeling that full life would have to wait for the day Augustus returned, if he did return.

Almost every time the ranger troop left Austin there would be a man among them who did not come back. It was a fact Clara couldn't forget; no woman could. And she had seen the anguish and the struggle that was the lot of frontier widows.

"If this is a joke it's a poor one," Augustus said, when he could find breath for speech.

But Clara was looking at him calmly, her honest eyes fixed on his. Of course she loved to tease him, and he would have liked to persuade himself that she was teasing him this time. But her eyes danced when she teased him, and her eyes were not dancing—not now.

"It ain't a joke, Gus," she said. "It's a fact. We're going to be married on Sunday."

"But . . . you kissed me," Augustus said. "When I came running in you called me your ranger, just like you always do."

"Why, you are my ranger . . . you always will be," Clara said. "Of course I kissed you . . . I'll always kiss you, when you come to see me. I suppose I have the right to kiss my friends, and I'll never be so married that I won't be a friend."

"But I'm a captain now," Gus said. "A captain in the Texas Rangers. Couldn't you have at least waited till I got home with the news?"

"Nope," Clara said firmly. "I've spent enough of my life waiting for you to get home from some jaunt. I don't like waiting much. I don't like going weeks not even knowing if you're alive. I don't like wondering if you've found another woman, in some town I've never been to."

At the memory of all her anxious waiting, a tear started in her eye.

"I wasn't meant for waiting and wondering, Gus," she said. "It was making me an old woman before my time. Bob Allen's no cavalier. He'll never have your dash—I know that. But I'll always know where he is—I won't have to be wondering."

"Hell, I'll quit the rangers if a stay-at-home is what you're looking for," Gus said, very annoyed. "I'll quit 'em today!"

He knew, even as he said the words, that it was a thing he had often offered to do, over the years, when Clara taxed him with his absences. But he never quite got around to quitting. Now he would, though, captain or no captain. What was being a captain, compared to being married to Clara?

To his dismay, Clara shook her head.

"No," she said. "It's too late, Gus. I gave Bob Allen my promise. Besides, being a captain in the rangers is what you've always wanted. You've talked of it many times."

"Well, I was a fool," Gus said. "Being a captain just means making a lot of decisions I ain't smart enough to make. Woodrow, he's always studying—let him make 'em!

"I'm quitting, I mean it!" he said, feeling desperate. He felt he had just as soon die, if he couldn't change Clara's decision.

"Hush that—it's nonsense," Clara said. "I'm promised now—do you think I'm so light a girl that I'd break my promise just because you quit a job?"

Augustus felt a terrible flash of anger. "No, if you promised, I expect you'll go through with it even if it ruins both our lives and his too!" he said.

"You shut up, Gus!" Clara said, with a flash to match his. "I've been telling you what I needed for ten years—if you'd wanted me enough to quit the rangers you would have quit long ago. But you didn't—you just kept riding off time after time with Woodrow Call. You could have had me, but you chose him!"

"Why, that's foolish—he's just my pard," Gus said.

"It may be foolish but it's how I felt and how I feel," Clara said.

She calmed herself with an effort. She had not called him into the street to fight over the disappointments of a decade—though it had not all been disappointment by any means.

Augustus didn't know what to do. Though it appeared to be a hopeless thing, he didn't know how to simply give up. The hope of someday marrying Clara had been the deepest hope of his life. What would his life be, with that hope lost? He could not even formulate a guess, though he knew it would be bleak and black.

"When will you be leaving?" he asked finally, in a flat voice.

"Why, Sunday," Clara said. "We're going to New Orleans and take the steamer up the Mississippi and the Missouri. It'll be chilly traveling, I expect—at least the last part of it will."

Gus felt such a weight inside him that he didn't know how he was even going to walk away.

"Then it's goodbye, I guess," he said.

"For a while, yes," Clara said. "My hope is that you'll visit, in about ten years."

"Visit you once you're married—now why would you want that?" Augustus asked, startled by the remark.

"Because I'd want you to know my children," Clara said. "I'd want them to have your friendship."

Augustus was silent for a bit. Clara was looking at him with something in her eyes that he couldn't define. Though she had just broken his heart, she still seemed to want something of him—what, he was not sure.

"You're just saying that now, Clara," he said, though he thought his throat might close up with sadness and leave him unable to speak.

"Bob, he won't be wanting me there, and you won't either, once you've been married awhile," he said finally.

Clara shook her head and put her arms around him.

"I can't claim to know too much about marriage yet, but there is one thing I know for sure—I'll never be so married that I won't need your friendship—don't you forget that," she said.

Then tears started in her eyes again—she turned abruptly and walked quickly back into her store.

Augustus stayed where he was for a bit, looking at the store. Whether staying or returning, looking at that store had long filled him with hope. The sight of the Forsythe store—just a plain frame building—affected him more powerfully than any sight on earth; for the store contained Clara. There he had met her; there, for years, they had kissed, quarreled, joked, teased; often they had made plans for a future together, a future they would now never have.

When he walked into the little room in the rough bunkhouse that he shared with Woodrow Call, what he felt in his heart must have showed in his face. Woodrow was just about to go out, but the sight of Gus stopped him. He had never seen Gus with quite such a strange look on his face.

"Are you sick?" Call asked.

Gus made no reply. He sat down on his cot and took off his hat.

"I have to pay a call, but I'll be back soon," Call said. "The Governor wants to see us again."

"Why? We done saw him, the fool," Gus asked.

"We're captains now," Call reminded him. "Did you think we were just going to see him that one time?"

"Yes, I had hoped I wouldn't have to look at the jackass again," Gus said.

"I don't know what's the matter," Call said, "but I hope it wears off quick. You needn't be sulky just because the Governor wants to see us."

Augustus suddenly drew back his fist and punched the center of the cot he sat on, as hard as he could. The cot, a spindly-legged thing, immediately collapsed.

"Dern it, now you broke your bed," Call said in surprise.

"Don't matter, I won't be sleeping in it anyway," Augustus said. "I wish that damn governor would send us off again today, because I'm ready to go. If I ain't rangering I mean to be out drinking all night, or else reside in a whorehouse."

Call had no idea what had come over his friend—before he could investigate, Augustus suddenly got up and walked past him out the door.

"I'll be down at the saloon, in case you lose my track," he said.

"I doubt I'll lose your track," Call said, still puzzled. By then Augustus was in the street, and he didn't turn.

32.

CALL, ABOUT TO LEAVE Maggie's, was in a hurry, aware that he was almost late for his appointment with the Governor, and he still had to find Gus and drag him out of whatever saloon he was in. He didn't at first understand what Maggie had just said to him. She had said something about a child, but his mind was on his meeting with the Governor and he hadn't quite taken her comment in.

"What? I guess I need to clean out my ears," he said.

Maggie didn't want to repeat it—she didn't want it to be true, and yet it was true.

"I said I'm going to have a baby," she said.

Call looked at Maggie again and saw that she was about to cry. She had just made him coffee and fed him a tasty beefsteak, the best food he had had in a month. She had a plate in her hand, but the hand that held the plate was not steady. Of course, she usually got upset when he had to leave, even if was just going to the bunkhouse. Maggie wanted him to live with her, a thing he could not agree to do. The part about the baby hardly registered with him until he saw the look in her eyes. The look in her eyes was desperate.

"The baby's yours, Woodrow," she said. "I'm hoping you'll help me bring it up."

Call took his hand off the doorknob.

"It's mine?" he asked, puzzled.

"Well, it's ours, I mean," Maggie said, watching his face as she said it, to see if there was any hope at all. For three weeks, ever since she was sure that she was pregnant, she had anguished over how to tell Woodrow. Over and over she practiced how she would tell him. Her best hope, her nicest dream, was that Woodrow would want the baby to be his and also, maybe, want to marry her and care for her as his wife.

Sometimes Maggie could imagine such a thing happening, when she thought about Woodrow and the baby, but mostly she had the opposite conviction. He might hate the notion—in fact he probably would hate it. He might walk out the door and never see her again. After all, he was a Texas Ranger captain now, and she was just a whore. He was not obligated to come back to see her, much less to marry her or help her with the child. Every time she thought of telling him, Maggie felt despair—she didn't know what it would mean for their future.

But she *was* pregnant, a truth that would soon be apparent.

Now the words were out—Woodrow just seemed puzzled. He had not flinched or looked at her cruelly.

"Well, Maggie," he said, and stopped. He seemed mainly distracted. Maggie had put on her robe but hadn't tied it yet; he was looking at her belly as if he expected to see what she was talking about.

"This is surprising news," he said, rather stiffly, but with no anger in his voice.

The fact was, Call had set his mind on the next task, which was locating Gus and getting on to the Governor's office. He had never been good at getting his mind to consider two facts at once, much less two big facts. Maggie was slim and lovely, no different than she had been the day he had ridden off to Fort Belknap. It occurred to him that she might just be having a fancy of some kind—Gus had told him that Clara often had fancies about babies. Maybe she had just got it into her head that she was having a baby. It might be something like Gus McCrae's conviction that he was going to stumble onto a gold mine, every time they went out on patrol. Gus was always poking into holes and caves, looking for his gold mine. But there wasn't a gold mine in any of the caves and there might not be a baby in Maggie, either.

What he didn't want to do was upset her, just when it was necessary to leave. She had been sweet to him on his return and had fixed him a tasty meal at her expense.

Maggie was a little encouraged by the fact that Woodrow didn't seem angry. He had an appointment with the Governor and was clearly eager to get out the door, which was normal. If he went on with his task, perhaps he would think about the baby and come to like the notion.

"You go on, I know you're in a hurry," she said.

"Why, yes, we can discuss this later," Call said, relieved that no further delay was required.

He tipped his hat to her before going out the door.

The minute he left, Maggie hurried over to the window so she could watch him as he walked down the street. She had always liked the way he walked. He was not a graceful man, particularly. Even when he was relaxed he moved a little stiffly—but his very awkwardness touched her. He needed someone to take care of him, Woodrow did, and Maggie wanted to be the one to do it. She knew she could take care of him fine, without ever letting him suspect that he needed to be taken care of. She knew, too, that he liked to feel independent.

Maggie just wanted her chance.

Despite herself, watching him walk away, her heart swelled with hope. He hadn't said anything bad, when she told him about the baby. He had not even looked annoyed, and he often looked annoyed if she asked him any question at all, or detained him even for a minute, when he was in a hurry to leave. An appointment with the Governor was important, and yet he had stopped and listened to her.

Maybe, after all, the whoring was over, she thought. Maybe Woodrow Call, the only man she had ever loved, would think about it all and decide to marry her. Maybe he was going to make her dream come true.

33.

INEZ SCULL, dressed entirely in black, was sitting in Governor Pease's office when Call and Augustus were ushered in. Bingham had come to fetch them and had not said a word on the buggy ride. What was more surprising to Call was that Gus had not said a word either. In the whole stretch of their friendship Call could not remember an occasion when Gus had been silent for so long—and the buggy ride only took ten minutes, not a long silence by normal standards.

"Are you sick, or are you so drunk you can't even talk?" Call asked, near the end of the ride.

Augustus continued to stare off into the distance. He did not speak a word. In his mind's eye he saw the woman he loved—the woman he would always love—steaming up a broad brown river with Bob Allen, horse trader of Nebraska. His rival had won; that was the bleak fact. He saw no reason to chatter just to please Woodrow Call.

Though Madame Scull was silent, she was a presence they could not ignore. When they stepped in, the Governor was busy with a secretary, so they stood where they were, hats in hand, just inside the door of the broad room. To their embarrassment Madame Scull got up and came and gave them a silent inspection, looking them over from head to foot. She was bold in her looking too, so bold that both men were made distinctly uncomfortable under her silent gaze.

"Here they are, Inez—our two young captains," the Governor said, when the secretary left. "They brought the troop home safe and rescued three captives besides."

"I'd say it's beginners' luck," Madame Scull said, in a tone that stung Gus McCrae to the quick.

"Excuse me, ma'am, but we ain't beginners," he said. "Woodrow and me have been Texas Rangers a good ten years already."

"Ten years!" Madame Scull said. "Then why haven't you learned to stand at attention properly? Your posture is a disgrace. It's a slouch, not a stance, and it doesn't bode well."

"And the other one needs barbering," she added, turning to the Governor. "I'm afraid I must decline to be impressed."

"But we ain't soldiers, we're rangers," Gus said, unable to restrain himself in the face of such insults.

"Now, McCrae, you hush," the Governor said. He knew that Inez Scull was capable of high, even cyclonic furies, and he did not want a cyclone to strike his office just then.

"This is Mrs. Scull," he added hastily. "She's upset that the Captain didn't come home with the troop."

"Shut up, Ed," Mrs. Scull said, to the young rangers' great shock. It couldn't be proper for a woman to tell a governor to shut up, even if she was the Captain's wife.

But the Governor immediately shut up.

"I am not so ill bred as to be upset," Inez said. "I'm angry. Do either of you have a notion as to where my husband is?"

"Somewhere along the Pecos River, I reckon, ma'am," Call said.

"I hope he drowns in it, then, the stumpy little mongrel," Madame Scull said, turning to the Governor—Governor Pease had retreated a step or two, and looked very out of sorts.

"He *is* rather a mongrel, you know, Ed," she said to the Governor.

"I don't follow you, Inez—he's a Scull and I believe they're a fine family," Governor Pease replied.

"Yes, but rather bred down, if you want the truth," Madame Scull said. "Inish is the only one left with any fight, and most of that comes from his mother—she was a Polish servant, I believe. Inish's father was Evanswood Scull. He rose rather high in Mr. Madison's government, but he *would* have the Polish maid. So Inish is a mongrel and that's that."

"Fight's worth more than breeding when you're policing a frontier," the Governor remarked.

"Perhaps, but *I* did not agree to police any frontiers," Inez replied. "I need my operas and my lapdogs and my fine shops. Given my shops and a little Italian singing I can get by rather well without that black mongrel of a husband."

Augustus wanted to look at Woodrow, to see how he was digesting all this, but Madame Scull stood right in front of them; he didn't dare turn his eyes.

"Did the ugly little brute give you any warning, or did he just sniff the air and walk off?" she asked. "Inish usually leaves at a moment of maximum inconvenience for everyone but himself. Did you wake up expecting him to leave, the morning he took himself away?"

"No, ma'am," both said at once.

"He just decided to go try to get his horse back," Call added.

"Bosh . . . the horse is just an excuse," Inez said. "Inish doesn't care about horses. Not even Hector. He'd just as soon eat one as ride one."

"But Inez, what other reason would he have to walk off like that?" the puzzled Governor asked, still nervous about the possible cyclone.

"I don't know and neither do these slouchy boys," Madame Scull said.

"We tried to talk him out of walking but he wouldn't listen," Call informed her.

"He was the captain—there wasn't much we could do," Augustus said.

"No, he's a damn restless mongrel—he wanted to walk off and he *did* walk off, leaving everybody, including me," Madame Scull said. "It's abominable behavior, I say."

"Ma'am, he left with Famous Shoes, who's a fine tracker," Call pointed out. "Famous Shoes knows the country. I expect he'll bring the Captain out."

"You don't know the man," Inez snapped. "He won't show up unless he's fetched. I expect he'll find his way to the sea, and the next thing I know there'll be a telegram from India, or somewhere, expecting me to pack up and follow. I won't have it, not this time!"

There was silence in the room. Madame Scull's last statement left everyone in doubt. Did she intend to go after the Captain herself? Her black eyes were so filled with anger that when she looked at Augustus he felt like stepping back a step or two, yet she was so forceful that he was afraid to move a muscle, and Woodrow was just as paralyzed. Governor Pease stared out the window, uncomfortable and silent.

"Will you fetch him for me, gentlemen?" she asked, softening her voice even as she raked them with her eyes. "If we can't catch him soon I might have to wait a year for news, and I won't tolerate it!"

"Of course you have my permission," the Governor quickly added. "I'd recommend taking a small force, perhaps four men besides yourselves."

"The sooner you get started, the better," Inez said.

In Gus's mind was the coming torment of Clara's wedding—he saw Madame Scull's request as a God-sent hope of escape.

"I'm ready, I can leave in an hour," Augustus said. "Or less, if it's required."

Call was very startled by his friend's wild statement. They had scarcely been back a day from a long expedition. The men were tired and the horses gaunt. Were they to set off without rest to find a man who might refuse to come back even if they found him, which was by no means a certain thing?

Before he could speak Mrs. Scull suddenly smiled at Augustus.

"Why, Mr. McCrae, such impetuosity," she said. "I wouldn't think of having you depart quite *that* soon. No doubt you have arrangements to make—a sweetheart to say goodbye to, perhaps?"

"I ain't got a sweetheart and I'm ready to leave as soon as possible I can clean my guns and catch my horse," Gus said. He didn't think he could endure being in Austin much more than another hour—not with the triumphant Bob Allen taking up all Clara's time, as he would for the rest of her life. If the boys couldn't leave at once, then he meant to leave anyway and camp somewhere along the route, with a bottle of whiskey to keep him company.

Call was astonished, but Gus's peculiar desire to depart at once wasn't the only thing that concerned him.

"What if we find him and he won't come back?" he asked.

"Oh, I'm sure if you tell him Inez is anxious he'll be happy to come back with you," the Governor said. His own main desire was get Inez Scull out of his office before she broke into a fit.

"Inish hates to be checked, particularly when he's running away from his duties," Inez said. "They may have to arrest him."

"Just find him and ask him politely to come back," Governor Pease said, remembering that Inish Scull himself was no slouch when it came to throwing fits. Besides, he was a popular hero, and not loath to act the part. Putting such a popular man under arrest might lead to political catastrophe—he might even lose the governorship, if Inish stood against him. It was too much to risk.

"Ask him politely—what good will that do?" Mrs. Madame Scull said. "Inish ain't polite."

"What'll we do then, ma'am, if we find him and he won't come back?" Call inquired.

"How should I know? I ain't a great Texas Ranger, I'm just a wife," she said. "But don't come back without him—I won't have it! Come along, Mr. McCrae."

She started for the door. Augustus wasn't sure he had heard correctly.

"Do what, ma'am?" he asked.

"Come along—are you deaf?" Madame Scull said, turning briefly. "I'd like you to walk me home, if you ain't too busy saying goodbye to your sweethearts."

"Ma'am, I just told you, I got no sweethearts to say goodbye to," Gus repeated.

"Capital!" Madame Scull said. "In that case I may ask you to stay for tea. Being abandoned by one's husband does make one so lonely."

Then she looked over at Call, with a little smile.

"I would ask you too, Captain Call," she said, "but I expect you're more of a ladies' man than Captain McCrae. I imagine you do have sweethearts who will expect you soon."

"Oh no, ma'am—Captain McCrae's the ladies' man," Call said, though Gus glared at him. "I guess I better go see which of the boys is in the mood to ride out again on short notice."

"I think I'd locate a barber first, sir, and let him clean you up a little," Mrs. Scull said. "I believe you'd be rather handsome if you were barbered properly."

"Thank you," Call said. "I intended to get barbered before I came to see the Governor."

"Then why didn't you, sir?" Inez asked. "You'd have made a far better impression if you'd gone to that little bit of trouble."

No wonder the Captain walked off, Call thought. He was not about to tell Madame Scull what he'd done instead of getting barbered and he resented that she had been so impertinent as to ask.

"Where do you think he went, Ed?" Madame Scull asked the Governor, her eyes fixed on Call, even though Augustus had gone to the door and was holding it open.

"Went? I don't know where he went," the Governor said impatiently. "I've just met Captain Call and am not familiar with his habits."

"I expect he went to a whore," Inez said, with a little laugh. "He looks like the kind of man who would put whoring before barbering. Don't you agree, Governor?"

Governor Pease had had enough—the woman *would* stay forever, it seemed; and he *was* the governor.

"Any man would put whoring before barbering, Inez," he replied. "It would be the normal thing."

"That's it! I knew you had starch, Ed Pease," Madame Scull said. "I expect I ought to ask you to my tea party instead of this green ear of corn here, but then you're the governor. You've got duties."

"I've got duties," Governor Pease agreed, as Madame Scull swept out the door.

Call glanced at Augustus, puzzled as to why he would twice say he had no sweetheart to say goodbye to, when Call himself had just seen him holding hands with Clara, outside the general store.

Gus, though, avoided his eye.

"I'll see you at the stables, Woodrow," he said, as he followed Inez Scull out the door.

"It's like eating green persimmons," the Governor remarked darkly, once the door was safely closed.

"What, sir?" Call asked.

"Uncharitable talk, Captain," Governor Pease said, with a sign and a smile. "Every time I talk to Inez I come away feeling like I've eaten a green persimmon—you know how they make your mouth shrink up?"

"I wouldn't know, I avoid green fruit!" Call said.

"I've got to send you out, Captain—I gave Inez my promise," the Governor said. "But it's up to you what to say to Inish, if you catch up with him."

"I might just tell him to keep on walking," Call said.

"That's right—let him wander," Governor Pease replied. "Why come back just to be et alive by your wife? If you've got to be et alive, let some cannibal Indian do it."

The more the Governor thought about Inez Scull, the more worked up he became.

"Damn rich women anyway," he said. "Particularly rich women from Birmingham, Alabama."

He looked out the window for a bit, gloomily.

"Inez Scull would try the patience of a saint, Captain," he said—and then he paced the room for a few minutes, evidently unable to leave the subject of Inez Scull alone.

"Not just a saint. Job!" he exclaimed. "Inez would even try the patience of Job!"

"I don't know Job, but she sure tried mine," Call said.

34.

As THEY WALKED up the steps of the Scull mansion Augustus began to feel timid and uneasy. Madame Scull had marched along, nearly half a mile, from the Governor's office to the slope where the castle stood, without saying a word to him. She had talked constantly while at the Governor's, but now she was mute as a jug.

Earlier in the day, in his vexation over Clara, Gus had kicked a large rock and broken his boot heel. He had been meaning to get it repaired when Woodrow showed up and stuck him in the Governor's buggy.

Now, as he was trying to keep up with the fast-striding Madame Scull, the wobbly boot heel broke off, which caused him to have to walk a little lopsided. His awkward, tilted stride seemed to amuse Madame Scull.

"I believe I embarrassed your friend by accusing him of being a whorer—would you say I did?" she asked.

"Yes, but it don't take much to embarrass Woodrow Call," he said. "He's still stiff as a poker when it comes to women."

"Stiff as a poker—do you mean that anatomically, sir?" Madame Scull asked, with a little laugh.

An old man with a rag was polishing the big brass knocker on the mansion's front door. The old man looked drunk, but he straightened up promptly when he saw Madame Scull.

"Hello, Ben, this is Captain McCrae, he's going to find Captain Scull and fetch him home," she said. "We'll be having tea in an hour—tell Felice we might appreciate a biscuit as well."

Augustus thought that was odd. Why would it take an hour to make tea? Once in the door, though, he forgot about it; he had never supposed he would be in such a grand establishment—everything in the house excited his curiosity. Just inside the door was a great hollowed-out foot of some kind that held umbrellas and parasols and canes and walking sticks.

"I sure wouldn't want to get stomped by a foot this big," he said.

"No, you wouldn't . . . it's an elephant's foot," Madame Scull said. "That tusk over the mantel came from the same beast."

Sure enough, a gleaming ivory tusk, a little yellowish and taller than a man, was mounted over the mantel. The whole house was full of curious objects and gadgets that he would have liked to look at, but Madame Scull gave him only a moment. In the next room a lovely yellow girl was polishing a long dining table with a cloth. He smiled at the girl but she didn't acknowledge his smile.

"Don't bring the tea into the bedroom, Felice, just leave it outside my door," Inez said. "And don't rush us, please. Captain McCrae and I have some serious matters to discuss. Do you take jam with your biscuits, Mr. McCrae?"

"Why, yes, I'd approve a little jam, if it's no trouble," he said.

"Why would it be trouble?" Madame Scull said. "Let us have a few dollops of jam, Felice."

"Yes, ma'am," the girl said.

Augustus wondered what it would be like to work with a blunt woman such as Madame Scull, but he was allowed no time to do more than nod at the girl. Madame Scull was ascending the long staircase and she seemed to expect him to follow.

On the second floor there was a long hall with high windows at both ends. A yellow bench stood against one wall. Gus was doing his best to hobble down the hall in his awkward boots when Madame Scull pointed at the bench and ordered him to sit.

"I've had enough of your hobbling, Captain, or may I call you Gus?" she asked.

" 'Gus' will do, ma'am," he said, taking the seat she pointed to.

"Let's get those boots off—I can't stand a hobbler," Madame Scull said.

"I can take 'em off, ma'am, but it won't be quick," he said, a little surprised. "They're tight as gloves."

"I'll help you, Gus . . . stick out your leg," the lady said.

"What, ma'am?" he asked, confused.

"Stick out your leg, sir," Inez demanded; when he obeyed she turned her back to him, straddled his leg, and took his boot in both hands.

"Now push," she demanded. "Push with your other foot."

Augustus did nothing of the sort; he was intensely embarrassed. Of course the rangers often helped one another off with recalcitrant boots by using that method—with a little pushing on the helpful ranger's backside, the boot would usually come off.

But Madame Scull wasn't a helpful ranger—she was the wife of Captain Scull. Besides, she was a female and a lady: he couldn't stick up a dusty boot and push on her backside.

"Ma'am, I can't, I'd be embarrassed," he said.

Inez Scull showed no inclination to relinquish the foot she held between her legs. Her black skirt was bunched up around Gus's ankle. Gus was so embarrassed he was blushing, but Inez Scull had her back to him and didn't see the blush.

"Push with your other foot and push now!" she demanded. "I'm damned if I'll tolerate any guff from you, Gus. I've helped Inish off with his boots a thousand times in this way. He says I'm better than a bootjack and I expect I am—so push!"

Gus wiped his foot a few times on the floor and gingerly set it against Madame Scull's backside. He pushed as commanded, but not very hard, as Madame Scull tugged.

"You're right, they're a close fit, push harder," Inez said.

Gus pushed harder, and Madame Scull tugged. To his relief the boot finally came off. She dropped his foot and he immediately withdrew his leg.

"The other one don't fit as close—I can get it off myself," he said.

Madame Scull was looking at him boldly—he had never had a woman look at him with quite such boldness.

"Give me the other foot and shut up!" she demanded. "Stick your leg out—let's have it!"

Again, she straddled his leg. Since he had only a sock on his other foot now, Augustus was not quite so reluctant to push—he thought the best thing to do was finish the business of the boot removal and hope it would soon be time for tea.

He pushed, and Madame Scull quickly got the second boot off and dropped it beside its mate. She didn't release his foot or his leg, though—not this time. Instead she held his foot tightly and began to rub herself against the leg that was now between hers. Augustus couldn't see her face, but, again, he was deeply embarrassed. Why would the woman forget herself in that way?

He didn't say a word. He preferred to pretend that his officer's wife wasn't astraddle him, rubbing his bony leg against herself. It was a predicament so unexpected that he could not think clearly.

Madame Scull continued with her activity for what seemed like several minutes. Gus began to hope, desperately, that a servant would wander upstairs on some chore, in which case surely she would stop her rubbing.

Just when he thought Madame Scull might be ready to stop she suddenly peeled off his sock. Once she had it off she stroked his bare foot for a minute and then threw the sock across the room.

"That sock's too filthy to wash," she said. "I'll give you a pair of Inish's, when you leave."

"Well, I guess I ought to get along and help Woodrow, pretty soon, ma'am," Gus said. He was beginning to be actively fearful, his suspicion being that Madame Scull was a madwoman—no doubt that was why Captain Scull had decided to leave.

Inez Scull didn't reply. Instead, to his horror, she pulled his bare foot up under her skirt and began to rub it against herself. Then she reached back, grasped his other foot, peeled the sock off, and stuck that foot under her too. She began to sway from side to side, rubbing herself with first one foot and then the other. Gus couldn't see her face, but he could hear her breathing, which was hoarse and raw.

Then Madame Scull dropped his feet and whirled on him. He had been pulled half off the bench by her exertions already. Before he could scoot back Madame Scull grabbed his belt and began to yank at it. She was breathing hoarsely and there was sweat on her forehead and cheeks.

"You said your friend Captain Call was stiff as a poker with the ladies—now let's see about you," she said.

Augustus suddenly realized what Inez Scull had been talking about when she made that remark in the yard. He felt feverish with embarrassment as Madame Scull proceeded to unbutton his pants. What would Clara think, if she knew?

But then, as Madame Scull opened his pants and began to probe in his long johns, Augustus remembered that Clara was getting married. In only two days she would be Clara Allen. What he did with Madame Scull or any woman would not be something she would want to know. The thought filled him with hopelessness, but, hopeless or not, Madame Scull was still there, hoarse and insistent. When he slipped down to the floor he thought, for a moment, that she might smother him with her skirts. But Clara was gone— gone forever. He had no reason to resist—in any case it was too late. Madame Scull managed to scoot them over onto a big green rug in front of a closet of some kind.

"This will be better, Gussie," she said. "We won't be bumping our knees on this hardwood floor."

"What about . . . ?" Gus said—he was still nervous about the servants; but he never got farther with his question. Madame Scull overrode it.

"Hush up, Gussie, let's trot!" she said. "Just be my ranger boy, and let's trot!"

35.

CALL WAS AT A LOSS to know what could be detaining Augustus. He had got himself well barbered, haircut and shave, and had a dentist look at a back tooth that had been bothering him from time to time. The dentist wanted to pull the tooth immediately, but Call decided to take his chances and keep it. He waited in Gus's favorite saloon for two hours, hoping Gus would appear and they could decide what men to take on their search for Captain Scull.

Mrs. Scull had said she might require Augustus to have tea with her—but why would it be taking so long to sip tea? He inquired of the old Dutch bartender, Liuprand, how long tea took to make, thinking there might be some ceremony involved, one he didn't understand.

"Tea . . . why, five minutes, if it's a big pot," Liuprand said. He was a small man with no skill at fisticuffs—in the course of trying to subdue unruly customers his nose had been broken so many times that it now bore some resemblance to the fat end of a squash.

Call had already decided that he wanted to take the black man, Deets, who had been the most useful member of the company on the recent trip north. Deets could cook and sew and even doctor a little, and had shown himself able to work whatever the weather.

He knew he could not linger over his choosing too much longer. The sun was setting; the men chosen would be expected to leave when it rose at daybreak. He wanted to ask Long Bill Coleman to go with them—there was no steadier man available than Long Bill Coleman—but he had just been reunited with his wife, Pearl, and might not feel like leaving her again, so abruptly. Even if Long Bill wanted to go, Pearl might not be willing to relinquish him again, so soon.

No more, for that matter, would Maggie want to see him leave again, so quickly. He dreaded having to go inform her of the order. She had brought up the subject of a baby, a problem he would hardly have time to consider, given all he had to do before leaving. In fact, he would have liked to linger with Maggie a few days and let her indulge him and feed him beefsteak. His dread at having to tell her the Governor was sending them off again was so strong that he had three whiskeys, an unusual thing for him. It was not something he would have done had Gus McCrae come promptly.

Call's suspicion was that Augustus was somewhere in the Forsythe store, spooning with Clara. It was a strong enough suspicion that he went outside and sent Pea Eye Parker across the street to check. Pea Eye had few friends; he was merely sitting in front of the barbershop when Call sent him on the errand. Call liked the tall lanky boy; he thought he might take him with them if Gus had no objection.

Pea Eye was back in the saloon before Call had had much time to even lift his glass.

"Nope, he ain't in the store—I asked the lady," Pea Eye said. "She ain't seen him since the two of you left for the Governor's, that's what she said to tell you."

"Now, this is a dern nuisance," Call said. "I need to pick the men and get them together. How can I make decisions with Captain McCrae if he's disappeared?"

Jake Spoon wandered into the saloon about then and heard the discussion.

"Maybe he got kidnapped," he said, mainly in jest.

"He just went to take tea with Madame Scull, I can't imagine what's detaining him."

"Oh," Jake said. He got a kind of funny look on his face.

"What's wrong, Jake? You look like you et a bug," Pea Eye said.

Jake was thinking that he knew exactly what Captain McCrae was doing, if he was with Madame Scull. He remembered his own hot actions with her, in the closet, all too well—the memories of their active lust were a torment to him at night.

"I ain't et no bug—I ain't that green," Jake replied. "I just swallowed wrong."

"But you ain't eating nothing," Pea Eye persisted. "What did you swallow, anyway?"

"Because I had air in my mouth, you fool," Jake said, irritated by Pea Eye's questioning.

"Captain, if you're going off again, can I go?" Jake asked, boldly. "There ain't much to do in town, with the boys gone."

The question took Call unprepared. In fact, the new assignment took him unprepared. The Governor, mainly to placate Madame Scull, had given them a task that seemed more ridiculous the longer he thought about it. There were thousands of miles to search, and the man they were looking for had the tracker with him. Captain Scull's departure had been wild folly to begin with, and now he and Augustus were being asked to compound the folly.

"I'll discuss it with Captain McCrae, Jake," Call said.

"I'm anxious to go if there's a place," Jake said. He thought it unjust that Pea Eye had got to go on the last expedition, while he had had to stay and run errands for Stove Jones and Lee Hitch, two rangers who had both suffered broken limbs from trying to ride half-broken horses. Though unable to travel, the two men were easily able to come up with twenty or thirty errands a day that they demanded Jake run. Mainly, they themselves stayed in their bunks and drank whiskey. On occasion they even tried to get him to fetch them whores.

Now there was another expedition forming, and Jake was determined to go; life in Austin had become so boresome that he'd even put his scalp at risk rather than stay. If the captains wouldn't take him, he meant to quit the rangers and try to get on as a cowboy on one of the big ranches down south of San Antonio.

Call grew more and more vexed. He was also a little drunk, thanks to Gus's lagging, and needed to get on with their decision making. He got up and left the barroom, meaning to walk up to Long Bill Coleman's house—or rather, Pearl's. Long Bill never had a cent to his name, but Pearl had been left a good frame house by her father, a merchant who had been ambushed and killed by the Comanches while on a routine trip to San Antonio. Call was on his way to see whether Long Bill had the appetite for more travel when he happened to spot Augustus, coming down the street in the deep dusk. Augustus usually strolled along at a brisk pace, but now he was walking slowly, as if exhausted. Call wondered if his friend had fallen ill suddenly—in the Governor's office he had been somber, but not sick.

"Where have you been? We need to be choosing our men and getting them ready," Call said, three hours of frustration bursting out of him.

"You choose, Woodrow, all I want is a bottle and a pallet," Augustus said.

"A pallet? Are you sick?" Call asked. "It's not even good dark."

"Yes, sick of Austin," Gus said. "I wish we were leaving right this minute."

Call was puzzled by the change in his old friend. All energy and spirit seemed to have drained out of him—and Gus McCrae was a man who could always be counted on for energy and spirit.

"You didn't say where you'd been," Call said.

Augustus turned and pointed up the hill, toward the Scull castle, its turrets just visible in the darkening sky.

"Up there—that's where I've been," Augustus said.

"Gus, it's been three hours—you must have drunk a fine lot of tea," Call remarked.

"Nope, we never got around to the tea," Augustus said. "Not the tea and not the biscuits, either. And while we're on the subject I don't think we ought to bring the Captain back."

"Why not?" Call asked. "That's the only reason we're going, to bring him back. Of course, we've got to find him first."

"You don't know Madame Scull, Woodrow," Gus said. "I'd say running off might be the Captain's only chance."

"I don't know what you're talking about," Call said. "I've no doubt they squabble, but they've been married nearly twenty-five years—the Captain told me that himself."

"He's a better man than me, then," Augustus said. "I wouldn't last no twenty-five years. Twenty-five days would put me under."

Then, without more comment, he walked off toward the bunkhouse, leaving Woodrow Call more puzzled than he had been before.

36.

WHEN CALL CAME IN with his saddlebags over his shoulder, Maggie's spirits sank. She was too disappointed to speak. Woodrow only brought his saddlebag into her rooms when he was leaving early—he was meticulous about checking his gear and would spend an hour or more at his task whenever he had to leave.

"You've only been here a day," she said sadly. "We haven't even talked about the baby."

"Well, you ain't having it tomorrow, and this may be a short trip," he said, not unkindly. "I expect we can discuss it when I come back."

What if you don't come back? she thought, but she didn't say it. If she spoke it would only anger him and she would risk losing the little sweet time they might have. Austin was full of widows whose husbands had ridden off one morning, like Pearl Coleman's father, and never come back. What Maggie felt was the fear any woman felt when her man had to venture beyond the settled frontier; and even the settled frontier was far from being really safe. Every year, still, settlers were killed and women and children stolen from their cabins, almost within sight of Austin. There was not much safety in town, but there was no safety where Woodrow had to go.

Worry about him sank deep in Maggie's gut, where it mixed with another grave worry: the question of what she would do if Woodrow refused to marry her, or accept her child as his. A woman with a child born out of wedlock had no hope of rising, not in Austin. If she wanted to raise the child properly she would have to move to another town and try to pass herself off as a widow. It would be hard, so hard that Maggie feared to think about it. Unless

Woodrow helped her she would be as good as lost, and the child as well.

But Maggie swallowed her questions and her doubts, as she had many times before. After all, Woodrow was there; he had come to her on his return and now again, on the eve of his departure.

He was there, not somewhere else; she did her best to push aside her worries and make the best of their time. The depth of her love for Woodrow Call gave him a power over her that was too great—and he didn't even know he had it.

"All right, I'll make you a meal—there's still two beefsteaks, if you want Gus to come," she said. It made Maggie happy if Woodrow brought Augustus home to eat with them: it was as if he were bringing his best friend home to eat his wife's cooking. She wasn't really his wife yet, but they were jolly on those occasions. Sometimes she and Gus could even tempt Woodrow into playing cards, or joining them in a singsong. He was a poor cardplayer and not much of a singer, but such times were still jolly.

"Gus went off to Madame Scull's and stayed three hours—that's why I'm late," Call said. "He just went to drink tea with her—I don't know why it took three hours. Now he's too tired to eat. I don't think I've ever seen Gus too tired to eat before."

Maggie smiled—everyone knew that Madame Scull took young men as lovers, the younger the better. She had taken Jake Spoon for a while; everyone knew that too. Lately Jake had come mooning around, wanting to make up to Maggie for his bad behavior. He had offered to carry her groceries twice, and had generally tried to make himself useful; but Maggie remained cool. She knew his kind all too well. Jake would be nice until he had what he wanted, and then, if she denied him a favor, he would pull her hair or slap her again. There was no changing men—not much, anyway; mainly men stayed the way they were, no matter what women did. Woodrow Call was not all she wanted him to be, but he had never raised a hand to her and would not think of pulling her hair. Jake could offer to carry her groceries if he wanted, but she would not forget what he did.

Call noticed her smile, when he mentioned Gus's fatigue.

"What's that grin for? What do you know?" he asked.

"It's just a smile, Woodrow—I'm happy because you're here," Maggie said.

"No, it was something else—something about Gus," he said. "If you've a notion of why he stayed at Madame Scull's so long I'd like to know it."

Maggie knew she was treading on dangerous ground. Woodrow had strict notions of what was right and what was wrong. But she was a little riled, too: riled because he was going away so soon, riled because he wouldn't talk about the baby, riled because she had to keep swallowing down the way she felt and the things she needed to say. If he wouldn't think about her baby, at least she could get his goat a little about their friend.

"I know why he's tired, that's all," she said, pounding the beefsteak.

"Why, then, tell me," Call asked.

"Because Madame Scull took his pants down—if you'd gone she would have tried to take yours down too," Maggie said.

Call flinched as if he had been slapped, or jabbed with a pin.

"Now, that's wrong!" he said loudly, but without much confidence in his own conclusion. "How could you know that?"

"Because that's what she does with any man who goes home with her, when the Captain's away," Maggie said. "It's the talk of all the barrooms and not just the barrooms—she don't care who knows."

"Well, she ought to care," Call said. "I expect the Captain would take the hide off her if he knew she was stirring up talk like that."

"Woodrow, it's not just talk," Maggie said. "I seen her kissing a boy myself, over behind some horses. One of the horses moved and I saw it."

"What boy?" Call said. "Maybe they were cousins."

"No, it was Jurgen, that German boy the Captain hung for stealing horses," Maggie insisted. "He couldn't even speak English."

"They could still have been cousins," Call said—but then he

gave up arguing. No wonder Gus had come down the hill looking as he sometimes looked when he had spent a day in a whorehouse.

"If it's true I just hope the Captain don't find out," Call said.

"Don't you think he knows?" Maggie asked. Sometimes Woodrow seemed so young to her, not young outside but young inside, that it made her fearful for him; it made her even more determined to marry him and take care of him. If she didn't, some woman like Madame Scull would figure out how young he was and do him bad harm.

"How could he know if she only does it when he's gone?" Call asked.

"You don't have to be with somebody every minute to know things about them," Maggie told him. "I'm not with you every minute, but I know you're a good man. If you was a bad man I wouldn't have to be with you every minute to know that, either."

Her voice quavered a little, when she said she knew he was a good man. It made Call feel a touch of guilt. He was always leaving Maggie just when she had her hopes up that he'd stay. Of course he left because it was his duty, but he recognized that that didn't really make things any easier for Maggie.

"Now you're risking your life because she wants somebody to go look for her husband, and she ain't even true to him," Maggie said bitterly.

When she thought of Madame Scull's dreadful behavior—kissing and fondling young men right in the street—she got incensed. No decent whore would behave as badly as Madame Scull, and yet she enjoyed high position and went to all the fanciest balls. More than that, she could send men into danger at her whim, as she was doing with Woodrow and the boys.

"I guess if it's true and Clara finds out about it, it'll be the end of her and Gus," Call said. "I expect she'll take an axe handle to him and run him out of town."

Maggie was silent. She knew something else that Woodrow didn't know—she had happened to be in the Forsythe store one day when Clara was trying on some of her wedding clothes, just the gloves and the shoes. But Clara had made no attempt to conceal the fact that she was marrying the tall man from Nebraska. The wedding was going to be in the church at the end of the street. Now that Augustus was back, surely Clara had told him; but evidently he hadn't got around to informing Woodrow. Perhaps Gus wasn't able. Perhaps talking about it made him too sad.

Maggie knew it wasn't her business to tell Woodrow this, and yet concealing things from him made her deeply uncomfortable. She knew he trusted her to tell him everything that might be important to the rangers, and the fact that Gus had lost Clara seemed pretty important to her.

"Woodrow, Gus ain't none of Clara's business anymore," she said nervously.

"Why isn't he?" Call asked, surprised. "He's been her business as long as I've knowed him, and that's years."

"She's marrying that horse trader," Maggie said. "The wedding's on Sunday."

Woodrow Call was stunned. The news about Madame Scull's faithless behavior was shocking and repulsive, but the news about Clara Forsythe hit him so hard that he almost lost his appetite for the juicy beefsteak Maggie had cooked him. He knew now why Augustus wanted to leave town so quickly: he wanted to be out of town when the wedding took place.

"I never expected her to marry anybody but Gus," he said. "This is a bad surprise. I doubt Gus expected her to marry anybody but him, either. I think he hoped his promotion would win her over."

To Maggie, his stunned comment was just more evidence that Woodrow was young inside. He wouldn't realize that Clara Forsythe wouldn't care a fig for Gus's promotion; nor did he realize that it didn't take a woman ten years to say yes to a man she meant to marry. She herself would have said yes to Woodrow in a matter of days, had he asked her. The fact that Clara had kept Gus waiting so long just meant that she didn't trust him. To Maggie it seemed that simple, and she knew that Clara was right. Gus McCrae could be plenty of fun, but trusting him would be the wrong thing to do.

Instead of saying those things to Woodrow she fed him some apple tarts she had saved up to buy from the bakery. They were such delicious apple tarts that he ate four of them, and, after a time, went to sleep. Maggie held him in her arms a long time. She knew there was much she could say to him, and perhaps *should* say to him, about the ways of women; but she only had one night and decided she had just rather hold him in her arms.

37.

THE TROOP did not make an auspicious appearance when they gathered in the lots at dawn and began to saddle their horses and tie on their gear. Call had decided to take the two boys, Pea Eye and Jake Spoon, plus Deets to do the cooking, Long Bill in case there was a desperate fight, and of course himself and Augustus—the latter had not appeared.

Long Bill was there, at least, dark circles under his eyes and a haggard look on his face.

"Didn't you sleep, Bill?" Call asked.

"No, Pearl cried all night—she ain't up to being consoled," Long Bill said.

"Women will just cry when the menfolk leave," Call said. His own shirt was wet from Maggie's tears.

"Did you hear about Clara? It's got me upset," Long Bill said. "I was looking forward to eating her cooking, once Gus married her, but I guess that prospect's gone."

"Have you seen him?" Call asked.

"No, but I heard he fought two Germans in a whorehouse last night," Long Bill said. "I don't know what the fight was about."

The two youngsters, Pea Eye and Jake, were nervous, Call saw. They kept walking around and around their horses, checking and rechecking their gear.

"Gus is late," Call observed. "Maybe he didn't win the fight."

"I imagine he won it," Long Bill said. "I suppose Gus could handle two Germans, even if he was heartbroken."

Call kept expecting to see Augustus ride up at any minute, but he didn't. They were all saddled up and ready. It was vexing to wait.

"His horse ain't here, Captain," Long Bill said. "Maybe he left without us."

"I can't get used to you calling me 'Captain,' Bill," Call said. It was an honest dilemma. He and Long Bill had been equal as rangers for years, and, in not a few instances, Long Bill, who was five years older than Call, had shown himself to be more than equal in judgment and skill. He was better with skittish horses than Call was, to name only one skill at which he excelled. Yet, through the whim of Captain Scull, he and Gus had been elevated, while Long Bill was still a common ranger. It was a troubling consideration that wouldn't leave his mind.

Long Bill, though he appreciated the comment, had no trouble with the shift in status. He was a humble man and considered himself happy in the love of his wife and the friendship of his comrades in arms.

"No, that's the way it ought to be," he said. "You're in this for the long haul, Woodrow, and with me it's just temporary."

"Temporary? You've been at it as long as I have, Bill," Call said.

"Yes, but Pearl and me are having a baby," Long Bill confided. "I expect that's one reason she was so upset. She made me promise this would be my last trip with you and the boys—that's a promise I have to keep. Rangering is mostly for bachelors. Married fellows oughtn't to be taking these risks."

"Bill, I didn't know," Call said, startled by the similarity of their circumstances. Long Bill had fathered a child and now Maggie was claiming he had done the same.

"You're welcome to stay if you feel you need to," he told Long Bill. "You've done your share of rangering. You did it long ago."

"Why, no, Captain. I'm here and I'll go," Long Bill said. "I mean to have one last jaunt before I settle down."

Just then they saw Augustus McCrae come around the corner by the saloon. Gus was walking slowly, leading his horse. Call saw that he was heading across the street toward the Forsythe store, which was not yet open, it being barely dawn. Call wondered if the matter of Clara's marriage was really as settled a thing as everyone seemed to think.

"There he is, headed for Clara's," Long Bill said. "Shall we wait for him?"

Call saw Gus turn his face toward where they sat, already mounted. Gus didn't wave, but he did see them. Though anxious to get started, Call hated to ride out without his friend.

"I guess he'll catch up with us—he knows which way we're headed," Jake Spoon said. He was anxious to get started before he grew any more apprehensive.

"If he lives he might," Long Bill said, looking at the man walking slowly across the street, leading his horse.

"Well, why wouldn't he live?" Jake asked.

Long Bill did not reply. What he knew was that Gus McCrae was mighty fond of Clara Forsythe, and now she was gone for good. He was not stepping high or jaunty, and Gus was usually a high-stepper, in the mornings. Of course Bill didn't feel like explaining it to a green boy such as Jake.

Call too saw the dejection in Gus's walk.

"I expect he's just going to say goodbye," Call said. "We better wait. He might appreciate the company."

38.

AUGUSTUS FELT QUEASY in his stomach and achy in his head from a long night of drinking, but he wanted one last word with Clara, even though he didn't expect it to improve his spirits much. But, since the day he had met her, every time he rode out of Austin on patrol he had stopped by to say goodbye to Clara. She wasn't quite a married woman yet—one more goodbye wouldn't be improper.

Clara was expecting him. When she saw him come round to the back of the store she went out barefoot to meet him. A wind whistled through the street, ruffling the feathers of some chickens that were pecking away on the little slope behind the store.

"It's cold, you'll get goose bumps," Gus said, when he saw that she was barefoot.

Clara shrugged. She saw that one of his eyes was puffy.

"Who'd you fight?" she asked.

"Didn't get their names," Gus said. "But they were rude. I won't tolerate rude behavior."

To his surprise he saw tears shining on Clara's cheeks.

"Why, now, what's the matter?" he asked, concerned. "I ain't hurt. It wasn't much of a fight."

"I'm not crying about the fight," Clara said.

"Then why *are* you crying?" he asked. He hitched his horse and sat down by her for a moment on the step. He cautiously put his arm around her, not knowing if that was still proper—Clara not only accepted it, she moved closer and clasped his hand, tight.

"It's hard to say goodbye to old boyfriends—especially you," she said. "That's why."

"If it's so dern hard, then why are you?" Gus asked her. "Where's the sense?"

Clara shrugged again, as she had when he told her she had goose bumps.

Then she put her head in her arms and cried harder, for a minute or two. Gus didn't know what to think, or what to say.

When Clara finished crying she wiped her eyes on her skirt and turned to him once more.

"Give me a kiss, now, Gus," she said.

"Well, that's always been easy to manage," he said. When they kissed he felt a salty wetness, from the tears on her cheeks.

As soon as the kiss was over, Clara stood up.

"Go along now," she said. "I hope to see you in Nebraska in about ten years."

"You will see me," Gus said. He looked up at her again. He had never seen her look lovelier. He had never loved her more. Unable to manage his feelings, he jumped on his horse, waved once, and trotted away. He looked back but didn't wave.

Clara stood up and dried her cheeks—despite herself, tears kept spilling out. Her father and mother would be up soon, she knew, but she didn't feel like facing them, just yet. She walked slowly around the store to the street in front of it. The six departing rangers were just passing. Call and Gus, both silent, were in the lead. Clara stood back in the shadows—she didn't want them to see her, and they didn't.

Along the street, also hidden in the shadow of buildings, two other women watched the rangers leave: Maggie Tilton and Pearl Coleman. Maggie, like Clara, had tears on her cheeks; but Pearl Coleman was entirely convulsed with grief. Before the rangers were even well out of town she began to wail aloud.

Maggie and Clara both heard Pearl's loud wailing and knew what caused it. Maggie knew Pearl from the old days, when she had been married to a bartender named Dan Leary, the victim of a random gunshot that killed him stone dead one night when he stepped outside to empty an overflowing spittoon. Some cowboys had been shooting off guns outside a bordello—one of the bullets evidently fell from the sky and killed Dan Leary instantly.

Clara too knew Pearl—she was a frequent customer at the store. She started up the street, meaning to try and comfort her, and was almost there when Maggie came out of the alley, bent on the same errand.

"Why, hello," Clara said. "I guess Pearl's mighty sad, because Bill's run off again, so soon."

"I expect so," Maggie said. She started to stop and leave the comforting to Clara, but Clara motioned for her to come along.

"Don't you be hanging back," Clara said. "This job is big enough for both of us."

Maggie, ever aware of her position, glanced down the street but saw only one man, an old farmer who was urinating beside a small wagon.

When they reached Pearl she was so upset she couldn't talk. She was a large woman wearing an old blue nightdress; her back shook, as she cried, and her ample bosom heaved.

"He's gone and he won't be back," Pearl said. "He's gone and this baby inside me will never have a father—I know it!"

"Now you shush, Pearl, that ain't true," Maggie said. "This trip they're taking is just a short trip. They'll all be back."

She said it, but in her own mind were fears for her own child, whose father also might never return.

Clara put her arm around Pearl Coleman, but didn't speak. People were always leaving, men mostly. The cold wind burned her wet cheeks. Soon she herself would be leaving with Bob Allen, her chosen husband, to start the great adventure of marriage. She was excited by the thought. She expected to be happy. Soon she would be living away from her parents, and Gus McCrae would not be riding in, dusty, every few weeks, to kiss her. A part of her life was gone. And there stood Maggie, crying for Call, and Pearl Coleman, wailing, bereft at the departure of her Bill.

For a moment Clara wondered whether life was a happier affair *with* men, or without them.

Pearl, who had calmed a little, was walking back and forth, looking down the road where the rangers had gone. Her face was the shape of a moon and now looked like a moon that had been rained on.

"My baby's a boy, I know it," she said. "He's going to need a pa." In a few more minutes the sun came up and the women parted. Pearl, somewhat relieved, went back to her house. Two or three wagons were in the street now—Maggie Tilton discreetly went home through an alley, and Clara Forsythe, soon to be Clara Allen, walked slowly back to her parents' store, wondering if, before the summer came, a child would be growing in her too.

Book II

1.

FOR THREE DAYS Buffalo Hump and his warriors rode south in a mass, singing and chanting during the day and dancing at night around their campfires. They were excited to be going to war behind their leader. Worm, the medicine man, made spells at night, spells that would bring destruction and death to the Texans. They flushed abundant game and ate venison and antelope when they rested. At night, when the half-moon shone, the warriors talked of killing, raiding, burning, taking captives, stealing horses. They were still well north of the line of settlements and forts—they were lords of the land they rode on and confident in their power. The young warriors, some of whom had never been in battle, did not sleep at night, from excitement. They knew their chance for glory lay at hand.

On the fourth morning Buffalo Hump stayed long at the campfire, watching some of the young men practice with their weapons. He was not pleased by what he saw. Many of the young warriors, his own son included, were not good with the bow. After he had watched for a while he called all the warriors together and issued an order that took everyone by surprise, even Worm, who knew what Buffalo Hump felt about the proper modes of warfare.

"Those of you who have guns, throw them down," Buffalo Hump said. "Put them here in a pile, in front of me."

More than two hundred warriors had firearms of some sort—old pistols or muskets, in most cases, but, in some instances, good, well-functioning repeating rifles. They prized their firearms and were reluctant to give them up. There were a few moments of silence and hesitation, but Buffalo Hump had planted himself before them and he did not look to be in a mood to compromise. Even Blue Duck, who far preferred the rifle to the bow, did not say anything. He did not want to risk being chastised by his father in front of so many warriors.

Buffalo Hump had not expected all the warriors to be happy with his order. He was prepared to have it challenged. Many of the warriors were from bands who scarcely knew him, over whom he held no authority—except the authority of his presence. But he had thought much about the great raid they had embarked on. He knew it might be his last chance to beat back the white man, to cleanse the land of them and make it possible for the Comanche people to live as they had always lived, masters of the llano and all the prairies where they had always hunted. He wanted the warriors who rode with him to fight as Comanches had always fought, with the bow and the lance—and there were reasons for his decision other than his devotion to the old weapons.

After he had faced the warriors for a time, Buffalo Hump explained himself.

"We do not need these guns," he said. "They make too much noise. They scare away game that we might need to eat. Their sound carries so far the bluecoat soldiers might hear it. There are bluecoat soldiers in all the forts but we do not want to fight them yet. We will spread out soon. We will slip between the forts and kill the settlers before the soldiers know we are there. We must slip down on the settlers and go among them as quietly as the fog. We want to kill them before they can run and get the bluecoats. Kill them with your arrows. Kill them with your lances and your knives. Kill them quietly and we can ride on south and kill many more. We will go all the way to the Great Water, killing Texans."

He stopped, so the warriors could think over what he had said. He had spoken slowly, trying to bring all his power into the words. His fear was that some of the young warriors would defy him and split off. They might make their own raid, shouting and raping, in the way of young warriors. But if such a thing occurred there could be no great raid into the large towns of the whites. There were many forts now, all along the Brazos and the Trinity. Unless they could get below the forts, into the country where white settlers were thick as sage, the soldiers would pour out of the forts and come after them. Then the Comanches would have to defend themselves, rather than bringing war to the settlements. It was not what he wanted, not what he had prayed for.

The half-moon was still visible in the morning sky. Buffalo Hump pointed to it.

"Tomorrow we will break into small parties," he said. "We will fan out, as far as the headwaters of the Brazos. Go quietly between the forts and kill all the settlers you find. When the moon is full we will come back through the hills to the Colorado and strike Austin, and then San Antonio. When we have killed as many Texans as we can, we will go on to the Great Water. If the bluecoats come after us we can go into Mexico."

The warriors listened silently. There was no sound in the camp except the stamping and snorting of horses. No one, though, had stepped forward to lay down his gun. Buffalo Hump feared, for a moment, that he was not going to be obeyed. The warriors were too greedy and too lazy to surrender a gun, even a poor gun. With guns they didn't have to hunt so hard and carefully. Too many of them had ceased to depend on their bows, or to practice with them. He decided he had better keep speaking to them.

"Now is the time to fight as the old ones fought," he said. "The old ones had no trouble killing Texans with our own weapons. It was only when we first tried to use guns that we lost battles to the Texans. The old ones believed in the power of their weapons. They fought so hard that they made the Texans run back down the rivers. We took their women and made their children captives. The Mexicans feared us worse than they feared their own deaths. Leave your guns here and let us make war like the old ones made it."

At that point old Yellow Foot pushed through the crowd and put his musket on the ground. The musket looked even older than Yellow Foot, one of the oldest warriors to come on the raid. He had wrapped buffalo sinew around the gun so that the barrel would not jump off the stock when he shot at something. It was such a bad gun that no one wanted to stand near Yellow Foot when he shot it, for fear that it might do more damage to them than to whatever Yellow Foot was shooting at.

Nevertheless, Yellow Foot was very proud of his gun and wasted many bullets shooting at game that was too far away to hit. Twice he had killed young horses because his vision was poor and he mistook them for deer. Buffalo Hump was pleased when he saw the old warrior come forward. Though a little crazy, Yellow Foot was much respected in the tribe because he had had over a dozen wives in his life and was known to be an expert on how to give women such extreme pleasure that they would remain jolly for weeks and not complain as other women did.

"I am leaving my gun," Yellow Foot said. "I don't want to smell all that gun grease anymore."

All the older warriors soon followed Yellow Foot's example and put their guns in a pile. Buffalo Hump said no more, but he did not move or look away, either. He looked from warrior to warrior, making them face and accept his command or else reject it in front of everybody. In the end only one warrior, a small, irritable man named Red Cat, refused to put his weapon on what had become a great pile. Though Blue Duck was almost the last man to lay his gun on the pile, he did finally put it there. Red Cat, who was indifferent to what any chief thought, kept his rifle.

Buffalo Hump did not want to make too big an issue of one gun.

"If you are going to keep that smelly gun, then raid far to the west, where the Brazos starts," he asked. "If there are any Texans out that way, you can shoot them. I don't think there are any bluecoats out there to hear you."

Red Cat made no answer, but he thought it was stupid of old Buffalo Hump to leave behind so many guns. He meant, when he had time, to slip back to where the guns were and pick out a new rifle for himself.

2.

WHEN FAMOUS SHOES saw that the tracks of the Buffalo Horse were going straight into the Sierra Perdida, he sat down on a rock to think about it. Scull was studying a small cactus, for reasons Famous Shoes could not fathom. Very often Scull would notice a plant he was not familiar with and would stop and study it for many minutes, sometimes even sketching it in a small notebook he carried. Sometimes he would ask Famous Shoes about the plant, but often it would be a plant Famous Shoes had no use for and knew little about. Some plants were useful and many were very useful, yielding up medicines or food or, as in the case of some cactus buds, yielding up important visions. But, as with people, some plants were completely useless. When Scull stopped for a long stretch to examine some fossil in the rocks or some useless plant, Famous Shoes grew impatient.

Now he was very impatient. The little cactus Scull was studying was of no interest at all—all anyone needed to know about it was that its thorns were painful if they stuck you. Now the situation they faced was apt to be far more painful than the thorns of any cactus. They were near the country of Ahumado, the Black Vaquero, a man who had wounded Scull once and who would do worse than wound him if he took him prisoner. Scull needed to recognize that their situation was perilous. Under such circumstances, studying a cactus was not the proper behaviour for a captain.

When Scull finally came over to where he sat, Famous Shoes pointed at the mountains.

"Kicking Wolf has taken your horse into the Sierra," he said. "Three Birds is still with him, but Three Birds does not want to go into the Sierra very much."

"I doubt that he does, but how can you tell that from a track?" Scull asked.

"I can't tell it from the tracks," Famous Shoes said. "I can tell it because I know Three Birds and he is not crazy. Only a crazy man would ride into the country of Ahumado."

"That qualifies me for the asylum, then, I guess," Scull said. "I went there once and got shot for my trouble and now I'm going again."

"Some of the *mexicanos* think Ahumado has lived forever," Famous Shoes said.

"Well, they're a superstitious people," Scull said. "I expect they have too many gods to worry about. The good thing about the Christian religion, if you subscribe to it, is that you only have to worry about the wrath of one God."

Famous Shoes didn't respond. Often he could only understand a small fraction of what Scull was talking about, and that fraction was of little interest. What he had just said made him seem a fool. No intelligent man would walk the earth long without realizing that there were many gods to fear. There was a god in the sun and in the floor, a god in the ice and in the lightning, not to mention the many gods who took their nature from animals: the bear god, the lizard god, and so on. The old ones believed that when eagles screamed they were calling out the name of the eagle god.

He thought that Scull would do well not to criticize Ahumado's gods, either—even if the Black Vaquero hadn't lived forever, he had certainly lived a long time. Men did not live to a great age in dangerous country without cleverness in placating the various gods they had to deal with.

"We are in Ahumado's country now," Famous Shoes said. "He may show up tomorrow. I don't know."

"Well, Kicking Wolf's ahead of us with my horse," Scull said. "If he does show up he'll have to take care of Kicking Wolf first."

"Ahumado is always behind you," Famous Shoes said. "That is his way. These mountains are his home. He knows trails that even the rabbit and the cougar have forgotten. If we go into his country he will be behind us."

Inish Scull thought the matter over for a moment. The mountains were blue in the distance, dotted with shadows. The way into them was narrow and craggy, he remembered that from his first assault. He picked up a small stick and began to draw figures in the dirt, geometric figures. He drew squares and rectangles, with now and then a triangle.

Famous Shoes watched him draw the figures. He wondered if they were symbols having to do with the angry Christian God. In Austin Scull sometimes preached sermons—he preached from the platform of the gallows that stood behind the jail. Many people gathered to hear Scull preach—white people, Indians, *mexicanos*. Many of them could not understand Scull's words, but they listened anyway. Scull would roar and stomp when he preached; he behaved like a powerful medicine man. The listeners were afraid to leave while he was preaching, for fear he would put a bad spell on them.

"I think you ought to find this man Three Birds and take him home," Scull said, when he had finished drawing the little shapes in the dirt. "He ain't crazy and you ain't either. What's left to do had best be done by crazy folks, which means myself and Mr. Kicking Wolf.

"If I was perfectly sane I'd be on a cotton plantation in Alabama, letting my wife's ugly relatives support me in high style," he added.

Famous Shoes thought he knew why Kicking Wolf was taking the Buffalo Horse to Ahumado, but it was a subtle thing, and he did not want to discuss it with the white man. It was not wise to talk to white men about certain things, and one of them was power: the power a warrior needed to gain respect for himself. He himself, as a young man, had been sickly; it was only since he had begun to walk all the time that his health had been good. Earlier in his life he had done many foolish things in order to convince himself that he was not worthless. Once in the Sierra Madre, in Chihuahua, he had even crawled into the den of a grizzly bear. The bear had not yet awakened from its winter sleep, but spring was coming and the bear was restless. At any time the bear might have awakened and killed Famous Shoes. But he had stayed in the den of the restless bear for three days, and when he came out the power of the bear was with him as he walked. Without risk there was no power, not for a grown man.

That was why Kicking Wolf was taking the Buffalo Horse to Ahumado—if he went into Ahumado's stronghold and survived he could sing his power all the way home; he could sing it to Buffalo Hump and sit with him as an equal—for he would have challenged the Black Vaquero and lived, something no Comanche had ever done.

There was nothing crazy in such behavior. There was only courage in it, the courage of a great warrior who goes where his pride leads him. When he was younger Buffalo Hump had often done such things, going alone into the country of his worst enemies and killing their best warriors. From such daring actions he gained power—great power. Now Kicking Wolf wanted great power too.

"You brought me where I asked you to bring me and you taught me to track," Scull said. "If I were you I'd turn back now. Kicking Wolf and me, we're involved in a test, but it's our test. You don't need to come with me. If you meet my rangers on your way home, just give them the news."

Famous Shoes did not quite understand the last remark.

"What is the news?" he asked.

"The news is that I'm off to the Sierra Perdida, if anyone cares to know," Scull said.

Then he walked away, following the tracks of his big horse, toward the blue mountains ahead.

3.

THEY HAD REMOVED the young caballero's clothes and were tying him to the skinning post outside the big cave when Tudwal came loping into camp with news he thought Ahumado would want to hear. Ahumado sat on a blanket outside the cave, watching old Goyeto sharpening his skinning knives. The blades of the old man's knives were thin as razors. He only used them when Ahumado wanted him to take the skin off a man. The young caballero had let a cougar slip into the horses and kill a foal. Though Ahumado never rode, himself—he preferred to walk—he was annoyed with the young man for letting a fine colt get eaten by the cougar.

Ahumado also preferred sun to shade. Even on the hottest days he seldom went into the big cave, or any of the caves that dotted the Yellow Cliffs. He put his blanket where the sun would shine on it all day, and, all day, he sat on it. He never covered himself from the sun—he let it make him blacker and blacker.

Tudwal dismounted well back from the skinning post and waited respectfully for Ahumado to summon him and hear his news.

Sometimes Ahumado summoned him quickly, but at other times the wait was long. When the old man was meting out punishment, as he was about to do, it was unwise to interrupt him, no matter how urgent the news. Ahumado was deliberate about everything, but he was particularly deliberate about punishment. He didn't punish casually; he made a ceremony of it, and he expected every-one in camp to stop whatever they were doing and attend to what was being done to the one receiving the punishment.

When the young caballero, stripped and trembling with fear, had been securely tied to the skinning post, Ahumado motioned for old Goyeto to come with him. The two men were about the same age and about the same height, but of different complexions. Goyeto was a milky brown, Ahumado like an old black rock. Goyeto had seven knives, which he wore on a narrow belt, each in a soft deerskin sheath. He was bent almost double with age, and only had one eye, but he had been skinning men for Ahumado for many years and was a master with the knives. He carried with him a little pot of blue dye to mark the places that Ahumado wanted skinned. The last man whose skin he had removed entirely was a German who had tried to make away with some rocks he had taken from one of Ahumado's caves. Ahumado did not like his caves disturbed, not by a German or anybody.

It was rare, though, for him to order a whole man skinned—often Goyeto would only skin an arm or a leg or a backside, or even an intimate part. Tudwal didn't expect him to be that hard on the young vaquero, who had only made a small, understandable mistake.

It soon developed that he was right. Ahumado took the little pot of dye and drew a line from the nape of the caballero's neck straight down to his heel. The line was not even an inch wide. Ahumado lifted the boy's foot, drew the line across the sole of his foot, and stepped around him to the other side. Then he carefully continued the line all the way up to the boy's chin.

Ahumado pulled the boy's face around so he could look right in his eye.

"I do not raise horses for cougars to eat," he said. "I am going to have Goyeto take an inch of your skin. Goyeto is so good with the knives that you may not feel it. But if you do feel it please don't yell too much. If you disturb me with too much yelling I may have him skin your *cojones* or maybe one of your eyeballs."

Then he walked back to his blanket and sat down. He could see that Tudwal was anxious to tell him something. Usually, while a torture was being performed, he made his couriers wait—it was hard to take in the news accurately when a man was screaming only a few feet away. But Tudwal had been sent north, toward the border, and it was never wise to ignore news from the border country.

He motioned to Tudwal, who came hurrying over. Just as he got there old Goyeto made a few cuts and began to peel the little strip of skin down the nape of the young caballero's neck. The boy, not understanding that he was being given only a light punishment, began to scream as loudly as he could. As Goyeto pulled and cut, pulling the strip below the boy's shoulder blades, the boy screamed so loudly that it was impossible to hear Tudwal's news. Before the strip of skin was pulled away past his hips the boy fainted, and Goyeto stopped and squatted on his heels. Ahumado did not approve of him skinning unconscious men.

"Two Comanches are coming," Tudwal said quickly. "They are almost to the Yellow Canyon now."

Ahumado was disappointed by the quality of news from the north. Two Comanches were worthless. He had been hoping that Tudwal might have spotted a party of rich travelers, or perhaps a small troop of *federales*. The rich people might have money and jewels with them; the soldiers they could torture.

He motioned for Goyeto to get on with things, so Goyeto pricked the caballero's *cojones* with the knives until he woke up. Soon he was screaming again, though not so loudly.

Of course Tudwal had known that Ahumado would not be excited to hear about the two Comanches; he decided to spring the news that he had been holding back.

"One of the Comanches is riding the Buffalo Horse," he said. "Scull's horse."

Ahumado had been watching the practiced way Goyeto twisted the boy's foot up and held it between his knees as he continued to peel the strip of skin across the sole. Goyeto's expert knife work was a pleasure to watch. It took a moment for Tudwal's information to register with him. The boy was screaming more loudly again.

"Scull's horse?" Ahumado asked.

"Scull's horse," Tudwal said. "I have more news too."

"You are a braggart," Ahumado informed him. "You are no better than a crow."

The old man's face was thin. His eyes were as flint when he was displeased, and he was often displeased.

"But I am the Crow-Who-Sees," Tudwal said. "I have seen the two Comanches and I have seen Scull. He is following the Comanches on foot, and he is alone."

"Scull wants to kill me," Ahumado mentioned. "If he is alone, why didn't you catch him?"

"I am only a crow," Tudwal said. "How can I be expected to catch such a fierce man?"

"I think Scull wants his horse back," Ahumado said. "There is no other horse like the Buffalo Horse."

"Maybe he wants his horse back, I don't know," Tudwal said. "Maybe he just wants to visit you."

Ahumado watched as Goyeto worked the strip of skin up the boy's leg. He worked with such delicacy that the wound hardly bled. Nonetheless, when the peel reached his hip, the young caballero fouled himself. Then, for the second time, he fainted.

"I am going to sell this boy as a slave, when he wakes up," Ahumado said. "He is too cowardly to work for me. If the *federales* caught him and squeezed his *cojones* he might betray me."

Tudwal agreed. Only a little skinning had reduced the young caballero to a sorry state.

"What do you think those Comanches want?" Ahumado asked. "I am asking you because you are the Crow-Who-Sees."

Tudwal knew he had better be careful. When Ahumado was disappointed in one of his men, his disappointment could turn into fury, but a cold fury. The old man kept his eyes hidden and spoke in soft tones, so that the man he was angry with could not see, until it was too late, that his eyes were like those of a striking snake. Someone would be struck, usually to the death, when Ahumado began to question things.

"One of the Comanches is a man called Kicking Wolf," Tudwal ventured. "He took the Buffalo Horse. Maybe he means to sell him to you."

The old man, the Black Vaquero, said nothing. Tudwal was scared, and when he was scared he spoke nonsense. Ahumado did not buy horses from the Comanches, or do anything else with them except kill them. The best any Comanche could expect from him was a quick death. The Comanche who was bringing him the Buffalo Horse was doing a foolish thing, or else he was playing a trick. The man could well be a trickster of some sort, allied with a witch. If he was just a plain man with horse trading on his mind, he was making a foolish mistake.

"Go eat," he told Tudwal. "Goyeto has to finish his work."

Relieved, Tudwal left at once. Goyeto peeled the strip of skin up the unconscious caballero's chest and up his neck to his chin. Then he cut it off and walked away with the thin, light strip. He meant to peg it out, salt it a little, and hang it in the big cave, with all the other human skins he had taken for Ahumado. On little pegs in the cave were more than fifty skins, a collection any skinner could be proud of. From time to time Ahumado would come into the big cave for a few minutes, take down the skins one by one, and admire them. He and old Goyeto would reminisce about the behavior of this captive or that. Some men, like the German who had tried to steal the rocks, behaved very bravely, but others, weak like the young caballero, were disappointing to work on. They broke down, fouled themselves, and bawled like babies.

Outside on his blanket, with the winter sun reflecting off the yellow walls of the canyon, Ahumado sat, thinking about the three men who were coming from the north—Big Horse Scull and the two Comanches. The notion that they had come for a visit was amusing. No one visited him in the canyon of the Yellow Cliffs.

When the time came for a visit, he would visit them.

4.

"WHAT WILL YOU SAY to the Black Vaquero when he catches us?" Three Birds asked.

They were camped in a long canyon with high walls, a place Three Birds didn't like. He had lived his life on the open prairie and didn't like sleeping beneath a cliff of rocks. Someone with the power to shake the earth could make one of the cliffs fall on them and bury them, a thing that could never happen on the plains. In his dream he had seen a great cliff falling and had awakened in a sweat.

Kicking Wolf had killed a small pig with spiky hair, a javelina, and was too busy roasting its bones to respond to Three Birds.

Then Three Birds remembered another bad story he had heard about the Black Vaquero, this one having to do with snakes. It was said that the old man had such power that he had persuaded the rattlesnake people to give up their rattles. It was said that Ahumado had many snakes with no rattles, who could crawl among his enemies and bite them without making a sound. Though Three Birds normally didn't fear the snake people, he didn't like the thought of rattlesnakes that made no sound. The pig they were eating was tasty, but not tasty enough to make him forget that the Black Vaquero had a number of evil ways.

"Have you heard about the snakes without rattles?" Three Birds asked. "There might be a few of them living in this canyon right here."

"If you are going to talk all night I wish you would go home," Kicking Wolf said. "I don't want to sleep tonight—I want to stay up and sing. If you want to sleep you had better go somewhere else."

"No, I will sing too," Three Birds said, and he did sing, far into the night. He had the feeling that they would be dead very soon and he wanted to sing as much as possible before death closed his throat.

The two Comanches sang all night and in the morning took pains to paint themselves correctly. They wanted to look like proud Comanche warriors when they rode into the camp amid the Yellow Cliffs, the camp of the hundred caves, where Ahumado had his stronghold.

Kicking Wolf was just about to mount the Buffalo Horse when he felt a change come. The sun had not yet struck the cliffs to the south; they were still filled with blue light. Three Birds had just finished painting himself when he felt the change. Sometimes, hours before a storm, the air would begin to change, though there was no sign of anything to fear.

That was how the air changed in the long canyon.

"I think he is here," Kicking Wolf said, coming over to Three Birds.

Just then Three Birds saw a rattlesnake without rattles going under a rock near where they had their blankets. He knew then that Ahumado must be near. He wondered if Ahumado's powers were such that he could turn himself into a snake and come near to spy on them. It might even have been Ahumado who crawled under the rock near where the blankets were. He didn't mention his suspicion to Kicking Wolf, though—Kicking Wolf didn't believe that people could turn themselves into animals, or vice versa, though he admitted that such things might have been possible in the old days, when the spirits of people had been more friendly with those of animals.

Then the Buffalo Horse snorted, and swung his head. He looked around the canyon, but didn't move.

"I don't want to camp in any more canyons," Three Birds observed—he was about to outline his objections when he turned and saw an old man sitting on a high rock a little distance behind them. The rock and the man were in shadow still; it was hard to see them clearly. He sat cross-legged on the rock, a rifle across his lap.

When the light improved a little they saw that he was as dark as an old plum.

Kicking Wolf knew that he was in great danger, but he also felt great pride. The old man on the rock was Ahumado, the Black Vaquero. Whatever his own fate might be, he had completed his quest. He had stolen the Buffalo Horse and brought him to the great bandit of the south; he had done it merely for the daring of doing it. If a hundred *pistoleros* rose up in the rocks and killed him, he would die happy in his courage and pride.

"I have brought you the Buffalo Horse," Kicking Wolf said, walking closer to the rock where the old man sat.

"I see him," Ahumado said. "Is he a gift?"

"Yes, a gift," Kicking Wolf said.

"He is a big horse," Ahumado said. "I shot him once but the bullet only scratched him. Why did you bring him to me?"

Kicking Wolf made no answer—there was no answer that could easily be put into words. He knew that at home, around the campfires, the young men would sing for years about his theft of the Buffalo Horse and his inexplicable decision to take him to Ahumado. Few would understand it—perhaps none would understand it. It was a thing he had done for no reason, and for all reasons and for no reason. He stood on his dignity as a Comanche warrior. He would not try to explain himself to an old bandit who was black as a plum.

"I will take this horse and the other one too," Ahumado said. "You can go home but you will have to walk until you get to Texas. Then you can steal another horse."

Kicking Wolf picked up his weapons. He and Three Birds started to walk out of the canyon past where Ahumado sat. But when Three Birds moved Ahumado made a motion with his rifle, pointing it directly at Three Birds.

"Not you," he said. "Your friend can go but you must stay and be my guest."

Three Birds didn't argue. What had happened was exactly what he had expected would happen. He had come to Mexico expecting to die, and now he was going to die. He was not upset; it was a moment he had been waiting for since the shitting sickness killed his wife and his three children. He had wanted to die then, with his family, but his stubborn body had not wanted to go. But some of his spirit had gone with his wife and his little ones and he had not been able to attend much to the things of the world, since then. Now he had had a good journey with his friend Kicking Wolf—they had traveled together to Mexico. He did not want the evil old man to do bad things to him, but, as to his death, that he was at ease with. He immediately stretched up his arms and began to sing his death song.

Though Three Birds wasn't upset, Kicking Wolf was. He did not like the disrespectful tone the old man had used when he addressed Three Birds. Even less did he like it that Ahumado meant to keep Three Birds a captive.

"This man helped me to bring you the Buffalo Horse," he said. "He has come a long way to bring you this gift."

Ahumado kept his rifle pointed at Three Birds. It was clear that he had no interest in what Kicking Wolf had just said.

Kicking Wolf was very angry. He had half expected to die when he had decided to bring the Buffalo Horse to Mexico. He knew that Ahumado was a very dangerous man who killed on whim, that death might be waiting for him in the canyon of the Yellow Cliffs. Besides, Three Birds had talked of little else on the trip except his conviction that Ahumado would kill them.

What he had not expected was that he would be spared and Three Birds taken. It angered him so that he had a notion to put an arrow through the old bandit immediately. Did he think a Comanche warrior would simply surrender his friend to torture and death? By that one stroke Ahumado made him seem a fool, the very thing Three Birds had been telling him he was, all the way south.

To make matters worse, Three Birds accepted the decision. He was already singing his death song and his eyes were looking far away.

252

As Kicking Wolf was about to draw his bow he saw three *pistoleros* to his left—they rose out of the rocks with their rifles pointed at him. Three more rose behind Ahumado.

"In my country rocks grow men," Ahumado said.

Kicking Wolf dropped his weapons and made a gesture of surrender. He could not simply walk out of the canyon and leave Three Birds to his death. If it was to be death for one, it would be death for both. But Ahumado made a gesture with his hand and several horsemen rode out of the rocks swinging horsehide ropes. Kicking Wolf tried to run but before he could escape three lassos caught him. The horsemen began to drag him over the rough ground, out of the canyon. He could not see Three Birds for the dust his own body raised as the men spurred their horses and pulled him faster. They pulled him through a field of big rocks. Then his head hit one of the big rocks, which sent him into a black sleep. But, even as he sank into the darkness he thought he heard someone singing a death song.

5.

WHEN BUFFALO HUMP came into the big store in Austin, some of the warriors had found an old woman upstairs and had pulled her and had thrown her down the steps. Now they were dragging her through some white flour. They had killed the old man who owned the store with one of his own axes and had used the axe to chop open a couple of barrels of white flour. Some of the young warriors had never seen white flour and took delight in throwing it in the air and covering themselves with it. They also liked dragging the old woman through it while she shrieked. Two of the young warriors outraged her while Buffalo Hump picked out a few hatchets and put them in a sack. Then he came over and waited for the warrior who was outraging the old woman to finish. The woman's husband was lying dead only a few feet away, while, outside, his warriors were setting buildings afire and killing people as they tried to escape the flames. Some warriors rode their horses into white people's houses and looted everything they could carry. Six Texans were shot down in the street and scalped where they fell. The people of Austin ran like chickens and the Comanches pursued them like wolves, killing them as they ran with lances, or arrows, or tomahawks.

The raid had begun just at dawn but now the sun was well up. Buffalo Hump knew it was time to leave. The young men would have to throw away much of the loot they carried; they would not be able to carry it if there was a fast pursuit. They had killed four rangers in one little house but had seen no soldiers.

When the warrior got off the old, flour-splotched woman Buffalo Hump stood over her and shot three arrows into her chest. He shot them with all the force of his bow, so that the arrows went through the woman and nailed her to the floor. The woman died immediately, but Buffalo Hump didn't scalp her. She was just an old woman whose thin hair was worthless.

He let his men take what baubles they wanted from the store, but told them to hurry. When he came outside he saw that some of his warriors had caught a blacksmith and were burning him to death on his own forge. One of them pumped the bellows and made the flames leap while the blacksmith screamed. The high flames set the man's hair on fire.

In the street a young man with no trousers was running, pursued by three warriors. They had stolen ropes from the big store and were trying to rope him, as a vaquero would rope a cow. But they were warriors, not ropers, and they kept missing. Finally, unable to rope the young man, the warriors began to whip him with their ropes.

Then Red Cat joined the fun. He had stolen an axe with a long handle from the store. While the young man was fleeing, Red Cat swung the axe and tried to cut the young man's head off. The blow killed him but his head was still on his neck. The warriors dragged him around for a while, to make sure he was dead. Then Red Cat finished cutting his head off and they threw his body in a wagon, along with some other bodies.

Buffalo Hump saw an old man rolling around in the street—he

was dying but not quite dead. He rode over and did what he had done with the old woman with flour on her: he shot three arrows into the old man so hard that they went through him and pinned him to the ground.

Buffalo Hump meant to do the same thing again, as they went south. At every farm or ranch he would put arrows through some Texan. He would leave them nailed to the floor, or to the ground.

It would be a thing the Texans would notice—a thing they would remember him by.

6.

WHEN MAGGIE WAS AWAKENED in the first gray light by the high, wild cries of the Comanche warriors, racing into Austin, she didn't even wait to look out the window. Their war cries had been in her nightmares for years. She grabbed a little pistol Woodrow had left her for her own defense and raced barefoot down the stairs. The house she boarded in was on the main street—she knew they would catch her if she stayed in it but she thought she might be able to squeeze under the smokehouse behind it. An old sow had rooted under the smokehouse so persistently that she had dug out a shallow wallow under the back corner of the shack. Maggie raced down the steps and, moments later, was squeezing herself under the smokehouse. There was room, too: the black sow was larger than she was. She clutched the pistol and cocked it to be ready. Woodrow had long ago taught her where to shoot herself, to spare herself torture and outrage.

Once Maggie had squeezed herself as far back under the house as she could get, she heard, from behind her somewhere, the buzz of a rattlesnake, at which point she stopped and remained motionless. The snake didn't seem close, but she didn't want to do anything to irritate it further.

She didn't want to kill herself, either. It would mean the end not only for herself but for the child inside her too. She knew what happened to women the Comanches took, though. Only yesterday she

255

had seen poor Maudy Clark, sitting on a chair behind the church, looking blank. The preacher was letting her sleep in a little room in the church until they located a sister in Georgia who might take her in. Her husband, William, had come one day in a wagon, taken the children, and left without speaking a word to Maudy. He had simply ridden away, as if his wife had ceased to exist: and his attitude was what most men's would be. Once fouled by a Comanche or a Kiowa or any Indian, a woman might as well be dead, for she would be considered so by respectable society.

Maggie didn't know that she could be befouled much worse by an Indian than she had been by some of the rough men who had used her; but, then, there were the tortures: she didn't think she could stand them. She clutched her pistol but otherwise didn't move. The snake's rattling slowly quieted—probably the rattler had crawled off into a corner. Slowly, very deliberately, Maggie squeezed herself a few more inches back. Then she put her face down; Woodrow had told her Comanches were quick to spot even the smallest flash of white skin.

Outside, the war cries came closer. She heard horses go right by the smokehouse. Three Indians went into the smokehouse, just above her—she heard them knocking over crocks and carrying off some of the meat that hung there. Something that smelled like vinegar dripped onto her through a fine crack in the floor.

But the Comanches didn't find her. Two braves stood not far from the hog wallow for a moment, but then mounted and loped off, probably to seek more victims. They didn't fire the smokehouse but they fired the rooming house. She could smell the smoke and hear the crackle of flames. She was afraid the rooming house might fall onto the smokehouse and set it on fire, but didn't dare come out. The Comanches were still there—she could hear their victims screaming. Horses dashed by and several more Comanches came into the smokehouse. Maggie kept her face down and waited; she was determined to hide all day if need be.

Then she heard a scream she recognized: it was Pearl Coleman screaming. Pearl screamed and screamed. The sound made Maggie want to stop her ears, and turn off her mind. She didn't want to think about what might be happening to Pearl, out in the street. At least Clara Forsythe was safe—married and gone to Galveston only five days before.

Maggie concentrated on keeping her head down; and she waited. Woodrow had warned her specifically not to be too quick to come out, in the event of a raid. Some of the Comanches would hold back after the main party left, hoping to snatch women or children who were brought out of hiding.

Maggie waited. One more Indian did come into the smoke-house, perhaps to snatch a ham or something, but he was there only moments. Maggie peeked briefly and saw the warrior's horse spill out turds, right in front of her.

The warrior left and Maggie waited for a long time. When she finally began to inch out, she thought it must be noon, at least. When she finally did come out, so did the snake that had buzzed at her earlier. The snake glided through a crack in the lower board and was soon under a bush.

Many of the buildings along the main street were burning; the saloon had burned to the ground. Maggie inched around the building, but soon decided there were no Indians still in the town. Several men lay dead in the street, scalped, castrated, split open. She heard sobbing from up the street and saw Pearl Coleman, completely naked and with four arrows sticking out of her, walking around in circles, sobbing.

Maggie hurried to her and tried to get her to stop weaving around, but Pearl was beyond listening. Her large body was streaked with blood from the four arrows.

"Oh, Mag," Pearl said. "They got me down before I could run. They got me down. My Bill, he won't want me now . . . if he gets back alive he'll be ashamed of me and put me out."

"No, Pearl, that ain't true," Maggie said. "Bill won't put you out."

She said it to cheer Pearl up a little, but in fact there was no predicting what Long Bill would do when he heard of his wife's defilement. She liked Long Bill Coleman but there was no knowing how a man would react to such news.

At that moment, through the drifting smoke, they saw three men with rifles coming cautiously up the street. The sight of them brought home to Pearl the fact that she was unclothed.

"Oh Lord, I'm naked, Maggie . . . what'll I do?" Pearl asked, trying to cover herself with her bloody hands. It it was only when she saw the blood on her own hands that she noticed an arrow in her hip. She put her hand on the arrow, which was only hanging by its tip, and, to her surprise, it came out.

"You got three more in your back, Pearl," Maggie said. "I'll get them out once I get you inside."

"Why, I'm stuck like a pincushion," Pearl said, trying to cover herself with her hands.

"Just turn around . . . those men don't see us yet," Maggie said. "I'll run in the Forsythe store and borrow a blanket for you to cover with."

Pearl turned around and hunched over, trying to make herself as small as possible.

Maggie ran across the street but slowed a little as she came up the steps to the Forsythe store. The windows had all been smashed—a barrel of nails had been heaved through one of them. The barrel had burst when it hit, scattering nails everywhere. Maggie, barefoot, had to pick her way carefully through the nails.

As soon as she stepped into the store she felt something sticky on one foot and assumed she must have cut herself on a nail; but when she looked down she saw that the blood on her foot was not hers. There was a large puddle of it just inside the door of the store. The display cases had all been smashed and flour was everywhere. Horse blankets, harness, ladies' hats, men's shoes had been thrown everywhere. The brown Pennsylvania crockery that Clara had been so proud of had been smashed to shards.

Maggie knew she had stepped in a puddle of blood, but it was dim in the store. She didn't know whose blood it was until she picked her way through the smashed crockery and scattered merchandise and then suddenly saw Mr. Forsythe, dead on the floor, his head split open as if it had been a cantaloupe.

Beyond him a few steps lay Mrs. Forsythe, naked and half covered with the white flour that had spilled out of the barrels. Three arrows had been driven into her chest, so hard that they had gone through her, pinning her to the floor.

Maggie felt such a shock at the sight that she grew weak. She had to steady herself against the counter. For a moment she thought her stomach might come up. Seeing the naked, spraddled woman with the arrows in her chest made her realize how lucky she was; and how lucky Pearl was, and Clara herself, and all the women who were still alive.

She herself wasn't even injured—she had to help those who were. It was no time to be weak.

Maggie picked her way back to where the blankets were—instead of taking one blanket she took three. One she carefully put over Mrs. Forsythe—the three arrows stuck up, but there was nothing she could do about that. The blanket didn't cover her well—it left the poor old woman's thin legs exposed, which seemed wrong. She went back, took another blanket, and used it to cover Mrs. Forsythe's legs. The men would have to deal with the arrows when they came to remove the bodies.

Then she put a nice blanket over Mr. Forsythe's split head and went outside to help her friend. One of the men with rifles was standing on the porch when she came out.

"How about the Forsythes?" he asked, peering in one of the smashed windows.

"They're both dead," Maggie told him. "She's got three arrows shot clear through her."

Then she opened the other blanket, picked her way through the nails, and wrapped the blanket around Pearl, who was still hunched down in the street. The three arrows were still in her back, but at least she was covered decently as Maggie walked her home.

7.

As soon as Inish Scull saw the horse in the distance he hid under a little shelf of rock and waited. The horse, still a long way off, seemed to be alone. Scull took out his binoculars and waited for the horse to come round a little closer, for the animal did not seem to be moving or grazing naturally. It moved slowly, and looked back over its shoulder frequently, odd behavior for a lone horse in empty country.

More than an hour passed before the horse was close enough for Scull to see that it was dragging a man behind it, an unconscious man and an Indian, securely tied at wrists and ankles and attached to the horse by a rawhide rope.

There was nothing to see on the vast spare desert except the one horse, walking slowly, dragging the man. Somebody had obviously wanted the horse to drag the man to death; that somebody, in Scull's view, was probably Ahumado. Famous Shoes had talked much about Ahumado's cruelty to captives. Being dragged to death by a horse was about as mild a punishment as Ahumado allowed anyone, if Famous Shoes was to be believed.

When the horse was only one hundred yards away, Scull crept down to take a closer look. As he came near he saw that the tied man's body was just a mass of scrapes, with very little skin left on it.

Scull watched the southern horizon closely, to be sure there were no clouds of dust in the air, such as riders would make; he also watched the bound man closely, to see if he was merely feigning unconsciousness. It seemed unlikely that a man so skinned and torn could be capable of threatening him; but many a fallen Indian fighter had been fatally lulled by just such reasonable considerations.

Once satisfied that it was safe to approach, Scull stopped the horse—he soon saw that the bound man was breathing. There were no bullet holes in him that Scull could see. On his back was a small quiver, with no arrows in it. There was a deep gash in his forehead. The beadwork on the little quiver was Comanche, Scull thought.

The thongs at his wrists and ankles had been pulled so tight that his flesh had swollen around the cords.

From a swift examination of the horse tracks Scull determined that the horse was one he had just been following for hundreds of miles. It was Three Birds' horse, but Scull didn't think it was Three Birds who was tied to it. Three Birds was skinny, Famous Shoes had told him, but the bound man was short and stocky.

"Kicking Wolf," Scull said aloud. He thought the sound of his name might wake the man up, but of course Kicking Wolf was only his English name; what his Comanche name was, Scull did not know. Scull would have dearly liked to know what had happened to Three Birds, and whether Ahumado was in the vicinity, but he could not expect to get such information from an unconscious man whose language he didn't speak.

Now that he was in the country of the Black Vaquero, Scull had taken to traveling mostly by night, letting the stars be his map. He knew that the canyon where Ahumado had his stronghold was crevassed and cut with many small caves, some of them no more than pockmarks in the rock but some deep enough to shelter a man nicely. Undoubtedly Ahumado would post guards, but Scull had been a commander too long to believe that any arrangement that required men to stay awake long hours in the night was foolproof. If he could sneak in at night and tuck himself into one of the hundred caves, he might, with patience, get a clean shot at Ahumado. Famous Shoes had told him that the old man did not like shade. He spent his days on a blanket and slept outside, by a small campfire, at night. The trick would be to get in a cave within rifle range. Of course, if he shot Ahumado, the *pistoleros* might swarm into his cave like hornets and kill him, but maybe not. Ahumado was said to be as cruel and unyielding to his men as he was to captives. Most of the *pistoleros* might only be staying with him out of fear. With the old man dead they might just leave.

It was a gamble, but Scull didn't mind—indeed, he had walked into Mexico in order to take just such a gamble. But first he had to get into the Yellow Canyon and find a well-situated cave. Famous

Shoes had warned him particularly about a man named Tudwal, a scout whose job it was to roam the perimeters of Ahumado's country and warn him of intruders.

"Tudwal will know you are there before you know it yourself," Famous Shoes assured him.

"No, that's too cryptic, what do you mean?" Scull asked, but Famous Shoes would not say more. He had given Scull a warning, but would not elaborate, other than to say that Tudwal rode a paint horse and carried two rifles. Scull put the man's reticence down to professional jealousy. Famous Shoes missed no track, and, evidently, Tudwal didn't either.

Meanwhile, dusk was turning into night and Scull had a horse and an unconscious man to decide what to do about. The Comanche very likely was the man Kicking Wolf, the thief who had stolen Hector. In other circumstances Kicking Wolf was a man he would immediately kill, or try to kill. But now the man was unconscious, bound, helpless. With or without Scull he might not live. With one swipe of his knife Scull knew that he could cut the man's throat and rid the frontier of a notable scourge, but when he did take out his knife it was merely to sever the rawhide rope that attached the man to the horse.

Then he quickly walked on toward the mountains, leaving the unconscious man tied but not dead.

"Tit for tat . . . Bible and sword," he said aloud, as he walked. Kicking Wolf's daring theft had freed him of a command he was tired of, presenting him with a fine opportunity for pure adventure—solitary adventure, the kind he liked best. He could match his skill against an unforgiving country and an even more unforgiving foe. That was why he had come west in the first place: adventure. The task of harassing the last savages until they were exterminated was adventure diluted with policy and duty.

The man who had been tied to the horse was a mystery, and Scull preferred to leave him a mystery. He didn't want to nurse him, nor did he want to kill him. He might be Kicking Wolf or just some wandering Indian old Ahumado had caught. By cutting the rope

Scull had secured the man a chance. If he came to he could chew his way free and try to make it to water.

But Inish Scull didn't intend to waste any of the night worrying the issue. The man could go if he was able. He himself had ten hours of fast walking to do and he wanted to be at it. The thought of what was ahead stirred his blood and quickened his stride. He had only himself to consider, only himself to depend on, which was exactly how he liked things to be. By morning, if he kept moving, he should be in the canyon of the Yellow Cliffs. Then he could lie under a rock and wait for the sun to complete its short winter arc. Perhaps when night fell again, if he made good progress, he could crawl through Ahumado's guard and work his way into the cliffs, where he might find a cave deep enough to shelter him for a day. If he could find a suitable cave he would then need to be sure that his rifle was in good order—he had walked a long distance with the rifle over his shoulder. The sights might well need adjusting. Ahumado was said to be quick, despite his age. Certainly he had been quick the first time Scull went after him. It was not likely that the old man would linger long in plain view, once Scull started shooting at him. He needed to cripple him, at least, with the first shot—killing him outright would be better still.

A brisk, nipping north wind rose during the night, but Scull scarcely noticed it. He walked rapidly, rarely slowing for longer than it took him to make water, for ten hours. Twice he startled small herds of javelina and once almost stumbled over a sleeping mule deer. Normally he would have shot the deer or one of the pigs for meat, but this time he refrained, remembering Tudwal, the scout who would know he was there even before he knew it himself. It would not do to go shooting off guns with such a man on patrol.

Toward dawn, Scull stopped. The closer he got to danger, the keener he felt. For a moment, pissing, he remembered his wife, Inez—the woman thought she could hold him with her hot lusts, but she had failed. He was alone in Mexico, in the vicinity of a merciless enemy, and yet he found it possible to doubt that there was a happier man alive.

8.

AT THE ENTRANCE to the camp in the Yellow Cliffs was a pile of human heads. Three Birds would have liked to stop and look through the heads for a while to see if any friends of his were represented in the pile. Ahumado had killed many Comanches, some of them his friends. Probably a few of their heads were in the pile. Many of the heads still had the hair on them, from what he could see. Three Birds was curious. He had never seen a pile of heads before and would have liked to know how many heads were in the pile, but it didn't seem a polite thing to ask.

"Those are just some heads he has cut off people," Tudwal said, in a friendly voice.

Three Birds didn't comment. His view was that Tudwal wasn't really as friendly as he sounded. He might be the man who skinned people. Three Birds didn't want to banter idly about cut-off heads with a man who might skin him.

"He won't take *your* head though," Tudwal said. "For you it will be the pit or else the cliff."

Three Birds soon observed that the camp they were coming to was poor. Two men had just killed a brown dog and were skinning it so that it could be put in the cook pot. A few women who looked very tired were grinding corn. An old man with several knives strung around his belt came out of a cave and looked at him.

"Is he the one who skins people?" Three Birds asked.

"We all skin people," Tudwal said. "But Goyeto is old, like Ahumado. Goyeto has had the most practice."

Three Birds thought it all seemed very odd. Ahumado was supposed to have stolen much treasure, in his robberies, but he didn't seem rich. He just seemed like an old, dark man who was cruel to people. It was all puzzling. Three Birds broke into his death song while puzzling about it. He wondered if Kicking Wolf would die from being pulled behind the horse they had tied him to.

Three Birds was soon taken off the horse and allowed to sit by one of the campfires, but nobody offered him food. Around him were the Yellow Cliffs, pocked with caves. Eagles soared high above the cliffs, eagles and buzzards as well. Three Birds was startled to see so many great birds, high above the cliffs. On the plains where he lived he seldom saw many eagles.

He had expected to be tortured as soon as he was brought into the camp, but no one seemed in any hurry to torture him. Tudwal went into a cave with a young woman and was gone for a long time. The great force of *pistoleros* that Ahumado was said to command were nowhere in evidence. There were only five or six men there. Ahumado walked over and sat on a blanket. Three Birds stopped singing his death song. It seemed foolish to sing it when no one was paying any attention to him at all. Two old women were making tortillas, which gave off a good smell. In the Comanche camp prisoners were always fed, even if they were to be promptly killed or tortured, but that did not seem to be the custom in the camp of Ahumado. No one brought him tortillas, or anything else.

When the day was almost passed Tudwal came and sat with him. A peculiar thing about the man, who was white but very dirty, was that his left eye blinked all the time, a trait that Three Birds found disconcerting.

"I have been with six woman today," Tudwal said. "The women are Ahumado's but he lets me have them. He is too old for women himself. His only pleasure is killing."

Three Birds kept quiet. It was in his mind that they might start his torture at any time. If that happened he would need all his courage. He did not want to weaken his courage by chatting with a braggart like Tudwal. He wondered how Kicking Wolf was faring. If the horse was still dragging him he was probably thoroughly skinned up.

Finally Ahumado stood up and motioned for Tudwal to bring the prisoner. Tudwal cut the throngs that bound Three Birds' ankles and helped him to his feet. Ahumado led them to the base of one of the high cliffs, where there was a big pit. Tudwal led Three Birds to the edge of the pit and pointed down. In the bottom Three Birds could see several rattlesnakes and also a rat or two.

"You can't see the scorpions and spiders but there are many down there," Tudwal said. "Every day the women go out and turn over rocks, to find more scorpions and spiders for the pit."

Without a word Ahumado turned toward the cliff and began to climb up a narrow trail of steps cut into the rock. The trail led higher and higher, toward the top of the cliff. Ahumado climbed the trail quite easily, but Three Birds, because his hands were bound, had some trouble. He could not use the handholds Ahumado used, and Tudwal. Because of his difficulty with the steps Tudwal began to insult him.

"You are not much of a climber," he said. "Ahumado is old but he is already almost to the top of the cliff."

That was true. Ahumado had already disappeared above them. Three Birds tried to ignore Tudwal. He concentrated on making his feet go up the trail. He had never been so high before. In his country, the beautiful country of the plains, even birds did not fly as high as he was being asked to climb. It seemed to him he was as high as the clouds—only it was a clear evening, with no clouds. Behind him Tudwal grew impatient with Three Birds' slow climbing. He began to poke him with a knife. Three Birds tried to ignore the knife, though soon both his legs were bloody. Finally he reached the top of the cliff. The Black Vaquero was standing there, waiting. The climb had taken so long that the sky was red with sunset. When Three Birds reached the top he found that his lungs were hurting. There didn't seem to be much air atop the old man's Yellow Cliffs.

Around him there was distance, though—a great distance, with the peaks of the Sierra Perdida, reddened by sunset, stretching as far away as he could see. Three Birds was so high he wasn't quite sure he was still on the earth. It seemed to him he had climbed into the country of the birds—the birds for which he was named. He was in the country of the eagles—it was no wonder he could hardly find air to breathe.

Near the edge of the cliff, not far away, there were four posts stuck in the ground, with ropes going from the posts over the edge of the cliff. Nearby four men, as dark as Ahumado, were squatting by a little fire. Ahumado made a motion and the dark men went to the first post and began to pull on the rope. Suddenly, as the dark men pulled, Three Birds heard a loud beating of wings and several great vultures swirled up over the edge of the cliff, almost into their faces. One of the vultures, with a red strip of meat in its mouth, flapped so close to Three Birds that he could have touched it.

Three Birds was wondering why the strange old man and his skinny *pistolero* had brought him so high on the cliff, but he did not have to wonder long, for the dark men pulled a cage made of mesquite branches tightly lashed together onto the top of the cliff. It was not a large cage. The dead man in it had not much room, while he was alive, but the vultures could easily get their heads through and eat the dead man, little by little. The man's bones were still together but a lot of him was eaten. There was not much left of the man, who had been small, like the dark men who raised the cage. As soon as the cage was on solid ground the dark men opened it and quickly pitched what was left of the stinking corpse over the cliff.

Now Three Birds knew why they had brought him to the top of the cliff. They were going to put him in a cage and hang him off the cliff. He walked to the edge of the cliff and looked down. There were three more cages, dangling below him.

"There is a vaquero down there who is still alive," Tudwal said. "We only put him in two weeks ago. A strong man, if he is quick, can stay alive a month, in the cages."

"Why does he need to be quick, if he is in a cage?" Three Birds asked.

"Quick, or he don't eat," Tudwal said. "Pigeons light on the cages. If the man inside is quick he can catch birds to eat. We had a card sharp once who lasted nearly two months—he was quick with his hands."

Old Ahumado walked over then. He did not smile.

"The cage or the pit?" he asked. "The snakes or the birds?"

"If I were you I would take the pit," Tudwal said. "It's warmer down there. There's some big rats you could eat, if they don't eat you first. Or you could eat a snake."

267

Three Birds was watching the dusk fill up the canyons to the south. He felt he was in the sky, where the spirits lived. Perhaps the spirits of his wife and children were not far away, or the spirits of his parents and grandparents, all dead from the shitting sickness. They were all in the high air somewhere, where he was. It might even be that Kicking Wolf was dead, in which case his spirit would be near.

"Choose," Ahumado said. "It is almost dark. It is a long way back down to the pit, if you want the pit."

"Don't you have a better cage to put me in?" Three Birds asked. "This is a filthy cage. It has parts of that dead man sticking to it. I don't think I will be comfortable in such a filthy cage."

Tudwal was astonished. He gave a nervous laugh.

"It is the only cage we have," he said. "Maybe it will rain and wash away some of that blood."

"It isn't the only cage you have," Three Birds pointed out, in a calm, reasonable voice. "There are three more cages down there. You showed them to me."

"They are full," Tudwal said. "There's that vaquero who's still alive, and two dead men."

"You could throw the dead men out," Three Birds pointed out. "Maybe one of those cages would be cleaner."

There was silence on the cliff. Tudwal was disconcerted. What did this Comanche think he was doing? It was crazy to bargain with Ahumado—it would only cause him to think up something worse to do to the prisoner.

"He doesn't like our cage," Ahumado said. "Take him back down. We'll let Goyeto skin him."

Before Tudwal could reach him Three Birds took two quick steps, to the very edge of the cliff. In only a second he could put himself beyond the reach of the old torturer and his blinking henchman. He only had to step backward and he would be gone forever, into the fine air where the spirits lived. For a while he would fly, like the birds he was named after; then he would be where the spirits were, without having wasted any time in the dirty pit or the filthy cage. Three Birds had always been a clean man; he was glad they had brought him to a high place, where the air was clean. In a moment he would go backward, into his final home in the air, but he wanted to speak to Ahumado and his henchman before he left them.

"You are stupid men," he said. "A child could fool you. Now Big Horse Scull is coming, and he is not a child. I imagine he will kill you both, and then you will not be skinning people and putting them in cages."

Three Birds saw, out of the corner of his eye, one of the dark men sneaking toward him along the cliff edge. The man was short, so short he must have thought no one could see him. But Three Birds saw him and decided he had lectured the two bandits long enough—somewhere behind him in the air, the spirits hovered, like doves. He began to cry out his death song and stepped backward off the cliff.

9.

WHEN KICKING WOLF came to he was almost too weak to move. The tight bonds made his limbs numb and his eyes were strange. Not far away he saw a horse that appeared to be two horses and a cactus bush that seemed to be two cactus bushes. The horse was Three Birds' horse, the one he had been tied to. It was only one horse, and yet, when Kicking Wolf looked at it, it became two, and the one bush became two. Some witch had distorted his vision so that he saw two things when there was only one. It must have been Ahumado or someone who worked for him.

Then he saw that the rope that had bound him to the horse had been cut. To his surprise, near his head, he saw Scull's footprint, a footprint he had often seen while he was following the rangers, before he stole the Buffalo Horse. Scull must have been the one who cut him loose, another puzzling thing.

Kicking Wolf's tongue was thick with thirst. When he sat up the world turned around. Three Birds' horse was still two horses, but the two horses were not far away. Kicking Wolf knew that if he could free himself he could catch the horse and ride it to water. There must be water nearby, else the horse would not have stayed.

Because of his thick tongue it took him a long time to chew through the bonds on his wrists. It was dark when the rawhide finally parted.

The vaqueros who had roped him had not taken his quiver—there were no arrows in it, so they had left it. But in the bottom of the quiver was a small flint arrowhead that had broken off one of his arrows. With the arrowhead he was able to cut quickly through the rawhide that bound his ankles. Flies were stinging him all over his body, where the skin had been taken off in the dragging. All he could do about the flies was throw sand on himself to cover the skinned areas. He found he could not hold his head up straight, either. Something had made his neck so sore that he had to keep his head tipped to one side or else a violent pain shot through him.

When it became dark Kicking Wolf felt a little less confused. In the dark he could not see two of everything. He made his way slowly to where the two horses that were one horse had been grazing and when he got there one of the horses melted into the other. As soon as he mounted, the horse went trotting north. Kicking Wolf found that the riding made him sick—it also made violent pains shoot through his head, but he did not stop and attempt to recover a little. He was still in the country of the Black Vaquero—in his weakness he would be easy to catch if Ahumado sent his men back after him. He remembered Three Birds, who had gallantly come with him to Mexico, although he had no business there. Probably Three Birds was being tortured, but Kicking Wolf knew there was nothing he could do about it. The pains shooting through his own head were as violent as torture. He had to slow the horse to a walk or he would have passed out. In such condition he could not go back to the Yellow Canyon and try to save his friend. Perhaps, later, he could go back with many warriors and avenge him—even

Buffalo Hump might join such a war party. He would not like it that the old man had tortured Three Birds to death. He might want to ride to the Yellow Cliffs and do some torturing himself.

Near morning the horse found water, a little trickling spring high in some rocks. The pool was only a few feet across but it was good water. Kicking Wolf let the horse drink and then tethered him securely. Then he lay down in the water and let it wash his wounds. It stung but it cleaned him. He drank a little, and then drank more, until his tongue became the right size again. He wanted to sleep by the little pool, but was afraid to. Ahumado's men would know of the water hole. They might catch him there. He rested an hour, let the horse drink, and then rode on through the day. It was sunny; he began, again, to see two things that were one. He saw a deer running and the deer became two deer. Kicking Wolf knew a bad witch must have made his eyes untrustworthy. The pain in his neck and head was still violent, but he kept riding. He wanted to get back across the Rio Grande. Besides the pain in his head there was also a sadness in his heart. He had had too much pride and because of it Three Birds was lost. Everyone had told him that his plan was folly; even a foolish man such as Slipping Weasel, who did stupid things every day, had been wise enough to warn him against taking the Buffalo Horse to Mexico. But he had done it, for his pride—but his pride had cost his friend's life and he would have to go home humbled and shamed. Ahumado had taken the Buffalo Horse, the great horse of the Texans, as if he had been given a donkey. He had not acknowledged Kicking Wolf's courage, or anything else. Even courage, the courage of a great warrior, didn't matter to the Black Vaquero.

It occurred to Kicking Wolf, as he rode north, that the problem with his eyes might not be the work of a bad witch; it might be the work of his own medicine man, Worm. The old spirits might have spoken to Worm and told him that Kicking Wolf had shamed the tribe by his insistence on taking the Buffalo Horse to Ahumado. The old spirits would know what happened to Three Birds—the old spirits knew such things. They might have come to Worm in a vision and insisted that he work a spell to punish this haughty man, Kicking Wolf. Because he had had too much pride, Worm might have made a spell to change his eyes so that they could never see accurately again. Always he might see two where there was one.

Kicking Wolf didn't know. His head hurt, his friend was lost, and he had many days of riding before he got home. When he got home—if he did—no one would sing for him, either.

Even so, Kicking Wolf wanted to be home. He wanted to see Worm. Maybe he was wrong about the old spirits. Maybe it was one of Ahumado's witches who had made the trouble in his eyes. Maybe Worm could cure him so that, once again, he would only see what was there.

10.

WHEN SCULL AWOKE Hickling Prescott was on his mind and the smell of cooking meat was in his nostrils. His mother, a Ticknor, had been a childhood friend of the great historian, whose house stood only a block down the hill from the great Georgian town house where Inish Scull had grown up. The world knew the man as William Hickling Prescott, of course, but Scull's mother had always called him "Hickling." As Inish Scull was leaving for the Mexican War he had gone by to pay his respects to the old man, then blind and mostly deaf. It was well to know your history when going off to battle, Scull believed, and certainly his mother's friend, Hickling Prescott, knew as much about the history of Mexico as anyone in Boston—or in America, for that matter. To Hickling Prescott, of course, Boston *was* America—as much of it, at least, as he cared to acknowledge.

Twice before, during the few weeks he had spent in Boston, Scull had made the mistake of taking Inez along when visiting the old man. But Hickling Prescott didn't approve of Inez. Although he couldn't see or hear and wasn't expected to feel, somehow Inez's determined carnality had impressed itself on the historian, who was not charmed. He didn't believe the sons of Boston should marry women from the South—and yet, to his annoyance, not a few sons of Boston did just that.

"Why, the South's just that riffraff John Smith brought over, Mr. Scull," the old man said. "Your wife smells like a Spanish harlot. I sat next to her at dinner at Quincy Adams's and I smelled her. Our Boston women don't smell—at least they smell very rarely. The Oglethorpes were low bred, you know, quite low bred."

"Well, sir, Inez is not an Oglethorpe, but I admit she can produce an odor once in a while," Inish said.

"There are several appealing misses right here in Boston," Hickling Prescott informed him crisply. "I hardly think you needed to root around in that Oglethorpe bunch just to find a wife."

He sighed. "But it's done, I suppose," he said.

"It's done, Mr. Prescott," Inish admitted. "And now I'm off to Mexico, to the fight."

"Have you read my book?" the old man asked.

"Every word," Inish assured him. "I intend to reread it on the boat."

"The Oglethorpes produced many fine whores," old Prescott said. "But, as I said, it's done. Now I'm working on Peru, and that *isn't* done."

"I'm sure it will be masterly, when it comes," Inish said.

" 'Magisterial,' I would have said," old Prescott corrected, sipping a little cold tea. "I don't expect we'll have to fight Peru, at least not in my time, and I have no advice to offer if we do."

"It's Mexico we're fighting, sir," Inish reminded him.

There was a silence in the great dim room, whose windows were hung with black drapes. Inish realized he had misspoken. William Hickling Prescott no doubt knew who the nation was about to go to war with.

"It was reading your great book that made me want to join this war," Inish told him, anxious to make up for his slip. "If I might say so, your narrative stirs great chords in a man. Heroism—strife—the city of Mexico. Victory despite great odds. The few against the many. Death, glory, sacrifice."

The historian was silent for a moment.

"Yes, there was that," he said dryly. "But this one won't be that way, Mr. Scull. All you'll find is dust and beans. I do wish you hadn't married that Southern woman. What was her name, now?"

"Dolly," Inish reminded him. "And I believe her people came over with Mr. Penn."

"Oh, that hypocrite," the historian said. "It must have been a great sorrow to your mother—your marriage, that is. I miss your mother. She was my childhood friend, though the Ticknors in general are rather a distressing lot. Your ma got all the shine in that family, Mr. Scull."

"That she did," Inish agreed.

There were no black drapes in the stony canyon where Scull had awakened, thinking of Hickling Prescott. The walls of the canyon were pale yellow, like the winter sunlight. Scull had slept without a fire and awoke stiff and shivering. On such a morning a little of Inez's unapologetic carnality would not have been unwelcome.

Of course, he was in Mexico, whose conquest Hickling Prescott had chronicled so vividly. Cortés and his few men had captured a country and broken a civilization. When Scull had gone to the old man's house on the eve of his departure for the war, he had meant to probe a little, to get the old man's thoughts on events which he probably understood as well as any living man, but the old man had been indifferent, opaque; what he knew was in his book and he did not see the point in repeating it to the young man.

"I ain't a professor, they've got some of them at Harvard," he had said.

"Whip 'em and get home, sir," he advised, showing Inish to the door. That he had actually risen from his chair and walked Inish to the door was, Inish knew, a great compliment—there was, after all, a butler to show visitors in and out. The compliment, no doubt, was inspired by the historian's fond memories of his mother.

"I'd leave that Oglethorpe girl down in Georgia, if I were you," the old man said, as he stood in the door, looking out on the Boston he could not see. "She won't do much harm if she's in Georgia—the Oglethorpe smell don't carry that far."

But it was a meaty smell, not the memory of the old, crabbed historian, that had awakened Inish Scull from his chilly sleep in the Yellow Canyon. What he smelled was meat cooking. He didn't take in the smell with every breath, but, intermittently, every few minutes, when there would be a certain shift in the wind, then came the smell.

Scull cautiously looked around. The land was broken and humpy. Perhaps someone else was camped behind one of the humps, cooking a deer or a pig. And yet, a fire would have meant smoke, and he saw no smoke.

It's dream meat, he told himself. I'm dreaming of venison and pork because I'm rumbling hungry. I'm so hungry I'm dreaming smells.

His only food the day before had been three doves—he had crept up on them in the early morning dimness and knocked them off their roost with a stick. He had seared the fat birds over a small fire and had eaten them before full daylight came. He knew he was in the domain of the old killer, Ahumado, and didn't want to be shooting his gun, not for a few days. Nor, ordinarily, did Inish Scull mind fasting. He had seen men killed in battle because fear and dread caused them to lose control of their stomachs or their bowels. In the time of battle a fighting man needed to stay empty, in his view; there would be time enough for feasting once the battle had been fought.

Still, he was human, and could not be fully immune to the smell of cooking meat. Then he saw movement to the west. In a moment a coyote came in sight, its ears pricked up, going toward the ridges to the south. The coyote was moving purposely; perhaps it smelled the cooking meat too. Perhaps, after all, it was a not a dream smell that had brought him awake in the Yellow Canyon.

Scull decided he might as well follow the coyote—it had a better nose than he did and would lead him to the meat, if there was meat.

He walked for two hours, keeping the coyote just in sight. For long stretches he lost the meat smell entirely, but then, faintly, if the wind shifted to the south, he would smell it again. Between one gray ridge and the next he lost the coyote completely. The country rose slightly; he was crossing a mesa, or tableland, almost bare of vegetation.

From being intermittent, the smell became constant, so constant that Scull could say with conviction that it was not a deer or a pig that was being cooked: it was a horse. He had eaten horse often in his trekking in the West and didn't think he could be mistaken. Somewhere nearby horsemeat was cooking—but why would the smell carry nearly a dozen miles, to the canyon where he had slept?

Then Scull began to notice tracks, many tracks. He was crossing the route of a considerable migration—there were a few horse tracks, but most of the migrating people were on foot. Some were barefoot, some wore moccasins. There were even dog tracks—it was as if a village had decided to move itself across the empty tableland.

Then Scull saw the smoke, which seemed to be rising out of the ground, a mile more ahead. The smoke rose as if from a hidden fire. He didn't know what to make of it, but he did know that he had begun to feel exposed. He was in plain sight on a bare mesa where a hundred people or more had just passed. Scull looked around quickly, hoping for a ridge, a hump of dirt, or patch of sage—anything that could conceal him, even a hole he could hide in until darkness fell, but there was nothing. Besides, he was marching in stout boots and his tread would stand out like a road sign to anyone with an eye for tracks.

Scull turned and hurried back toward the last cover, doing his best to erase or at least blur his track as he went. Suddenly he felt more exposed than he ever had, in all his years of soldiering; a kind of panic seized him, an overwhelming need to hide until dark came. Then he could come back and unravel the mystery of the smoke and the smell of cooking meat.

Scull hurried back, scrubbing out his tracks as best he could, as he walked—the last ridge had been rocky; he felt sure he could dig under one of them and stay safely hid until dark.

Then he saw the old man, coming toward him along his own track. The minute he saw him he remembered something Famous Shoes had said.

"Ahumado is always behind you," Famous Shoes had told him. "Don't look for him in front. When he wants you he will appear, and he will be behind you."

The memory came too late. The Black Vaquero was following the plain track left by his boots. The old man seemed to be alone, but Scull knew his men had to be somewhere nearby. The old man had not lived to a great age by being a fool.

Scull decided he would just keep walking, with his head down, pretending he hadn't seen Ahumado, until he was in rifle range. He shot best from a prone position. When the distance was narrowed sufficiently he would just drop to the ground and fire. With one well placed shot he could eliminate the Black Vaquero, the old bandit who had harassed the settlers of the border as ferociously as Buffalo Hump had the settlers along the northern rivers.

Of course, the *pistoleros* would probably run him down and kill him, but then it was not the Scull way to die at home. His brother had been yanked off a whaling ship in the Hebrides and drowned. His Uncle Fortescue had drunk poisoned kvass in Circassia, and his father had been attempting to ice-skate on the frozen Minnesota River when he was overwhelmed by a band of Cree Indians. The Sculls died vividly, but never at home.

Scull had only a hundred yards to walk before he was in rifle range of Ahumado. He didn't mean to risk a long shot, either. The one hundred yards might take him three minutes; then he would have to decide between certain martyrdom and very uncertain diplomacy. If he chose to risk the diplomacy he would have to live until Ahumado chose to let him die, which might be after days of torture. It was a choice his forebears had not had to make. His brother hadn't meant to get jerked out of the whaleboat, his Uncle Fortescue had no idea the kvass was poisoned, and his father had merely been skating when the Cree hacked him down.

Scull walked on; Ahumado came in range; Scull didn't shoot.

Too curious about that smoke, he told himself. Maybe he'll consider me such a fine catch that he'll ask me to dinner.

Then he saw, to Ahumado's right, four small dark men. To his left a tall man on a paint horse had appeared. The Black Vaquero, indeed, had not been alone.

For a moment, Scull wavered. Only six men opposed him. Ahumado carried no weapon—the only gunman was the skinny man on the paint horse; he could shoot him, grab the horse, and run. His fighting spirit rose. He was about to level his rifle when he glanced over his shoulder and saw, to his amazement, that four more of the dark men were just behind him, within thirty yards. They had risen as if from the earth and they carried *bolos*, the short rawhide thongs with rocks at each end that Mexicans threw at the legs of cattle or deer, to entwine them and bring them down.

Scull did not level his rifle; he knew he had waited too long. Now it would have to be diplomacy. The fact that the dark men had simply appeared was disturbing. He had looked the terrain over carefully and seen no one; but there they were and the die was cast.

Ahumado came to within ten feet of Scull before he stopped.

"Well, hello from Harvard," Scull said. "I'm Captain Scull."

"You have come just in time, Captain," the old man said.

The man on the paint horse rode up behind him. He had a blinking eye. The dark men stood back, silent as rocks.

"Just in time for what, sir?" Scull asked.

"To help us eat your horse," Ahumado informed him. "That's what we are cooking, over there in our pit."

"Hector?" Scull said. "Bible and sword, you must have a big pit."

"Yes, we have a big pit," Ahumado said. "We have been cooking him for three days. I think he is about cooked. If you will hand this man your rifle we can go eat him."

The tall *pistolero* rode close. Scull handed him the rifle. With the dark men walking behind him, Inish Scull followed Ahumado toward the rising smoke.

11.

SCULL STOOD ON THE EDGE of the crater, astonished first by the crater itself and then by what he saw in it. From rim to rim the crater must be a mile across, he judged. Below him, at the bottom of it, were the hundred or more people whose tracks he had seen—men and women, young and old. There were all waiting. The smoke rose from a pit in the center of the crater. Hector, whose head was missing, had been cooked standing up, in his skin.

The old man, Ahumado, had scarcely looked at Scull since his surrender. His eyelids drooped so low that it was hard to see his eyes. Men had shoveled away the bed of coals that had covered the pit for three days. The coals were scattered in heaps around the pit—many of them still glowed red.

"We have never cooked a horse this big," Ahumado remarked.

"He appears to be thoroughly charred," Scull observed. "You might as well let the feast begin."

He felt chagrined. The old man treated his arrival as casually as if he had received a letter announcing the date and arrival time. He had walked into Mexico, convinced that he was proceeding with extreme stealth, and yet Ahumado had read his approach so precisely that he had finished cooking Hector in time for Scull to say grace, if he wanted to.

Now the need he had always had to be as far as he could get from Boston—not just Boston the place but Boston as a way of being—had landed him in a crater in Mexico, where a hundred dark people were waiting to eat his horse.

Ahumado made a gesture and the squatting, waiting people rose like a swarm and crowded into the pit around the smoking horse. Knives flashed, many knives. Strips of skin were ripped off, exposing the dark flesh, which soon dripped blood from a hundred cuts. Some who had no knives tore at the meat with their fingers.

"They are hungry but your horse will fill them up," Ahumado said. "We will go down now. I have saved the best part for you, Captain Scull."

"This is a big crater," Scull said, as they were walking down. "I wonder what made it?"

"A great rock—Jaguar threw it from the sky," Ahumado said. "He threw it long ago, before there were people."

"I expect we'd call it a meteor, up at Harvard College," Scull said.

Then he saw four men shoveling coals out of another, smaller pit. This pit was modest, only a few scoops of coals in it. When the coals were scattered the men lifted something out of it on two long sticks, something that steamed and smoked, although wrapped in heavy sacking. They carried their burden over to a large flat rock and sat it down. Ahumado took out a knife, walked over, and began to cut the sacking away.

"Now this is a treat, Captain," Tudwal said. "You'd do best to eat hearty before we put you in the cage."

"I will, sir, I've never lacked appetite," Scull assured him. "I ate my own pig, as a boy, and now I expect I'll eat my horse."

He did not inquire about the cage he was going to be put in.

Ahumado cut away the last of the sacking: Hector's steaming head stared at him from the flat rock. Smoke came from his eyes. The top of his skull had been neatly removed, so that his brains would cook.

"Now there's a noble head, if I ever saw one," Scull said, as he approached. "Hector and I harried many a foe. I had expected to ride him back north, when the great war comes, but it's not to be. You were his Achilles, Señor Ahumado."

Now the dark men carried machetes. Ahumado gestured for them to move back a few steps.

Scull glanced back at the larger pit. Hector was rapidly being consumed. The dark people in the pit looked as if they had been in a rain of blood.

So it must have been when the cavemen ate the mastodons, Scull thought.

Then he turned back, pulled out his knife, and began to cut bites of meat from the cheeks of his great horse.

12.

ONCE INISH SCULL was securely shut in the cage of mesquite branches, Tudwal reached in and offered to cut the thongs that bound his hands and feet. Scull had been stripped naked too. Both the binding and the stripping were indignities he didn't appreciate, though he maintained a cheerful demeanor throughout.

"Stick your feet over near the bars and I'll cut you loose," Tudwal offered. "Then I'll do your hands. You won't be able to catch no pigeons with your hands tied like that. You'd starve in ten days, which ain't what he has in mind. When he hangs a man in a cage he expects him to last awhile."

"I have never cared much for squab," Scull said. "I suppose I can learn to like it, if there's nothing else."

"A Mexican we hung off this cliff caught an eagle once," Tudwal said. "But the eagle got the best of him—pecked out one of his eyes."

"I notice you blink, sir—what happened?" Scull said. "A sparrow get you?"

"Nothing. I was just born ablinking," Tudwal said.

The insult, as Scull had feared, didn't register.

"But you weren't born in Mexico," Scull said. "You sound to me like a man who was probably born in Cincinnati or thereabouts."

Tudwal was startled. How did the man know that? He had, in fact, been born on the Kentucky River, not far from Cincinnati.

"You're right, Captain—but how'd you know that?" Tudwal asked.

"I suppose it's your mellow tone," Scull said. He smiled at the man, hoping to lull him into a moment of inattention. The cliff they were about to lower him over seemed to fall away for a mile. Once they lowered him his fate would be sealed. He would hang there in space, with half of Mexico to look at, until he froze or starved. He didn't relish hanging there for days or weeks, surviving on the occasional bird he could yank through the bars. Ahumado, an old Mayan come north to prey on ignorant people, white and brown, had not proved susceptible to Harvard charm; but Tudwal, the blinking man, did not seem overly intelligent. If he kept talking he might yet fool him into making a mistake. He had obediently held his feet near the bars and Tudwal had freed his ankles. His wrists came next, and there lay the opportunity.

Tudwal looked puzzled when Scull mentioned the mellow tone. Actually, the man had a nasal voice with little mellowness in it.

"Yes sir, I've been sung to often by Ohio maidens—some of them may not quite have been maidens at the time. The whores in the fine town of Cincinnati have lullabied me to sleep many times. Have you heard this old tune, sir?"

He struck up the old ballad of Barbara Allen:

> In London town where I was born
> There was a fair maid dwelling . . .

Tudwal nodded. Someone far back in his life had once sung that song, a grandmother or an aunt, he was not sure. He forgot, for a moment, that Captain Scull was about to be dangled to his death. The song took him away, into memory, into thoughts of his mother and his sister, when he had led a gentler life.

As Scull sang he held his hands close to the bars so that Tudwal could cut the rawhide thongs. He sang softly, so that Tudwal would lean forward as he cut. The moment the bonds parted Scull grabbed Tudwal's wrist and whacked it so hard against the mesquite bars that he broke it. The knife fell into the cage: he had one weapon. Then he caught Tudwal by the throat and pulled him close enough to the cage that he could reach with the other hand and yank the man's Colt pistol out of its holster. Now he had two weapons. He would have preferred to conserve bullets by strangling Tudwal, but the man was too strong. Before Scull could get his other hand on Tudwal's throat he twisted away, forcing Scull to shoot him dead, the sound echoing through the Yellow Canyon.

The four dark men who had been waiting to lower the cage immediately took their machetes and trotted away. Ahumado was still back at the crater, where the feast was being held, waiting on his blanket; he would have heard the shot.

"There, you Cincinnati fool, I warbled you to death," Scull said.

His situation had improved dramatically. He had a knife and a gun, and five bullets. On the other hand he was in a flimsy cage, on top of a five-hundred-foot cliff, and he was naked.

The bindings that held the mesquite cage together were hardened rawhide. Scull began to hack at them but the knife was dull and the rawhide hard as iron. Tudwal's horse stood near. If he could cut himself free he might have a chance, but the rawhide was so resistant and the knife so dull that it might take an hour to free himself—and he didn't have an hour.

"You goddamned fool, why didn't you sharpen your knife?" Scull said. "Not only did you have a Cincinnati voice, you had a goddamned weak Kentucky brain."

It annoyed him. He had worked a miracle, killed his captor, and yet he wasn't free. Then, with a moment to breathe, he remembered another of Papa Franklin's fine sayings: "Haste makes waste." He looked more closely at the jointure of the wrappings. He didn't need to hack the cage apart—if he could just break the wrappings at one corner of the cage he could squeeze out and run. He still had five bullets; it seemed good policy to sacrifice one or two of them to free himself. He immediately tested the decision and was well pleased with the result: two bullets and the wrappings blew apart, and he squeezed through and stood up.

His fighting spirit rose; by God, he was out! He squatted briefly over the body of Tudwal, but found only two more bullets, in a pocket of the man's dirty tunic. But the man at least wore clothes; Scull hastily stripped him and pulled on his filthy pants and tunic. They were too large, but they were clothes!

The paint horse stood not thirty feet away. Its ears were up—it looked at Scull nervously. Steady the yardarm, light on the throttle, Scull told himself. Haste makes waste. He had to approach calmly and slowly; he could not afford to spook the skittish animal. Without the horse the dark men would soon run him to earth.

The fact that he wore Tudwal's clothes was an advantage. The man's smell lingered in the filthy garments; he could plainly smell it, and no doubt the horse could too.

"Bible and sword, that's good of you, boy," he said, walking slowly toward the horse. "Be a good nag now, be a good nag. You're an ugly nag but I'll overlook that if you'll just carry me to Texas."

The horse pawed the ground once, but did not retreat. Scull came on, steadily, and soon had the bridle rein in his hand. In another moment he had Tudwal's rifle out of its scabbard and was in the saddle. Then, to his intense annoyance, the horse began to crow-hop. Scull had no skill with broncos, as the Texans called bucking horses. He had to grab the horse's mane, to keep from being thrown, and in the process, to his intense vexation, dropped the rifle. Finally the crow-hopping stopped but by then Scull was not sure where the rifle was—he saw a line of men on the horizon and knew that he had no time to search for the gun. He sawed the reins until he had the paint pointed north, and then urged him into a dead run. I'm gone, he thought—I'm gone. But then he heard the whirl of bolas as the dark men rose up from behind a low ridge. The running horse went down hard—Scull flew a good distance and lit on his shoulder. As he rose, more bolas were flying at him. One wrapped around his legs. He quickly shot two of the dark men but a third dashed in and hit him on the head with the flat side of a machete. The sky swirled above him as it might if he were on a fast carousel.

This time Ahumado supervised the caging.

The three other cages were pulled up and the pecked-at corpses in them flung over the cliff. Scull was put in the strongest cage. He was dazed from the blow to his head and made no resistance. Ahumado let him keep the clothes he had taken from Tudwal.

"I have no one to put in these cages," the old man said. "You will be alone on the cliff."

"It's a fine honor, I'm sure," Scull said. His head rang so that it was a chore to talk.

"It is no honor—but it means that many birds will come to you. If you are quick you can catch these birds. You might live a long time."

"I'll be quick but you ain't smart, señor," Scull said. "If you were smart you'd ransom me. I'm a big *jefe*. The Texans might give you a thousand cattle if you'd send me back.

"Your people could live a good spell on a thousand cattle," he added.

Ahumado stepped close to the cage and looked at him with a look of such contempt that it startled Inish Scull. The look was like the slice of a machete.

"Those are not my people, they are my slaves," Ahumado said. "Those cattle in Texas are mine already. They wandered there from Jaguar's land, and Parrot's. When I want cattle I go to Texas and get them."

He stopped, and stepped back. The force of his contempt was so great that Scull could not look away.

"You had better try to catch those fat pigeons when they come to roost," the old man said. Then he gestured to the dark men, and turned away.

The dark men put their shoulders against the cage and nudged it outward, over the lip of the great cliff. Slowly the men who stood at the post began to lower it into the Yellow Canyon. The cage twisted a little, as it was lowered; it twisted and swayed. Inish Scull held tightly to the mesquite bars. The height made him dizzy. He wondered if the rope would hold.

Far below him, great black vultures soared and sank. One or two rose toward him, as the cage was lowered, but most of them pecked at the remains of the corpses that had just been thrown off the cliff.

13.

AUGUSTUS MCCRAE, brokenhearted because of Clara's marriage, resorted much to the bottle or jug as the six rangers proceeded west in search of Captain Inish Scull. It was vexing to Call—damn vexing. He was convinced they were on a wild goose chase anyway, trying to find one man in an area as large as west Texas, and a man, besides, who might not appreciate being found even if they *did* find him.

"It's two men, Woodrow," Augustus reminded him. "Famous Shoes is with him."

"Was with him—that was a while ago," Call said. "Are you too drunk to notice that time's passing?"

They were riding through the sparsely grassed country near the Double Mountain Fork of the Brazos, well beyond the rim of settlement. They had not even come upon a farm for over a week. All they saw ahead of them was deep sky and brown land.

"I ain't drunk at all, though I would be if there was whiskey to be had in this country," Gus said. "I doubt if there's a jug of whiskey within two hundred miles of here."

"That's fine," Call said. "You were drunk enough to last you while it *was* available."

"No, Woodrow—it didn't last," Gus said. "Maybe Clara didn't really marry. She likes to joke, you know. She might have just been joking, to see what I'd do."

Call didn't answer. The conjecture was too foolish to dignify. Augustus had lost his girl, and that was that.

The other rangers were jolly, though—all except Long Bill, who had not expected to leave his Pearl so soon. Imagining domestic delights that he was not at home to experience put Long Bill in a low mood.

Young Jake Spoon, though, was so jolly that he was apt to be irritating. The mere fact that he had survived two weeks in the wilderness without being scalped or tortured convinced him that rangering was easy and himself immortal. He was apt to babble on endlessly about the most normal occurrence, such as killing an antelope or a cougar.

The weather had been warm, which particularly pleased Pea Eye; he did most of the camp chores with will and skill, whereas young Jake had adequate will but little skill. The third morning out he girthed Gus's young horse too tightly. Gus was too hung over to notice; he mounted and was promptly bucked off, a circumstance that didn't please him. He cussed young Jake thoroughly, plunging the young man into a state of deep embarrassment.

Deets, the black man, was the happiest and least troublesome member of the troop. Deets liked being a scout far better than he liked being in town, the reason being, Call suspected, was because in town there were always men who might abuse him because of his color.

"Why are you so dern hard to convince, Woodrow?" Gus asked. "I've known you forever and I've never been able to convince you of a single thing."

"No, you've convinced me of one thing for sure," Call said, "and that's that you're foolish about women.

"I expect Clara turned you down because she knew you were too fond of whores," he added.

"Not a bit of it!" Gus retorted. "She knew I'd give up whores in a minute if she'd marry me."

Nonetheless, the thought that what Call said might be true made Augustus so unhappy that he wanted to get down and beat his head against a rock. They had only been in Austin two days: what happened with Clara happened so fast that, when he thought back on it, it was more like a visit in a dream than something real. He wanted to believe that when they returned to Austin again, things would be as they had always been, with Clara in her father's store, unmarried, waiting for him to rush in and kiss her.

Long Bill Coleman rode up to the two captains in hopes of getting some things clarified. He had quickly come to regret his gallantry in allowing himself to be conscripted for the new expedition. Adjusting to the racket of domestic life was hard for him, after a long trip; it might have been a little quieter had Pearl not insisted on keeping her chickens in the kitchen, but Pearl couldn't stand to be parted from her chickens; so there was the racket to contend with, on top of which Pearl was a fervent woman who liked to make up his absences by lots of fervor—an overwhelming amount of fervor at times, in fact. Thus Long Bill was subjected to conflicting feelings: part of him wanted Pearl and her fervor, while another part longed for the peace of the prairies.

For the moment he seemed to have the peace of the prairies, though there was no guarantee that the peace would hold. Several times, moving west along the rivers and creeks, they had struck Indian sign—enough Indian sign to make Long Bill nervous. His opinion of the matter, now that he was too far west to do much about it, was that he ought to have stayed with his wife. The chickens, after all, could be tolerated; better chickens than Comanches.

"Shut up, Bill—I don't know where we are and neither does Woodrow," Gus said, when he saw Long Bill riding up, an interrogative look on his face.

"I never asked a question," Long Bill pointed out.

"No, but you were about to—I seen it in the way you was holding your mouth," Gus said.

"I just wanted to know when we give up on finding the Captain," Long Bill said. "I got chores to do at home."

"You're a ranger and that comes first," Gus said tartly. "Your wife's big and stout. She can do the confounded chores."

"Well, but she's got a baby in her—that will slow some women down," Long Bill said.

"Rather than arguing, we need to be paying attention to the trail," Call said. With Augustus in such an uncertain temper he wanted to cool things before the argument became a fistfight.

"What trail?" Gus said. "There's no trail. We're just following our noses and our noses are pointed west."

"That's what it looks like to me," Long Bill said. "Captain Scull's got clean away. When do we go back?"

"I guess we'll go back when we've gone far enough," Call said, aware that it was no answer.

"Well, but what's far enough?" Jake Spoon asked, thrusting himself into the conversation—and not for the first time, either. Pea Eye Parker would never have intruded when his elders were talking. Pea Eye offered an opinion only when asked for one, which was seldom. He tried to determine correct procedure by watching his elders. Jake Spoon didn't think in terms of elders or superiors. It never occurred to him that there were times when the two captains might not want to be bothered with a youngster. Jake just barged in and asked his question.

"We're not to the Pecos yet," Call said. "If we don't strike his trail between here and the Pecos, I expect we ought to go back."

"I think we ought to look in Mexico, myself," Augustus said.

"Why?" Call said. "We had no orders to look in Mexico."

"No, but there's whores and tequila in Mexico," Gus said. "Bill and me, we could drown our sorrows."

"I ain't going all the way to Mexico just so you two can drown your sorrows," Call said.

"Woodrow always changes the subject when the talk turns to women," Augustus said.

"I didn't know the talk was even about women," Call said. "I thought we were talking about when to give up on the Captain and go back home."

Long Bill Coleman, to his own surprise and Call's, suddenly burst out with an opinion that he had been holding in for months.

"A man ought to marry, Captain," Long Bill said. "It's a lonely life not having no woman to hold on to when you bunk down at night."

Call was so startled by the remark that he hardly knew what to say.

"I'm usually working at night, Bill—I don't spend much time in a bunk," he replied, finally.

Long Bill's Adam's apple was quivering and his face was red. Call had seen him fight several fierce engagements with the Comanches and exhibit less emotion.

"I don't know that little Maggie Tilton too well, but I do know she wasn't meant to be no whore," Long Bill said. "She was meant to be a wife and she'd make a fine one."

Then, embarrassed by what he had said, he abruptly shut up and rode away.

"Amen," Gus said. "Now you see, Woodrow—the sooner you marry Maggie, the happier the rest of us will be."

Call was amazed—here they were in the middle of the wilderness, on a dangerous assignment, and Long Bill Coleman, the solidest man in the troop, had seen fit to deliver a public lecture, urging him to get married! Surely the decision to marry was a private matter that need only be discussed between the couple who were thinking of marrying.

Worrying about it while patrolling the Double Mountain Fork of the Brazos struck him as highly inappropriate. It would only distract them from the business at hand, which was rangering. While on patrol he liked to give his full attention to the landscape, the men, the horses, tracks, sign, the behavior of the birds and animals they spotted, anything that might help keep a troop of men alive in a country where a Comanche raiding party could swoop down on them at any moment. It was no time to be clouding the mind with issues of marriage or lustful thoughts—and the mention of slim Maggie Tilton *did* lead to lustful thoughts. Many a night, on guard, he had been distracted by the thought of Maggie. It was just good luck that he hadn't come under sudden attack at such a moment.

Long Bill, embarrassed by his own impertinence, avoided Call for the rest of the day. Augustus, as surprised by Long Bill's statement as Call had been, thought it best to avoid the subject of marriage for the rest of the day.

That evening, as soon as he'd had coffee and his bite, Call walked away from the campfire and sat by himself all night.

"I doubt he'll marry her, Gus," Long Bill whispered to Gus McCrae.

"I doubt it too," Gus said. "He ought to, though. You're right about that, Bill."

14.

IN THE MIDDLE of the next afternoon they heard the crack of gunshots from some low, rocky hills to the north. Then a dog bayed, a hound of some kind. They had just watered their horses at a thin trickle of creek, with a few wild plum bushes scattered along it. While the horses were taking in water and the men relieving themselves of it, Deets hurried up and down the little creek, looking at the plum bushes. Of course it was too early in the year for plums yet, but he liked to make note of such things in case they passed that way in June, when the sweet plums would be mature.

When the shots rang out, Deets came hurrying back. There were two shots and then silence, except for the hound.

Since the party was so small, Call and Augustus decided they had best stay together. They could not afford to send one man to scout—he might be surrounded and cut down.

"That ain't a real hound," Augustus ventured. "It's a damn Comanche, imitating a hound. They can imitate anything, you know—Indians can."

All during his years as a ranger, Augustus had been prone to anxiety because of the Indians' well-known ability to perfectly mimic birdsongs and animal sounds. He had never actually caught an Indian imitating a bird, but he knew they could.

Long Bill Coleman shared this particular anxiety.

"That's Indians for sure, Captain," he said. "They're trying to make us think there's a hound over in those rocks."

Call didn't share the anxiety. Deets himself could mimic several animals and most birds—he could perfectly imitate the snuff an armadillo makes when startled, and Deets wasn't an Indian. Besides, there was an abundance of wildlife, birds and animals, that did an excellent job of making their own sounds.

The ridge of shaley rock where the shots had come from looked uninviting, though. The ridge wrinkled the prairie for miles and could easily shelter an ambushing war party.

"They're there, Woodrow," Augustus said. "They're just waiting till we get closer. Look to your weapons, boys."

Young Jake Spoon was so terrified that he felt frozen. He put his hand on his pistol but was too scared to pull it out. If an Indian did come running at him Jake felt the fright alone would kill him. He realized he had been wrong not to stay in town. He felt as good as dead and just hoped the termination would be as quick and pain-less as possible.

"Well, if that's a Comanche, he not only sounds like a dog, he looks like a dog," Call said—a large gray hound had just appeared, trotting back and forth amid the rocks.

Long Bill felt immediate relief.

"Why, I know that dog," he said. "That's old Howler, Ben Lily's dog. Ben probably shot a bear. That's all he does, shoot bears."

"I doubt there's many bears out in this country," Gus said.

"There's one less now—Ben Lily, he's deadly on bears."

The sight of the large gray dog dispelled the general apprehen-sion. As they drew closer to the rocky ridge the hound started howling again, a dismal sound, Pea Eye thought. He had never been overly fond of the canine breeds.

Sure enough, when they clattered over the rocks that covered the ridge, they came upon a large, stooped man in buckskin clothes, skinning a young brown bear. The man's thick hair and long beard were evidently strangers to the comb or the brush. He favored them with a quick glance and then went on with his work.

"Howdy, Mr. Lily," Long Bill said. "What are you doing out here on the baldies?"

He had intended the remark to be jocular, but Ben Lily took it literally.

"Skinning a bear," he said.

"That bear's not much bigger than a cub," Augustus said. "If his ma's around here I expect she'll be wanting to eat us."

"Shot her yesterday," Ben Lily said. "Took us a day to catch up with the cub. Howler and me, that's us."

Call thought the man looked daft. What use was a dead bear, in a place so remote? Of course he could eat some of the meat, but why take the skin, which was heavy and awkward to transport? Where would he take it, anyway? Yet the man seemed content at his task. He even began to whistle as he skinned, and he clearly had no interest in the rangers.

"Well, if you shot his ma, where's *her* skin?" Augustus asked. He too was puzzled by the skinning. How many bearskins could a man use?

"Buried," Ben Lily said, a little testily. "I bury skins. Then if I get caught in a blizzard I can dig up one of my skins and wrap up."

"You best be worrying about Indians, not blizzards, Mr. Lily," Long Bill said. "If Buffalo Hump was to catch you I expect he'd throw you on a campfire and cook you."

Ben Lily disregarded that remark completely. He finished with his skinning and sat down on a rock. He plunged his hunting knife into the ground to cleanse it, then took out a whetstone and began to sharpen the knife. The fact that his task was concluded seemed to put him in a sociable mood.

"You can have this bear meat," he informed them. "I don't eat much bear."

Deets had been hoping for such an offer. He immediately got down and began to inspect the carcass, meaning to secure the tenderest cuts. But what was tender, on a bear?

"We've been sent to look for Captain Inish Scull," Call said. "He was last seen going south with one scout. Have you seen or heard of him?"

The name "Scull" seemed to excite the man—he looked at the group with interest for the first time.

"I know Scull," Ben Lily said. "Took on a hunt once, over east.

He wanted to shoot bear and we shot 'em. One bear got into the canebrakes and Scull crawled in after him and shot him. He was a small fellow. He went right into that cane and shot that quick little bear."

"That's him, he's a hunter," Augustus said. "We need to find him if we can."

Ben Lily was carefully folding the bloody bearskin.

"Ain't seen Scull since that hunt over east," he said. "I'd know him if I seen him, but I ain't seen him. I expect they took him in the big raid."

All the rangers were startled by the remark.

"Big raid? What big raid?" Gus asked.

Ben Lily looked at them with genuine astonishment.

"The big raid," he repeated. "Ain't you seen any dead? I buried six dead just yesterday, back up this creek. Six dead—trying to farm where they oughtn't to farm. Took me all morning to bury them. I'd have caught this cub sooner if I hadn't had to do that burying."

"We've been on the trail for two weeks," Call said. "We don't know anything about a raid. Was it Comanches?"

"It was Buffalo Hump," Ben Lily said. "He came down off the plains with a passel of warriors—a thousand or more."

"A thousand braves—I doubt it," Call said. "People always think there's more Indians than there are, when the Comanches attack."

Ben Lily hoisted his bearskin onto one shoulder, and picked up his gun. Then he whistled for his dog.

"Go east," he told them. "See how many dead you find. There's dead along ever creek. I don't know how many men he came with but he struck Austin and nearly burned it down. This wasn't just a few scalp snatchers. Buffalo Hump came for war, and he made it."

All the rangers were stunned by his last statement.

"Struck Austin, are you sure?" Long Bill said.

"Struck it and burned most of it," Ben Lily repeated. "Kilt everybody he saw—that's what I heard."

Then, without waiting for further comment or discussion, he

took his gun and his bearskin and walked away. He took no more interest in the troop of rangers.

"Do you believe him, Woodrow?" Long Bill asked. "My wife's in Austin—my Pearl."

"I don't know why he'd lie to us," Call said.

"Clara," Gus said. "My Lord. I wonder if she was gone when they struck."

I wonder if Maggie hid where I told her to, Call thought.

"Woodrow, we have to go back," Augustus said. "If they burned Austin, Clara might be dead."

Long Bill remembered the captive they had rescued, Maudy Clark, now demented. What if the Comanches caught Pearl and left her in the same state?

"Captain, let's go back," he said.

Augustus looked across the emptiness they had just crossed—now they would have to recross it, riding for days and days in great anxiety.

"Lord, I wish I was a bird," Gus said. "I wish I could just fly home."

"You ain't a bird, Gus," Call said. All the rangers, even Deets, seemed stunned by Ben Lily's news. An Indian force large enough to strike Austin and burn most of it was a calamity greater than they could immediately comprehend. Call felt stunned, too. The first time he and Augustus had gone into the Pecos country, with a small surveying troop, nine Comanches led by Buffalo Hump had attacked them, killed three men, and captured their ammunition. None of the nine Comanches had been so much as grazed by a ranger bullet. If a thousand warriors had indeed come into the settlements, there might be little to defend, by the time they reached Austin.

"You ain't a bird," he said, again, to Gus. "We can't fly it—we'll have to ride it, and we don't want to wear out these horses, because horses won't be easy to find, on the way back. Buffalo Hump's probably run off most of the horses from the ranches out this way."

"I don't care about the dern horses, I just hope he ain't took my wife," Long Bill said. "Took her or kilt her. I don't think I can do without my Pearl. I should never have left her, not to come on no silly chase like this."

Augustus, though heartsick himself, saw the anguish on Long Bill's face and thought if he joshed him a little it might help.

"Now, Billy, don't worry," he said. "Pearl's too bossy to steal. She'd argue those Comanches to a frazzle. I expect she'll be there ready to boss you, when we get back."

The witticism had no effect. Long Bill looked no less anguished. The rangers sat in silence while Deets finished taking what he hoped was tender cuts of the bear meat.

"I guess Captain Scull will have to find his own way back," Call said, looking south.

Then he turned his horse and the little troop began the long ride home, every man wondering what they would find when they got there.

15.

BUFFALO HUMP took only one man with him when he went on to the Great Water. He took Worm, the medicine man. The glory of the great raid was over; the Comanches had harassed and murdered the Texans in town after town, and had even defeated a company of bluecoat soldiers who charged at them foolishly, not realizing how many warriors they faced. By then the Comanches were driving more than a thousand stolen horses; the bluecoats managed to separate off a few of the horses but then they had to leave them and flee for their lives. One soldier whose horse went lame fell behind—when his gun misfired Blue Duck killed him with a lance, a thing that would have made Buffalo Hump proud had Blue Duck not spoiled his coup by bragging about it excessively around the campfire that night. It was no great feat to kill a white soldier whose horse was lame and whose gun wouldn't shoot. Blue Duck also bragged excessively about his rapes.

Buffalo Hump had meant to take Blue Duck and a few warriors on to the Great Water, but after listening to Blue Duck brag he decided to leave the boy—let him fight his way back to the plains. He did not want such a braggart with him. Many of the warriors were still crazy for blood; they did not want to stop killing just to see water.

The morning after the chase with the bluecoat soldiers Buffalo Hump decided to leave the war party and go, alone with Worm, to the Great Water. The raid had been a fine triumph—all the Texans knew again that the Comanche power was still great. The Texans were scattered and frightened. They had their dead to bury, their wounded to heal. The bluecoat soldiers would come, in time, to the llano but it would not be soon.

Buffalo Hump spoke to some of the chiefs who had joined the raid with their warriors. He advised them to break into parties of forty or fifty and filter back up to the plains along the old trails. The whites, if they pursued at all—which he doubted—would wear themselves out trying to decide which party to chase.

When Blue Duck saw his father preparing to leave, with only old Worm for a companion, he loped over and watched his father filling his quiver with arrows; Buffalo Hump had worked on the arrows most of the night, making sure that the arrowheads were tightly set.

"I will come with you," Blue Duck said. "You might need me."

"No, you go with the horses," Buffalo Hump instructed. "Keep them together and travel fast. Take them to the canyon and don't lose any. I will come in a few days, with Worm."

Blue Duck was annoyed. He was a warrior now—he had killed a bluecoat—and yet his father treated him like a horse herder.

"What if the Texans trap you?" he asked. "You will not get much help from that old man."

"I will not need much help," Buffalo Hump said. It wearied him to have to be always arguing with his son. The boy never accepted any command simply, as an obedient son should. He always had words of his own to say about every request. Because Blue Duck was so rude, Buffalo Hump had to keep reminding himself that he was also brave—he was one of the bravest young men in the tribe.

He too had been brave and daring, when he was young, yet he had not been disrespectful. His own father was named Two Arrows—he had once killed the largest grizzly bear anyone had ever seen with only two arrows. Buffalo Hump would never have dared question anything Two Arrows told him to do. He seldom spoke to his father, unless Two Arrows asked him something. He would not have dared be rude, as Blue Duck was rude.

Blue Duck did not like being sent home with the horses. He sulked and pouted, and insulted two young warriors, hoping to provoke a fight. Buffalo Hump saw it all, but he ignored it. He gathered his things, motioned to Worm, and left the camp. It was a relief to go. He had taken pride in being able, once more, to gather so many warriors that the whites could not stand before them; but now he felt the need to be alone, to move quietly across the land and just take care of himself, without having to mediate disputes and make decisions for so many warriors.

Worm was old; he was a man of silence. He could speak prophecy and make spells, but mostly he was quiet and alert, a pleasure to travel with. For two days they traveled through the thick brush country, a country where there were many armadillos. Worm was particularly fond of armadillo meat—also, the little scaly animals seemed to amuse him. Sometimes he would catch an armadillo that was half in its hold and would have to tickle its testicles to make it come out. When he cooked an armadillo he carefully preserved the scaly case that had been the beast's defense; soon he had several armadillo shells dangling from his pack.

"Why do you like that meat so much?" Buffalo Hump asked him one night—they were only one camp from the Great Water. He himself had killed a javelina that afternoon and was eating it. In his view pig was tastier by far than armadillo.

Worm rarely answered a direct question directly.

"The armadillo people are from a time before the Comanche," Worm said. "They were here when we were not. They are so old that they have learned to grow shells, and yet they are not slow, like turtles."

298

Worm paused. He was studying the paw of one of the armadillos he had killed.

"If we could learn to grow shells we would be safe in battle," he said. "If I eat enough of these armadillos maybe I will grow a shell."

"You have eaten several and I don't see any shell on you," Buffalo Hump commented.

Worm was silent. He preferred to think his own thoughts about the armadillo people.

The next day they came to a country where the trees were low and inward bent, from the constant push of the sea wind. The air was so salty Buffalo Hump could lick salt off his lips. The land became swampy, with tall reeds higher than a horse growing in dense thickets; there were inlets of water here and there, with cranes and great storks standing in them. As they grew nearer the sea both the land and the air were alive with birds: geese and ducks in great numbers floated on the inlets or waddled through the grass. There were white gulls that rose and dipped. But the most interesting to Buffalo Hump were the great cranes—they came from far in the north and did not stop in the Comanche country. Once, in Nebraska on the Platte River, he had seen a few of the great cranes, but in the swamps and inlets near the Great Water there were thousands of them.

Worm seemed in awe of the birds. His old eyes widened when the storks flapped into the air, or when the herons sailed down to the water on their wide wings. He turned his head from side to side and listened when the sea gulls spoke; it was as if he were trying to learn their language. Worm had only half an upper lip—the other half had been cut off years before, in battle. When he was excited, he licked his half lip; it was a thing he did, too, when his interest in a woman was high. The women of the tribe joked about it. They could always tell when old Worm needed a woman because he licked his lip. All his wives had died of one illness or another. There was a story about him from the old days that the old women told the young women, to inform them about the vengefulness of men. Worm had once had a wife who would not open her legs when he wanted her; to teach her obedience Worm had made a great black cactus grow out of her womb, a cactus with thorns so sharp that the woman could never close her legs again, but had to walk with them widespread even when she was only doing chores.

Buffalo Hump had heard the story from Hair-on-the-Lip and did not believe it.

"I have been with this tribe since I was born," he said. "I have never seen a woman waddling around with a cactus sticking out of her."

"Oh no, a bear took that woman—you were just a child then," Hair-on-the-Lip assured him.

Buffalo Hump still did not believe her, but he did like most of the stories Hair-on-the-Lip told. Many of her stories were about things that happened to humans while they were coupling—such stories seldom failed to amuse him.

After wading through several inlets, frightening many birds off the water, Buffalo Hump and Worm at last came to the long strip of sand that bordered the Great Water. They rode along the edge of the Great Water for many miles. Buffalo Hump liked to ride on the wet sand, so close to the sea that the waves foamed over the hooves of his horse, as the waves died.

Worm, though, would not come near the Great Water. He kept his horse far back at the edge of the sand, where sand gave way to grass. He tried repeatedly to point out to Buffalo Hump that the Great Water was unsafe to approach, but Buffalo Hump ignored him. He rode where he wanted to ride.

"There are great fish in the water, and snakes as long as the tallest pine tree," Worm insisted. "One of those snakes might wrap its tongue around you and pull you under."

Buffalo Hump paid no attention to Worm and his talk. Despite Worm's protest he camped that night on the sandy beach. The air at night was warm and salty. He built a small fire of driftwood and sang as the fire died. Worm finally came and sat with him; they shared a little of the javelina meat. Worm still worried that the water might somehow engulf them.

"That water is never still," he told Buffalo Hump suspiciously. "It is always moving."

Buffalo Hump shrugged. He liked it that the water moved, that the waves came in and went out. He liked the sound it made, a sound that came from depths he could not see.

"I like the land—it doesn't move," Worm said. "This water sighs like a woman who is sad."

There was some truth in that comment, Buffalo Hump thought. The ocean did sigh like a woman, as she sighed in sorrow, or at the slowing of her passion.

"There are great fish in that water with mouths so wide they can swallow buffalo," Worm worried. Buffalo Hump sang over Worm's droning, his complaints. He sang much of the night, in the warm salt air.

In the gray mist before the dawn Buffalo Hump got on his horse and sat waiting for the sun. On impulse he forced the horse into the water and made him swim until the small waves broke over them. Then he swam back to land. Worm was beside himself when he saw Buffalo Hump in the water. He was worried about the snake as long as a pine tree, but Buffalo Hump had no such worry. He merely wanted to watch the sun rise out of the water. All his life he had watched the sun rise upward out of the prairie; now he wanted to see it come out of the water. When it came, at first it was only a faint glow in the grayness of water and sky.

"We had better move back there in those trees," Worm said, when Buffalo Hump came out.

"Why?" Buffalo Hump asked.

"They say the sun rides all night on the back of a great fish," Worm said. "When it is time for morning the great fish brings it back so it can shine on the people of the land and make them warm."

In the mist it was hard to see the sun clearly. Buffalo Hump wondered if there was a great fish so large that it could carry the sun. He watched the surface of the water and saw no great fish, though that didn't mean that the story was untrue. The sun was now well up. Maybe the great fish that carried it had gone back to its home in the deep water. Maybe the fish slept all day, while the people of the land enjoyed the sun. He didn't know.

What Buffalo Hump did know was that the ocean was a great mystery. In his country the stars and the moon were the great mysteries; he had been studying them all his life, and yet he knew nothing of the stars and the moon. The ocean was such a mystery, too. He could live his life on the sand, as the Indians of the seaside did, and yet never know the secrets of the ocean—why its waves moved in and out, why it sighed like a woman. Perhaps the ocean was even more powerful than the moon and stars. After all, it had called him to it, across hundreds of miles of land. Although the fighting had been good, he had finally grown restive with it; he did not want to delay any longer his trip to the Great Water.

When the sun was high Buffalo Hump rode back to Worm, who was crouched nervously over the little campfire. Often Worm could be irritating, a cranky man with half an upper lip and many fears and complaints. But Worm, for all his complaining, was a powerful prophet, and sometimes his clearest prophecies were called forth by his fears.

Buffalo Hump wanted a prophecy—all through the fighting he had wanted one, for his feelings were not good. Although he had felt again the excitement of war and the thrill of running down and killing his enemies, there had been a sadness in him through it all. At night as the young men sang and bragged of their killing, he had felt apart and could not make the sadness leave. In his life he had had many victories; the young men bragging and singing were as he had been in his youth, brave and unthinking. They expected that they would live their life as warriors and have many victories over the whites and the Mexicans. In their dreams and in their songs they saw themselves as Comanche warriors always, men of the bow and of the horse.

Buffalo Hump knew, though, that for most of them, it would not be that way. A warrior skilled with the lance and the bow might, if he were bold, prevail over a man with a gun; but a thousand men with guns, whether they were skilled or not, would win in a battle against

302

even the bravest warriors with bows. His son, Blue Duck, though foolish and rude, would have to fight with the gun if he were to live. Buffalo Hump knew that the bluecoat soldiers would come in thousands someday. Their defeat would sting; they would try to reverse the Comanche victory. They would not come this year, but they would come; there were as many of them as there had once been buffalo. It was a bitter truth, but a truth. The young warriors who were even then stringing white scalps on their lances would either die in battle or end their days as old Slow Tree had predicted, growing corn on little patches of land the white men let them keep.

Buffalo Hump wanted to see the ocean because the ocean would always be as it was. Few things could stay forever in the way they were when the spirits made them. Even the great plains of grass, the home of the People, would not be always as it had been. The whites would bring their plows and scar the earth; they would put their cattle on it and the cattle would bring the ugly mesquite trees. The grass that had been high forever would be trampled and torn. The llano would not be always as it had been. The ocean and the stars were eternal, things whose power and mystery were greater than the powers of men.

Long before, when Buffalo Hump was a boy, his own grandmother had predicted the end of the Comanche people. She thought it would come through sickness and plague; and, indeed, sickness and plague had carried off almost half the People. Now, looking at the Great Water, Buffalo Hump wanted to know if Worm had a prophecy that would tell him how the next years would be.

He got off his horse and sat for a few minutes with the old man, Worm. It was Worm who had said that the pox and the shitting sickness were caused by gold. He had a vision in which he saw a river of gold flowing out of a mountain to the west. The whites ran through their country like ants, seeking the gold, and left their sicknesses behind them.

"I will take you away from this water you dislike so much if you will tell me a prophecy," Buffalo Hump said. "I won't let a great fish get you, either, or a snake as long as a pine tree."

"I have the vision now," Worm said. "Last night I could not sleep because I heard too many horses squealing in my head."

"I heard no horses squeal," Buffalo Hump said. Then he realized he had made a foolish comment. Worm was not talking about their horses, but about the horses in his vision.

"It was not these horses with us," Worm said. "It was the horses we have taken in the raid, and the others, the horses at home."

"Why did they squeal—was there a cougar near?" Buffalo Hump asked.

"They were squealing because they were dying," Worm said. "The white men were killing them all, and the sky was black but it was not a storm. The sky was black because all the buzzards in the world had come to eat our horses. There were so many buzzards flying over that I could not see the sun. All I could see were black wings."

"It that the whole prophecy?" Buffalo Hump asked.

Worm merely nodded. He seemed tired and sad.

"That is a terrible prophecy—we need our horses," Buffalo Hump said. "Eat a little of this meat. Then we will go."

"We will have to slip along at night," Worm said. "All the whites will be looking for us now."

"Eat your meat," Buffalo Hump said. "Don't worry about the whites. I am going to take you up the Rio Grande. Once we are far enough up it we can go home along the old war trail we used to ride, when we went into Mexico and caught all those Mexicans. I don't think we will see many whites out that way—if we do see whites I will kill them."

Worm was relieved. They had traveled far on the great raid, all the way from the llano to the sea. He did not care for the sea, he was tired, and he had no more armadillo meat to eat. But Buffalo Hump gave him a little of his pig meat and he ate it.

When Worm had eaten, Buffalo Hump mounted and led him inland, back through the twisted trees, toward Mexico.

16.

"IT'S SUCH A FAR WAY BACK, Woodrow," Augustus said. "I swear I wish we hadn't gone so far from town."

He said it at night, as they were burying two men whose scalped and cut-open bodies they found just at dusk, at the foot of a small hill. The two men had been traveling in a little wagon, with nothing much in it except axes. The Indians hadn't destroyed the wagon, but they had used the axes to hack the two men open.

"It's far yet, and we can't make no time for burying folks," Long Bill observed. The three older rangers watched as Pea Eye, Deets, and Jake Spoon dug the grave.

The day before, they had found a family slaughtered by a poor little tent. Evidently they had intended to start a farm. There were two women among the six dead. Seeing the women, whom they wrapped in blankets and buried properly, put Gus in mind of Clara, Long Bill in mind of his Pearl, and Call in mind of Maggie. It would be many days before they knew whether their womenfolk had suffered the fate of the two young women just buried, and the anxiety was tiring them all. For three days they had pushed the horses to their limits, and yet they were still ten days from home. At night none of the older men could sleep. Images rose up in their minds, images that kept them tense. Call usually went off with his rifle and sat in the darkness. Long Bill and Gus stayed by the fire, talking about anything they could think to talk about. Pea Eye, Jake, and Deets, with no one at home to worry about, said little. Jake had thrown up at the sight of the mutilated bodies.

"I never seen how a person looks inside themselves before," he said to Pea Eye, who didn't reply.

Pea Eye was afraid to talk about the deaths for fear that he would cry and embarrass himself before the older men. The sight of dead people made so much sadness come in him that he feared he couldn't contain it. In death people looked so small—the dead adults looked like sad children, and the dead children looked like dolls. The fury that found them was so great that it reduced them as they died.

"Why will people come out here, Captain?" Jake asked, as they were burying the two men who were traveling in the small wagon. "This ain't farm country . . . what could you grow, out here?"

Call had often wondered the same thing himself. Over and over, rangering, he and Augustus had come upon little families, far out beyond the settlements, attempting to farm country that had never felt the plow. Often such pioneers didn't even *have* a plow. They might have a churn, a spindle, a spade, and a few axes, an almanac, and a primer for the children. Mainly what they had, as far as Call could tell, was their energies and their hopes. At least they had what most of them had never had before: land they could call their own.

"You can't stop people from coming out here," Call said. "It's open country now."

Later, Call and Augustus walked off from the group a little distance to discuss the problem of Long Bill, who was so distraught at the thought that his Pearl might have been killed or kidnapped that he seemed to be losing his mind.

"Bill's always been steady," Call said. "I wouldn't have expected him to get this bad."

"He's bad, Woodrow," Gus said. "I guess he's as crazy about Pearl as I am about Clara."

The fact was, Call himself had had a number of disquieting thoughts about Maggie since hearing about the raid. Maggie had tried three times to talk about the baby she was carrying, a baby she claimed was his, but in his haste to round up his troop and get them started he had put her off, a rudeness he regretted. Now Maggie might be dead, and the child too, if there really was a child.

"I mean to leave Texas forever, if Clara's dead," Augustus told him. "I wouldn't want to live here without my Clara. The memories would be too hard."

Call refrained from commenting that the woman Gus was talking about wasn't his anymore. If Clara had left Austin before the big raid it was because she had married Bob Allen.

"Let's get off the damn Brazos tomorrow," Gus suggested.

"Why?" Call asked. "There's always abundant water in the Brazos."

"I know it—that's why," Augustus said. "Where there's water, there's farmers—or people who were trying to be farmers. It means more people to bury. Me, I'd like to get on home."

"It's wrong to leave Christian folk unburied," Call told him.

"It ain't if we don't even see 'em," Gus said. "If we get away from all this watered country we won't happen on so many."

It was a still, windless night, and very dark. The three young grave diggers had to bring burning sticks from the campfire, in order to determine if they had the grave deep enough. The spades they were digging with had belonged to the two men who were murdered.

"We could start a hardware store with all the spades and axes scattered around out here," Gus remarked.

Long Bill had not come out with them to the grave site. They could see his tall form, pacing back and forth in front of the campfire, making wavy shadows.

"Oh, Saint Peter!" they heard him exclaim. "Oh, Saint Paul!"

"I wish Billy would hear of some new saints to pray to," Gus said. "I'm tired of hearing him pray to Peter and Paul."

"He can't read—I guess he's forgot the other saints," Call said. The grave diggers had paused for a moment—they were all exhausted, from hard travel and from fear.

Call felt sorry for Long Bill Coleman. Seldom had he seen a man so broken by grief, though Pearl, the woman he grieved for, might well be alive and well. Pearl, though large, did not seem to him exceptional in any way. She had none of Clara's wit or spirit, nor Maggie's beauty of face.

"Pearl must be a mighty good cook, for him to take on about her so before he even knows if she's dead."

"No, she ain't," Augustus said. "I've et Pearl's cooking and it was only fair. I expect it's the poking."

"The what?" Call asked, surprised.

"The poking, Woodrow," Gus said. "Pearl was large and large women are usually a pleasure to poke."

"Well, you would think that," Call said.

17.

IN THE AFTERMATH of the great raid, much to her distress, Maggie's business increased. No one knew exactly where the Comanches were, but rumors of widespread carnage swept the town. Some said that Buffalo Hump had killed three hundred people in San Antonio, and one hundred more in Houston. Then a counter-rumor reversed those numbers; others thought he had burnt Victoria, while someone had heard that he was already in Mexico. There was a general fear that he might come back through Austin and finish what he had begun. Men went about heavily armed, draped with all the weapons they could carry. At night the streets were empty, though the saloons still did a good business. Men were so scared that they drank, and, having drunk, discovered that they were still too nervous to sleep.

So they came to Maggie—a stream of men, knocking on her door at all hours of the day or night. She couldn't protest, but she was not welcoming, either. She had been sickly of a morning lately, and was often nauseous or queasy during the day. Her belly had begun to swell visibly, yet none of the men seemed to notice. They were so scared that only what she sold them could bring them a little peace. Maggie understood it. She was scared herself. Some nights she even went down and hid in the crawl space under the smokehouse. It brought her a little relief, both from fear and from the men.

Maggie longed for Woodrow to show up, with the boys. Once Woodrow was there, the men would leave her be. Although they were only two men, they were respected; the townspeople took much comfort from their presence, just as she did.

Every morning at first light Maggie looked out her window,

toward the corrals where the rangers kept their horses. She was hoping to see Woodrow's buckskin, Johnny. If she could just spot Johnny she would know that he was back.

But, morning after morning, there was no sign of the rangers. Maggie found Call's absence almost too much to bear, at such a time, with the baby in her. Just as she was hoping to give up whoring forever, all the men wanted her to do was whore, and she was afraid to refuse. The dark thought struck her that Woodrow might be dead. He had left with only five men, and the Comanches numbered more than five hundred, some said. The rangers might all be dead, and likely were.

Even to think it made Maggie feel hopeless. If Woodrow was dead she would have no father for her baby. Then the whoring wouldn't stop: the men at the door, the men on top of her, the men who counted out money and waited for her to lay back and pull up her skirt. She would go on laying there, lifting her skirt to men who were none too clean, who stank and vomited, who had violence in their eyes, until she got sick, or was too old to be worth the money they counted out.

She thought she could have borne all the worry and all the doubt a little better if Woodrow had just had time to talk to her about the baby, to give her some hope that he would marry her, or at least help her with the child. He hadn't seemed to be angry about it; just a few words would have been enough. But he had been in a hurry, usually was. Maggie could not find it in her to tax Woodrow too hard for his failure to speak; she rarely taxed Woodrow too hard about any of the things that bothered her. He was a captain now and had many responsibilities. Her hope was that he would come round to liking the idea of a child, or at least to not minding it much. When Woodrow Call did get angry with her a coldness showed in him that made her question whether happiness would ever be hers. He could be so cold, when angered, that Maggie wondered how she had ever come to care for him anyway. He had only been a customer, after all, a young man with quick needs, like many another. The older whores had all warned her not to get attached to customers. One named Florie, who had taught her something of the business, had been emphatic on that score.

"I've known whores to marry, but it's a seldom thing," Florie said. "It's one of those things that if you look for them you won't find them."

"Well, I ain't looking," Maggie declared—she had been much younger then. It wasn't entirely true: she had already met Woodrow Call and already knew she liked him.

"I looked once, but not no more," Florie said. "I just take their money and give 'em a few jerks. It don't take much longer than it takes to wring out a mop, not if you set your hips right."

The next year Florie stumbled coming down her own steps and broke her neck. She had a big basket of laundry in her arms—it was the laundry that caused her to misstep. She was lying dead at the bottom of the steps with her eyes wide open when they found her. A goat had wandered over and was eating her laundry basket, which was made of coarse straw.

Maggie, despite Florie's advice, had gone on and got attached to Woodrow Call, so attached that she would sometimes put her hand on her belly and imagine that there was a little boy inside, who would look just like him.

One morning when she had gone out early to draw a bucket of water, she was surprised to see the sheriff limping up her stairs. The sheriff was named Gawsworth Gibbons; he was a large man and, in the main, kindly. Several times he had taken Maggie's side in disputes with drunken customers, a rare thing for a sheriff to do.

Despite Gaw Gibbons's kindly attitude, Maggie was always a little disturbed to see a sheriff coming up her stairs—it could mean she was going to be asked to move, or some such thing.

The sheriff had a bad limp, the result of a wound sustained in the Mexican War. It took him some time to mount the stairs—all Maggie could do was stand and wait, wondering what she could have done to prompt a visit from the sheriff.

"Why, what is it, Gaw?" she asked. She had known Gawsworth Gibbons long before he became a sheriff; before the Mexican War he had made his living shoeing horses.

"Has somebody complained?" she asked.

Gawsworth Gibbons smiled his large, kindly smile and followed Maggie into her room before answering.

"No complaints, Mag," he told her. "All that's wrong is just what's apt to be wrong with any feller."

To her shock, Maggie saw that he had money in his hand—he was coming to her as a customer, something that had never happened in the years she had known him. It took her a moment to adjust to the notion.

The sheriff, out of consideration, turned his back as he lowered his pants. Even from the back, though, Maggie saw that the skin on his legs was twisted in a strange way. The skin had black specks in it, as if Gaw Gibbons had been peppered.

Then she recalled that what she had heard about his war wound was that he had been severely burned—a keg of gunpowder had blown up while he stood near it, blowing gunpowder and bits of the barrel into his legs.

"My wife, she's about give up on me, Mag," the sheriff said. "I expect she just can't tolerate these burned legs no more."

"Oh, Gaw," Maggie said.

The fact that he spoke so sorrowfully when he mentioned his wife made the business at hand a little less hard.

18.

INISH SCULL quickly discovered that Ahumado didn't want him to starve too soon or too easily. Every second day one of the dark men whose duty it was to watch the cages lowered him a small jug of water. Though dizzied at first by the height and the space and the constant swaying of the cage—the lightest wind seemed to move it—Inish Scull gradually persuaded himself that the old man wanted him to live. Why else the water? Perhaps upon consideration the notion of a large ransom became more appealing; though, in view of Ahumado's searing contempt, to think thus was probably to think too optimistically.

Far from wanting him to live, Ahumado may only have wanted him to starve more slowly—thus the fresh, cool water. The first jug tasted as good as a meal.

In thinking about his situation—hung off a cliff, a two-hundred-foot drop below him, and an infinite space before him—Scull soon concluded that, whatever the Black Vaquero might want, *he* wanted to live. He was in good health, had sustained no wounds, was of sound mind. Thinking about the matter soberly, he realized that he had often felt more hopeless in his wife's arms than he did in Ahumado's cage. He was of the mental temperament to relish extreme situations—in fact, had spent much of his career seeking them out. Now he had found himself in as extreme a situation as any man could well want. Few of his Harvard brethren had sought the extreme quite so successfully; it would make a good story to tell in the Yard, next time he was there.

Of course, in order to have the pleasure of telling, he first had to meet the challenge of surviving. In practical terms that meant securing the food most likely to be available, which meant birds. The only possible alternative was worms. His experience as a naturalist taught him that earthworms were to be found almost everywhere—he might be able to scratch a few out of Ahumado's cliff, but probably too few.

Of birds there was no scarcity. The cage attracted them, not merely eagles and vultures but others. On the first morning he caught a pigeon and two mourning doves. The pants he wore, once Tudwal's, were ragged things. Scull unraveled one leg a bit and hung the three birds with threads from the pants leg; in the Scull family game was always hung before it was consumed, the customary period of hanging being three days. There was no reason to abandon the family's standards, that he saw.

Far below, he could see the people of the village; few of them looked up. They had, no doubt, seen many people hang and die in the cages.

Every day Ahumado sat on his blanket, and he did look up, not with his naked eye, though. Scull saw the glint of sun on glass and realized Ahumado was watching him through binoculars, no doubt taken from some murdered officer or traveler. This knowledge perked him up. Contempt or no contempt, at least he had caught the old man's interest. Scull had a spectator now; he meant to give the man on the ground a good show.

When Scull searched the pockets of Tudwal's filthy garments he found a small tool that he had missed when searching the clothes for bullets. The tool was a file of the sort used to improve the sights on a rifle or cut the head off a nail. It wasn't much, but it was something. Although the cage he swung in had a solid bottom, there were cracks in it. Scull took great care not to drop his file—as long as he had it there were ways he could employ his mind. He could keep a calendar by scratching lines on the rock of the cliff, and he immediately began to do so.

Scull knew a bit of geology. He had heard Mr. Lyell lecture on his first visit to America and had even sat with the great man at a luncheon in Washington. It occurred to him there might be fossils or other geological vestiges in the stony cliff behind him—vestiges he could investigate. To make sure that he didn't drop the file he unthreaded another cord from his pants leg and used it to secure the little tool, tying one end of the thread to the file and the other end to a bar of the cage.

Fortunately he was small enough to get his legs through the bars of the cage—wiggling them vigorously was the best he could do by way of exercise. It amused him to consider what Ahumado must think, watching him wiggle his legs. He had caught a curious prisoner this time, one a little more resourceful than the miscreant peasants he had been wont to cage.

If his diet was limited, Scull told himself, at least his view was magnificent. In the morning he could see the mist lift off the distant peak as the red sun rose. The nights, though chilly, produced a fine starlight. Scull had not made much progress in astronomy, but he did know his constellations, and they were there to be viewed, in sharp and peaceful clarity, every night.

The fourth day was cloudy—it sprinkled in the morning, which was welcome; it allowed Scull to wash himself. But a mist ensued so thick that he could not see the ground, a fact which dampened his spirits considerably. He liked to look down, observe the life of the camp, and watch Ahumado watch him. It was a competition they were in, the Bostonian and the Mayan, as he saw it. He needed to observe his opponent every day. Now and then, through the mist, he would see one of the great vultures sail by. One vulture flew so close that he saw the bird turn its head and look at him—the bird's old eye reminded him in that instance of Ahumado's. The resemblance was so sharp that it spooked Scull, for a moment. It was as if the old Mayan had turned himself into a bird and flown by to taunt him.

Scull felt sour all day, sour and discouraged. For all his skill at catching birds, his calender keeping, his feet wiggling, he was still hung in a cage off a cliff, with no way down. The contest wasn't for a day or a week; it was for as long as he could convince himself it was worth it to hang in a cage and eat raw birds, at the whim of an old man who sat on a blanket, far below.

The next day, though, was one of brilliant sunlight and Scull's spirits improved. He spent much of the morning in close inspection of the cliff above him. They had lowered him some seventy feet, he judged, and the rope that held the cage seemed sound. But the ascent, if he decided to try one, was sheer. He could saw the bindings of the cage with his precious file and break out; but if he chose the climb he knew he had better do it quickly, while he still had his strength. In a week or two poor diet and cramped quarters would weaken him to such an extent that he could never make the climb, or escape the dark men and their machetes if he did.

For most of the day Scull weighed his chances. He studied the cliff face; he looked down at Ahumado. In the afternoon he saw some young women filing out of camp with laundry on their heads, making for a little stream not far from camp. Some vaqueros were there, watering their horses. The young women took the laundry far upstream from the men and the horses. Now and then Scull would hear a rill of laughter as the young women pounded the clothes on the wet rocks. The vaqueros mounted and rode away. As soon as they were gone the women began to sing as they worked. Scull could only faintly catch the melody, but the sight of the young women cheered him, nonetheless. It was a fine joke, that his adventuring had finally got him hung off a cliff in Mexico, but it didn't stop the laughter of women, or their flirtations with men.

As the day waned Scull fingered his file, wondering how long it would take him to file through the bindings of the cage, if he chose to try the climb. While he was looking up and down, considering, he saw a brilliant flash of color coming toward the cage; the brilliancy turned out to be the red-and-green plumage of a large parrot, which flew past his cage and turned its head, for a moment, to look at him. Again, Scull was startled—the parrot's eye reminded him of Ahumado's. The impression was so strong that he dropped his file, but fortunately the string he had attached it to saved it.

Later, when the sun was down and the canyon lit by strong starlight, Scull decided he must be having altitude visions. He knew from his experiences in the Alps that high air could make a man giddy, and prone to false conclusions. The parrot and the vulture were just birds. No dove and no pigeon had lighted on his cage that day—Scull put it down to his jumpiness, his indecision, his nerves. He knew he had better get his thoughts under control and regain some calm or the fowl of the air would avoid him and he would starve.

The next morning he fixed his mind on a task, which was to remember his Homer. He took his file and began to scratch a Greek word on the surface of the rock behind him. By noon he had completed a hexameter. All day he worked on, scratching Greek into the rock. The giddiness left his head, and the nervousness his limbs.

"Hard and clear," he told himself. "Hard and clear."

The rock was not easy to work. Scull had to press the file hard to give the Greek letters the graceful shape they deserved. His fingers cramped, from gripping the file so hard; now and then he had to stop and flex them.

Below, old Ahumado was watching him through the binoculars. In the stream the girls were spreading wet clothes again. Scull's nerves no longer put off the birds. In the afternoon he caught two pigeons and a dove.

"That takes care of the larder," he told himself, but he did not pause long enough to hang the birds or pluck them.

By evening the great words were there, each letter as distinct as Scull could make it, words hard and clear, to remind him that brave men had battled before:

OI ΔE MEΓA ΦΠONEONTEΣ EΠI ΠTOΛEMOIO
   ΓEΦΨΠAΣ
EIATO ΠANNΨΞIOI, ΠΨΠA ΔE ΣΦIΣI KAIETO
   ΠOΛΛA.
ΩΣ Δ OT EN OΨΠANΩI AΣTΠA ΦAEINHN
   AMΦI ΣEΛHNHN
ΦAINET AΠIΠEΠEA, OTE T EΠΛETO
   NHNEMOΣ AIΘHΠ.
EK T EΦANEN ΠAΣAI ΣKOΠIAI KAI
   ΠONEAKΠOI
KAI NAΠAI. OΨΠANOΘEN Δ AΠ ΨΠEΠΠAΓH
   AΣΠETOΣ AIΘHΠ,
ΠANTA ΔE EIΔETAI AΣTΠA, ΓEΓHΘE ΔE TE
   ΦΠENA ΠOIMHN.
TOΣΣA MEΣHΓΨ NEΩN HΔE ΞANΘOIO
   ΠOAΩN
TΠΩΩN KAIONTΩN ΠΨΠA ΦAINETO IΛIOΘI
   ΠΠO.
ΞIΛI AΠ EN ΠEΔIΩI ΠΨΠA KAIETO, ΠAΠ ΔE
   EKAΣTΩI

ΕΙΑΤΟ ΠΕΝΤΗΚΟΝΤΑ ΣΕΛΑΙ ΠΨΠΟΣ
    ΑΙΘΟΜΕΝΟΙΟ.
ΙΠΠΟΙ ΔΕ ΚΠΙ ΛΕΨΚΟΝ ΕΠΕΤΟΜΕΝΟΙ ΚΑΙ
    ΟΛΨΠΑΣ,
ΕΣΤΑΟΤΕΣ ΠΑΠ ΟΞΕΣΦΙΝ, ΕΨΘΠΟΝΟΝ ΗΩ
    ΜΙΜΝΟΝ.

It was Homer enough for one day, Scull felt. He had put the
words of a Greek on the face of a cliff in Mexico. It was a victory, of
sorts, over the high air and the old dark man. The words had
calmed him—the fowl of the air had come back to perch on his
cage. Another night or two, maybe he would file through the
rawhide bindings and climb the rope. This night, though, he curled
up against the chill and slept, while, far below, the Mexican campfires glittered, bright as the campfires of old Troy.

19.

EASTWARD, AS THE RANGERS hurried home along the valley of the
Brazos, they came upon scene after scene of devastation. Six times
they stopped to bury families, some of them so decomposed as to be
hardly worth burying. They saw not a single Comanche, though
several times a day they crossed the tracks of the retreating war parties. Most of the raiders were driving horses before them—sometimes sizable herds of horses.

"They must have stolen half the horses in south Texas," Augustus said.

"Kilt half the people, too," Long Bill said, in a low tone. Convinced by all the corpses that his wife could not possibly have survived, Long Bill had sunk into a state of dull resignation. He
scarcely ate and seldom spoke.

Call grew more and more vexed as the Indian sign multiplied.

"Our main job is to fight Indians and here we rode off and missed
the biggest Indian fight in history."

"We didn't ride off. We was *sent* off, Woodrow—sent by the Governor," Augustus reminded him.

"He might have tried to recall us, but if he did, the Comanches probably got the messengers," Call said, grimly.

As they rode into Austin they passed near the cemetery—they could see from the number of crosses that there were many fresh graves. Tears began to stream down Long Bill's face, at the thought of having his conviction about Pearl confirmed. In all there were nearly thirty fresh graves—Long Bill stumbled from cross to cross, but none had "Pearl Coleman" written on them.

"It may mean they took her," Long Bill said, still anxious.

Augustus found two crosses with the name "Forsythe" on them—the sight made him tremble; tears came and he sank to his knees.

"Oh God, I knowed it," he said. "I went away and she's dead."

It was Call, looking more closely, who saw that it was her parents, not Clara, who lay buried in the cemetery.

"No, Gus, she ain't dead—it's her father and mother," Call said.

"Well, I swear . . . I wonder if she knows," Augustus said, bending closer so he could see the two names more clearly. Though he knew it was a terrible blow to Clara—both her parents dead and her a new bride—he felt a relief so powerful that for a time it made him weak. He stayed on his knees in the cemetery, fingering a clod or two of the fresh dirt, while the others tried to make out who was buried in all the fresh graves.

"They got the blacksmith," Call said. "Here's the preacher and his wife—got them both."

He walked on, stopping over every new grave.

"Oh Lord, boys," Call said. "Here's Neely and Finch and Teddy—I guess Ikey must be alive."

"My God, Neely," Gus said, coming over to look.

As they rode on into town, past a grove of live oak or two, they saw house after house that showed evidence of burning; and yet most of the houses still stood. Only the church and one saloon seemed to have been burned to the ground.

"They didn't kill Governor Pease—there he stands," Augustus said, as they turned into the main street. "I expect he'll be glad to see us back."

"We didn't do what we was sent to do—he may fire us," Call said.

"I doubt that," Gus said. "He won't have nobody who can fight at all, if he fires us."

The Governor stood in shirtsleeves and black suspenders on the steps of what had been the Forsythe store. He was loading a shotgun when they rode up, and he looked grim.

"Hello, Governor," Call said. "Are the Indians still around?"

"No, but the coons are," the Governor said. "The coyotes got most of my hens, after the raid. The coons don't bother the hens but they're ruining me in the egg department."

He sighed, and cast a quick glance at the little troop.

"Lose any men?" he asked.

"No sir, but we didn't find the Captain," Call said. "When we heard about the raid we thought we better just get home."

The Governor's buggy stood in the street, but Bingham, who usually drove him, wasn't in it.

"I just came down to get some shotgun shells," the Governor said. "I need to do something about those coons."

Governor Pease was usually clean shaven, but now had a white stubble on his cheeks; he looked tired.

"Where's Bingham, Governor?" Augustus asked.

"Dead . . . they killed most of our niggers," Governor Pease said. "They stole that yellow girl who worked for Inez Scull—she was down by the springhouse and they took her."

Just then Long Bill gave a yell. They all turned and saw why. Pearl, the wife he had given up for dead, was in plain view far up the street, hanging out washing.

"It's my Pearl, she ain't dead!" Long Bill said. The cares of the last weeks fell away from him in an instant—he wheeled his horse and was off in a run.

"That's one happy ending, I guess," Augustus said.

319

The Governor did not smile. "She's alive but she was outraged," he said, before going to his buggy. He drove off holding his shotgun, his eggs on his mind.

Call saw that the house where Maggie lived was partially burned but still standing, which was a relief. He thought he glimpsed someone at her window but could not be quite positive. Maggie was ever discreet. She would never lean out her window and look down at him—she didn't feel it was right. He quickly crossed the street and saw her coming down the steps behind the house. She looked so glad to see him that he had to dismount and hug her; when he did she cried so hard that she wet the front of his shirt, just as she had when he was leaving.

"Now hush, I'm back," he said.

He had never before touched her outside her room. After a moment he got nervous, and Maggie did too.

"They didn't get you . . . that's good . . . and they didn't get Pearl, either . . . Bill's been about worried to death," he said.

Maggie's face clouded, for a moment. "They shot four arrows into her, and that ain't all," she said. "But they didn't touch me—I hid where you told me, Woodrow."

"I'm glad you hid," Call said. Maggie didn't say more. She still had tears in her eyes.

Call went back to the rangers, who were still in the street, where he had left them. Gus had dismounted and was sitting on the steps in front of the Forsythe store, a dejected look on his face.

"We ought to get the boys settled and see to the horses," Call said. Jake Spoon and Pea Eye Parker both looked as if they might go to sleep in their saddles. Even Deets, who seldom flagged, looked very weary.

"You do it, Woodrow," Gus said. He stood up and handed his bridle reins to Deets as he went by him. Call turned and followed Gus a step or two, curious as to what was the matter.

"I guess you're going drinking," he said.

"By God, you're a genius, Woodrow," Augustus said. "I ain't even close to a saloon, but you figured it out."

Call knew it was Clara, or the fact that she was absent, that caused Gus to look so low. It was usually Clara at the bottom of Gus's dark moods.

"She's alive, at least," he said. "You ought to be glad she's alive."

"Oh, I *am* glad she's alive," Gus said. "I'm mighty glad. But the point is, she ain't here. Your girl is here, Billy's wife is alive, but my girl's married and gone to Nebraska."

Call didn't argue—there would be no point. He turned back to the rangers, and Augustus McCrae went on across the street.

20.

AHUMADO HAD NEVER had a captive who behaved like the small *americano*, Captain Scull. Most captives despaired once they realized they were in a place they could never get out of, except by death. In his experience, Americans made poor captives. He had had old Goyeto try to skin several Americans—traders, miners, travelers who happened to travel the wrong road—but they all died before Goyeto had got very far with the skinning. Even if he only skinned an arm or a leg the Americans usually died. They were weak captives, the whites. Once he had had a small Tarahumara Indian from the north who had stood at the skinning post without making a sound while Goyeto took his whole skin off—that Tarahumara had been an exceptional man. Ahumado decided to shelter him and feed him well—he thought it was possible that the man might grow a new skin; but the man took no food and didn't profit much from the shade he was given. He died after three days, without having grown any new skin.

Once or twice Ahumado had tried sticking Americans on the sharpened trees, but there again they had turned out to be disappointing captives, dying after much screaming before the sharpened tree had penetrated very far into their bowels. The Comanches and Apaches he captured on the whole did much better, although it was not unknown for one of them to disgrace himself. Once, though, he put an Apache who had stolen a woman on the sharpened tree and the Apache lived for two days even after the sharp point of the tree had come out behind his shoulder blade. No Comanche and so far no whites had done so well.

It was clear, though, that the white man Scull, the ranger, was an *americano* of a different order. Scull had mettle, so much mettle that Ahumado was surprised; and surprise was a thing he rarely experienced.

As for men in the cage, the best survivor had been an old Yaqui man who had been both exceptionally tough and exceptionally lucky. It had rained often while the old man was in the cage, so the man had moisture. Also, since he was a Yaqui of the hot desert, he wasn't used to eating much. In his days in the cage he cleverly peeled all the bark off the bars of his cage and ate it—the old Yaqui seemed to like the taste of dry bark better than the taste of raw bird meat. Later the blind woman Hema, the *curandera*, told Ahumado that the bark kept the old man from feeling hunger.

Even this Yaqui, skilled at going without food, was not as adept at living in the cage as the white man Scull. No one before Scull had ever put his legs through the cage and wiggled them. Ahumado spent a good deal of time watching Scull through some binoculars he had taken off a dead *federale*. Once he even let old Goyeto look through the binoculars and Goyeto was so astonished at what he saw that he did not want to give the binoculars back to Ahumado. He called them the Two-Eyes-That-Made-Things-Large—their ability to make things large left Goyeto speechless, and he was a man who usually chattered a lot. Even when Goyeto was skinning a person and the person was screaming, Goyeto would often be running on, talking about things of little interest or importance. Goyeto had always lived in the mountains, close to the Yellow Canyon. Though he was an old man he had only seen Jaguar once. Sometimes it amused Ahumado to startle Goyeto with trinkets he had stolen from the whites. Some whites carried watches that made sounds, and these sounds never failed to impress Goyeto, who thought they were magical.

Goyeto did not understand mechanical things; even guns were

too complicated for him. He understood only knives—with knives he was better than anyone Ahumado had ever known.

Once Ahumado had even had Goyeto skin a great rattlesnake alive—a snake that was more than eight feet long. The reason for skinning the snake alive was that it had bitten Ahumado's favorite mare, a fleet gray filly that could outrun the Comanche horses. The snake had bitten the filly right in the nose; when the nose swelled up her air could not get through. She struggled so hard to breathe that her heart gave way. Ahumado saw the old snake lying insolently only a few yards from where he had killed the mare. Because the old snake was insolent Ahumado caught him with a crooked stick and nailed him to the ground. Then he instructed Goyeto to skin him, and Goyeto did, turning the snake carefully until it was naked of skin. Then, once it was skinned, Ahumado threw it into a pit of hot coals and cooked it. He did not want to turn it loose because snakes were better than humans at growing new skins. If he let the snake go it might grow a new skin and kill another filly. Some of the *pistoleros* were made nervous by this treatment of the snake. Many of them feared the vengeance of the snake people, and, indeed, the very next day, a *pistolero* was bitten when he rolled on a rattlesnake in his sleep. But Ahumado was indifferent to such worries. Any man should be able to watch out for snakes. He had the skin of the big snake made into a fine quirt.

After Scull had been in the cage three days Ahumado noticed that he had acquired a small tool of some kind. By watching closely with the glasses he saw that it was a small file that Tudwal had once used to sharpen things. It did not surprise Ahumado that Scull had managed to kill Tudwal, who was not a smart man; but he was curious as to what Scull meant to do with the file now that he had it. Of course he could use the file to saw through the bindings of the cage, but where would that leave him? He would either fall to his death or have to climb the rope to the top of the cliff. Ahumado suspected that climbing was what Scull had in mind—he immediately sent word to the dark men to watch the rope carefully, day and night. If Scull did make it to the top of the cliff the dark men were instructed to chop off his feet with their machetes. A lack of feet would quickly put an end to his travels.

Ahumado noticed, though, that Scull did not seem to be interested in filing through the bindings, at least not in daylight. One day Scull spent the whole day scratching at the rock face with his file. It was the most puzzling thing he had done since his capture—Ahumado watched closely but could not make out the purpose of the scratching. Scull was so absorbed by his scratching that he did not even try to catch several fat pigeons that lit on the cage while he was working. Most men, once in the cage, made desperate efforts to catch any bird that came near, fearing that they would starve if they didn't. But Scull seemed confident that he could catch birds when he needed them. Hunger didn't seem to worry him.

It occurred to Ahumado one day that Scull might be a witch. He had had that suspicion from the beginning, but the suspicion increased when Parrot appeared one day from the south and soared close to Scull's cage. Ahumado was not one who thought much about witches. He didn't believe there were very many witches—most vision people, in his view, were just charlatans, full of foolish talk.

That did not mean, though, that there were no witches at all. Ahumado believed there were only a few witches, but those few possessed powers that enabled them to do very unusual things. It was possible that the small ranger, Scull, was just such a rare thing: a witch.

Fortunately the old blind *curandera*, Hema, knew something about witches. Hema was a woman of the desert who knew more than anyone else about plants that could heal. Ahumado went to her and asked her what she thought Scull might be doing, scratching on the rock with Tudwal's file. Hema of course could not see Scull but she had an acquaintance with witches. Her own sister had been a famous witch who had been taken by the Apache Gomez many years before. Hema was not a witch herself, but she was skilled with herbs and plants. She could help barren women, and old men who could no longer couple pleasantly with their wives. One woman, barren for years, had come to Hema and borne four babies, one of which was carried off by a she-wolf. She was able to brew concoctions that made the organs of aging men stiffen again when they went to their wives.

Sometimes Ahumado talked to Hema when he needed to know about things which were beyond sight. Scull, of course, was not really beyond sight; Ahumado could see him clearly, through the binoculars he had secured by killing the *federale*. But the fact that Scull was scratching on the rock with a file was worrisome. Why did he scratch on the mountain? Ahumado knew that whites could find things in the earth that others couldn't see. Sometimes they would dig into a mountain at a certain place and come out with gold. Some Indians believed that whites could make the earth shake; they might even be able to make whole mountains fall. In the war with the *americanos* Ahumado himself had seen the little cannons of the whites knock down a great church and several smaller buildings. When the cannonballs hit the earth they tore it up terribly. Ahumado was a child of the earth; he didn't like the way the guns of the whites could scar it and disturb it.

Now the fact that Captain Scull chose to scratch on the mountain annoyed Ahumado. The more he watched it and wondered about it, the more it annoyed him. What if the white man knew how to open a hole or tunnel into the mountain? Then he could simply file through the bindings on the cage and escape. He knew that the whites opened great holes in the mountains when they mined; then they walked into the earth, through the holes. A white man such as Scull might even be able to make the whole cliff fall all at once, like the church that had been knocked down during the war.

Ahumado soon developed such a strong curiosity about what Scull was doing on the cliff that he considered having himself lowered down beside him in one of the other cages, in order to watch Scull closely. He himself had no fear of heights and would not have minded being in a cage. But he soon rejected the notion of having himself lowered in a cage because of the dark men. Though they were obedient if he ordered them to chop off someone's feet, the truth was that they hated him. Once they got him in a cage they might simply cut the rope and let him fall; or they might just leave him in the cage to starve and go home to their villages in the south. Though very curious about what Scull was up to, Ahumado was not so foolish as to put himself at the mercy of the dark men.

One day he went to the hut where blind Hema sat, and told her his fears about the white man Scull opening a hole in the mountain. He wanted her to go up to the top and be lowered to the place where Scull was, in hopes that she could determine what he was doing. Though blind, Hema had hearing so sharp that she could tell what sort of bird was flying just by listening to its wing beats. Ahumado wanted her to listen to the rock and see if the rock was all right. If she thought the earth might be about to move he would have to shift his campsite. Ahumado had become convinced that Scull was not a normal man. He did not put men in cages so that they could enjoy themselves, and yet Scull seemed to be enjoying himself. While Scull scratched on the rock he sang and whistled so loudly that everyone looked up at him. That in itself was highly unusual. Most of the men put in the cages quickly lost their spirit; they did not sing and whistle. They might yell down pleas, and beg for a day or two, but after that they usually sat quietly and waited for their deaths.

Blind Hema listened closely to what Ahumado said. Then she got up and moved slowly to the base of the cliff. She moved along the cliff for an hour or more, putting her ear close to the rock and listening. The longer she moved along, listening to the cliff, the more agitated she became. When she came back to where Ahumado waited, she was trembling—in a moment her teeth began to chatter and froth came out of her mouth. Ahumado had known the old blind woman for many years and had never seen her so upset that froth came out of her mouth.

"He is calling the Serpent," old Hema said. "That is what he is doing when he scratches on the rock. He is sending signals to the great snake that lives in the earth. He wants the Serpent to shake the mountain down on us."

Then the old blind woman stumbled around the camp until she found someone who would give her tequila. Soon she became drunk—very drunk, so drunk, finally, that she fell on her face in the dust. She could not stand up, for drunkenness, but had to crawl around the camp on all fours. Seeing her on her hands and knees, some of the *pistoleros* began to tease her. They pulled up her skirts and pretended that they wanted to couple with her in the manner of dogs—of course it was only a joke. Hema was an old woman, too old for a man to be interested in.

Ahumado paid no attention to the teasing, and not much attention to what old Hema said about the Serpent. There were many people who believed that there was a great serpent in the center of the earth whose coilings and uncoilings caused the earth to move. These were not beliefs Ahumado shared. He had seen many large snakes in his youth, in the jungles of the south, but no snakes large enough to move the earth, and he did not believe that there was a serpent god who lived within the earth. Even if there was such a serpent in the earth there would be no reason for it to respond to the scratchings of a small *americano*.

The gods Ahumado believed in were Jaguar and Parrot; the thing that worried him most about Scull was that Parrot had flown by his cage and looked at him. None of the spirits were as intelligent as Parrot, in his view. In his youth in the jungles he had often seen parrots who could speak the words of men. Though men could imitate the calls of many birds, no man could speak to a bird unless the bird was Parrot. Parrot was to be feared for his brain, Jaguar for his power. Jaguar was not interested in the human beings; he might eat one but he would not talk to one. In his youth Ahumado had been like Parrot; he talked to many men—now that he was old he had become like Jaguar. Rather than talk to men he merely had Goyeto skin them, or else thrust them onto the sharpened trees.

In the morning old Hema stumbled back to her hut. She had forgotten her words about the Serpent. She had forgotten that her teeth chattered and that froth came out of her mouth. Still, Ahumado kept a close watch on Scull, up in his cage. Scull was still scratching on the rock with the little file that had been Tudwal's, but Ahumado no longer cared about that very much. He only wanted to know if Parrot would come again.

21.

WHEN KICKING WOLF was halfway home he began to encounter signs of the great raid. He crossed the tracks of many bands of warriors, all of them going north. The bands traveled in a leisurely way—they drove many horses ahead of them and they were not being pursued. At first he thought that only a few bands had been raiding, but then, as he saw more and more tracks, all flowing north, he began to realize that a great raid had been launched against the whites. Twice he came upon the bodies of white children who had died in travel. Several times he saw pieces of garments that had been torn off captive women, either by thorny brush or by warriors who had outraged the women and left their clothes.

By good luck he even came upon three stray horses and was able to catch one of them. The sorrel horse of Three Birds had traveled a long way in rocky country. Its hooves were in poor condition. Kicking Wolf had been about to abandon him and go home on foot; it was a boon to find the three horses.

The night after he caught the fresh horses Kicking Wolf heard the faint sound of singing from a camp that was not too distant. Even though at first he could scarcely hear the singing he recognized the voice of one of the singers, a brave named Red Hand, from his own band. He had often raided with Red Hand and did not think he could mistake his voice, which was deep, like the bellow of a bull buffalo. Red Hand was the fattest man in the tribe, and the biggest eater. When there was meat Red Hand ate until he fell back in sleep; when he woke up he ate some more. He was something of a braggart, who, when he was not eating, sang of his own exploits. Though fat, Red Hand was quick, and deadly with the bow. He had three wives who complained that he didn't lie with them enough. When Red Hand was at home he devoted himself to eating, and to the making of arrows.

Kicking Wolf was tired, but he was also hungry. Ahumado had left him no weapons and he had had a hard time getting anything to eat on his trip north. He survived on roots and wild onions and several fish he speared with a crude spear when he was crossing the Rio Grande. He had been so hungry that he had been almost ready to kill Three Birds' horse and eat him.

Though he had been about to sleep he decided it was better to go on to the camp where Red Hand was singing. There would probably be food in the camp, unless Red Hand had eaten it all.

The camp was farther away than he thought, but Red Hand and a few others were still singing when Kicking Wolf appeared on his new horse. There were almost twenty warriors in the party; they had two captive girls. The warriors were so confident that they hadn't even posted guards. When Kicking Wolf appeared they all stopped singing and stared at him, as if he were someone they didn't know. Red Hand had been eating venison but he stopped when he saw Kicking Wolf.

"If you are a ghost please go somewhere else," Red Hand said politely.

Several of the warriors looked at Kicking Wolf as if they thought he might have come from the spirit world, the place of ghosts.

"I am not a ghost," Kicking Wolf assured them. "I hope you don't mind if I eat some of this deer meat. I have been on a long trip and I am very hungry."

He could tell that some of the warriors still thought he might be a ghost, but after they watched him eat for a while they got over their suspicions. Then they all wanted to brag about the great raid they had been on. Several warriors talked so fast that Kicking Wolf had to delay his eating in order to listen politely. They were men of his own band, and yet he felt like a guest. The warriors had been off fighting together, whereas he had been on a quest of a different kind. His own vision was still damaged; he still saw two where there was one. The men talked to him about all the whites they had killed and all the captives they had taken.

"I don't see so many captives," Kicking Wolf said. "There are only two girls and one of them looks as if she might die tonight."

Then he looked at Red Hand.

"I found you because you were singing so loudly," he said. "If the bluecoat soldiers were after you they could find you too. You didn't even put out a guard. The bluecoats could sneak up and shoot you all down with rifles. Buffalo Hump would not be so careless if he were here."

"Oh, he went to the Great Water, with Worm," Red Hand said. "We don't have to worry about the bluecoat soldiers. They tried to fight us and we chased them away."

Red Hand had an arrogant side that was apt to come out when he was questioned or criticized. Once Buffalo Hump had hit him in the head with a club when he was talking arrogantly. The blow would have killed most warriors but it only made a lump on Red Hand's head.

"I am only telling you what any warrior should know," Kicking Wolf said. "You ought to post a guard. Though I have traveled a long way and am tired I will be your guard tonight if no one else wants to."

Before anyone could speak or offer to stand guard Red Hand started talking about the rapes he committed while on the raid. While Kicking Wolf was listening he happened to glance across the fire and when he did he got a shock: he thought he saw Three Birds sitting there—the sight was so startling that Kicking Wolf began to shake. He thought perhaps the men had been right at first to consider him a ghost. Perhaps he *was* a ghost. He was becoming more and more disturbed when the warrior who seemed to be Three Birds stood up and went to make sure that the captive girls were tied well. At that point Kicking Wolf saw that the warrior was not Three Birds, but his brother, Little Wind. The two brothers looked so much alike that it was confusing. But the warrior seeing to the girls' bonds was Little Wind. He had been away on a hunt when the Buffalo Horse was stolen—he might not even know that his brother, Three Birds, had helped Kicking Wolf take him.

"Your brother, Three Birds, did a brave thing," he told Little Wind, when the man came back and sat down.

Little Wind received this news modestly, without comment. Like Three Birds he seldom spoke, preferring to keep his sentiments to himself.

"He helped me steal the Buffalo Horse from Big Horse Scull," Kicking Wolf informed him.

"Yes, everybody knows that," Red Hand said rudely. "The two of you went away with the Buffalo Horse and missed the great raid.

"None of us had time to go look for you," Red Hand added, in such a rude tone that Kicking Wolf would have hit him with a war club if one had been handy.

"You be quiet! I have to tell Little Wind that his brother is dead," he said, a statement that caused Red Hand to shut up immediately. The death of a warrior was serious business.

"I hope he died bravely," Little Wind said. "Can you tell me about it?"

"I did not see him die," Kicking Wolf said. "He may even be alive but I don't think so. He went with me to Mexico, to the Yellow Cliffs where the Black Vaquero has his camp."

The warriors who had been moving around, doing small chores, stopped at this moment. The camp became silent. There were no more rude comments from Red Hand. All the warriors knew that to go willingly to the country of Ahumado required great courage. It was a foolish act, of course, for any warrior who wanted to continue with his life; but it was the valor of the act, not its wisdom, that stilled the warriors now. They stood or sat where they were, quiet, in awe. For two warriors to go alone into Mexico and put themselves at the mercy of the Black Vaquero was a thing of such manliness that the warriors wanted to be quiet for a time and think about it.

Kicking Wolf waited a bit, in silence, for the news of what he was saying to be absorbed.

"I stole the Buffalo Horse and took him to Mexico," he said. "I took him to Ahumado—I wanted to do it."

He saw that the warriors understood him. Many warriors would leave the band for a few weeks, to go on a quest, or see someplace they wanted to see. Such journeys became a part of the strength of a warrior.

"Ahumado caught us," he said. "He tied me to a horse and made the horse run away. He wanted to kill me but Big Horse Scull found me while I was in the blackness and cut me loose."

"Ah's!" came then from several warriors—exclamations and looks of puzzlement. Why would Big Horse Scull do such a thing?

"I did not see him," Kicking Wolf said. "I only saw his track. But now I see two things where there is one."

Little Wind waited patiently for Kicking Wolf to tell him more about his brother.

"Three Birds decided to go with me to the Yellow Canyon," Kicking Wolf said. "Even though I told him I would seek Ahumado, he decided to come. When we found Ahumado he was behind us. He tied me to a horse and made the horse run. That is the last time I saw Three Birds. Ahumado kept him."

The warriors continued to be silent. All of them had heard what Ahumado did to Comanches when he caught them. They knew about the cages, the pit, and the sharpened trees. Little Wind felt proud of his brother, for doing such a brave thing. In his life with the tribe Three Birds had never been considered especially brave. He did not lead the hunt when buffalo were running in a great stampede. He had never gone off alone to kill a bear or a cougar, though such a thing was common enough. Several of the warriors at the campfire had done such acts of bravery. Three Birds was seldom in the front of a charge, when there was an attack. His main skill as a warrior had been his ability to move quietly—that was why Kicking Wolf had chosen him to help steal the Buffalo Horse.

Since his wives and children had all died of the sickness Three

Birds had been sad—Little Wind knew. He still had his quietness of movement, but he did not join in things. Little Wind thought his brother's sadness might explain why he had decided to do such a brave thing.

When Kicking Wolf finished talking he stood up to go sit on guard, as he had offered to do when he arrived and found that the camp was unguarded. But, when he stood up, Red Hand quickly gestured for him to sit again. Red Hand had always liked Kicking Wolf and was ashamed that he had been rude to him, earlier. Kicking Wolf had done a great thing, a thing that would be sung about for many years. He should not have to listen to rudeness. It was just that his sudden appearance had startled everyone a lot. Some had taken him for a ghost. Red Hand had sought to challenge the ghost with his rudeness. But, now that he had heard Kicking Wolf's story, he was eager to make amends.

"I see that you are hungry," Red Hand said. "You should eat some of this deer meat. I will stand guard tonight."

Kicking Wolf politely accepted Red Hand's offer. He stayed where he was, but did not eat much of the deer meat. Now that he was back with the warriors of his own band, a great tiredness came over him. He lay down in the warm ashes of the fire and was soon asleep.

22.

PEARL COLEMAN pushed down her sadness every morning and tried to make her husband a sizable and tasty breakfast. She sat Long Bill down to a good plate of biscuits and four tasty pork chops. Then she told him, as she had every morning since his return, that she wanted him to quit the rangers and quit them now.

"I can't stand you going off in the wilds no more, Bill," she said, beginning to weep at the memory of her recent ordeal. "I can't stand it. I get so scared my toes cramp up when I get in bed. I can't get to sleep with my toes cramping up like that."

Though he appreciated the biscuits and the pork chops, Long

Bill let his wife's remarks pass without comment—he also let her tears flow without trying to staunch them. Tears and entreaties for him to quit the rangers had become as predictable a part of the morning as the sunrise itself.

"There's worse things than cramped toes, Pearl," he answered, a biscuit in one hand and an unhappy look on his face.

He said no more than that, but Pearl Coleman felt exasperation growing. For the first time in her marriage she felt herself in opposition to her husband, and not casual opposition either. About the need for him to quit the rangers immediately she was right and he was wrong, and if she couldn't get Bill to accept her view then she didn't know what to think about their future as husband and wife.

"I'd be the one to know what's bad better than you," she told him. "I was here. I had four arrows shot into me, and I lost our baby from being so scared. I got so scared our baby died inside me."

Long Bill's own view was that the raping Pearl had endured had probably killed the baby, but he didn't say so; he ate another biscuit and held his peace. The overwhelming relief he felt when he saw that Pearl was alive had subsided, drained away by the new problem of adjusting to what had happened to her.

One thing Long Bill had to face immediately was that Pearl had been raped by several Comanches. On his anguished long, nervous ride home he had half expected to have to cope with the knowledge of rape; but once he got home and discovered that Pearl actually *had* been raped he was so shocked that, so far, he had not even attempted the conjugal act that in normal circumstances he looked forward to so much.

Not only that, Pearl didn't want him to attempt it.

"They done it and you wasn't here to help me," she told him, weeping, the first night he was back. "I can't be a wife to you no more, Bill."

All that night, and every night since, Pearl lay beside her husband, her legs squeezed together, so desperately unhappy that she wished one of the Comanche arrows had killed her.

Long Bill, beside her, was no less unhappy. He and the rangers had buried thirteen people on the ride back to Austin. Now, lying beside his unhappy wife, he thought of all the battles he had been in and reflected that a single well-placed bullet could have spared him such a painful dilemna.

"How many done you?" he asked Pearl, finally.

"Seven," Pearl admitted. "It was over quick."

Long Bill said no more, then or ever, but if seven Comanches had violated his wife then it didn't seem to him that it could have been over very quick.

Since his return, day by day, life had gotten harder. Pearl cooked him lavish, delicious meals, but, in bed, lay beside him with her legs squeezed shut, and he himself had no desire to persuade her to open them.

Through the long, anxious nights on the trail he had wanted nothing more than to be home and in bed with his wife. Now, though, he left the house the minute supper was over, to sit late in the saloon every night, drinking with Augustus McCrae. Gus drank to ease his broken heart, Long Bill to blur his own vivid and uneasy thoughts. Sometimes they were even joined by Woodrow Call, who had his own worries but wouldn't voice them—the most he would do was take a whiskey or two. By this time everybody in Austin knew that Maggie Tilton was pregnant, and many people assumed the baby was Woodrow Call's, a fact not of much importance to anyone except the young couple themselves.

Austin had the great raid to recover from. Most of the towns-people had homes or businesses to repair; they also had griefs to grieve. The fact that a young Texas Ranger had got a whore preg-nant was in the normal order of things, and no one thought the worse of Woodrow or of Maggie, because of it. Few had the leisure to give the matter more than an occasional thought.

Night after night the three of them, Long Bill, Gus, and Call, sat at a table in the back of the saloon, all three troubled in mind because of difficulties with women. Augustus had lost the love of his life, Long Bill's wife had been shamed by the red Comanches, and Woodrow's girl was carrying a child she insisted was his, a child he could not find it in him to want, or even to acknowledge.

"How would a whore know if a child is one man's or another's?" he asked one night. Long Bill was nodding, so the question was mainly directed at Gus, but Long Bill snapped to attention and answered.

"Oh, women know," he said. "They got ways."

To Call's annoyance, Augustus casually agreed, though he was so drunk at the time that he could scarcely lift his glass.

"If she says it's yours, it's yours," Gus said. "Now don't you be fidgeting about it."

Call had asked Gus because Gus had made a study of women, more or less, while he himself had devoted more attention to the practicalities of ranger life on the frontier. Since Maggie had immediately claimed the baby was his, and had remained firm in her opinion, he thought there might be some medical or scientific basis for her conviction, and if there was he was prepared to do his duty. But he wanted to know the science of it, not merely be told that women knew about such things.

"Maggie's honest, that's the point, Woodrow," Gus reminded him. Though drunk, he meant to see that Woodrow Call did not evade the responsibilities of fatherhood.

"I know she's honest," Call replied. "That don't mean she's right about everything. Honest people make mistakes too.

"I'm honest, and I've made plenty," he added.

"I even make mistakes," Long Bill admitted, ruefully. "And I'm as honest as the day is long."

"Pshaw, you ain't!" Gus said. "I expect you told Pearl you was standing guard at night, so you lied within the hour. Ain't that true?"

"It's not so much a lie as that Pearl don't need to know everything," Long Bill replied. It was true that he lied to Pearl about his evenings in the saloon, but he didn't think Pearl minded. In fact she might even prefer to have him out of the house until it was time for them to sleep. Otherwise, they would have nothing to do but sit in their chairs or lay in their bed and brood about the fact that they were no longer husband and wife as they had been.

"The point is, Maggie ain't a mistake," Gus told Call. "She's a blessing and you're dumb not to see it."

"I am right fond of Maggie," Call said. "But that don't mean the child is mine. I'd just like to know if there's a way she can be sure about the father."

Gus, in a poor mood anyway, was annoyed by the very tone of Woodrow Call's voice.

"If I say it's yours and Bill says it's yours and Maggie says it's yours, then that ought to be enough for you," he said hotly. "Do you need the dern Governor to say it's yours?"

"No," Call said, making an earnest effort to stay calm about the matter. "I just want to know for sure. I expect any man would want to know for sure. But you can't tell me for sure and Bill can't either. I don't know what the Governor has to do with it."

Silence followed. Augustus saw no point in pursuing the matter further. He had been in many arguments with Woodrow Call but had never, so far as he could recall, succeeded in changing his mind. Long Bill must have felt the same. He stared at his whiskey glass and said nothing.

Call got up and left. He had taken to walking by the river for an hour or more at night, but, on this occasion, had left his rifle in the bunkhouse and strolled back to get it. Since the raid no one ventured out of town, day or night, without a rifle.

"Woodrow's hard to convince, ain't he?" Long Bill said, once Call left.

Augustus didn't reply. Instead he reached in his pocket and took out a letter he had received the day before, from Clara. He had already memorized the letter but could not resist looking at it again:

Dear Gus,
    I write in haste from St. Louis—tomorrow a boat will take us up the Missouri River. I trust that you are safe. If you are in

Austin when you get this letter you will have heard that Ma and Pa were killed in the big raid.

I only got the news two days ago. Of course it's hard, knowing that I will never see Ma and Pa again.

As you are my oldest and best friend I would like you to do this for me: go and see that they are well buried in the cemetery, there by Grandma Forsythe. I would appreciate it if you would hire someone to care for their graves. It is not likely, now that I am a married woman, that I will return that way for many years, but it would be a comfort for me to know that their graves are being cared for. Perhaps a few flowers, bluebonnets maybe, could be planted above them in the spring. My Ma was always taken with bluebonnets.

I hope you will do this for me, Gus, and not be bitter about Bob. Once we are settled in Nebraska I'll send money for the caretaker.

It's hard to write you, Gus—we've always just talked, haven't we? But I mean to practice until I get the hang of it. And you need to write me too, so that I'll know you're safe and well.

Your friend,
Clara

She don't know, Augustus thought, as he carefully folded the letter and put it back in its envelope. Merely seeing her writing caused such yearning to swell up in him that he didn't think he could stand it. Despite himself tears welled in his eyes.

"I reckon we can tell about that baby of Maggie's once it's born," Long Bill said. He spoke mainly to cover his friend's embarrassment—merely getting a letter from Clara had brought tears to his eyes.

Gus, though, didn't seem to be listening. He put the letter back in his pocket, scattered some money on the table, and left.

Long Bill sat alone for a while, drinking, though he knew it was about time he went home to Pearl. No doubt she'd be in bed with her Bible, trying to pray away troubles that just weren't willing to leave. Gus's girl had married someone else, as women would. Maggie Tilton had become pregnant, as women would. But his wife had been shamed by seven Comanche warriors, causing her to lose a baby that had been legally and pleasurably conceived.

Now he wasn't sure that there would be any more such pleasure for himself and Pearl. Her ample flesh, which had once drawn him to her night after night, now repelled him. He didn't mind that Pearl kept her legs squeezed together. Every night now he scooted farther and farther from her, in the bed. Even her sweat smelled different to him now.

He didn't know what to do, but one thing he did not intend to do was resign from the rangers, which was the very thing Pearl wanted most. That very morning, before starting in about it, Pearl had run out in the yard and grabbed up a fat hen that he wasn't even too sure was their hen; she had wrung its neck before he could even raise the question of whose hen it might be, and then started talking about the rangers.

"Pearl, I wish you'd stop talking about me quitting the rangers," he told her bluntly. He didn't think he could survive his sorrows without the companionship of the boys in the troop; besides that, he had to make a living and had few marketable skills. How did the woman expect him to feed her if he quit the job he was best at? They'd have to poach some neighbor's chicken every day if he did that.

"But Bill, I need you to quit, I can't help it!" Pearl said.

"Don't be complaining at me today, Pearl," he said. "I've got to help Pea Eye shoe the horses, and that's tiring work." He had just come down the stairs in time to see the chicken die. Pearl was already gutting it—she flung a handful of guts toward the woodpile where several hungry cats soon descended on them.

Pearl knew Long Bill was tired of her trying to get him to quit the rangers, but she couldn't stop herself. Sometimes at the thought of him going away again she felt such distress that she felt her head might burst, or her heart. She and Long Bill had been so happy before the raid; they hardly ever fussed, except over the crease in his pants, which she could never seem to iron well enough to suit him. They had been happy people, but a single hour of horror and torment had changed that. Pearl didn't know how to get their happiness back but she knew it would never be possible unless Bill moved her to a place where she felt there were no Indians to threaten her. If he wouldn't move to a safer town, then the least he could do was stay home and protect her. The thought of Bill leaving made her so scared that, twice recently, just walking down the street, she had grown so nervous that she wet herself, to her great shame. She had no confidence now, and knew she had none. The Comanches had come once and done as they pleased with her. There was no reason to think they wouldn't come again.

Long Bill paid for his whiskey and walked home under a thin March moon. There had been a spurt of snow the day before, and a little of it lingered in the shaded places near the buildings. It crunched under his feet as he approached the house where he and Pearl lived.

It was late, past midnight. Long Bill had hoped to find his wife asleep, but when he tiptoed in he saw that the lamp by the bed was still lit. There lay Pearl, propped up on a pillow with the lamp lit and a Bible in her lap.

"Pearl, if you've been praying, that's enough of it, let's blow out the lamp and get to sleep," he said.

Pearl didn't want to. For hours, while Bill drank in the saloon to avoid coming home to her—Pearl knew that was what he was doing and knew that the rapes were what had driven him out—she had been praying to the Lord to show her a way to get their happiness back; finally, only a few minutes before Bill stepped in the door, a vision had come to her of what that way was—a vision so bright that it could only have come from the Lord.

"Billy, it's come to me!" she said, jumping out of bed in her excitement.

"Well, what has, Pearl?" Long Bill asked, a little taken aback by his wife's sudden fervor. He had been hoping to slip into bed and sleep off the liquor he had just drunk, but that clearly was not going to be easy.

"I know what you can do once you quit the rangers," Pearl said. "It came to me while I was praying. It's a vision from the Lord!"

"Pearl, I've learnt rangering and I don't know how to do anything else," Long Bill said. "What's your notion? Tell me and let's get to bed."

Pearl was a little hurt by her husband's tone, which was brusque. Also, he was swaying on his feet, indicating a level of drunkenness that she could not approve. But she hadn't lost hope for her God-sent vision—not quite.

"Billy, you could preach to the multitudes!" she said. "Our preacher got killed in the raid and his wife too. There's a church open right here in town. I know you'd make a fine preacher, once you got the hang of it."

Long Bill was so stunned by Pearl's statement that he dropped, a little too hard, into their one chair, causing a loose rung to pop out, as it often did. In his annoyance he threw the rung out the open window.

"We need a better chair than this," he said. "I'm tired of that damn rung popping out ever time I sit down."

"I know Bill, but the Forsythes are dead and the store ain't open," Pearl said, horribly disappointed in Bill's response to her suggestion. She had convinced herself that he would be delighted to become a preacher, but he clearly wasn't delighted at all. He just looked annoyed, which is how he had looked most of the time since his return.

"Didn't you hear me?" she asked. "Handsome as you are, I know you'd make a fine preacher. The town needs one, too. One of the deacons has been holding church, but he can't talk plain and he's boresome to have to listen to."

Long Bill felt a good deal of exasperation. In the first place, Pearl had no business being up so late; now she had caused him to break their chair, and all because of a notion so foolish that if he had been in a better mood he would have laughed.

"Pearl, I can't read," he pointed out. "I've heard some of the Bible read out, but that was a long time ago. The only verse I can recall is that one about the green pastures, and even that one's a little cloudy in my mind."

Long Bill paused, noticing that his wife was on the verge of tears; Pearl did not cry thimblefuls, either. Once she got started crying it was wise to have a bucket handy, or at least a good-sized rag.

"I do not know how you got such a notion, honey," he said, in the gentlest tone he could manage. "If I was to put myself up to be a preacher, I expect the boys would laugh me out of town."

Pearl Coleman wasn't ready to give up her God-sent vision, though. Faith was supposed to move mountains—it was just a question of convincing Bill that faith and his handsome looks was all he would need to start out on a preaching career.

"I can read, Billy," she said. "I can read just fine. I could read you the text in the morning before church and then you could preach on it."

Long Bill just shook his head. He felt a weariness so deep he thought he might go to sleep right in the chair.

"Would you help me off with my boots, Pearl?" he asked, stretching out a leg. "I'm tired to the bone."

Pearl helped her husband off with his boots. Later, in bed, as silently as possible, she had her cry. Then she got up, went out into the street, and managed to locate the chair rung Long Bill had flung out the window. There was no telling how long it would be before the store opened again, and, meanwhile, they had to have their chair.

23.

OLD BEN MICKELSON had been so badly frightened during the great Comanche raid that, as soon as it was clear that he had survived it, he attempted to give notice and leave.

"Leave and go where?" Inez Scull asked him, a moment or two before she took the long black bullwhip to him.

In the Scull mansion, of course, there was little room to employ a bullwhip properly, and old Ben, when it became a question of his hide, proved surprisingly nimble, darting through the halls and managing to keep the heavy furniture between himself and his enraged mistress. The best Inez managed was to strike the old butler a few times across the shoulders with the coiled whip before driving him outside, where she cornered him on the high porch.

"Leave and go where, you scabby old fool?" Inez said, waving the whip back and forth.

"Why, back to Brooklyn, madame," Ben Mickelson said; he was calculating the risk of jumping off the porch—it wasn't *that* high but neither was it *that* low, and he had no desire to break an ankle or any other limb.

"There's no red Indians in Brooklyn," he added. "A man needn't fear mutilation, not in honest Brooklyn."

"You'll get worse than mutilation if you think you can give notice on me," Inez hissed at him. "Where do you suppose I can get another butler, in these wilds? If you leave, who do you suppose will serve the brandy and the port?"

She swung the whip, but clumsily—mostly she employed the bullwhip more as a club than a whip, in her fights with Inish. Old Ben Mickelson deflected the blow and leapt off the porch. He failed to make a clean landing, though; one ankle twisted beneath him so painfully that when Inez Scull followed him and attempted to apply a sound lashing Ben Mickelson was forced to crawl away.

That was the sight that greeted Augustus McCrae as he came trotting up from the town. Old Ben Mickelson was crawling down the long slope toward the springhouse, while Inez Scull followed, attempting to whack him with the bullwhip. Nothing that happened at the Scull mansion surprised Augustus very much; the one thing that was obvious in the present encounter was that Madame Scull could have done the old butler more damage if she'd used a quirt and not a bullwhip. He arrived just in time to hear her deliver a final comment.

"If you attempt to leave me again, Ben, I'll put it out that you stole my emeralds," she said. "You won't have to worry about red Indians if I do that, because the sheriff will haul you off and hang you."

"All right! Let me be! I'll stay and serve your damned port," old Ben said, standing up but favoring his ankle.

Inez promptly whacked him again.

"Damned port, indeed," she said. "Don't you presume to swear at your mistress!"

Augustus watched with amusement. Lately he and Ben Mickleson had become allies in crime. Before going upstairs to engage in what Inez Scull described as a good trot, he and old Ben would often sneak in and raid the cabinet where Captain Scull kept his fine whiskeys and brandies. At first he had underestimated the potency of the brandy to such an extent that he represented himself poorly, once he got to the boudoir, a fact which never failed to draw a stinging reproach from Madame Scull.

"It looks as if you've crippled Ben," he said to the lady, watching the old butler limp away.

"The scabby old beast attempted to quit, just because a few Comanches chased through town," she said. "I won't have desertion—you should bear that in mind yourself, Captain McCrae."

Her face was fiery red and she flung him a look of contempt.

"I detest contrary servants," she said. "Ben Mickelson has too much damned gall to think he could just walk in and quit."

Augustus got off his horse, a nervous filly. He thought it best to walk along with Madame Scull until she calmed down. Sometimes a jumpy horse would start bucking even if it only heard a voice it didn't like. Woodrow Call had some skill with bucking horses, but he himself had none. Three jumps and he usually went flying; better to dismount and walk when Inez Scull was waving her bullwhip around.

"Your husband's in Mexico—that's the news," he told her. "Or at least that's the rumor."

"Not interested in rumors and not especially interested in where

Inish is," Inez said. "Anyway, I doubt he's that close. Inish usually goes farther afield when he strays—I expected him to be in Egypt, at least. Who says he's in Mexico?"

"It's a thirdhand rumor," Augustus said. "A miner heard it from a Mexican, and the Governor heard it from the miner."

"Does the news disturb you, Gussie?" she asked, smiling at him suddenly and taking his arm as they walked. Then she lifted his hand and gave his finger a hard bite; she set her teeth into it and looked at him as she bit.

"I suppose we'll have to leave off trotting if Inish shows up," she said. "He's a very jealous man. I have no doubt he'd find a reason to hang you if he knew we'd been doing all this fine trotting."

"Well, but who would tell him?" Augustus asked. He had never known quite such a devilish woman. Clara Forsythe could be extremely vexing, but her contrariness was done mostly in play, whereas Inez Scull's devilment had anger in it, and defiance, and even lust; it wasn't a thing done in play, as Clara's was. Inez had just bitten his finger so hard there was blood on her front teeth. He wiped his finger on his pants leg and walked on with her toward the big house.

"I might tell him myself if you displease me," Inez said. "I do rather like to be the center of attention when I choose a man, and I can't say you're lavish with your attention. My Jakie was much more attentive, while he lasted."

"Jake Spoon, that pup!" Gus said. "Why, he is barely dry behind the ears."

"I wasn't interested in his ears, Captain," Mrs. Scull said. "I've a notion that you're not sorry that Inish is returning."

"Ma'am, I didn't say he was returning," Gus said. "I just said he's in Mexico—you didn't let me finish my report."

"Why wouldn't he return, if he's in Mexico?" Inez asked. "I hardly think those brown whores would interest him for long."

"We heard he was a captive," Gus told her. "We think the Black Vaquero caught him."

"Oh well, no one keeps Inish a captive long, he's too troublesome," Inez said. "You don't really like me, do you, Gussie?"

"Ma'am, I'm walking along with you—ain't that a sign that I like you?" Augustus asked. He wanted to curse her, though, for being so bold as to ask such a question. The fact was, he didn't like her; it was just that he had an emptiness in him, an emptiness that hadn't been there until Clara left. It was the emptiness that brought him up the hill to Madame Scull. Being with her invariably left a bad taste in his mouth, yet he kept coming.

"You coward, why can't you say it? You despise me!" Inez said, with bitter scorn. "You'd be happy to see Inish back. Then you could just drink whiskey all day and moon about that Forsythe girl. I'm jealous of that girl, I can tell you that. I've more to offer than any girl who works in a store, and yet you've had her on your mind the whole time I've known you."

Gus didn't answer. He wondered how women so easily found out what men were feeling. He had never so much as mentioned Clara's name to Inez Scull—how did she know it was Clara on his mind? Women could smell feelings as a dog could smell a fox. He had just told Madame Scull that her husband was a prisoner of the cruelest man in Mexico, and yet she hadn't turned a hair. She was far more disturbed by the fact that he loved Clara Forsythe and not her. Even in their passion, though he seemed to be there, he wasn't, and Mrs. Scull knew it.

"Well, I better just go," he said. "I mainly came up to give you the news."

"Liar," Inez said, slapping him. "You're a liar and a coward—if I hadn't dropped my bullwhip I'd cut you to ribbons. You didn't come up to tell me about Inish. You came here because I know more about certain things than any whore you can afford on your puny little salary."

She was red in the face again—Gus's nervous young horse was backing away.

"You and your village maiden, I despise you both!" Inez said. "You and your calf love. You come to me, though, with your mangy

346

grin—and Inish will come for the same reason, when he's through wandering."

"What's the reason?" Augustus asked, annoyed by the woman's violent tone—a tone that even scared his horse.

"Lust, sir . . . free lust!" Inez said. "Do you hear me? Lust!"

She yelled the last so loudly that anyone within half a mile could have heard her. It made him nervous. Lust was one thing—telling the whole town about it was something else. He decided he could leave, but when he stepped toward his horse Madame Scull struck at him with the coiled bullwhip.

"There, go along, you coward," she said. "In your whole life you'll never find a woman who will make herself so free—and yet you're too callow to appreciate it."

With that she turned and stalked off toward her mansion, while Gus stroked and soothed his agitated mount. He thought of following Madame Scull into the house, but, in the end, mounted and rode back down the hill toward town.

The first person he saw when he reached the lots was young Jake Spoon, idle as usual, though there was plenty of work available. Deets, Pea Eye, and Long Bill Coleman were struggling to subdue a stout young gelding, so they could shoe him. Jake, though, sat on an empty nail keg playing a game of solitaire, using an overturned wheelbarrow for a table. It evidently didn't bother Jake to play while others worked, a fact that annoyed Gus so that he walked over and kicked the nail keg out from under—it sent him sprawling. Then, not satisfied, he bent over, grabbed Jake by his curly hair, and knocked his head against the ground a time or two.

Jake saw from Gus's face that he was very angry—he had no idea why Gus had chosen to take it out on him, but he knew better than to resist. Gus McCrae was fully capable of doing worse.

"There, you better play possum or I'll have your damn gizzard," Gus said.

The three men struggling with the mustang noticed the little altercation. They stopped what they were doing, to watch, but there was nothing more to see. A little wind swirled through the lots, blowing several of Jake Spoon's cards off the wheelbarrow. Gus left Jake on his back in the dust and walked over to the horseshoeing crew.

"Jake's a lazy one, ain't he?" Long Bill said. "The whores like him, though. They fancy that curly hair."

"Jakie," Mrs. Scull called him, Gus remembered. Probably she too had fancied his curly hair. The thought brought the bad taste back to his mouth.

Jake Spoon picked himself up, but cautiously. He left the windblown cards to lie in the dust. Gus McCrae looked as if he were in the mood to give someone a thorough licking. The men resumed working with the horse, but they kept one eye on Gus, who stood with his back to them. It was clear that it wouldn't take much to set him off.

But when Gus turned it was to motion for Deets to come with him.

"You, there," he said to Jake, "leave them cards alone and help the boys shoe that horse."

Long Bill started to protest the order. Deets was handy with a hasp and a horseshoe nail, and there was nothing in the way of labor that Jake was handy with. But he saw that Gus was upset, and held his tongue.

Augustus walked Deets out of town to where the cemetery lay, in a curve of a stream. They could hear the water rushing before they reached the stream. Once amid the live oaks that bordered the river Gus felt a little relief from his sour mood, a mood mostly caused by Inez Scull. He didn't like the woman, but she exuded a strong nectar, too strong to easily ignore.

Deets followed Gus quietly, glad to be relieved of the horseshoeing. When they came to the cemetery he took off his hat, an old felt Captain Call had given him only the day before. It had belonged to one of the rangers killed in the raid. Deets was mighty proud of his hat, but he took it off quickly when they came to the graveyard. It wouldn't do to be disrespectful of the dead.

Augustus walked him carefully through the fresh graves until he came to those of Clara's mother and father. He knew Deets couldn't read the names on the wooden crosses, so he wanted him to take care to note exactly where the two graves were.

"These are the Forsythes," he told Deets. "They were parents of a good friend of mine. I aim to put up good stone headstones when I get time—she'd want me to, I expect."

The thought of Clara entrusting him with the care of her parents' graves left him briefly overcome. He knelt down and didn't try to speak.

"Deets, can you garden?" he asked, when the mood passed and he had better control of his voice.

"I can garden," Deets assured him. "Kept a big one, back home. Lord, we grew the string beans."

Augustus realized he knew almost nothing about the young black man. Deets had just shown up one day, as people did—black people, particularly. Their owners died and they were set to wandering.

"Where was back home, Deets?" Gus asked.

"Louisee, I believe," Deets said, after a moment. "It was in Louisee, somewhere on the river."

"Oh, Louisiana, I guess you mean," Gus said. "I want you to tend these graves like you would a garden. Only you don't need to grow no string beans, just flowers. My friend's mother was partial to bluebonnets, particularly. I'd like you to get some flowers growing on these graves, come spring."

It was clear to Deets that Mr. Gus had a powerful affection for the friend he mentioned. When he mentioned her his voice shook. As for flowers, that was easy.

"The flowers be coming soon," he said. "I'll get some of the bluebonnets and put them on these graves."

"I'll see you get a wage for it—a fair wage," Augustus said. "I want you to keep tending these two graves as long you're in these parts. Just these two, now. You don't have time to be flowering up other people's graves."

"No sir," Deets said. "I see which two. I'll make 'em pretty."

"You tend them, come what may," Gus said. "That's how my friend wants it."

He paused—he seemed to have difficulty with his voice. Deets waited.

"You'll need to be keeping them pretty, year after year," Gus said, with a glance at the young black man who knelt, hat in hand, a few feet away.

"You'll need to do it whatever happens to me," Gus said, looking down at the clods of brown earth on the fresh grave.

These last words startled Deets. It was clear that Mr. Gus was mighty concerned about the upkeep of the two graves. Deets could not but feel proud that he had been selected, from all the company, to be the one to see that the burial places were well maintained.

But now Mr. Gus was concerning him a little. What did he mean, whatever happened to him? It sounded as if he might be intending to leave, which was startling and upsetting. Of all the rangers only Pea Eye, a young man like himself, had been as kind to him as Mr. Gus.

"I expect you be seeing for yourself what a good job I do, Captain," Deets said. He tried to pick his words carefully, for the matter clearly meant a lot to Mr. Gus.

"But if I ain't here to see it for myself, you tend these graves anyway," Gus said, with force in his voice suddenly. "You make 'em pretty anyway, Deets, even if I'm dead and in a grave myself."

It had suddenly come to Augustus that he might die without ever seeing Clara again—or, even worse, Clara herself might die before they could ever have another moment together with one another. It was a terrible thought to think, and yet men and women died every day on the frontier; and Nebraska, where Clara had gone, was no less a frontier than Texas. Thirty people, all of them alive when he and Call left Austin, lay buried under the freshly turned earth just before him.

"I ain't guaranteed tomorrow—you ain't either," he told Deets.

"If I should fall I wouldn't want my friend to have to be . . . worrying about these graves not being tended."

Deets had never heard Mr. Gus speak so. He realized he had been given a solemn responsibility.

"I'll be seeing to the graves, Captain," he said.

Mr. Gus nodded. He was looking away; it was as if he were thinking of a far place, a place well distant from the little graveyard outside of Austin. He nodded, but he didn't speak. Deets thought it might be best just to leave him alone, to do his looking away. He walked out of the graveyard, put his hat back on, and began to inspect some of the first spring flowers, to see if any of them might do for prettying up the two graves.

24.

MAGGIE NOW seldom went out. The baby was growing inside her, its kicks stronger every day. Even with her coat on it was obvious to everyone who saw her that she was with child. Fortunately her room was light, with a good south breeze blowing through it most of the time. Woodrow had started taking most of his meals with her, which meant that she did have to go out and shop a little in the market. Since the raid beef had become scarce and pricey. There were plenty of cattle but few hunters bold enough to go into the brush country to slaughter them, for fear of encountering Comanches. Fortunately, Woodrow liked goat, which was available and cheap. Sometimes Gus McCrae would come up and eat with him—he was always tipsy, it seemed.

"I fear my partner will end up a drunkard," Woodrow said, one night after Gus had left. They stood by the window and watched him make straight for a saloon.

"That's because of Clara," Maggie said. "He had his heart set on her."

"Yes, but she's gone," Call said. "He needs to let it go and find himself another girl."

"He can't," Maggie said. "Some folks can't just bend their feelings that way."

"Well, he ought to try," Woodrow said. "There's plenty of girls that would make him a decent wife if he'd just give them a chance."

Then he picked up his rifle and left to walk the river, as he did most every night. He scarcely lingered with Maggie ten minutes now, after taking his meal; when he returned it would be nearly dawn. He would merely sleep an hour or two with her, before going down to the rangers.

Each night's departure left Maggie feeling empty and sad. She wanted to say to him what he had just said about the girls Gus might marry: I could make you a decent wife, if you'd just give me the chance. Already, she tried to treat Woodrow as she would treat a beloved husband, yet all it seemed to get her was the hastiest attentions. The thing that seemed to please him most was that she kept his clothes clean and nicely pressed. As the weather grew warmer, Maggie sometimes felt faint, ironing in the heat, and yet she kept on because Woodrow liked to dress neatly and his pleasure in wearing well-placed clothes was a kind of bond they had, a stronger one than their pleasure even. Anyway the pleasure had become hasty and more and more intermittent. Woodrow seemed to feel that much indulgence in the carnal appetites would be medically inadvisable; or perhaps he was merely put off by her swelling body. He withdrew and walked the river; Maggie felt sad, but continued to do her best.

The baby that was so visibly there inside her she had given up mentioning at all. That she was pregnant was a fact of their existence, yet a fact they both ignored. Maggie longed for a good chance to talk to Woodrow about the baby; but he was careful in his speech and never gave her one.

Best wait, she thought—best wait until it's here. Her hope was that once the child was born Woodrow would see it and take to it. In her daydreams she imagined him pleased by the little child, so pleased that he would want everybody to know he was its father. And yet, at night, alone, with Woodrow gone, she couldn't keep herself from wondering if it would really be that way. One day she would be hopeful, the next day despairing. She could well understand why Gus McCrae had turned to drink, from missing Clara Forsythe, now Clara Allen. Maggie missed her too. Although circumstance had not permitted much conversation to pass between them, Maggie felt that Clara liked her. Sometimes, sweeping the boardwalk in front of the store, Clara would look up at Maggie's window and smile and wave. When some small need took Maggie into the store, Clara was invariably friendly and welcoming. Knowing that Maggie had a yearning for fine goods, gloves or shoes often well beyond her purse, Clara would sometimes mark a little off an item, so that Maggie could have at least a few things that pleased her.

Having Clara there broke the loneliness; now there was no one with such a fine spirit who might break it. Maggie had once talked to Pearl Coleman now and then, but since the raid Pearl herself had become too despondent to chatter in the light way she once had. Maggie saw her almost every day, in the market, but Pearl barely responded to her hello. From being an aggressive customer, willing to haggle tirelessly and loudly over the price of a pepper or a squash, Pearl had become indifferent, merely raking a few foodstuffs into her basket and paying the price without dispute.

Seeing Pearl Coleman, a woman who had always been cheerful and well able to take care of herself, so despondent made Maggie reflect on how precarious life was, in such a place. Thirty people had lost their lives, and several women had had their marriages destroyed by the rapes they endured; most of the children had stopped going to school for fear that the Indians would come back and take them, and the men were nervous about venturing much beyond the outskirts of Austin. Maggie herself felt like going to a safer place—San Antonio, perhaps, or one of the towns on the coast. But she knew that if she moved she would lose all hope of marriage to Woodrow Call. The rangers were quartered in Austin and he had been promoted to captain. He would not be likely to leave.

One good thing about the promotion was that Woodrow had

started giving her six dollars a month toward her housekeeping expenses.

"Woodrow, what's this for?" Maggie asked, very startled, the first time he gave her the money.

"Take it—it will be easier for you to make ends meet," Call said. The fact was, he lived frugally and seldom spent all his salary; a factor in his modest prosperity was that Maggie fed him several meals a week and looked after his laundry. Nobody gave her the food she served him, and she could scarcely do much whoring with her belly so swollen. He felt that he was an expense Maggie could ill afford. Mainly he would just put the money on the table, or by the cupboard; often he would leave it at night, before he left to walk the river.

When Maggie saw the six dollars on her table something stirred in her, something mixed. She realized it was as close as Woodrow could come to admitting that he lived with her. On the other hand, she had always cared for herself. She might long for a man who might marry her and want to support her—and yet she could not convince herself that Woodrow really *did* want to support her. He just felt he ought to; it was his conscience, not his heart, which moved him to put the six dollars on her table every month.

Sometimes Maggie left the money on the table a day or two before she picked it up. The sight of it made her feel both better and worse; it made her feel that she was being kept by a man who, though he might care for her, had no true desire to keep her, much less marry her and claim their child.

Still, Woodrow Call, with his nightly absences and the six dollars a month which he punctually left, was still the best that life offered, or was likely to offer, in the place where Maggie was. Sometimes she felt so defeated that she wondered if she ought to give up on the idea of respectability altogether. She might as well just whore and whore and whore, until she got too old. Even if she only saw a few customers, now and then, she could still make a lot more than six dollars a month.

25.

THEY HAD TRAVELED up the Rio Grande almost to the crossings on the great war trail when they saw the Old One. Worm at once became upset and began to shake and to speak incoherently, although the Old One was merely squatting by a little fire, carefully removing the quills from a large porcupine he had shot.

The Old One, whose long white hair touched the ground when he squatted, was devoting careful attention to the dead porcupine. He did not want to break any of the porcupine quills—one by one he took them out and laid them on a little strip of buckskin he had unfurled and placed on a rock by his campfire. The big wolf that traveled with the Old One gave one howl when he smelled Buffalo Hump and Worm, and loped away into the bed of the river.

Buffalo Hump stopped, respectfully, a good distance away. The Old One turned his head briefly and looked at them; then he went back to the careful extraction of the porcupine quills.

"We must not stay here," Worm said, in a shaky voice. "The wolf can hide in a dream. In the dream it will be a bird, or a woman you want to couple with. But when you do, the wolf will come out of the dream and open your throat."

"Be quiet," Buffalo Hump said. "I am not afraid of any wolf. If we are respectful, the Old One might give us some of those nice quills."

"No, we cannot take the quills," Worm protested. "The Old One might witch them. They might turn into scorpions while you carry them. Nothing about the Old One is as it seems."

Buffalo Hump was beginning to wish he had sent Worm home after the great raid. Worm had become too nervous to make good company. Everything he had seen on their ride up the river seemed malign to him. At the mouth of the river, where the water was salt, they had caught a young alligator that had got into the wrong waters somehow. Worm made a big fuss over the alligator. Later they came upon a dead eagle and Worm made a big fuss about that too. Now they had stumbled on the Old One and Worm was terrified. Once Worm had been a competent medicine man but now everything seemed to scare him or upset him.

"The Old One is just an old man," Buffalo Hump said. "I have seen him several times and he has never witched me. He probably found that wolf when it was a pup and raised it as we would a dog.

"The Old One is not a fighting man now," he added, but Worm was still not reassured.

"He is too old," Worm contended. "He belongs to death and he brings death with him. His breath is the breath of death."

Buffalo Hump decided just to ignore Worm. If Worm didn't want to visit with the Old One, then Worm could take himself home.

"The Old One isn't dead," he pointed out. "He belongs to the river, and he has killed a fine porcupine. It is hard to find a porcupine on the llano now. I want some of those quills for my wives—they always like porcupine quills."

He rode slowly on down to where the Old One was working—Worm hung back, but he did not leave for home. Buffalo Hump knew all the stories about Ephaniah, the Old One, the man who walked with a wolf. It was said that he had come to the West with the first whites, the ones who took the beaver. One story was that he had bathed in a stream where the river was born, in a place no one else had ever found, and that the water in that place had made him unable to die. It was said that he would only die when the world died. That was why he called himself the Lord of the Last Day. Because the sacred waters of the spring of life had bathed him he had been able to escape the dangers that had long ago finished all the other white men who took the beaver. Once, it was said, the fastest warriors the Blackfeet could muster got after the Old One for taking their beaver; they ran him hard for a hundred miles. Though the warriors were young and fleet, Ephaniah was faster. He ran on and on and could not be overtaken. It was said, too, that he had made a pact with the beaver people, so that they would let him hide in their houses when he was in danger. Worm believed that the Old One could breathe in water, like a fish. He bathed in the icy water of the high streams and did not seem to be affected. Some thought his power was in his hair, and that if he could be scalped he would die like other men. But no one yet had been able to take his hair, though he had more hair than any woman. Others thought that he could speak the language of animals and birds and even fish. Some had seen him put his head under water; they believed that he could call the fish and make them come to him when he was hungry. He was often seen eating fish when others could find no fish.

It was certain that the Old One knew the languages of many tribes; it might be that he knew the language of fish and birds as well, or the language of wolves. Buffalo Hump neither believed the stories nor disbelieved them. He was not a man who felt that he always knew the truth of things. He liked to watch and listen. A man such as the Old One must know things that other people had forgotten. It might be that the Old One had stumbled on the spring of life and could not die, but was that good? In life was much pain; what man would want to bear it forever? Besides, any man who was curious would want at last to enter the mystery, to walk the plains of the spirit land. Buffalo Hump was in no hurry to have his own life end, and yet the knowledge that it *would* end someday and that he would go to where the spirits were brought a kind of peace, after struggles and warfare and wounds and the quarrels of women.

And yet, what he had noticed the few times he had come across the Old One was that he seemed to be a cheerful man, and practical. His first request was always for tobacco, and so it was now.

"Those are fine quills you are taking from that porcupine," Buffalo Hump said, once he had dismounted at the Old One's camp.

"Leave off the talk, I'm counting and don't want to lose my count," Ephaniah said, which amused Buffalo Hump no end. Worm was a long distance back, quivering and trying to make a protective spell of some kind, while the Old One with the long white hair was merely counting the quills of his porcupine.

Buffalo Hump accepted his rebuke and sat quietly by the campfire as the old man plucked out each quill carefully and laid it on the buckskin. He worked with ease and skill; not once, while Buffalo Hump watched, did he break a single quill. Now and then Buffalo Hump turned and gestured for Worm to come to the camp, but Worm was too fearful. Soon the dusk hid him. When darkness filled the sky, with only the small speckle of firelight to interrupt it, the old man put the porcupine aside. He had not been able to finish his work before dark and evidently did not want to jeopardize it by working when the light was poor.

"That's a thousand and one, so far," Ephaniah said. "I'm stopping till daylight. Got any tobaccy?"

Buffalo Hump had none but Worm had plenty. He had filled several pouches with it during the great raid; once back with the tribe he meant to trade it for a young woman who belonged to old Spotted Bull, a warrior with a great taste for tobacco who was much too decrepit to need the young woman.

"Worm will give you some when he comes to the camp," Buffalo Hump said. "Right now he is scared you will witch him so he is staying back."

The Old One, Ephaniah, seemed to be amused by this comment. He cupped his hands around his mouth and produced the howl of a wolf. It was such a good howl that Buffalo Hump himself was startled for a moment—then, from the darkness, there came an answering howl, from the wolf that had trotted away when the two Comanches appeared.

It was only a few minutes later that Worm came into the camp. He did not enjoy being alone by the river with wolves howling all around. He did not want to fall asleep in a place where a wolf might come out of his dream and rip his throat.

Once he discovered that the Old One wanted some of his tobacco, Worm forgot about being witched; since the Old One was their host he had to give him *some* tobacco, or else be thought a bad guest, but he only offered him the smallest of the many plugs of tobacco he had looted from the Texans. The Old One accepted the plug without comment, but Buffalo Hump frowned.

"If you would be a little more generous the Old One might give us some of these nice porcupine quills," he said. "My wives would be pleased if they had such nice quills."

"You know Spotted Bull," Worm said. "He won't give me that woman unless he gets a lot of tobacco."

"You have enough tobacco to buy five or six women," Buffalo Hump told him. "If you can't talk Spotted Bull out of that woman, buy someone else. What you are doing is impolite. If you can't be a better guest than this, you deserve to have the dream wolf come and eat you."

Worm did not enjoy being spoken to so sternly. Buffalo Hump was a man whose moods were uncertain, and they were still a long way from home. Worm was torn; he very much wanted the young wife of Spotted Bull, yet he did not want to make an enemy of Buffalo Hump, not while they had such a way to travel. In the end he gave the Old One three more plugs of tobacco. The old man took them without comment.

In the morning, though, in the clear sunlight, he continued to remove quills from the hide of the porcupine.

Buffalo Hump sat in silence, watching. The great wolf who traveled with the Old One stood on a little bluff to the east. Worm would have liked to ask the Old One a few questions; he wanted particularly to know if the Old One could speak to fish. But Buffalo Hump discouraged him. He did not want the old man to be bothered while he was extracting the porcupine quills.

When the last quill had been coaxed from the porcupine's hide and laid on the little piece of buckskin, the Old One quickly separated about a quarter of the quills and offered them to Buffalo Hump, who nodded in thanks. The Old One then carefully folded the rest of the quills into the buckskin, put them in a little pouch he carried, and then went down to the cold river to wash his face.

While the two Comanches watched he put his head under the water. When he stood up he shook water off his long hair, as a dog might.

"I think he was just talking to the fish people," Worm said.

"What did he say to them?" Buffalo Hump asked. "He is an old white man. I think he just likes to wash himself."

Worm was stumped by the question. He had no idea what the Old One might have said to the fish. But he was convinced there was witching involved—witching of some kind. He was also wishing he had not given away so much tobacco. It would tell against him when he began his trade with Spotted Bull.

26.

THE SECOND TIME the young Comanches caught him, Famous Shoes thought it was probably going to be his time to die. He had found his grandmother at a poor little camp near the Arkansas but did not have a very good visit. His grandmother had immediately set in complaining about his grandfather and had kept up her complaining for two days. Every time Famous Shoes tried to get her to consider more important things, such as how the Kickapoo people had come to be, his grandmother grew irritated and brushed aside his question. Everybody knew of course that the Kickapoo people had come out of a hole in the earth at the time when there were only buffalo in the world. The Kickapoo had been chosen by the buffalo to be the first human beings; Father Buffalo himself had pawed open the hole and allowed the Kickapoo to come up from their deep caves. Everybody knew about the hole and Father Buffalo and that the Kickapoo had become human beings at a time before rain clouds, when all creatures received their moisture from the dew; they knew that rain had only begun to fall out of the sky once the Kickapoo people had made a prayer that caused the sky to let down its waters.

But what no one knew, or, at least, what his grandmother could not be bothered to tell him, was where the hole was that the Kickapoo had come out of.

The reason Famous Shoes wanted to find the hole so much was because he was convinced there were still underground people who lived somewhere in the earth. At night, when he slept with his ears close to the ground, the underground people spoke to him in dreams. Over the years he had come to want badly to go visit the underground people and learn the important things they knew. After all, they were the oldest people. His interest in tracks had only made him more interested in the underground people. Over the years he had become convinced that the underground people were watching the tracks that were made on the earth; sometimes, out of mischief, they altered the tracks of animals and made the tracks vanish. Quite a few animals that he tracked had simply ceased to make visible tracks; they vanished. These odd vanishings had happened so often that it occurred to him that perhaps the underground people had a way of opening the earth, so that animals being pursued could come down with them for a time, and rest.

Famous Shoes had no proof that the underground people could open the earth and take animals into it. He didn't know. He just knew that tracks sometimes stopped—it was one of the mysteries of his work. He thought that if he could find the hole the Kickapoo people had come out of he might be able to go down into the earth for a few days and see if there was someone there who could explain these matters to him.

When, on the third day, his grandmother finally grew tired of complaining about his grandfather's habit of wandering off and leaving her just when she needed him most, she listened to him explain his theory of the underground people and told him it was nonsense.

"There are no underground people," she informed him brusquely. "All the Kickapoo people came out of the hole except one old woman who was our mother, and she died and let her spirit go into the rocks. She is Old Rock Woman. Those dream people you hear when you sleep on the ground are witch people, and the reason you think those animals vanish is because you have been witched. The witch people take away the power of your eyes. The tracks are still there but you can't see them."

Then she cut up a polecat she had caught and started making polecat stew. While the stew was cooking his grandmother made clear to him that she thought it was time he was on his way.

"You can't eat polecat stew," she informed him. "The skunk people are your enemies. If you eat polecat stew you will shit too much and your eyes will grow even weaker."

Famous Shoes took the hint and left. He didn't believe his eyes were weak—it was just that his grandmother was stingy with her polecat stew.

It was while he was headed for a place on the caprock where there were many snake dens that the young Comanches caught him. Famous Shoes knew there were Comanches about because he saw the tracks of their horses, but he wanted to go to the snake-den place anyway and look for the hole that led into the earth. He didn't believe his grandmother's story about Old Rock Woman—it was just a way of getting rid of him. He thought his own theory made better sense and he wanted to spend a few days in the place of snake dens, looking for the hole that the Kickapoo people had come out of.

Of course he knew of Buffalo Hump's great raid long before Blue Duck and the other Comanche boys caught him. Six buffalo hunters were the first to tell him about it. They were well armed, but they were hurrying to get north of the Comanche country, out of fear. The Comanches were strong in their pride again—they were apt to kill any whites they encountered.

When Blue Duck and his haughty young friends spotted Famous Shoes they were on their way to try and trade a captive to old Slow Tree. The captive was a white boy who looked as if he had only a few more days of life in him. The young braves ran over and immediately pointed guns at Famous Shoes. They thought he would be better trading material than a white boy who was sick and near death.

"Slow Tree wanted to torture you before, so I will give you to him," Blue Duck told Famous Shoes. Blue Duck was arrogant and boastful; even as his friends were tying Famous Shoes' wrists Blue

Duck was trying to impress him with stories of his rapings on the raid. He poked Famous Shoes three or four times with his lance, not deep, but deep enough to draw blood. Famous Shoes didn't bother pointing out to the young man that his father, Buffalo Hump, had told him in front of many warriors that Famous Shoes was to be left alone. Such a reminder might only inflame Blue Duck—he was of an age to be defiant of his father.

"You should just leave this white boy and let him die," he told Blue Duck, but no one paid any attention. Once they had Famous Shoes securely tied they fell to quarreling about what to do with him—several of the braves wanted to torture him right there. One, a stout boy named Fat Knee, the grandson of old Spotted Bull, thought the best course would be to bury Famous Shoes in the ground, with only his head sticking out, and then ride off and leave him. Fat Knee was afraid of what Buffalo Hump might do when he found out they had delivered the man to Slow Tree—after all, Buffalo Hump had explicitly said he was to be let alone. Fat Knee had seen Buffalo Hump kill men over small disputes—he did not want to be killed over Famous Shoes. His argument was that if they just buried him and rode off, some animal would kill him; Buffalo Hump might never know about it.

"If we bury him good and poke out his eyes he won't last long," Fat Knee said.

Blue Duck was contemptuous of the suggestion—he was determined to have his way about the disposal of the prisoner.

"We are going to the camp of Slow Tree," he insisted pompously.

So Famous Shoes was put on a horse behind Fat Knee, and the braves hurried on to the camp of the old chief, a camp that lay below the caprock thirty or more miles to the south. Famous Shoes would have preferred to walk; he had never liked the pace of horses very much. It seemed to him that a man who bounced around on the back of horses risked injury to his testicles—indeed, he had known men whose testicles were injured when their horses suddenly jumped a stream or did something else injurious to the testicles.

But he was a prisoner of several hotheaded Comanche boys. Under the circumstances it would have been foolish to complain. Such boys were apt to change their minds at the slightest provocation. If he argued with them they might do what Fat Knee suggested, in which case he would be blind and unable to follow tracks that interested him. It was better to keep quiet and hope that Fat Knee didn't jump his sorrel horse over too many creeks.

27.

IT WAS ON THE DAYS when Ahumado paid him no attention, never once raising his binoculars to the Yellow Cliffs, that Scull came closest to despair. As long as Ahumado watched, Scull could feel that he was in a fair contest of wills. When Ahumado watched, Scull immediately responded. Though he had given up scratching Greek hexameters, or anything else, on the rock wall, he grabbed his file and pretended to be scratching something. If that didn't hold the old man's interest then Scull tried singing. He roared out the "Battle Hymn" at the top of his lungs—then, hoping to puzzle Ahumado, he warbled a few snatches of Italian opera, an aria or two that he knew imperfectly but that might fool the old dark man who sat on the blanket far below him. It was all a bluff, but it was his only chance. He had to keep Ahumado interested in order to stay interested himself; otherwise he was just a man hanging in a cage, eating raw birds and waiting to die. One book might have saved him; a tablet to write on might have saved him. He tried recalling his Shakespeare, his Pope, his Milton, his Virgil, his Burns—he even tried composing couplets in his head; he had always been partial to the well-rhymed couplet. But his memory, stretch as it might, would only get him through two or three hours of the day. His memory wasn't weak, he could snatch back much of the poetry that he had read, and not just poetry either. Lines came to him from Clarendon's *History*, from Gibbon, even from the Bible. His memory was vigorous and Scull enjoyed exercising it; but he wasn't at war with it and war was what he needed: someone or something to fight. For days he studied the cliff above and below him, thinking he might fight it. But the thought of the dark men, waiting with their machetes, made him hesitate about the climb.

Most of all, what he needed was Ahumado's attention. The Black Vaquero was a man worth fighting—Scull warbled and howled, sometimes yelling out curses, anything to let Ahumado know that he was still an opponent, a challenger, a captain. Ahumado heard him, too—often he would train the binoculars on the cage. Sometimes he would study Scull for many minutes—but Ahumado was sly. Often he would do his studying while Scull was napping, or distracted by the effort to catch some bird that was nervous and would not quite settle on the cage. Ahumado wanted to watch but not be watched in turn; it was another way of being behind, in a position to surprise his opponent. He was subtle with his attention; perhaps he knew that Scull drew his energy from it.

What Scull wanted was some way to trigger Ahumado's anger, as he had triggered it when he suggested a ransom. Ahumado's hatred would give him something to challenge and resist: not just the endless swinging over an abyss. Confinement induced torpor, and from torpor he could easily slip to passivity, resignation, death. He needed a fight to keep his blood up. He had been three weeks in the cage, long enough to grow sick of the sight and taste of raw fowl—yet long enough, too, that news of his plight might have reached Texas—such news would travel quickly, across even the most seemingly deserted country. A peon would mention something to a traveler and that single comment would radiate outward, like sunlight. Soldiers in the northern forts would soon hear of things happening below the border—of course the information might be distorted, but that was to be expected. Even well-informed journalists, writing for respectable papers, were not free of the risk of distortion.

Even now, for all Scull knew, the Governor of Texas might have got wind of his peril; with luck a rescue party might already be on the way.

While rescue was still a possibility, it was all the more imperative that he keep his blood up, which he could do best by reminding the old man on the blanket that he, Inish Scull, was still alive and kicking, still a fighter to be reckoned with.

Hardest were the days when Ahumado failed to lift the binoculars, when he seemed indifferent to the white man hanging in the cage. On those days, the days when Ahumado did not look, the birds seemed to know that Scull was losing. The great vultures roosted in a line on the cliff above him, waiting. Pigeons and doves, the staple of Scull's diet, rested in numbers on the cage itself; he could, with a little stealth, have caught a week's supply, and yet he didn't.

On such days it was often only the evening light that brought Scull out of despair. The space before him would grow golden at sunset, leaving the distant mountains in haze until the glow faded and they became blue and then indigo. Staring into the distance, Scull would slowly relax and forget, for a time, the struggle he had to wage.

It was on such an evening that he began to file away the bindings on the side of the cage that faced outward, away from the cliff. If the vast echoing space was to be his balm and his ally, he didn't want bars interfering with his relation to it. The bars were ugly anyway, and stained with bird droppings. He didn't want them between himself and the light of morning or evening.

Once, long before, as a youth, walking in Cambridge, he had seen a man of the East, a Buddhist monk who sat cross-legged in bright orange robes by the Charles River; the man was merely sitting, with his robe covering his legs and his hands folded in his lap, watching the morning sunlight scatter gold over the gray water.

The memory came back to Scull as he cut through the bindings at the front of his cage. The Buddhist had been an old man, with a shaven head and a long drooping wisp of beard; he had attentive eyes and he seemed to be thoughtfully studying the air as it brightened amid the buildings of Cambridge.

Scull, high on his cliff, thought he might emulate the old Buddhist man he had seen only that once, on a Cambridge morning, by the Charles River. When it came to air, he had, before him, a grander prospect for study than the old man had by the Charles. Before him, indeed, was a very lexicon of air, a dictionary or cyclopedia that would be hard to exhaust. He could study the gray air of morning, the white air of the bright noon, the golden air of evening. He wanted no bars to interfere with his contemplation, his study of the airy element—and to that end he sawed and sawed, with his little file, well into the deep Mexican night.

28.

AHUMADO HAD JUST walked out of the cave when Scull gave a great yell. At first Ahumado didn't look up. He knew well that the white man, Scull, craved his attention—the stronger prisoners always craved his attention, or, at least, the attention of the people in the camp. They didn't want to be forgotten by the people who were alive—they wanted to remind everyone that they were still of the living.

But then one of the vaqueros shouted and Ahumado looked up in time to see Scull heave the front of the cage as far as he could pitch it. The people sitting with coffee or tobacco jumped up when they saw what was happening—they got out of the way of the piece of cage that was falling. The only thing that didn't get out of the way was a red hen; the falling piece of cage hit the hen and caused her to flop around for a minute of two—then she died.

Ahumado picked up the binoculars and looked up at the man in the cage—for a moment he was annoyed because he supposed Scull had decided to commit suicide, as the sly Comanche had. With the front of the cage gone Scull could jump to his death at any time, which was a thing not to be tolerated. Ahumado did not put prisoners in the cage in order to provide them with a choice in the matter of their own deaths.

Yet, when Ahumado looked, he saw that Scull did not seem to be getting ready to jump. He was sitting comfortably in the cage, singing one of the songs he was always singing. This penchant for song was another annoying thing about the man. It made the villagers restive. Many of them considered Scull to be a powerful witch. There were a few, probably, who thought that Scull might prove to be more powerful than Ahumado. Why was he singing? Why wouldn't he just die? The most logical answer was that Scull was a witch. Ahumado had carefully considered that possibility when Scull began scratching on the rock, and he was still a little uneasy about it. The notion that Scull might make the mountain fall had come to him in a dream, and dreams of that sort were not to be lightly disregarded. Although time passed and the mountain didn't fall, Ahumado did not forget his dream and continued to be suspicious of Scull. Witches were often known to bide their time. An old witch from the south, who had a grudge against his father, had caused a tumor to grow in his father's stomach. Though they caught the old witch and cut her throat, the tumor continued to grow in his father's stomach until it killed him. It was a thing Ahumado had never forgotten. He knew better than to underestimate the patience of a powerful witch.

Now Scull had cut open his cage—he could leap out if he wanted to. The old woman Hema, the one who had foamed at the mouth when she was listening to the mountain, came hobbling over, carrying the red hen that the fallen cage had killed.

"We should cut open this hen and look inside her," Hema said. "He might have put a message in her."

"No," Ahumado said, "if we look inside her we will only find chicken guts."

In his view vision people who tried to see the future by looking at the entrails of animals were frauds. The future might be visible in the smoke that rose from a campfire, if only one knew how to look into the smoke, but he didn't believe that the spirits who made the future would bother leaving messages in the guts of goats or hens.

He gave old Hema the hen, to get rid of her, but before she left she came out with another prophecy, one that was a little more plausible.

"A great bird is going to come and get the white man soon," old

Hema said. "The great bird lives on a rock at the top of the world. The reason the white man cut away the front of his cage is because the great bird will soon be coming to fly him back to Texas."

"Go away and eat your hen," Ahumado said. She was a long-winded old woman and he did not want to waste his mornings listening to her. Still, his mind was not entirely easy where Scull was concerned. Once or twice, when he looked up and saw the white man sitting there in the open cage, he considered taking his Winchester and shooting the man right where he hung. That would end his worry about the mountain falling down. The mention of the great bird was worrisome too; there were many stories about a great bird that lived at the top of the world. Perhaps the white man's strange singing was in the language of the birds. Perhaps he was telling the eagles that flew around the cage to go to the top of the world and bring the great bird. The language that Scull sang in was not the language of the Texans; perhaps it was the language of the birds.

To make matters even more uncertain, that very afternoon the largest vulture that anyone had ever seen came soaring over the cliff and flew down past the cage. The vulture was so large that for a moment Ahumado thought it might *be* the great bird. Though it proved to be only an exceptionally large vulture, its appearance annoyed him. Big Horse Scull was proving to be the most troublesome prisoner he had ever captured; Scull did so many things that were witchlike that it might be better just to kill him.

That evening, by the campfire, he discussed the matter with old Goyeto, the skinner. Usually old Goyeto had only one response when asked about a prisoner; he wanted to skin the prisoner at once. This time, though, to Ahumado's surprise, Goyeto took a different tack.

"You could sell him to the Texans," Goyeto said. "They might give you many cattle—nobody around here has very many cattle."

Ahumado remembered that Scull had mentioned a ransom. He had never bargained with the Texans—he had only taken from them, in the way of a bandit. But the old simpleminded skinner,

Goyeto, had made a good point. Perhaps the Texans would want Big Horse Scull so badly that they would bring them a lot of cattle. Scull had said so himself—because he had said it, Ahumado had scorned the idea. He did not like suggestions from prisoners.

Besides, he had supposed that Scull would soon lose heart, like other men in the cage. But Scull was not like other men, and he had not lost heart. He had boldly cut away the front of his cage, he scratched on the face of the mountain, he sang loudly, and he ate raw birds as if he liked them. All this was annoying behavior, so annoying that Ahumado was still tempted just to shoot the man—then if the great bird came to free him he would only find a corpse.

There had not been much to eat lately, in the camp. The thought of cattle made Goyeto's mouth water, but, of course, he still wanted to use his sharp skinning knives on Big Horse Scull. It would be vexing to send him home without skinning even a little part of him. Goyeto knew that would vex Ahumado too.

It was then that Goyeto remembered the small *federale*, Major Alonso, a strong fighter they had been lucky to catch alive. Major Alonso had killed six of their *pistoleros* before one of the dark men caught him with a bola. When they tied Major Alonso to the skinning post, Goyeto had had one of his most brilliant ideas. Without even telling Ahumado what he had in mind he had delicately removed the Major's eyelids. Tied to the skinning post, with no eyelids or any means of shielding his eyes, the Major had to bear the full light of the August sun for a whole day, and by the end of it he was insane. It was as if the sun had burned away his brain. Major Alonso gibbered and made the sounds of a madman.

Ahumado was so pleased by Goyeto's inventiveness with Major Alonso that he did not bother to torture the man more. Why torture a man whose brain had been burned up? They merely took away the Major's clothes and chased him out into the desert. He stumbled around with no eyelids until he died. A vaquero found his body only a few miles from camp.

"I could take his eyelids and we could leave him in the sun until the Texans come with the cattle," Goyeto suggested, to Ahumado. "I guess he would be crazy, like that *federale*."

"Ah," Ahumado said.

It was rare that the Black Vaquero exclaimed. It usually meant that he was impressed. Goyeto was pleased with himself, for having had such a timely idea. That very afternoon Ahumado dispatched a caballero that he trusted, Carlos Diaz, to Texas to tell the Texans that they could have Scull if they brought a thousand cattle to a grassy place below the river, where Ahumado's vaqueros would take them.

Ahumado then wasted no time hauling Scull up the cliff. The dark men swarmed over him before he could run, although he did stab one of them fatally with the small file he had concealed—he shoved the file straight into the dark man's jugular vein, causing him to lose so much blood that he died. Scull was taken down the cliff and pinioned securely to the skinning post—Goyeto finally got to use his knives. He took away Big Horse Scull's eyelids with even more delicacy than he had managed with the *federale*, Major Alonso. Scull fought his bonds and cried out curses but there was so little pain involved in the operation that he didn't moan or groan. Ahumado seemed pleased by the skill with which Goyeto worked.

But then, before the sun could begin to bring its searing heat into Big Horse Scull's brain, clouds, heavy and dark, begin to roll in from the west. Thunder shook the cliffs and hard rain fell. Before the little stream of blood from the cuts died on Scull's cheeks the rain washed the blood away. The thunder was so loud that some of the people started to run away. They were more than ever convinced that Scull might bring the mountain down on them because of what had been done to his eyes. Goyeto thought so too, for a time. He began to regret that he had even had such a crazy idea. Why had he ignored all the signs that Scull was a witch? If the mountain fell on them he would be dead, and even if it didn't, Ahumado might kill him for exercising such bad judgment in regard to Big Horse Scull.

The mountain didn't fall, though the sun was not seen for three days, during which time nothing bad at all happened to Captain Scull's brain. Ahumado, though, exhibited no doubt—he had another cage made for Scull and put it right in the center of the village, not far from where he sat on his blanket. He wanted all the people to see the man without eyelids. Scull did not curse anymore. The women were instructed to feed him, and he ate. He was silent, watching Ahumado out of eyes he could not close.

On the fourth day the sun came back and Scull was immediately tied to the skinning post, so he could not shield his eyes. Even so, Goyeto worried. It was only May. The sun was not strong, as it had been in August, when he had removed Major Alonso's eyelids.

"I don't know," Goyeto said. "This is not a very strong sun."

Ahumado was getting tired of the old skinner and his endless anxieties. He wished Goyeto had a wife to distract him, but unfortunately Goyeto's wife had grown a tumor almost as large as the one that had killed his own father. Not many women were willing even to couple with Goyeto, because he smelled always of blood. Probably some of the women were afraid he might skin *them*, if he got angry.

"This is the only sun there is," Ahumado pointed out. "Do you think you can find another?"

"I can't find another," Goyeto said meekly. "There is only this sun. What if it doesn't make him crazy before the Texans come with all those cattle?"

"Then I may let you skin the rest of him," Ahumado said.

Then he gave Goyeto a hard look, the kind of look he gave people when he wanted them to go away and do so promptly.

Goyeto knew what that look meant. He had talked too much. Immediately he got up and went away.

29.

WHEN SLOW TREE saw Famous Shoes bounced into camp on the back of Fat Knee's sorrel horse, he looked severely displeased, but Blue Duck, not Famous Shoes, was the object of his displeasure.

Instead of yanking the Kickapoo off the horse and marching him straight to the torture post, as Blue Duck had supposed he would do, Slow Tree took a knife and cut Famous Shoes' bonds himself.

Then the old chief did worse. To Blue Duck's intense annoyance, Slow Tree apologized to Famous Shoes.

"I am sorry you were disturbed," Slow Tree said. "I hope you were not taken too far from where you wanted to be."

At this point, Blue Duck, a rude and impatient boy, interrupted.

"He was only looking in snake holes," he said. "I caught him and brought him here so you could torture him. He is a Kickapoo and should be tortured to death."

Slow Tree paid no attention to the rude young man.

"Were you catching snakes?" he asked Famous Shoes, in mild tones.

"Oh no," Famous Shoes said. "I was looking for the hole the People came out of. I thought some snakes might have found the hole and started living in it."

"Oh, that hole is far to the north," Slow Tree said, in a pompous tone, as if he knew perfectly well which of the many holes in the earth the People had come out of.

"I thought it might be around the caprock somewhere," Famous Shoes replied, in a mild tone. He wanted to be as polite with Slow Tree as Slow Tree was being with him. As he was not of the Comanche tribe, certain courtesies had to be respected, but, once these courtesies had been observed, Slow Tree might turn back into a cruel old killer and torture him after all. The chief didn't appear to be in a torturing mood, but he was a crafty old man and his mood could always change.

Blue Duck, though, continued to behave with poor manners. He looked scornfully at Slow Tree, who was, after all, one of the most respected of the chiefs of the Comanche people. He spoke scornfully, also. So far he had not even bothered to dismount, a serious discourtesy in itself. All the other Comanche boys had immediately dismounted. But Blue Duck still sat on his prancing horse.

"When you saw this Kickapoo in my father's camp you wanted to torture him," Blue Duck said. "You wanted to put scorpions in his nose. We caught him and brought him to you, though it was out of our way. We were going after antelope when we saw this man. I would not have brought him to you if I had known you would only turn him loose. I would have killed him myself."

Blue Duck's tone was so rude that even his own companions looked unhappy. Fat Knee walked away—he did not want to be associated with such rude behavior.

Slow Tree looked up at Blue Duck casually, with no expression on his face. It was as if he had just noticed the loud-spoken boy who had not had the manners to dismount. He looked Blue Duck up and down and his eyes became the color of sleet. He still had a knife in his hand, the one he had used to set Famous Shoes free.

"You are not a Comanche, you are a *mexicano*," Slow Tree said. "Get out of my camp."

Blue Duck was shocked—it was as if the old man had slapped him. No one had ever offered him such an insult before. He wanted to kill old Slow Tree, but the chief was backed by more than thirty warriors, and his own friends had dismounted and quickly walked away from him. They were all being so polite it disgusted him; it made him think they were cowards. He was sorry he had ever ridden with them.

"Go on, leave," Slow Tree said. "If your father has any sense he will listen to the elders and make you leave his camp too. You are rude like the *mexicanos*—you don't belong with the Comanche."

"I am a *Comanche!*" Blue Duck insisted, in a loud voice. "I went on the great raid! I killed many whites and raped their women. You should give me food at least."

Slow Tree, not amused, stood his ground.

"You will get no food in my camp," he said.

"Then I will take my prisoner!" Blue Duck said, riding toward Famous Shoes, who stood just where he had been standing when Slow Tree released him.

"You have no prisoner," Slow Tree said. "Your father granted this man protection. I heard him say so myself, with my two ears. You were there. You heard the same words I heard, and they were your father's words. Your father said not to interfere with this man, and you should have obeyed."

"You are afraid of my father," Blue Duck said. "You are old."

Slow Tree didn't answer, but several of his warriors scowled. They did not like hearing their chief insulted.

Slow Tree just stood, looking.

"You have no prisoner," he repeated. "You had better be gone."

Blue Duck saw that the situation was against him. His own friends had walked away. He could not reclaim his prisoner without fighting the whole camp. Fat Knee had been right to begin with. They should have tortured the Kickapoo themselves. He himself had insisted that they take him to Slow Tree, never supposing that Slow Tree would consider that he was bound by Buffalo Hump's instructions regarding the Kickapoo tracker. He thought Slow Tree might be so happy to get the Kickapoo to torture that he would reward him with a fine horse, or, at least, a woman. Now he had lost his prisoner and had been insulted in front of the whole camp. He was angry at his father, at Slow Tree, and at Famous Shoes, all three. He had expected to gain much respect, from bringing Slow Tree such a desirable prisoner; but Slow Tree was more interested in remaining at peace with Buffalo Hump. Instead of gaining respect, and perhaps a horse and a woman, he had been humiliated by an old fat chief.

Without another word he turned his horse and rode out of Slow Tree's camp. He didn't look back, or wait for his companions to join him. He didn't even know if they *would* join him. Probably they, too, were only interested in staying in good with his father, Buffalo Hump.

When Blue Duck rode away, only Fat Knee chose to follow him. The other boys made themselves at home in Slow Tree's camp.

Famous Shoes watched the two young Comanches ride away— he did his best to maintain a calm demeanor. He figured the only reason he was alive was because Slow Tree, who still had sleet in his eyes, did not want trouble with Buffalo Hump, not when Buffalo Hump had just led the great raid that all the warriors were talking about—and all the travelers too. Famous Shoes was still a Kickapoo, in the camp of Comanches—and some of the young warriors were undoubtedly more reckless than Slow Tree. They didn't have a chief's responsibilities, and most of them probably didn't care what Buffalo Hump thought. They were free Comanches and would feel that they had every right to kill a Kickapoo if they could catch one.

"I think I will go now," Famous Shoes said. "I want to keep looking for that hole where the People came out."

Slow Tree no longer looked at him so politely. Though he felt obliged to respect Buffalo Hump's wishes in this matter, he did not look happy about it. The braves who stood behind him didn't look friendly, either.

"That hole is to the north, where the great bears live," Slow Tree said. "If you are not careful one of those bears might eat you."

Famous Shoes knew that Slow Tree himself was the bear most likely to eat him—or at least to do something bad to him. It was not a place to linger, not with the old chief so moody. He got his knife and his pouch back from the Comanche boy who had taken them, and trotted out of the camp.

30.

CALL FOUND GUS MCCRAE asleep by the river, under a bluff that looked familiar. Long before, when the two of them were young rangers, Augustus had stumbled off that very bluff one night and twisted his ankle badly when he hit. Then, because of Clara Forsythe, Gus had been too agitated to watch where he was going; now, an hour after sunup, he was snoring away and probably hung over because he pined for the same woman. In a boat, turning slowly in the middle of the river, an old man was fishing. An old man had been fishing the night Gus hurt his ankle—for all Call knew, it might even be the same old man, in the same boat. Years had worn off the calendar, but what had changed? The river still flowed, the old man still fished, and Augustus McCrae still pined for Clara.

"Get up, the Governor wants to see us," Call said, when he got back to where his friend was sleeping. Gus had stopped snoring; he was nestled comfortably against the riverbank with his hat over his eyes.

"It's too early to be worrying with a governor," Gus said, without removing his hat.

"It ain't early, the sun's up," Call said. "Everybody in town is up, except you. The barber is waiting to give you a good shave."

Gus sat up and reached for an empty whiskey bottle by his side. He heaved the bottle out into the river and drew his pistol.

"Here, don't shoot," Call said. "There's an old man fishing, right in front of you."

"Yell at him to move, then, Woodrow," Augustus said. "I'm in the mood for target practice."

He immediately fired three shots at the bottle, to no effect. The bottle floated on, and the old fisherman continued to fish, unperturbed.

"That fisherman must be deaf," Call said. "He didn't realize he was nearly shot."

Gus stood up, shot twice more, and then heaved his pistol at the bottle, scoring a solid hit. The bottle broke and sank, and the pistol sank with it.

"Now, that was foolishness," Call said.

Gus waded into the river and soon fished out his gun.

"Which barber did you hire to shave me?" he inquired.

"The small one, he's cheaper," Call said, as they walked back toward town.

"I don't like that short barber, he farts," Gus said. "The tall one's slow but he don't fart as often."

They were almost to the barbershop when a shriek rent the calm of the morning. The shriek came from the direction of the Colemans' house—one shriek followed by another and another.

"That's Pearl," Gus said. "Nobody else in town can bellow that loud."

The shrieks caused a panic in the streets. Everyone assumed that the Comanches had come back. Men in wagons hastily grabbed their weapons.

"It might not be Indians—it might just be a cougar or a bear that's strayed into town," Gus said, as he and Call, keeping to what cover there was, ran toward the Colemans' house.

"Whatever it is you best load your gun," Call said. "You shot at that bottle, remember?"

Gus immediately loaded his pistol, which still dripped.

Call happened to glance around, toward the house where Maggie boarded. Maggie Tilton stood on her landing in plain view, looking at whatever caused Pearl Coleman to shriek. Maggie had her hands clasped to her mouth and stood as if stunned.

"It ain't Indians, Gus," Call said. "There's Maggie. She ain't such a fool as to be standing in plain sight if there's Indians around."

Yet the shrieks continued to rake the skies, one after another.

"Could she be snakebit?" Gus asked. "I recall she was always worried about snakes."

"If she's snakebit, where's Bill?" Call said. "I know he's a sound sleeper, but he couldn't sleep through this."

Two more women were in sight, two laundresses who had been making their way back from the well with loads of laundry. Like Maggie they were looking at something. Like her, they had clasped their hands over their mouths in horror. They had dropped their laundry baskets so abruptly that the baskets tipped over, spilling clean laundry into the dirt.

"It might just be a big bear," Call said. On occasion bears still wandered into the outskirts of town.

The shrieks were coming from behind the Coleman house. There was a big live oak tree a little ways back from the house—in happier days Gus and Long Bill had spent many careless hours in its shade, gossiping about women and cards, cards and women.

As the two men approached the corner of the Coleman house,

pistols drawn, they slowed, out of caution. Pearl Coleman shrieked as loudly as ever. Gus suddenly stopped altogether, filled with dread, such a dread as he had not felt in years. He didn't want to look around the corner of the Coleman house.

Woodrow Call didn't want to look, either, but of course they had to. In the streets behind them, men were crouched behind wagons, their rifles ready. Whatever it was had to be faced.

"Somebody's dead or she wouldn't be shrieking like that," Gus said. "I fear something's happened to Bill. I fear it, Woodrow."

Both of them remembered Long Bill's doleful face, as it had been for the last few weeks; no longer was he the stoical man who had once walked the Jornada del Muerto and eaten gourd soup.

Call stepped around the corner, his pistol cocked, not knowing what he expected, but he did not expect what he saw, which was Long Bill Coleman, dead at the end of a hang rope, dangling from a stout limb of the live oak tree, a kicked-over milking stool not far from his feet.

Pearl Coleman stood a few yards away, shrieking, unable to move.

The pistol in Call's hand became heavy as an anvil, suddenly. With difficulty he managed to uncock it and poke it back in its holster.

Gus stepped around the corner too.

"Oh, my God . . ." he said. "Oh, Billy . . ."

"After all we went through," Call said. The shock was too much. He could not finish his thought.

The townspeople, seeing that there was no battle, rose up behind wagons and barrels. They edged out of stores, women and men. The barbers came out in their aprons; their customers, some half shaven, followed them. The butcher came, cleaver in hand, carrying half a lamb. The two laundresses, their work wasted, had not moved—the clean clothes were still strewn in the dirt.

Above them, Maggie Tilton, clearly pregnant and too shocked to trust herself to walk down her own steps, stood sobbing.

Augustus holstered his gun and came a few steps closer to the swaying body. Long Bill's toes were only an inch off the ground; his face was purple-black.

"Billy could have done this easier if he'd just taken a gun," he said, in a weak voice. "Remember how Bigfoot Wallace showed us where to put the gun barrel, back there years ago?"

"A gun's noisy," Call said. "I expect he done it this way so as not to wake up Pearl."

"Well, she's awake now," Gus said.

The silent crowd stood watching as the two of them went to the tree and cut their old friend down.

31.

TOGETHER CALL and Augustus cut Long Bill down, pulled the noose from his neck, and then, feeling weak, left him to the womenfolk. One of the laundresses covered him with a sheet that had spilled out when her basket overturned. Maggie came down the steps and went to Pearl, but Pearl was beyond comforting. She sobbed deep guttural sobs, as hoarse as a cow's bellow. Maggie got her to sit down on an overturned milk bucket. The two laundresses helped Maggie as best they could.

"I don't want him going to heaven with his face so black," Pearl said suddenly. "They'll take him for a nigger."

Maggie didn't answer. The undertaker had been killed in the raid—funerals since then had been hasty and plain.

Call and Gus caught their horses and rode on to the Governor's. Though the distance was not great, both felt too weak to walk that far.

"What are we going to say to the Governor, now that this has happened?" Augustus asked.

"He's the Governor, I guess he can do the talking," Call said, as they rode up the street.

When informed of the tragedy, Governor Pease shook his head and stared out the window for several minutes. A military man was with him when the two captains came in, a Major Nettleson of the U.S. Cavalry.

"That's three suicides since the raid," Governor Pease said. "Raids on that scale have a very poor effect on the nerves of the populace. Happens even in the army, don't it, Major?"

"Why, yes, we sometimes have a suicide or two, after a violent scrap," the Major said. He looked at the rangers impatiently, either because they were late or because they were interrupting his own interview with the Governor.

"Bill Coleman had been with us through it all, Governor," Call said. "We never expected to lose him that way."

Governor Pease turned from the window and sighed. Call noticed that the Governor's old brown coat was stained; since the raid he had often been seen in an untidy state. He had grown careless with his tobacco juice, too. Judging from the carpet, he missed his spittoon about as often as he hit it.

"It's one more murder we can charge to Buffalo Hump," the Governor said. "A people can only tolerate so much scalping and raping. They get nervous and start losing sleep. The lack of sound sleep soon breaks them down. The next thing you know they start killing themselves rather than worry about when the Comanches will show up again."

Just then Inez Scull came striding into the room. Major Nettleson, who had been sitting, hefted himself up—he was a beefy man. Madame Scull merely glanced at him, but her glance caused the Major to flush. Augustus, who was merely waiting dully for the interview to be over, noted the flush.

"Why, there you are, Johnny Nettleson," Inez said. "Why'd you leave so early? I rather prefer for my house guests to stay around for breakfast, though I suppose that's asking too much of a military man."

"It's my fault, Inez," the Governor said quickly. "I wanted a word with the Major—since he's leaving, I thought we'd best meet early."

"No, Johnny ain't leaving, not today," Madame Scull said. "I've planned a picnic and I won't allow anything to spoil it. It's rare that I get a major to picnic with."

Then she looked at Governor Pease defiantly. The Governor, surprised, stared back at her, while Major Nettleson, far too embarrassed to speak, stared solemnly at his own two feet.

Augustus suspected that it was stout Major Nettleson that Madame Scull was trotting with now; the picnic she was anxious not to have spoiled might not be of the conventional kind. But this suspicion only registered with him dully. His mind was on the night before, most of which, as usual, he had spent drinking with Long Bill Coleman. It was a close night, and the saloon an immoderately smelly place. During the raid a bartender had been stabbed and scalped in a rear corner of the barroom; the bartender had been murdered, and so had the janitor, which meant that the bloody corner had been only perfunctorily cleaned. On close nights the smells made pleasant drinking difficult, so difficult that Gus had left a little early, feeling that he needed a breath of river air.

"Come along, Billy, it's late," he said to Long Bill.

"Nope, I prefer to drink indoors, Gus," Long Bill replied. "I'm less tempted to seek whores when I drink inside."

Augustus took the comment for a joke and went on out into the clean air, to nestle comfortably by the riverbank all night. But now the remark about whores, the last words he would ever hear from Long Bill Coleman, came back to mind. Had Bill, so deeply attached to Pearl, really been seeking whores; or was it, as he had supposed, a joke?

He didn't know, but he did know that he hated being in the Governor's office, listening to Inez Scull banter with her new conquest, Major Nettleson. Long Bill's death was as much a shock as Clara's marriage. It left him indifferent to everything. Why was he there? What did he care about rangering now? He'd never stroll the streets of Austin again, either with the woman or the friend; at the thought, such a hopeless sadness took him that he turned and walked out the door, passing directly in front of the Governor, the Major, and Madame Scull as he went.

"I'll say, now where's McCrae going?" the Governor said in surprise. "The two of you have just got here. I haven't even had a moment to bring up the business at hand."

"I expect he's sad about our pard—he'd ridden with the man for many years," Call said.

"Well, but he was your friend too, and you ain't walked out," Governor Pease said.

"No," Call said, though he wished the Governor would get down to business. He thought he knew how Gus felt, when he walked out.

The Governor seemed momentarily thrown off by Gus's departure—he bent right over the spittoon but still managed to miss it with a stream of tobacco juice. Madame Scull had relaxed, but Major Nettleson hadn't.

"Was there something in particular, Governor?" Call asked finally. "Long Bill will be needing a funeral and a burial soon. I'd like to arrange it nice, since he was our friend."

"Of course, excuse me," Governor Pease said, coming back to himself. "Arrange it nice and arrange it soon. There's work waiting, for you and McCrae and whatever troop you can round up."

"What's the work?" Call asked.

"Ahumado has Captain Scull," the Governor said. "He's offered to exchange him for a thousand cattle, delivered in Mexico. I've consulted the legislature and they think we better comply, though we know it's a gamble."

"The U.S. Army cannot be involved—not involved!" Major Nettleson said, suddenly and loudly. "I've made that plain to Governor Pease and I'll make it plain to you. I'm trying to train three regiments of cavalry to move against the Comanche and finish them. I've no men to spare for Mexico and even if I did have men, I wouldn't send them below the border—now that there *is* a border, more or less. Not a man of mine will set foot across the Rio Grande—not a man. I must firmly decline to be involved, though of course I'd be happy to see Captain Scull again if he's alive."

Both the Governor and Call were nonplussed by this stream of talk. Madame Scull, however, was merely amused.

"Oh, shut up, Johnny, and stop telling lies," she said, with a flirtatious toss of her head.

"What lies? I'm merely pointing out that the U.S. Army can't put itself out every time a bandit demands a ransom."

"No, the lie was that you'd be happy to see Inish again," Madame Scull said. "You weren't happy to see him when he was your commanding officer, I seem to recall."

"Not happy . . . I fail to understand . . . really, Madame," Major Nettleson protested, turning cherry red from embarrassment.

"Inish always thought you were a fat-gutted fool," Madame Scull said. "He said as much many times. The only man in the whole army Inish thought had any sense was Bob Lee, and Bob Lee's a little too stiff-necked for my taste."

Then she looked at Governor Pease, who was staring at her as if she was insane.

"Close your mouth, Ed, before a bug flies down your gullet," she said. "I'm taking Johnny off to our picnic now. I've managed to find virtues in him that Inish never suspected."

As Madame Scull was about to leave she paused a moment and looked at Call.

"A thousand cattle is a good deal more than Inish is worth," she said. "I wouldn't give three cats for him myself, unless the cats were mangy. If you see that yellow gal of mine while you're looking for Inish, bring her back too. I have yet to find a match for that yellow gal. She had the Cuba touch."

"I doubt we'll spot her, ma'am," Call said. "The Comanches went north and we're going south."

"And you think life is that simple, do you, Captain?" Inez Scull said, with more than a little mockery in her tone. "You think it's just a matter of plain north or south, do you?"

Call was perplexed. He could not clear his mind of the image of Long Bill Coleman, hanging dead by his own hand from a live oak limb. More than ten years of his life had been bound up with Long Bill Coleman—now he was dead. He found it hard to attend to the mocking woman in front of him—his mind wanted to drift backward down the long river of the past, to the beginning of his ranger-ing days. He wished Madame Scull would just go away and not be teasing him with questions.

"I hope you'll come to tea with me before you leave, Captain," Madame Scull said. "I might be able to teach you that there's more to life than north and south."

With that she turned on her heels and left.

"Can't interfere with Mexico, not the U.S. Cavalry," Major Net-tleson said. Then he left, putting on his military hat as he went through the door.

Governor Pease spat once more, inaccurately, at the brass spit-toon.

"If I had a wife like that I'd run farther than Mexico," the Gov-ernor said, quietly. His own wife had only raised her voice to him once in twenty years of marriage, and that was because the baby was about to knock the soup pot off the table.

Call didn't know what to say. He thought he had best stick to simple, practical considerations and not let himself be sidetracked by what Madame Scull felt, or didn't feel, about her husband.

"You mentioned a thousand head of cattle, Governor," Call said.

"Yes, that's the demand," Governor Pease said, in a slow, weary voice. "A thousand head—we have a month to make the delivery."

"What if the Captain's already dead?" Call asked.

"Why, that's the gamble," the Governor said. "The man might take our cattle and send us Inish's head in a sack."

"Or he might just take the cattle and vanish," Call said.

"Yes, he might—but I have to send you," the Governor said. "At least I have to ask you if you'll go—I'm not forgetting that I just sent you off on a wild-goose chase just when we needed you here the most. But Ahumado has Inish and he's set a price on him. Inish is still a hero. They'll impeach me if I don't try to get him back."

"Where will we get the cattle?" Call asked.

"Why, the legislature will vote the money for the cattle, I'm sure," the Governor said.

Call started to ask a practical question, only to have his mind stall. He saw Long Bill's black face again and couldn't seem to think beyond it. The Governor talked and the Governor talked, but Call was simply unable to take in what he was saying, a fact Governor Pease finally noticed.

"Wrong time—you've got your friend to bury," he said. "We can talk of these arrangements tomorrow, when your sad duty has been done."

"Thanks," Call said. He turned and was about to leave, but Governor Pease caught his arm.

"Just one more thing, Captain Call," he said. "Inez mentioned having you to tea—don't go. The state of Texas needs you more than she does, in this troubled hour."

"Yes sir, I expect it does," Call said.

32.

When Call got back to the ranger corrals he heard the sound of hammering from behind the barn. Ikey Ripple, the oldest ranger left alive, was making Long Bill a coffin—or, at least, he was supervising. Ikey had never advanced much in the ranks of the rangers due to his taste for supervising, as opposed to actually working. He and Long Bill had been sincere friends, though, which is why he stood beside Deets to supervise the sawing of every plank and the driving of every nail.

"Billy was particular and he'd want to be laid out proper," Ikey said, when Call joined the group, which consisted of the entire ranger troop, such as it then was.

Augustus sat on one end of the wagon that was to haul Long Bill to his grave: he was silent, somber, and drunk. Deets put the coffin together meticulously, well aware that he was being watched by the whole troop. Lee Hitch and Stove Jones had spent a night of insobriety in a Mexican cantina; they were so hung over as to be incapable of carpentry. Stove Jones was bald and Lee Hitch shaggy—they spent their evenings in the cantina because they had ceased to be able to secure adequate credit in the saloons of Austin. Call noticed that neither man was wearing a sidearm.

"Where's your guns?" he asked them.

Lee Hitch looked at his hip and saw no pistol, which seemed to surprise him as much as if his whole leg were missing.

"Well, where is it, damn it?" he asked himself.

"I don't require you to swear," Call said. "We've a mission to go on soon and you'll need your weapons. Where's yours, Stove?"

Stove Jones took refuge in deep, silent solemnity when asked questions he didn't want to answer. He stared back at Call solemnly, but Call was not to be bluffed by such tactics, forcing Stove to rack his brain for a suitable answer.

"I expect it's under my saddle," he said finally.

"They pawned their guns, Woodrow," Augustus said. "I say just let them fight the Comanches with their pocketknives. A man who would sink so low as to pawn his own pistol deserves a good scalp-ing, anyway."

"It's not the Comanches," Call told him. "It's Ahumado. He's got Captain Scull and he's offered to ransom him for a thousand cattle."

"That lets me out—I ain't got a thousand cattle," Gus said.

"The state will buy the cattle. We have to deliver them and bring back the Captain," Call told him.

"Well, that still lets me out because I ain't a cowboy," Gus said. "I have no interest in gathering cattle for some old bandit. Let him just come and steal them. He can leave off the Captain if he wants to."

Call noted that the coffin was almost finished. He saw no reason to pursue an argument with Gus at such a time. In his present mood Gus would easily find a reason to disagree with anything he might say. The men were all stunned by Long Bill's suicide. The best pro-cedure would probably be to go on and hold the funeral, if the women were up to it. With no undertaker and no preacher, funerals were rude affairs, but they were still funerals. The womenfolk could sing, and the ceremony would draw the men away from the saloons for a few minutes. Once their old *compañero* was laid to rest there would be time to consider the matter of Ahumado and the thousand cattle.

"We don't have to worry about the mission right this minute," Call said. "We've got a month to deliver the cattle. Let's go see how the womenfolk are doing, while Deets finishes the coffin."

"Nearly done," Deets said, wondering if he was expected to go to the funeral—or if he would even be allowed to. He worked carefully on the coffin; one of the laundresses had brought over an old quilt to line it with. Deets took special care to see that the lining was laid in smoothly. He knew that the spirits of suicides were restless; they were more likely than other people to float out of their graves and become spooks, harassing those who had offended them in life. He was not aware that he had offended Long Bill—he had helped him with quite a few chores, but all that might be forgotten if he then built him an uncomfortable coffin, a coffin his spirit could not be at rest in. Mr. Bill, as Deets had always called him, had rangered far in his life; it would be too bad if his spirit had to keep rangering, for want of a comfortable resting place.

"We ought to caulk this coffin, I expect," Ikey Ripple said, rendering his first judgment on the matter. The coffin was sitting on two sawhorses. He bent over and peered underneath it, an action that aggravated his rheumatism. It was a coffin that could profit from a good caulking, in his view.

"I doubt we have anything to caulk it with," Call said.

"It won't hold out the worms or the maggots no time, if we don't give it a caulking," Ikey insisted.

"Well, the store's closed, I don't know where we could get any caulking," Call said. With the Forsythe store still out of operation, everyone in town was constantly discovering that they needed some small necessity which there was no way to procure.

"Billy Coleman was a fine fellow," Ikey went on. "He deserves better than to be bloated up with screwworms before he's hardly in his grave. The dern state of Texas ought to have some caulking, somewhere."

Mention of screwworms at a moment of such solemnity made everyone queasy, even Call, for they had all seen the dreadful putrefaction that resulted when screwworms infested a deer or a cow. The thought that such might happen to Long Bill Coleman, a comrade who had been walking among them only yesterday, made everyone unhappy.

"Shut up talking about worms and maggots, Ikey," Augustus said. "Long Bill's just as apt to be up in heaven playing a harp as he is to be having screwworms infect him."

Ikey Ripple considered the remark obtuse—and, besides that, it was made in an unfriendly tone, a tone particularly unwelcome for having come from a raw youth such as Gus McCrae. Ikey had passed his seventieth year and considered anyone under fifty to be callow, at best.

"I don't know what happens in heaven but I do know what happens when you stick a coffin in the ground that ain't caulked," Ikey said. "Worms and maggots, that's what."

Deets had just finished the coffin lid, which fitted snugly.

"Ikey, stop your griping," Gus said. "Plenty of our fine rangers have been buried without no coffin at all."

"Them boards are thin—I expect the worms will get in pretty soon even if you do caulk it," Stove Jones observed.

"Worms and varmints—a hungry varmint will dig up a coffin unless it's buried deep," Lee Hitch added.

"You are all too goddamn gloomy," Augustus said. "I say let's bury Billy Coleman and go get soundly drunk in his memory."

He got off the wagon and began to walk toward the Coleman house.

"I expect we'll just have to do without the caulking," Call said. "Just load the coffin in the wagon and bring it to the house. I believe it would be best to get this burying done."

Then he followed Gus, who was walking slowly. Ahead, a knot

of women stood around the back porch of the Coleman house. Call looked for Maggie but didn't see her at first. When he did spot her she was not with the women on the porch—they were respectable women, of course. Maggie sat alone on the steps going up to her rooms. She had her face in her hands and her shoulders were shaking.

"Mag's upset," Gus said. "I expect one of these old church biddies ran her off from the mourning."

"I expect," Call said. "Maggie's close to Pearl. She took the arrows out of her after the raid, she said. The doctor was busy with the serious wounds."

When Call walked over and asked Maggie if one of the ladies had been rude to her, Maggie shook her head. She looked up at him, her face wet with tears.

"It's just so hard, Woodrow," she said. "It's just so hard."

"Well, but there's easy times, too," Call said awkwardly; he immediately felt he had said something wrong. He could never come up with the right words, when Maggie cried. His remark was true enough—there were easy times—but the day of Long Bill's death was not one of them.

Not for me, Maggie wanted to say, when he mentioned easy times. She wanted to go be with Pearl Coleman, but she couldn't, because of her position. It was hard, not easy, but there was no point in trying to make Woodrow understand how hard it was for her.

"It's sunny, at least," Call said. "Bill hung himself on a mighty pretty day."

That didn't sound right either, although it was true: the day was brilliant.

To his dismay, Maggie began to cry all the harder. He didn't know whether it was the standoffish women, or Long Bill's death, or his ill-chosen remarks. He had thought to comfort her, but he didn't know how. He stood awkwardly by the steps, feeling that he would have been wiser just to go along with Gus and see that Bill was wrapped up proper and ready for the coffin.

"Hush, Woodrow, you don't have to talk," Maggie said, grateful that he had come to stand beside her. It was the first time he had done such a thing, when there were people watching.

Just then the rangers came around the corner with the coffin in the wagon. Old Ikey Ripple, who had once pestered Maggie endlessly, drove the wagon. The other rangers rode behind the wagon. All of them saw Call standing by Maggie at the bottom of the steps.

"I best go—will you be coming?" Call asked.

"Yes, I'll follow along," Maggie said, surprised that he asked.

33.

THERE WAS GREEN spring grass in the little graveyard when they buried Long Bill Coleman. Trees were leafing out, green on the distant slopes; fine clear sunlight shone on the mourners; mockingbirds sang on after the hymn singing stopped and the mound of red dirt was shoveled back in the grave. Maggie, fearing censure, hadn't followed very close. Pearl Coleman, bereft, heaved her deep cow sobs throughout the brief service.

"I'm a poor talker, you talk over him," Call whispered to Augustus, when the time had come for someone to speak a few words over the departed.

Augustus McCrae stood so long in thought that Call was afraid he wouldn't find it in him to speak. But Gus, hat in hand, finally looked up at the little crowd.

"It's too pretty a day to be dying, but Long Bill's dead and that's that," he said. "I recall that he liked that scripture about the green pastures—it's spring weather and there'll be green grass growing over him soon."

He paused a minute, fumbling with his hat. When he spoke again he had some trouble controlling his voice.

"Billy, he was a fine pard, let's go home," he said finally.

Pearl Coleman had a brother, Joel, who was stout like her. Joel helped his sobbing sister back down the path toward town. The ladies who liked Pearl and had come to support her in her hour of grief followed the brother and sister away. The other townspeople trickled away in twos and threes but the rangers were reluctant to leave. In the heat of battle they had surrendered many comrades to death, often having no opportunity to bury them or take note of their passing at all. But this death had not occurred in battle; it occurred because Long Bill, a man who had been stouthearted through much violent strife, wanted it.

"I wish we'd had time to caulk the coffin," Ikey Ripple said. "I expect it'll be worms and maggots for Billy, pretty soon."

The others cast hard glances at him, causing Ikey to conclude that his views were not appreciated. He decided to seek a saloon, and was joined in his search by Lee Hitch and Stove Jones, men disposed to overlook his views of worms and maggots.

"Reckon Bill would change his mind, if he had a chance to?" Gus asked Call. They were the last to leave, although Pea Eye was not far from them on the path.

Call had been asking himself the same question all day. The last conversation he had had with Long Bill Coleman had been a casual one about the relative merits of mares and geldings, as saddle horses. Long Bill argued for geldings, as being more stable; Call argued for mares, for their alertness. Long Bill talked fondly of a horse he had favored in earlier years, a sorrel gelding named Sugar who had carried him safely on many patrols. Call reminded Bill of a time when Sugar had shied at a badger and run away with him. They had a chuckle, remembering the runaway.

It had been an easy conversation about horses, of the sort he had often had with Long Bill over the years. Sugar grew old and had to be put out to pasture, but Long Bill, from time to time, would have another gelding whose virtues he would brag about, just as Call, from time to time, would acquire an exceptional mare. They would often talk about horses, he and Bill—whatever troubles might be elsewhere in their lives never dampened their interest in the pleasure to be had with good horses.

"He can't change his mind, Gus—it's foolish to even think that way," Call said. "Gone is gone."

"I know it," Gus said—yet he could not stop wondering about Long Bill. In the saloon the night before Long Bill had seemed somber, but not more somber than he had been on many a night. Augustus couldn't get the business of hanging out of his mind. Hanging wasn't simple, like shooting oneself. Shooting he could imagine. A momentary hopelessness, such as he himself had felt several times since Clara's marriage, could cause a man to grab a pistol and send a bullet into his brain. A few seconds, rushing by so fast they gave one no time for second thoughts, would allow a man to end the matter.

But hanging was different. A rope had to be found, and a stool to climb on. Long Bill had watched the hanging of quite a few thieves and miscreants in his years of rangering; he knew the result was often imperfect, if the knot was set wrong. The hanged man might dangle and kick for several minutes before his air supply was finally cut off. Care had to be taken, when a hanging was contemplated. A good limb had to be chosen, for one thing. Limbs that looked stout to the eye would often sag so far in practice that the hanged man's feet would touch the ground. Long Bill had never been skilled with his hands, thus his quick failure as a carpenter. It taxed him to tie a simple halter knot. The more Gus thought about the physical complications involved in hanging, the more perplexed he felt that his friend had been able to manage his final action successfully. And why? Had there been a sharp quarrel? Had a nightmare afflicted him so powerfully that he lost his bearings? It seemed that Long Bill was so determined to be free of earthly sorrow that he had gone about the preparations for his death with more competence than he had been capable of when only the chores of life were involved. He had even done it all in the dark, perhaps fearing that if he saw the bright sunrise he might weaken in his resolve and not do it.

"I just wonder what Bill was thinking, there at the end," Gus said.

"You can wonder all you want to," Call said. "We'll never know that. It's just as well not to think about it."

"I can't help thinking about it, Woodrow—can you?" Gus asked.

"I was the last man to drink with him. I expect I'll think about it for years."

They had walked back almost to the steps that led to Maggie's rooms.

"I think about it," Call admitted. "But I ought to stop. He's dead. We buried him."

Call felt, though, that the comment had been inadequate. After all, he too had been friends with Long Bill for many years. He had known several men who had lost limbs in battle; the men all claimed that they still felt things in the place where the limb had been. It was natural enough, then, that with Bill suddenly gone he and Gus would continue to have some of the feelings that went with friendship, even though the friend was gone.

"I can't be thinking about him so much that I can't get the chores done, that's what I meant," Call added.

Augustus looked at him curiously, a look that was sort of aslant.

"Well, that's you, Woodrow—you'll always get the chores done," Augustus said. "I ain't that much of a worker, myself. I can skip a chore now and then, if it's a sunny day."

"I don't know what sunny has to do with chores—they need to be done whether it's sunny or not," Call said.

Augustus was silent. He was still thinking about Long Bill, wondering what despair had infested his mind while he was looking for the rope and setting the milking stool in place.

"It's funny," he said.

"What is?" Call asked.

"Billy was the worst roper in the outfit," Augustus said. "If you put him in the lots with a tame goat, the goat would die of old age before Billy could manage to get a loop on it. Remember?"

"Why, yes, that's true," Call said. "He was never much of a roper."

"It might take him six or seven tries just to catch his own horse," Augustus said. "If we was in a hurry I'd usually catch his horse for him, just to save time."

Call started to go up the stairs to see Maggie, but paused a moment.

"You're right," he said. "The only thing the man ever roped on the first try was himself. That's a curiosity, ain't it?"

"Why yes," Augustus said. "That's a curiosity."

Call still had his hat in his hand; he put it on and went up the steps to Maggie.

Woodrow's lucky and he don't know it, Augustus thought. He's got a girl to go to. I wish I had a girl to go to. Whore or no whore, I wouldn't care.

34.

WITH NO WAY to shade his pupils, Scull began to pray for rain—or, if not rain, at least a cloud, anything that might bring his eyes relief. Even on cool days the white light of the sun at noon brought intense headaches. The light was like a hot needle, stabbing and stabbing into his head. Rolling his eyes downward brought a few moments of relief, but not enough—day after day the white light ate at his optic nerve. Even though he heard the caballero Carlos Diaz tell Ahumado that the Texans had agreed to send the cattle for his ransom, Scull felt little hope. He might be blind or insane before the cattle arrived; besides, there was no certainty that Ahumado would honor the ransom anyway. He might take the cattle and kill the Texans—if he respected the bargain it would be mere whim.

From the noon hour each day until the sun edged behind the western cliffs, Scull felt himself not far from madness, from the pain in his eyes. The only thing that saved him, in his view, was that the season was young and the days still fairly short; also, Ahumado had pitched his camp in a canyon, a deep slot in the earth. In the canyon the sun rose late and set early; it only burned at his eyes for some six hours a day, and often spring thunderheads drifted over the canyon and brought him some minutes of relief.

As soon as the sun went behind the canyon wall Ahumado took him from the skinning post and put him back in the cage. Scull then covered his head with his arms, to make a cave of darkness for his throbbing eyes. Sometimes, instead of drinking the water they brought him, he poured a little in his palms and wet his throbbing temples. He could hear the rippling of the little stream that ran not far away; at night he dreamed of thrusting his head in the cool water and letting it soothe his eyes.

He no longer sang or cursed, and when, now and then, he tried to remember a line of verse, or a fragment of history, he couldn't. It was as if the white light itself had burned away his memory, so that it would no longer give back what was in it. The old bandit was clever, more clever than Scull had supposed. He might take the Texans' cattle and send them back their captain—only the captain he sent back would be blind and insane.

The one weapon Scull had left to him was his hatred—always, throughout his life, hatred had come easier to him than love. The Christian view that one should love his brethren struck him as absurd. His brethren were conniving, brutish, dishonest, greedy, and cruel—and that judgment included, particularly, his own brothers and most of the men he had grown up with. From the time he first hefted a rifle and swung a sword he had loved combat. He sought war and liked it red. His marriage to Inez was a kind of war in itself, which was one reason he stayed in it. Several times he had come close to choking her to death, and once he even managed to heave her out a window, unfortunately only a first-floor window, or he would have been rid of the black bitch, as he sometimes called her. He had no trouble hating any opponent, any prey: red Indians, bandits, horsethieves, card cheats, pimps, bankers, lawyers, governors, senators. He had once pistol-whipped a man in the foyer of the Massachussetts statehouse because the man spat on his foot.

All his earlier hatreds, though, seemed casual and minor when compared to the hatred he felt for Ahumado, the Black Vaquero. There was nothing of chivalry in Scull's hatred—no respect for a worthy opponent, none of the civilities that went with formal warfare. Scull dreamed of getting Ahumado by the throat and squeezing until his old eyes popped out. He wanted to saw off the top of the man's head and scoop out his brains, as they had scooped out the steaming brains of Hector, his great horse. He wanted to open his belly and strew his old guts on the rocks for carrion birds to peck at.

Ahumado had outsmarted him at every turn, had caught him easily, stripped him, hung him in a cage, taken his eyelids; and he had done it all with light contempt, as if it were an easy, everyday matter to outsmart Inish Scull. The old man didn't appear to want his death, particularly; he could have had that at any time. What he wanted was his pride, and taking the eyelids was a smart way to whittle it down. When the sun shone full in his face, Scull's pupils seemed as wide as a tunnel, a tunnel that let searing light into his brain. At times he felt as if his own brains were being cooked, as Hector's had been.

The hatred between Scull and Ahumado was a silent thing now. For most of the day the two men were no more than fifty feet apart. Ahumado sat on his blanket; Scull was either in his cage or tied to the skinning post. But no words passed between them— only hatred.

Scull tried, as best he could, to keep track of days. He lined up straws in the corner of his cage. Keeping a crude calendar was a way of holding out. He needed to keep his hatred high, to calculate when he might expect the Texans. Once the season advanced, once spring gave way to summer, the sun would burn even hatred out of him. He knew it. The old dark man sitting a few feet away would become meaningless. The sun would cook away even hatred—and when hatred was gone there would be nothing left.

While he could, though, he lined up straws in the corner of his cage and imagined revenge. One morning it rained, a blessed rain that continued to fall for eight hours or more. They did not bother tying him to the skinning post that day—there was no sun to afflict him. Scull scraped at the puddles in his cage and made a paste of mud, which he plastered over his sore eyes. The relief was so great that he wept, beneath his mud poultices. All day he kept on, putting the mud poultices over his eyes. No one came near him. Ahumado, who hated rain, stayed in his cave. Later, when the rain had subsided to a cool drizzle, Scull heard two vaqueros talking. The vaqueros wanted to kill him—they were convinced he was a witch. What he did with the mud was a thing a witch would do. The vaqueros had long believed that Scull was a witch and were annoyed at Ahumado for allowing a witch to live in their midst; he might cause someone to be struck by lightning; he might even cause the cliff to fall and bury them all alive. They wanted to take out their guns and shoot many bullets into Scull, the witch in the cage. But they could not because Scull belonged to Ahumado, and only Ahumado could order his death.

When Scull overheard the conversation, he felt his strength revive a little. Because of the rain and the mud, he was saved for a little time. Perhaps he *was* a witch—at least, perhaps, he could play on the vaqueros' superstition. At once, in his croak of a voice, he began to sing in Gaelic, a sea ditty a sailor had once taught him in Boston. He couldn't sing loud and had forgotten most of the Gaelic song, but he sang anyway, with mud plastered over his eyes.

When he took the plasters off Scull saw that the vaqueros and everyone else in the camp had moved as far away from him as they could get. He had witched them back, and if the mud puddles would just last a few days he might keep witching them until the Texans came with the cattle—at least it was something to try.

Ahumado even came out of his cave for a moment, although he disliked rain. He wanted to watch the strange white man who put mud on his eyes.

35

WHEN BUFFALO HUMP and Worm were only two days from the canyon, they met up with Fat Knee and two other boys. One of the boys, White Crow, was so good with snares that he had caught several wild turkeys. Of course they were glad to share the turkey meat with their chief. Buffalo Hump ate the turkey happily but Worm refused it, believing that turkey meat might affect his brain; turkeys were easily confused, and so might be the people who ate them, Worm reasoned. Buffalo Hump thought the notion was ridiculous and tried to joke Worm out of his silly belief.

"*You* are confused," he told Worm, "but if I ate you I would still be smart."

Fat Knee had always been afraid of Buffalo Hump—the sight of the great hump made him fearful. While Buffalo Hump was eating a wild turkey hen, Fat Knee blurted out the business about Blue Duck and Famous Shoes. He was afraid that if he waited Blue Duck might try to put the blame for the whole episode on him. Blue Duck was a good liar; he was always managing to get other people blamed for his mistakes. Also, of course, he was Buffalo Hump's son. Fat Knee assumed that Buffalo Hump would more likely believe his own son than an insignificant young warrior named Fat Knee.

But when he blurted out the admission that he and Blue Duck had tried to trade Famous Shoes to Slow Tree, Buffalo Hump didn't seem particularly interested.

"You should change your name," the chief suggested. "Your parents gave you that name because when you were young a snake bit you on the knee and made your knee fat. Now you are grown and your knee isn't fat. If I were you I would change my name."

Fat Knee was relieved that Buffalo Hump wasn't angry about the business with Famous Shoes. He had been worrying about Buffalo Hump's reaction to that business for many days. In fact, though, Buffalo Hump seemed more annoyed with Worm for his reluctance to eat turkey meat than he was about the matter of Famous Shoes and Slow Tree.

As they were riding north, Buffalo Hump brought up the matter of his name again.

"People who are named for parts of the body can only be jokesters and clowns," Buffalo Hump told him. "Look at Straight Elbow—his name ruined him. If you were named for your scrotum it would be the same. No matter how hard you fought in battle, people would get tickled when they said your name. Soon you would forget about being brave. It would be enough that you were funny. You would only be a clown."

Fat Knee recognized that what Buffalo Hump said might be true, but he had no idea what he should change his name to. His father had named him Fat Knee, and his father, Elk Shoulders, was an irascible man. If he went to his father and announced that he wanted to change his name, his father might hit him so hard with a club that his brains would spill out like clotted milk.

Still, Buffalo Hump was the chief. It would not do to ignore his suggestion completely. Buffalo Hump was known to hold grudges, too. He had been known to kill people over incidents or embarrassments that had occurred so long ago that most people had forgotten them. Often the warrior who suddenly found himself being killed would be dispatched so quickly that he could not even remember what he had done to deserve the knife or the lance.

As they were riding north Fat Knee rode up beside Buffalo Hump and put a question to him.

"If I change my name from Fat Knee, what will I change it to?" he asked.

Buffalo Hump gave the matter only a moment's thought.

"Change it to Many Dreams," Buffalo Hump suggested. "The name will make you dream more. If you can learn to dream enough we might make you into a medicine man."

While Fat Knee was thinking about the name "Many Dreams," which pleased him, they saw an Indian sitting on the edge of a low butte not far to the west. The butte was not high—it was no more, really, than a pile of rocks. Buffalo Hump immediately recognized the warrior's horse, a small gray gelding.

"That is Red Hand's horse," he said. "Why is Red Hand sitting on that pile of rocks?"

No one had any idea—Red Hand was a gregarious man who usually stayed in camp so that he could couple frequently with his wives. He liked to lie on soft elk skins and have his wives rub his body with buffalo tallow. He also liked to wrestle but was hard to throw because his wives had made him slippery with the tallow. He had never been known to sit on a pile of rocks far from camp.

When they came to where the gray horse stood, Red Hand was staring up into the sky. His body was shaking. He did not look at them. He kept his face turned up to the sky.

"He is praying—we had better just leave him to his prayers," Worm said. Worm wanted very much to be back in camp; too many things that he had seen on this trip did not seem right to him. The sight of the Old One had unnerved him badly. Now they were almost home and Buffalo Hump was slowing them down again, just because of Red Hand.

The delay was one thing too many for Worm, who did not hide his impatience, forgetting that Buffalo Hump could be impatient too. Before Worm realized the danger he had pushed too hard. Buffalo Hump whirled on him—he did not raise his lance or draw his bow, but the death he could deal with them was there, in his eyes.

"I want you to wait until Red Hand has finished his prayer," he said. "He might need to talk to you. He would not come so far to pray unless it was important. Once he has finished and we have all talked to him, then we will go home."

Worm restrained himself with difficulty. He did not like to be corrected. Red Hand was a man of no judgment; probably he was just sitting on a rock pile praying because his wife had refused him, although it was true that Red Hand was shaking as if his life were about to end.

Worm composed himself and waited. Fat Knee caught a mouse and he and the other boys amused themselves with it for a while, catching it under a cup and then releasing it, only to catch it again before it could get to a hole.

Finally Red Hand stopped shaking so much. His eyes had been turned up to the sky—he had been seeing only what was inside his prayer. When he lowered his head and saw several people waiting for him he looked very surprised.

"I came here to pray," he said. Then he could not seem to think of more words. He got to his feet, moving like an old man, and mounted his gray horse.

"This is a new place you have found to pray," Buffalo Hump pointed out. "Many people find good places to pray in the canyon."

He was trying to be patient. After all, a man's prayers were serious. He himself had chosen a difficult place on a high rock when he had prayed for the success of the great raid. Red Hand had every right to pray on a rock pile if he wanted to. Buffalo Hump was merely curious as to why he had chosen this particular rock pile as his praying place.

What Red Hand wanted to do was change the subject. What had driven him to the rock pile to pray was the fact that one of his wives had got her blood on him—they had been coupling when her impure time came. When he pulled away from his wife and saw that he was red with blood he was so upset that he jumped on his horse and left the village. Red Hand was no longer a youth; he had four wives and he coupled with them as frequently as possible, but never before had he coupled with one of his wives when she was impure. The wife it happened with was known as High Rabbit because she stepped so high in the dance—also her legs were thin like a jackrabbit's. High Rabbit was not an immodest woman; in fact she was the most circumspect of his wives. She insisted on a great deal of privacy before she would let Red Hand couple with her. High Rabbit was also horrified by what had happened. She ran quickly to her mother to find out what her fate would be. Sometimes women were driven out of the tribe or even killed for allowing men to come near them when they were impure.

Red Hand didn't know what High Rabbit's mother might have told her, because he had left the village immediately and had not been back. As soon as he came to a stream he washed himself many times, though he knew the washings would do little good. The impurity would strike him inside, where he couldn't wash it away. His assumption was that he would die soon; he wanted to pray as much as possible before his end came, and the rock pile seemed as good a place as any. In his mind contact with impure blood meant death and he wanted to hurry to a praying place and start praying. Some rattlesnakes had been around the rock pile when he arrived, but they soon went away. Probably even the rattlesnakes knew of his impurity and hurried to their dens to dissociate themselves from it.

To Red Hand's surprise, he didn't die; now Buffalo Hump, leader of the great raid, had come upon him and seemed to find it amusing that he had chosen to pray on a rock pile. Of course Buffalo Hump didn't know about the dire thing that had occurred in Red Hand's lodge.

Red Hand would have liked a few words with Worm about the matter of impure blood, but Worm had never liked him very much. Probably he would just tell him to go away and die if he knew about the blood.

Under the circumstances Red Hand thought it best to talk about something beside his choice of places to pray. Buffalo Hump was not a great chief for nothing. He might find out that Red Hand had come to the rock pile because he was stained.

"Kicking Wolf is back," Red Hand said. "He was very weak when he found us and he sees two deer where there is one."

Buffalo Hump was not concerned with Kicking Wolf's vision problems.

"Where is the Buffalo Horse?" he asked.

"I don't know about that, but the worst thing is that Three Birds did not return," Red Hand said. "The Black Vaquero got him."

"If he got Three Birds, how did Kicking Wolf get away?" Buffalo Hump asked.

Then Red Hand realized that he *did* know what had happened to the Buffalo Horse—he returned in his mind to an earlier part of the story; he was so upset about his impurity that he could not remember events in a straightforward way. Now he suddenly remembered about the Buffalo Horse—an Apache had told Slipping Weasel about him. The Apache had heard the story from a man who was wandering.

"Wait, I was in my prayer, I forgot this," Red Hand said. "They cooked the Buffalo Horse in a great pit, but they took away his head and cooked it somewhere else. It took a whole village to eat him. I think Ahumado ate his head. They also caught Big Horse Scull and hung him in a cage."

"I was wanting to know about Kicking Wolf," Buffalo Hump said, without impatience. He could tell that Red Hand's mind was in a disordered state. He was talking rapidly, although there was no need to hurry their talk.

"Ahumado did catch Kicking Wolf," Red Hand said. "He tied him to a horse and the horse almost dragged him to death. But Big Horse Scull cut him loose."

"What did Ahumado do with Three Birds?" Worm asked.

"There are some stories about Three Birds but I don't know if they are true," Red Hand said. "An Apache said that Three Birds flew off the Yellow Cliff. He did not want to go in the cage where they put Scull."

"I don't think Three Birds could fly," Buffalo Hump said. "I will ask Kicking Wolf about it myself. He may know more than that Apache."

"He may, but since the horse pulled him he sees two deer where there is one," Red Hand told him.

On the ride home Buffalo Hump asked Worm about the things Red Hand had said, but Worm was not very informative. He was annoyed that Kicking Wolf had taken the Buffalo Horse to Mexico, to be eaten by a village.

"We could have cooked it in a pit ourselves," Worm said. "We could have eaten it as quickly as that village."

Later, in camp, Buffalo Hump mentioned Worm's complaint to Kicking Wolf. The latter was having his hair greased by one of his wives, at the time.

"Worm thinks you should have let *us* eat the Buffalo Horse," Buffalo Hump said.

"If Worm had stolen it he could have eaten it, but I stole it and I wanted to take it to Mexico," Kicking Wolf said. "Anyway, Apaches are liars. The Buffalo Horse may still be alive."

Buffalo Hump saw that Kicking Wolf was in a quarrelsome mood. He had been about to tease Kicking Wolf a little—after all, the man had missed the great raid—but he decided to let it be, mainly because he was anxious to see Lark and his other wives. Fat Knee had ridden ahead to let them know he was coming, so they would probably have cooked him something good. He wanted to eat. Kicking Wolf he could tease anytime.

"How about Three Birds?" he asked, before going on to his tent. "Do you think he is still alive too?"

At that Kicking Wolf merely shook his head. He didn't think Three Birds was alive, and it was a sorrow to him.

"I didn't want him to go to Mexico," he told Buffalo Hump. "I was going to take the horse myself. I wanted Three Birds to go home, but he came to Mexico anyway. He wanted to be brave."

Though Buffalo Hump had always considered Three Birds a fool, there was no doubt that what he had done had been very brave.

"He got his wish," Buffalo Hump said. "He was brave. When your eyes are better we will sing for him, some time."

36.

WHEN THE WILD BLACK COW came popping out of a thicket of mesquite and chaparral, she was on them and had gored Deets's horse badly in the flank before the rangers even knew what kind of beast they were dealing with. The horse squealed and fell over, throwing Deets almost under the cow, whose horn tips were red with the horse's blood. The cow lowered her head when Call and Gus shot her, firing almost at the same time. The bullets knocked the cow to her knees but didn't kill her. Even on her knees she tried to go for Deets—it took a bullet to the head to kill her.

Deets was shaking, as much from surprise as from fright. His horse gushed blood from its torn flank.

"My horse dying," Deets said, stunned.

"Well, where'd she come from?" Pea Eye asked. All he could remember was that a black streak with short shiny horns came popping out of the brush—he had had no time to make precise observations.

"She came out of *that!*" Augustus said, pointing to what seemed to be an impenetrable thorny brush. The mesquite and chaparral grew out above a solid floor of green prickly pear.

"Maybe she had hydrophobie," Stove Jones volunteered. "I've lived with cows and such all my life, but I've never seen a cow charge a bunch of men like that."

"Just be glad it wasn't one of them tough little black bulls," Lee Hitch said. "One of them little black bulls would have done for about half of us.

"You can't kill a bull with no pistol bullet," he added. "Not even with ten pistol bullets."

A mile or two farther—Deets was now riding double with Jake Spoon, who had the stoutest horse—they came upon three of the small black bulls Lee Hitch had described. Everyone in the troop drew their rifles, expecting to have to defend themselves, but the bulls were content to paw the earth and snort.

Then, just as they were about to stop for coffee and a bit of bacon, a second cow came shooting out of the brush behind them. This time the rangers were primed, but even so it took three rifle shots to bring the cow down.

In midafternoon it happened a third time. A red cow came charging directly at them, breathing froth and bellowing. All the rangers shot this time and the cow went down.

Call, though profoundly startled by the violent behavior of the wild south Texas cows, held his counsel, meaning to talk the development over with Augustus privately, when they camped.

Gus McCrae couldn't wait for a private parley. They were scarcely south of San Antonio and had just been attacked three times, with the loss of one horse. They had seen no ranches or ranchmen who might advise them on the bovine behavior they were encountering. The rangers were jumpier now than they would have been if they had been crossing the *comanchería*—in the space of an afternoon they had come to fear cattle more than they feared Indians. And it was the cattle of the country, hundreds of them, that they were supposed to round up and deliver to Mexico.

"This is pointless traveling," Gus said. "How are we going to deliver a thousand cattle to that old bandit if we have to shoot ever damn cow we see?"

Call accepted the point. It was obvious they had been presented with a difficult mission.

"There must be tamer cattle down here somewhere," he said. "There's ranches down this way—big ranches. They ship cattle to New Orleans regular, I hear. The boats come to Matagorda Bay. They don't shoot ever cow. There's got to be cowboys down here who know how to handle this stock."

The rangers listened in silence, but his words made little impression compared to their fresh memories of the mad, frothing cows.

"Livestock ain't supposed to be this hostile," Stove Jones commented.

"We're Indian fighters, Woodrow," Augustus pointed out. "Indian fighters and bandit chasers. We ain't vaqueros. If I tried to go into one of them thickets after a cow I'd be lucky not to get scratched to death. We'd just as well try to deliver a thousand deer. At least deer don't come charging at you.

"That damn governor's betrayed us again," he added in disgust.

Call couldn't really disagree. Governor Pease had given them a flowery letter to show to the ranchers in south Texas. The letter bound the state of Texas to compensate the ranchers for cattle sufficient to make a herd of one thousand head. There was no mention, however, of a price per head. When Call pointed this out to Governor Pease, the Governor had merely shrugged.

"Our south Texans are patriotic men," he said. "They'll be glad to let you take a few head of stock if it will get our hero back.

"Speak to Captain King," he added—two harried clerks were

following him around at the time, hoping to get his attention. "Captain Richard King. He'll help you. I expect that goddamn old black bandit has stolen at least that many cattle from him already."

"Where do we find Captain King?" Augustus asked. "I've never met the man."

"Why, just ask, Captain McCrae—just ask," Governor Pease said. "Captain King is well known along the coast."

The Governor's office was bustling that day—besides the clerks and an army man or two, there were three benches packed with legislators, all of them evidently hoping for an audience with the Governor. As a lot they looked dusty and drunken.

"Look at them ramshackly senators," Augustus said, as they left the office. "Maybe we ought to change jobs, Woodrow. We could make laws instead of enforcing them."

"I can barely read," Call reminded him. "I'd be a poor hand at making laws."

"Why, you wouldn't need to read," Gus said. "We could hire a clerk to do the scribbling. All it takes to make laws is good sense. I could probably make better laws than that whole bunch sitting in there half drunk."

"Maybe," Call said. "Maybe not."

Governor Pease handed them the letter and sent them away. As they left, several of the legislators were attempting to crowd in his door.

Now, faced with the fact that they were barely out of sight of the Alamo and had already had to shoot three cows, Call remembered the Governor's advice.

"I expect we better try and find Captain King," Call said. "Maybe he'll want to lend the state of Texas some vaqueros for a week or two."

"I don't know, Woodrow," Gus said. "When I'm given a job that's downright impossible, my practice is to find a whorehouse and stay in it until my funds run out."

"We don't need to find a whorehouse, we need to find a ranch house," Call said. "This is Captain Scull we're trying to rescue.

Captain Scull led us for quite a few years and got us out of plenty of hard spots. Now he's in a hard spot and we've got to do the best we can to bring him back."

"Well, the fool *would* walk off to Mexico," Augustus said. He reloaded his rifle and kept a wary eye on the thickets, as they passed them.

The next day they did find a ranch house, but there was no one there except three womenfolk, some babies and small children, and two old Mexican men who had been left to do the chores.

A lanky woman with a baby at her breast and two toddlers clinging to her skirts just looked unhappy when asked where the menfolk were.

"They're off branding cattle," she said. "I expect they're south. They've been gone three weeks—I've been looking for them back but they ain't here."

"South's a big place," Augustus remarked.

The woman just smiled a tired smile. "It's a brushy place too— you'll find that out once you leave here," she said. "I got goat and I got frijoles—you won't get much except goat and frijoles, not in this part of the country."

The men ate outside, at a long table shaded by a great mesquite tree whose limbs seemed to spread over an acre. The woman who greeted them was named Hannah Fogg—she had a pretty younger sister who helped with the serving. Though the younger sister was shy as a deer, Gus did get her to reveal that her name was Peggy. Gus stole several glances at her during the meal and lingered over his coffee so he could steal several more.

As the men ate, Augustus began to notice children, peering out shy as mice, one under the porch, another behind a bush, two more who had managed to climb the big tree. Two, at least, were under the wagon.

"Why, there's a passel of children here," he said to Peggy—it was an excuse to speak to her. "Are all these little tykes Mrs. Fogg's?"

But Peggy ducked her head and wouldn't say.

Hannah Fogg was not lying about the difficulties of the country south of her ranch house. For a day and a half more the rangers zigged and zagged in a southerly direction, proceeding from little clearing to little clearing. They were seldom long out of sight of cattle, but no more cows charged—these cattle fled like deer the moment they saw the riders.

In the afternoon of the second day they heard the sound of men working and came upon the rancher Denton Fogg and his branding crew, which numbered more than twenty vaqueros. The cattle were held in a large clearing. Ropers slid into the herd and soon came out, dragging the animal to be branded. Denton Fogg himself, drenched in sweat and lugubrious in appearance, applied the iron himself; he was not happy to be interrupted in his hot work by a party of Texas Rangers with a letter from the Governor asking for a donation of cattle to be driven into Mexico in return for Inish Scull.

He did *read* the letter, though, holding it carefully so his sweat wouldn't drip on it.

"This is a piece of worthless foolery, sir," he declared, handing the letter back to Call. "The Mexicans steal half our cattle anyway and Ed Pease does nothing about it. Now he wants us to give them a thousand more? No thank you, sir—not my cattle."

Call didn't like the man's tone.

"He's not asking you to *give* anything," he pointed out. "The state will pay you for your cattle."

"If the state intended to pay for the cattle it should have provided you with cash money," the rancher said. "Have you got cash money, sir?"

Augustus didn't care for the man's tone either.

"We're in a hurry to rescue our captain," he said. "We couldn't wait for a bunch of money to be gathered up. Don't you even trust the state of Texas?"

"Nope, not the state and not Ed Pease, either," Denton Fogg replied. "I wouldn't give either one of them a cow. But I will sell cattle for cash on the barrelhead. Come back with the money and I can have a thousand head ready for delivery within the week."

With that he walked off and picked a hot iron out of the branding fire.

"The fool, I feel like shooting him," Augustus said.

"We can't shoot a man just because he doesn't want to give away his cattle," Call said—he was not without skepticism about the state's willingness to pay for the cattle.

"Well, he's out here branding ever cow he can catch," Augustus pointed out, "Who said he could take these cattle?"

"I guess that's just how you build up a ranch," Call said. "The cattle belong to the man who gets to them first."

"Hell, we could be ranchers ourselves then," Gus said. "We could hire a few ropers and buy some branding irons and get to work. Pretty soon we'd be big livestock men too."

"Where'd we put the cattle once we branded them?" Call asked. "We don't own any land. We don't even own the horses we're riding. All we own are our guns and our clothes.

"And the saddles," he added. "We do own our saddles."

The comment depressed Augustus to an unusual degree. He liked to think of himself as prosperous, or at least prospectively prosperous—but the fact was he was just short of being a pauper. All he owned was three guns, a fairly well made saddle, and some clothes. He had no house, no land, no wife, no livestock. He had ridden all day in the blazing sun, through thorny country, threatened by dangerous bovines and possibly even wild Indians, and for what? A paltry salary that would scarcely see him through a month of whoring and imbibing.

"I say we quit the rangers," he said abruptly. "There's a fortune in cattle down here in this brush and we're letting fools like that one beat us to it."

"If you want to get rich ranching you'll have to work as hard as that fellow Fogg—I doubt myself that you'd enjoy working that hard," Call said.

He rode over to where Denton Fogg was working—smoke rose from a brand he had just slapped on a large yearling.

"Do you know a man named Richard King? Captain King?" Call asked.

"I know him," Fogg said, but did not continue—he moved on to the next yearling while the iron was still hot enough to impress a brand.

"Well, would you know where we could find him?" Call asked. "The Governor thought he might advance us the cattle we need."

At that Denton Fogg stopped dead. He looked at Call for a moment and smiled—he even slapped his leg, in amusement.

"Dick King, give up a thousand cattle?" he said. "Dick King didn't get what he's got by giving away cattle."

"He wouldn't be *giving* them, sir," Call said, trying his best to curb his impatience. "The state will pay him. I'd appreciate it if you would just tell me where I can find him."

"I don't keep up with Dick King," Denton Fogg said, still amused. "There's a fellow in Lonesome Dove that knows him. You might ask him."

Before he had quite worked through his amusement, he was off to the nearest branding fire, to select a fresh iron.

"Is Lonesome Dove a place?" Call asked. "I confess I'm not familiar with it."

"You don't seem to be familiar with anything, Captain," Denton Fogg told him. "This is branding season—every cattleman who's got any sense is off branding every animal he can get his rope on. Dick King's branding, like the rest of us. I wish I had as many cattle as he does, but I don't, and I never will if I have to stand here all day giving directions to Texas Rangers. Just go due south to the Rio Grande and turn left. You'll eventually come to Lonesome Dove. There's a man there named Wanz who might know where Dick King and his men are branding."

"Let's go," Call said to the troop. "That man's too busy branding cattle to bother with us."

"The fool, I'd arrest him if there was a jail nearby," Augustus said.

"No, he's not a criminal, let's go," Call said. For a moment he keenly missed Long Bill Coleman. Though not a professional tracker, such as Famous Shoes, Long Bill had a good instinct for routes, and what they needed just then was to hold a true route south, to the Rio Grande.

But it was more than Bill's usefulness that Call missed—the man had been reassuring company, and a frontiersman whose opinion was always useful to have. The thought that he would never have it again made Call low spirited, for a time. If they were lucky enough to strike another ranch house he meant to try and hire an old vaquero to guide them through the brush.

"I've a notion to go back and marry that fellow's sister-in-law," Augustus said. "Being married to her would be better than having this goddamn brush scratch your eyes out."

"It's odd to be traveling without Billy Coleman, ain't it?" Call said. "It's the first time since we took up rangering that Billy ain't been along."

Augustus started to agree, but before he could speak memory rose in him so powerfully that he choked on his words. There was no more Long Bill to ride with. Memories of the missions they had been on together passed through his mind in a vivid parade; but then, to his dismay, the parade was interrupted by images of Clara. One second he would be remembering the tall, lanky man, white with dust, on their march as captives across the Jornada del Muerto—but then it would be Clara smiling, waiting for him on the back porch of the Forsythe store in her pretty gingham dress; Clara laughing, teasing, kissing. She had grown a little fuller in the bosom over the years, but otherwise she had been the same girl, from the moment in the muddy street when he had kissed her for the first time until he had bidden her goodbye, in the morning mist, behind the same store, only a few weeks ago. Clara hadn't gone where Bill was. It had already occurred to him that, life being the dangerous business that it was, she might be a widow someday; but, by then, his own life might have ended, or he might be in jail or in a war somewhere; anyway, even if Clara were once more to be free, she might turn him down again, as she just had.

"Why would the man hang himself, Woodrow?" Augustus asked, trying to force his mind back to the original topic.

"I know it's best not to think about it, but I can't stop thinking about it," he went on. "There are times at night when I'd give a year's wages just to ask Billy one question."

"Well, but he's gone where wages don't help you," Call said. "The best thing is just to try and do the job we have to do."

"I doubt we *can* do this job—where are we going now?" Gus asked.

"To the Rio Grande," Call replied.

"To the Rio Grande and then what—is Captain King a fish?" Gus asked.

"No, but there's a town there where we might be able to find him," Call said. "At least I guess it's at a town."

"Well, if it's a town, is it on a map—does it have a name?" Gus asked, impatiently. "Is it on this side of the river, or is it an island or what?"

"It's probably a town," Call said. "There's a saloon there owned by a man named Wanz—I think he's a Frenchman."

"Oh, if it's got a saloon, let's go," Augustus said. "In fact, let's hurry. We'll give the saloon a thorough inspection—then we'll worry about Captain King. What's the name of this place?"

"Lonesome Dove—that's its name," Call said.

37.

THE CAPTIVES, three men and a woman, were brought in a little after sunrise, in an oxcart. Muñoz, the bandit Ahumado had assigned to do the job Tudwal once did, ambushed them in their fine coach three days to the east. All their finery, rings, watches, and the like he put in a little sack, for Ahumado to inspect. The first thing the old man did, before he so much as glanced at the captives, was take the sack from Muñoz and carry it to his blanket. He emptied the sack and carefully inspected every item before he turned his attention to the prisoners, all of whom were large and fleshy, as hidalgos and their women tend to be, and all of whom, with good reason, were terrified.

Scull watched the proceedings from his cage, shielding his eyes with his hands. On days when they tied him to the skinning post his vision became a blur—he could distinguish motion and outlines but not much else. The rains had stopped and the sun was blinding, but Ahumado only now and then tied him to the skinning post. Often he would be left for three or four days in his cage—when free to shade his eyes, his vision gradually cleared.

Also, to his puzzlement, Ahumado instructed the women to feed him well. Every day he was given tortillas, frijoles, and goat meat. Ahumado himself ate no better. Scull suspected that the old man wanted to build him up for some more refined torture later, but that was just a guess and not one that impeded his appetite. Live while you're alive, Bible and sword, he told himself. He observed that from time to time the Black Vaquero was racked with coughing, now and then bringing up a green pus. It was enough to remind Scull that the old bandit was mortal too. He might yet die first.

That was not a thought likely to bring comfort to the fat new captives. As soon as Ahumado had inspected the booty he had the four prisoners lined up in the center of the camp. He did not speak to them or question them; he just made them stand there, through the hot hours of a long day. The people of the village stared at them, as they went about their work. Vaqueros or *pistoleros* who rode in from time to time stared at them.

Scull judged the captives to be gentry of some sort—their dusty garments had once been expensive. Provincial gentry, perhaps, but still from a far higher sphere than the peasants who peopled the camp. The prisoners were used to being pampered; they spent their lives sitting, eating, growing fatter. They were unaccustomed, not merely to being prisoners, but to being required to stand up at all. They were too scared to move, and yet they longed to move. They were offered neither food nor drink. Muñoz, a thin man with a pocked face, was clearly proud of his catch. He stood close to them, waiting for Ahumado's order. The standing was a torture in itself,

Scull observed. In the afternoon the woman, desperate, squatted and made water; she was well concealed behind heavy skirts but still Muñoz laughed and made a crude joke. Later the three men made water where they stood, in their pants.

Scull watched Ahumado—he wanted to know what the old man would do with his prize catches. The old skinner, Goyeto, sat beside him, clicking his finely sharpened knives, one of them the knife that had taken off Scull's eyelids.

A little before sundown, trembling with fatigue, the woman passed out. She simply fell facedown—in a faint, Scull supposed. Ahumado did not react. Muñoz had just filled his plate with food; he went on eating.

A few minutes later the three men were prodded at knifepoint to the edge of the pit of snakes and scorpions and pushed in. The bottom of the pit was in darkness by this time. The captives had no idea how deep the pit was. They were merely led to the edge of a hole and pushed off the edge. All of them screamed as they fell, and two of them continued screaming throughout the night. One of the men screamed that his leg was broken. He pleaded and pleaded but no one listened. The peasants in the camp made tortillas and sang their own songs. Scull decided that the third captive must have broken his neck in the fall—there were only two voices crying out for help.

In the morning, when Ahumado and Goyeto went to look in the pit, Scull heard the old skinner complaining.

"I thought you were going to let me skin one of them," he said.

Ahumado ignored the complaint—he usually ignored Goyeto, who complained often. He stood on the edge of the pit, looking down at the captives and listening to them beg him and plead with him; then he returned to his blanket.

When an old woman brought Scull a little coffee and two tortillas, he asked her about the men in the pit. He had noticed several of the women peeking in.

"Is one of the men dead?" he asked.

"Sí, dead," the old woman said.

The woman who fainted lay through the night in the place she had fallen. It had grown cold; Scull noticed that someone had brought her a blanket during the night. She was not tied. After the sun had been up awhile the woman rose and hobbled hesitantly over to one of the little campfires. The poor women of the camp made a place for her and gave her food. She thanked them in a low voice. The women did not respond, but they allowed her to sit by the fire. Ahumado took no further interest in her. A week later, when all three of the men in the pit were dead, the woman was still there, unmolested, eating with the women of the camp.

38.

WHEN BLUE DUCK saw that his father was angry, he thought it might be because of the captive woman. The woman, who was young and frail, had been found dead that morning; but in fact she had been sickly when they took her. There had been some beating and raping but not enough to kill her. She had been sick all along, spitting blood night after night on the trail—now she had died of her sickness, which was not his doing or his fault.

As a chief, Buffalo Hump had always been touchy about the matter of captives; he expected to control the disposal of all captives. He might order them tortured or killed, he might sell them into slavery with another tribe, or he might let them live and even on occasion treat them well. The fate of a captive brought to Buffalo Hump's camp depended on reasoning Blue Duck did not understand. Even though he felt blameless in the matter of the dead woman, he was also scared. Everyone feared Buffalo Hump's angers, and with good reason.

The words his father said, though, shocked him. They were not what he had expected, not at all.

"You should have left Famous Shoes alone, as I ordered," Buffalo Hump said. "Now you have to leave the tribe. You can take five horses but you cannot come back to my camp again. If you do I will kill you myself."

At first Blue Duck could not believe his father meant what he was saying. Was he going to banish him from the tribe because of a little foolery with a Kickapoo tracker? The Kickapoo had not even been harmed. Blue Duck had fought bravely on the great raid, killing several Texans in close combat. No young warrior had done better on the great raid, or fought more bravely.

He said as much, but Buffalo Hump merely stood and looked at him, a chill in his eye.

"We didn't hurt the Kickapoo," Blue Duck said. "We merely teased him a little. I thought Slow Tree might want him but he didn't so we let him go."

Buffalo Hump didn't change expression. He was not interested in arguments or explanations. He had his big lance in his hand.

"Slow Tree heard me tell you to leave the Kickapoo alone," Buffalo Hump said. "He did not want to assist you in your disobedience. Now I am telling you to go. You have never been obedient and I have no time to argue with you or to correct your ways. If you stay I will kill you soon, because of what is in you that will not obey. You have courage but you are rude. Take the five horses and go away now. Any warrior who sees you near this camp after today has a duty to kill you."

Blue Duck had not expected such a terrible judgment to fall on him so quickly. Yet it had fallen. Though he didn't really like many people in their band, it was the camp where he had always lived. He had always been where the tribe was; his roaming had seldom lasted more than a week. When he could not kill game there would be food in the camp. He felt a terrible anger at the Kickapoo, for having brought such a judgment on him. The next time he saw Famous Shoes he would kill him, and he would also like to kill Slow Tree, the fat chief who had been unwilling to torture Famous Shoes merely because Buffalo Hump had forbidden it.

But he could not think much about such things, not then, when his father still stood before him. He had his rifle in his hand; perhaps he should shoot his father right there. But he didn't shoot, or do anything at all. As always, when confronting his father, he felt a weakness in his legs and his belly. The weakness paralyzed him. He knew that if he tried to raise his gun and shoot, Buffalo Hump would be quicker. His father would shove the big lance into him. Blue Duck thought of murder but did nothing.

Buffalo Hump watched his son for a minute and then turned away. A little later he saw the boy ride out to the horse herd, to select his five horses. He looked dejected, but Buffalo Hump did not relent. He had returned home tired, only to have to listen half the night to stories of Blue Duck's bad behavior. The boy had beaten Hair-on-the-Lip severely, though he had no right to. Hair-on-the-Lip was still sore and could not move well. Also, Blue Duck had followed Lark when she went into the bushes to make water, and had spoken to her rudely. Also he had raced a fine young horse that belonged to Last Horse's father. In the race he put the horse off a cutbank and it broke both its front legs. Of course it had to be killed and eaten; the old man was indignant and wanted a high price for the horse that had been lost.

Buffalo Hump had never been able to like his son and now he wanted to see him gone. He had never been obedient to the Comanche way, and never would. The bluecoat soldiers would be coming onto the llano to fight them soon, in a year or two; Buffalo Hump didn't want anyone in the camp who was only disposed to make trouble, as Blue Duck had.

Soon word of the banishment spread around the camp. Buffalo Hump was with Lark for a long time; when he came out he discovered that the men and women who came to visit him were more cheerful. All of them approved of what he had done. A few brought him new stories of Blue Duck's bad behavior, mostly with women. Buffalo Hump was not especially disturbed by these stories. Many young warriors strutted too much with women and were not careful about marriage customs—he himself had almost been banished in his youth because of his lusts.

Later that day Fat Knee came hesitantly up to Buffalo Hump— it seemed that Blue Duck wanted Fat Knee to accompany him into exile. Blue Duck planned to go north and east, into a territory where renegades and exiles from many tribes gathered. There were slavers there, and bandits. They watched the Arkansas River and picked off people who traveled in boats, or freighters who hauled goods in wagons. Blue Duck told Fat Knee they would soon be rich if they joined the renegades, but Fat Knee was hesitant.

"Isn't he gone yet?" Buffalo Hump asked.

"No," Fat Knee said. "He is still looking at the horses. He wants to take the best five."

A wind had come up. Sand was blowing through the camp. It had been warm for several days but a cold wind was bringing the sand.

"You stay in camp," Buffalo Hump said. "I will go drive him away."

He found the whole business vexing. The fact that Blue Duck was still prowling around the horse herd was annoying, so annoying that Buffalo Hump caught his own horse, took his lance, and immediately rode out to the horse herd. Blue Duck's delay was merely one more example of his disobedience. Buffalo Hump thought it might be wiser just to kill the boy—talking to him that morning, his arm had tensed twice, as it did when he was ready to throw his lance. But he had held off—exile should be enough—but now the boy had angered him by not leaving.

When he reached the horse herd the only person who was there was Last Horse—one of his mares had just foaled and he was watching for a bit, to see that no coyote slipped in and killed the foal.

"I thought Blue Duck was here," Buffalo Hump said.

Last Horse merely pointed upward to the rim of the canyon. A rider with five horses in front of him had climbed out of the canyon and was following the horses along the rim.

Buffalo Hump could barely see the rider through the blowing sand, but he knew it was Blue Duck, leaving.

39.

"Whoa, now . . . stop, boys!" Augustus said.

Far down the river, in the shallows, he saw something he didn't like; something blue. The creature was a good distance away, but it was rolling in the shallow water; Gus judged it to be an aquatic beast of some sort. Few land animals worried him, but he had long been afflicted with an unreasoning fear of aquatic beasts—and now one had appeared in the muddy Rio Grande, where, up to then, they had seen nothing more threatening than the occasional snapping turtle.

The rangers immediately stopped and yanked out their rifles. Thanks to the hostility, as well as the volatility, of the south Texas cattle, they had become well accustomed to yanking out their rifles several times a day. Gus McCrae was known to have exceptional eyesight; if he saw something worth calling a halt for, then it was best to look to their weapons.

"What is it?" Call asked. All he saw ahead of them was the brown Rio Grande. An old Mexican with three goats whom they came upon half an hour earlier assured them that they were nearly to the town of Lonesome Dove—Call was anxious to hurry on, in hopes that Captain King would be there. But Augustus apparently saw something that made him nervous, something Call could not yet see.

"It's blue and it's in the edge of the water, Woodrow," Gus said. "I expect it might be a shark."

"Oh Lord, a shark," Stove Jones said, wishing suddenly that he had never left the cozy cantinas of Austin.

"It was a shark that swallowed Jonah, wasn't it?" Lee Hitch inquired.

"Shut up, you fool—that was a whale, and this river's too small for a whale to be in."

Augustus kept his eyes on the blue object thrashing in the shallow water. It was an aquatic beast of some kind, that was for sure—now and then he thought he glimpsed the limb of a body; it might be that the shark was eating somebody, right before their eyes, or before *his* eyes at least. None of the other rangers could see anything, other than the river, but they had grown accustomed to accepting Gus's judgment when it came to the analysis of distant events.

"If it's a shark, why are we stopped?" Call said. "It's in the water and we ain't. Sharks don't walk on land, that I recall."

"It might jump, though," Augustus said.

"If it jumped out of the water then it would die," Call pointed out. "Let's go."

Call was about to ride past him when they suddenly heard brush popping from the Mexican bank of the river. In a moment two men and a bull emerged from the brush and plunged into the river. In a minute the bull, a large brown animal wearing a bell that clanged with even step, came out of the river and trotted straight into a thicket of brush, popping their limbs liberally as he went.

One of the riders was an American, a short man riding a fine bay gelding; the other was an old vaquero on a buckskin mare.

The short man pulled up in surprise when he saw the rangers but the old vaquero went right on into the brush, behind the bull. The rangers, who had been stopped by the brush a number of times in the last week, were as amazed by the vaquero's ability to penetrate the thicket as they were by the size of the bull that had just swum out of Mexico.

The American had bushy sideburns and a short, stiff beard. He surveyed the rangers carefully if quickly before he trotted up to where they were stopped.

"You're Call and McCrae, aren't you? And these are your wild ranger boys, I expect," the man said. "I'm Captain King. So you want a thousand cattle, do you?"

Though Call had already suspected the short man's identity—several of the ranchers had described him, mentioning that he was partial to fine horses—he was surprised that Captain King not only knew who they were but what they wanted of him.

"Yes, but not as a gift," Call said. "The state will pay you for them."

"I doubt that, but let's see the letter," Captain King said.

He observed that Gus McCrae seemed to be considerably less interested in the matter of the thousand cattle than was Captain Call. Gus McCrae was looking downriver, in the direction of Lonesome Dove.

Call produced the letter, which he had wrapped in oilcloth—two or three violent rainstorms had doused them lately. Inasmuch as the letter was their only hope of getting the cattle they needed, he wanted to make sure it didn't get wet.

"That was my bull Solomon you just saw—you'll not see his equal in America," Captain King said, taking the letter from Call. "He strayed off last night—tempted by a Mexican heifer, I suppose."

He started to read the letter but then looked again at Gus.

"McCrae, you seem jumpy as a tick," he said. "What do you see that's upset you so?"

"It's down the river and it's blue, Captain," Gus said. "I expect it's a shark."

Captain King glanced at what Gus pointed at and immediately burst out laughing—just as he did a gust of wind took the Governor's letter out of his hand and blew it into the river. Before anyone could move it sank.

Call jumped off his horse and ran into the river—he was not a little vexed at Captain King, who sat astride his horse enjoying a fit of laughing. Call was able to pull the letter from the water, but not before it had become a sodden mess.

Call felt like giving Captain King a good dressing down, for being so careless with an important document, but it was hard to dress down a man who was laughing; and, anyway, Captain King was the one man who might help them succeed in their mission.

"I wish you'd read it before you let it blow in the river," Call said. He spread the letter on a good-sized rock, thinking it might dry if given time.

"I beg your pardon, Captain," Captain King said, attempting to control his amusement. "I don't usually throw letters into the river, particularly not if they're letters from a high potentate like Ed Pease. But I must say this is the best laugh yet. Captain McCrae here has mistook our blue sow for a shark."

"Sow . . . what sow?" Gus asked, annoyed by the man's jocular tone.

"Why, *that* sow," Captain King said, with a wave of his hand. "She probably caught a snake—a moccasin, perhaps. There's not much to Lonesome Dove but at least it's mainly clean of snakes. The sow eats them all—she's thorough, when it comes to snakes."

"But Captain," Gus said, appalled by his mistake. "Whoever heard of a blue pig? I ain't."

Captain King evidently didn't welcome challenges to his point of view—he looked at Augustus sharply.

"That's a French pig, sir," he said. "She's silvery in the main, though I suppose she does look bluish in certain lights. She comes from the region of the Dordogne, I believe. In France they use pigs to root up truffles, but you'll find very few damn truffles in this part of the world—so mainly she roots up snakes. Madame Wanz brought her over, and a fine boar too. I expect the boar is off girling, like my bull Solomon. When you get a closer look you'll find she's unusually long legged, that sow. She ain't low slung, like these runty little Texas pigs. The long legs are for climbing hills, to seek out the truffles, which don't flourish in low altitudes."

Call was listening carefully, impressed by Captain King's quick manner. Gus had had the rangers half spooked, with his talk of sharks, when it was only a pig in the water, downriver. He didn't know what a truffle was, or why one would need to be rooted up.

"What *is* a truffle, Captain?" he asked, putting up the rifle he had pulled during the alarm.

"Truffles are edible delicacies, Captain," Richard King said. "I have not had the pleasure of digesting one myself, but Therese Wanz swears by them, and she's as French as they come."

"If she's French, why is she here? This ain't France," Gus said. He was a good deal embarrassed by the matter of the shark that was only a sow; he felt sure he would be ribbed about it endlessly by the other rangers, once they got to town—if there really was a town.

"She should have stayed in France, and her pig too!" he said, in a burst of annoyance. "They've got no call to be disturbing the local stock!"

Captain King had been about to turn his fine bay horse and ride down the river, but he paused and looked at Gus sharply again.

"As to that, sir, *you've* got no call to be coming down here asking me for cattle when I'm hellish busy selecting worthy wives for my bull Solomon," Captain King said. "When was the last time you had a drink of whiskey, Captain?"

"More than a week's passed—I last touched liquor before we struck this dern brush," Gus said.

"No wonder you're surly, then," Captain King said. He pulled a flask out of his saddlebag and offered it to Gus. Gus was startled—he politely wiped the top of the flask on his sleeve before taking a good swig and handing the flask back to Captain King. Lee Hitch and Stove Jones looked on enviously.

"Thank you, Captain," Augustus said.

"A man needs his grog," Captain King said. "I'm goddamn surly myself, when deprived of my grog."

Call was annoyed with Gus. Why would he say a woman he had never met should have stayed in France? It was rude behavior, though Captain King was mainly right about the grog. Gus McCrae was scarcely able to be good company now unless he had had his tipple. He was anxious, though, that the rude behavior not obscure the fact that they needed Captain King's help if they were to secure the thousand cattle.

"Captain, what about the cattle?" he asked—but Richard King was too quick for him. He had already turned his horse and was loping down the river toward where the blue pig lay.

40.

WHEN THE RANGERS finally rode into Lonesome Dove, the town they had been seeking, thicket by thicket, for several days, the wet blue sow, who was indeed large and long legged, followed them at a trot, dragging a sizable bull snake she had just killed.

"I wouldn't call this a town," Augustus McCrae said, looking around disappointed. There were four adobe buildings, all abandoned—despite what Captain King had just said about the sow's efficiency as a snake killer, the buildings all looked snaky to him.

"No, but it's a nice-sized clearing," Call said. "You could put a town in it, I guess."

On the west side of the clearing a large white tent had been erected—near it, construction was under way on what was evidently meant to be a saloon. A floor had been laid, and a long bar built, but the saloon, as yet, had no roof. One table sat on the floor of the barroom-to-be; a small man dressed in a black coat sat at it. There was a tablecloth on the table, as well as a bottle of whiskey and a glass, although the small man did not seem to be drinking.

Outside the tent a small plump woman whose hair hung almost to the backs of her knees was talking volubly to Captain King.

"Do you reckon that bar's open, Gus?" Ikey Ripple asked.

Augustus didn't immediately comment. He was watching the blue sow suspiciously—on the whole he didn't trust pigs—but Stove Jones spoke up.

"Of course it's open, Ike," he said. "How could you close a saloon that don't have no roof?"

Before the matter could be debated further, Captain King came back.

"That tent belonged to Napoleon once," he said. "At least that's Therese's line. That's Xavier, her husband, sitting there at his table. I guess the carpenters ran off last night. It's put Therese in a temper."

"Run off?" Gus said. "Where could a person run off to, from here?"

"Anywhere out of earshot of Therese would do, I expect," Captain King said. "The carpenters in these parts ain't used to the French temperament, or French hair, either. They think Therese is a witch."

Call looked with interest at the tent. He had not made much progress in the book Captain Scull had given him about Napoleon, but he meant to get back to it once his reading improved. He would have liked to have a look inside the tent, but didn't suppose that would be possible, not with a talky Frenchwoman in it.

"It's a nuisance," Captain King admitted. "Now I'll have to go try to corral the carpenters—I expect it could take half a day."

Just then a flock of white-winged doves flew over the clearing, a hundred or more at least. Mourning doves were abundant too—the one thing that wouldn't need to be lonesome in such a remote place were the doves, Augustus concluded.

"Even if there was a town here I don't see why it would be called Lonesome Dove," he said. "There's dove everywhere you look."

Captain King chuckled. "I can tell you the origin of that misnomer," he said. "There used to be a traveling preacher who wandered through this border country. I knew the man well. His name was Windthorst—Herman Windthorst. He stopped in this clearing and preached a sermon to a bunch of vaqueros once, but while he was preaching a dove lit on a limb above him. I guess Herman took it as a holy omen, because he decided to stop wandering and start up a town."

Captain King gestured toward the four fallen-in adobe huts.

"Herman was holier than he was smart," he said. "He lived here a year or two, preaching to whatever vaqueros would stop and listen."

"Where is he now?" Gus asked.

"Why, in heaven I expect, sir," Captain King said. "Herman preached his last sermon about five years ago. He thought he had a nice crowd of vaqueros but in fact it was Ahumado and some of his men who stopped to listen. As soon as Herman said 'Amen' they shot him dead and took everything he had."

Captain King fell silent for a moment, and so did the rangers. Mention of the Black Vaquero reminded them of their dangerous mission.

"But they still call it Lonesome Dove—the name stuck," Call said.

"Yes sir, that's true," Captain King said. "The preacher's gone, but the name stuck. It's curious, ain't it, what sticks and what don't?"

"I better get after those carpenters," he went on. "I need to get a roof on this saloon. There's a fine crossing of the river, there—I can do some business in this town, once it gets built. We need that roof—otherwise it will shower one of these days, and if Xavier ain't quick it will get his tablecloth wet."

Augustus looked at the small man in the black coat, sitting stiffly with the bottle of whiskey, at the one table.

"What's he need a tablecloth for?" he asked. "Why worry about a tablecloth if you ain't even got walls or a roof?"

"He's French, sir," Captain King said. "They order things differently in France."

Without further explanation he turned his horse and rode off.

"I wish he could have waited until we talked to him about the cattle," Call said, disappointed.

"I don't," Augustus said.

"Why not?" Call asked. "We've been at this two weeks and we don't have a single cow. We need to get some and go."

"*You* need to, Woodrow," Gus said. "I don't. All I need is to see if that fellow with the tablecloth will sell this thirsty bunch some whiskey."

Call was annoyed with Captain King for leaving before they could discuss the business at hand, and annoyed, as well, with Gus McCrae, for being so quick to seize every opportunity to loaf.

All the rangers dismounted and the older men headed for the roofless bar.

On impulse, Call loped after Captain King, thinking perhaps they could negotiate for the cattle while looking for the carpenters—it might speed things up a little.

Lee Hitch and Stove Jones began to feel anxious when they saw Call leaving.

"Now Woodrow's leaving . . . what'll we do, Gus?" Lee asked.

"I'd like to get drunk, myself . . . I suppose you can do as you like, Lee," Gus said.

It occurred to Lee that there weren't many of them. What if the *pistoleros* who finished the preacher came back and went for them? With Call gone and Gus drunk, they might all be massacred.

"Yes, but then what?" he asked.

"Why, then, nothing, Lee," Gus said. "I guess we can all sit around and watch that French pig eat snakes."

41.

"INISH SCULL'S just a Yankee adventurer," Richard King said directly, when Call overtook him. "He went up against Ahumado once with a strong force and he lost. What the hell made him go back alone?"

"I can't say, Captain," Call admitted. "We were on our way home and he just peeled off, with the tracker—the next thing we heard he was captured."

"Speaking of peeling, what do you think of Madame Inez?" Captain King asked. "I hear she peels the pants off the lads quicker than I could core an apple."

Call had managed to depart Austin without having accepted Madame Scull's invitation to tea. He knew what Maggie thought about her, but what Madame Scull did was none of his business. He had no intention of gossiping about her with Captain Richard King.

"I scarcely know her," Call said. "I believe the Governor introduced us once. I suppose she's anxious to have her husband back."

"Possibly," Captain King said, eyeing Call closely. "Possibly not. As long as she has lads to peel she might not care. You're a circumspect man, ain't you, Captain?"

Call was not familiar with the word.

"Means you don't gossip about your superiors, Captain—that's a

429

rare trait," Captain King said. "I wish you'd quit the rangers and work for me. I need a circumspect man with ability, and I believe you have ability to go with your circumspection."

Call was surprised by the statement. He knew little about Captain King—just that he owned a vast stretch of land, south along the coast. The two of them had met scarcely an hour ago. Why would the man try to hire him on such short acquaintance?

Captain King, though, did not seem to expect a reply, much less an acceptance. The trail narrowed, as it entered the thick mesquite. The two of them had been riding side by side, but that soon ceased to be possible. Call fell in behind the Captain, who kept a brisk pace, ducking under the larger limbs and brushing aside the smaller. Call, less experienced in brush, twice had his hat knocked off. He had to dismount to retrieve it and in the process fell some ways behind Captain King. Fortunately the trail was well worn. He pressed on, as fast as he could, but, despite his best efforts, could not draw in sight of the Captain, or hear him, either. He was beginning to feel anxious about it—perhaps the trail had forked and he had missed the fork. Then he heard shouts from his left. Suddenly a large form came crashing at him, through the brush. His horse reared and threw him against the base of a mesquite tree just as Solomon, Captain King's great brown bull, passed in front of them with a snort. Call just managed to hang on to his rein and stop his horse from bolting up the trail. As he fell a thorn had caught his shirt and ripped it almost off him, leaving a cut down one side. The cut didn't worry him but it was a nuisance about the shirt because he only had one other with him. The shirt was so badly torn he didn't think it could be mended, even though Deets was adept with needle and thread.

The great bull had passed on, its head up, its testicles swinging. The trees over the trail were so low that Call didn't immediately remount. He walked, leading his horse. Then he heard a sound and turned in time to see the old vaquero Captain King had put in charge of the bull slipping through the brush, in close pursuit of the great animal.

It was all puzzling to him: why would anyone try to raise cattle in a place where you could scarcely see twenty feet? Even if you owned ten thousand cattle, what good would it do if you couldn't find them? He wondered why Texas had bothered taking such brushy country back from Mexico. In his years of rangering he had become competent, or at least adequate, in several environments. He could ranger on the plains, or in the hills, or even in the desert; but now he had been thrust into yet another environment, one he was not competent in at all. Captain King could move through the brush, the vaqueros could move through it, Solomon, the great bull, could move through it, but so far all he had done was get lost and ruin his shirt. He would have done better to have stayed with Gus and got drunk.

Just as Call was beginning to wonder if he should try to retrace his steps and at least get back to Lonesome Dove, he heard voices ahead of him. He went toward the voices and soon came into a sizable clearing. Captain King was there, talking to four black men who were sitting on the thick lower limb of a big live oak, their feet dangling.

"Why, there you are, Captain, what happened to your shirt?" Captain King asked.

"Thorns," Call said. "Are these the lost carpenters?"

"Yes, Solomon kindly treed them for me," Captain King said. "They're not eager to come down while Solomon's in the vicinity. They don't think the treeing was kindly meant."

"I don't blame them," Call said. "He nearly treed me."

"Nonsense, that bull is gentle as a kitten most of the time," Captain King said. "I expect it was those Mexican heifers that stirred him up. Anyway, Juan is taking him home. It's unfortunate about your shirt, Captain."

The black men did not seem at all inclined to leave their limb. While they watched, Solomon trotted quickly through the clearing, with the old vaquero, Juan, right behind him. The bull did not look their way.

"See there, men, Juan's taking Solomon home," Captain King

said. "He won't chase you no more. It's perfectly safe to come down."

The black men listened respectfully, but didn't move.

"Now, this is vexing, I don't know if Lonesome Dove will ever get built, though there's a fine river crossing there to be taken advantage of," Captain King said. "Between the bull and the French witch, these men are badly spooked. I don't suppose I could persuade you to lead them back to Lonesome Dove, could I, Captain?"

"Well, I guess I could take them back, if they ever decide to come down," Call said. "But what about the cattle to ransom Captain Scull?"

Captain King simply ignored the question.

"I've decided to proceed to my headquarters," he said. "I'd be obliged if you'd take these men back. They've got a saloon to build, and then a house. Therese Wanz will not be wanting to bivouac in Napoleon's tent forever."

The black men, evidently feeling that the bull was now gone, began to edge off the limb.

Call was hoping that Captain King would at least make some proposal regarding the cattle. After all, the Governor had asked, even if his letter did get a little wet. It was annoying that Captain King felt he could simply disregard it. He seemed far more interested in the carpenters than in the fate of Captain Scull.

One by one the carpenters edged down the bole of the live oak tree. They were all elderly men, each carrying a small sack of possessions—not much.

"Captain Scull is my captain," Call said. "I'm obliged to try and rescue him if I can."

Captain King only looked at him the more severely.

"I'm a blunt man, Captain," he said. "I know Scull's rank and I know your mission. In my opinion you and those tipplers back in Lonesome Dove could no more drive a thousand head of cattle to the Sierra Perdida than you could a thousand jackrabbits. I won't give you a cow, and besides that, I'm in the midst of the branding season and can't spare my vaqueros, either. Were that not enough,

I happen to know that the state of Texas is broke, and I am not the sort of man who enjoys giving away livestock."

"Well, Mr. Fogg said as much," Call told him.

"Oh, Denton Fogg, that gloomy fool," Captain King said. "He'll starve out in another year or two and have to take those spavined women back east."

"You won't sell us any cattle, then, Captain?" Call asked.

Captain King, whose mind seemed to be elsewhere, swung his severe gaze back to Call.

"You're a persistent man, I see, Captain," he said. "Do you like Inish Scull?"

"What, sir?" Call asked, surprised by the question.

"It's a simple question, Captain," Richard King said. "Do you *like* Inish Scull?"

Call resented the question so much that it was all he could do to keep from simply riding off with the black carpenters. He *didn't* like Inish Scull, as it happened: the man had been rude to him too often. But that was his business, not Captain King's.

"The Governor gave us orders," he said. "I mean to carry them out, if I can. I'd appreciate your help, but if I can't get it I've still got my orders to carry out."

"I should have asked McCrae," Captain King said. "I expect I would have got an answer from McCrae. You do like McCrae, don't you, Captain? Will you admit that much?"

"I had better take these men and head back to Lonesome Dove, Captain," Call said. "I don't want to get caught in this brush after dark."

"I'm glad you didn't take me up on that job offer, Captain Call," Richard King said. "I fear we'd quarrel."

"We would if you asked about things that are none of your business," Call said.

Captain King's look grew dark.

"Everything that happens in Texas is my business, Captain Call," he said. "*Everything!* I trust you'll remember that."

Without another word or look he turned his horse and left, disappearing into the brush at the point where the bull and the old vaquero had been.

Call found himself no wiser in the matter of the ransom than he had been when he left Austin. They had no cattle, and could find no one who would let them have any. Yet another mission was tending toward failure.

Besides that, he was in the midst of the south Texas brush country, with four elderly black men who did not seem happy to have been left with him. He suddenly realized that he had failed to ask Captain King whether the men were slave or free. If they were free he had no right to insist that they go back to Lonesome Dove with him. He decided just to ask them if they would come.

"I'm ready to go, men—are you coming with me?" he asked.

All the men nodded—they clearly didn't want to be caught in the brush after dark either.

"Missus Therese gonna whip us, though," the oldest of the men said.

"Oh, does she whip you, then?" Call asked. To his surprise the four men all smiled broadly.

"She get after us with the buggy whip," one said.

"Mister Xavier too, though," another commented. "She get after Mister Xavier worse."

"Her husband, you mean," Call asked.

The old black man nodded; the others looked suddenly fearful, as if they might have said too much.

Call didn't question them further—it would only embarrass them. As he rode back down the narrow trail he recalled that Madame Scull was said to go after the Captain with a bullwhip, when in a temper. Now here was another wife who whipped her husband—it struck him as strange. Though he and Maggie were not married, he could not imagine her behaving so.

"Well, at least it's just a buggy whip," he said.

None of the black men said anything.

42.

"GET UP, MONSIEUR. Make the liquors. The customer is here!" Therese Wanz said, flinging each word at her husband as if it were a small stone. Xavier Wanz, her husband, seemed to be thinking thoughts of his own; he continued to sit at the table with the white tablecloth, staring at his glass.

Therese, in only a few moments in her tent, had managed to sweep her abundant brown hair up on her head in an appealing mound; the gown she wore did not quite conceal her plump shoulders. Augustus McCrae, who had not expected to see a woman, much less an attractive woman, for several years, if ever, found that the sight of Therese brought an immediate improvement in his mood.

She stood in the middle of the barroom floor, hands on her hips, looking at the rangers cheerfully.

"See, already the customers," she said to Xavier. "Vite! Vite! Make the liquors."

Xavier Wanz compressed his lips, and then, as if propelled by a spasm of fury, jumped from his chair and strode over to the tent, beside which a sizable mound of goods was covered by a large wagon sheet. Xavier dove under the sheet like a rat seeking cover; for a moment, only his rump was visible, but, in the space of a minute, he emerged with two bottles of whiskey and several glasses. He hurried to the bar, set the bottles and glasses on it, and paused to straighten his cuffs.

"Messieurs," he said, bowing slightly, "the pleasures are mine."

"If the bar's open I expect a few of those pleasures might be ours, too," Gus said.

Pea Eye declined the liquor and Deets wasn't offered any, but in a few minutes the other rangers, including young Jake Spoon, were all seated around the table where Xavier had sat. At Therese's strident urging Xavier had applied himself again to the mound under the wagon seat and come out with several chairs.

"These glasses are clean," Gus said, in astonishment. "You could

435

spend a week in the saloons of Austin and never encounter a clean glass."

As soon as each glass was emptied, a process that didn't take long, Xavier appeared with a bottle, poured, and bowed.

"Monsieur," he said, invariably.

Ikey Ripple, who had passed easily and quickly into a state of profound inebriation, found himself a little put off by the bowing.

"Why's he bowing to us?" Ikey asked.

"To be polite—why shouldn't he bow?" Augustus asked.

"That's right, a bartender ought to bow," Lee Hitch said—although, so far as he could remember, none of the bartenders of his acquaintance had ever bothered to bow to him before.

"I say it's a goddamn trick," Ikey declared. "I think he means to get us drunk and steal all our money."

"Ikey, if you've got cash money on you, you don't need to wait for a Frenchman to steal it," Gus said. "Loan it to me and I'll invest it for you."

"Invest it in whores—that's all you know about, Gus," Ikey said.

"Well, that way you wouldn't have to be anxious about it," Gus told him.

Therese Wanz, a smile on her lips, seemed to be studying the rangers closely. Pea Eye had elected to help Deets with the horses, but Jake Spoon had boldly taken his place at the table and was drinking whiskey as if he had a right to, a fact that annoyed Gus McCrae a good deal. Even more annoying was the fact that the Frenchwoman was looking at Jake with interest.

"Jake, you ought to be helping with the horses," Gus said, in an irritable tone.

Jake knew well that when Gus was out of temper it was better to walk small. He saw the Frenchwoman watching him, but didn't connect it with Gus's angry tone. After all, the woman's husband was standing right behind her.

Therese decided right away that she liked Monsieur McCrae, but she saw nothing wrong with flirting a little with the curly-headed boy. Opportunities to flirt were limited in Lonesome Dove.

Opportunities to make money were no less rare, and Therese liked money. Captain and Therese liked money. Captain King assured her there would soon be a brisk trade in the town—he seemed to think that merchants would rush to Lonesome Dove in order to take advantage of the fine river crossing, but, so far, very few merchants had appeared, a fact which frustrated Therese's commercial instincts severely.

Now, at the sight of the tired, dusty, unshaven men, Therese began to think in terms of money. She quickly decided that the first task would be to barber them—they could all use shaves and two or three of them needed haircuts as well.

"Xavier! The woods, monsieur!" she said crisply, with a glance at her husband. "I want to shave these men and give them the hair-offs."

Xavier Wanz, severely depressed as he was by the many differences between Texas and France, walked over to a campfire that smoldered in front of the tent. He would have preferred, himself, to sit at the table all day, enjoying the seemliness of his clean table-cloth, and perhaps drinking just enough liquor to blind himself to the ugliness of the mesquite trees that surrounded the clearing where, if Captain King was to be believed, a town would one day exist.

Therese, of course, had her own ideas; every day Lonesome Dove presented some new challenge to her energies, and her energies were not small. Every day, in this new land, Therese arose, impatient; every day Xavier was the man who bore the brunt of her impatience. Yesterday, Therese's impatience had overflowed and scared away the carpenters; today, at least, there were these men to occupy her, these rangers. If she wanted to barber them it was fine with him.

With his foot he nudged a few more sticks of firewood into the fire, before returning to his bar.

"Hair-offs—hair-offs!" Therese said, coming to the table. "You first, monsieur," she said, tapping Augustus on the shoulder.

"All right, I'll volunteer—do I get a shave too?" Gus said.

Therese didn't answer—she had already marched off to her tent. When she emerged, carrying a razor, a razor strop, and several other tools of the barbering trade, she pulled another chair from under the wagon sheet and insisted that Gus sit on it.

The rangers, most of them now drunk, watched with interest as Therese vigorously stropped her razor.

"I'm shaggier than Gus, she ought to have barbered me first," Stove Jones complained.

"What you complaining about? I'll be lucky to even get a shave," Lee Hitch said, well aware that his bald head offered little incentive to a barber.

Jake Spoon gulped down what was left of the whiskey and went off to sit with Pea Eye and Deets. It *was* vexing that Gus McCrae seemed to get the first attentions, if a woman was around. Now the woman was wrapping Gus in a sheet and cooing over him as if he were something special. The sight put Jake in such a hot mood that he picked up three clods and threw them at the blue sow, who had consumed the bull snake and had flopped down under a small bush to rest. The clods missed but Xavier Wanz noticed and immediately walked over to Jake.

"Monsieur!" he said sternly. "Do not disturb the pig."

"That's right, it ain't your pig, don't be chunking it," Gus said, from his barber chair. "That pig's the pride of the community—it needs its rest."

His pride stung, Jake walked straight past Pea Eye and on toward the river. He had merely thrown three clods at a sow. What right had Gus to speak to him in such a tone? He felt like quitting the rangers on the spot. He could hammer and saw; maybe the French couple would hire him to carpenter. With Gus gone the French-woman might even come to like his curly hair, as Madame Scull once had. Perhaps she would take him up and teach him the language; he imagined how chagrined Gus McCrae would be if, the next time the rangers stopped in Lonesome Dove, he and Madame Wanz were chattering in French.

"Where do you suppose he's going?" Pea Eye asked, when Jake walked past.

"Could be going to take a wash," Deets said.

"Now you've run Jake off, picking on him," Lee Hitch remarked.

"The pup, he's welcome to drown himself for all I care," Gus said, well aware that he was the envy of the troop, by virtue of having been chosen to receive the first haircut.

Therese Wanz, though flirtatious in her approach to barbering, was all seriousness when she got down to the business itself. She decided to start with the shave and promptly lathered Gus's face liberally with a nice-smelling soap.

"Boy, this beats that old lye soap," Gus said, but Therese rapped his head sharply with her knuckles, indicating that the time for talk was over. Therese then shaved him carefully and expertly, not omitting to do some careful work under his nose. Then she wrapped his face in a hot towel and began the haircut, moving his head this way and that, touching him, making him sit up straighter, or insisting that he turn one way or another. With the hot towel steaming on his face and Therese's deft hands working it with scissors and comb, Gus drifted into a kind of half sleep, in which he allowed himself to imagine that it was Clara doing the barbering. On occasion, dissatisfied with the work of the local barbers, Clara *had* barbered him, sitting him down on the steps behind the store and scissoring away until she had him looking the way she wanted him to look, a process that took much squinting and inspecting.

Therese Wanz, more expert than Clara, was also more decisive. When she took the hot towel off his face she produced some small tweezers and began to yank the hairs out of his nose. Gus had never had his nose hairs interfered with before. He was relaxed, half asleep, and a little drunk—the first extraction took him so completely by surprise that he yelped.

His companions had been watching the barbering operation closely, all of them filled with envy. When Therese yanked out the first nose hair Gus's reaction struck them as the funniest thing they had ever seen. They howled with laughter. Lee Hitch was so amused that a chair could not hold him—he lay on his back on the floor of the saloon, laughing violently. Stove Jones laughed nearly as loud. Far down the street, Jake Spoon heard the laughter and turned, wondering what could be so funny.

Pea Eye and Deets, who had been trimming a gelding's hoof, had not been paying too much attention to the barbering. When they saw the Frenchwoman pulling hairs out of Gus's nose they began to laugh too.

Augustus McCrae, who had been in a pleasurably relaxed state, found that he had suddenly become an object of wild amusement to the men. Therese, though, brooked no resistance; she finished his nose to her satisfaction and began to yank hairs out of his ears, oblivious to the laughter from the saloon. She proceeded briskly with her tweezers, seizing a hair and extracting it with the same motion.

Xavier Wanz, standing stiffly behind a bar, thought the men he was serving must be crazy. He had never heard such desperate laughter, and at what? Because his wife was giving their captain the hair-offs? Not knowing quite what to do, he contented himself with folding and refolding his little white towel several times.

The hairs out, Therese began to rub Gus with an unguent whose smell she liked. The young monsieur had nice hair; she felt she might enjoy entertaining him in her tent for a bit, if only Xavier could be distracted, which didn't seem likely.

Meanwhile, there was business. Once she had combed Gus's hair the way she considered that it ought to be combed, she took the sheet off him and announced that he could stand up.

"One dollars, monsieur," she said. "Now you look like a fine cavalier."

Augustus was somewhat startled by the price; he had not expected to pay more than fifty cents for his barbering, in such a place. Many a whore would cost little more than the haircut. But Therese smiled at him and whisked him off with her little brush. He liked her plump shoulders—why be tight?

"A bargain at the price, ma'am," he said, and paid her the dollar.

43.

WHEN CALL CAME BACK to Lonesome Dove with the four carpenters he was surprised to find that the whole troop had been barbered and shaved. Pea Eye was just rising from the chair when he rode up. Only Deets, watching silently from a seat on a stump, had not been worked on. All the men were preening as if they had just come out of church. Therese Wanz, the woman who had clipped the considerable pile of hair that was around the barber chair, was bent over a large washtub, wringing out a towel.

"Ma'am, you need to strop your razor—here's one more," Gus said. "I'll take your horse, Woodrow—you've got a treat in store."

Madame Wanz was evidently a woman of cheerful temperament. She sat Call down and poured out a torrent of French.

"Do you know what she's saying?" he asked Augustus.

"Just keep still and do your duty, Woodrow," Gus said.

Madame Wanz made a little bow when she sat Call in the barber's chair. He felt a touch of embarrassment; he had heard of women barbers but had never been worked on by one before. All of the men were in high good humor. They looked more presentable than they had looked in months.

"I expect you better shear me," Call said. "It'll probably be a good spell before I see a barber again."

Call had relaxed and slipped into a half-doze by the time Therese Wanz got around to the extraction of his nose hairs. He jumped so violently at the first jerk of the tweezers that he turned the barber chair over—all the men, who had been watching for just such a reaction, exploded with laughter. Augustus laughed so hard he had to hold his side. Even Call had to smile. It must have been funny, seeing him tip over a barber's chair.

"I wish we had old Buffalo Hump here," he said. "I expect he'd think this was a pretty fancy torture."

Therese, undeterred, sat him down again and applied the tweezers until his nose was plucked clean of hairs.

Later, when they were all cleaned up enough to look almost as respectable as Xavier Wanz's tablecloth, Therese proved that she was as skilled a cook as she was a barber. A sizable flock of half-wild chickens chirped amid the crumbling adobe huts. Therese snatched four of them, collected a great number of eggs, and made them all a feast which included potatoes. The men ate so much they could scarcely stumble off the floor of the saloon-to-be, where the feast had been served on a folding table Xavier had produced from under the wagon sheet.

"If people knew they could get fed like this, Lonesome Dove would be a town in no time," Gus said. "I wouldn't mind moving here myself. It would save the expense of all that high-priced Austin liquor."

"Yes, but what would you do for cash?" Call asked. "It's fine eating, but there'd be no one to pay you a wage."

Therese had put two candles on the folding table. Other than their flickering light, the only illumination came from the high moon.

"Captain King expects there'll be businesses here someday, because of the fine river crossing," Gus said. "If there's businesses here, I guess we could have one too."

"Speak for yourself," Call said. "I'm a Texas Ranger and I aim to stay one."

"Now that's a damn boresome point of view," Gus said. "Just because we started out being rangers don't mean we have to stay rangers all our lives. The army will whip out the Indians in a few more years and there won't be much to do, anyway."

"Maybe, but there's plenty to do right now," Call said.

"Mr. Xavier, now he's a curious fellow," Gus said. "He's been standing behind that bar all day and he's still standing behind it."

Call looked. Sure enough, Xavier still held his position behind the long bar, although all the rangers had either fallen asleep or left the floor of the saloon.

"Between the barbering and the liquor they made a pretty penny on us today," Call said. "I expect they'll soon prosper."

The two of them strolled away from the unbuilt saloon and the camp where their comrades slept, and meandered toward the river. They heard the water before they saw it, and, when they did see it, it was only the flicker of moonlight here and there on the surface.

"Lonesome Dove will need a whore or two, otherwise it won't grow," Augustus allowed. "Prosperous businessmen won't long tolerate the absence of whores."

"You can't tolerate it, you mean," Call said. "That's one reason you'll never be a prosperous businessman."

"Well, I just wasn't meant to work at one trade all my life," Augustus said. "I'm too fond of variety."

"If you like variety I don't see how you can beat rangering," Call said. "A month ago we were freezing on the plains, trying not to get scalped, and now we're off to Mexico, where we'll be hot and probably get shot."

"Is the Captain sending the cattle?" Gus asked. "If he is, I hope they don't come for a day or two. A little more of that woman's cooking might improve my cowboying."

"He's not sending the cattle—no interest," Call said.

"No interest?" Gus said, astonished. "No cattle? What are we going to do, Woodrow?"

They both stood looking across the river, at Mexico, the dark country.

"Maybe the Captain's already escaped," Gus said. "He's sly, the Captain. He could be halfway home by now."

"He might be halfway dead, too," Call pointed out.

"If we can't raise the cattle, what do we do?" Augustus asked. "Go after him anyway, or give up again?"

"You're a captain, same as I am," Call said. "What do you want to do? The two of us might go in alone and sneak him out."

"Why, yes, and pigs might cuss," Gus said. "What'll happen is we'll get caught too—and the state of Texas won't bother sending no expedition after *us*."

Still, once he thought about it, something about the adventure of trying to rescue Captain Scull appealed to him, and the thought of a herd of cattle did not.

"It's getting to be the fly season, Woodrow," Gus said.

Call waited. Augustus didn't elaborate.

"What's your point?" Call asked, finally. "We can't stop the seasons from turning."

"No, but we could avoid cattle during the fly season," Gus said. "A thousand cattle would attract at least a million flies, which is more flies than I care to swat."

"We don't have them anyway," Call said. "And if Captain King won't give them to us, nobody will. Anyway, he's right. We could no more drive a thousand cattle across Mexico than we could a thousand jackrabbits."

"That's right, we ain't vaqueros," Gus said.

The two of them fell silent, looking across to Mexico. Though they quarreled frequently, they were often tugged by the same impulses, and so it was at that moment by the slow river. The longer they looked across it, the more strongly they felt the urge to attempt their mission alone—without cattle and without the other men.

"We could just do it, Woodrow—the two of us," Augustus said. "We'd have a better chance than if we take the cattle *or* the troop."

Call agreed.

"I'm game if you are," he said. "I think it's about time we made something of ourselves, anyway."

"I'd just like to travel with less company, myself," Gus said. "I don't know about making something of ourselves."

"Buffalo Hump's held the plains ever since we've been rangers," Call pointed out. "We've never whipped him. And Ahumado's held the border—we've never whipped him either. We can't protect the plains or the border either—that's poor work in my book."

"Woodrow, you're the worst I've ever known for criticizing yourself," Gus said. "We've never rangered with more than a dozen men at a time. Nobody could whip Buffalo Hump or Ahumado with a dozen men."

Call knew that was true, but it didn't change his feeling. The Texas Rangers were supposed to protect settlers on the frontier, but they hadn't. The recent massacres were evidence enough that they weren't succeeding on their job.

"You ought to give up and open a store, if you feel that low about it," Augustus suggested. "There's a need for a store, now that the Forsythes are dead. You could marry Mag while you're at it and be comfortable."

"I don't want to run a store or marry either," Call said. "I'd just like to feel that I'm worth the money I'm paid."

"No, what you want is to take a big scalp," Gus said. "Buffalo Hump's or Ahumado's. That's what you want. Me, I'd take the scalp too, but I don't figure it would change much."

"If you kill the *jefe* it might change *something*," Call argued.

"No, because somebody else just as mean will soon come along," Gus said.

"Well, we rarely agree," Call said.

"No, but let's go to Mexico anyway," Augustus said. "I'm restless. Let's just saddle up and go tonight. There's a fine moon. Without the boys to slow us down we could make forty miles by morning."

Call felt tempted. He and Augustus at least knew one another's competencies. They *would* probably fare better alone.

"What's your hurry?" he asked Gus. "Why tonight?"

"If I stay around I expect that Frenchwoman might fall in love with me," Gus said. "Her husband might fight me—it'd be a pity to get blood on that nice tablecloth."

"Do you suppose the boys can find their way back to Austin, if we leave?" Call asked.

"Ikey Ripple claims to have never been lost," Augustus reminded him. "I expect it's a boast, but I think we should put him to the test. If the other boys don't want to try it with Ikey, they can stay and help build the saloon. The town would grow quicker if they had a saloon that didn't expose you to the weather—if the saloon had a roof and there was a whore or two and a livery stable, Lonesome Dove might be a place somebody might want to live."

"The boys will be right surprised, when they wake up and find us gone," Call said.

445

"A little startlement would be better than being caught by Ahumado," Gus pointed out. "From what I've heard, he ain't gentle."

The white moon soared over Mexico. The longer the two men looked, the stronger beckoning they felt from the unknown land.

"If we had cattle I'd try it the way we were supposed to," Call said. "But the fact is we don't."

When they got back to the saloon the two candles had been blown out and the Wanzes had retired to their tent.

"I doubt that tent really belonged to Napoleon," Call said. "He was the emperor. Why would he give it up?"

"He might have just liked Therese, if he'd met her," Augustus said. "I like her myself, even if she did pull hairs out of my nose."

Deets was the only man awake when the two of them were saddling their horses and selecting a few provisions. At first he supposed the two captains were just going off on a scout; when Call came over and informed him that they were going to try and rescue Captain Scull themselves, Deets's eyes grew wide. He knew it was not his place to question the action of his two captains, but he could not entirely suppress his apprehension.

"We way down here in the brush," he said.

It wasn't that Deets felt exactly lost—it was just that he didn't feel exactly safe. The big Indian with the hump might come—or, if not him, someone just as bad.

Call felt a little guilty as he gathered up his gear. He was usually the one impatient to leave, but this time it was Augustus who was in a sweat to get started. Call felt he ought to wake up one or two of the men and let them know what was happening, but Augustus argued against it.

"These men have been drinking ever since we got here," he pointed out. "They're drunk and they're asleep—let's just go. They ain't new calves, they're grown men. I doubt we'll be gone more than a few days. If they don't want to head back to Austin, they can stay here and wait for us."

Several loud snores could be heard, as they talked.

Call felt that they ought to leave instructions, but again Gus protested.

"You don't always have to be telling people every single thing to do, Woodrow," he complained. "They need to work up some independence anyway. If we wake 'em up they might quarrel and start punching one another."

"All right," Call said. It didn't feel quite right, but there was logic in what Gus said.

Pea Eye woke up, as the two captains talked. He saw them mount and ride out of camp; in a minute or two he heard their horses take the river. But it was not an unusual thing. Captain Call particularly often rode off at night, to scout a little. Pea Eye supposed it was no more than that, and went back to sleep.

44.

WHEN AHUMADO SAW the small hole in his leg, with the little ring of rot around it, he knew that Parrot had been at work. Parrot had sent the small brown spider who hides to bite him; when he first saw the hole, which was in the lower part of his leg, he was surprised. He had always been respectful of Parrot, as he had of Jaguar. It was hard to know why Parrot would have the Spider-Who-Hides bite him—but the evidence was there. When Ahumado bent over he could smell the rot, and he knew it would get worse. Soon he might have no leg; he might merely have a bone where the leg had been. The flesh of his leg would rot and turn black. Parrot liked to joke—what had happened might only be Parrot's joke. Parrot was older than humans, and had no respect for them. He was capable of complicated jokes, too. The whites had always called Ahumado the Black Vaquero, despite the fact that he had no interest in cows. He only bothered taking them to annoy the Texans, who prized cows highly. He didn't like horses, either, except to eat, yet the whites considered him a great horsethief, though he only stole horses to trade them for slaves. Still, all the whites called him the Black

Vaquero. Parrot knew such things—so now Parrot had sent Spider-Who-Hides to make his leg black. It was one of Parrot's jokes, probably. The Black Vaquero would at least have a black leg.

Ahumado did not reveal his injury to anyone. He sat on his blanket, as he always did, watching the great vultures soar across the face of the Yellow Cliffs. There were fewer vultures now, because Ahumado had stopped hanging men in the cages, men the vultures could eat. Only a few of the vultures, or the eagles, still flew along the cliff, waiting to see if Ahumado would cage a man for them to eat.

Ahumado sat as he had always sat, listening, saying little. The wound in his leg was very small yet; no one had noticed it, or smelled the rot that would soon spread. Once he had thought the matter over for a day or two, Ahumado realized that it was more than just one of Parrot's jokes. Parrot had sent Spider to call him home; Parrot and Jaguar wanted him to leave the Yellow Cliffs, to stop harrying the whites with their thin cattle; Parrot and Jaguar wanted him to return to his home, to the jungle, where great serpents rested in the vine-covered temples. There was a broad tree near one of the temples, a tree with a great hole in it. Lightning had hit the tree and burned it away inside, so that there was a space in the tree large enough for a person to live in. When Ahumado was young an old woman had lived in the tree: her name was Huatl and she was a great *curandera*, so great that she could even cure the bite of the Spider-Who-Hides. In his youth Ahumado had often seen old Huatl; she lived in the split tree, near his home. She had told him that he would live long but that in his old age it would be his duty to return to the place of the split tree. When it was time for him to finish with his life as a human being, he was to lie near the tree with the hole in it; then he would sink into the earth and become a root. Lightning would come again and burn the great tree where Huatl lived. That tree would burn up but another tree would grow from the root that had once been the man Ahumado. That tree would live for a thousand years and become the tree of medicines. The people would come in their weakness or illness to the tree of medicines and be cured. In that tree would be all knowledge, all that Huatl and all the other great healers knew.

For three days Ahumado watched the tiny hole in his leg become larger; he watched as the ring of rot spread. On the third day he heard a sound deep in his ear and looked up to see Parrot fly like a red streak across the face of the cliff. He thought the sound in his ear was from Jaguar, who was somewhere near.

Ahumado knew then that he had been summoned. He was spending his last day in the canyon of the Yellow Cliffs. None of the people in the camp knew this, of course. The women went on with their work, washing clothes in the stream and making tortillas. The men played cards, drank tequila, quarreled over dice, and tried to get the women to couple with them. Scull crouched in his cage, sheltering his lidless eyes from the sun. It was hundreds of miles to the jungle, to the place of temples. Ahumado knew he had better get started. He wanted to get across the first mountains before his leg became too bad. He knew that by the time he reached the home of Jaguar he would have no leg. He meant to take a good hatchet with him, so he could make himself a crutch when his leg failed. That night he would crawl through a hole that only he knew about—the hole would take him through the belly of the cliff; it would take him past the dark men. He told no one; he would merely vanish—in the morning there would be no Ahumado. He would travel over rocks and leave no track. None of the people would know where he went. He would simply be gone.

There was only one thing left for Ahumado to do, in the canyon of the Yellow Cliffs, and it involved old Goyeto, the skinner.

"Sharpen your knives," he told Goyeto. "You had better get them as sharp as you can. They need to be very sharp today."

Goyeto brightened, when he received those instructions. They had taken no captives lately; there had been no one to skin. But now Ahumado wanted him to make the knives sharp. He wanted the knives to be very sharp. It must mean that he had at last decided to let him skin the white man, Scull. There was no one else who was a candidate for skinning.

So Goyeto set about to make his little knives sharp—while Ahumado sat on his blanket, Goyeto whetted his knives, with skill. When they were ready he brought them to Ahumado, who tested them one by one. He used fine threads from his blanket, cutting the threads with the mere touch.

"Are we going to skin the white man?" Goyeto asked. "I'll have him tied to the post, if you want."

When Ahumado turned to face him Goyeto's heart almost stopped, from the look that was in Ahumado's eyes. Goyeto did not even have the strength to stammer. He knew he had been discovered; an old sin, one he had committed many years before with one of Ahumado's women, on a blanket amid the horses, had been found out. Goyeto had long feared discovery—Ahumado was jealous of his women—but Ahumado had been one hundred miles away, on a trip to catch slaves, when the woman coaxed him onto the blanket. She was a lustful woman; she had tried to coax him onto the blanket many times, but Goyeto had been too fearful of Ahumado's vengeance. He had only coupled with the woman that once.

When Ahumado turned his snakelike look on him, Goyeto knew who the knives had been sharpened for. He jumped up and tried to run, but the vaqueros quickly caught him. At Ahumado's command they took all his clothes off and tied him to the post where he had practiced his delicate art for so long. Goyeto felt such a fear that he wanted to die. No one but himself knew how to skin a man—if one of the crude young *pistoleros* tried to skin him it would just be butchery; they would hack his flesh off, with his skin.

Then Ahumado himself rose from his blanket and took the knives. He stuck them one by one into the post above Goyeto's head, so that, as one became dull, he could take another.

"Parrot told me what you did with my woman," Ahumado said. "He told me in a dream. I have watched you skin people for many years. I am your pupil in this matter. Now we will see if I have learned well."

Goyeto didn't plead. He was so frightened that all words left his mind and became screams. Ahumado began at his armpits and began to work downward. Old Goyeto had a big stomach—Ahumado thought such a stomach would be easy to skin, but it wasn't. Goyeto screamed so loudly that people became confused and began to flee the camp. It was not merely the loudness of the screams that confused them, either. Ahumado was skinning the skinner—no one knew what it meant. It might mean that he was tired of them, that he meant to skin them all. If they ran he might merely shoot them, which would be better than being skinned.

Goyeto's voice wore out long before Ahumado worked downward to the part that had been active in committing the sin, years before on the horse blanket. Goyeto's mind broke; he spewed liquids out of his mouth that mixed with his blood. Ahumado tried to skin one of his ears but Goyeto didn't feel it. He died in the afternoon, well before the sun touched the rim of the Yellow Cliff. Disappointed, Ahumado stuck all of Goyeto's skinning knives in him, and walked away.

There were only a few people left in the camp by then; a few old women, too crippled to run, and one or two of the older vaqueros; all of them hated Goyeto and wanted to see how long he would last. Like Ahumado, they were disappointed.

The other person left was the white man, Scull. He had not watched the skinning. It was a bright day. He had to crouch with his arms over his head to keep the brightness from burning his brain. Scull knew what happened, though. Ahumado had seen him glance once or twice at the skinning post. Scull noticed that people were leaving the camp. It was only when dusk fell and deep shadows filled the canyon that Scull could look. Ahumado had returned to his blanket—a few old women sat by the fires.

In the night, when the camp slept, Ahumado went to the cage where Scull was kept. Scull flashed his white eyes at him but didn't speak. Neither did Ahumado. Goyeto, dead, hung from the skinning post. Even some of the old women had begun to hobble away. Ahumado pulled the cage, with Scull in it, toward the pit of snakes and scorpions and, without delay, pushed it over the edge. He heard it splinter when it hit the floor of the pit. There was no sound from Scull, but Ahumado heard the buzz of several rattlesnakes as he walked away.

Ahumado took his rifle and his blanket and moved quickly until he found the hole that led through the belly of the mountain.

By morning, when old Xitla woke and began to stir the campfire, the vultures had begun to curl down into the camp, to feast on Goyeto; but Ahumado, the Black Vaquero, was gone.

45.

As SCULL LISTENED to old Goyeto's screams he wondered what had occurred. The skinner was being skinned, that much he could see, although he only glanced up once or twice. He could not risk more; not with the sun so bright. But Ahumado was doing the skinning and, to judge from the intensity of Goyeto's screams, doing it badly on purpose. Where the skinner, Goyeto, had only taken skin, Ahumado pulled away strips of flesh, and did it so cavalierly that Goyeto soon wore out his voice and his heart. He died well before sunset, only partially skinned.

Once the shadows came Scull could risk more looks—he saw that almost all the people in the camp were leaving, unnerved by the unexpected execution of Goyeto.

Then, once it was dark, Ahumado suddenly appeared and began to push the cage toward the pit. He didn't speak; Scull didn't either. The two had contested in silence so far; let it stay silent, Scull thought, though he was disturbed by what was occurring. He had seen men hurled into the pit and had heard their dying screams. He didn't know how deep the pit was—perhaps he would be killed or crippled by the drop. He knew there were snakes in the pit because he could hear them buzzing; but he didn't know how many snakes, or what else might be there. Once Ahumado appeared there was no time to reflect or plan. Ahumado didn't even glance at him, or speak words of hatred and triumph. He just pushed the cage a few feet and, without ceremony, shoved it over the edge of the pit.

The darkness Scull fell into was soon matched by the darkness in his head. He heard snakes buzzing and then he heard nothing. The cage turned in the air—he landed upside down and struck his head sharply on one of the wooden bars.

When he came to, it was night—in the moonlight he could see the opening of the pit above him. Scull didn't move. He heard no buzzing, but didn't consider it prudent to move. If there was a snake close by he didn't want to disturb it. In the morning he could assess matters more intelligently. There was dried blood on his cheek; he assumed he had cut his head when the cage hit bottom. But he was alive.

At the moment his worst affliction was the stench. The rich Mexicans who had died in the pit were still there, of course, and they were fragrant. But *he* was alive, Bible and sword; under the circumstances, phenomenal luck. It could easily have been himself, and not Goyeto, at the skinning post.

The *pistoleros*, the vaqueros, the young men of the camp, and the young women seemed to have gone. Always at night there would be singing around the campfires; there would be laughter, quarrels, the sounds of flirtation, drunkenness, strife. Sometimes guns were fired; sometimes women shrieked.

But now the camp above him was silent, a fact which bothered Scull considerably. To be alive, after such a drop, was exhilarating; but after relief and euphoria came terrible thoughts. What if they had all left? The old man might just have pushed him into the cage and left him to starve. The walls of the pit looked sheer. What if he couldn't scale them? What would he survive on? What if no rains came and he had no water?

From exhilaration he slid toward hopelessness; he had to will himself to stop, to collect his thoughts. Intelligence, intelligence, he told himself. Think! The fact that he was in a hard situation didn't mean the final doom was come. At least in the pit he could shade himself, and the rangers might be well on their way with the cattle. With Ahumado gone all they would have to do was ride in and hoist him out of the pit.

Slowly, Scull's panic subsided. He reminded himself that in the pit there was shade; the torture of sunlight would be avoided.

Finally a gray light began to filter into the air above the pit. The stars faded. Scull looked first for the snakes and saw none. Perhaps they were hiding in crevices. The dead men were far gone in rot. Fortunately his cage had splintered and he soon freed himself of it. The stench all but overcame him; he thought his best bet to contain it would be to scoop dirt over the bodies. If he could cover them over with dirt it would cut at least some of the smell. He pulled loose a couple of bars, from his cage, to use as digging instruments. He could dig at the side of the pit until he had enough dirt to cover the bodies. Though not particularly fastidious, he felt that a day or two of the stench might unhinge his mind.

He was just about to begin digging at the wall of the pit when he heard the buzzing again and realized he had been wrong about the snakes. The light was gray and so was the dust in the pit—in the gray dust the snakes were almost invisible. One large rattler had been resting not a yard from where he stood. The snake started to crawl away, only rattling a little, not coiling, but Scull leapt at it and crushed its head with his stick. He knew he had to be careful. His eyes were apt to water when he focused too long on one thing. He couldn't see well enough to spot the snakes. He edged around the perimeter of the pit and killed three more snakes before he was done. Then he began to dig at the walls. By noon, when he had to quit and hide his eyes, the dead Mexicans lay buried under sizable mounds of earth. Before burying the men Scull held his nose with one hand and forced himself to investigate their pockets. He was hoping Ahumado had overlooked a pocketknife, or another file, but in that he was disappointed. All he got off the corpses was their belts.

From time to time he dug, heaping more dirt on the corpses, but his time in the cage had weakened him; he could not dig long at a stretch, and no matter how careful he was, dirt got into his lidless eyes. The dust and dirt felt as painful as if it were gravel. Finally he took off his shirt, tied it over his eyes, and dug at the walls blindly.

By the afternoon, exhausted, he huddled in the shade. One of his ankles was inflamed. He had seen several scorpions and wondered if he had been bitten by one during the night, when he was unconscious. He saw no sign of a bite, but the ankle was very sore, which chastened him. The pit seemed to be only fifteen feet deep, only some three times his size. Perhaps he could dig a few handholds and pull himself out. But his throbbing ankle, coupled with his exhaustion and the beginnings of a fever, brought home to him again the desperate character of the situation. No sound at all came from what had been, only the day before, a bustling camp. There might be no one left to bring him water or food. The rangers might not have been able to get the cattle; no help might be coming. The pit he was in, though not really deep, was just deep enough to constitute the perfect trap for a man in his condition. Even if he could dig the handholds, he might not have the strength to climb out; his ankle would scarcely bear his weight. He could eat the snakes he had killed, but, after that, he would have nothing. Every day he would get a little weaker, and have less and less hope of effecting his own escape. Barring a miracle, Ahumado had beaten him after all. The old man had even robbed him of time. As soon as Ahumado noticed that Scull was keeping a little calendar of twigs, he moved the cage and scattered the twigs. It was a thing to brood about. Ahumado had known that time meant something special to his prisoner. Now and then he would approach the cage and say, "Do you know what day it is, Captain?"

Scull refused to answer—but Ahumado knew that Scull's hold on time had been broken.

"I know what day it is," he would say quietly, before returning to his blanket.

That night, as Scull's fever rose, he dreamed of a flood. He dreamed that water filled the pit to its brim, cool water that allowed him to float free. "Forty days and forty nights," he mumbled, but he awoke to dry sunlight and pain in his eyes. The dirt he had got in them the day before left them swollen.

"Noah," Scull said, aloud. "I need what Noah had. I need a flood to raise me up."

His own words sounded crazy to him. As his mind swirled, touching the edges of madness, he suddenly thought of Dolly, his Dolly—Inez to the world but always Dolly to him. Even at that moment, as he lay starving in a scorpion pit in Mexico, she probably was in a bed or a closet, stoking her own fires with some stout illiterate lad.

"The black bitch!" he said.

Then, anger pulsing through him, he yelled the words as loudly as he could: "The black bitch! The bitch!" The sound echoed off the cliffs, where a few buzzards still circled.

Then, dizzy from his own spurt of anger, Scull sat back against the wall of the pit, exhausted. In his mind he saw exactly how the handholds should be dug, in an ascending circle around the pit. He stood five foot two; he only needed to raise himself a bit over ten feet to escape—nothing to what Hannibal had faced with his elephants at the base of the Alps. Yet it was those ten feet that would defeat him. His eye saw the way clearly, but his body, for the first time in his life, would not respond.

Scull dozed; the heat of the day began to fill the pit. Soon it felt hot as a stovepipe to him. His fever rose; he felt chill even as he sweated. Once he thought he heard movement above him. He thought it might be a coyote or some other varmint, inspecting the camp, hoping to find a scrap to eat. He yelled a time or two, though, on the off chance that it might be a human visitor.

His yells produced no answer. Scull stood up, to test his ankle, but immediately sat back down. His ankle would bear no weight. Then he began to get the feeling that he was not alone: someone was above him, waiting where he couldn't see them. But the person, if it was a person, waited quietly, making no sound. Through the afternoon he turned his sore eyes upward a few times, but saw no one.

Then, as dusk was approaching, he saw what he had sensed. A face, as old and brown as the earth, was visible above him. Then he remembered the old woman. He had seen her often during his days of captivity in the cage, but had paid her little mind. Most of the day the old woman sat under a small tree, silent. When she rose to do some chores she walked slowly, bent almost double, supporting herself with a heavy stick. He rarely saw anyone speak to her. No doubt the people of the camp had left her to die—crippled as she was, she would have been an impediment to travel.

"*Agua!*" he said, looking up at her. The sight of a human face made him realize how thirsty he was. "*Agua! Agua!*"

The old face disappeared. Scull felt a flutter of hope. At least one human knew where he was, and that he was alive. There was no reason for the old woman to help him—she was probably dying herself. But she was there, and people were unpredictable. She might help him.

Above him old Xitla crept about the camp. She was glad the people had left—the camp was hers now. She had spent the day looking for things people had dropped as they were leaving. People were so careless. They left things that they considered had no use, but old Xitla knew that everything had a use, if one were wise enough to know the uses of things. In a few hours of looking she had already found a bullet, several nails, an old shirt, and a rawhide string. These things were treasures to Xitla. With each find she hobbled eagerly back to her tree and put her treasure on her blanket.

In her years in Ahumado's camp Xitla had been careful never to tell him her name. She knew he would kill her immediately if he knew that her name was Xitla and that she was the daughter of Ti-lan, a great *curandera* who had known him in his youth in the south. Her mother had insisted that she take the name "Xitla" because it would protect her from Ahumado. When he was a baby, her mother told her, the elders had put a poisoned leaf under Ahumado's tongue and sent him out in the world to do evil. Though Ahumado did not know it, he and Xitla had been born on the same minute of the same day, and their mothers were sisters—thus their destinies were forever linked together. They would die on the same moment of the same day too—in killing Xitla, Ahumado would have killed himself. But Ti-lan, her mother, when she sent Xitla away, warned her that she was never to tell Ahumado her real name, or the circumstances of her birth. If Ahumado knew he would try to challenge his destiny by putting Xitla to death in some cruel fashion. He bore the legacy of the poisoned leaf and would do much evil as a result.

A few years back Xitla thought Ahumado had found her out. He seldom rode a horse, yet one day for no reason Ahumado mounted a strong horse and rode the horse right over her, injuring her back, so that she could never again stand straight. He had never explained his actions. He had merely ridden over her and left her in the dust. Then he dismounted and was never seen on a horse again. He had forbidden the people to help her, too. Xitla had crawled away on her hands and knees and found roots and leaves that helped her pain to be less.

Around the camp, Xitla was known as Manuela. Because it was understood that Ahumado disapproved of her, she had few friends. Sometimes drunken vaqueros, men so debased that they would use any woman, or even a mare or a cow, came and pawed at her in the night. She had been small and dark but very beautiful; the vaqueros saw something of her beauty and still pawed at her, even though she had passed her time as a woman.

One or two of the other old grandmothers in the village spoke to her; they were too old to care about Ahumado or his wrath. Xitla's one companion was a small white cat. The little cat grew and became her hunter. It brought her the fattest rats and even, now and then, a baby rabbit, a delicacy Xitla cooked in her pot, seasoned with good spices. Her cat was Xitla's companion. It slept next to her head at night, and its thoughts went into her brain. The cat wanted her to leave the camp and go to a nearby village. But Xitla was afraid to go. She moved so slowly that it would take her many days to reach the village—once Ahumado knew that she was gone he might send his *pistoleros* to catch her and put her on one of the sharpened trees—that was the penalty for those who left without permission.

A few weeks later her cat left the camp to hunt and never came back. A woman told her, much later, that Ahumado had caught it and given it to a great rattler he kept in a cave—Xitla never knew whether the story was true. Even though she was old many women in the camp were jealous of her, because of her great beauty. Sometimes in the night Xitla felt her cat trying to send its thoughts into her brain, but its thoughts were not clear. Another woman told her that the story about the great rattler was nonsense; there had been an old cougar living near the camp; the cougar had probably eaten her cat.

This old woman, Cincha, had merely wanted gossip, Xitla thought. Like everyone else in the camp, Cincha was curious about Xitla and Ahumado. They wanted to know why the Black Vaquero hated Xitla so much; and why, if he hated her, didn't he just kill her. None of them knew about the sisters, or the poisoned leaf, nor did they know the real reason for Ahumado's hatred, which was simple. Once in his youth Ahumado had tried to come to her in the way of a man and she had stuck him in his member with a green thorn. She had been using the thorn to sew and had merely stuck Ahumado with it because she did not want to be with him in that way.

The green thorn had poison in it and the poison went into Ahumado's member. He had several wives, but none of them were happy—there were stories and stories, but Xitla didn't know if they were true. She just knew that Ahumado hated her so badly that he had run over her with a horse.

Now, to her surprise, Ahumado had been the one to leave the camp. He told no one that he was leaving. There was much speculation but no one really knew why Ahumado did the things he did. Within a day, all the other people in the camp left too. No one offered to take Xitla. They had simply left her on her blanket. The women were particularly anxious to leave her—they did not like it that Xitla had such beauty of face still.

Xitla had been asleep, dreaming of Parrot, when Ahumado pushed the white man into the pit. When she awoke she heard the white man speaking to himself and knew that he was still alive. The white man had survived as Ahumado's captive for many weeks—

he had a strong spirit in him; he might yet find a way to escape the pit. She could not resist peeking at him, in the pit, and it was then that he asked her for water.

There were three or four pots laying around the camp, pots people had left in their careless haste. Xitla took one of the pots and filled it with water from the stream. Then she searched though her treasures until she found enough rawhide string to make a cord long enough to lower the water to the white man. It would please her to help the prisoner in the pit, but when she lowered the water and looked at the man she realized it would not be easy to save him—he was very weak. He was on the point of giving up, this man, but Xitla hoped that a little cool water and some food would bring his spirit back its strength.

It took Xitla a long time to get the water, moving slowly as she did, and she was careful when she lowered it into the pit. When the white man stood up to catch the jug Xitla saw that one of his ankles was injured. He could not put his foot on the ground without pain, a fact which complicated his escape. It would be hard for him to climb out of the pit with such a sore ankle.

Xitla decided to take her blanket and go to the little cornfield by the stream. The corn was young, but it was the only food close to the camp that she might bring him. She would pile some of the soft corn on her blanket and drag it to the pit, so that the man would have something to eat. She could stay alive on very little, and the white man could too or he would have already starved.

"*Gracias, gracias,*" Scull said, when the water jug was safely in his hands. He took the water in little sips, just a drop or two at a time, to soothe his swollen tongue. His tongue was so thick that he could barely speak his words of thanks.

It was a good sign that Scull was careful with the water, Xitla thought. He was disciplined; if she could get him a little corn his spirit might revive.

That night Xitla listened carefully to the animal noises around the camp. She wanted to be awake in case Ahumado came back. He had always been a night raider; he struck at the most peaceful hour, when people were deep in restful sleep. Young women, dreaming of lovers, would not know anyone was there until the hard hands of the *pistoleros* took them away into slavery, far from their villages and their lovers. People were not alert enough to sense the approach of Ahumado, but animals could sense it. All the animals knew that Ahumado had been given the poison leaf, and did evil things. Sometimes he made Goyeto tie up animals and skin them, for practice. The animals knew better than to let such an old man catch them. The coyotes stayed away, and the skunks and even the rats. The night birds didn't sing when Ahumado was around.

Xitla listened carefully, and was reassured. There were plenty of animals out that night, enjoying the bright moon. Just beyond the cornfield where she meant to go in the morning with her blanket there were some coyotes playing, yipping at one another, teasing and calling out. She watched a skunk pass by, and heard an owl from a tree near the cliff.

Hearing the sounds of the animals made Xitla feel peaceful, content to doze by her little fire of twigs and branches. She didn't know where Ahumado had gone, or why, but it was enough, for the moment, to know that he was far away. In the morning she would go to the cornfield with her blanket and pick some young corn for the white man, Captain Scull.

46.

THERESE WANZ was much put out when she emerged from the white tent and discovered that Captain Call and Captain McCrae had left Lonesome Dove in the night. She had been up early, gathering eggs in her basket from hens' nests in the crumbling house left by Preacher Windthorst. She liked the two young captains; having them there was a fine change from the company of her husband, Xavier, a man disposed to look on the dark side of life, a man who had little natural cheer in him or even a satisfactory amount of the natural appetites all men should have. Frequently, due to his

461

gloom, Therese had to sit on Xavier in order to secure her conjugal pleasures. Xavier was convinced they would starve to death in the Western wilderness they had come to, but Therese knew better. In only one day, with the rangers there, they had made more money than they would have made in France in a month, doling out liquor in their village for a few francs a day.

All day the rangers had drunk liquor and paid them cash money, a fact not lost on Xavier, who threw off his gloom long enough to accord Therese a healthy dose of conjugal pleasure without her having to go to the trouble of sitting on him.

She sprang up early, ready to make the rangers a fine omelette and collect a few more of their dollars, only to discover that the two rangers she liked best had ridden off to Mexico. Only the black man had seen them leave; the other rangers were as startled as Therese to discover they were gone.

"You mean they left us here?" Lee Hitch asked.

"Yes sir," Deets said. "Gone to get the Captain."

"That's all right, Lee," Stove Jones said. "I imagine they expect us to wait, and at least we'll be waiting in a place where the saloon don't close."

"It'll close if Mr. Buffalo Hump shows up," Lee said, with an apprehensive look around the clearing. Toward the river the blue sow and the blue boar were standing head-to-head, as if in conversation. Xavier Wanz was attempting to fasten a bow tie to his collar, a task that soon reduced him to a state of exasperation.

At the mention of Buffalo Hump, Jake Spoon came awake with a start.

"Why would he show up, Lee?" Jake asked. "There ain't a town here yet—he wouldn't get much if he shows up here."

"My tooth twitched half the night, that's all I know," Lee Hitch said. "When my tooth twitches it means Indians are in the vicinity."

"Goddamn them, why did they go?" Jake said, annoyed at the two captains for leaving them unprotected. Since the big raid on

Austin his fear of Indians had grown until it threatened to spoil his sleep.

Pea Eye was shocked that Jake would use such language in talking about Captain Call and Captain McCrae. They were the captains—if they left, it was for a good reason.

Then, to Pea Eye's surprise, the Frenchwoman began to wave at him, beckoning him to come help her prepare the breakfast. She was breaking eggs into a pan, and swirling it around; her husband, meanwhile, took out his tablecloth, from a bag where he kept it, and spread it on the table, smoothing it carefully. The man had on a bow tie, which struck Pea Eye as unnecessary, seeing as there was only a rough crew to serve.

"Quick, monsieur, the woods!" Therese said, when Pea Eye bashfully approached. He saw that the cook fire was low and immediately got a few good sticks to build it up. As Therese swirled the eggs in the pan her bosom, under the loose gown, moved with the swirling motion. Pea Eye found that despite himself his eyes were drawn to her bosom. Therese didn't seem to mind. She smiled at him and, with her free hand, motioned for him to bring more sticks.

"Hurry, I am cooking but the fire is going lows," she said.

Though it was so early that there were still wisps of ground fog in the thickets, Lee Hitch and Stove Jones presented themselves at the bar, expecting liquor. To Pea Eye's amazement Jake Spoon stepped right up beside them. Only the night before Jake had confided in him that he didn't have a cent on him—he had lost all his money in a card game with Lee, a man who rarely lost at cards.

Xavier Wanz put three glasses on the bar and filled them with whiskey; Jake drank his down as neatly as the two grown men. Both Lee and Stove put money on the bar, but Jake had none to put, a fact he revealed with a smile.

"You'll stand me a swallow, won't you, boys?" he asked. "I'm a little thin this morning, when it comes to cash."

Neither Lee nor Stove responded happily to the request.

"No," Lee said bluntly.

"No one invited you to be a drunkard at our expense," Stove added.

Jake's face reddened—he did not like being denied what seemed to him a modest request.

"You're barely weaned off the teat, Jake," Lee said. "You're too young to be soaking up good liquor, anyway."

Jake stomped off the floor of the saloon, only to discover another source of annoyance: the Frenchwoman had summoned Pea Eye, rather than himself, to help her with the cook fire. The woman, Therese, was certainly comely. Jake liked the way she piled her abundant hair high on her head. Jake sauntered over, his hat cocked back jauntily off his forehead.

"Pea, you ought to be helping Deets with the horses—I imagine they're restless," Jake said.

To his shock the Frenchwoman suddenly turned on him, spitting like a cat.

"You go away—ride the horses yourself, monsieur," she said emphatically. "I am cooking with Monsieur," she said emphatically. "I am cooking with Monsieur Peas. You are in the way. *Vite! Vite!*

"Young goose!" she added, motioning with her free hand as if she were shooing away a gosling that had gotten underfoot.

Mortified, Jake turned and walked straight down to the river. He had not expected to be rudely dismissed, so early in the day; it was an insult of the worst kind because everybody heard it—Jake would never suppose such a blow to his pride would occur in such a lowly place.

It stung, it burned—the high-handedness of women was intolerable, he decided. Better to do as Woodrow Call had done and form an alliance with a whore—no whore would dare speak so rudely to a man.

The worst of it, though, was having Pea Eye chosen over him, to do a simple chore. Pea Eye was gawky and all thumbs; he was always dropping things, bumping his head, or losing his gun—yet the Frenchwoman had summoned Pea and not himself.

While Jake was brooding on the insult he heard a splashing and looked down the river to see a group of riders coming. At the thought that they might be Indians his heart jumped, but he soon saw that they were white men. The horses were loping through the shallows, throwing up spumes of water.

The man in the lead was Captain King, who loped right past Jake as if he wasn't there. The men following him were Mexican; they carried rifles and they looked hard. He turned and followed the riders back toward the saloon.

When he arrived Captain King had already seated himself at the table with the tablecloth, tucked a napkin under his chin, and was heartily eating the Frenchwoman's omelette. One of the vaqueros had killed a javelina. By the time Jake got there they had the little pig skinned and gutted. One of the men started to throw the pig guts into the bushes but Therese stopped him.

"What do you do? You would waste the best part!" Therese said, scowling at the vaquero. "Xavier, come!"

Jake, and a number of the other rangers too, were startled by the avid way Therese and Xavier Wanz went after the pig guts. Even the vaquero who had killed the pig was taken aback when Therese plunged her hands to the wrists in the intestines and plumped coil after coil of them on a tray her husband held. Her hands were soon bloody to the elbow, a sight that caused Lee Hitch, not normally a delicate case, to feel as if his stomach might come up.

"Oh Lord, she's got that gut blood on her," he said, losing his taste for the delicious omelette he had just been served.

Captain King, eating *his* omelette with relish, observed this sudden skittishness and chuckled.

"You boys must have spent too much time in tea parlors," he said. "I've seen your Karankawa Indians, of which there ain't many, anymore, pull the guts out of a dying deer and start eating them before the deer had even stopped kicking."

"This is fine luck, Captain," Therese said, bringing the heaping tray of guts over for him to inspect. "Tonight we will have the tripes."

"Well, that's fine luck for these men—while they're eating tripe

I'll be tramping through Mexico," he said. "Some thieving caballeros run off fifty of our cow horses, but I expect we'll soon catch up with them."

"You could take us with you, Captain," Stove Jones said. "Call and McCrae, they left us. We ain't got nothing to do."

Captain King wiped his mouth with his napkin and shook his head at Stove.

"No thanks—taking you men would be like dragging several anchors," he said bluntly. "Call and McCrae were unwise to bring you—they should have left you to the tea parlors."

He spoke with such uncommon force that none of the men knew quite what to say.

"It was the Governor sent us on this errand," Lee Hitch said finally.

"He just wanted to get rid of you so he could claim he'd tried," Captain King said, with the same bluntness. "Ed Pease knows that few Texas cattlemen are such rank fools as to deliver free cattle to an old bandit like Ahumado. He takes what livestock he wants anyway."

"It was to ransom Captain Scull," Stove Jones reminded him.

Captain King stood up, wiped his mouth, scattered some coins on the table, and went to his horse. Only when he was mounted did he bother to reply.

"Inish Scull is mainly interested in making mischief," he said. "He got himself into this scrape, and he ought to get himself out, but if he can't, I imagine Call and McCrae will bring him back."

"Well, they left us," Lee Hitch said.

"Yes, got tired of dragging anchors, I suppose," the Captain said.

He motioned to his men, who looked dismayed. They had cut up the javelina and prepared it for the fire, but so far the meat was scarcely singed.

"You will have to finish cooking that pig in Mexico," he informed them. "I cannot be sitting around here while you cook a damn pig. I need to get those horses back and hang me a few thieves."

With that he turned and headed for the river. The vaqueros hastily pulled the slabs of uncooked javelina off the fire and stuffed them in their saddlebags. A couple of the slabs were so hot that smoke was seeping out of their saddlebags as they rode away.

Therese and Xavier Wanz began to cut up the pig guts, stripping them of their contents as they worked. Xavier had taken off his black coat, but he still wore his neat bowtie.

Lee Hitch and Stove Jones were both annoyed by Captain King. In their view he had been rude to the point of disrespect.

"Why does he think we sit around in tea parlors?" Stove asked.

"The fool, I don't know—why didn't you ask him yourself?" Lee said.

47.

"LORD, MEXICO'S a big country," Augustus said. It was a warm night; they had only a small campfire, just adequate to the cooking they needed to do. Just after crossing the river, Call had shot a small deer—meat for a day or two at least. They were camped on a dry plain, and had not seen a human being since coming into Mexico.

"The sky's higher in Mexico," Gus observed; he felt generally uneasy.

"It ain't higher, Gus," Call said. "We've just traveled sixty miles. Why would the sky be higher, just because we're in Mexico?"

"Look at it," Gus insisted. He pointed upward. "It's higher."

Call declined to look up. Whenever Gus McCrae was bored and restless he always tried to start some nonsensical argument, on topics Call had little patience with.

"The sky's the same height no matter what country you're in," Call told him. "We're way out here in the country—you can just see the stars better."

"How would you know? You've never been to no country but Texas," Gus commented. "If we was in a country that had high mountains, the sky would *have* to be higher, otherwise the mountains would poke into it."

Call didn't answer—he wanted, if possible, to let the topic die.

"If a mountain was to poke a hole in the sky, I don't know what would happen," Gus said.

He felt aggrieved. They had left in such a hurry that he had neglected to procure any whiskey, an oversight he regretted.

"Maybe the sky would look lower if I had some whiskey to drink," he said. "But you were in such a hurry to leave that I forgot to pack any."

Call was beginning to be exasperated. They were in deserted country and could get some rest, which would be the wise thing.

"You should clean your guns and stop worrying about the sky being too high," he said.

"I wish you talked more, Woodrow," Augustus said. "I get gloomy if I have to sit around with you all night. You don't talk enough to keep my mind off them gloomy topics."

"What topics?" Call asked. "We're healthy and we've got no reason to be gloomy, that I can see."

"You can't see much anyway," Gus said. "Your eyesight's so poor you can't even tell that the sky's higher in Mexico."

"The fact is, I was thinking about Billy," Augustus said. "We've never gone on a rangering trip without Billy before."

"No, and it don't feel right, does it?" Call agreed.

"Now if he were here I'd have someone to help me complain, and you'd be a lot more comfortable," Augustus said.

They were silent for a while; both stared into the campfire.

"I feel he's around somewhere," Augustus said. "I feel Billy's haunting us. They say people who hang themselves don't ever rest. They don't die with their feet on the ground so their spirits float forever."

"Now, that's silly," Call said, although he had heard the same speculation about hanged men.

"I can't stop thinking about him, Woodrow," Gus said. "I figure it was just a mistake Billy made, hanging himself. If he'd thought it over a few more minutes he might have stayed alive and gone on rangering with us."

"He's gone, though, Gus—he's gone," Call reminded him, without reproach. He realized he had many of the feelings Augustus was trying to express. All through the bush country he had been nagged by a sense that something was missing, the troop incomplete. He knew it was Long Bill Coleman he missed, and Augustus missed him too. It *was*, in a way, as if Long Bill were following them at an uncomfortable distance; as if he were out somewhere, in the thin scrub, hoping to be taken back into life.

"I hate a thing like death," Augustus said.

"Well, everybody hates it, I expect," Call said.

"One reason I hate it is because it don't leave you no time to finish conversations," Gus said.

"Oh," Call said. "Was you having a conversation with Billy that night before . . . it happened?"

Augustus remembered well what he and Billy Coleman had been talking about the night before the suicide. Bill had heard from somebody that Matilda Jane Roberts, their old traveling companion, had opened a bordello in Denver. Matty, as they called her, had ever been a generous whore. Once, on the Rio Grande, bathing not far from camp, she had plucked a big snapping turtle out of the water and walked into camp carrying it by its tail. He and Long Bill always talked about the snapping turtle when Matilda's name came up.

"We was talking about Matty, I believe she's in Denver now," Gus said.

"I guess she never made it to California, then," Call said. "She was planning to go to California, when we knew her."

"People don't always do what they intend, Woodrow," Gus said. "Billy Coleman had it in mind to turn carpenter, only he couldn't drive a nail."

"He was only a fair shot," Call remembered. "I guess it's a wonder he survived as a ranger as long as he did."

"You survive, and you're just a fair shot yourself," Augustus pointed out.

"He married," Call said. He remembered how anguished Long Bill had been after he learned that Pearl had been outraged by the

Comanches. That discovery changed him more than all their scrapes and adventures on the prairies.

"He's out there now, Woodrow—I feel him," Gus said. "He's wanting to come back in the worst way."

"He's in your memory, that's where he is," Call said. "He's in mine too."

He did not believe Long Bill's ghost was out in the sage and the thin chaparral; it was in their memories that Long Bill was a haunt.

"Rangers oughtn't to marry," he said. "They have to leave their womenfolk for too long a spell. Things like that raid can happen."

Augustus didn't answer for a while.

"Things like that happen, married or not," he said finally. "You could be a barber and still get killed."

"I just said what I believe," Call said. "Rangering means ranging, like Captain Scull said. It ain't a settled life. I expect Bill would be alive, if he hadn't married."

"I guess it's bad news for Maggie, if you feel that way, Woodrow," Gus said. "She's needing to retire."

"She can retire, if she wants to," Call said.

"Yes, retire and starve," Gus said. "What would a retired whore do, in Austin, to earn a living? The only thing retired whores can do is what Matty just did, open a whorehouse, and I doubt Maggie's got the capital. I imagine she could borrow it if you went on her note."

Call said nothing. He was being as polite as he could. They would need to be at their best, if they were to rescue Captain Scull. They ought not to be quarreling over things they couldn't change. He believed what he had just said: rangers ought not to marry. The business about going on Maggie's note was frivolous—Maggie Tilton had no desire to open a whorehouse.

"I doubt Captain Scull is even alive," Gus said. "That old bandit probably killed him long ago."

"Maybe, but we still have to look," Call said.

"Yes, but what's our chances?" Gus asked. "We'll be looking for one man's bones—they could be anywhere in Mexico."

"We still have to look," Call said, wishing Augustus would just quiet down and go to sleep.

48.

ON THE THIRD DAY the rangers came into terrain that looked familiar—they had crossed the same country before, when Inish Scull had first pursued Ahumado into the Sierra Perdida.

"We've got to be alert now," Call said. "We're in his country."

In the afternoon they both had the feeling that they were being watched—and yet, as far as they could see, the country was entirely empty of human beings. The mountains were now a faint line, far to the west. Augustus kept looking behind him, and Call did too, but neither of them saw anyone. Once Gus noticed a puff of dust, far behind them. They hid and waited, but no one came. Gus saw the puff of dust again.

"It's them," he said. "They're laying back."

Too nervous to leave the problem uninvestigated, they crept back, only to see that the dust had been kicked up by a big mule deer. Gus wanted to shoot the deer, but Call advised against it.

"The sound of a gun would travel too far," he said.

"The sound of my belly rumbling will too, pretty soon, if we don't raise some more grub," Gus said.

"Throw your knife at him—I don't object to that," Call said. "I think it's time we started traveling at night."

"Aw, Woodrow, I hate traveling at night in a foreign country," Augustus said. "I get to thinking about Billy being a ghost. I'd see a spook behind every rock."

"That's better than having Ahumado catch you," Call told him. "We're not as important as Captain Scull. They won't send no expeditions after us."

"Woodrow, he ain't important either," Augustus said. "None of these ranchers let us have a single cow—I guess they figure the Captain's rich enough to pay his own way out."

They rode all night and, the next day, hid under some overhanging rocks. Gus thought to amuse himself by playing solitaire, only to discover that his deck of cards was incomplete.

"No aces," he informed his companion. "That damn Lee Hitch stole every one of them. What good is a deck of cards that don't have no aces?"

"You're just playing against yourself," Call pointed out. "Why do you need aces?"

"You ain't a card-playing man and you wouldn't understand," Gus said. "I always knew Lee Hitch was a card cheat. I mean to give him a good licking once we get back to town."

"I'd suggest hitting him with a post, if you want to whip him," Call said. "Lee Hitch is stout."

As dusk approached they started to edge into the foothills and immediately began to see tracks. People had been on the move, some on horseback, some on foot, and all the tracks led out of the Sierra. Gus, who considered himself a tracker of high skill, jumped down to study the tracks but was frustrated by poor light.

"I could read these tracks if we'd got here a little earlier," he said.

"Let's keep going," Call said. "These tracks were probably just made by some poor people looking for a better place to settle."

As they passed from the foothills into the first narrow canyon, the darkness deepened. Above them, soon, was a trough of stars, but their light didn't do much to illuminate the canyon. The terrain was so rocky that they dismounted and began to lead their horses. They had but one mount apiece and could not risk laming them. They entered an area where there were large boulders, some of them the size of small houses.

"There could be several *pistoleros* behind every one of those big rocks," Augustus pointed out. "We might be surrounded and not know it."

"I doubt it," Call said. "I don't think there's anybody here."

When they had ridden into the Yellow Canyon before, there had been no army of *pistoleros*, just three or four riflemen, shooting from caves in the rock. Only their Apache scout had seen Ahumado lean out briefly and shoot Hector and the Captain. No one else saw

472

him. Ahumado was not like Buffalo Hump—he didn't prance around in front of his enemies, taunting them. He hid and shot; he was only seen by his enemies once he had made them his prisoner.

As they walked their horses deeper and deeper into the Sierra Perdida, Call became more and more convinced that they were alone. From years of rangering in dangerous territory he had gained some confidence: he believed he could sense the presence of hostiles before he saw them. There would be a sense of threat that could not be traced to any one element of the situation: the horses might be nervous, the birds might be more noisy; or the threat might be detectable by the absence of normal sounds. Even if there was nothing specific to point to, he would tense a little, grow nervous, and rarely was his sense of alarm without basis. If he felt there was about to be a fight, usually there would be a fight.

Now, in the canyon that led to the cliff of caves, he felt no special apprehension. Few landscapes were more threatening, physically—Gus was right about the boulders being a good place for *pistoleros* to hide—but he didn't believe there were any *pistoleros*. The place felt empty, and he said so.

"He's gone," he said. "We've come too late, or else we've come to the wrong place."

"It's the place we came to before, Woodrow," Augustus said. "I remember that sharp peak to the south. This is the same place."

"I know that," Call agreed, "but I don't think anybody's here."

"Why would they leave?" Gus asked. "They'd be pretty hard to attack, in these rocks."

Call didn't answer—he felt perplexed. They were only a few miles from the place where they expected to find the Captain, but they had heard nothing and seen nothing to indicate that anyone was there.

"Maybe we came all this way for nothing," he said.

"Maybe," Gus said. "We've had a lot of practice, going on expeditions for nothing. That's how it's mostly turned out. You ride awhile in one direction and then you turn around and ride back."

In the rocky terrain they had several times heard rattlesnakes sing, so many that Augustus had become reluctant to put his foot on the ground.

"We'll just get snakebit if we keep tramping on in the dark like this," he said. "Let's stop, Woodrow."

"We might as well," Call agreed. "We can't be more than a mile or two from the place where the camp was. In the morning we can ride in and see what we see."

"I hope I see a whore and a jug of tequila," Gus said. "Two whores wouldn't hurt, either. I'm so randy I might wear one of them down."

Now that he didn't have to march through rattlesnakes, Augustus felt a little more relaxed. He immediately took off his boots and shook them out.

"What was in your boots?" Call inquired.

"Just my feet, but I like to shake my boots out regular," Gus said.

"Why?"

"Scorpions," Gus replied. "They crawl around everywhere, down here in Mexico. One could sneak off a rock and go right in my boot. They say if a Mexican scorpion bites you on your foot it will rot all your toes off."

They hobbled the horses and kept them close by. There was no question of a fire, but they had a few scraps of cold venison in their saddlebags and ate that.

"What was in your boots?" Call inquired.

"Just my feet."

"Why would he ask for a thousand cattle if he was planning to leave?" Call asked.

"Maybe he didn't," Gus suggested. "That vaquero who showed up in Austin might have been lying, hoping to get a thousand free cattle for himself. I expect he just wanted to start a ranch."

"If so, he was a bold vaquero," Call said. "He came right into Austin. We could have hung him."

"The more scared I get, the more I feel like poking a whore," Augustus said.

"How scared are you?" Call asked.

"Not very, but I could still use a poke," Augustus said.

When he thought about the matter he realized that he had almost no apprehension, even though they were close to the Black Vaquero's camp.

"I know why I ain't scared, Woodrow," he said. "Long Bill ain't haunting us no more. He was following along for a while but he's not here now."

"Well, he never liked Mexico," Call observed. "Maybe that's why."

"Either that or he just decided it was too far to travel," Augustus said.

49.

IT WAS AFTER the old crippled woman began to bring him food that Scull's mind slipped. At first the food she brought him was only corn—ears of young corn which she pitched down into the pit. The kernels were only just forming on the corn, it was so young; but Scull ate it greedily, ripping off the husks and biting and sucking the young kernels for their milky juice. The cobs he threw in a pile. He had been so hungry he was about to eat the dead snakes; the corn and the cool water revived him; it was then, though, with his strength returning and his ankle not so sore, that he began to speak in Greek. He looked up at the old woman to thank her, to say "*gracias*," and instead reeled off a paragraph of Demosthenes that he had learned at the knee of his tutor, forty years ago. It was only later, in the night, when the pit was dark, that he realized what he had done.

At first his lapse amused him. It was a curious thing; he would have to discuss it with someone at Harvard, if he survived. He believed it was probably the eyelids. The sun, unobstructed, burned through forty years of memory and revealed, again, a boy sitting in a chilly room in Boston, a Greek grammar in his lap, while a tutor who looked not unlike Hickling Prescott put him through his verbs.

The next morning it happened again. He woke to the smell of

tortillas cooking—then the old woman rolled up a handful and lowered them to him in the jug that she used to bring him water. Scull hopped up and began to quote Greek—one of Achilles' wild imprecations from the *Iliad*, he couldn't recall which book. The old woman did not seem startled or frightened by the strange words coming from the filthy, almost naked man in the pit. She looked down at him calmly, as if it were a normal thing for a white man in a pit in the Mexican mountains to be spouting Greek hexameters.

The old woman didn't seem to care what language he spoke, English and Greek being equally unintelligible to her; but Scull cared. It wasn't merely damage done by the sun that was causing him to slip suddenly into Greek; it was the Scull dementia, damage from the broken seed. His father, Evanswood Scull, intermittently mad but a brilliant linguist, used to stomp into the nursery, thundering out passages in Latin, Greek, Icelandic, and Old Law French, a language which it was said that he was the only man in America to have a thorough mastery of.

Now the aberration of the father had reappeared in the son, and at a most inconvenient time. In the night he suddenly woke up twitching in the brain and poured out long speeches from the Greek orators, speeches he had never been able to remember as a boy, an ineptness that caused him to be put back a form in the Boston Latin School. Yet those same speeches had been, all along, imprinted in his memory as if on a tablet—he had merely to look up at the old woman to ask for water to pour out, instead, a speech to the citizens of Athens on some issue of civic policy. He couldn't choke off these orations, either; his tongue and his lungs worked on, in defiance of his brain.

Scull began to try and curb himself; he needed to devise a way to get out of the pit before Ahumado came back, or, if not Ahumado, some other *pistolero* who would shoot him for sport. His tongue might soar with the great Greek syllables, but even that noble language wasn't going to raise him fifteen feet, to the pit's edge. He thought he might encourage the old woman to look around—maybe someone had left a length of rope somewhere. If she could find a rope and anchor it somehow, he felt sure he could pull himself up.

He was handicapped, though, by the insistent Scull malady. When he saw her old face above him he would try to make a polite request in Spanish, of which he knew a sufficiency, but before he could utter a single phrase in Spanish the Greek would come pouring out, a cascade, a flood, surging out of him like a well erupting, a torrent of Greek that he couldn't check or slow.

She'll think I'm a devil, he thought. I might yet get free if I could just choke off this Greek.

Xitla, for her part, leaned over the edge and listened to the white man as long as he wanted to talk. She could make no sense of the words but the way he spoke reminded her of the way young men, heart-stricken by her beauty, had sung to her long ago. She thought the white man might be singing to her in a strange tongue he used for songs of love. He spoke with passion, his thin body quivering. He was almost naked; sometimes Xitla could see his member; she began to wonder if the white man was in love with her, as all men had been once. Since Ahumado had run over her with the horse and broken her back, few men had wanted to couple with her—a regret. Always Xitla had had men to couple with her; many of them, it was true, were not skilled at coupling, but at least they wanted her. But once the men knew that Ahumado hated her, they withdrew, even the drunken ones, for fear that he would tie them to the post and have Goyeto skin them. Xitla had not been ready to stop coupling when the men began to ignore her; she did not want to be like the other old women, who talked all day about the act that no one now wanted to do with them. Xitla had coupled happily with many men and thought she could still do so pleasurably if only she had a man with a strong member to be with.

The only possibility was the white man, but before any coupling could take place she would have to get the white man out of Ahumado's scorpion pit and feed him something better than the young green corn.

Xitla didn't know how she was going to do either thing until she remembered Lorenzo, a small caballero who was more skilled than anyone else at breaking horses. About a mile south of the cliff was a spot of bare, level ground, where Lorenzo took the young horses he worked with. There was a big post in the center of the clearing; often Lorenzo would leave the horses roped to the post for a day or two, so that they would have time to realize that he, not they, was in control. Lorenzo left a long rope tied to the snubbing post; perhaps it was still there. With such a rope she could help the white man get out of the pit.

It was a gamble, though. Xitla knew it would take her all day to hobble to the post and back. There was an irritable old bear who lived somewhere down the canyon, and an old cougar too. If the old bear caught her he would probably eat her, which would put an end to her coupling, for sure.

Still, Xitla decided to try and secure the rope. With all the people gone the old bear might come into camp and eat her anyway. In the early morning she lowered the white man some tortillas and a jug of water and set out for the place where Lorenzo trained his horses. By midday she regretted her decision. Her bent back pained her so badly that she could only hobble a few steps at a time. Xitla realized she could not go to the post and make it back to the camp by nightfall. The hunting animals would be out—the bear and the puma—if one of them smelled her they would kill her; the pumas in the great canyon were particularly bold. Several women had been attacked while waiting by the cliffs for their lovers to appear.

All day, Xitla crept on, stopping frequently to rest and ease her back. She did not want to be eaten by a puma or a bear. Long before she reached the spot where Lorenzo trained the horses the shadows had begun to fill the canyon. When she got to the place Xitla saw at once that she had not traveled in vain: the rope that was used to restrain the young horses was still tied to the hitching post. It was a good long rope, as she had remembered. She could tie one end to the skinning post and throw the other end to the white man, so that he could pull himself up. Maybe he would continue to sing his strange love song to her; maybe his member would rise up with the song.

On the way back, though, hobbling slowly through the darkness with the coiled rope, Xitla felt a deep fear growing in her. At first she thought it was fear of the bear or the puma, but, as she crept along, pain from her back shooting down her leg, Xitla realized she had made a terrible mistake. She had allowed the white man's strange love song to drive judgment and reason out of her head; an old vanity and the memory of coupling had driven out her reason just as the shadows were driving the last light out of the canyon. Because she remembered a time when vaqueros would ride one hundred miles just to look on her beauty, she had forgotten that she was an old bent woman nearing the end of her time.

Now that Xitla was caught in the darkness, far from camp, she realized that she had been a fool. What was it to couple with a man anyway? A little sweat, a jerk, a sigh. The pain shooting down her legs grew more intense. Now she had put herself at the mercy of Bear and Puma, that was bad; but now, as she crept along, a worse fear came, the fear of Ahumado. He was dying somewhere. Xitla knew he must have gone to the south, to their home, to seek the Tree of Medicines; but something was eating at his leg and he would not reach the tree. The pain in her leg came from Ahumado; perhaps Spider had bitten him, or Snake, or Scorpion. A poison was killing Ahumado; those who tasted the poison leaf died of poison when their time arrived. But Ahumado's time was Xitla's time too, and she would suffer it without even the protection of her little shelter at the camp. It was Ahumado who had made the prisoner show her his member and turn her head, Ahumado who had made the white man sing her love songs in the old tongue—perhaps the words Scull used were in the language of the first human beings, words which no one could resist. Because of it, she had been lured away, far from her little store of herbs and plants, things that might have helped her scare away Bear and Puma—all for a rope to save the white man, for a jerk and a sigh. Ahumado had made it all happen, so that, as he was dying, a death more cruel than his own would come to Xitla.

She crawled faster, carrying the rope, although she knew well that such haste was foolish. Her fear grew so strong that she threw away the rope she had come so far to get. The rope was only another trick of Ahumado's; its loop was the loop of time that would close and catch her soon. It was all a joke of Ahumado's, Xitla realized. He had put the white man in the pit to tempt her, to awaken her loins again, to draw her away from camp, where she had herbs and leaves to protect her. She had the black leaves that made a bad smell when burned—if she put them in the fire, then Puma would let her alone. Puma did not like the smell the black leaves made when they were burned.

Xitla was only halfway back to camp when the night began to end. She had traveled slowly; often she had to stop and rest. Now the light of day was beginning to whiten the sky overhead; when the light sank into the canyon Xitla saw something near the canyon wall, not far ahead. At first she thought it was Puma. She yelled and yelled at it, hoping to scare it away. Puma would sometimes run from people who yelled.

It was not until the animal began to glide toward her that Xitla saw it wasn't Puma, it wasn't Bear: it was Jaguar. Around her neck she had a little red stone; the stone had hung around her neck all her life. The red stone was Parrot. Xitla clutched it in her hand as Jaguar came. Xitla knew that Jaguar would not stop for Parrot. Jaguar was coming to eat her. But Ahumado too was dying—dying of poison somewhere to the south. He would not reach the Tree of Medicines. Xitla clutched the red stone tight and sent a message to Parrot. She wanted Parrot to find the body of Ahumado and peck out his eyes.

50.

WHEN SCULL REALIZED the old woman was no longer in the camp above him, he fell, for the first time, into raw panic, a kind of explosion of nerves that caused him to hop wildly around the floor of the pit, cursing and yelping out strange words; he emitted cries and bursts of language as if he were farting fear out of his mouth. He became afraid of himself; if he could have bitten himself to death at that time, he would have. He leapt on top of the mound of earth he had heaped over the three corpses and sprang at the wall of the pit several times, hoping to claw his way out of it by main force.

But it was hopeless. He could not leap out of the pit. When he exhausted himself he fell back, his eyes raw and stinging with the dirt that fell in them when he leapt at the walls of the pit.

Scull tried to calm himself but could not stifle his panic. He knew the old woman's absence might be only temporary; perhaps she had had to hobble a little farther than usual to gather the corn she brought him. Perhaps she had even journeyed to another village, to bring back someone who would help him out of the pit. He used all his force of mind to try and find a rational reason why the old woman's absence was temporary, but it was no use; the panic was violent and strong, so strong that he could not stop hopping around the pit, gibbering, mewling, cursing. There were many reasons why the old woman might only be gone temporarily, but Scull could not calm himself even for a second by thinking of them. He knew the old woman was dead, she would never be back, and he was alone, in a stinking pit in Mexico. His heart was beating against his ribs so hard he thought it might burst, and hoped it would; or that the arteries of his brain would pop and bring him a quicker death than starving, day by day, amid the scorpions and fleas—for fleas were one of the worst torments of the pit. They were in his hair, his armpits, everywhere. If he sat still and focused he could see them hopping on his bare leg. From time to time, crazed, he tried to catch them and squeeze them to death, but they mostly eluded him.

With the old woman there Scull could manage a little hope, but now his nerves told him all was lost. The old woman was dead; he was stuck. He knew he should resign himself, but for hours he was fired with panic, like a motor, a dynamo. He jumped and jumped; it was as if lightning ran through him. He could not make himself stop jumping; he saw himself soaring with one miraculous jump all the way up, out of the pit. He jumped and gibbered all day, until dusk.

Then he collapsed. When the sunlight of a new day woke him,

he was too drained to move. He still had a little water, and a few scraps of food, but he didn't drink or eat, not for several hours; then, in a rush, he choked down all the food, drank all the water. Though he knew there would be no more he didn't care to ration what there was. He wanted to put sustenance behind him. He had, he thought, fought well; he had held out against torturous circumstances longer than many a man of his acquaintance would have, excepting only his second cousin Ariosto Scull. But the fight was over. He had seen many men—generals, captains, privates, bankers, widowers—arrive at the moment of surrender. Some came to it quickly, after only a short sharp agony; others held to their lives far longer than was seemly. But finally they gave up. He had seen it, on the battlefield, in hospital, in the cold toils of marriage or the great houses of commerce; finally men gave up. He thought he would never have to learn resignation, but that was hubris. It was time to give up, to stop fighting, to wait for death to ease in.

Now he even regretted killing all the rattlesnakes. He should have left one or two alive. He could have provoked one or two to strike him; while not as rapid as the bite of the fer-de-lance that had killed his cousin Willy in a matter of seventeen minutes, three or four rattlesnake bites would probably be effective enough. Scull even went over and examined the dead snakes, thinking there might be a way to inject himself with the venom; it would ensure a speedier end. But he had beaten the snakes until their heads were crushed and their fangs broken; anyway, the venom must have long since dried up.

After his day of hopping and jumping, raging and gibbering, clawing at the walls and spewing fragments of old orations and Greek verse, Inish Scull settled himself as comfortably as he could against the wall of the pit and did nothing. He wished he had the will to stop his breath, but he didn't. Whether he wanted it or not, his breath came. It was a bright day; to look up at all with his lidless eyes was to invite the sun into his brain. Instead, he kept his head down. His hair was long enough to make a fair shade. He wanted to let go the habit of fighting, to die in calmness. He remembered again the Buddhist, sitting calmly in his orange robes by the Charles River. He had no orange robes, he was not a Buddhist, he was a Scull, Captain Inish Scull. He thought he had fought well in every war he had been able to find, but now was the day of surrender, the day when he had to snap the sword of his will, to cease all battling and be quiet, be calm; then, finally, would come the moment when his breath would stop.

51.

CALL AND GUS were moving cautiously into the canyon of the Yellow Cliffs when a great bird rose suddenly from behind a little cluster of desert mesquite. Five more rose as well, great bald vultures, so close to the two men that their horses shied.

"I hope it wasn't the Captain they're eating," Augustus said. "It'd be a pity to come all this way and lose him to the buzzards."

"It wasn't the Captain," Call said— through the thin bushes he glimpsed what was left of the body of an old woman. The vultures were reluctant to leave. Two lit on boulders nearby, while the shadows of the others flickered across the little clearing where the body lay.

"Must have been a cougar, to up her up like that," Gus said. "Would a cougar do that?"

"I guess one did," Call said. "See the tracks? He was a big one."

They dismounted and inspected the area for a few minutes, while the vultures wheeled overhead.

"I've never seen a lion track that big," Augustus commented.

A rawhide rope lay not far from the corpse.

"Why would an old woman be way out here alone?" Gus wondered. "All she had was this rope. Where was she going?"

"I guess we could pile some rocks on her," Call said. "I hate just to leave a body laying out."

"Woodrow, she's mostly et anyway," Gus said. "Why spoil the buzzards' picnic?"

"I know, but it's best to bury people," Call said. "I believe she was crippled—look at her hip."

While they were heaping rocks on the corpse Call got an uneasy feeling. He couldn't say what prompted it.

"Something's here, I don't know what," he said, when they resumed their cautious ride into the canyon.

"It might be that cougar, hoping for another old woman," Gus said.

A few moments later, Augustus saw the jaguar. He was not as convinced as Call that Ahumado and his men had left, and was scanning the rocky ledges above them, looking for any sign of life. Probably if the old bandit *had* gone, he would have left a rear guard. He didn't want to be ambushed, as they had been the first time they entered the Yellow Canyon, and he took particular care to scan the higher ledges, where a rifleman could hide and get off an easy shot.

On one of the higher ledges he saw something that didn't register clearly with his eye. There was something there that was hard to see—he stopped his horse to take a longer look and when he did the jaguar stepped into full view.

"Woodrow, look up there," he said.

Call could not immediately see the jaguar, but then the animal moved and he saw him clearly.

"I think it's a jaguar," Augustus said. "I never expected to see one."

"I imagine that's what got the old woman," Call said.

For a moment, surprised, they were content to watch the jaguar, but their mounts were far from content. They put up their ears and snorted; they wanted to run but the rangers held them steady.

The jaguar stood on the rocky ledge, looking down at them.

"Do you think you can get off a shot?" Call asked. "If we don't kill it, it might get one of these horses, when it comes nightfall."

Augustus began to lift his rifle out of the scabbard. Though both men were watching the jaguar, neither saw it leave. It was simply gone. By the time Augustus raised his rifle there was nothing to shoot.

"He's gone—it's bad news for the horses," Call said.

"I'll never forget seeing him," Augustus said. "He acted like he owned the world."

"I expect he does—this world, at least," Call said. "I've never seen an animal just disappear like that."

All afternoon, as they worked their way carefully through the narrow canyon, they often looked upward, hoping for another glimpse of the jaguar—but the jaguar was seen no more.

"Just because we don't see him don't mean he's not following us," Call said. "We have to keep the horses close tonight."

Suddenly the canyon opened into the space they remembered from the time they were ambushed. The cliffs above them were pitted with holes and little caves. They stopped for a few minutes, examining the caves closely, looking for the glint of a rifle barrel or any sign of life.

But they saw nothing, only some eagles soaring across the face of the cliff.

"We ought to walk in, but we can't leave the horses," Call said. "That jaguar might be following us."

"I think this camp is deserted," Augustus said. "I think we came too late."

They rode slowly into the deserted camp, a sandy place, empty, windy. Only a ring of cold campfires and a few scraps of tenting were left to indicate that people in some numbers had once camped there.

Besides the tenting and the campfires there was one other thing that suggested the presence of humans: the skinning post, with a crossbar at the top, from which a badly decomposed, mangled, and half-eaten corpse still hung.

"Oh my Lord," Augustus said. He could barely stand to look at the corpse, and yet he couldn't look away.

"They say Ahumado had people skinned, if he didn't like them," Call said. "I supposed it was just talk, but I guess it was true."

"I ain't piling no rocks on *that*," Gus said emphatically. The bloated thing hanging from the crossbar skinning post bore little resemblance now to anything human.

"I'll pass myself, this time," Call said. He did not want to go near the stinking thing on the post.

In the pit, not far from where the two rangers stood, Inish Scull had slipped into a half-sleep. Many times he had dreamed of rescue, so many that now, when he heard the voices of Call and McCrae, in his half sleep, he discounted the words. They were just more dream voices; he would not let them tempt him into hope.

"We ought to search these caves," Call said. "They might have had the Captain here. If we could find a scrap of his uniform or his belt or something at least it would be a thing we could take to his wife."

"You look in the caves, Woodrow," Gus said. "I'll stand guard, in case that jaguar shows up."

"All right," Call said.

As Call started for the largest of the caves at the base of the cliff, Augustus noticed the pit. Because of the shadows stretching out from the pit it had been hard to see from where they entered the camp.

Curious, Augustus took a step or two closer—a stench hit him, but a stench less powerful than that which came from the swollen black flesh hanging from the skinning post. He stepped to the edge of the pit—from the stench it seemed to him that the pit might be a place where Ahumado tossed his dead. It could be that Captain Scull's body might be there; or what was left of it.

He looked into the pit but did not at first see the small, almost naked man sitting with his head bent down in the shadows near one wall of the pit. Augustus saw some dead snakes, a broken cage, and a mound of dirt with the dirt not piled thickly enough to shut out the stench of death. He was about to turn away, disappointed, when the man sitting against the wall suddenly rolled two white lidless eyes up at him from beneath a long dirty mat of hair.

"Oh Lord! Woodrow . . . Woodrow!" Gus yelled.

Call, almost at the entrance to the first cave, turned at once and came running back.

"We found him, Woodrow! It's the Captain!" Augustus said.

Inish Scull was still in his-half sleep, listening listlessly to the dream voices, when he felt a shadow slant across the pit. With his eyes exposed he registered shadows even when he was looking down or trying to shield his eyes. If a vulture or an eagle soared above the camp he saw its shadow.

But the shadow that slanted across the pit was not a shadow made by a bird's wings. Scull saw a man looking at him from the edge of the pit; the man looked like the ranger Augustus McCrae. At the sight, panic stormed Scull's nerves again. He vowed to be calm, but he couldn't. He leapt to his feet and sprang at the wall, hopping from one side of the pit to the other. When a man appeared who looked like the ranger Woodrow Call, Scull sprang all the harder. He spewed out words in Greek and English, jumping frenziedly about the pit and at the walls. Again and again he jumped, ignoring the rangers' words of calm. He jumped like a flea, like one of the thousands who had tormented him. He had become a flea, his duty to jump and jump, hopping up at the wall, hopping across the pit. Even when ranger Call slid down a rope into the pit and attempted to quiet him, to let him know that he was saved, Inish Scull, the Boston flea, continued to jump and jump.

52.

BUFFALO HUMP let the summer pass, resting with his wives, climbing to the spire of rock to pray and meditate. At night around the fire the warriors made songs about the great raid. Hair-on-the-Lip died suddenly; something went wrong inside her. Word came that Blue Duck was the leader of a gang of renegades, white and half-breed, who killed and robbed along the Sabine River. In July Buffalo Hump went on an antelope hunt far north, near where he had taken the great buffalo whose skull he had used for his shield. He had heard that the antelope were thick in the north, and it was true. In one day he killed seven antelope with the bow. Worm made a prophecy about the feat. There was no fighting with the whites. The story came from an Apache that Gun-in-the-Water and his friend McCrae had rescued Big Horse from the camp of Ahumado. The Apache said that Big Horse Scull was insane; he jumped around like a flea. The Apache mentioned that Ahumado had cut off Scull's eyelids, which was what had made him insane.

"No eyelids, what a clever torture," Buffalo Hump said to Slow Tree—it was Slow Tree who had brought him this gossip. When asked about Ahumado, though, Slow Tree grew vague. There were many stories, much speculation, but it had all come from Apaches and Apaches were all liars, Slow Tree reminded him.

"Tell me the stories anyway," Buffalo Hump said.

"No one has seen Ahumado all summer," Slow Tree said. "He left his camp at night, through a hole in the mountain. They think he went back to the place he came from, in the south. Most people think he died."

"What else?" Buffalo Hump asked.

"Two white men were found stuck on the sharpened trees," Slow Tree said. "No one does that but Ahumado."

"Anyone can do it if they want to," Buffalo Hump said. "All they have to do is sharpen a tree and catch a white man, or any man. An Apache could do it. You could do it, if you wanted to. It doesn't mean that Ahumado is alive."

"They say a jaguar lives in his camp now," Slow Tree said. "The Texans took away Big Horse Scull and the jaguar came. Some people think he ate Ahumado."

"Ho!" Buffalo Hump said. "I have never seen a jaguar. Have you?"

Slow Tree was reluctant to answer. He had never seen a jaguar, either, but he was reluctant to admit this to Buffalo Hump. He liked people to think that he was the wisest and most experienced chief, a man who had tasted every plant and killed every animal. He did not like to confess that he had never seen a jaguar.

"They are very shy," Slow Tree pointed out. "They can make themselves invisible, so you cannot see them. They have much power, jaguars."

"I know they have much power but I don't think they can make themselves invisible—they are just good at hiding," Buffalo Hump said. "I think I will go south and see this jaguar. Would you like to come with me?"

Slow Tree was surprised by Buffalo Hump's invitation. Buffalo Hump had never offered to hunt with him before. Now he was offering to ride with him all the way to Mexico, to see a jaguar. Slow Tree decided on the spot that it was a plot to kill him. Probably Buffalo Hump knew that Slow Tree would kill him, if he ever got a chance to drive a lance through his big hump. But Buffalo Hump was wary: he never slept in Slow Tree's presence, and rarely turned his back to him, even for a moment. Slow Tree knew that Buffalo Hump didn't really like him or respect him; even now Buffalo Hump looked at him with hooded eyes, smiling a little. Buffalo Hump was mocking him, only doing it politely, with just enough regard for ceremony and custom that Slow Tree could not challenge the mockery without appearing to be more touchy than a great chief should be.

Slow Tree knew that he did not want to go to Mexico with Buffalo Hump—that would be a fatal mistake. He regretted even telling Buffalo Hump the story about the jaguar—once again his own tongue had got him into difficulties.

Thinking quickly, Slow Tree produced several reasons why it would be imprudent for him to leave on a long trip just then. The buffalo would have to be hunted soon, and they were scarce. Also, one of his wives was dying and he did not want to leave her. Buffalo Hump himself had just lost Hair-on-the-Lip—he knew how important it was to stay with a valued wife while she was dying.

Buffalo Hump pretended to be surprised when Slow Tree began to pile up reasons for not going to Mexico with him.

"I thought you wanted to see a jaguar," he said, and quickly changed the subject. Of course he hadn't wanted Slow Tree to go in the first place, but it was nice to embarrass him and make him think up lies.

Later, when Slow Tree left the camp, Buffalo Hump sought out Kicking Wolf—the great horsethief had become discouraged since losing his friend Three Birds. Kicking Wolf hardly left the camp all summer, only going out now and then to hunt. He had not stolen a horse since the theft of the Buffalo Horse; though his vision had improved he still complained, now and then, that he saw two where there was one.

Buffalo Hump had often found Kicking Wolf irritating, but there was no denying that he was a good horsethief. In the fall it might be wise to raid again, to put more fear in the Texans, but Buffalo Hump suddenly felt like traveling. He wanted to go somewhere, and a chance to see a jaguar was not to be missed. Even if the jaguar was no longer there it would be good to go to Mexico—if Ahumado was gone there might be some villages worth raiding near the Sierra Perdida.

He found Kicking Wolf not far from his tent, sitting alone, watching some young horses frolic. Two of his wives, both large, stout women not noted for their patience, were drying deer meat. Kicking Wolf was braiding a rawhide rope. The rawhide came from three cows Kicking Wolf had found on the llano, thin cows he had killed and skinned. He was good at braiding rawhide into ropes and hobbles.

"I have heard of a jaguar—I think we should go try and kill it," Buffalo Hump said. "If we killed such a beast it might clear up your sight."

Kicking Wolf had been prepared to be annoyed with Buffalo Hump; the comment took him by surprise. He looked at Buffalo Hump gratefully; they had been good friends when they were boys, but, as they grew older, rivalry made them touchy with one another.

"My sight is still uncertain," Kicking Wolf acknowledged. "If we were able to kill a jaguar it might clear up."

"Then go with me," Buffalo Hump said. "I want to leave right now, before the women try to stop us."

Kicking Wolf smiled. "Where is this jaguar?" he asked.

"In Mexico," Buffalo Hump said. "It lives near where you took the Buffalo Horse."

"Slow Tree told me the same thing," Kicking Wolf said. "He is a liar, you know. He makes up stories and claims he heard them from

Apaches, but he never kills these Apaches, which is what he should be doing."

"I know all that," Buffalo Hump assured him. "Let's go anyway. If we don't find the jaguar we can steal some horses on the way back."

Kicking Wolf immediately got up and coiled up his rawhide. He seemed eager to leave off braiding the rope.

"If the jaguar lives in Ahumado's old camp, as Slow Tree claims, where is Ahumado?" he asked.

"They say he is gone," Buffalo Hump said.

"Do you believe it?" Kicking Wolf asked.

"I don't know," Buffalo Hump said. "He may be gone or he may be waiting for us."

"I will go with you," Kicking Wolf said. "I want to see the jaguar and I want to know what happened to Three Birds."

"How will you know that—he went with you in the winter," Buffalo Hump pointed out. "If he is dead there won't be much left of him by now."

"I intend to look, anyway," Kicking Wolf said.

Heavy Leg knew Buffalo Hump much better than did his young wife, Lark. Heavy Leg could tell by the way her husband moved, and by the way he looked at the horses, when he was wanting to leave. By the time he came back with Kicking Wolf she had already filled a pouch with dried deer meat, for him to take on his journey. She was not allowed to touch his bow or his lance, but she got his paints ready, in case he had to paint himself and go into battle.

Buffalo Hump was a little surprised when he saw what Heavy Leg had done. Though Heavy Leg had been his wife for a long time, it still startled him that she could anticipate his intentions so accurately. His young wife, Lark, by contrast, had no idea that he was in a mood to leave. She was putting grease on her black hair and had not even noticed what Heavy Leg was doing. Buffalo Hump was almost ready to mount before Lark awoke to the fact that he was leaving. Though he depended on Heavy Leg and respected her for providing him what he would need on his journey, he sometimes wished she were a little dumber, like Lark. He was not sure he trusted a wife who could read his thoughts so clearly.

Kicking Wolf's wives were indignant that he was leaving them on such short notice, but Kicking Wolf ignored them. It had been a long time since he had traveled with Buffalo Hump—it pleased him that Buffalo Hump had asked him to come on the journey to Mexico.

By sunset the two warriors had left the camp. Eager for travel, singing a little, they climbed out of the canyon and rode all night.

53.

FOR TWO DAYS, as they approached the canyon of the Yellow Cliffs, Buffalo Hump and Kicking Wolf saw no game, though there had been an abundance of antelope and deer as they traveled south. Soon after crossing the Rio Grande they discovered a small herd of wild horses, a discovery that excited them both. They were small horses, mustangs—as soon as they saw the Comanches, they fled.

Kicking Wolf wanted to chase them awhile; at the sight of the quick, hardy wild horses, animals able to live where there was little water and almost no grass, his appetite for catching horses revived a little.

But Buffalo Hump was intent on one purpose, which was to go to the canyon of the Yellow Cliffs and see the jaguar.

"We know where those horses are now," he told Kicking Wolf. "We can come back and track them anytime. If we chase them they might move into Apache country."

"The Apaches don't like horses," Kicking Wolf said.

"Not to ride, but they like to eat them," Buffalo Hump said. "I would like to have a few of them. The jaguar must have eaten all the deer and antelope but he has not been able to catch those horses."

Kicking Wolf was growing very excited. His passion for horses was very great, and these horses did not even have to be stolen, they only had to be caught. Buffalo Hump wouldn't listen to him, though, so he reluctantly had to leave the mustangs, for the moment.

All Kicking Wolf talked about for a whole day was the wild horses they had found near the Rio Grande.

The next day he led Buffalo Hump to the place where he and Three Birds had been ambushed.

"Ahumado was behind us," Kicking Wolf said. "He walks as quietly as I do when I go into a herd of horses."

"I don't think he is here," Buffalo Hump said, "but if he is I don't want him behind me."

He started to reveal the prophecy of the hump, but caught himself. Kicking Wolf was a gossip—if he knew of the prophecy the whole camp would soon know.

"Let's go high on the rocks," he said. "If he is here I would rather be above him than below him."

They picked their way up to the high plateau that led to the Yellow Cliffs. To their surprise there was a declivity on the plateau, a great crater whose sides were steep. Near the center of the crater was a pit, with some charred and broken horse bones in the bottom of it, laying in the deep ashes. Kicking Wolf knew at once whose bones he was looking at.

"This is the place where they ate the Buffalo Horse," he said. "Why did they eat him?"

"Why does anyone eat any horse?" Buffalo Hump said. "They were hungry."

Kicking Wolf stayed a long time by the pit, looking at the bones of the Buffalo Horse. That Ahumado would kill and eat such a beast, rather than keeping him as a prize, astonished him. He jumped down into the pit and came back with one of the great rib bones.

Buffalo Hump spent some time riding around the rim of the crater, trying to understand how it had come to be. The rocks in it were black, the walls steep. He knew that the great hole with the black rocks in it was a place of power, a place where people came to pray and perform their spirit ceremonies. Some of the old ones thought that such holes were the footprints of the first spirit people to visit the world. His own view was that it might be the hole where the People first came out of the earth; only, in time, it had silted over, so that the People could not go back into the darkness they had left.

Buffalo Hump put a few of the black rocks in his pouch, to show to Worm and a few of the old men when he got home. It occurred to him that the reason Ahumado had so much power was because he had put his camp near the place of the black rocks. He was said to be black himself, like the rocks.

The crater was such a powerful place that Buffalo Hump was reluctant to leave it; but they had come to look for the jaguar that had been eating all the game.

In the afternoon they rode across the plateau to the Yellow Cliffs. They found the place where the posts were, and the cages, all but one of which had human remains in them. From the cliffs they could see far south, down the range of peaks. Several eagles soared along the cliff edge. Buffalo Hump wanted badly to shoot an eagle. He waited until dusk with his arrows ready, but none of the eagles flew close enough for him to risk an arrow.

"In the morning I will hide myself better," he said. The eagles were the large eagles of the south; he thought if he was patient he might kill one.

They camped on the plateau. In the morning the sun and moon were in the sky together, one to the east and the other to the west.

Both men knew that it was time to be careful, when the two powers, sun and moon, were in the sky together. At such times unexpected things could happen. Below them the cliff was pocked with caves. Buffalo Hump wondered if the jaguar lived in one of them. It soon became clear that no people were in the old camp. Three jackrabbits were nibbling at the bushes near the edge of the clearing, a thing that would not happen if the people were still nearby.

As he stood on the cliff looking down, Kicking Wolf suddenly had a memory of his friend Three Birds—a memory so strong that he began to tremble.

"What's wrong—why are you shaking like that?" Buffalo Hump asked.

"I was thinking of Three Birds," Kicking Wolf said.

Although Buffalo Hump waited, Kicking Wolf did not say more, but he continued to tremble for some time.

Though Buffalo Hump hid himself well near the edge of the cliff, he soon realized that the eagles were not going to come anywhere near him, certainly not close enough that he could kill one with an arrow. One eagle did dip close enough to tempt him, but it was merely a trick on the eagle's part. He tilted and let the arrow pass under his wing—it fell all the way to the bottom of the cliff, so far that Buffalo Hump lost sight of it.

"Let's go down," he said to Kicking Wolf. "I want to find my arrow."

Once they rode into the camp at the base of the Yellow Cliffs they saw that no people had been there for some time.

"The jaguar was here," Buffalo Hump said. "The Apache who spoke with Slow Tree did not lie."

Near one of the little caves they found some scat, and, everywhere, there were tracks. But the scat was old and none of the tracks were fresh. The jaguar had slept in a little cave near where the people had been. He had left some of his hairs on the rock. Carefully the two men collected as many hairs as they could—the hair of a jaguar would be very useful to Worm or the other medicine men.

While Buffalo Hump finished collecting the hairs, and some of the scat to be used in medicine, Kicking Wolf walked a good distance along the base of the cliff, looking for any trace of his friend. They had looked in the smelly pit and determined that the hastily buried bodies in it were Mexican. There was nothing of Three Birds in the pit, and it was not he rotting from the post in the center of what had been the camp. Yet Kicking Wolf felt that Three Birds would not have come to him so powerfully in memory if his remains, or at least some part of them, were not near the cliff somewhere.

"Be careful," Buffalo Hump told him. "The jaguar might be clever. He might be hiding."

Kicking Wolf did not answer. He wanted to be away from Buffalo Hump for a while. Buffalo Hump was so strong in himself that when you were with him it was hard to think about other people, even such an old friend as Three Birds.

Kicking Wolf thought that if he just got away from Buffalo Hump for a while he might receive another strong memory and be able to locate some trace of his friend; his thinking was correct. Near the base of the cliff, below where the cages hung, Kicking Wolf found the bones of the Comanche Three Birds. The bones were scattered and most of them broken, with only a little skin clinging to them here and there, but when Kicking Wolf found the skull he knew that he had located his friend. Three Birds had a knot, a little ridge of bone, located just below his left temple. As a boy he had been hit in the head with a war club while playing at war with the other boys: the blow left the little ridge or knot of bone behind his temple.

Kicking Wolf looked up at the cliff, so high that it was hard to see the top—there two eagles were soaring. He wondered if Ahumado had had Three Birds thrown from the cliff, or if he had fallen out of one of the cages. It might be that he had jumped, in hopes of becoming a bird as he was falling to his death.

Kicking Wolf knew that he would never know the answer to that question, but at least he had found what he had journeyed to Mexico to find.

He went back to his horse and got a deerskin he had brought just for that purpose; then he wrapped the bones of Three Birds carefully in the deerskin and tied them securely with a rawhide thong. Buffalo Hump came to him as he was working. When Kicking Wolf showed him the skull and the hand he merely said, "Ho!" and helped Kicking Wolf search the site so they would not miss any bones. It was Buffalo Hump who found one of Three Birds' feet.

The next day the two of them left the canyon of the Yellow Cliffs. Kicking Wolf carried the bones of Three Birds tied safely in the deerskin. He meant to take them to Three Birds' brother.

"We must come back soon and catch those wild horses," he said to Buffalo Hump, as they were crossing the river, back into Texas.

"I have never known a man who wanted horses so much," Buffalo Hump said.

BOOK III

1.

AUGUSTUS MCCRAE was sitting at the bedside of his second wife, Nellie, when Woodrow Call tapped lightly on the door. Bright sunlight poured through the window, but, to Gus's eye, the sunlight only pointed up the shabbiness of the two poor rooms where Nellie was having to die. There was no carpet on the floor, and the curtains were dusty; the windows faced on Austin's busiest street—horses and wagons were always throwing up dust.

"Come in," Augustus said. Call opened the door and stepped inside. The sick woman was pale as a bedsheet, as she had been for several weeks. He thought it could not be long before Nellie McCrae breathed her last.

Augustus, weary and confused, held one of the dying woman's hands.

"Well, what's the news, Woodrow?" he asked.

"War—civil war," Call said. "War between the North and the South. The Governor just found out."

Augustus didn't answer. Nellie was in a war, too, at the moment, and was losing it. Thought of a larger war, one that could split the nation, seemed remote when set beside Nellie's ragged breathing.

"The Governor would like to see us, when you can spare a moment," Call said.

Augustus looked up at his friend. "I can't spare one right now, Woodrow—I'm helping Nellie die. I don't expect it will be much longer."

"No—it's not likely to," Call agreed.

A bottle of whiskey and a glass with a swallow or two left in it sat on a little table by the bed, along with two vials of medicine and a wet rag that, now and then, Augustus used to wipe his wife's face.

"Captain Scull predicted this war years ago," Call said. "Do you remember that?"

"Old Blinders—I expect he's already enlisted on the Yankee side," Gus said.

Once they had returned Captain Scull from captivity, his mind recovered, though not immediately. For months he was still subject to bursts of hopping, which could seize him in the street or anywhere. He soon invented a kind of goggle, containing a thin sheet of darkened glass, to protect his lidless eyes from the sunlight. The goggles gained him the nickname "Blinders" Scull—he and Madame Scull were soon as intemperately married as ever, yelling curses at one another as they raced through town in an elegant buggy the Captain had ordered.

Then, overnight, they were gone, moved to Switzerland, where a renowned doctor attempted to make Scull usable eyelids, using the skin of a brown frog; rumor had it that the experiment failed, forcing the Captain to get by with his goggles from then on.

"Yes, I expect he's signed up," Call said. It was not likely that Inish Scull would sit out a war, eyelids or not.

Call put his hand on Gus's shoulder for a moment and prepared to leave, but Gus looked up and stopped him.

"Sit with me for a minute, Woodrow," he said, feeling sad. It was not much more than a year ago that his first wife, Geneva, had been carried off by a fever.

"You've no luck with wives, Gus," Call said. He sat back down and listened as the sick woman drew her shallow breaths.

"I don't, for a fact," Augustus said. "Geneva barely lasted four months and it's not yet been a year since Nellie and I wed."

He was quiet for a bit, looking out the window.

"I guess it's a good thing Clara turned me down," he said. "If we'd married, I fear she would have died off years ago."

Call was surprised that Gus would bring up Clara, with Nellie dying scarcely a yard away. But the sick woman didn't react—she seemed to hear little of what was said.

Neither of the two women Gus *had* married had been able to survive a year. Call knew it had discouraged his friend profoundly.

Unable to secure a healthy wife, he had already gone back to the whores.

"I wish Nell could go on and go," Gus said. "She ain't going to get well."

"I would prefer to be shot, myself, if I get that sick," Call said. "Once there's no avoiding death I see no point in lingering."

Augustus smiled at the comment, and poured himself a little more whiskey.

"We're all just lingering, Woodrow," he said. "None of us can avoid dying—though old Scull did the best job of it of any man I know, while that old bandit had him."

"Do you have an opinion about the war?" Call asked. "One I could take to Governor Clark?" The hubbub in the streets had already grown louder. Soon the citizens of Austin, some of whom sided with the Yankees and more of whom sided with the South, might decide to begin a war at the local level, in which case there would soon be more people dying than Gus McCrae's wife.

"No opinion—and the Governor has no right to press me, at a time like this," Augustus said.

"He just wants to know if we'll stay," Call told him. In the last few years he and Augustus had been the twin mainstays of frontier defense. Naturally a governor wouldn't want to lose his two most experienced captains, not at a time when most of the fighting men in the state would be going off to fight in the great civil war.

"I don't know yet—you vote for me, Woodrow," Augustus said. "Once Nellie dies I'm going to want to go drinking. When Nellie's buried and I'm fully sober again, I'll get around to thinking about this war."

Call smiled at the comment.

"I've known you a good many years and I've rarely seen you fully sober," he remarked. "I wouldn't be surprised if this war is fought and finished before that happens.

"The whole nation might kill itself before you're fully sober," he added.

He smiled when he said it, and Gus returned a weary glance.

"You go on and manage the Governor, Woodrow," he said. "I've got to manage Nellie."

Hearing gunfire in the street, Call hurried out, to discover that it was only a few rowdies shooting off their guns. They wanted to celebrate the fact that, at long last, war had come.

2.

CALL MADE SLOW PROGRESS up the street. Every man he saw wanted his opinion about the war; but the sight of Gus and his Nellie, in the poor cheap bedroom, left him feeling melancholy—it was hard to deal with the war question because he couldn't get his mind off Gus and Nellie. He had not known Nellie well—Gus had married her on only a week's acquaintance, but she seemed to be a decent young woman who had done her best to settle Augustus down and make him comfortable with the little they had. The only thing he knew about Nellie McCrae was that she was from Georgia; the only fondness he had ever heard her express was for mint tea. Now Lee Hitch and Stove Jones came crowding up with war questions, when all Call could think about was the sadness Gus must feel at having married twice, only to lose both wives.

"When are you leaving to fight the Yankees, Captain?" Stove Jones asked—it was only at that moment, when he saw Lee Hitch draw back in shock, that Stove realized he and Lee might favor different sides. It dawned on him too late that Lee Hitch hailed from Pennsylvania, a Yankee state, as well as he could remember.

Call didn't have to answer. Lee and Stove were looking at one another in astonishment. The two old friends agreed about almost everything; it had not occurred to either of them that they might be divided on the issue of the war that had just begun.

"Why, are you a Reb, Stove?" Lee asked, in puzzlement.

"I'm a Carolina boy," Stove reminded him; but his appetite for discussion of the coming conflict had suddenly diminished.

"We've still got the Comanches to fight, here in Texas," Call reminded them. "I suppose they're Yankees enough for me."

"But everybody's going to war, Captain—that's the talk, up and down the street," Stove Jones said. "There'll be some grand battles before this is settled."

"Some grand battles and some grand dying," Augustus said. He had come quietly up to where Call and the two men were talking. His arrival, so soon, took Call by surprise, though Augustus did not seem quite as sad as he had been in the rooming house.

"Nell's gone," Gus added, before Call could ask. "She opened her eyes and died. I never had a chance to ask her if she needed anything. Why will people die on days this pretty?"

Sunlight poured down on them; the sky was cloudless and the air soft. No one had an answer to Gus's question. Darkness and death seemed far away; but war had been declared between South and North, and Nellie McCrae lay dead not two blocks away.

"What are you, Gus, Yank or Reb?" Lee Hitch asked, putting the question cautiously, as if afraid of the answer he might receive.

"I'm a Texas Ranger with a good wife to bury, Lee," Gus said. "Will you go find Deets and Pea for me? I'd like to get them started on the grave."

"We'll find them—we'll help too, Gus," Lee assured him.

Call and Augustus walked briskly to the lots and caught their horses. It was a short walk to the Governor's office, but if they walked everybody they met would try to sound them out about the war, an intrusion they wanted to avoid.

"Remember what Scull said, when he first told us war was coming?" Call asked.

" 'Brother against brother and father against son,' that's what I remember," Augustus replied.

"He was accurate too," Call said. "It's happened right here in the troop, and the news not an hour old."

Augustus looked puzzled.

"You mean there's Yankees in the company?" he asked.

"Lee Hitch," Call said. "And Stove is a Reb."

"My Lord, that's right," Augustus said. "Lee's from the North."

Governor Clark stood by a window, looking out at the sunlit hills, when the two rangers were admitted to his office. He was a spare, solemn executive; no one could remember having heard him joke. He was patient, though, and dutiful to a fault. No piece of daily business was left unfinished; Gus and Call themselves had seen lamplight in the Governor's office well past midnight, as the Governor attended, paper by paper, to the tasks he had set himself for the day.

In the streets, men, most of them Rebels, were rejoicing. All of them assumed that the imperious Yankees would soon be whipped. Governor Clark was not rejoicing.

"Captain McCrae, how's your wife?" the Governor asked.

"She just died, Governor," Gus said.

"I would have excused you from this meeting, had I known that," Governor Clark said.

"There would be no reason to, Governor," Gus said. "There's nothing I can do for Nellie now except get a deep grave dug."

"If I had money to invest, which I don't, I'd invest it in mortuaries," the Governor said. "Ten thousand grave diggers won't be enough to bury the dead from this war, once it starts. There's a world of money to be made in the mortuary trade just now, and I expect the Yankees will make the most of it, damn them."

"I guess that means you're a Reb, Governor," Gus said.

"Up to today I've just been an American citizen, which is what I'd prefer to stay," Governor Clark said. "Now I doubt I'll have the luxury. Do you know your history, gentlemen?"

There was a long silence. Call and Augustus both felt uneasy.

"We're not studied men, Governor," Call admitted, eventually.

"I'm so ignorant myself I hate to talk much," Augustus said. The remark annoyed Call—in private Augustus bragged about his extensive schooling, even claiming a sound knowledge of the Latin language. When Captain Scull was around, Augustus moderated his bragging, it being clear that Captain Scull *was* extensively schooled.

Augustus was not confident enough, though, to attempt a display of learning with Governor Clark looking at him severely.

"Civil wars are the bloodiest, that's my point, gentlemen," the Governor said. "There was Cromwell. There were the French. People were torn apart in the streets of Paris."

"Torn to bits, sir?" Gus asked.

"Torn to bits and fed to dogs," the Governor said. "It was as bad or worse as what our friends the Comanches do."

"Surely this will just be armies fighting, won't it?" Call asked. Though he had read most of his Napoleon book, there was nothing in it about people being torn to bits in the streets.

"I hope so, Captain," the Governor said. "But it's war—in war you can't expect tea parties."

"Who do you think will win, Governor?" Call asked. He had lived his whole life in Texas. The work of rangering had taken him to New Mexico and old Mexico and, a time or two, into Indian Territory; but of the rest of America he knew nothing. He did know that almost all their goods and equipment came from the North. He assumed it was a rich place, but he had no sense of it, nor, for that matter, much sense of the South. He had known or encountered men from most of the states—from Georgia and Alabama, from Tennessee and Kentucky and Missouri, from Pennsylvania and Virginia and Massachusetts—but he didn't know those places. He knew that the East had factories; but the nearest thing to a factory that he himself had ever seen was a lumber mill. He knew that the Southern boys, the Rebs, without exception assumed they could whip the Yankees—rout them, in fact. But Captain Scull, whose opinion he respected, scorned the South and its soldiers. "Fops," he had called them. Call was not sure what a fop was, but Captain Scull had uttered the word with a sort of casual contempt, a scorn Call still remembered. Captain Scull seemed to feel himself equal to any number of Southern fops.

"Nobody will win, but I expect the North will prevail," the Governor said. "But they won't win tomorrow, or next year either, and probably not the year after. Meanwhile we've still got settlers to defend and a border swarming with thieves."

The Governor stopped talking and looked at the two men solemnly.

"There won't be many men staying here, not if they're ablebodied, and not if the war lasts as long as I think it will," he said. "They'll be off looking for glory. Some of them will find it and most of the rest of them will die in the mud."

"But the South will win, won't it, Governor?" Augustus asked. "I would hate to think the damn Yankees could whip us."

"They might, sir—they might," the Governor said.

"Half the people in Texas come from the Northern part of the country," Call observed. "Look at Lee Hitch. There's hundreds like him. Who do you think they'll fight for?"

"There will be confusion such as none of us expected to have to live through," the Governor said. "That could have been prevented, but it wasn't, so now we'll have to suffer it."

He paused and gave them another solemn inspection.

"I want you to stay with the rangers, gentlemen," he said. "Texas has never needed you more. The people respect you and depend on you, and we're still a frontier state."

Augustus let bitterness fill him, for a moment; bitterness and grief. He remembered the cheap dusty room Nellie had just died in.

"If we're so respected, then the state ought to pay us better," he said. "We've been rangers a long time now and we're paid scarcely better than we were when we started out. My wife just died in a room scarcely fit for dogs."

You could have afforded better if you'd been careful with your money, Call thought, but he didn't say it; in fact Augustus's criticism was true. Their salaries were only a little larger than they had been when they were raw beginners.

"I wouldn't go to no war looking for glory," Gus said. "But I might go if the pay was good."

"I take your point," the Governor said. "It's a scandal that you've been paid so poorly. I'll see that it's raised as soon as the legislature sits—if we still have a legislature when the smoke clears."

There was a long pause—in the distance there was the sound of gunshots. The rowdies were still celebrating.

"Will you stay, gentlemen?" the Governor asked. "The Comanches will soon find out about this war, and the Mexicans too. If they think the Texas Rangers have disbanded, they'll be at us from both directions, thick as fleas on a dog."

Call realized that he and Augustus had not had a moment to discuss the future, or their prospects as soldiers, or anything. They had scarcely had a minute alone, since Nellie McCrae got sick.

"I can't speak for Captain McCrae but I have no wish to desert my duties," Call said. "I have no quarrel with the Yankees, that I know of, and no desire to fight them."

"Thank you, that's a big relief," the Governor said. "I recognize it's a poor time to ask, but what about you, Captain McCrae?"

Augustus didn't answer—he felt resentful. From the moment, years before on the llano, when Inish Scull abruptly made him a captain, it seemed that, every minute, people had pressed him for decisions on a host of matters large and small. It might be trivial—someone might want to know which pack mules to pack—or it might be serious, like the question the Governor had just asked him. He was from Tennessee. If Tennessee were to join the war, he might want to fight with the Tennesseeans; not having heard from home much in recent years, he was not entirely sure which side Tennessee would line up with. Now the Governor was wanting him to stay in Texas, but he wasn't ready to agree. He had lost two wives in Texas—not to mention Clara, who, in a way, made three. Why would he want to stay in a place where his luck with wives was so poor? His luck with cards hadn't been a great deal better, he reflected.

"I assure you there'll be an improvement in the matter of salaries," the Governor said. "I'll raise you even if I have to pay you out of my own pocket until this crisis passes."

"Let it pass—there'll just be another one right behind it," Augustus said, irritably. "It's just been one crisis after another, the whole time I've been rangering."

Then he stood up—fed up. He felt he had to get outside or else choke.

"I've got to get my wife decently buried, Governor," he said. "She won't keep, not with the weather this warm. I expect I'll stay with Woodrow and go on rangering, but I ain't sure. I just ain't sure, not right this minute. I agree with Woodrow—Yankees are still Americans, and I'm used to fighting Comanche Indians or else Mexicans."

He paused a moment, remembering his family.

"I've got two brothers, back in Tennessee," he added. "If my brothers was to fight with the Yankees, I wouldn't want to be shooting at them, I know that much."

Governor Clark sighed.

"Go home, Captain," he said. "Bury your wife. Then let me know what you decide."

"All right, Governor," Augustus said. "I wish there was a good sheriff here. He ought to arrest those fools who are shooting off their guns in the street."

3.

INISH SCULL—Hoppity Scull, as he was known in Boston, because he was still occasionally seized by involuntary fits of hopping; they might occur at a wedding or a dinner party or even while he was rowing, in which case he hopped into the chilly Charles—was walking across Harvard Yard, a copy of Newton's *Opticks* in his hand, when a student ran up to him with the news that war had been declared.

"Why the Southern rascals!" Scull exclaimed, after hearing of the provocation that had occurred.

His mind, though, was still on optics, where it had been much of the time since Ahumado had removed his eyelids. He had just spent three years making a close study of the eye, sight, light, and everything having to do with vision—Harvard had even been prompted to ask him to teach a course on optics, which is what he had been doing just before news of the Southern insurrection reached him. He was wearing his goggles, of course; even in the thinner light of Boston a chance ray of sunlight could cause him intense pain; the headaches, when they came, still blinded him for days. He was convinced, though, from his study of the musculature of the eye, that his experiment with the Swiss surgeon and the frog membrane need not have failed. He had been planning to go back to Switzerland, armed with new knowledge and also better membranes, to try again.

But the news that the spindly student had brought him, once it soaked in, drove optics, in all their rich complexity, out of Inish Scull's mind. The excitement in Cambridge was general; even the streets of Boston, usually silent as a cemetery, rang with talk. Scull rarely walked home, but today he did, growing more excited with every step. He still had his commission in the army of the United States; the thought of battle made a sojourn in Switzerland seem pallid. He longed to lead men again, to see the breaths of cavalry horses condense in white clouds on cold mornings, to ride and curse and shoot under the old flag, Bible and sword.

When he flung open the door of the great house on Beacon Hill, the house where he had been born and been raised, the sight that greeted him was one to arouse ardor, but not of a military kind. Inez Scull, entirely bored with Boston, was striding up and down the long, gloomy entrance hall, naked from the waist down, slashing at the Scull family portraits with a quirt. Lately she had begun to exhibit herself freely, mostly to shock the servants, good proper Boston servants all, very unused to having their mistress exhibit her parts in the drawing room or wherever she happened to be, and at all hours of the day, as well.

Hearing the door open, Entwistle, the butler, appeared—old

Ben Mickelson had been sent to the house in Maine, to dodder and tipple through the summer. Without giving Madame Scull so much as a glance, Entwistle took the master's coat.

"So there, Inez, I hope you're satisfied," Inish said.

"I'm very far from satisfied, the stable boy was hasty," Inez said, turning her red face toward him as she continued to quirt the portraits.

"Entwistle, would you find a towel for Madame?" Scull said. "I fear she's dripping. She'll soil the Aubusson if she's not careful."

"You Bostonians are so beggarly," Inez said. "It's just a rug."

"Sack the stable boy, if you don't mind, Entwistle," Scull added. "He's managed to anger me while not quite pleasing Madame."

Then he looked at his wife.

"I wasn't talking about the success—or lack of it—of your amours, Inez, when I said I hoped you were satisfied," he informed her. "The fact is, your imbecile cousins have gotten us into a war."

"The darlings, I'm so glad," Inez replied. "What did they do?"

"They fired on us," Scull said. "The impertinent fools—they'll soon wish they hadn't."

At that point Entwistle returned with a towel, which he handed to Madame Scull, who immediately flung it back in his face. Entwistle, unsurprised, picked up the towel and draped it over the banister near where Madame Scull stood.

"Find that stable boy?" Scull asked.

"No, he didn't, and he won't," Inez said, before Entwistle could answer.

"Why's that, my dear?" Scull asked, noting that a whitish substance was still dripping copiously down his wife's leg. Happily, though, her quirtings had done little damage to the Scull portraits, which hung in imposing ranks along the hallway.

"Because I've stowed him in a closet, where I mean to keep him until he proves his mettle," Inez said.

"I should shoot you on the spot, you Oglethorpe slut," Scull said. "No Boston jury would convict me."

"What, because I had a tumble with the stable boy, you think that's grounds for murder?" Inez asked, coming at him with menace in her eyes.

"No, of course not," he said. "I'd do it because you embarrassed Entwistle. You don't embarrass butlers, not here in our Boston."

"My cousins will soon put you to rout, you damn Yankee hounds," Inez said, starting up the stairs.

"Hickling Prescott suspects you of Oglethorpe blood—did you hear me, you dank slut?" Inish yelled after her.

Inez Scull did not reply.

Before he could say more he was taken with a fit of hopping. He was almost to the kitchen before Entwistle and the parlor maids could get him stopped.

4.

MAGGIE CONSIDERED IT a happy turnabout that she now had a position in the store that had once been the Forsythes'. She did the very jobs that Clara had once done: unpacking, arranging goods on the shelves, helping customers, writing up bills, wrapping the purchases that required wrapping. She thought often of Clara, and felt lucky to have, at last, a respectable job. Clara, she thought, would have understood and approved. The store's new owner, Mr. Sam Stewart, was from Ohio, and a newcomer to Austin. He knew little of Maggie's past, and what he knew he ignored. Fetching and competent clerks were not plentiful in Austin—Mrs. Sam Stewart was glad to accept the fiction that Maggie was a widow, and Newt the son of a Mr. Dobbs, killed by Indians while on a trip. Sam Stewart had a few irregularities in his past himself and was not disposed either to look too closely or to judge too harshly when Maggie applied for the job, though he did once mention to his formidable wife, Amanda Stewart, that Maggie's boy, Newt, then four, bore a strong resemblance to Captain Call.

"I'd mind your own business, if I were you, Sam," Amanda informed him. "I'm sure Maggie's done the best she could. I'll nail your skin to the back door if you let Maggie go."

"Who said anything about letting her go, Manda?" Sam asked. "I have no intention of letting her go."

"Scoundrels like you often get churchly once they're safe from the hang rope," Amanda informed him. She said no more, but Sam Stewart went around for days wondering what skeleton his wife thought she had uncovered now.

It was while clerking in the store that Maggie made friends with Nellie McCrae. Nellie often came in to purchase little things for Gus, but rarely spent a penny on herself, though she was a fetching young woman whose beauty would have shone more brightly if she had allowed herself a ribbon, now and then, or a new frock.

That Nellie was not strong had always been clear—once or twice she had become faint, while doing her modest shopping; Maggie had had to insist that she rest a bit on the sofa at the back of the store before going home.

Then Nellie commenced dying, and was seen in the store no more. Maggie sorrowed for her and sat up all night rocking Newt, who had a cough, when news of the death came.

She was dressing to go to the funeral when Graciela, the Mexican woman who watched Newt while Maggie worked, came hobbling in in terror—Graciela was convinced she had been bitten by a snake.

"Was it a rattler?" Maggie asked, not without skepticism—the day seldom passed without nature striking some near-fatal blow at Graciela.

Graciela was far too upset to give an accurate description of the snake; though Maggie could find no fang marks on her leg, or anywhere else, Graciela was convinced she was dying. She began to pray to the saints, and to the Virgin.

"You might have stepped on a snake but I don't think it bit you," Maggie said, but Graciela was sobbing so loudly she couldn't hear. It was vexing. Maggie thought the best thing to do was take Newt to the funeral with her. He was a lively boy and might escape Graciela and be off—if there *was* a rattlesnake around, Newt might be the one to find it.

While Maggie was buttoning Newt into the nice brown coat he wore to church, Graciela, in her despair, turned over a pot of beans—a small river of bean juice was soon flowing across the kitchen floor.

"If you don't die, clean up the beans," Maggie said, as she hurried Newt out the door. Then she regretted her sharpness: Graciela was a poor woman who had lost five of her twelve children; she had suffered so many pains in life that she had become a little deranged.

Maggie could already hear the strains of the new church organ—it had just arrived from Philadelphia the week before. Amanda Stewart, who had some training in music, had been enlisted to play it.

"Will we see Captain Woodrow?" Newt asked, as his mother hurried him along.

"Yes, and Jake too, I expect," Maggie said. "Maybe Captain Woodrow would walk with us to the graveyard."

Newt didn't say anything—his mother was always hoping that Captain Woodrow would do things with them that the Captain seldom wanted to do.

Jake Spoon, though, was always jolly; he came to their house often and played with him, or, sometimes, even took him fishing. Jake had even given him an old lariat rope, Newt's proudest possession. Jake said every ranger needed to know how to rope, so Newt practiced often with his rope, throwing loops at a stump in the backyard, or, if his mother wasn't looking, at the chickens. He thought roping birds would be safe, though he was careful not to go near old Dan, the quarrelsome tom turkey that belonged to Mrs. Stewart.

"Old Dan will peck you, Newt," Mrs. Stewart warned, and Newt didn't doubt. Old Dan had pecked Graciela, causing her to weep for several days.

Though Newt, like his mother, hoped that Captain Woodrow would come and do things with them, the occasions when he did come frightened little Newt a little. Captain Woodrow didn't play with him, as Jake did, and had never taken him fishing, though, on rare occasions, he might give Newt a penny, so that he could buy sassafras candy at the store where his mother worked. Jake Spoon's visits usually ended with Newt laughing himself into a fit—Jake would tickle him until he went into a fit—but nothing like that happened when Captain Woodrow came. When the Captain came he and Newt's mother talked, but in such low voices that Newt could never hear what they were saying. Newt tried to be on his best behavior during Captain Woodrow's visits, not only in the hope of getting a penny, but because it was clear that Captain Woodrow expected good behavior.

Newt was always a little glad, when Captain Woodrow got up to go, but he was always a little sorry, too. He *wanted* Captain Woodrow to stay with them—his mother was never more pleased than when Captain Woodrow came—but he himself never quite knew what to do when the Captain was there. He had a whistle which he liked to blow loudly, and a top he liked to spin, and a stick horse he could ride expertly, even though the stick horse bucked and pitched like a real bronc, but when the Captain came he didn't blow his whistle, spin his top, or ride his stick horse. Newt just sat and tried to be well behaved. Almost always, after Captain Woodrow came, his mother cried and was in a bad temper for a while; Newt had learned to be cautious in his playing, at such times.

Maggie and Newt hurried across the street and crept into the back of the church just as the brief service began.

"Ma, I can't see," Newt whispered. He didn't like being in church, which required him to be still, even more still than he was used to keeping during Captain Woodrow's visits. At the moment all he could see was a forest of backs and legs.

"Shush, you be quiet now," Maggie said, but she did hoist Newt up so he could see Amanda Stewart play the new organ. All the rangers were there but Deets, one of Newt's favorites. Deets was skillful at devising little toys out of pieces of wood or sacking and whatever he could find. So far he had made Newt a turkey, a bobcat, and a bear. Of course, Deets was black; Newt was not sure whether he was exactly a ranger—in any case he could not spot him in the church.

Then his mother whispered to him and pointed out a thin man standing with the rangers.

"That's the Governor," she said. "It's nice that he came."

Newt took no special interest in the Governor, but he was careful to squeeze his eyes shut during the prayer. Graciela had made it clear to him that he would go to hell and burn forever if he opened his eyes during a prayer.

When the praying was finished the rangers went past them out of the church, carrying a wooden box, which they set in the back of a wagon. Jake Spoon was helping carry the box; when he went past Newt he winked at him. Newt knew that winking at such a time must be bad, because his mother colored and looked annoyed.

Maggie *was* annoyed. Jake ought to have better manners than to wink while carrying a coffin. Newt adored Jake; it was not setting the boy a good example to wink at such a solemn time. What made it worse was that Gus McCrae looked so low and sad.

Sometimes Maggie wondered why she had fixed her heart on Call, and not on Gus—she and Gus were more adaptable people than Woodrow ever had been or ever would be. She thought she could have stayed alive and done nicely by Augustus, had she felt for him what a wife should feel for a husband; and yet, through the years, it was Woodrow she loved and Jake she tolerated. Even then, walking up the street behind the wagon, Maggie felt her spirits droop a little because Woodrow, mindful of the solemnity of the occasion, had walked past them without a nod or a glance.

The hope Maggie held, above all, was that her son would be able to live a respectable life. She herself might manage to die respectable, but she had not lived respectable, not for much of her life; she placed a high value on it and wanted it for her son. He might never manage to be a hero, as his father was; he might never even be called to do battle—Maggie hoped he wouldn't. But it wasn't necessary to fight Indians or arrest bandits to be respectable. Respectability was a matter of training and guidance—learning not to wink in funerals, for example, or keeping one's eyes closed during prayer.

There was no managing Jake Spoon, though; there never had been. Maggie knew it, and it was bittersweet knowledge, because, for all his faults, Jake did his best to help her, and had for the whole time she had had Newt. It was Jake who carried her groceries home, if he noticed that she was heavily laden; Jake that tacked up a little shelf in her kitchen, to hold the crockery—Jake Spoon did the chores that Woodrow Call would rarely unbend to do, even if he had the time. Maggie knew her own weaknesses: she could not do entirely without a man, could not be alone always, could not survive and raise her son well without more help than Woodrow Call gave her.

Call and Gus were not heroes to the people for nothing; they were constantly on patrol along the line of the frontier. Skirmishes with the Comanches were frequent, and the border was very unsettled. Call and Gus were always gone but Jake Spoon was usually left at home—he had had the prudence to take a course in penmanship and wrote the neatest hand in the company. There was a man in the legislature, a senator named Sumerskin, who considered the rangers profligate in the matter of expenses. He hectored Call and Gus to produce accountings down to the last horseshoe nail, a vexation that both captains found hard to tolerate. Though Jake Spoon could shoot and might occasionally produce a dashing bit of derring-do during a fracas, he was also lazy, careless of his tack, and prone to exhausting the troop by leading singsongs all night. His main use when they were after bandits was that he could tie the most elegant hang knots in the troop. Bandits hung with one of Jake's nooses rarely danced or kicked more than a few seconds.

Call, though, could barely tolerate Jake's laziness—Augustus, though an inspired fighter, provided more than enough laziness for any one troop, Call considered, so, usually, Jake got left at home to keep the company records in his elegant hand. He would wad up page after page of ledger paper until he had his columns exact and the loops and curves of his letters precisely as he wanted them to be.

Where Woodrow Call was concerned, Maggie's hopes shrank, year by year, to one need: the need to have Call give Newt his name. She no longer supposed, even in her most hopeful moments, that Woodrow would marry her. It wasn't that he scorned her because of her past, either; the bitter truth Maggie slowly came to accept was that Woodrow Call liked being alone; he liked his solitude as much as Gus and Jake liked female company.

"Woodrow just ain't the marrying kind, Mag," Augustus said to her, on more than one occasion, and he was right.

Still, every time Maggie saw Woodrow her heart fluttered, although she knew that a fluttering heart could not change such things. She ceased mentioning marriage to him; even, in time, ceased to think about it. It had been the central hope of her life, but it wasn't to be. What she didn't cease to think about was Newt. Newt was the spitting image of his father: the two of them walked alike, talked alike, had the same smile and the same forehead, yet Call would not give Newt his name. The resemblances Maggie catalogued—resemblances that were obvious to everyone in Austin—didn't convince him; or, if they did convince him, he hid the realization from himself. Often Maggie could not contain her bitterness at his refusal; she quarreled with him about it, sometimes loudly. Once on a hot still day they quarreled so loudly that their argument woke Pea Eye, who had been dozing below them, in the shade of the building. Maggie knew Pea Eye overheard them; she happened to look out the window and saw his startled face turned up in surprise.

That Newt would someday bear his father's name was the one hope Maggie would not relinquish, though she came to realize that no effort of hers would make it happen. Her hope, she felt, lay with Newt himself—as the boy grew, his own sweetness might have an effect on Woodrow that she herself had not been able to have. All the rangers liked Newt; they kept him with them whenever they could. They sat him on their horses, whittled him toy guns, let him pet the crippled possum that Lee Hitch found in the hay one morning and adopted. As Newt grew they taught him little skills, and Newt was a quick pupil. All of them, Maggie was convinced, knew he was Call's.

Now, in the strong sunlight, the crowd followed the wagon with the coffin in toward the green cemetery by the river. Maggie heard, all about her, murmurs about the war. She scarcely knew herself what it meant; she longed for a moment with Woodrow, so he could explain it. But he had not, as she hoped, dropped back to walk with her. Instead, it was Jake Spoon who dropped back, when they were almost to the graveyard. Jake had a habit of touching her in public that Maggie despised; she worked in a store now, she had a respectable job, but even if she hadn't she would not have wanted Jake to touch her in public. Even in private her acceptance of him had some reluctance in it. When he attempted to touch her arm Maggie drew away.

"You oughtn't to be winking at Newt—not at a funeral," she reproached him.

Jake, though, could not be managed. He turned to Newt and winked again.

"Why, the preaching was over," he said. "There's no harm in a wink. Nobody noticed, anyway. All they can think about is the war. It's a wonder anybody even came to see Nellie buried.

"Gus does have poor luck with wives," he added. "If I was a woman I'd think twice before hitching up with him—it'd be a death sentence."

"I wish you'd be nice," Maggie whispered. "I just wish you'd be nice. You can be nice, Jake, when you try."

Maggie knew that Jake Spoon wasn't really bad; but neither was he really good, either. Though he was capable of sweetness, at times, she often felt that she would be better off having no man than a man like Jake; but, if she sent him away, Newt would be the lonelier for it. She never completely turned Jake out, though she was often tempted to. It vexed her that she was spending so much of her energy on a large child, when there was a better man, one she had long loved, not one hundred yards away—yet, there it was.

"I see Deets," Newt whispered, as the procession reached the little graveyard. Sure enough, Deets and two other Negroes, men who had worked for Nellie McCrae or her family, stood deferentially, waiting, near a grove of trees.

Newt was wondering if Graciela had died of the snakebite, in which case they might have to bury *her*, too, when they got back home. He did like Graciela; she gave him honey cakes and taught him how to tie little threads on grasshoppers' legs and make them pull sticks along, like tiny wagons. But if Graciela *had* died and they had to go through the singing and praying again, it would be a long time before he got to play. Besides, the brown coat his mother was so proud of scratched his neck. There was more singing, and the grownups all gathered around a hole in the ground. Newt seemed sleepy—the brown coat made him hot. He held his mother's hand, put his head against her leg, and shut his eyes. The next thing he knew, Deets, who carried him home, was setting him down in his own kitchen. Graciela, who was still alive, helped him take off the scratchy coat.

5.

ONCE HE HAD become a rich man, Blue Duck began to think of killing his father. Getting rich had been easy—the whites were on the roads in great numbers, and they were careless travelers. They traveled as if there were no Comanches left—most of these whites did not even post guards at night. Blue Duck supposed they must be coming from lands where the Indians were tame, or where they had all been killed. Otherwise the whites would long since have been robbed and killed. They drank at night until they passed out, or else lay with their women carelessly. They were easy to kill and rob, and even the poorest of them had at least a few things of value: guns, watches, a little money; some of the women had jewels hidden away. Often there would be a horse or two Blue Duck could add to the herd he was building at his camp near the Cimarron River.

Few of his father's band hunted that far east; Comanches didn't bother him, nor did the Indians to the east, the Cherokees or Choctaws or other tribes that the whites had driven into the Indian Territory. Those Indians were not raiders anyway: they tried to build towns and farms. They hunted a little, but they had few horses and did not go after the buffalo. A few renegades from those tribes tried to join up with Blue Duck, but the only one he allowed into his band was a Choctaw named Broken Nose, who was an exceptional shot with the rifle. Blue Duck wanted only Indians who were skilled horsemen, like his own people, the Comanches. Sometimes he liked to strike deep into the forested country, where the whites had many little settlements; for such work he needed men who could ride. He wanted to raid as the Comanches raided, only in the eastern places, where the whites were numerous and careless.

Blue Duck had five women, two who were Kiowa and three white women he had stolen. There were many other stolen women that he let his men play with for a while, and then killed. He wanted the whites to know that once he had one of their women, the woman was lost. Ermoke, the first man to join up with him once he had left his father's band, was very lustful, so lustful that he had to be restrained. Blue Duck wanted wealth but Ermoke only wanted women—he would raid any party if he saw a woman that he wanted.

Soon there were fifteen men in the camp on the Cimarron; they had many guns, a good herd of horses, and many women. Sometimes Blue Duck would get tired of all the drinking and quarreling that went on in the camp. Once or twice he had risen up in fury and killed one or two of his own men, just to quiet the camp. He had learned from his father that the way to deal death was to do it quickly, when people were least expecting death to be dealt. Blue Duck kept an axe near the place where he spread his robes. Sometimes he would spring up and kill two or three renegades with his axe, before they could react and flee.

At other times he would simply ride away from the camp for a few days, to rest his mind, and when he left he always rode west, toward the Comanche lands. It rankled him that he had been made an outcast. He would have liked to ride again with the Comanche, to live again in the Comanche way. He missed the great hunts; he missed the raids. The renegades he commanded seldom took a buffalo, or any game larger than a deer. Once or twice Blue Duck rode north alone and took a buffalo or two—he did it for the meat, but also because it reminded him of a time he had gone hunting with Buffalo Hump and Kicking Wolf and the other Comanche hunters. The knowledge that he had been driven out, that he could never go back, filled him sometimes with anger and other times with sadness. He did not understand it. He had done no worse than many young warriors; he had only been trying to prove his bravery, which it was right to do.

Blue Duck decided that the real reason for his exile was that the old men feared his strength. They knew he would be a chief someday, and they feared for themselves, just as the renegades on the Cimarron were afraid for themselves.

He decided too— one night when the sleet was blowing and he was eating buffalo liver, far north of the Canadian River—that his father also feared his strength. Buffalo Hump was older; soon his strength would begin to fade. But he had been war chief of his band for a long time; he would not want to surrender his power, to a son or anyone. His power would have to be taken, and Blue Duck wanted to be the one to take it.

In the cold morning he skinned the buffalo he had killed and took the hide back to the camp on the Cimarron, for the women to work. Only the two Kiowa women knew how to work with skins; the stolen white women had no such skills. The women were inept and so were many of the men. They were adequate when raiding white farmers, travelers with families, and the like, but in battle none of them were equal to the Comanches. They had no skill with any weapon except the rifle, and most of them were cowards, as well. A few Comanche warriors could make short work of them, a thing Blue Duck knew well.

He meant to kill his father, but it was not a thing he would attempt hastily. His father was too alert, and too dangerous. He might have to wait until his father weakened; perhaps an illness would strike Buffalo Hump, or a white soldier kill him; or perhaps he would just grow careless when on a hunt and die of an accident.

As the years passed Blue Duck's fame spread, thanks to his random and merciless killings. He was a wanted man in the eastern country, the country of trees. In Arkansas and in east Texas or Louisiana his name was feared by people who had never heard of Buffalo Hump; people who had no reason to fear a Comanche attack feared Blue Duck. He became expert at working the line between the wild country and the settled. He knew where there were effective lawmen and where there were not. Many of his renegades were shot, and not a few captured, tried, and hung, but Blue Duck shifted away. He robbed at night, then went north into Kansas; few white lawmen had ever seen him, but all knew of him.

His restlessness did not leave him, or his frustration. He was a Comanche who was not allowed to live as a Comanche, and the injustice rankled. Many times he went back to the Comanche country, sometimes camping in it for days, alone. He was careful, though, to stay well away from his father's people. He didn't fear Slow Tree, but he knew that if he gave Buffalo Hump enough provocation Buffalo Hump would come after him and hunt him to death, if he could.

Blue Duck, cool in the attack, but impatient in most other aspects of life, knew that he needed to be patient in the matter of his father. He was the younger man; he had only to wait until time weakened his father, or removed him. Now and then his hot blood urged him not to wait, to challenge his father and kill him. But in cooler moments he knew that was folly. Even if he killed Buffalo

Hump there were other warriors who would hunt him down and kill him.

In the east, among the forests, the name of Blue Duck was most feared. Even on the much-traveled army roads few travelers felt safe. The gun merchants in Arkansas and Mississippi sold many guns to travelers who hoped to protect themselves from Blue Duck, Ermoke, and their men.

Many of those travelers died, new guns or no; Blue Duck's wealth grew; but, despite it, he still went back, every few months, to ride the *comanchería*, the long plains of grass.

6.

THE MORNING AFTER Nellie's funeral, Augustus McCrae disappeared. He had been seen the night before, drinking in his usual saloon, but when morning came he was nowhere to be found. His favorite horse, a black mare, was not in the stables, and there was no sign that he had been back to the room where he had lived with Nellie.

Call was surprised, and a little disturbed. When Geneva, his first wife, died, Gus had sought company wherever he could find it. He stayed in the saloons or the whorehouses for over two weeks, and was hardly fit for rangering duties once he did resume them. On a trip to Laredo, where banditry had been especially rife, he had been thrown from his horse three times, due to inebriation. The fact that he had chosen a half-broken, untrustworthy horse for the ride to Laredo was evidence that his mind was not on his work. Augustus had always been careful to choose gentle, well-broken mounts.

Call was annoyed by his friend's sudden disappearance. Even allowing for grief, and Gus *had* seemed sadly grieved, it was unprofessional behavior in view of the unsettled state of things. Call supposed, himself, that the war fever would soon abate at least a little. Texas wasn't in the war yet, and when the eager volunteers discovered how far they would have to travel to get into a battle, many of them, he suspected, would develop second thoughts. Many would elect to stay at home and see if the war spread in their direction. It wasn't like the Mexican conflict, where men could ride south for a day or two and join in battle.

Still, it was a *war*, and the Governor's concern about the local defenses was justified. Governor Clark had an assistant, a man named Barkeley, a small man who fancied that he was a large cog in the machinery of state government. Augustus McCrae had promised the Governor an answer regarding his intentions, and Mr. Barkeley wanted it.

"Where's McCrae? The Governor's in a hurry and so am I," Barkeley wanted to know, presenting himself at the ranger stables with an air of impatience.

"He's not here," Call said.

"Where is he, then? This is damned inconvenient," Barkeley snapped.

"I don't know where he is," Call admitted. "He just buried his wife. He may have wanted to take a ride and mourn a little."

"We're all apt to have to bury wives," Barkeley replied. "McCrae has no business doing it on state time. Can't you send someone to find him?"

"No, but you're welcome to go look yourself," Call said, piqued by the man's tone.

"Go look, what do you mean, sir?" Barkeley said. "Look where?"

"He was here yesterday, I expect that means he's still somewhere in the state," Call informed the man, before turning on his heel.

By midafternoon, with Augustus still gone, Call became genuinely worried. He had never married and could not claim to know the emotions that might torment a man at the loss of a wife; but he knew they must be powerful. In the back of his mind was the sad fate of Long Bill Coleman, whose wife had not even been dead. Long Bill had seemed to be a troubled but stable man, only the day before he killed himself—and Augustus, if anything, was a good deal more flighty than Long Bill. The thought kept entering Call's mind that Augustus might have done something foolish, in his grief.

The Kickapoo tracker, Famous Shoes, the man so trusted by Captain Scull, lived with his wives and children not far north of Austin. Though Famous Shoes preferred the country along the Little Wichita, the Comanches had been violent lately in that region, killing several Kickapoo families. Famous Shoes had brought his family south, for safety. The army, hearing of his skill, tried to hire him to track for them on several expeditions, but their present leader, Colonel D. D. McQuorquodale, insisted that all scouts be mounted, a form of travel that Famous Shoes rejected. Colonel McQuorquodale refused to believe that a man on foot could keep up with a column of mounted cavalry, despite numerous testimonials to Famous Shoes' speed and ability, one of them by Call himself.

"He not only keeps up, he gets three or four days ahead, if you don't keep him in sight," Call assured the Colonel. "He's the best I've ever seen at finding water holes, Colonel."

"You'll need the water holes, too," Augustus said. He had a contempt for soldiers, but had been eavesdropping on the conversation while whittling on a stick.

"I have every confidence in my ability to find water, sir," Colonel McQuorquodale said. "I run the scouts, and they'll travel the way I tell them to, if they expect to work for Dan McQuorquodale."

On the Colonel's next expedition west, sixteen cavalry horses starved to death and several men came close to it, saved only by a heavy spring rain. Despite this evidence of the variability of water sources on the western plains, Colonel McQuorquodale refused to relax his requirements, and Famous Shoes continued to refuse to ride horses, the result being that he was in his camp, surrounded by his wives and children, when Call and Pea Eye sought him out. Call wanted to know if Famous Shoes was available to conduct a quick search for Augustus. When they arrived Famous Shoes was holding the paw of a small animal of some sort, studying it with deep curiosity. His wives were smiling as if they shared some joke, but Famous Shoes was only interested in the paw.

"We've lost Captain McCrae," Call said, dismounting. "Are you busy, or could you find the time to go look for him?"

"Right now I am wondering about this paw," Famous Shoes said. "It is the paw of a ferret my wives killed, but they cooked it when I was away. I did not get to look at the ferret."

"Why would you need to look at it, if it was tasty?" Pea Eye asked. Over the years he had grown fond of Famous Shoes—he liked it that the Kickapoo was curious about things that other men didn't even notice.

"This ferret did not belong here," Famous Shoes informed him. "Once I went to the north and I saw many weasels like this near the Platte River. This ferret was black, but all the ferrets around here are brown. This is the kind of ferret that ought to be up by the Platte River."

Famous Shoes' penchant for diverting himself for days in order to investigate things that didn't particularly require investigation was one of the things that tried Call's patience with him.

"Maybe it was just born off-color," Pea Eye suggested. "Sometimes you'll see a litter of white pigs with one black pig in it."

"This paw is from a ferret, it is not a pig," Famous Shoes said, unpersuaded by Pea Eye's suggestion. He saw, though that Captain Call was impatient—Captain Call was always impatient—so he put the ferret's paw in his pouch for future study.

"Captain McCrae went by this morning early," Famous Shoes said. "It was foggy here. I did not see him but I heard him say something to his mare. He is on that black mare he likes, and he is going west. I saw his track while I was looking for some more of these ferrets."

"His wife died, I expect he's just grieving," Call said. "I'd be obliged if you'd track him and see if you can get him to come back."

Famous Shoes considered the matter in silence for a moment. He could not do anything about the fact that Captain McCrae's wife had died—if Captain McCrae had a wife to mourn he had probably gone away so he could mourn her without anyone interfering with him too much. Also, he himself now had an interesting problem to study, the problem of the black ferret; he was comfortably settled in with his wives and children and did not particularly want to go anywhere. But Captain Call had helped him with the army, when the Colonel who wanted all scouts to ride horses had decided to put him in jail because he refused to ride. Famous Shoes had carefully explained to the Colonel, and to his captains and lieutenants, his views on horses; there were several reasons why it was not wise for Kickapoos to ride horses; besides those reasons there was a simple reason that should have been apparent to the Colonel and his men, which was that it was impossible to track expertly from the back of a horse, a tracker needed his eyes close to the ground if he were to see the fine details that would tell him what he needed to know. The qualities of dust and dirt were important to a tracker; no one could know what the dust revealed without kneeling often to feel it and study it.

The white colonel had not been interested in any of that—he had promptly put Famous Shoes in jail for disobedience. Fortunately Captain Call heard about the matter quickly and soon got him out. He and Captain McCrae had complained to the white colonel, too—Captain McCrae had even yelled at the Colonel; he let him know that Famous Shoes was needed by the Texas Rangers and was not to be interfered with.

In view of the help he had received, Famous Shoes thought he ought to lay aside the problem of the black ferret for a bit and go locate Captain McCrae. He had known Captain McCrae for a number of years and knew that he did not behave like most white men. Captain McCrae's behavior reminded him of some friends he had who were Choctaw. Captain Call was very much a white man; he lived by rules. But Captain McCrae had little patience with rules; he lived by what was inside him, by the urgings of his heart and his spirit—and now, grieved by the death of his wife, Captain McCrae's spirit urged him to get on his black mare and go west. Already, that morning, Famous Shoes had the feeling that something unusual was happening with Captain McCrae. He was not going away to do some chore that he would be paid for. He was going away for a different reason. Famous Shoes got up and led the two rangers over to the stream, to show them the tracks where the black mare had crossed.

"I will go find him—I think it will take me many days," Famous Shoes said.

Captain Call looked displeased, but he didn't disagree with the statement. He himself probably felt that something unusual was happening with his friend.

"Why would it take so many days if he just left?" Pea Eye asked. Tracking was a mystery to him. He liked to watch Famous Shoes as he did it, but he didn't understand the process involved. The track he saw by the stream just told him that a horse had passed. Which horse, and where it was going, and how heavy a rider it was carrying were all obvious to Famous Shoes but not obvious to Pea Eye. Even more puzzling was Famous Shoes' ability to predict things about the traveler, his mood or circumstance, that he himself could not have guessed even if he were with the traveler and looking him right in the eye. Captain McCrae himself had been doubtful of the scout's ability to figure out such things, and said so often.

"He's just guessing," Augustus said. "When he's right it's luck and when he's wrong nobody knows about it because whoever he's guessing about gets away."

"I don't think he's guessing," Call had protested. "He's got nothing to do but track, and think about tracking—and he ain't young. He's learned it. He gathers information that we can't see, and puts it together."

Pea Eye thought Captain Call probably had the better of the argument. The tracker's very next comment was a case in point.

"He's looking for peace and cannot find it here along the Guadalupe," Famous Shoes said. "I think he will have to go a long way to find it. He may have to go to the Rio Pecos."

"The Pecos!" Call exclaimed. "The Governor will fire him if he goes that far."

"I don't think the Captain will care," Famous Shoes said.

"No, you're right," Call said, once he had considered. He thought the matter over for a minute, looking west into the hills.

"I'm going to send Corporal Parker with you," he told Famous Shoes. There were no graded ranks in the rangers, but he and Gus had taken to calling Pea Eye "Corporal" because they liked him. He was not a confident young man—it flattered him a little to be thought of as a corporal.

"We can leave now," Famous Shoes said. "Maybe we can spot another of those black ferrets while we are tracking Captain McCrae."

Pea Eye was startled but pleased—traveling with Famous Shoes would be instructive. The man was already trotting west; he did not seem to think it necessary to go back and speak to his wives.

"Stay with him, Corporal," Call said.

"I'll stay with him, Captain," Pea Eye said.

He had no more than said it when he looked around and noticed that Famous Shoes, the man he had just promised to stay with, had disappeared. The hilly country was patched with clumps of cedar, juniper, live oak, chaparral, and various other bushes. Pea Eye felt something like panic. He had not taken even one step westward and had already lost the man he was traveling with—and Captain Call was right there to see it.

Call noticed Pea Eye's confusion, and remembered how annoyed he had been at first, and how confused, when Famous Shoes would just disappear, often for days.

"There he is," Call said, pointing at Famous Shoes, who was crossing a little hillock some two hundred yards to the west.

"I expected he just squatted behind a bush to look at a track," he added.

"Maybe it was a ferret track," Pea Eye said, much relieved. "He's got a powerful interest in ferrets.

"What is a ferret, Captain?" he asked—he wasn't quite sure and did not want to appear ignorant, as he traveled with Famous Shoes.

"Well, it's a varmint of the weasel family, I believe," Call said. "You best catch up with Famous Shoes and ask him. He might lecture you on ferrets all the way to the Pecos, if you have to go that far.

"I don't know why Gus would want to go all the way to the Pecos," he said, but Pea Eye had his eye fixed on Famous Shoes, clearly worried that he might disappear again.

"I'm going, Captain, before I lose him," Pea Eye said.

He put his horse in a lope and was soon beside the tracker, who neither stopped nor looked around.

Watching them go, Call felt both relief and envy: relief that Famous Shoes had accepted the job; envy because he wished he could be as young and unburdened with duties as Pea Eye Parker. It would be nice to be able to forget the Governor, and Barkeley, and the ledger keepers and just to ride west into the wild country. Perhaps, he thought, as he turned back, that was what Augustus wanted: just to be free for a few days, just to saddle his horse and ride.

7.

WITHIN AN HOUR of leaving Captain Call, Pea Eye began to wish fervently that they would soon find Augustus McCrae, mainly because he had no confidence that he could stay with Famous Shoes. It wasn't that Famous Shoes traveled particularly fast—though it was certainly true he didn't travel slow. The problem was that he traveled irregularly, zigging and zagging, slipping into a copse of trees, loping off at right angles to the track, sometimes even doubling back if he spotted an animal or a bird he wanted to investigate. No matter how hard Pea Eye concentrated on staying with him, Famous Shoes continually disappeared. Every time it happened Pea Eye had to wonder if he would ever see the man again.

Famous Shoes was amused at the young ranger's frantic efforts to keep him in sight, a thing, of course, which was quite unnecessary. The young man looked worried and nervous all day and was so tired when they made camp that he was barely capable of making a decent fire. Famous Shoes liked the young man and thought it might help a little if he instructed Corporal Parker in the ways of scouting.

"You do not have to follow me or stay close to me," he told Pea Eye. "I do not follow a straight trail."

"Nope, you don't," Pea Eye agreed. He had been almost asleep, from fatigue, but the strong coffee Famous Shoes brewed woke him up a little.

"I have many things to watch," Famous Shoes told him. "I do not think we will catch up with Captain McCrae for a few days. I think he is going far."

"Can you tell how far he's going just from the tracks?" Pea Eye asked.

"No—it is just something I am thinking," Famous Shoes admitted. "He has lost his wife. Right now he does not know where to be. I think he is going far, to look around."

In the night Pea Eye found that he could not sleep. It occurred to him that he had never been alone with an Indian before. Of course, it was only Famous Shoes, who was friendly. But what if he wasn't *really* friendly? What if Famous Shoes suddenly got an urge to take a scalp? Of course, Pea Eye knew it was unlikely—Captain Call wouldn't send him off with an Indian who wanted to take his scalp. He knew it was foolish to be thinking that way. Famous Shoes had scouted for many years and had never scalped anybody. But Pea Eye's mind wouldn't behave. The part of it that was sensible knew that Famous Shoes meant him no harm; but another part of his mind kept bringing up pictures of Indians with scalping knives. He was annoyed with his mind—it would be a lot easier to do his task well if his mind would just behave and not keep making him scared.

Late in the night, while the young ranger dozed, Famous Shoes heard some geese flying overhead, and he began to sing a long song about birds. Of course he sang the song in his own Kickapoo tongue, which the young white man could not understand. Famous Shoes knew that the words of the song would be mysterious to the young man, who had awakened to listen, but he sang anyway. That things were mysterious did not make them less valuable. The mystery of the northward-flying geese had always haunted him; he thought the geese might be flying to the edge of the world, so he made a song about them, for no mystery was stronger to Famous Shoes than the mystery of birds. All the animals that he knew left tracks, but the geese, when they spread their wings to fly northward, left no tracks. Famous Shoes thought that the geese must know where the gods lived, and because of their knowledge had been exempted by the gods from having to make tracks. The gods would not want to be visited by just anyone who found a track, but their messengers, the great birds, were allowed to visit them. It was a wonderful thing, a thing Famous Shoes never tired of thinking about.

When Famous Shoes finished his song he noticed that the young white man was asleep. During the day he had not trusted enough, and had worn himself out with pointless scurryings. Perhaps even then the song he had just sung was working in the young man's dreams; perhaps as he grew older he would learn to trust mysteries and not fear them. Many white men could not trust things unless they could be explained; and yet the most beautiful things, such as the trackless flight of birds, could never be explained.

The next morning, when the first gray light came, Pea Eye awoke to find that he had not been scalped or hurt. He felt so tired and so grateful that he didn't move at once. Famous Shoes squatted by the campfire, bringing the coffee to a boil. Pea Eye wanted to be helpful, but he felt as if his joints had turned to glue. He sat up, but he felt incapable of further movement.

Famous Shoes drank his coffee as if he were drinking water, although, to Pea Eye's taste, the coffee was scalding.

"I am leaving now," Famous Shoes said. "You do not have to go where I go. Just travel to the west."

"What? I won't see you at all?" Pea Eye asked. Never since joining the rangers had he spent a whole day alone, in wild country. Even if he hadn't been feeling that his joints had melted, the prospect would have alarmed him. If he met a party of Comanches, he would be lost.

"You haven't seen no Indian sign, have you?" he asked.

Famous Shoes was not in the mood for conversation just then. There was a ridge to the north that had some curious black rocks scattered around it; he wanted to examine those black rocks. The sky to the east was white now—it was time to start.

"No, there are no Indians here, but there is an old bear who has a den in that little mountain," he said, pointing toward a small hill just to the west. "You should be careful of that bear—he might try to eat your horse."

"The rascal, I'll shoot him if he tries it," Pea Eye said, but with his joints so gluey he didn't feel confident that he could kill a bear.

Determined to make a show of competence, he stood up.

"I will find you when the evening star shines," Famous Shoes said. "Bring the coffeepot."

Then he slipped into the grayness. Pea Eye sipped his coffee, which was still barely cool enough to drink; but he kept his hand on his rifle while he sipped, in case the surly old bear was closer than Famous Shoes thought.

8.

WHEN AUGUSTUS LEFT Austin he had no aim, other than to ride around for a while, alone. To be in Austin was to be under orders: the Governor was always summoning them or sending them off, consulting with them or pestering them about details of finance that Augustus had not the slightest interest in.

As a rule he did not, like his friend Call, enjoy solitude. Woodrow was virtually incapable of spending a whole evening in the company of his fellow men—or women either, if Maggie's account was to be trusted. At some point in the evening Woodrow Call would always quietly disappear. He would slip off in the night, ostensibly to stand guard, when there was not a savage within one hundred miles. Prolonged stretches of company seemed to oppress him.

With Augustus it was the opposite. When night fell, if he was in town, he wanted company, the livelier the better; he sought it and he found it, whether it involved a card game, a few talky whores, a singsong, or just a session of bragging and tale-telling with whatever gamblers and adventurers happened to be around. He had never particularly liked to sleep, and rarely did for more than three or four hours a night. Even that necessity he begrudged. Why just lay there, when you could be living? A little rest at night was needful, but the less the better.

Now, though, his lovely Nellie's death had arrested, for the moment, his taste for company; it seemed to him that he had been under orders for his entire life, and he was tired of it. Once it had been captains who ordered him around; now it was governors, or legislators or commissioners. The war in the East was barely started and already the Governor was pressing him and Call to pledge themselves to stay in Texas.

Augustus didn't want it; he had been ordered around enough. The war could wait, the Governor could wait, Woodrow could wait, and the whores and the boys in the saloons could wait. He was going away because he felt like it, and he would come back when he felt like it, *if* he felt like it, and not because of some governor's summons.

He rode all the first day in brilliant weather, not thinking of Nellie or the war or Call or anything much. His black mare, Sassy, was a fine mount, with a long easy trot that carried them west mile after mile through the limestone hills. He had not rushed off improvidently this time, either; he had four bottles of whiskey in one saddlebag, some bullets and a good slab of bacon in another. He was not much of a hunter, and he knew it. Stalking game was often boresome work. He would cheerfully shoot any tasty animal that presented itself within rifle range, but he seldom pursued his quarry far.

Despite the Comanches, the country west of Austin was rapidly settling up. Those settlers who had survived the great raid of 1856 had by now rebuilt and remarried; cabins were scattered along the valleys, or anywhere there was sufficient water. Several times Gus had heard a large animal in the underbrush and pulled his rifle, expecting to flush a bear or a deer, only to scare out a milk cow or a couple of heifers or even a few goats.

A little before dusk he smelled wood smoke and saw a faint column rising from a copse of cedar to the southwest. He knew there must be a settler's cabin there, but, on this occasion, decided to ride on. The grub at these rude little homesteads was apt to be uncertain; frequently the families lived on nothing but corn cakes. He didn't feel inclined to sit for an hour, making conversation with people he didn't know, only to eat corn cakes or mush. A good many of the new settlers were Germans, who spoke only the most rudimentary English; also many of them were, to Augustus's way of thinking, excessively pious. Some kept no liquor in their houses at all, and, on several occasions when he had been invited in for a meal, the grace was said at such length that he had all but lost his appetite before anyone was allowed to eat.

This night, he decided not to gamble on the cabin. A dog began to bark but Augustus left it to its barking and slipped on by. He rode only another few miles before making camp. It was rocky country, the footing in some places so uncertain that he felt he risked laming the black mare if he traveled farther. In any case, he was not going anywhere in particular and was on no schedule except his own. The cedarwood and low mesquite burned nicely; he soon had a fragrant fire going. It was not cold; he only fed the fire a stick now and then because he liked to have a fire to look at.

Over the last years he had looked into many campfires and only seen one face: Clara's. His fat wife, Geneva, and his skinny wife, Nellie, were dead; the memory of their forms and faces didn't disturb him. That night when he looked into the fire he saw no one. Women had been constantly in his thoughts since his youth, but that night he was free of even the thought of them. He thought he might just keep on riding west, into the desert, where there were neither governors nor women. His absence would vex Woodrow Call, of course, but he didn't see that he needed to live like a bound servant, just to spare Woodrow Call a little vexation. The bright stars above him seemed to act like a drug. He dreamed of floating on air like a gliding bird, gliding into a slumber so deep that, when he woke, the stars had faded into the light of a new day. At the edge of sleep he heard a clicking sound, the sort a tin cup might make, or a coffeepot; the first thing he saw when he opened his eyes was a pair of legs standing by his campfire, which blazed beneath the coffeepot.

"The coffee's hot, I suggest you rouse yourself up, Captain," a voice said. Recognizing that his visitor was none other than Charlie Goodnight, Augustus immediately did as the man suggested.

"Howdy—I'm glad it was you and not Buffalo Hump, Charlie," Gus said. "I may have taken ill. Otherwise I fail to understand why I would sleep this late."

"You don't look ill to me, just idle," Goodnight observed. He was a stout man, a little past Gus's age, fully as forceful in speech as he was in body. He had been at times a superlative scout and ranger, but lately his interest had shifted to ranching; he now only rode with the rangers when the need was urgent. He was known for being as tireless as he was gruff. Conversations with Charlie Goodnight were apt to be short ones, and not infrequently left those he was conversing with slightly bruised in their feelings.

"Heard about the war?" Augustus asked.

"Heard," Goodnight said. "I'd appreciate a bite of bacon if you have any. I left in a hurry and took no provisions."

"It's in my saddlebag, with the frying pan," Gus said. "You'll pardon me if I don't offer to cook it. I prefer to contemplate the scriptures in the morning, at least until the sun's up."

Goodnight got the bacon and the pan. He didn't comment on the war, or the scriptures. Gus saw that a fine sorrel gelding was nibbling mesquite leaves, alongside his mare. Not only had he not heard the man approach, he had not heard the horse, either. It was fine to be relaxed, as he had been last night, but in wild country there was such a thing as being too relaxed.

Goodnight's silence irked him a little: what good was a guest who consumed bacon but didn't contribute conversation?

"Do you fear God, Charlie?" Augustus asked, thinking he might pursue the religious theme for a moment.

"Nope, too busy," Goodnight said. "Are you a God-fearing man? I would not have supposed it."

"I expect I ought to be," Gus said. "He keeps taking my wives, I suppose he could take me at any time."

"He might as well, if you're going to sleep till sunup," Goodnight said. He had already cooked and eaten fully half of Gus's bacon. He stood up and returned the rest to the saddlebag.

"Are you going somewhere?" Goodnight asked.

"Why yes, west," Augustus said. "How about yourself?"

"Colorado," Goodnight replied. "There's a lively market for Texas beef in Denver, and an abundance of beef on the hoof down here in Texas."

Augustus considered the two remarks, but in his groggy state failed to see how they connected.

"Have you got a herd of cattle with you, Charlie?" he asked. "If so, I guess I'm blind as well as deaf."

"Not presently," Goodnight said. "But I could soon acquire one if I could find a good route to Denver."

"Charlie, I don't think this is the way to Colorado," Augustus said. "Not unless your cattle can drink air. There's no water between here and Colorado, that I know of."

"There's the Pecos River—that's a wet river," Goodnight said. "If I could just get a herd as far as the Pecos, I expect the moisture would increase, from there to Denver."

Mention of Denver reminded Gus of Matilda Roberts, one of his oldest and best friends. In the old days everyone had known Matty, even Goodnight, though as one of the soberer citizens of the frontier he had no reputation as a whorer.

"You remember Matty Roberts, don't you, Charlie?" Gus inquired.

"Yes, she's a fine woman," Goodnight said. "She's in the love business but love ain't been kind to her. I've not visited her establishment in Denver but they say it's lavish."

"What do you mean, love ain't been kind?" Gus asked. He realized that he had no recent information about his old friend.

"Matilda's dying, that's what I mean," Goodnight said. He had unsaddled his horse, so the sorrel could have a good roll in the dust; but the sorrel had had his roll and in a few minutes Goodnight was ready to depart.

"What—Matty's dying—what of?" Augustus asked, shocked. Now another woman of his close acquaintance was about to be carried off. The news struck him almost as hard as if he had been told that Clara was dying. Even Woodrow Call would admit a fondness for Matty Roberts; he would be shocked when he heard the news.

"I don't know what of," Goodnight informed him. "I suppose she's just dying of living—that's the one infection that strikes us all down, sooner or later."

He mounted and started to leave, but turned back and looked down at Augustus, who still sat idly at the campfire.

"Are you poorly today?" Goodnight asked.

"No, I'm well—why would you ask, Charlie?" Gus said.

"You don't seem to be in an active frame of mind today, that's why," Goodnight said. "You ain't ready to die, are you?"

"Why, no," Augustus said, startled by the question. "I'm just a little sleepy. I was sitting up with Nellie quite a few nights before she passed away."

Goodnight did not seem to be satisfied by that answer. The sorrel was nervous, ready to leave, but Goodnight held him back, which was unusual. When Charlie Goodnight was ready to go he usually left without ceremony, seldom giving whomever he was talking to even the leisure to finish a sentence. He had never been one to linger—yet, now, he was lingering, looking at Augustus hard.

"If you were under my orders I'd order you home," he said bluntly. "A man who can't get himself in an active frame of mind by this hour has no business traveling in this direction."

"Well, I ain't under your orders and I never will be," Augustus retorted, a little annoyed by the man's tone. "I ain't a child and nobody appointed you to watch over me."

Goodnight smiled—also a rare thing.

"I was concerned that you might have lost your snap, but I guess you ain't," he said, turning his horse again.

"Wait, Charlie . . . if you're bound for Denver I've got something for you to take to Matty," Gus said. The news that she was dying struck him hard—he was beginning to remember all the fine times he had had with the woman. He went to his saddlebag and pulled out the sock where he kept his loose money. The sock contained about sixty dollars, which he promptly handed to Goodnight. As he did his face reddened, and he choked up. Why were all the good women dying?

"I was always behind a few pokes with Matilda," he said. "I expect I owe her at least this much. I'd be obliged if you'd take it to her, Charlie."

Goodnight looked at the money for a moment and then put it in his pocket.

"How long have you owed this debt?" he asked.

"About fifteen years," Augustus said.

"If you were going toward the Pecos I'd accompany you until your mind gets a little more active," Goodnight offered.

"I ain't, though," Gus said. He did not want company, particularly not company as prickly as Charles Goodnight.

"I'm bound for the good old Rio Grande," he said, although he wasn't.

"All right, goodbye," Goodnight said. "If I plan to find a way to get my cattle to Colorado, I better start looking."

"Charlie, if you do see Matty, tell her she's got a friend in Texas," Augustus said—he was still choked up.

"Done, if I get there in time," Goodnight said.

9.

WHEN FIVE DAYS PASSED with no word from Augustus McCrae or the two men who had been sent to find him, Governor Clark waxed so indignant that he was hot to the touch. Call, impatient himself, thought the Governor's indignation unwarranted. The rangers had no urgent mission at the moment, in light of which Augustus's absence did not seem exceptional. Governor Clark himself was a hunter, often gone from Austin for a week at a time killing deer, antelope, or wild pig. Call began to find the Governor's complaints irksome, and said so to Maggie one evening over a beefsteak which she had been kind enough to cook him. The boy, Newt, had scampered downstairs on his arrival and was blowing his whistle at some chickens who belonged to the lady next door.

"I expect Gus is just grieving," Maggie said. "If I ever had a husband and he died, I'd want to go off someplace to do my grieving. It wouldn't be fair to Newt to do too much moping at home."

"Being a ranger's getting to be like being a policeman," Call said. "Nowadays they want you on call all the time."

He noticed that Maggie's arms were freckled to the elbows. Probably she had spent a little too much time in the sun, working the little garden plot she had planted with Jake Spoon's help. In the warm months Maggie was never without vegetables.

It was a fine thing, in Call's view, that Maggie had gained respectable employment at last. He had been in the store one day while Maggie was writing up an inventory and was surprised to see that her penmanship was excellent.

"Why, you write a hand as fine as Jake's," he said. "They'll be asking you to teach school next. I doubt there's a teacher in town who writes that pretty."

"Oh, it just takes practice," Maggie said. "Jake lent me his penmanship book and showed me how to do some of the curls."

As Call was finishing his beefsteak he noticed Jake's penmanship book on a table by Maggie's bed; then he noticed a bandana that he

542

thought was Jake's hanging over the bedpost at the foot of Maggie's bed.

He had known, of course, that Jake and Maggie had a friendship; the two of them were often seen working in the garden. Jake's skills as a gardener were such that a number of local women pestered him for his secrets or showed up to watch when he was working in the garden. Jake basked in the attention of all the local ladies—Call had no doubt that many of them would have envied Maggie her penmanship lessons.

"Why, Jake's left his bandana on the bedpost," Call said, as Maggie was taking his plate to the wash bucket.

"Yes, he left it," Maggie said. At that point young Newt burst in, crying and holding up an injured hand; in his pursuit of the chickens he had wandered too close to old Dan, the turkey, and had been soundly pecked.

"That ain't the first time Dan's pecked you—why *won't* you avoid that turkey?" Maggie said. "Go down to the mud puddle and daub a little mud on that peck—it'll soothe it."

When Newt went down Maggie excused herself for a moment and went with him—she wanted to run the old turkey off before it did damage to her garden.

While Maggie was gone Call looked around the room. A pair of Jake's spurs were on the floor by the little sofa and his shaving brush and razor were by the washbasin.

Call knew it was none of his business where Jake kept his razor, or his spurs, or his bandana, and yet the sight of so many of Jake's things in Maggie's room disturbed him in a way he had not expected. When she came back he thanked her for the beefsteak, gave Newt a penny for some sassafras candy—Newt was a well-behaved little boy who deserved an occasional treat—and left.

Call got his rifle and started to take a short walk down by the river. He had been twice to the Governor that day and had spent the afternoon going over the company accounts with Jake, a task that always tired him. He didn't intend to walk long.

As he came out of the bunkhouse he saw Jake Spoon leave a saloon across the street and angle off toward Maggie's rooms. Ordinarily he would have thought nothing of it, but that night he *did* think of it. He didn't wait to see if Jake went up the stairs to the room he himself had just left; he felt that would be unseemly. Instead, he walked out of town, disquieted without quite knowing why. He realized he had no right to boss Maggie Tilton at all. She had her employment and could do as she pleased.

The thought that disturbed him—right or no right—was that Jake and Maggie were now living together. That notion startled him greatly. Maggie was a respectable woman now, with a child who was well liked. She needed to be thinking of her work and her child and not risk her respectability for any reason—certainly not for the irresponsible Jake Spoon.

Call walked out of Austin on the wagon road that led to San Antonio. He wished Gus were back, not because the Governor wanted him back but so he could ask his opinion about the matter of Maggie and Jake. Of course, he knew nothing definite—all he knew was that what he was feeling left him too agitated for sleep.

In what seemed like a matter of minutes Call was surprised to see, at a curve in the wagon road, a big live oak tree that had been split by lightning some years before. The reason for his surprise was that the live oak was ten miles from town. In his confusion he had walked much farther than he had meant to—usually he only strolled two or three miles and went to bed. But he had walked ten miles without noticing, and would have to walk another ten to get back to the bunkhouse.

The walk back went slower—it was almost dawn when he got back to the bunkhouse. Across the way, Maggie's window was dark. Was Jake sleeping there? And what if he was? He had long since put the whole question of Maggie and men out of his mind. Now, suddenly, it was very much in his mind, and yet he had no one to discuss the matter with and was far from knowing even what he felt himself.

Old Ikey Ripple, retired now except for ceremonial appearances, was sitting on a nail keg rubbing his white hair when Call walked up, in the first light.

"Hello, you're up early," Call said to the old man. Ikey, of course, was always up early.

"Yep, I don't like to miss none of the day," Ikey said.

Ikey was a snuff dipper; he had already worked his lip over a good wad of snuff.

"Where have *you* been, Captain?" he asked. "It's too early for patrol."

"Just looking around," Call said. "Someone saw three Indians west of town yesterday. I don't want them slipping in and running off any stock."

"Will you be going off to the war, Captain?" Ikey asked.

Call shook his head, which seemed to reassure the old man.

"If you was to go off to that war I expect the Indians would slip in and get all the stock," Ikey said.

Ikey looked around and saw only the morning mist. The mention of Indians to the west was unwelcome. Those same Indians could be hidden by the mist—they might be lurking anywhere in which case he was more than glad to have Captain Call with him.

"I've been skeert of Indians all my life," Ikey said, feeling the sudden need to unburden himself in the matter. "I expect I've woke up a thousand times, expecting to see an Indian standing over me ready to yank off my scalp. But here I am eighty and they ain't got me yet, so I expect it was wasted worry."

"I imagine you'll be safe, if you just stay in town," Call told him. "You need to be careful, though, if you're off fishing."

"Oh, I don't fish no more—give it up," Ikey said.

"Why, Ikey?" Call asked. "Fishing is a harmless pursuit,"

"It's because of the bones," Ikey said. "Remember Jacob Low? He was that tailor who choked on a fish bone. Got it stuck in his gullet and was dead before anybody knew what to do. Here I've survived the Comanches near eighty years—I'm damned if I want to take the risk of choking on a bone from one of them bony little perch."

"I don't recall that you've been married, since I've known you," Call said.

But he left the remark hanging—just a remark, not quite a question. He felt absurd suddenly. Maggie Tilton had wanted, for years, to marry him, but he had declined, preferring bachelorhood—why was he talking about marriage to an eighty-year-old bachelor who had little to do but gossip? Though fond of Maggie, he had never wanted to marry and didn't know why he was so disturbed to discover that she was keeping closer company with Jake than he had supposed.

"Illinois," Ikey Ripple said. "I sparked a girl once—it was in Illinois."

Though Captain Call didn't question him further, Ikey thought back, across sixty years, to the girl he had sparked in Illinois, whose name was Sally. They had danced once in a hoedown; she had blue eyes. But Sally had fallen out of a boat on a foggy morning, while crossing the Mississippi River on a trip to St. Louis with her father. Her body, so far as he could recall, had never been found. Had her name been Sally? Or had it been Mary? Had her eyes been blue? Or had they been brown? He had danced with her once at a hoedown. Was it her father she had been with on the boat trip? Or was it her mother?

Captain Call, who had seemed interested, for a moment, in Ikey's past with women, walked off to seek breakfast, leaving Ikey to sit alone, on his nail keg. As the morning sun burned away the mist in the streets of Austin, the mist in Ikey's memory deepened, as he tried to think about that girl—was it Mary or Sally, were her eyes blue or brown, was it her mother or her father she was in the boat with?—he had danced with at a hoedown long ago.

10.

BY THE TENTH DAY of travel Pea Eye had given himself up for lost. There was so little vegetation that he had let his horse go at night, in hopes that he would find enough grazing to survive. Often, when he awoke in the gray dawn, neither the horse nor Famous Shoes would be anywhere in sight. All he would see, as the sun rose, was an empty, arid plain, almost desert. There was seldom a cloud, just a great ring of horizon, with nothing moving within it. The freezing plains to the north had been just as empty, but he had only ventured onto the llano with a troop of men; now, for most of the day, he was alone. He had long since stopped believing that they would find Gus McCrae—why would Gus leave the cozy saloons of Austin to come to such a place?

After the first week, Pea Eye's days were spent struggling against his own sense of desperation. Sometimes he would not see Famous Shoes until the evening. He rode west, west, west, feeling hopeless. It was true that Famous Shoes always returned, as promised, when the evening star shone; but, every day, Pea Eye became more anxious that the man would abandon him. When Famous Shoes did appear, Pea Eye's relief was intense but short lived; soon it would be morning again, and Famous Shoes nowhere to be seen.

Sometimes it took Pea Eye an hour just to locate his horse—the animal would be nibbling leaves or small plants in some little dip or gully. Then, all day, he would plod to the west, seeing no one. All day he longed for company, any company.

On the tenth evening, when Famous Shoes rejoined him, Pea Eye could not hold back his doubts.

"Gus ain't out here, is he?" he asked. "How would he get this far? Why would he want to cross so much of this poor country?"

Famous Shoes knew the young ranger was scared. Nothing was easier to detect in a man than fear. It showed even in the way he fumbled with his cup while drinking coffee; and it was normal that he would be afraid. He didn't know where he was, and it must puzzle him that Captain McCrae would choose to go so far into the desert. The young ranger was not old enough to understand the things men might do when they were uncertain and unhappy.

"He is ahead of us, just one day," Famous Shoes said. "I have not lost his track, and I won't lose it."

"By why would he come so far?" Pea Eye asked. "There's nothing here."

Famous Shoes had been wondering about the same thing. The journeys that people took had always interested him; his own life was a constant journeying, though not quite so constant as it had been before he had his wives and children. Usually he only agreed to scout for the Texans if they were going in a direction he wanted to go himself, in order to see a particular hill or stream, to visit a relative or friend, or just to search for a bird or animal he wanted to observe.

Also, he often went back to places he had been at earlier times in his life, just to see if the places would seem the same. In most cases, because he himself had changed, the places did not seem exactly as he remembered them, but there were exceptions. The simplest places, where there was only rock and sky, or water and rock, changed the least. When he felt disturbances in his life, as all men would, Famous Shoes tried to go back to one of the simple places, the places of rock and sky, to steady himself and grow calm again.

Though he had not talked with Captain McCrae about his journey, Famous Shoes had the feeling that such a thing might be happening within him because of the loss of his wife. Captain McCrae might be going back to someplace that he had been before, hoping he would find that it was the same and that it was simple. Every day Famous Shoes followed his track and noted that the Captain was not wandering aimlessly, like a man too distracted to notice where he was going. Captain McCrae knew where he was going—that much Famous Shoes did not doubt.

"I think he is going back to a place he has been before," Famous Shoes said, in answer to Pea Eye's question. "He is pointed toward the Rio Grande now. If he stops when he comes to the river we will find him tomorrow."

Famous Shoes suspected that the young ranger did not believe what he had just said—he was not old enough to understand the need to go back to a place where things were simple. He had no happiness in his face, the young ranger; perhaps he had never had a place where things were simple, a place he could think about when he needed to remember happiness. Perhaps the young ranger had been unlucky—he might have no good place or good time to remember.

Famous Shoes himself had begun to feel the need to live in a simpler place. The plains were filled with white travelers now, all heading west. The Comanches were more irritable than ever, because their best hunting grounds were always being disturbed. The buffalo had moved north, where there were fewer people. The old life of the plains, the life he had known as a boy, was not there to be lived anymore. The great spaces were still there, of course, but they were not empty spaces, as they had once been; the plains did not encourage his dreams, as they once had.

Lately he had been thinking of moving his family even farther south, to a simpler, emptier place, such as could be found along the Rio Grande, in the place of the canyons. There was not much to eat along the river there; his wives would have to keep busy gathering food, and they would also have to learn to eat things that people of the desert ate: rats, mesquite beans, corn, roots of various kinds. But his wives were young and energetic—he was sure they could find enough food if he beat them a little, just enough to convince them that the lazy years were over—people who lived in the desert had to work. The food was not going to come to them.

One of the reasons he had agreed to track Captain McCrae was because once the job was finished he could go on and investigate the river country a little—he wanted a place where he would not be bothered by irritable Comanches or the continual movement of the whites. He was hoping to find a place with a high mountain nearby.

He thought it might be good to sit high up once in a while. If he was high enough there would be nothing to see but the sky and, now and then, a few of the great eagles. He thought living in a place where there were eagles to watch might encourage some pretty good dreams.

11.

AUGUSTUS HAD ALWAYS enjoyed calendars and almanacs—he rarely journeyed out of Austin without an almanac in his saddlebag. If he did any reading at night around the campfire it was usually just a page or two of the current almanac. Often he would discover that, on the very day he was living, the signs of the zodiac were in disorder, causing dire things to be predicted. If the predictions were especially dire—hurricanes, earthquakes, floods—Gus would amuse himself by reading aloud about the catastrophes that were due to start happening at any moment. If he saw a heavy cloud building up he would inform the men that it was probably the harbinger of a forty-day flood that would probably drown them all. Many of the rangers were unable to sleep, after one of Gus's readings; those who knew a few letters would borrow the almanac and peer at the prophetic passages, only to discover that Augustus had not misread. The terrible predictions were there, and, inasmuch as they were printed, must be true. When nothing happened, no flood, no earthquake, no sulphurous fire, Augustus suavely explained that they had been spared due to a sudden shifting in the stars.

"Now you see the planet Jupiter, right up there," he would say, pointing straight up into the million-starred Milky Way; he knew that most of the men would not want to admit that they had no idea which star Jupiter might be.

"Well, Jupiter went into eclipse—I believe it was a double eclipse—you won't see that again in your lifetime, and it's all that saved us," he would conclude. "Otherwise you'd see a wall of water eighty feet high coming right at us," he would remark, to his awed listeners, some of whom thought that the mere fact that he was a captain meant that he understood such things.

Pea Eye had that belief, for a while, and worried much about the floods and earthquakes, but Call, who put little stock in almanacs, reproached Gus for scaring the men so.

"Why do you want to tell them such bosh?" Call would ask. "Now they'll lose such little sleep as we can allow them."

"Tactics, Woodrow—tactics," Gus would reply. "You need to finish that book on Napoleon so you'll understand how to use tactics, when you're leading an army."

"We ain't an army, we're just ten rangers," Call would point out heatedly, to no avail.

Since Augustus was traveling alone this time, he didn't try to frighten himself with dire predictions, but he did keep a close calendar as he traveled west. He wanted to know how many days from home he had come, in case he developed a strong nostalgia for the saloons and whorehouses of Austin and needed to hurry home.

On the twelfth day, with a few mountain crags visible to the north, Augustus picked his way along the banks of the Rio Grande, to the campsite where, long before, as a fledgling ranger, traveling far from the settlement for the first time, he and Call, Long Bill, and a number of rangers now dead had camped and waited out a terrible dust storm. A fat major named Chevallie had been leading them; Bigfoot Wallace and old Shadrach, the mountain man, had been their scouts. In the morning before the storm struck, Matty Roberts, naked as the air, had picked the big snapping turtle out of the river, carried it into camp, and threw it at Long Bill Coleman and One-eyed Johnny Carthage, both of whom owed her money at the time.

Augustus recognized the little scatter of rocks by the water's edge where Matty had found the turtle; he recognized the crags to the north and even remembered the small mesquite tree—still small—where he and Call had snubbed a mustang mare they were trying to saddle.

No trace of the rangers' presence remained, of course, but Augustus was, nevertheless, glad that he had come. Several times in his life he had felt an intense desire to start over, to somehow turn back the clock of his life to a point where he might, if he were careful, avoid the many mistakes he had made the first time around. He knew such a thing was impossible, but it was still pleasant to dream about it, to conjure, in fantasy, a different and more successful life, and that is what he did, sitting on a large rock by the river and watching the brown water as it rippled over the rocks where Matty had caught the turtle. While he sat Gus noticed a number of snapping turtles, no smaller than the one Matty had captured; at least things were stable with the turtles.

While the river flowed through the wide, empty landscape a parade of dead rangers streamed through the river of his memory—Black Sam, Major Chevallie, One-eyed Johnny, Bigfoot Wallace, Shadrach, the Button brothers, and several more. And now, by Goodnight's account, Matty Roberts herself was dying, which of course was not wholly surprising: whores as active as Matty had been were seldom known to live to a ripe old age. For a moment he regretted not going with Goodnight, over the dry plains to Denver. He would have liked to see Matty again, to lift a glass with her and hear her thoughts on the great game of life, now that she was about to lose it. She had always hoped to make it to California someday, and yet was dying in Denver, with California no closer than it had been when she was a girl.

"If I could, Matty, I'd buy you a ticket on the next stage," Augustus said, aloud, overcome by the same regretful emotion he had felt when he pressed the sixty dollars into Charles Goodnight's hand.

Later in the day Gus walked away from the camp, attempting to locate the rocky hillock where he had first come face-to-face with Buffalo Hump. It had been stormy; the two of them had seen one another in a lightning flash. Gus had run as he had never run in his life, before or since, and had only escaped because of the darkness.

Because it had been so dark, he could not determine which of the rocky rises he was looking for, though no moment of his life was so clearly imprinted on his memory as the one when he had seen, in a moment of white light, Buffalo Hump sitting on his blanket. He could even remember that the blanket had been frayed a little, and that the Comanche had a rawhide string in his hand.

When he tired of his search he caught the black mare and rode on west a few miles, to the high crag of rock where the Comanches had lured them into ambush. A few warriors had draped themselves in white mountain-goat skins, and the rangers had taken the bait. Gus himself had only survived the ambush because he stumbled in his climb and rolled down the hill, losing his rifle in the process.

Augustus tied his horse and climbed up to the boulder-strewn ridge where the Comanches had hidden. In walking around, he picked up two arrowheads; they seemed older than the arrowheads the Comanches had used that day, one of which had to be extracted from Johnny Carthage's leg, but he could not be sure, so he put the arrowheads in his pocket, meaning to show them to someone more expert than himself. It might be that the Comanches had been fighting off that crag for centuries.

As Augustus was walking back down the hill to his horse, his eye caught a movement far to the east, from the direction of the old camp on the river. He stepped behind the same rock that had shielded him long ago and saw that two men approached, one on horseback and one on foot. He didn't at first recognize the horse and rider, but he did recognize the quick lope of the man on foot—Famous Shoes' lope. His first feeling was annoyance: Woodrow Call had had him tracked at a time when all he wanted was a few days to himself.

A moment later Augustus saw that the rider was young Pea Eye Parker, a choice which amused him, since he knew that Pea Eye hated expeditions, particularly lone expeditions across long stretches of Indian country. On such trips Pea Eye scarcely slept or rested, from nervousness. Now Call had sent the boy hundreds of miles from home, with no companion except a Kickapoo tracker who was known to wander away on his own errands for days at a stretch.

Augustus waited by his horse while the horseman and the walker came toward him from the river. While he was waiting he dug the two small arrowheads out of his pocket and studied them a little more, but without reaching a conclusion as to their age.

"You have gone far—I don't know why," Famous Shoes said, when he came to where Augustus waited.

"Why, I was just looking for arrowheads," Augustus said lightly. "What do you make of these?"

Famous Shoes accepted the two arrowheads carefully and looked at them for a long time without speaking. Pea Eye came up and dismounted. He looked, to Gus's eye, more gaunt than ever.

"Hello, Pea—have you slept well on your travels?" he asked.

Pea Eye was so glad to see Captain McCrae that he didn't hear the question. He shook Gus's hand long and firmly. It was clear from his tense face that travel had been a strain.

"I'm glad you ain't dead, Captain," Pea Eye said. "I'm real glad you ain't dead."

Augustus was a little startled by the force of the young man's emotion. The trip must have been even more of a trial to him than he had imagined.

"No, I ain't dead," Augustus told him. "I just rode off to think for a few days, and one of the things I wanted to think about was the fact that I ain't dead."

"Why would you need to think about that, Captain?" Pea asked.

"Well, because people die," Augustus said. "Two of my wives are dead. Long Bill Coleman is dead. Quite a few of the men I've rangered with are dead—three of them died right on this hill we're standing on. Jimmy Watson is dead—you knew Jimmy yourself, and you knew Long Bill. A bunch of farmers and their families got massacred that day we found you sitting by the corncrib."

Pea Eye mainly remembered the corn.

"I was mighty hungry that day," Pea Eye said. "That hard corn tasted good to me."

Now that Captain McCrae had reminded him, Pea Eye did remember that there had been three dead bodies in the cabin where he found the scattered corn. He remember that the bodies had arrows in them; but what he remembered better was walking through the woods for three days, lost, so hungry he had tried to eat the bark off trees. Finding the corn seemed like such a miracle that he did not really think about the bodies in the cabin.

"I guess people have been dying all over," he said, not sure how to respond to the Captain's comments.

Augustus saw that Pea Eye was exhausted, not so much from the long ride as from nervous strain. He turned back to Famous Shoes, who was still looking intently at the two arrowheads.

"I was in a fight with Buffalo Hump and some of his warriors here, years ago," Gus said. "Do you think they dropped these arrowheads then, or are they older?"

Famous Shoes handed the two arrowheads back to Augustus.

"These were not made by the Comanche, they were made by the Old People," he said.

Famous Shoes started up the hill Augustus had just come down.

"I want to find some of these arrowheads too," he said. "The Old People made them."

"You're welcome to look," Gus said. "I mean to keep these myself. If they're so old they might bring me luck."

"You already have luck," Famous Shoes told him—but he did not pause to explain. He was too eager to look for the arrowheads that had been made by the Old People.

"I guess you're here to bring me home, is that right, Pea?" Augustus asked.

"The Governor wants to see you—Captain Call told me that much," Pea Eye said.

Though Augustus knew he ought to go light on the young man, something about Pea Eye's solemn manner made teasing him hard to resist.

"If I'm under arrest you best get out your handcuffs," he said, sticking out his hands in surrender.

Pea Eye was startled, as he often was by Captain McCrae's behavior.

"I ain't got no handcuffs, Captain," he said.

"Well, you might have to tie me, then," Gus said. "I'm still a wild boy. I might escape before you get me back to Austin."

Pea Eye wondered if the Captain had gone a little daft. He was holding out his hands, as if he expected to be tied.

"Captain, I wouldn't arrest you," he said. "I just came to tell you Captain Call asked if you'd come back. The Governor asked too, I believe."

"Yes, and what will you tell them if I decide to slip?" Gus asked.

Pea Eye felt that he was being given a kind of examination, just when he least expected one.

"I'd just tell them you didn't want to come," he said. "If you don't want to come back, you don't have to, that's how I see it."

"I'm glad you feel that way, Pea," Augustus said, letting his hand drop, finally. "I fear I'd be uncomfortable traveling with a man who had a commission to arrest me."

"I was not given no papers," Pea Eye said—he thought a commission must involve a document of some kind.

Augustus looked past the crag of rock toward El Paso del Norte, the Pass of the North.

"I guess I've traveled long enough in a westerly direction," he said. "I believe I'll go back with you, Pea—it'll help your career."

"My what?" Pea Eye asked.

"Your job, Pea—just your job," Augustus said, annoyed that he was unable to employ his full vocabulary with the young man. "You might make sergeant yet, just for bringing me home."

12.

FAMOUS SHOES was so excited by the old things he was finding on the hill of arrowheads that he did not want to leave. All afternoon he stayed on the hill, searching the ground carefully for things the

Old People might have left. He looked at the base of rocks and into holes and cracks in the land. He saw the two rangers leave and ride back toward the camp by the river, but he did not have time to join them. After only a little searching he found six more arrowheads, a fragment of a pot, and a little tool of bone that would have been used to scrape hides. With every discovery his excitement grew. At first he spread the arrowheads on a flat rock, but then he decided it would be wiser not to leave them exposed. The spirits of the Old People might be nearby; they might not like it that he was finding the things they had lost or left behind. If he left the arrowheads exposed, the old spirits might turn themselves into rats or chipmunks and try to carry the arrowheads back to the spirit place. The objects he was finding might be the oldest things in the world. If he took them to the elders of the tribe they could learn many things from them. It would not do to leave them at risk, particularly not after he found the bear tooth. Famous Shoes saw something white near the base of the crag and discovered, once he dug it out with his knife, that it was the tooth of a great bear. It was far larger than the tooth of any bear he had ever seen, and its edge had been scraped to make it sharp. It could be used as a small knife, or as an awl, to punch holes in the skins of buffalo or deer.

Famous Shoes knew he had made a tremendous discovery. He was glad, now, that he had been sent after Captain McCrae; because of it he had found the place where the Old People had once lived. He wrapped his finds carefully in a piece of deerskin and put them in his pouch. He meant to go at once to find the Kickapoo elders, some of whom lived along the Trinity River. While the elders studied what he had found, which included a small round stone used to grind corn, he meant to come back to the hill of arrowheads and look some more. There were several more such hills nearby where he might look. If he were lucky he might even find the hole in the earth where the People had first come out into the light. Famous Shoes thought it possible that he had been acting on wrong information in regard to the hole of emergence. It might not be near the caprock at all. It might be somewhere around the very hill he was standing on, where the Old People had dropped so many of their arrowheads.

The possibility that the hole might be nearby was not something he meant to tell the rangers. When darkness fell he left the hill and went toward their campfire, which he could see winking in the darkness, back by the river. He thought it would be courteous to tell Captain McCrae that he had to leave at once, on an errand of great importance. Captain McCrae was not lost, and would not need him to guide them home.

When Famous Shoes reached the camp he saw that the young ranger who had traveled with him was already asleep. In fact he was snoring and his snores could be heard some distance from the camp. The snores reminded Famous Shoes of the sounds an angry badger would make.

"Snores awful, don't he?" Augustus said, when Famous Shoes appeared. He had been enjoying a little whiskey—he had used his supply only sparingly, so as not to run out before he got back to a place where he could count on finding a settler with a jug.

"He did not snore like that while he was with me," Famous Shoes said. "He did not snore at all while we were looking for you."

"I doubt he slept, while he was with you," Augustus said. "It's hard to snore much if you're wide awake. I expect he was afraid you would scalp him if he went to sleep while he was with you."

Famous Shoes did not reply. He knew that Captain McCrae often joked, but the discoveries he had just made were serious; he did not have the leisure to listen to jokes or to talk that made no sense.

"Did you find any more of them old arrowheads?" Gus asked.

"I have to go visit some people now," Famous Shoes said. He did not want to discuss his findings with Captain McCrae. Even though Captain McCrae had shown him the old arrowheads, Famous Shoes still thought it was unwise to discuss the Old People and their tools with him. He himself did not know what was sacred and what wasn't, with such old things—that was for the elders to interpret.

"Well, you ain't chained, go if you like," Augustus said. "I'll tell Woodrow Call you done your job proper, so he won't cut your pay."

Famous Shoes did not answer. He was wondering if all the hills beyond the Pecos had old things on them. It would take a long time to search so many hills. He knew he had better get busy. It had been windy lately—the wind had blown the soil away, making it easier to see the arrowheads and pieces of pots. He wanted to hurry to the Trinity and then come back. Some white man looking for gold might dig in one of the hills and disturb the arrowheads and other tools.

Augustus saw that Famous Shoes was anxious to leave but he didn't want him to go before he could attempt to interest him in the great issue of mortality, the problem he had been pondering in the last two weeks, as he rode west. His efforts to interest Pea Eye in the matter of mortality had met with complete failure. Pea Eye was mindful that he might die sooner rather than later, from doing the dangerous work of rangering, but he didn't have much to say on the subject. When Augustus tried to get his opinion on factors that prevailed in life or death situations such as Indian fights, he found that Pea Eye had no opinion. Some men died and some men lived, Pea Eye knew that, but the why of it was well beyond his reasoning powers; even beyond his interest. When questioned on the subject, Pea Eye just went to sleep.

"Before you go loping off, tell me why you think I'm lucky," Augustus asked. "Is it just because I found them arrowheads?"

"No, that was not luck, you have good eyes," Famous Shoes said. "No arrow has ever found you—no bullet either—though you have been in many battles. No bear has eaten you and no snake has bitten you."

"Buffalo Hump's lance bit me, though," Augustus said, pointing. "It bit me right out there on those flats."

"It only bit your hip a little," Famous Shoes reminded him—he had heard the story often.

"I admit that I was lucky it was so dark," Gus said. "If it had been daylight I expect he would have got me."

In Famous Shoes' opinion that was true. If the encounter with Buffalo Hump had occurred in daylight Captain McCrae would probably be dead.

"If I have all this luck, why do my wives keep dying?" Augustus asked.

It seemed to Famous Shoes that Captain McCrae was wanting to know the answer to questions that had no answer. Though it was sometimes possible to say why a particular woman died, it was not possible to say why one man's wives died while another man's lived. Such things were mysteries—no man could understand them, any more than a man could understand the rain and the wind. In some springs there were rain clouds, in other springs none. In some years frost came early, in other years it came late. Some women bore children easily, others died in the effort. Why one man fell in battle while the man fighting right beside him lived was a thing that could not be known. Some medicine man might know about the arrowheads he had found, and about the scraper, or the pots, but no medicine man or wise man knew why one man died and another lived. Wise men themselves often died before fools, and cowards before men who were brave. Famous Shoes knew that Captain McCrae enjoyed discussing such matters, but he himself could not spare the time for extended conversation, not when he had such a great distance to travel, on such an urgent errand.

"It was good that you showed me those arrowheads that were not from the Comanche," Famous Shoes said. "That was a good place to look for old arrowheads. I found some for myself."

"I've heard they sell arrowheads, back east," Augustus told him. "The Indians back east have forgotten how to make them—I guess they've got too used to guns. Back in Carolina and Georgia and them places, the only way folks can get arrowheads is to buy them in a store."

Famous Shoes was feeling very impatient. Captain McCrae was one of the most talkative people he had ever known. Sometimes, when there was leisure for lengthy conversation, he was an interesting man to listen to. He was curious about things that most

560

white men paid no attention to. But everyone was curious about death—Famous Shoes didn't feel he could spend any more time discussing it with Captain McCrae, and he had no interest in discussing tribes of Indians who were so degenerate that they no longer knew how to make arrowheads.

"I will see you again when I have time," he said.

"Damn it, I wish you wasn't always in such a hurry," Augustus said, but his words simply floated away. Famous Shoes was already walking toward the Trinity River.

13.

AUGUSTUS COULD NOT restrain his amusement that Woodrow Call, stiff and nervous, confided his suspicion that Maggie Tilton had an involvement with Jake Spoon that went beyond the friendly.

"Didn't you ever notice Jake carrying her groceries, or helping her with her garden?" Augustus asked.

"I noticed," Call said. "But a man ought to help a woman carry groceries, or help her with a garden if he knows anything about gardens. I'm ignorant in that field myself."

"Not as ignorant as you are in the woman field," Augustus said. "If Maggie was the sun you'd have to carry around a sundial to let you know if it's a cloudy day."

"You can hold off on the fancy talk, Gus," Call said, annoyed. It had taken him a week to work up to confiding in Augustus and he did not appreciate the flippant way his confidence was being treated.

"I think he bunks there," he added, so there would be no doubt as to the nature of his suspicions.

Augustus realized that his friend was considerably upset. With effort he held in his amusement and even passed up a chance to make another flowery comparison in regard to Woodrow's ignorance about women—an ignorance he believed to be profound. He knew there were times when Call could be safely teased and times when he couldn't; in his judgment much more teasing in the present situation might result in fisticuffs. Woodrow appeared to be drawn about as tightly as it was safe to draw him.

"Woodrow, you're correct—Jake's been bunking with Maggie for a while," Augustus said, keeping his tone mild.

It was the news Call had feared; yet Augustus delivered it as matter-of-factly as if he were merely announcing that he needed a new pair of boots. They were standing by the corrals in bright sunlight, watching Pea Eye try to rope a young gelding, a strawberry roan. The boy Newt watched from a perch atop the fence.

Pea Eye caught the gelding on the third throw and dug in his heels as the young horse began to fight the rope.

"Pea's getting trained up to a point where he can almost rope," Gus said. "I can remember when it took him thirty throws to catch his horse."

Call was silent. He wasn't interested in how many throws it took Pea Eye to catch a horse, nor was he interested in the six young horses the rangers had just purchased from a horse trader near Waco, though he had approved the purchase himself and signed the check. Normally the arrival of six new horses, acquired at no small cost, would have occupied him immediately—but what occupied him then was Augustus's acknowledgment that Jake was living with Maggie Tilton and her son, Newt—or, if not fully living with her, at least bunking with her to the extent that suited his pleasure and hers.

Augustus saw that his friend was stumped, if not stunned, by the discovery of a situation that had been no secret to most of the rangers for well over a year. It was a peculiar oversight on Woodrow's part, not to notice such things, but then Woodrow Call always had been able to overlook almost everything in life not connected with the work of being a Texas Ranger.

"If you knew about this why didn't you tell me?" Call asked.

Augustus found himself finally having the conversation he had been dreading for a year. He had long known that Woodrow was more attached to Maggie Tilton than he allowed himself to admit. He wouldn't marry her or claim as a son the nice little boy sitting on the fence of the corral; but neither of those evasions meant that Woodrow Call wasn't mighty fond of Maggie Tilton—even though he knew that Call had stopped visiting her as a lover about the time Newt was born. Call had known Maggie longer than he himself had known Clara Allen. It was a long stretch of time, during which Woodrow had displayed no interest, serious or trivial, in any other woman. Augustus knew, too, that the fact that Woodrow was awkward about his feelings didn't mean that his feelings were light— Maggie Tilton, he felt sure, knew this as well as anyone.

Evidence that Woodrow Call harbored no light feeling for Maggie was right before him: Call looked blank and sad, not unlike the way survivors looked after an Indian raid or a shoot-out of some kind.

"I suppose I am a fool," Call said. "I would never have expected her to accept Jake Spoon."

"Why?" Gus asked. "Jake ain't a bad fellow, which ain't to say that he's George Washington, or a fine hero like me."

"He's lazy and will shirk what he can shirk," Call replied. "I will admit that he writes a nice hand."

"Well, that's it, Woodrow—that's accurate," Augustus said. "Jake's just a middling fellow. He ain't really a coward, though he don't seek fights. He's lazy and he'll whore, and I expect he cheats a little at cards when he thinks he can get away with it. But he helps ladies with their groceries and he's handy at gardening and will even paint a lady's house for her if the lady is pretty enough."

"Maggie's pretty enough," Call replied.

"She is, yes," Augustus said. "I will have to say I ain't noticed Jake doing too many favors for the ugly gals."

"Damn it, he's taken advantage of her!" Call said. He could think of no other explanation for the situation.

"No, I don't think he has," Gus said. "I think Jake's been about as good to Maggie as he's able to be."

"Why would you say that?" Call asked—of course it was like Augustus to take the most irritating position possible.

"I say it because it's true," Gus said. "He's been a damn sight more helpful to her than you've ever been."

There was a silence between the two men. Neither looked at one another for a bit—both pretended they were watching Pea Eye, who had managed to get the gelding snubbed to the heavy post in the center of the corral.

Call started to make a hot reply, but choked it off. He knew he wasn't really much help to Maggie—as his duties as a ranger captain had increased, he had less and less time to devote to the common chores that Maggie, like everyone else, might need help with. He didn't carry her groceries or help her with her gardening; the fact was, rangering or no rangering, he had never felt comfortable doing things with Maggie in public. If they met in the street he spoke and tipped his hat, but he rarely strolled with her or walked her home. It was not his way. If Jake or Gus or any decent fellow wanted to do otherwise, that was fine with him.

But what Jake was doing now—or seemed to be doing—went well beyond giving Maggie a hand with her groceries or her garden. It bothered him, but he was getting no sympathy from Augustus; what he was getting, instead, was criticism.

"I have no doubt you think I'm in the wrong," Call said. "You always do, unless it's just rangering that's involved."

"You're always fussing at me about my whoring and drinking," Augustus reminded him. "I suppose I have a right to fuss at you when the matter is crystal clear."

"It may be crystal clear to you, but it's damn murky to me," Call said.

Augustus shrugged. He nodded toward Newt, who still sat on the fence, absorbed by the struggle between Pea Eye and the gelding. The boy loved horses. The rangers took him riding, when they could, and there was talk about finding him a pony or at least a small gentle horse.

"That boy sitting there is yours as sure as sunlight, but you won't claim him or give him your name and you've been small help with his raising," Augustus pointed out. "Pea Eye's more of a pa to him than you've been, and so am I and so is Jake. Maggie would like to be married to you, but she ain't. The only thing I don't understand about it is why she tolerates you at all. A man who won't claim his child wouldn't be sitting in my parlor much, if I was a gal."

Call turned and walked off. He didn't need any more conversation about the boy; in particular he was sick of hearing how much the boy resembled him. The business about the resemblances annoyed him intensely: the boy just looked like a boy. Discussing such matters with Augustus was clearly a waste of time. Augustus had held to his own view for years, and was not likely to change it.

He heard the whirl of a grindstone behind the little shed where the rangers did most of their harness repair and handiwork. Deets was there, sharpening an axe and a couple of spades. The cockleburs were bad in the river bottom where the horses watered—Deets sharpened the spades so he could spade them down and spare the rangers the tedious labor of pulling cockleburs out of their horses' tails, an annoyance that put them all out of temper.

"Deets, would you go get Newt and walk him to his mother?" Call asked. "It's a hot day, and he won't stay in the shade. He'll get too hot if he just sits there in the sun."

"That boy need a hat," Deets observed. The grindstone was the kind that operated with a pedal, but the pedal had a tendency to stick. He had a cramp in his calf from working the old sticking pedal most of the day; but he had an impressive pile of well-sharpened tools to show for his effort: four axes, seven hatchets, an adze, five spades, and a double-bladed pickaxe. Walking a little with Newt would be a nice relief. Captain Call had promised to get him a better grindstone at some point, but so far the money for it hadn't been made available. Captain Augustus said it was the legislature's fault.

"That legislature, it's slow," Augustus often said.

Deets thought probably the reason the legislature was so slow to provide a grindstone was because so many of the senators were drunk most of the time. Deets had had one or two senators pointed out to him and later had seen the very same man sprawled out full length in the street, heavily drunk. One senator had even lost a hand while sleeping in the middle of the street on a foggy morning. A wagon came along the street and a rear wheel passed over the senator's wrist, cutting off his hand as neatly as a butcher or a surgeon could have. Deets had been struggling to extract a long mesquite thorn from the hock of one of the pack mules at the time: he still remembered the senator's piercing scream, when he awoke to find that his hand was gone and his right wrist spurting blood into the fog. The scream had such terror in it that Deets and most of the other people who heard it assumed it could only mean an Indian attack. Men rushed for their guns and women for their hiding places. While the rushing was going on the senator fainted. While the whole town hunkered down, waiting for the scalping Comanches to pour in among them, the senator lay unconscious in the street, bleeding. When the fog lifted, with no one scalped and no Comanches to be seen, the local blacksmith found the senator, still fainted, and, by that time, bled white. The man lived, but he soon stopped being a senator. As Deets understood it, the man decided just to stay home, where he could drink with much less risk.

Now the Captain was wanting him to carry Newt home to his mother, a task he was happy to undertake. He liked Newt, and would have bought him a good little hat to shade him on sunny days, if he could have afforded it. Mainly, though, Deets was just given his room and board and a dollar a month toward expenses—in his present situation he could not afford to be buying little boys hats.

The boy still sat on the fence, watching Pea Eye trying to rope a second gelding, the first one having been firmly snubbed to the post. Call stood watching—not at the boy or the roper; just watching generally, it seemed to Deets.

"Newt wishing he could be a roper," Deets said. "A roper like Mr. Pea."

Call had just watched Pea Eye miss the skinny gelding for the fourth time; he was not pleased.

"If he ever is a roper, I hope he's better at it than Pea Eye Parker," he said, before he walked away.

14.

"Yes, he stays here, when I can keep him out of the saloons," Maggie said, when Call asked her if Jake was sleeping at her house.

She didn't say it bashfully, either. Newt had an earache; she was warming cornmeal in a sock, for him to hold against his ear. Graciela had told her she ought to drip warm honey in Newt's ear, but Maggie didn't think the earache was severe enough to risk making that big a mess. In fact, she wondered if it was an earache at all, or just a new way Newt had thought of to get himself a little more attention. Newt enjoyed his minor illnesses. Sometimes he could persuade his mother to let him sleep with her when he was a little sick, or could pretend to be. Maggie suspected that this was only a pretend earache, but she warmed the cornmeal anyway. She did not appreciate Woodrow Call's question and didn't bother to conceal how she felt. For years she had concealed most of what she felt about Woodrow, but she had given up on him and had no reason to conceal her feelings anymore.

"Well, I am surprised," Call said cautiously. He felt on unfamiliar ground with Maggie; possibly infirm ground as well. She didn't look up when she informed him that Jake was sleeping there.

"I ain't a rock," Maggie said, in reply, and this time she did look up.

Call didn't know what she meant—he had never suggested that she was a rock.

"I guess I don't know what you're trying to say," he said cautiously. "I can see you ain't a rock."

"No, I doubt you can see it," Maggie said. "You're too strong, Woodrow. You don't understand what it's like to be weak, because you ain't weak, and you've got no sympathy for those who are."

"What has that got to do with Jake bunking here?" Call asked.

Maggie turned her eyes to him; her mouth was set. She didn't want to cry—she had done more than enough crying about Woodrow Call over the years. She might do more, still, but if so, she hoped at least not to do it in front of him. It was too humiliating to always be crying about the same feeling in front of the same man.

"I need somebody here at night," Maggie said. "Not every night, but sometimes. I get scared. Besides that, I've got a boy. He needs someone around who can be like a pa. You don't want to stay with me, and you don't want to be a pa to Newt."

She paused; despite her determination to control herself, her hands were shaking as she spooned the hot cornmeal into the old sock.

It always seemed to come back to the same thing, Call thought. He wasn't willing to be her husband and he wasn't willing, either, to claim Newt as his son. He knew that might give him a limited right to criticize, and he hadn't come to criticize, merely to find out if his suspicion about Maggie and Jake was true. It seemed that it was true; he had merely been honest when he said the fact surprised him.

"If it makes you think the less of me, I can't help it," Maggie said. "Jake ain't my first choice—I reckon I don't have to tell you that. But he ain't a bad man, either. He's kind to me and he likes Newt. If I didn't have someone around who liked my son, I expect I would have given up the ghost."

"I don't want you to give up the ghost," Call said at once; he was shocked by the comment.

"The rangering does keep me busy," he adding not knowing what else to say.

"You wouldn't help me if helping me was the last thing in the world you had to do," Maggie told him, unable to hold back a flash of anger. "You don't know how to help nobody, Woodrow—at least you don't know how to help nobody who's female.

"You never have helped me and you never will," she went on, looking him in the eye. "Jake wants to help me, at least. I try to give him back what I can. It ain't much, but he's young. He may not know that."

"Yes, young and careless," Call said. "It would be a pity if he compromised you."

Without hesitating Maggie threw the panful of hot cornmeal at him. Most of it missed but a little of it stuck to the front of his shirt. Woodrow looked as startled as if an Indian with a tomahawk had just popped out of the cupboard; as startled, and more at a loss. An Indian he could have shot, but he couldn't shoot her and had no idea what to say or do. He was so surprised that he didn't even bother to brush the cornmeal off his shirt.

Maggie didn't say anything. She was determined that he would at least answer her act, if he wouldn't answer her need. She set the pan back on the stove.

"Well, that was wasteful," Woodrow Call said finally. He recovered sufficiently to begin to brush the cornmeal off his shirt. Maggie didn't seem to be paying much attention to him. She dipped a cup into the cornmeal and scooped out enough to replace what had been in the pan.

Graciela had been dozing on her little stool at the back of the kitchen—she was often there, making tortillas, such good ones that Newt was seldom seen without a half-eaten tortilla in his hand or his pocket. Something had awakened Graciela, Call didn't know what, for Maggie had not raised her voice before she threw the cornmeal. Graciela looked shocked, when she saw him with cornmeal on his shirt—she put a hand over her mouth.

"I see that I have upset you," Call added, perplexed and a good deal shocked himself. One reason he had grown fond of Maggie Tilton, and a big reason he stayed fond, was that she behaved so sensibly. In that respect he considered her far superior to Gus's old love Clara, who never behaved sensibly and was rarely inclined to restrain her emotions. Certainly Clara had been competent at arithmetic—he had never caught her in an error on a bill—but that didn't keep her from being prone to wild rages and fits of weeping. Maggie had always been far more discreet about her feelings; she had mainly managed to keep her sorrows and even her annoyances to herself.

Now, though, she had done something foolish, and, to make matters worse, had done it in front of Graciela. He knew that Mexican women were prone to gossiping—white women, of course, were hardly immune to such activity—and he was vexed to think that the story of what Maggie had just done, an act most uncharacteristic of her, would soon be talked about all over town.

But the fact was, she had; the deed was done. Call picked up his hat and sat a coffee cup that he had been holding on the counter.

"I regret that I upset you," he said. "I suppose I had better just go."

He waited a minute, to see if Maggie would apologize, or explain her action in any way; but she did neither. She just went on with her task. Except for a spot of red on each cheekbone, no one would suppose that she was feeling anything out of the ordinary. Call had rather expected that she would quickly regret her action and come over and brush the cornmeal off his shirt and trousers; but she showed no inclination to do that, either.

Newt opened his eyes and saw Captain Woodrow with what looked to be meal on his shirt—but he was so sleepy that he felt that what he was seeing must be part of a dream. He yawned and turned over, hoping that Captain Woodrow would offer him a penny for sassafras candy when his dream ended.

Call went out and started down the long flight of stairs that angled down the back of Maggie's house to the ground. When he was almost down he got an uncomfortable feeling and turned to look back; Maggie had come outside and stood above him, on the landing. Sunlight flecked the cornmeal on her hands and forearms—a visitor might have thought that her hands and forearms were flecked with gold dust.

"*You* compromised me, Woodrow, not Jake!" Maggie said, with a sharpness that he had never heard in her voice before. "*You* compromised me and I hope that you'll be thinking about what you did and about how you betrayed our little son for the rest of your life, right up till the day you die. You don't deserve Newt! You don't even deserve me!"

Call said nothing. Maggie went back through the door. Later, when Call thought about that moment, he remembered that the sunlight made cornmeal look like gold dust on Maggie's hands and arms.

15.

AFTER WOODROW LEFT, Maggie went in her bedroom and cried. She was tired—more than tired—of crying about Woodrow Call; but, once again, she couldn't help it. The best she could do was hide in her bedroom and cry, so Newt wouldn't see her in tears, if he woke up. He had seen her sobbing far too often as it was, and it upset him. All too often she cried after his father left, which was worrisome to her. Although Call had brought her sorrow, he *was* Newt's father, even though Newt didn't know it. She didn't want Newt associating his father with her tears and her pain. No one could know what might happen in life. Someday Woodrow might unbend, recognize that he had a fine son, and claim him publicly. The two of them might yet find some happiness as father and son. She didn't want to blight that chance.

Graciela came in while Maggie was attempting to dry her tears. Graciela had been mightily shocked by what she had seen in the kitchen. She didn't know Captain Call very well, but she knew he was a Texas Ranger. For a woman to throw cornmeal on a Texas Ranger was a serious thing. They might hang Maggie, for such an offense. At the very least, the man would beat her.

"That was a bad thing you did," Graciela said. She was in the habit of speaking quite frankly to Maggie, who didn't seem to mind.

"Not very bad," Maggie said. "I could have hit him with the frying pan. All I did was throw a little cornmeal on him."

"Now he will beat you," Graciela said. "How will you work in the store if he beats you badly?

"I need to get my wages—I have my grandbabies to feed," she added.

"He won't beat me, Graciela," Maggie said. "He has never hit me and he never will. I doubt we'll see any more of him around here."

"But you got his shirt dirty," Graciela said. "He will beat you. The last time my husband beat me I could not move for two days. He beat me with an axe handle. I could not have worked in a store, after such a beating."

"This cornmeal is getting hot," Maggie said. "Would you put some in a sock and give it to Newt for his earache?"

"I do not think his ear is sick," Graciela said.

"I don't either, but give him the sock anyway," Maggie said. "It won't hurt to humor him."

Graciela did as she was told, but she was both annoyed and uneasy. The boy wasn't sick; he had no fever. Why waste good cornmeal, when it was attention he wanted, anyway? She could not always be fixing poultices for a boy who wasn't sick. She was still uneasy about the beating, too. In her opinion Maggie still had a lot to learn about the ways of men. Because Maggie wanted Captain Call, and loved him, she was trying to pretend that he was better than other men—that he was above beating a woman. Graciela had had to marry three times before she could get a husband who knew how to stay alive. All her husbands had beaten her, and all the husbands of her sisters and her friends beat their women. It was a thing men did, if they were provoked a little, or even if they were not provoked at all. The slightest drunkenness could cause a man to beat a woman—so could the slightest rebuke. Graciela had only married poor men—men who had to struggle and who had many worries—but two of her sisters had married men of wealth, men who did little all day except gamble and drink. The wealthy men had beaten her sisters just as often as the poor men had beaten her.

Graciela was a little shocked by Maggie's innocence about men and women—it was not wise to take lightly or discount the violence that was in men.

But, before she could discuss the matter further, Newt woke up.

"I don't need that hot sock, my ear don't hurt now," he said, just as Graciela finished getting the poultice ready. Such a boy deserved a good thump on the head, but before Graciela could administer the thump, Newt smiled at her so sweetly that she thought better of it and gave him one of her good tortillas instead.

16.

"I HAVE NEVER BEEN no place this naked, Pea," Jake Spoon confided, staring with some trepidation into the bleak dusk. They had made a poor camp, waterless, shelterless, and dusty, out on the plain somewhere, a plain so vast that the sun, when it set, seemed to be one hundred miles away.

Captain Call had gone ahead, with six rangers, including Charlie Goodnight. The force at the waterless camp consisted of Deets, Pea, Jake, Captain McCrae, Major Featherstonhaugh, a fat lieutenant named Dikuss, and six soldiers. The purpose of the little scouting expedition was to seek out the Comanches in their winter strongholds and determine how many were left. The army wanted to know how many bands were still active and how many warriors they could put into the field.

Jake Spoon had never been able to stifle his tendency to complaint, unless Captain Call was in hearing; Jake said as little as possible around Captain Call. It was obvious to all the rangers that Captain Call didn't like Jake and preferred to avoid his company.

Pea Eye considered it a puzzling thing. He didn't know why the Captain had such a dislike for Jake, but, at the moment, with no water and just a little food, he had more pressing things to worry about. Pea had developed the habit of counting his cartridges every night—he wanted to know exactly how many bullets he could expend in the event of an Indian fight. Every ranger was supposed to travel with one hundred rounds, but Pea Eye had only been given eighty-six rounds, the result of some confusion in the armory the day the bullets had been handed out. It worried Pea considerably that he had started on the trip fourteen bullets shy of a full requisition. Fourteen bullets could make all the difference in the world in the event that all his companions were killed, while he survived. If he had to walk all the way back to Austin living on what game he could shoot he would have to be careful. His marksmanship was not exceptional; it sometimes took him four or five bullets to bring down a deer, and his record with antelope was even worse. Also, he could shoot at Indians fourteen more times, if he had those bullets. The lack preyed on his mind; his count, every night, was to assure himself that no bullets had slipped away in the course of a day's travel.

With his bullets to count, and the light poor on the gloomy plain, Pea Eye could not waste time worrying about why Captain Call found it hard to tolerate Jake Spoon. Captain McCrae, who knew practically everything, may have known the reason, but if so he wasn't saying.

At the moment Captain McCrae was discussing with Major Featherstonhaugh the difficulty of counting Comanches with any accuracy.

"Several men I know have got haircuts they didn't want while counting Comanches," he informed the Major, a skinny man with a sour disposition.

"Of course there's no risk to Dikuss here," Augustus added. "He's a bald man—he's got no hair to take. They'd have to find something else to cut off, if they took Dikuss."

Augustus liked the fat lieutenant and teased him when possible. He was less fond of the dour Featherstonhaugh, though he was not especially more dour than the few army men who found themselves stuck in dusty outposts in the remote Southwest while the great war raged to the east. Featherstonhaugh and his men were missing out on the glory, and they knew it; and for what? To attempt to subdue a few half-starved Comanches, scattered across the Texas plains?

"It seems a poor exercise, don't it, Major?" Augustus said. "You could be back home fighting with Grant or Lee, according to your beliefs. I expect it would be better employment than counting these poor Comanches."

Major Featherstonhaugh received that comment soberly, without change of expression. He did not welcome jocularity while in the field, but Captain McCrae, a skilled and respected ranger, seemed unable to avoid the jocular comment.

"I am from Vermont, Captain," Major Featherstonhaugh informed him. "I would not be fighting with General Lee, though I admire him. He once fought in these parts himself, I believe, in the war with Mexico."

"Well, I didn't notice," Augustus said. "I was in love while that scrap was going on. I was younger then, about Lieutenant Dikuss's age. Are you in love, Lieutenant?"

Lieutenant Dikuss was mortified by the question, as he was by almost every question Captain McCrae asked him. In fact he was in love with his Milly, a strong buxom girl of nineteen whose father owned a prosperous dairy in Wisconsin. Jack Dikuss nursed the deepest and tenderest feelings for his Milly, feelings so strong that tears came into his eyes if he even allowed himself to think of her. He had not been meaning to think of her—indeed, had been cleaning his revolver—when Captain McCrae's unexpected and unwanted questions brought her suddenly and vividly to mind. Lieutenant Dikuss was only just able to choke back tears; in the process of choking them back his neck swelled and his large face turned beet red, a fact fortunately lost on the rangers and soldiers, who were tending to their mounts, their saddles, or their guns, while Deets made a small campfire and got the coffee going. Lieutenant Dikuss made no reply at all to Captain McCrae's question, being well aware that if he attempted to speak he would burst into tears and lose what little authority he had over the rough soldiers under his command, whorers all of them, with scant respect for tender sentiments of the sort he harbored for his Milly.

Augustus noticed the young man's discomfort and did not press his enquiry. He wished he had a book, some whiskey, or anything to distract him from the fact that he was camped in a cold, dusty place with a bunch of military men, while on an errand that he considered foolish. Lately he had begun to delve into the Bible a little, mainly because Austin was so thick with preachers—there were at least seven of them, by his count—that he couldn't walk down the street without bumping into one or two of them. One, an aggressive Baptist, had the temerity to tax him one day about his whoring; in response Augustus had bought a small Bible and began to leaf through it in idle moments, looking for notable instances of whoring or, at least, of carnal appetite among the more distinguished patriarchs of old. He soon found what he was looking for, too, and meant to use his findings to confound the preachers, if they dared challenge him again.

The print in his Bible was small, however, and the circumstance of a dim evening on the plains, with only a flicker of campfire, did not encourage biblical studies just then. He wished he had something to do besides tease nice boys such as Lieutenant Dikuss, but offhand he couldn't think what it might be. It was a pity, in his view, that Charlie Goodnight had insisted on going with Call on the advance scout; he could always raise a debate with Charlie Goodnight, a man disposed to think that he knew everything. Of course, one of the things Charlie Goodnight *did* know was where the principal bands of Comanches hunted; Goodnight was now in the cattle business and needed to keep track of the Comanches in order to keep them from running off his saddle horses.

It was obvious to Augustus that little in the way of conversation was likely to be coming from Major Featherstonhaugh, the Vermonter who would not be fighting with General Lee. Major Featherstonhaugh had been in Texas only a few months; this expedition was his first into the Texas wilds and, so far, he had yet to lay eyes on a wild Comanche. It annoyed Augustus extremely that the military kept its personnel rolling over and over, like clothes wringers—each commander who came out of the East seemed to be less experienced and less knowledgeable about the geography and the terrain than the one before him. He and Call were constantly vexed by the ignorance of the military, though there *had* been one intelligent captain, named Marcy, who had conducted an excellent survey of the Red River country; Captain Marcy knew the country and the ways of the native tribes as well as anyone, but at the present time he was elsewhere and they were stuck with Major Featherstonhaugh, a man so ill informed that he seemed surprised when told there might be problems finding water on their trip across the llano.

"But gentlemen, I was assured there was an abundance of fine springs in Texas," the Major stated, when Call brought up the matter of water, the day before they departed.

"Oh, there's plenty of healthy springs in Texas," Augustus assured him. "I could find you a hundred easily, if we was in the right part of the state."

"Isn't it Texas we're going to be journeying in?" the Major asked.

"Yes, but it's a big place, Major," Call said. "We're going to be crossing the Staked Plain. There may be springs there, but if there are, nobody but the Comanche know where to find them."

That comment was greeted by an expression of polite disbelief on the face of Major Featherstonhaugh, whose only response was to instruct his men to be sure to fill their canteens.

Neither Augustus nor Call chose to press the matter—they had yet to meet a military man, other than the smart Captain Marcy, who was willing to take advice from Texas Rangers, or, for that matter, from Indian scouts either.

"It's a waste of energy to argue with a man like that," Call said, as they left Fort Phantom Hill.

"Agreed," Augustus said. "Let the plains do the arguing."

They were only four days out, but already the point had been made—Major Featherstonhaugh had begun to absorb some hard lessons about west Texas aridity. The Major was neat to a fault—he could not abide soiled linen, or dust on his face, and had carelessly drained his own canteen by the end of the second day, wetting his kerchief often in order to swab the dust off his face. Though Augustus didn't comment, he was amused—the Major would no sooner wash his face than a dust devil or small whirlwind would sweep over the troop and get him dusty again. Now, impatient for the coffee to boil, he seemed indisposed to conversation of any kind; Augustus suspected that an offer to play a hand of cards would not be well received.

"How far ahead do you suppose Captain Call's party is?" the Major asked the next morning, as he was sipping coffee.

"I can't really say, Major," Augustus said. "We're the slow wing of this procession."

"We've come quite a distance from that fort, sir," the Major said. "Why do you think we're slow?"

"Because we still stop and sleep at night," Augustus said. "Sleep does slow a troop down, unless you sleep in your saddle, and Mr. Goodnight is the only one of us who's skilled at saddle snoozing. Call don't sleep at night, neither does Goodnight, and neither does Famous Shoes. I imagine some of the men with them are so tired they'd be willing to get scalped if only they could have a good nap afterwards."

Major Featherstonhaugh seemed unconvinced by the remark—or, if not unconvinced, uninterested.

"It's time to give out the prunes now," he said. "We mustn't forget the prunes, Captain."

Major Hiram Featherstonhaugh was a firm believer in the efficacy of prunes, as an aid to regularity for men on the march. One of the pack mules carried two large sacks of prunes; leaving nothing to chance, the Major had Deets open one of the sacks each morning, so that he himself could dispense the prunes. He personally handed each man in the company six prunes, which, after some experimentation, he had concluded was the number of prunes most likely to ensure clear movements in a troop of men on the march.

"Here now, have your prunes, gentlemen," the Major said, as he went briskly around the troop. "Clear movements now, clear movements."

Augustus, the last man to receive his morning allotment, waited until the Major's back was turned and dropped his back in the sack.

He did not insist that the rangers eat prunes, but he urged them not to throw them away, either.

"We might get to a place out here on the baldies where a prune would taste mighty good," he said. "Just wait till the Major ain't looking and put them back in the sack."

Pea Eye particularly hated prunes; he had carelessly eaten one the first morning and had been unable to rid himself of the pruny taste all day.

"What kind of a tree would grow a prune?" he asked.

"A Vermont kind of tree, I reckon," Augustus said. "The Major says he grew up eating them."

"Maybe that's why he don't never smile," Pea Eye said. "They probably shrunk up his mouth till he can't get a smile out."

"Or it might be that he's got nothing to smile about, particularly," Augustus said. "Here he is in Texas, which he don't like, trying to count Indians he can't find and couldn't whip if he did find."

Within an hour of breaking camp the rangers found themselves riding into a brisk north wind. The long horizons quickly blurred until there was no horizon, just blowing yellowish dust. The rangers tied their bandanas over their noses and their mouths, but the soldiers lacked bandanas and took the stinging dust full in the face. The wind that whirled across the long spaces sang in their ears, unnerving some of the soldiers, recent arrivals who had never experienced a full norther on the plains. The howling wind convinced some of the young recruits that they were surrounded by wolves or other beasts. The rangers had told them many stories of Comanche torture, but had said nothing about winds that sounded like the howling of beasts.

"On a day like this it's good that the Major don't smile," Pea Eye said to Jake. "If he did it would just let in the grit."

In the afternoon the wind, which had been high to begin with, increased to gale force. Increasingly, it was difficult to get the horses to face it; also, the temperature was dropping. Augustus tried to persuade Major Featherstonhaugh of the wisdom of stopping until the norther blew itself out.

"It won't blow like this long, Major," he said. "We could take shelter in one of these gullies and wait it out. Out here it's risky to travel when you can't see where you're going. We might ride off a cliff."

Major Featherstonhaugh was unmoved by the advice. Once started, he preferred not to stop until a day's march had been completed, however adverse the weather conditions.

"I don't need to see where I'm going, Captain," he said. "I have a compass. I consult it frequently. I can assure you that we're going north, due north."

An hour later the half-blinded troop stumbled into and out of a steep gully; in the rock terrain, half peppered by blowing sand, the Major dropped his compass, but didn't immediately register the loss. When, at the half hour, he reached for it, meaning to take his bearings, as he always did twice hourly, he discovered that he no longer had his compass, a circumstance which vexed him greatly.

"I must ask you to stop the troop and wait, Captain," he said. "I must have dropped my compass when we were crossing that declivity—what do you call it?"

"A gully, Major," Gus said.

"Yes, that's probably where it is," the Major said. "It's back in that gully. I'll just hurry back and find it."

"Major, I doubt you'll find it," Augustus said. "The sand's blowing so thick you can barely see your horse's ears. That compass will be covered up by now, most likely."

"Nonsense, I'm sure I can find it," the Major said. "I'll just retrace my steps. You give the men a few prunes, while you're waiting. Important to avoid constipation, Captain—an army can't fight if it's constipated."

"Major, I've got a compass, take it," Augustus said, horrified by what the man planned to do. He was convinced that if the Major rode off in such a storm they would probably never see him again.

"I know mine probably ain't as good as yours, but it will point you north, at least," he assured the Major, holding out his own compass.

"I don't want your compass, Captain—I want my own," Major

Featherstonhaugh said firmly. "It was my father's compass—it was made in Reading, England—it's our family compass. It's made the trip around the Cape. I'm not going to leave it in some declivity in west Texas. I'd never be able to face Pa. He expects me to have this compass when I come home, I can assure you of that, Captain McCrae. Prunes, men, prunes."

With that, the Major turned and was gone.

Augustus was nonplussed. He knew he ought to send someone with the Major, to help him find his way back, but he had no one to send except himself and he did not feel it wise to leave the troop, in such a situation. The men were huddled around him—in the blowing sand they seemed spectral, like gray ghosts. His rangers, veterans of many severe northers, were stoical, but the army boys were nervous, stunned by the abrupt departure of their commander.

"I guess I should have roped him, but it's too late now," Augustus observed. The sandstorm had promptly swallowed up the Major.

"Now he's rode off and left me in command," Lieutenant Dikuss said, appalled at being thrust into a position of responsibility under such conditions, at such a time and in such a place.

Augustus smiled. He could not help being amused by the large lieutenant from Wisconsin. At that moment Lieutenant Dikuss was staring hopelessly at the wall of sand into which his commanding officer had just disappeared.

"It must have been a mighty good compass," Jake Spoon said. "It would have to be made of emeralds for me to go looking for it in a wind like this."

"I doubt you'd know an emerald if you swallowed one, Jake," Augustus said, dismounting. "That compass was made in Reading, England, and besides, the Major's got his pa to think about."

"I don't know what to do, Captain," Lieutenant Dikuss admitted, looking at his gray, cold, gritty men.

"Well, one thing we can do is let the prunes be," Augustus said. "Myself, I'd vote for a cup of coffee over a goddamned prune."

17.

THE SANDSTORM raged until sunset; the whirling sand seemed to magnify the sun as it sank—for a time the sand and dust even made it seem that the sun had paused in its descent. It seemed to hang just above the horizon, a great malign orb, orange at the edges but almost bluish in the center. Some of the young army men, newcomers, like their Major, to the country of sand and wind, thought something had gone wrong with nature. One private, a thin boy from Illinois, almost frozen from a day in the biting wind, thought the bluish sun meant that the world was coming to an end. He had a memory of a church in Paducah, Illinois, where he had lived as a boy, saying that the world would end with the setting of a blue sun.

The boy's name was Briarley Crisp; he was the youngest man in the troop. His mother and all his sisters wept when he left home; they all expected Briarley to be killed. Briarley had been eager, at the time, to get gone into the army, mainly to escape the plowing, which he detested. Now, looking at the ominous blue sun, its edges tinged with the orange hues of hellfire, and with the sand piling up on his eyelids so heavy he could hardly focus his eyes, Briarley knew he had made a terrible, fatal mistake. He had come all the way to Texas to be a soldier, and now the world was ending. He began to shiver so violently that his shaking caught the eye of Lieutenant Dikuss, who, though nervous himself, felt it was now his responsibility to see that morale did not falter within the troop.

"Stop that shaking, Private Crisp," he said. "If you're chilly get a soogan off the pack mule and wrap up in it."

"I ain't shivering from the chill, Lieutenant," Briarley Crisp said. "I see that old blue sun there—a preacher told me once the world would end the night the sun set blue, like that one's setting."

"I doubt that that preacher who upset you had spent much time along the Pecos River," Augustus said. "I've seen the sun set blue many a time in these sand showers, but the world hasn't ended. What I do doubt is that we'll see any more of Major Featherstonhaugh this evening—him or his compass either."

They didn't. To Briarley Crisp's relief the sun finally did set; the night that followed saw the temperatures drop so far that the men slept beneath white clouds of frozen breath. Toward midnight the sandstorm finally blew out—by four the stars were visible again. Augustus debated with himself whether to take advantage of the faint starlight to conduct a quick search for Major Featherston-haugh; but, in the end, he didn't. The morning promised to be clear—they could easily find the Major then, assuming he had survived the chilly night.

They were not long in doubt on that issue. There was still so much sand in the air that the sun rose in haze, with a fine nimbus around it. To Private Crisp's joy, the world was still there and still dry. Augustus had just picked up his coffee cup when he saw a moving dot to the south, a dot that soon became Major Featherston-haugh, cantering briskly toward them on his heavy white mare. Augustus had advised against the mare, not because of her heft but because she was white. The Comanches they were supposed to be scouting particularly loved a white horse.

"If Kicking Wolf gets sight of her that's one more horse the army won't have to feed, Major," Augustus had informed him, but the Major had only returned a chilly stare.

Now, though, he was simply relieved that Major was alive—it would have been a task to locate him, if he had lost himself on the llano.

"Good morning, Major—I hope you found that compass," Augustus said when Featherstonhaugh trotted up, his uniform caked with dust.

"Of course I found it—that was why I went back," Major Featherstonhaugh said. Dusty as he was he still seemed startled by the suggestion that he might *not* have found the compass.

"It was made in Reading, England," he added. "My father took it around the Cape."

"I wish I had a bath to offer you, Major," Augustus said. "You look like you've been buried and dug up."

"Oh, it was weathery," the Major admitted. "I thought I might find one of those springs and have a wash, but I couldn't find one—of course I had to wait for daylight before I could locate my compass."

The Major dismounted and took a little coffee, carefully inspecting his compass while he breakfasted.

"I wish it would snow," he remarked, to Lieutenant Dikuss. "I'm accustomed to snow when it's this weathery."

Lieutenant Dikuss regarded it as a miracle that the Major had reappeared at all; the absence of snow, of which there was an abundance in Wisconsin, did not disturb him.

"You can melt snow, and once it's melted you can heat the water and have a wash," the Major said. "Does it ever snow here, Captain?"

"It snows, but not too many people care to wash in it, Major," Augustus said. "I doubt that washing's as popular in this country as it is in Vermont."

An hour later, pressing on north with the aid of Major Featherstonhaugh's compass, Augustus spotted a rider coming toward them across the long sage flats.

"That's Charlie Goodnight—I expect he's got news," Augustus said.

Major Featherstonhaugh and Lieutenant Dikuss both looked in the direction Augustus was pointing but they could see nothing, just high clouds and wavery horizon. The Major could think of very little besides how much he desired to wash. He was sixty-one years old and never, in his more than three decades of soldiering, had he felt as thoroughly soiled as he felt at the moment. During the weathery night the blowing sand had worked its way into his skin to a depth no dust had ever been allowed to penetrate before. Besides that, his canteen was empty; he could not even wet his kerchief and wipe the dust off his face; his lips were so cracked from the dryness that he would have been hard put to eat even if they had more palatable food; all day the men talked of game, but they saw no game. The Major had once been offered a favorable position in a dry goods firm in Baltimore, but had turned it down out of a distaste for the frivolity of town life. As he stared at the Texas plain, dirt under his collar, incapable of seeing the rider that Captain McCrae could not only see but identify, the Major could not help wondering if he had been wise to turn down that position in the dry goods firm. After all, he could have resided outside of Baltimore and ridden in a buggy—if nothing else there would have been plenty of fine, meltable snow.

"How can you tell who it is?" Lieutenant Dikuss asked. He had finally been able to detect motion in the sage flats to the north, but he could not even tell that the motion was made by a human on a horse. Yet Augustus McCrae could see the horse and even identify the rider.

"Why, I know Charlie," Augustus said. "I know how he rides. He comes along kind of determined. He don't look fast, but the next thing you know he's there."

Events soon bore out Augustus's point—the next thing the troop knew, Goodnight was there.

"I expected you to be farther along, Captain," Goodnight said. "I suppose the military had a hard time keeping up."

Goodnight nodded at Major Featherstonhaugh and promptly turned his horse, as if assuming that the company would immediately respond and follow him. His impatience with military behavior was well known.

"Nope, this is a speedy troop, Charlie," Augustus said. "The fact is the Major dropped his compass in that sandstorm yesterday and had to go back for it. It's a prominent compass, made in Reading, England."

Major Featherstonhaugh, though startled by the man's manner, did not intend to let himself be deflected from his original purpose by mere frontier rudeness; he was dusty as an old boot and felt that his efficiency as a commander would soon diminish if he could not secure a good wash.

"Any springs ahead of us, sir?" he asked Goodnight. "The sand has been plentiful the last two days—I think we could all profit from a good bath."

"I imagine our weapons need cleaning as well," he added—it had just occurred to him that the blowing dust might have gummed up mechanisms to their pistols and rifles and revolvers.

Military ignorance did not surprise Goodnight.

"There's a fine spring about three hundred miles due north of here, Major," he said. "I expect you could reach it in a week if you don't lose your compass again."

"Sir, three hundred miles?" Major Featherstonhaugh asked, aghast.

"That is, if you can get through the Comanches," Goodnight added.

"How many Comanches, and how far ahead?" Augustus asked.

The soldiers, some of whom had been grimly amused by Goodnight's brusque treatment of Major Featherstonhaugh—he was not a popular leader—ceased to be amused; mention of Comanches was enough to quell all merriment in the troop and replace it with dread. The thought of Comanches called into their minds scenes of torture and dismemberment. They had all heard too many stories.

"Charlie, have you run into our red foes?" Augustus inquired again.

"Crossed their trail," Goodnight said. "It's a hunting party. They're about thirty miles ahead of us, but they're lazing along. I think we can overtake them if we hurry. They've got nearly fifty stolen horses and I expect a captive or two."

"Then let's go," Augustus said. Before putting spurs in his horse and following Goodnight, who had already left—he had reached down and accepted a tin cup full of coffee from Deets and drained it in three swallows—Augustus looked back at the few dirty, discouraged, ignorant, and ill-paid men that constituted the troop, all of whom, including Major Featherstonhaugh, looked as if they wished they could be somewhere else in the world.

"We're going after the Comanches—don't lame your horses," Gus said. "It's lucky you dropped your compass, Major. The horses got a night's rest and that might make the difference."

Then he turned and rode. It was cruel to press men as hard as it would be necessary to press them now, but the alternative was to lead a futile expedition that would accomplish nothing. With war raging among the whites, the Comanches had grown bold again— in some places the line of white settlement had been driven back almost one hundred miles. Only those settlers brave enough to live in homemade forts and risk death every day as they worked in their fields farmed the western country now. He and Call had had to abandon the border to banditry; answering raids on the northwestern frontier took all their time and resources. Lately they had scarcely been in town long enough to launder their clothes.

The rangers were too few in number to overwhelm the war parties, but their guns had improved and their marksmanship as well. They would sometimes demoralize their attackers by killing a few prominent warriors—as fighting men they had become a match for the Comanches, but their horses, for the most part heavy and slow, were rarely capable of keeping up with the leaner, faster Comanche ponies.

Goodnight, in his brief time in the soldiers' camp, had quickly sized up the state of the horses. When Augustus caught up with him he did not hold back his assessment.

"Those horses are just glue buckets with legs," he told Augustus. "I doubt they've got fifty miles in them."

"I doubt they've got forty," Gus agreed. Goodnight, of course, was well mounted, on a gelding with sure feet and abundant wind; Augustus, likewise, had taken care to provide himself with a resilient mount. But most of the troopers were not so fortunate.

"We're fighting horse Indians, not walking Indians," he himself had pointed out, to more than one governor and many legislators, but the rangers were still mounted on the cheapest horseflesh the horse traders could provide, an economy that cost several rangers their lives.

"Who are we chasing? Do we know?" he asked Goodnight—he had come to know the fighting styles of several Comanche chiefs rather well.

"Peta Nocona and some of his hunters," Goodnight said. "That's what I think, and Famous Shoes agrees."

"I wonder if Buffalo Hump is still alive," Augustus said. "You'll still hear of Kicking Wolf taking horses now and then, but we ain't had to engage Buffalo Hump since the war started."

"He's alive," Goodnight said.

"How do you know?" Gus asked.

"Because I'd hear of it if he died," Goodnight said. "So would you. He led two raids all the way to the ocean. No other Comanche has done that. They'll be singing about him, when he dies."

Goodnight had a disgusted look on his face.

"I guess you're mad at me, Charlie, for not keeping up," Augustus ventured.

"No, but I won't come back for that major again," Goodnight said. "If he can't keep hold of his compass then I'd rather he went home."

18.

BUFFALO HUMP was slow to recover from the shitting sickness—the cholera; for the first time in his life he was forced to live with weakness in his limbs and body. For two months he could not mount a horse or even draw a bow. His wives fed him and tended to him. A few of the warriors still came to confer with him for a while, but then they began to avoid him, as the strong always avoid the weak. Kicking Wolf was stealing many horses from the Texans, but he did not ask Buffalo Hump to raid with him, anymore.

No one asked Buffalo Hump to raid with them now, although warriors from many bands raided frequently. Many whites had gone to fight other whites, in the East; there were few blue-coated soldiers left, and few rangers to defend the little farms and settlements. The young warriors killed, tortured, raped, and stole, but they did not take Buffalo Hump with them, nor did they come to him to brag of their courage and their exploits when they returned from the raids with horses or captives.

They did not ask Buffalo Hump, or brag to him, because he was not young anymore. He had lost his strength, and, with his strength, lost his power. Buffalo Hump was resentful—it was not pleasant to be ignored or even scorned by the very warriors he had trained, the very people he had led—but he was not surprised. Many times he had seen great warriors weaken, sicken, grow old, lose their power; the young men who would have once been eager to ride with them quickly came to scorn them. The young warriors were cruel: they whispered and snickered if one of the older men failed to make a kill, or let a captive escape. They respected only the strong men who could not be insulted without a price being paid in blood.

When Buffalo Hump saw that the time had passed when he could be a powerful chief, he had his wives move his lodge into a cleft in the canyon some distance from camp. He wanted to be where he would not have to listen to the young men brag after each raid—even the screams of tortured captives had begun to irritate him. Buffalo Hump would not be scorned, not in his own camp; if he heard some young warrior whispering about him he would fight, even if it meant his death. But he thought it was only a foolish man who put himself deliberately in the way of such challenges. He took himself away, too far from the main camp for the shouting and dancing to disturb him.

Then he instructed his wives, Lark and Heavy Leg, how to make good snares—it was a craft he expected them to learn. There was little large game in the canyon now, but plenty of small game: rabbits, skunks, ground squirrels, prairie dogs, quail and dove, possums, and fat prairie hens. He wanted his wives to work their snares and catch what food they needed. When his strength returned, so that he could draw his bow and throw his lance, he meant to journey alone with his wives north to the cold rivers where the buffalo still lived. He would take two pack horses and kill enough meat to last all winter.

The shitting sickness had not affected his eyes, though, or his ears. He saw the young men riding south, murder in their hearts, singing their war songs; and he could count, as well. He saw how many young men rode out and he saw how many came back. In his days of raiding he rarely lost more than one or two warriors to the guns of the Texans. If he lost more than three men he did not claim victory; and, always, he recovered and brought back the bodies of the fallen warriors, so they could have a proper burial. Now, though, when the young men came back, claiming victory, they had sometimes lost five or six men; once they even lost eight, and, another time, ten. Seldom, in those battles, did they recover more than one or two bodies to bring home. Many warriors were left unburied, a thing that in his time would have shamed any chief or warrior who led a raid.

But it did not seem to shame the young men—they spoke only of the Texans they had killed and said nothing about the warriors who were lost and whose bodies had been abandoned.

Usually, after such a raid, a few of the old men would come to Buffalo Hump in his new camp, to discuss the shameful losses and the even more shameful abandonment of bodies. Some of the elders, old Sunrise in particular, wanted Buffalo Hump to speak to the young men; they wanted him to ride with them on a raid, to instruct them of the correct way to behave toward the dead; but Buffalo Hump refused: he would not ride with warriors who didn't want him. The young men had no use for him now—they made that clear by the arrogant looks they gave him when he walked through the camp or rode out to the horse herd to watch the young horses.

When the old men came to him with their complaints he listened but did not say much in reply. He had led the band for a long time, but now could not. Let the young men decide who should be chief; let them do without a chief, if they could not decide. After all, any warrior could follow anyone he wanted to—or follow no one, if that was his choice. Buffalo Hump did not like what he saw, but he could do little about it. His own time was short—it had almost ended in the weeks of his sickness—and he did not intend to use it giving advice to young men who did not want it.

With Kicking Wolf, though, he sometimes did talk and talk frankly about what the large losses meant.

"The Texans have learned to fight us," he said. Heavy Leg had caught a fat coon in a snare and was cooking it.

"Some have," Kicking Wolf admitted. "Some are fools."

"Yes, some are fools, but Gun-in-the-Water is not a fool, and neither is McCrae," Buffalo Hump said. "They don't get scared now just because we yell at them—their men wait until we are close and then they shoot us. They have better guns now—if they had better horses they would follow us and kill us all."

"Their horses are too fat and too slow," Kicking Wolf agreed.

"That is because you have stolen so many of the good ones," Buffalo Hump told him. Though Kicking Wolf had often annoyed him, it was clear that he was the best horsethief the tribe had ever produced. Now he felt annoyed again, but it was not because Kicking Wolf had been rude. Kicking Wolf had always been rude. What was annoying was that he was younger—he had not been sick, and the hand of age had not touched him. The young men made a little fun of him, but not much. They didn't fear him as a fighter, but they respected him as a thief.

"Slow Tree has sat down with the white man," Kicking Wolf informed him one day. "So have Moo-ray and Little Cloud. They are all going to the place the whites want to put them, near the Brazos. The Texans have promised to give them beef."

That news came as no surprise to Buffalo Hump. He had never sat down with the white men and never would, but it did not surprise him that Slow Tree and others, worn out by the difficulty of feeding their bands, would talk with the whites and go to the places the white men wanted to put them.

"It is because the buffalo have left," Kicking Wolf said, a little apologetically. Buffalo Hump was looking angry. He did not like the news that Comanches were giving in to the white men, ceasing to fight or be free. Yet he knew how thin the game was; he saw that the buffalo were gone.

"The buffalo haven't left the world," Buffalo Hump told him.

"They have only gone to the north, to be away from the Texans. If we go north we can still kill buffalo."

"Slow Tree and the other chiefs are too old," Kicking Wolf said. "They don't like to go into the snows."

"No, I see that," Buffalo Hump said. "They had rather sit with the Texans and make speeches. They had rather be given beef than steal them, although cattle are easy to steal."

Kicking Wolf was sorry he had mentioned that the chiefs were too old. It brought anger to Buffalo Hump's face. He was fingering his knife, the cold look in his eyes. Kicking Wolf understood that the anger was because Buffalo Hump himself was now old—he could not ride the war trail again. It was known that he planned to go north, to hunt buffalo alone. Kicking Wolf thought that was foolish but he didn't say anything. There were many whites to the north and they *did* have good guns.

"Would you let the whites tell you where to live?" Buffalo Hump asked him. "Would you let them buy you off for a few of their skinny beeves?"

"No, I would rather eat horsemeat than beef," Kicking Wolf said. "I can eat the horses I steal. I will never sit down with the whites."

There was a long silence. The coon had been chopped up—it was bubbling in the pot. The flesh sagged on Buffalo Hump's arms and his torso was thin now—his hump seemed as if it would pull his body over backward.

"Doesn't Slow Tree have horses he could eat?" Buffalo Hump asked. "Doesn't Moo-ray?"

"They have some horses," Kicking Wolf said. "I think they are just tired of fighting. Many of their young men have been killed, and their women are unhappy. They have been fighting for a long time."

"We all have been fighting for a long time," Buffalo Hump reminded him. "We have been fighting for our whole lives. That is our way."

He was silent again. He had begun to think that it was time for him to leave his people—perhaps even leave his wives. If, one by one, the chiefs of the various bands were giving up, making peace with the white men, then the time of the free Comanche was over—and so was his own time. Perhaps he should go away, alone, and seek a place to die. The greatest warriors inconvenienced no one when their time was ending. They simply went away, alone or with one old horse. Of course it was a thing rarely done now, a custom that was almost forgotten; the Texans had made it hard for any man to survive long enough to come to the natural end of his time. Now so many warriors fell in battle that few could survive until they could die with dignity, in the old way.

Buffalo Hump did not want to discuss this possibility with Kicking Wolf. He wanted only one more piece of information: he wanted to know about Quanah, the young chief of the Antelope band, the Comanches who lived the farthest west, in the barren llano. These Comanches had never sat down with the whites. They survived in their harsh land even when the buffalo didn't come. The Antelope Comanches would live on roots and grubs, on weeds and prairie dogs and bulbs they dug from the earth. Buffalo Hump himself had only been among the Antelope Comanches once or twice in his life; they lived too far away, and were not friendly—the fact that they were not friendly was something he had come to admire. They lived in their own place, in the old way, hunting, moving as the game moved, finding enough water to survive in a place where no one else could find water. The Antelope rarely fought the whites, because the whites could not find them. When the whites came the Antelope merely retreated deeper and deeper into the long space of the llano. Always, the whites ran out of food and out of water before they could attack them. Antelope knew their country and could survive in it; the whites didn't know it, and feared it. Even Famous Shoes, the Kickapoo who went everywhere, did not try to follow the Antelope Comanches to their watering holes. Even he found the llano too hard a test.

Now Buffalo Hump had heard that there was a young chief of the Antelope band—his name was Quanah. Though scarcely more than a boy he was said to be a great fighter, decisive and terrible in battle, a horseman and hunter, one who had no fear either of the whites or of the country. The talk was that Quanah was half white, the son of Peta Nocona and the captive Naduah, who had been with the Comanche for many years. She had been taken in a raid near the Brazos when Buffalo Hump himself had been young. Naduah had been with the People so long that she had forgotten that she was a captive—now her son led the Antelope Comanches and kept his people far from the whites and their councils.

When Buffalo Hump asked about Quanah, Kicking Wolf did not answer immediately. The subject seemed to annoy him.

"I took him four good horses but he didn't want them," he said, finally.

"Did you try to fool him?" Buffalo Hump asked. "I remember that you used to try and trade me bad horses. You only wanted to trade the horses there was something wrong with. Maybe Quanah is too smart for you. Maybe he knew those horses had something wrong with them."

Kicking Wolf immediately rose and prepared to leave.

"There was nothing wrong with the horses I took him, or with the horses I traded you, either," he said. "Someday Quanah will wish he had horses as good as those I took him."

Then he walked away, to the embarrassment of Heavy Leg and Lark, who had been preparing to offer him some of the coon—that was the polite thing to do. When Buffalo Hump visited Kicking Wolf he always politely ate a little of what Kicking Wolf's wives had prepared. He was a good guest—he did not simply get up and leave just as the meal was ready. Lark and Heavy Leg were afraid they might have done something to offend their guest. Perhaps he was forbidden to eat coon? They didn't know what to think, but they were fearful. If they had erred, Buffalo Hump would surely beat them—since his sickness he was often in a bad temper and beat them for the smallest errors in the management of the lodge. They knew that the beatings mainly came about because Buffalo Hump was old and ill, but they were severe beatings anyway, so severe that it behooved them to be as careful as possible.

This time, though, Buffalo Hump merely ate his food; he said nothing to his wives. It amused him that Kicking Wolf was annoyed with Quanah, the young war chief of the Antelopes, just because he was a good judge of horseflesh. It only impressed Buffalo Hump more, that Quanah had refused to trade with Kicking Wolf. Living where he lived, on the llano, where the distances to be traveled were great and the forage sparse, a war chief could not afford to make mistakes about horses. If a horse's feet were poor it might imperil the success of a hunt, and the People's survival depended on the hunt.

Of course, Kicking Wolf was notorious—and had been throughout his whole career as a thief—for attempting to trade off horses that looked like fine horses but that had one hard-to-detect flaw. Perhaps a given horse was deficient in endurance, or had no wind, or had hooves that were prone to splitting. Kicking Wolf was skilled at glossing over flaws that only a man with an experienced eye could see. There was a way of knowing that some men had and some men didn't. Kicking Wolf could watch a horse graze for a few minutes and know whether he was watching a good horse. But fewer and fewer could do that. Buffalo Hump had never been an exact appraiser of horseflesh himself. What he knew was that Kicking Wolf was tricky and that he ought to be wary of the horses that Kicking Wolf praised the most.

It amused him to think that this boy, this half-white war chief, Quanah, might know the same thing: that Kicking Wolf was sly, too sly to be easily trusted when it came to horses.

19.

NADUAH WAS NURSING the child when the other women began to scream. She had been dreaming while the little girl nursed, dreaming of the warm lodge they could build if Peta was successful in the hunt and brought some good skins for her to clean and tan. The men had left early, to hunt—only an hour before, Peta had been there.

There were a few slaves in the camp, young Kickapoos who had been caught only a week before. The white men charging at them on the horses were shooting the young slaves, thinking they were warriors. Before Naduah could run, the Texans were all around her. Her little girl, Flower, was a speedy child; she was almost two years old and could run as fast as any of the little children in the camp.

Before Naduah could flee, Flower dropped the breast and ran, crazed with fear of the Texans. She almost ran under one of the charging horses, but the rider pulled up just in time. The wind was up—dust swirled through the camp. In the confusion, with the dust blinding them, the Texans were shooting at anyone who ran, whether woman or slave. Naduah only wanted to catch her child before one of the horses injured her. Her hope was that Peta and the other hunters would hear the shooting and come back to attack the Texans.

Just as Naduah caught up with her little girl she turned and saw two men aiming rifles at her. They were going to shoot her down. The wind blew her clothes away from her legs. She held tightly to Flower, regretting that there was no time to hide her. If she could just hide the child well, then even if she herself were killed the men would return and find her. Flower would live.

Naduah thought death was coming, but the first man suddenly lifted his rifle and put out his hand to keep the other Texan from shooting. The first rider jumped off his horse and grabbed Naduah, to pull her aside so that none of the Texans would ride her down or shoot her. Some of the other women had been killed, and others were fleeing with their children. Naduah tried to pull free and run, but the man who held her was strong; though she fought and scratched she could not break free.

When the shooting stopped several of the Texans gathered around her—their smell was terrible. They peered into her eyes and rubbed her skin. One even lifted her garments to stare at her legs. Naduah thought rape was coming, the rape that many women experienced when a camp was invaded. The Texans kept rubbing her skin, arguing with one another. Naduah thought they were only arguing about who would rape her first, but the men didn't rape her. Instead, they began to make plans to take her with them—when Naduah saw what they were about she began to scream and try to free herself. She could not stand the touch of a Texan: their breath smelled like the breath of animals and their eyes were cruel. Naduah screamed and fought; when she got a hand free she began to rake at herself, clawing at her breast to make herself bloody and ugly, so the Texans would leave her to run away with the other women. She knew Peta would come back, if she could only find a hiding place where she could wait for him.

The Texans would not free her, though. They tied her hands and put her on a horse, but Naduah immediately rolled off and ran a few steps before the Texans caught her again. This time, when they put her on the horse, they tied her feet under the horse's belly, so she could not get free. Some of the men rode off rapidly toward the west, in the direction Peta had gone with the other hunters. Naduah hoped that Peta was too far away for the Texans to catch. There were too many Texans for Peta and the few hunters to fight. Other warriors had already taken the stolen horses north—it was mainly the horses that the Texans wanted.

Soon the riders came back and the Texans began to ride south. Naduah screamed and struggled with her bonds. She wanted the Texans to leave her. Two women lay dead at the edge of the camp, shot by the Texans in the first charge. But Naduah was tied to the horse and could not escape. She wished she could be dead, like the women whose bodies she had seen. She thought it would be better to be dead than to be taken by the Texans, men whose breath smelled like the breath of beasts.

20.

"SHE MIGHT BE the Parker girl," Goodnight said, as they rode away from the Comanche camp. The blue-eyed woman tied to the horse behind them screamed as if her life were ending. Call had his doubts about taking the woman back; even Goodnight, who led the horse she was on, seemed to have his doubts. All of them had seen what happened when captive white women were returned to white society. Grief was what happened, and the longer the captivity the less likely it was that the women could accept what they would have to face, or be accepted even by the families who had wanted them back. Most of the returned captives soon died.

"The Parker girl was taken twenty-five years ago," Call reminded Goodnight. "Comanche women themselves mostly don't live that long. I doubt any white woman could survive it."

"I know I couldn't survive twenty-five years in one of their camps," Augustus said. "If I couldn't get to a saloon now and then I'd pine away."

He said it in jest, hoping to lighten the general mood, but the jest failed. The mood was grim and stayed grim. They had killed six Comanche women as they charged into the camp; they had also killed three Kickapoo captives who were only boys. It was not their practice to kill women or the young, but the men were frightened, the dust was bad, and they knew there was a band of Comanche hunters in camp or not far away. At such times fear and blood lust easily combined—it was impossible to control nervous, frightened men in such a situation; men, in particular, who had good reason to hate all Comanches. Except for the new soldiers there was scarcely a man in the troop who had not lost loved ones in the Comanche raids.

Killing women left a bad taste in the mouth. But the deed was done: they had killed six. The women were dead. There was nothing to do but go home.

They were all troubled by the woman's screaming, and by the way she ripped at her breast when she saw that they meant to take her. Despite her blue eyes and white skin, the poor woman *thought* she was Comanche; she wanted to stay with the people she felt and believed to be her own. Taking captive women back was not a duty any of the men could be sure of or be easy with. Of course, leaving a white woman with the Comanches would have been just as hard and left them just as uneasy.

"She doesn't know English," Goodnight said. "She's been with them so long she's forgot it."

"In that case it would be a mercy to shoot her," Call said. "She'll never be right in the head."

"I don't know why you think she's the Parker girl, Charlie," Augustus said. "That girl was taken before I was even a ranger, and I can't even remember what I was before I started being a ranger."

"You were a loafer," Call said, though he agreed with Gus's point. Sometimes Goodnight's opinions irritated him. The poor woman could be anybody, yet Goodnight had convinced himself that she was the long-lost Parker girl, the mother, some said, of Quanah, the young war chief of the Antelope band, a warrior few white men had ever seen.

"I know the Parkers, that's why I think it," Goodnight said. "I've been around Parkers ever since I came to Texas, and this woman looks like Parker to me."

"Even if she was born a Parker, she's a Comanche now—and she's got a Comanche child," Augustus said. "Call's right—it would be a mercy to shoot her."

Goodnight didn't argue further. He saw no point; there was no clear right to be argued. The captive was a white-skinned woman with blue eyes; she had not been born a Comanche. They could neither shoot her nor leave her. He knew, as did Call and McCrae, that only sorrow awaited her in the settlements of the whites. It was a hard thing. The white families, of course, thought they wanted their captive loved ones back—they thought it right up until the moment when rangers or soldiers did actually return some poor, ragged, dirty, wild captive to them, a person who, likely as not, had not been washed, except by the rains, since the moment they had been stolen. If the captivity had lasted more than a month or two, the person the families got back was never the person they had lost. The change was too violent, the gap opened between new life and old too wide to be closed.

Call said no more about the white woman, either. He knew they were saving her merely to kill her by tortures different from those the Indians practiced. He could take no pride in recovering captives, unless, by a rapid chase, the rangers were able to recover them within a few days of their capture; only those who had been freshly taken ever flourished once they were returned.

As usual he rode homeward off the plains with a sense of incompletion. They had fought three violent skirmishes and acquitted themselves well. Some livestock had been recovered, though most of the stolen horses had escaped them. Several Comanche warriors had been killed, with the loss of only one ranger, Lee Hitch, who had lagged behind to pick persimmons and had strayed right into a Comanche hunting party. They shot him full of arrows, scalped him, mutilated him, and left; by the time his friend Stove Jones went back and found him the Comanches had cut the track of the ranger troop and fled to the open plains, joining the horsethieves in their flight. Stove Jones was incoherent with grief—in the space of an hour he had lost his oldest friend.

"Them persimmons weren't even ripe yet, either," Stove said—he was to repeat the same bewildered comment for years, whenever the name of Lee Hitch came up. That his friend had got himself butchered over green persimmons was a fact that never ceased to haunt him.

Call regretted the loss too. An able ranger had made a single mistake in a place where a single mistake was all it took to finish a man. It was the kind of thing that could have happened to Augustus, if whiskey bottles grew on bushes, like persimmons.

What troubled him continually was the impossibility of protecting hundreds of miles of frontier with just a small troop of men. The government had been right to build a line of forts, but now the civil war was rapidly draining those forts of soldiers. The frontier was almost as unprotected as it had been in the forties, when he and Augustus had first taken up the gun.

The Comanches had been in retreat, demoralized, sick, hungry—a few aggressive campaigns would have eliminated them as a threat to white settlement; but now, because of the war, progress had been checked. With so few fighting men to oppose them, the

Comanches would raid again at will, picking and choosing from the little exposed ranches and farms. There had just been reports that a young chief had even ridden down the old war trail into Mexico, destroying three villages and costing the Mexicans many children.

It left Call with such a sense of futility that he and Augustus had even begun to talk of doing something else. They rarely had even fifty men under their command at any one time. Though the Comanches were comparatively weak, the rangers were weaker still.

Meanwhile, to the south and west, the banditry raged unchecked. The more prominent cattlemen of south Texas—men such as Captain King—were virtually at war with their counterparts in Mexico, forced to employ large bands of well-mounted and well-armed riflemen in order to hold their ground.

To the east, where the war raged, the tide of battle was uncertain; no one could say whether North or South would win. Even those partisans in Austin who regarded General Lee as second only to the Almighty had muted their bragging now. The struggle was too desperate—no one knew what would happen.

What Call did know was that his own men were tired. They had more ground to cover than any one group of men could reasonably be expected to cover, and, despite many promises, their mounts were still inadequate. Governors and legislators wanted the hostiles held in check and the bandits hung, but they wanted it all to be done with the fewest possible men on the cheapest possible horses. It irritated Call and infuriated Augustus.

"If I could I'd strike a deal with old Buffalo Hump," Augustus said at one point—admittedly he was well in his cups—"I'd bring him down and turn him loose in the legislature. If he scalped about half the damn senators I have no doubt they'd vote to let us buy some good horses."

"How could they vote if they were dead?" Call asked.

"Oh, there'd soon be more legislators," Gus said. "I'd make the new ones dig the graves for the old ones. It would be a lesson to them."

Meanwhile, the captive woman had not ceased or abated her shrieking. It was a cold, cloudy day, with a bitter wind. The woman's wild shrieking unnerved the men, the younger ones particularly. As Pea Eye watched, the woman tried to bite her own flesh, in order to pull her wrists free of their rawhide bonds. She bit herself so violently that blood was soon streaming down her horse's shoulders. Of course it did no good. Jake Spoon had tied the knots, and Jake was good with knots. It was Jake, of all the rangers, who seemed most disturbed by the woman's screaming.

"I wish we could just shoot her, Pea," Jake said. "If I had known she was going to bite herself and carry on like that I would have shot her to begin with."

"I wouldn't want to shoot no woman, not me," Pea Eye said. He wished the sun would come out—after violent skirmishes his head was apt to throb for hours; it was throbbing at the time. He had a notion that if the sun would just come out his head might get a little better. His horse had a hard trot, which made his head pound the worse.

Jake Spoon, who was delicate and prone to vomits at the sight of dead people, couldn't tolerate the woman's shrieks. He plugged his ears with some cotton ticking he kept in his saddlebags for just such a purpose. Then he loped ahead, so he wouldn't have to see the blood from the woman's torn wrists dripping off her horse's shoulders.

"What's wrong with that boy?" Goodnight asked, when he saw the tufts of cotton sticking out of Jake Spoon's ears.

"Why, I don't know, Charlie," Augustus said. "Maybe he's just tired of listening to all this idle conversation."

21.

IDAHI HAD RIDDEN all the way from the Big Wichita to the Arkansas River, looking for Blue Duck and his band of renegades; he wanted to join the band and become a renegade himself, mainly so he could go on killing white people and stealing their guns. Idahi would kill anybody, Indian or white, if they had guns that he wanted to shoot. He didn't consider himself a harsh or a particularly bloodthirsty man—it was merely that killing people was usually the easiest way to get their guns.

To his annoyance Idahi missed Blue Duck as he was traveling toward the Arkansas. Several people had told him Blue Duck was camped on the Arkansas, when in fact he was camped on a sandy bend of the Red River, well east, where the river curved into the forests.

"Quicksand," Blue Duck informed him, when Idahi finally found his camp and asked why he was camping on the Red River. "There's bad sand along this stretch of the river. If the law tries to come at us from the south they'll bog their horses. We can shoot them or let them drown. Five or six laws from Texas have drowned already."

"If they drown, do you get their guns?" Idahi asked. He was from the Comanche band of Paha-yuca, whom Blue Duck had known long ago, when he was still welcome among the Comanche people. But Paha-yuca had agreed to take his people onto a reservation the whites had promised him. Paha-yuca was old; what had made him agree to go onto the reservation was the news that the big war between the whites might soon end. The white soldiers were said to have reached an agreement to stop killing one another. At least that was the rumor, though there had been other such rumors in the last few years and they had not been accurate. But it was Paha-yuca's opinion that once the white soldiers stopped killing one another they would start killing Comanches again. The bluecoat soldiers would return to the empty forts stretching westward along the rivers. Many bluecoats would come, and this time they would come onto the llano and press the fight until there were no more free Comanches left to kill.

Paha-yuca was not a coward, nor was he a fool. Idahi knew that he was probably right in his assessment, right when he said that the People would no longer be able to live in the old ways. If they wanted to live at all they would have to compromise and live as the whites wanted them to. Also, they would have to stop killing whites—they could no longer just kill and scalp and rob and rape whenever they came across a few whites.

It was that injunction that caused Idahi to leave and seek out Blue Duck, the outcast, the man not welcome in the lodges of the Comanches—Blue Duck continued to kill whites wherever he met them. He also hated Kiowas because they had denied him a woman he wanted—he killed Kiowas when he could, and also Kickapoos and Wichitas.

Idahi had known Blue Duck when the latter was still with his people; they had ridden together and practiced shooting guns. They both thought it was foolish to try and kill people or game with bows and arrows, since it was so much easier to kill them with bullets. The two had been friends, which is why Idahi decided to seek him out when Paha-yuca made his decision.

Fortunately Blue Duck was at the camp on the Red River when Idahi rode up—the camp was a violent place, where strangers were not welcome. Everyone stopped what they were doing when they saw a horseman approaching; they all picked up their guns, but Blue Duck recognized Idahi and immediately rode out to escort him into camp, a signal to all the renegades that Idahi enjoyed his protection.

"All the people are going on reservations now," Idahi said, when Blue Duck greeted him. "I do not want to live that way. I thought I would come and fight with you."

Blue Duck was glad to see Idahi—no other Comanches had ever come to join his band. He remembered Idahi's love of guns and immediately presented him with a fine shotgun he had taken from a traveler he killed in Arkansas. Idahi was so delighted with his present that he immediately began to shoot off the shotgun, a disturbance hardly noticed in the camp of Blue Duck, where a lot of loud activity was going on. At the edge of the Red River, where the bad sand was supposed to be, two renegades were dragging a white woman through the water. They seemed to be trying to drown her. One man was on horseback—he was dragging the woman through

604

the mud on the end of a rope. The other man followed on foot. Now and then he would jump on the woman, who was screaming and choking in fear.

Idahi saw to his astonishment that there was a half-grown bear in the camp, tethered by a chain to a willow tree. The bear made a lunge and caught a dog who had been unwary enough to approach it. The bear immediately killed the dog, which seemed to annoy Blue Duck. He immediately grabbed a big club and beat the bear off the corpse of the dog—Blue Duck took the dog's tail and slung the dead dog in the direction of a number of dirty women who were sitting around a big cook pot. Two half-naked prisoners, both skinny old men, lay securely tied not far from the women. Both had been severely beaten and one had had the soles of his feet sliced off, a torment the Comanches sometimes inflicted on their captives. Usually a captive who had the soles of his feet sliced off was made to run over rocks for a while, or cactus, on his bloody feet; but the old man Idahi saw looked too weak to run very far. The two prisoners stared at Idahi hopefully; perhaps they thought he might rescue them, but of course Idahi had no intention of interfering with Blue Duck's captives.

The dog the bear had killed was the only fat dog in the camp, which was no doubt why Blue Duck took it away from the bear and gave it to the women to cook.

"A fat dog is too good to waste on a bear," Blue Duck said. "You and me will eat that dog ourselves."

"What does the bear eat?" Idahi asked. Personally he thought it was bad luck to keep a bear in camp; he had been shocked when Blue Duck casually picked up the club and beat the young bear until blood came out of its nose. He had been raised to believe that bears were to be respected; their power was as great as the power of the buffalo. Seeing Blue Duck beat the bear as casually as most men would beat a dog, or a recalcitrant horse, gave Idahi a moment of doubt—if Blue Duck had forgotten the need to respect the power of the bear, then he might have been foolish to come to Blue Duck's camp. Though Idahi had left the Comanches he had only done so a few days ago; he had not forgotten or discarded any of the important ways or teachings of his people. But Blue Duck had been a renegade for years. Perhaps the old teachings no longer mattered to him. It was a thought that made Idahi uneasy.

A little later, while the dog was cooking, Blue Duck dragged the old man whose soles had been sliced off over to where the bear was. He wanted the bear to eat the old man, who was so terrified to be at the mercy of a bear that he could not even scream. He lay as if paralyzed, with his lips trembling and his eyes wide open. But the bear had no interest in the old man, a fact which annoyed Blue Duck. He picked up the club and beat the bear some more; but, though the bear whimpered and whined, he would not touch the skinny old captive.

The second beating of the bear was too much for Idahi. He took his new shotgun and walked away, beside the Red River, pretending he wanted to hunt geese; he was a new guest and did not want to complain, but he knew it was wrong for Blue Duck to beat the bear. Behind him, he heard screams. The two renegades who had been playing at drowning the woman had brought her back to camp and were tormenting her with hot sticks. Idahi walked away until the sounds of the camp grew faint. The thought of finding Blue Duck had excited him so much that he had ridden all the way to the Arkansas River and then back to the Red. But what he found, now that he was in Blue Duck's camp, troubled him. He didn't know if he wanted to stay, even though Blue Duck had already given him a fine shotgun and would certainly expect him to stay. But Blue Duck's treatment of the bear discouraged him. Idahi knew that Blue Duck had formed a company of raiders, but he had thought that most of them would be Kiowa or men of other tribes who had joined Blue Duck in order to keep killing the whites in the old way. But the men in the camp were mostly white men; some were mixed blood, and all of them, he knew, would kill him without a qualm if they could do it without Blue Duck knowing. They didn't like it that Blue Duck had ridden out especially to escort him in, and the longhaired half-breed Ermoke liked him least of all. Idahi felt

Ermoke's angry eyes following him as he walked around the camp. Even the women of the camp, all of them filthy and most of them thin from hunger, looked at him hostilely, as if he were only one more man who had come to abuse them.

It was not what Idahi had expected; but, on the other hand, he had not expected his own chief, Paha-yuca, to agree to take his people onto a reservation. He knew he could not live on a reservation and be subject to the rules of a white man. He did not want to wait like a beggar by his lodge for whites to give him one of their skinny beeves. He had left his three wives behind, in order to join Blue Duck—already he missed his women, and yet he had no intention of bringing them to such a filthy camp, where the men had no respect for anything, not even a bear.

The longer Idahi walked the more troubled and confused he became. He did not know what to do. He was a hunter and a warrior; he wanted to hunt on the prairies and fight his enemies until he was old, or until some warrior vanquished him. There was no shame in defeat at the hands of a good fighter—Idahi knew that in many of the battles he had fought, but for a lucky move at the right moment, he would have been killed. He did not fear the risks of a warrior's life; he respected the dangers such a life entailed. But Idahi wanted to remain a warrior and a hunter; he did not want to become a mere bandit. He wanted to steal from his enemies, the Texans, but he did not intend to steal from the people who had always been *his* people. The men in the camp of Blue Duck had no such qualms, he knew. They would steal from anyone. If they saw a Comanche riding a fine horse, or carrying a fine gun, or married to a pretty plump woman, they would, if they could, kill the Comanche and take the horse, the gun, or the woman.

Fine gun or no fine gun, Idahi knew he could not live with such men. After all, he himself had a fine shotgun now; several of the men in camp had looked at his gift with envious eyes—someday, if Blue Duck happened to be gone, one of the renegades would kill him for it, or try to.

Idahi considered the problem through a long afternoon. Many

ducks and geese landed on the Red River and then flew away again, but Idahi did not shoot them. He was thinking of what he had done, and, by the time the sun set, he had reached a conclusion. It was clear that he had made a mistake. He could not live as Blue Duck lived. Where he would go he was not sure. The way of his chief, Paha-yuca, was not a way he could follow any longer. He would have to give back the fine shotgun and leave. He had begun to feel wrong when he saw Blue Duck beat the bear—now he felt he didn't want to stay where such things happened.

When Idahi walked back to camp it was almost dark. One of the skinny old white men had been killed while he was gone; someone had clubbed him to death. Blue Duck was sitting alone, eating the dog meat the women had cooked. Idahi went to him and handed him back his shotgun.

"What's this—I thought you were going to bring us a goose?" Blue Duck said.

"No, I wasn't hunting," Idahi told him. "This is a fine gun, though."

"If it is such a fine gun, why are you giving it back to me?" Blue Duck asked, scowling. He did not like having his gift returned. Idahi knew that what he had done was rude, but he had no choice. He wanted to leave and didn't want the renegades following him in order to kill him and take the gun.

"When you gave me this gun I thought I could stay here," Idahi said. "But I am not going to stay."

Blue Duck stared at him, a dark look on his face and coldness in his eyes. Idahi remembered that Buffalo Hump had once stared at people like that, when he had been younger; and then, usually, he killed the people he had been staring at with eyes like sleet. Idahi wanted to get his horse and leave. He did not want to fight Blue Duck, in his own camp, where there were so many hostile renegades. He knew, though, that he might *have* to fight. Blue Duck had gone out of his way to welcome him as a guest, and he was going to think it rude of Idahi to go away so soon.

"Eat a little of this dog—it's tasty," Blue Duck said. "You just got here. I guess you can leave in the morning if you're determined to go."

Idahi did as he was asked. He had not changed his mind—he meant to go—but he did not want to be rude, and it was very rude to refuse food. So he sat down by Blue Duck and accepted some of the dog. He had not been eating much on his travels and was happy to have a good portion of dog meat to fill him up.

While they were eating Blue Duck seemed to relax a little, but Idahi remained wary. In deciding to go away he had made a dangerous decision.

"What about my father?" Blue Duck asked. "Is he going to the reservation too, with his people?"

"No, only Paha-yuca is going now," Idahi said. "Slow Tree has already taken his people in, and so has Moo-ray."

"I didn't ask you about them, I asked about Buffalo Hump," Blue Duck said.

"He is old now—people do not speak of him anymore," Idahi said. "His people still live in the canyon. They have not gone to the reservation."

"I want to kill Buffalo Hump," Blue Duck said. "Will you go with me and help me?"

Idahi decided at once to change the subject. Blue Duck had always hated Buffalo Hump, but killing him was not a matter he himself wanted to discuss.

"I wish you would let the bear go," Idahi said. "It is not right to tie a bear to a tree. If you want to kill him, kill him, but don't mistreat him."

"I drug that bear out of a den when he was just a cub," Blue Duck informed him. "He's my bear. If you don't like the way I treat him, you can go kill him yourself."

He said it with a sly little smile. Idahi knew he was being taunted, and that he was in danger, but, where the bear was concerned, Idahi suffered no doubt and had to disregard such considerations.

"He's my pet bear," Blue Duck added. "If I was to turn him loose he wouldn't know what to do. He doesn't know how to hunt anything but dogs."

Idahi thought that was a terrible comment. No bear should have its freedom taken away in order to be a pet. He himself had once seen a bear kill an elk, and he had also had two of his best stallions killed by bears. It was right that bears should kill elk and stallions; it was a humiliating thing that a bear should be reduced to killing dogs in a camp of sullen outlaws. Idahi didn't know what life he was going to have now, anyway. He had left his people and did not intend to go back. He could go to one of the other free bands of Comanches and see if they would accept him and let him hunt and fight with them, but it might be that they would refuse. His home would be the prairie and the grasslands; he might not, again, be able to live with his people. It seemed to him that he ought to do what he could to see that a great animal such as a bear was treated in a dignified manner, even if it meant his own death.

"If you would turn him loose I wouldn't have to kill him," Idahi said.

"It's my bear and I ain't turning him loose," Blue Duck said. "Kill him if you want to."

Idahi decided that his life was probably over. He got up and began to sing a song about some of the things he had done in his life. He made a song about the bear that he had seen kill an elk. While he sang the camp grew quiet. Idahi thought it might be his last song, so he did not hurry. He sang about Paha-yuca, and the people who would no longer be free.

Then he walked over to his horse, took his rifle, and went to the willow tree where the bear was chained. The bear looked up as he approached; it still had blood on its nose from the beating Blue Duck had given it. Idahi was still singing. The bear was such a sad bear that he didn't think it would mind losing its life. He stepped very close to the bear, so he would not have to shoot it a second time. The bear did not move away from him; it merely waited.

Idahi shot the bear dead with one shot placed just above its ear.

Then, still singing, he took the chain off it, so that it would not have, in death, the humiliations it had had to endure in its life.

Idahi expected then that Blue Duck would kill him, or order Ermoke or some of the other renegades to kill him, but instead Blue Duck merely ordered the camp women to skin the bear and cut up the meat. Idahi went on singing until he was well out of camp. He didn't know why Blue Duck had let him go, but he went on singing as loudly as he could. He made a song about some of the hunts he had been on in his life. If the renegades were going to follow him he wanted them to know exactly where he was: he didn't want them to think he was a coward who would slink away.

That night he thought he heard a ghost bear, far away on the prairie, howling in answer to his song.

22.

THOUGH ERMOKE KNEW IT was dangerous to question Blue Duck, he was so angry at what he had seen Idahi do that he went to him anyway, to complain about his lax behavior with the Comanche from the south. One of the rules of the band was that there could be no visitors; those who came either stayed or were killed. Blue Duck had made the rule himself, and now had broken it, and broken it flagrantly. Within the space of a single day a man had ridden in, surveyed the camp, and ridden out.

That Idahi had killed the bear also bothered Ermoke. No one liked the bear, a coward whose spirit Blue Duck had broken long ago. When they tried to use it to make sport with captives the bear only whimpered and turned its back. Once they had even convinced a terrified white woman that they were going to force the bear to mate with her, but of course the bear did not mate with her or even scratch her. Besides, even though it was a skinny bear, it had to be fed from time to time. The bear was only a source of discontent. Sometimes, just to flaunt his authority, Blue Duck would feed the bear choice cuts of venison or buffalo that the men in camp would have liked to eat themselves. It galled them to see a bear eating meat while they had to subsist on mush or fish.

What infuriated Ermoke was that the Comanche, Idahi, had been in the camp long enough to count and identify every man in it. Besides, he knew exactly where the camp was; if he cared to sell his knowledge to the white law, the white law would make him rich. It was to prevent that very thing from happening that Blue Duck had made the rule regarding visitors.

Ermoke marched up to Blue Duck in a fury, which was the safest way to approach him in the event of a dispute. Blue Duck showed the timid no mercy, but he was sometimes indulgent of angry men.

"Why did you let the Comanche go?" Ermoke asked. "Now he can tell the white men where we are and how many of us there are."

"Idahi does not like white men," Blue Duck said.

"People are not supposed to come and go from our camp," Ermoke insisted. "You said so yourself. If people can come and go someone will betray us and we will all be dead."

"You should go help those women skin that bear—I don't think they know how to skin bears," Blue Duck said. It was an insult and he knew it. If Ermoke helped the women do their work he would soon be laughed out of camp. He thought the insult would make Ermoke mad enough that he would kill one or two of the filthy, cowardly white men—they were men who would betray anyone if they could do so profitably. There were always too many people in the camp. Men drifted in, hoping for quick riches, and were too lazy to leave. There was never enough food in the camp, or enough women. Several times Blue Duck had killed some of the white men himself; he would merely prop a rifle across his knees and start shooting. Sometimes the men would sit, stupefied and stunned, like buffalo in a herd, while he shot such victims as caught his eye.

"I wish I could follow that man and kill him," Ermoke said. "I don't like it that he knows where our camp is."

Blue Duck looked at Ermoke in surprise. He saw that the man was angry, so angry that he didn't care what he did. Usually when Ermoke was angry he took his anger out on captive women. He was very lustful. But the one woman captive in the camp had already been abused so badly that she offered no sport—so now Ermoke had decided to be angry at Idahi. Blue Duck thought Ermoke was a fool. Idahi was a Comanche warrior, Ermoke just a renegade. If the two men fought, Idahi would not be the one who lost his scalp.

But Blue Duck had another reason for letting Idahi leave the camp without challenge, a reason he did not intend to share with Ermoke. He had asked Idahi to help him kill Buffalo Hump. Of course, Idahi had refused, but Idahi was a gossip. Soon all the Comanches would know that Blue Duck intended to kill Buffalo Hump. Blue Duck knew that when a chief was old and had lost his power he could expect little help from the young warriors. Old chiefs were just old men—they could expect no protection as they waited to die.

Blue Duck wanted Idahi to spread the word that he intended to kill his father—that was why he had let Idahi go. The nice thing was that Idahi had even given him back the shotgun. He had lost nothing from Idahi's visit except the bear, and the bear had become more trouble than it was worth.

Ermoke still faced him, still hot.

"If you want to kill somebody, go kill that other old man," Blue Duck said. "I'm tired of looking at him—go club him out. But don't bother my friend Idahi. If you bother him I'll club you out."

Ermoke didn't like what he was told—he didn't like it that a Comanche was allowed to come and go, just because he was a Comanche. There was little food in the camp. Tomorrow he meant to take a few of the better warriors and try to find game. He thought he might follow the Comanche while he was at it. He didn't know. He was angry, but not angry enough to start a fight with Blue Duck, not then. To relieve his anger he got a club and beat the old white man until he had broken most of his ribs. Several of the renegades watched the beating, idly. One of them, a short whiskey trader with a bent leg named Monkey John, began to upbraid the women for doing such a crude job of skinning the bear. They had got the skin off but it was cut in several places. The bear lay on its back, a naked pile of meat. When Monkey John got tired of yelling at the cowering women he took his knife and cut off the bear's paws, meaning to extract all the claws. Some of the half-breeds put great store in bear claws—Monkey John meant to use them as money and gamble with them.

In the night the old man who had been so severely beaten coughed up blood and died. One of the half-breeds dragged him into the river, but the river was shallow. The old man didn't float far. He grounded on a mud bank, a few hundred yards from camp. In the morning the mud bank was thick with carrion birds.

"Buzzard breakfast, serves him right," Monkey John said. He rattled his bear claws, hoping to entice some of the renegades into a game of cards.

23.

JAKE SPOON'S decision to leave the rangers and go north caught everyone by surprise except Augustus McCrae, who, as he grew older, laid more and more frequent claims to omniscience. Gus had stopped allowing himself to be surprised; when something unexpected happened, such as Jake abruptly quitting the troop, Augustus immediately claimed that he had known it was going to happen.

Augustus's habit of appearing all-knowing weighed on everybody, but it weighed heaviest on Woodrow Call.

"How did you know it?" Call asked. "Jake said himself he only made up his mind last night."

"Well, but that's a lie," Augustus said. "Jake's been planning to leave for years, ever since you took against him. It's just that he's a lazy cuss and was slow to get around to it."

"I didn't take against the man," Call said, "although I agree that he's lazy."

"Would you at least agree that you don't like the man?" Gus asked. "You ain't liked him a bit since he started bunking with Maggie—and that was back about the time the war started."

Call ignored the comment. It had been some years since he had been up the steps to Maggie's room. If he met her on the street he said a polite hello, but had no other contact with her. The boy, Newt, was always around where the rangers were, of course; Pea Eye, Deets, and Jake had made a kind of pet of the boy. But what went on between Jake Spoon and Maggie Tilton had long ceased to be any concern of his.

"I don't regard him highly, will that satisfy you?" Call said.

"No, but I have passed the point in life where I expect to be satisfied," Augustus said. "At least I don't expect to be satisfied with much. When it comes right down to it, Woodrow, I guess my own cooking beats anything I've come across in this life."

Lately, due to a dissatisfaction with a succession of company cooks—Deets no longer had the time to cook, due to his duties with the horses—Augustus had mastered the art of making sourdough biscuits, a skill of which he was inordinately proud.

"I will allow that Jake has done a fair job with the bookkeeping," Call said. "That will be your job, once he leaves, and you need to be strict about it."

They were sitting in front of a little two-room shack they had purchased together, at the start of the war, to be their living quarters. Augustus, after the death of his Nell, vowed never to marry again; Call gave marriage no thought. The house cost them forty-five dollars. It consisted of two rooms with a dirt floor. It beat sleeping outdoors, but not by much, particularly not in the season when the fleas were active.

"Bookkeep yourself," Gus said. "I will leave too before I'll waste my time scribbling in a ledger."

Across the way, at the lots, they could see Jake Spoon, standing around with Deets and Pea Eye and several other rangers. His horse was saddled but he seemed in no hurry to leave. He sat on the top rail of the corral, with Newt, dangling his feet.

"He said he was leaving this morning, but it's nearly dark and he's still here," Call said.

"Maybe he just wants to spend one more night in safe company," Augustus suggested. "With the war ending I expect he'll have to put up with a lot of thieving riffraff on the roads."

"I expect so," Call said, wishing Jake would go on and leave. Some of the rangers were using his departure as an occasion for getting thoroughly drunk.

"The question ain't why Jake's leaving, it's why *we're* staying," Augustus said. "We ought to up and quit, ourselves."

Call had been thinking along the same lines, but had not pushed his thoughts hard enough to reach a conclusion. The distant war had ended but the Comanche war hadn't; there was still plenty of rangering to do—yet the thought of quitting had occurred to him more than once.

"If we don't quit pretty soon we'll be doing this when we're ninety years old," Augustus said. "Some young governor will be sending us out to catch rascals that any decent sheriff ought to be able to catch."

"And that will have been life," he added. "A lot of whoring and the rest of the time spent catching rascals."

"I would like to see the Indian business through," Call replied.

"Woodrow, it's through," Augustus said.

"The settlers up in Jack County don't think so," Call said. There had been a small massacre only the week before—a party of teamsters had been ambushed and killed.

"I have no doubt a few more firecrackers will go off," Augustus said. "But not many. The Yankee military boys will soon come down and finish off the Comanche."

Call knew there was truth in what Gus said. Most of the Comanche bands had already come in—only a few hundred warriors were still free and inclined to fight. Still, it was too soon to say it was over; besides that, there was the border, as chaotic from the standpoint of law and order as it had been before the Mexican War.

Augustus, though, was not through with his discourse on the Indian question.

"In six months' time we'll have the Yankees here, giving us

orders," he said. "We're just Rebs to them. They won't want our help. We'll be lucky if they even let us keep our firearms. They'll probably have to issue us a pass before we're even allowed on the plains."

"I don't think it will be that bad," Call said, but he spoke without conviction. The Confederacy had been defeated, and Texas had been part of the Confederacy. There was little telling what the future of the rangers would be. What Augustus had proposed on the spur of the moment—quitting the rangers—might not merely be something they ought to consider; it might be something they would *have* to consider.

"We've done this since we were boys," he said to Gus. "What would we do, if we quit?"

"I don't care, as long as we go someplace that ain't dull," Augustus said. "Remember that town that wasn't quite there yet, by the river? I expect that Frenchwoman has got the roof on that saloon by now. Not only could she cook, she could barber. Lonesome Dove—wasn't that what they called it? It might be booming now. It wouldn't hurt us to ride down that way and take a look."

Call didn't reply. He saw that Jake Spoon was shaking hands with all concerned. Probably he had decided to leave that night, after all. Augustus noticed and stood up, meaning to saunter over and say goodbye.

"Coming, Woodrow?" he asked.

"No—he's got half the town to say goodbye to as it is," Call said—but Augustus, to his surprise, insisted that he come.

"You've been his captain since he was a boy," Gus said. "You mustn't let him go off without a goodbye."

Call knew Augustus was right—it would puzzle the boys who were staying if he held aloof from Jake's goodbye. He walked over with Augustus and shook Jake's hand.

"Take care on the roads, Jake, and good luck," he said.

Jake Spoon was so surprised that Call had come to see him off that he flushed with gratitude. It had been four years or more since Call had spoken to him, other than to issue the briefest and simplest commands—mostly, for the whole term of the civil war, Captain Call had treated him as if he were not there. It was such a surprise to receive a handshake from him that Jake was speechless, for a time.

"Thanks, Captain," he managed to mumble. "I aim to go prospecting for silver."

Call saw no need to extend the courtesies further. Even though Jake was mounted, Augustus produced a bottle and passed it around; soon the whole troop would be too drunk to notice whether he was polite to Jake Spoon or not. He noticed to his surprise that several of the rangers had been crying—to Pea Eye and Deets and several of the younger men, Jake was a pard, a friend who had rangered with them and shared the anxieties of youth. Jake had ever been a merry companion, except when he was scared; why wouldn't they mist up a little, now that he was going?

Call walked away, back across the street, past the house where Maggie Tilton still boarded. He wondered, for a moment, what she was thinking, now that the man who had carried her groceries and tended her garden was going. He seldom thought much of Maggie now, though, sometimes, from habit, crossing beneath her window at night, he would look up to see if her lamp was lit.

In the dusk, by the lots, the men were urging Jake to stay at least until morning. Newt could not control his emotions—tears kept leaking out of his eyes. He kept turning his back to wipe them away, so that Pea Eye and Deets and the others would not see him crying. Jake was his best pard and his mother's best friend. With his mother sickly and Jake leaving, Newt hardly knew what he would do; he would have to try and do all the things that Jake did, when it came to helping his mother. He didn't know much about gardening, but thought he could manage the firewood, at least.

Pea Eye, too, was disturbed. Jake had been talking about leaving the rangers the whole of the time Pea Eye had known him; he supposed it was just the kind of dreamy talk men indulged in when they were restless or blue; but now his horse was saddled and all his goods packed on a mule he had bought with some saved-up wages.

Pea Eye considered the move a dreadful mistake—but no one could argue Jake out of it.

Deets said only a brief goodbye. The comings and goings of white men were beyond his understanding and concern. Now and then, though, he saw things in the stars he didn't like, things that suggested Mr. Jake might be having some trouble, someday. No doubt his leaving would make Miss Maggie sad.

When Augustus learned that Jake had purchased a mule to carry his tack, he was indignant.

"Why, Jake, you scamp—you've been hoarding up money," he said. "Your job was to bring out your money and lose it to me in a fair game of poker. Now that I know you're a hoarder I ain't so sorry you're leaving."

Jake had taken a good amount of liquor in the course of his goodbyes. In fact, he had been drunk for the last three days, attempting to work himself up to departing. No one could understand why he wanted to leave at such a time, with the war just ended. Jake hadn't wanted to be a soldier in that war, but he *did* want to get rich. He had seen a little booklet about the silver prospects in Colorado and the thought of discovering silver had given him a bad case of wanderlust. Besides, Texas was poor, impoverished by the war; the Indians were still bad, and Woodrow Call didn't like him—all reasons for leaving. Even if Call *had* liked him there would have been no way to get rich in Texas—Jake had a longing for fine clothes that would never be satisfied if he stayed in Texas.

Of course, there was Maggie and Newt—they'd been a family to him for a few years, although Maggie had refused him the one time he suggested marriage. Later, Jake was relieved by the refusal. Maggie was not well, and, even if she had been, it was too hard to earn a living in a poor place such as Texas.

Besides, he had heard a rumor that the Yankee military meant to come in and hang all the Texas Rangers, as being sympathizers with the Rebs. He didn't want to hang, so now he was leaving, but it wasn't an easy thing. He had bidden goodbye to Maggie three times now, and to Newt; he had said several goodbyes to Pea Eye and the boys. It was time to go, and yet he lingered.

"Go on now, Jake, if you're going," Augustus said, finally. "I can't afford no more goodbye toasts."

With no further ado, Augustus walked away, and the rangers, after a final farewell handshake, wandered off to the part of town where the whores plied their trade. Jake felt lonely, suddenly—lonely and confused. Part of him had hoped, until the end, that someone would come out with an argument that would cause him to change his mind and stay. But now the street was empty; the boys had blandly accepted his decision to leave and it seemed he must go. If he waited until morning and announced that he had changed his mind the boys would only scorn him and take him for an irresolute fool.

Sad and unsteadied, Jake managed to secure the lead rope attached to the pack mule. Now that he actually had to leave, the fact of the mule irritated him. It had already proven itself to be an annoying beast, but if he waited until morning and tried to sell it back to the horse traders they would only offer him a pittance. He decided to sell the mule in Fort Worth, instead. Perhaps there was a shortage of good mules up there—he would see.

In leaving he passed beneath Maggie's window. If the lamp had been lit he would have hitched his animals and rushed up for one more farewell, perhaps even one more embrace; but the window was dark. Tears rushed out at the thought that he was leaving his Mag, but Jake didn't stop. He knew Newt wanted him to stay, but he wasn't so sure about Maggie. She didn't chatter much with him anymore; perhaps it was her illness. In any case there were said to be merry women in Colorado, and Colorado was where he was bound.

Above him in the dark room, Maggie watched him leave. Newt had come in sobbing and cried himself to sleep. Maggie watched out the darkened window as Jake made his extended farewells. She left the light off deliberately, so that Jake would not rush at her again, confused, sad, importunate; one minute he wanted her to bless his departure, the next he wanted her to marry him and keep him in Austin. In either mood he sought her welcome, wanted her to lie with him. It had been months since Maggie had felt well. She had a cough that wouldn't leave her. She did her job and tended her child, but she rarely had the energy now to deal with Jake Spoon's confusions, or his needs.

Though Maggie knew she would miss Jake—she felt a certain sadness as he passed beneath her window—she also felt relieved that he was going. Though he was as helpful as he knew how to be, having him with her was like having two children, and she no longer had the energy for it. She had never been able to be quite what Jake wanted, though she had tried; though she would now have no one to carry her groceries or help her with her garden, she would also be free of the strain involved in never being quite what a man wanted.

Her true regret was for Newt. Jake had been what father Newt had; Newt's life would be the poorer, for his leaving. Maggie was glad that all the ranger boys liked her son; they let him stay with them all day, when they were in town. The fear that haunted Maggie, that seized her every time she coughed, was that she would die before Newt was grown. What would happen to Newt then? Sometimes Maggie imagined that with her death Woodrow would soften and accept his son, but it was not a thing she could be confident of. Many nights she scarcely slept. She tried to evaluate her own coughing; she wondered what her son would do, if she died. At least she knew he was welcome with the ranger boys, Augustus and Pea Eye and Deets. Newt had grown up with those men; they had all had a hand in his raising. Ikey Ripple was like a grandfather to the boy. Maggie knew Augustus well enough to know that, with all his whoring and his drinking, he would see to it that Newt was well cared for. Gus wouldn't desert him, nor would Deets or Pea—even without her, Newt would be better off than many of the orphaned children adrift in the country now, children whose parents the war had taken.

But such reflections didn't end Maggie's fears. Augustus McCrae was not immortal, and neither were the others. What if they had to leave Texas to earn a living, as Jake was doing? What if they were all killed in an Indian fight?

The worry about Newt and his future was a worry Maggie could not entirely put down—it made her determined to last. If she could just last a few more years Newt would be old enough that someone might employ him—she knew that many cowboys were no more than twelve or thirteen when they first gained employment on the many ranches to the south.

The streets of Austin were empty: Jake was gone. Maggie sat by the window a long time, thinking, hoping, looking down at the silent street.

Then, just as she was about to go to bed, she saw Pea Eye roll out of the wagon where he had been napping. Maggie watched, expecting him to walk off—she had never known Pea Eye to be drunk, but then old friends such as Jake Spoon didn't leave the troop every day. It was late in the night and chilly; it had begun to drizzle. Maggie waited, thinking Pea Eye would wake up, stand up, and make his way to the shelter of the bunkhouse.

But he didn't wake up. He lay as he had fallen, flat on his face in the street.

Maggie went to bed, telling herself that Pea Eye was, after all, a grown man—as a roving ranger he had no doubt slept out of doors in far worse weather, and in more dangerous places than the streets of Austin.

Maggie's reasoning failed to convince her—the thought of Pea Eye kept sleep from coming. No doubt he had slept out of doors in worse weather, but, on those occasions, she hadn't been in sight of him. Finally she got up, took a heavy quilt out of her cedar chest, went down the stairs, walked the few steps, covered Pea with the quilt, and pulled him around so that his legs were no longer sticking into the street where a wagon could run over them, as in the case of the senator who lost his hand.

The next morning, when Maggie went down to recover her

quilt, Pea Eye was seated with his back to the wagon wheel, looking like a man in shaky health and spirits.

"I wish I could take my head off," he said, to Maggie. "If I could take it off I'd chuck it far enough away that I couldn't feel it throb."

"Many a man has ruined his health for good, drinking whiskey with Gus McCrae," Maggie informed him sternly.

Pea Eye didn't dispute the opinion.

"Gus? He can hold more liquor than a tub," he said. "Is this your quilt?"

"Yes, I thought I better cover you," Maggie said.

"I had an awful dream," Pea Eye said. "I dreamed a big Comanche held me up by my legs and scalped me."

"That wasn't a Comanche, that was me," Maggie said. "Your legs were sticking into the street—I was afraid a wagon would run over you, so I pulled you around."

"Jake's gone off to Colorado to find a silver mine," Pea Eye said.

Maggie didn't answer. Instead, to Pea Eye's consternation, she began to cry. She didn't say anything; she just took her quilt and walked home with it, crying.

Pea Eye, never certain about what women might do, got up at once and walked back to the bunkhouse. He resolved in future never to get drunk and fall asleep where a woman might spot him. That way there would be no tears.

"Maybe I shouldn't have talked about my dream," he said, a little later, discussing the incident with Deets.

"Do you think it would upset a woman to hear about my dream?" Pea asked.

"Don't know. I ain't a woman and I ain't had no dream," Deets said.

24.

INISH SCULL—General Scull now, thanks to a brilliant, some would say brutal, series of victories in the long conflict with the South—

had just settled into his study, with the morning papers and a cup of Turkish coffee, when his nephew Augereau, a wispy youth with French leanings, wandered in with an annoyed look on his face.

"It's a damn nuisance, not having a butler," Augereau said. "Why *would* Entwistle enlist?"

"I suppose he didn't want to miss the great fight," General Scull replied. "I didn't so much mind his enlisting—the real nuisance is that the man got himself killed, and within two weeks of the armistice too. If the fool had only kept his head down for another two weeks you wouldn't be having to answer the door, would you, Augereau?"

"It *is* rather annoying—I ain't a butler," Augereau said. "I was reading Vauvenargues."

"Well, Vauvenargues will keep, but what about the fellow at the door? I suppose it was a fellow," Scull said.

"Yes, I believe he's a colonel," Augereau said.

"There's no reason to expect. Either he is or he isn't," Scull said. "Would it discommode you too much to show him in?"

"I suppose I could show him in, since he's here," Augereau said. "I say, will Auntie Inez be back soon? It's a good deal more jolly when Auntie Inez is here."

"Your aunt just inherited a great deal of money," Scull informed him. "She's run off to Cuba, to buy another plantation. I don't know when she'll be returning. Her tropical habits ain't exactly suited to Boston."

"Oh what, the masturbation?" young Augereau said. "But there was a lap robe and they were in a carriage. What's the bother?"

"Augereau, would you mind going and getting that colonel?" Scull said. "We can discuss your dear Auntie's behavior some other time."

Augereau went to the door, but he didn't quite exit the study. He stood for almost a minute right in the doorway, as if undecided whether to go out or stay in.

"The fact is, I don't much care for Vauvenargues," he said. "I do care for Auntie—hang the bloody masturbation!"

Then, before Scull could speak to him again about the colonel he had misplaced somewhere in the house, Augereau turned and drifted off, leaving the door to the study ajar, a lapse that irritated Scull intensely. He liked doors, drawers, shutters, windows, and cabinets to be closed properly, and, on balance, was more annoyed with his impeccably trained butler, Entwistle, for getting himself shot at an obscure depot in Pennsylvania than he was at Inez for masturbating old Jervis Dalrymple in an open carriage injudiciously parked near Boston Common. Somehow the lap robe had slipped during the operation; to Inez's annoyance the policeman who happened to be passing was a tall Vermonter, well able to look into the carriage and witness the act, which resulted in a charge of public fornication, not to mention much fuss and bother.

"Really, you Yankees!" Inez remarked in annoyance. "I was only doing off his pizzle in order to calm him down. I couldn't take him into Mr. Cabot's tea party in that state, now could I? He might have thrust himself on some innocent young miss."

"I have no doubt your action was well intended," Scull told his wife, "but you might have been more careful about where you parked."

"I'll park where I please—this is a free country, or at least it was until you filthy Yankees won the war," Inez told him, her fury rising. "It was no worse than milking a cow. I suppose next I'll be arrested if I decide to milk my Jersey in public."

"Your Jersey and a Dalrymple pizzle are not quite the same thing, not in the eyes of Boston," Scull informed her. He had recently been forced to turn all the Scull portraits face to the wall, to prevent Inez from ruining them with her wild quirtings.

Young Augereau never reappeared, but, after a bit, Scull heard a tread in the hallway, a hesitant and rather unmilitary tread. He put down his Turkish coffee and stepped out of the study just in time to stop a thin, stooped colonel in the United States Army from proceeding along the almost endless hallway.

"I'm here, Colonel—we lost our butler, you know," Scull said.

"I'm Colonel Soult," the man said. "We met not long after Vicksburg, but I don't suppose you remember. That's S-o-u-l-t—it's often confused with 'salt.' In my youth I was called 'Salty' because of the confusion."

Scull had no memory of the man, but he did recall seeing the name 'Soult' on a muster roll or document of some sort.

"Samuel Soult, is it?" he inquired, only to see a flush of delight come to the man's sallow features.

"Why, yes, that's me, Sam Soult," he said, shaking Scull's hand.

"What brings you to our old Boston, Colonel Soult?" Scull asked, once the two of them were settled in his study. A sulky cook had even been persuaded to bring Colonel Soult a cup of the strong Turkish coffee General Scull now favored.

Scull wore the multilensed dark glasses he had worn throughout the war—glasses which got him the nickname "Blinders" Scull. With a touch of his finger he could regulate the tint and thickness of the lenses to compensate for whatever intensity of light prevailed. The study, at the time, was rather a litter. Scull could see that the disorder offended the neat colonel a little; but, by the end of the war, he was in a fever of impatience to get back to the book he had just started writing when the conflict broke out: *The Anatomy and Function of the Eyelid in Mammals, Reptiles, Fish, and Birds.* At the moment he was plowing through the classical authors, noting every reference to the eyelids, however slight. A towering pile of papers, journals, books, letters, photographs, and drawings had had to be dumped out of the chair where Colonel Soult was by now rather cautiously sitting.

"I was sent, sir—sent by the generals," Colonel Soult said. "You did leave the front rather quickly, once the peace was settled."

"True, I'm not a man to wait," Scull said. "The fighting was over—the details can be left to the clerks. I had a book to write, as you can see—a book on the eyelid, a neglected subject. Until I lost my own I didn't realize how neglected. I was eager to get to it—still am. I hope you've not come all this way to try and pull me away from my researches, Colonel Soult."

"Well, I *was* sent by the generals," Colonel Soult admitted. "They believe you're the man to take the West—I believe that's the general view."

The Colonel was almost stuttering in his anxiety.

"*Take* the West? Take it where?" Scull asked.

"What I meant to say was, administer it," the Colonel said. "General Grant and General Sherman, they're of the view that you're the man to do it."

"What did General Sherman think about this scheme?" Scull inquired. He knew that the rough Sherman was not likely to sponsor or support his candidacy for such an important post.

"Don't know that Sherman was consulted," the Colonel admitted. "If you won't take the West, would you at least take Texas? The savages there require a firm hand and the border is not entirely pacified, if reports are to be believed."

"No, the savages in Texas are broken," Scull said firmly. "I don't doubt that there are a few free remnants, but they won't last long. As for the border, my view is that we should never have bothered stealing it from Mexico in the first place. It's only thorn and mesquite anyway."

He let that opinion sink in and then pointed his thick blinders directly at the quaking colonel and let fly.

"You're a poor specimen of colonel, Sam Soult," Scull said. "First you offer me the West and then you reduce me to Texas before I even refused the first offer. All I did was inquire about General Sherman's opinion, which you evidently can't provide."

"Oh, beg pardon, General—I suppose I'm not used to this sweet coffee," the Colonel said, aghast at the blunder he had just committed. "Your tone when I offered the West was not encouraging— of course, if you *would* take the whole West, the generals would be delighted."

"No sir, I pass," Scull said. "Let General Sherman run the West. I expect the Sioux and the Cheyenne will lead him on a merry chase for a few more years."

"I don't believe he wants it either," the Colonel said, with a droop in his tone. "General Sherman has not declared his intentions."

"If Sherman won't take it, give to whoever you want," Scull said. "I doubt the northern tribes will last ten years, if they last that long."

"But General, what about Texas?" the lugubrious colonel asked. "We have no one to send. The President was particularly hopeful that you'd take Texas."

Inish Scull clicked his lenses a few times, until he came to the last lens, the one that shut out all light, and insured perfect darkness. Behind his black lens he could no longer see the Colonel, which was how he preferred it. He wanted to think for a few minutes. Inez hated the black lens; she knew he could click the black lens and make her vanish from view.

But Colonel Soult was not in on the secret; he didn't know that he had just vanished from view. All he could tell was that Blinders Scull, victor in fifteen engagements with the Rebs, was staring at him from behind the very blinders that had produced his nickname.

It made Colonel Soult distinctly uncomfortable, but no more uncomfortable, he felt sure, than having to journey back to Washington with the news that Scull had refused everything. The refusal would undoubtedly be taken as the result of his own inadequate diplomacy; he was unhappily aware that he had blundered by offering General Scull Texas before he had quite refused the whole West. If word of that misspeaking leaked out, the Colonel knew that his own next posting was not likely to be one that would appeal to Mrs. Soult; if it happened to be west of Ohio, Mrs. Soult would be disturbed, it being her firm belief that Ohio was the westernmost point at which a civilized existence could be sustained. She had heard once of a frontiersman who, faced with a howling blizzard, had actually torn pages out of one of Mrs. Browning's books in order to start a fire; Mrs. Soult herself wrote a little poetry, mostly of a devotional nature—the report of the frontiersman and the fire struck her as evidence enough that, beyond Ohio, there was only barbarism and blizzards.

General Scull, secure behind his blinders, was reflecting on the fact that he had abruptly stopped hopping during the siege of Vicksburg. The flea malady, as he called it, that had seized him while in Ahumado's pit had left him because of a particularly loud cannon blast one gray morning in Mississippi. He had been hopping uncontrollably, to the bewilderment of his troops, when the cannon boomed in his ear; since then he had not indulged in a single hop.

Now he had been offered the West, land of distances and sky, the place where the last unpacified aboriginal people dwelled. He had been at a conclave once attended by a few Cheyenne and thought he had never seen a handsomer people. The necessity of blasting and starving them into line with territorial policy did not appeal to him. It was a job he could happily refuse.

When he remembered Texas, though, he found himself unable to be quite so immediate or so categorical in his refusal. He had enjoyed tramping the plains at the head of his ranger troop—it beat mowing down his cousins from the Carolinas, or Inez's cousins from Georgia. He remembered his sharp engagements with Buffalo Hump, an enemy he had never even really seen, at close range. He remembered the daring thievery of Kicking Wolf, and the loquacity of the tracker Famous Shoes. In particular Scull remembered Ahumado, the Black Vaquero, the pit, the cages, the raw pigeons, and the blistering his brain suffered once the old Mayan had taken off his eyelids.

His friend Freddie Catherwood and his companion Johnnie Stephens had regaled him several times with tales of Chiapas and the Yucatan. Catherwood had even given him a portfolio of drawings of lost temples in the Yucatan, made on his last journey with Johnnie Stephens.

Ahumado, he recalled, had been a man of the south, of the very regions Catherwood and Stephens had explored. Scull felt he might go someday and see the jungles and the temples, the place that had spawned his shrewdest foe.

But Ahumado, if alive, was in Mexico, whereas Texas was the theater he was being offered. He wondered which of the men he had once led were still alive, and whether Buffalo Hump still held the great Palo Duro Canyon. Scull had kept up, as best he could, with the battle reports from Texas, but it had been years since he had seen Buffalo Hump's name mentioned in connection with a raid. Like most great chiefs, his name had simply dropped from history, once he grew old.

It occurred to him, as he hid behind his blinders, that the one good reason for going back to Texas was Inez. Since there was no way to control her it was no doubt better to turn her loose on a frontier than in the somber streets of Boston. The cattle business was booming, from what he could read. With cowboys and cattle barons to amuse her Inez might be content, for a year or two.

But Inez was in Cuba, mistress now to the greatest plantation on the island. There was no telling when or if she would return, and, in any case, experience persuaded him that it was seldom wise to return to a theater he had left. There were far too many places in the world that he hadn't seen to waste his years revisiting those he had already been to. Johnnie Stephens had been to Persia and was enthusiastic about it, going on and on about the blue mosques and the long light.

Then there was the impediment of his book. All during the war sentences and paragraphs had boiled up in his brain; he had scribbled them down on every imaginable article, including, on occasion, his saddlebags. He had worn out a whole set of Pickering's excellent little Diamond Classics, thumbing through them during intervals in battle for chance references to eyelids.

When at last he clicked his lenses and brought Colonel Soult back into focus he saw that the man was almost shaking with anxiety. Battle itself could have hardly unnerved him more than his hour in the dim old mansion on Beacon Hill.

"They thought if I came myself, to bring you their respects in person, maybe you would consider a command in the West," Colonel Soult said. "Some part of the West, at least, General."

The Colonel saw from the set of General Scull's jaw that he was about to deliver a refusal. Sam Soult had not served as a subordinate to seven generals not to know when he was about to get a no rather than a yes.

"Thank them kindly, Colonel, but as you can see I'm a man of the library now," Scull said. "I've just served five years in a great war—the only struggle that still interests me is the conflict with the sentence, sir—the English sentence."

Colonel Soult had got the refusal he expected, but the grounds the General gave confused him.

"Excuse me, General—the sentence?" Colonel Soult replied.

Scull seized a blank sheet of foolscap and waved it dramatically in front of Colonel Soult's face—it might make the man's job easier if he could be sent back to Washington with the conviction that the great General Inish Scull was a little teched.

"See this page of paper? It's blank," Scull said. "That, sir, is the most frightening battlefield in the world: the blank page. I mean to fill this paper with decent sentences, sir—this page and hundreds like it. Let me tell you, Colonel, it's harder than fighting Lee. Why, it's harder than fighting Napoleon. It requires unremitting attention, which is why I can't oblige the President, or the generals who sent you here."

Then he leaned back and smiled.

"Besides, they just want me to go back and eat dust so they won't have to," he said. "I won't do it, sir. That's my final word."

"Well, if you won't, you won't, General," Colonel Soult said. It was a dictum he was to repeat to himself many times on the somber train ride back to Washington. General Scull had said no, which meant that he himself could look forward to a posting well west of Ohio, where Mrs. Browning's books were considered little better than kindling. Sam Soult knew well that it would greatly dismay his wife.

25.

FAMOUS SHOES was traveling by night, covering as much ground as he could, when he heard the singing to the south. At first, when he was far from the singer, he thought the faint sound he heard might be a wolf, but as he came closer he realized it was a Comanche, though only one Comanche. All that was very curious. Why would a single Comanche be singing by himself at night, on the llano?

He himself had been to the Cimarron River, where a few old people of his tribe still held out. He had been showing some of the flints he had found while tracking Captain McCrae to some of the oldest of the Kickapoos. Over the years since his discovery he had shown the flints to most of the oldest members of his tribe, and they had been impressed. He had been back several times to the place where he found the flints, and had located so many arrowheads and spearheads that he had to take a sack with him, to carry them. He had found a fine hiding place, too, on the Guadalupe River, a small cave well concealed by bushes, which is where he hid the flints that had been made by the Old People.

His one disappointment was that he had never found the hole where the People emerged from the earth. He had talked about the hole so much that the Kickapoos had come to consider him rather a bore. Of course, the hole where the People had emerged was important, but they themselves did not have time to look for it and had lost interest in talking to Famous Shoes about it.

It was while returning from his trip to the Cimarron that Famous Shoes had the misfortune to run into three of Blue Duck's half-breed renegades. They had just ambushed an elderly white man who was riding a fine gray horse. It was the white man Famous Shoes saw first. He had been shot two or three times, stripped of all his clothes, and left to die. When Famous Shoes spotted him he had just stumbled into a little gully; by the time Famous Shoes reached him he was staring the stare of death, though he was still breathing a little.

Then the renegades themselves came riding down into the gully. One of them rode the old man's fine horse and the others had donned pieces of his clothing, which was better clothing than their filthy rags.

"Leave him alone, he is ours," one of the renegades said insolently.

Famous Shoes was startled by the bad tone the renegades adopted. Apparently they had decided to torture the dying man a little, but before they could start the man coughed up a great flood of blood, and died.

"He is not yours now," Famous Shoes pointed out. "He is dead."

"No, he is still ours," the renegade said. The three renegades were drunk. They began to hack the old man up—soon they had blood all over the clothes they had taken from him.

While the renegades were cutting up the old man, Famous Shoes left. They were in such a frenzy of hacking and ripping that they didn't notice him leaving. He was a mile away before one of the drunken killers decided to pursue him. It was not the bandit who had taken the gray horse; that man was called Lean Head. The man who pursued Famous Shoes was a skinny fellow with a purple birthmark on his neck. Birthmarks brought either good luck or bad, and this bandit's did not bring him good luck. Famous Shoes noticed the other two bandits riding off in the direction the old man had come from. No doubt they wanted to scavenge among his possessions a little more thoroughly.

Because the skinny renegade was alone, and his companions headed in the other direction, Famous Shoes saw no reason not to kill his pursuer, which he did with dispatch. He had a bow and a few arrows with him which he used to provide himself with game. When the renegade loped up behind him Famous Shoes turned and put three arrows in him before the man could catch his breath. In fact, the renegade never did catch his breath again. He opened his mouth to yell for help, but before he could yell Famous Shoes pulled him off the horse and cut his throat—then he grabbed the horse's bridle and cut the horse's throat too. The horse was as skinny as the rider; Famous Shoes left them together, their lifeblood ebbing into the prairie. He left the arrows in the dead man—there were so many guns on the plains now that it was becoming rare to see a man killed with arrows. The renegades might be so ignorant that they could not tell Kickapoo arrows from any other; they might conclude that their friend had been killed by a passing Kiowa.

The renegades, though, were not quite so ignorant. By the middle of the afternoon Famous Shoes saw their dust, far behind him. Once he knew they were pursuing him he turned due west, onto the llano. He was soon into a land of gullies—he skipped from rock to rock and walked so close to the edge of the gullies that the pursuers could not follow his steps without riding so close to the gullies that they risked falling in.

That night he only rested for an hour. However drunken or foolish the renegades might be, pursuit was likely to make them determined, or even bold. They would think that he was a rabbit they could run to ground. They would never think that since he had killed one of them he might kill them too. In general he preferred to avoid killing men, even rude, ignorant, dangerous men, for it meant setting a spirit loose that might become his enemy and conspire against him with witches. He ran west into the llano all night and most of the next day, not merely to evade his pursuers but to put as much distance as possible between himself and the spirit of the dead man. Now that the skinny man was dead Famous Shoes began to worry about the birthmark, which might mean that the man had had an affinity with witches.

It was as he moved deeper into the waterless llano that he heard the faint singing, at night, and determined that it was made by a single Comanche. Famous Shoes thought he ought to just pass by the Comanche, but the closer he came to the singing, the more curious he felt. Though he knew it was dangerous to approach a Comanche, in this case he could not resist. As he eased closer to the singer it became clear to him that the man was singing the song of his life. He was singing of his deeds and victories, of his defeats and sorrows, of the warriors he had known and the raids he had ridden on.

As he came closer Famous Shoes saw that the man was indeed alone. He had only a tiny fire, made of buffalo dung, and a dead horse lay nearby. The song he sang was both a life song and a death song: the warrior had decided to leave life and had sensibly decided to take his horse along with him, so that he could ride comfortably in the spirit world.

Famous Shoes decided that he wanted to know this warrior, who had chosen such a fine way to leave life. He didn't think the Comanche would turn on him and kill him—from listening to the life song that was a death song he knew that the warrior would probably not be interested in him at all.

He knew, though, that it was not polite to interrupt such a song. He waited where he was, napping a little, until the gray dawn came; then he stood up and walked toward the warrior, who was poking up his fire a little.

The warrior by the small fire did not rise when he saw Famous Shoes coming. His voice was a little hoarse, from all his singing. At first, when he saw Famous Shoes approaching, his look was indifferent, like the look of warriors so badly wounded in battle that their spirits were already leaving their bodies, or like the look of old people who were looking beyond, into the spirit home. The warrior was very thin and very tired. He had not eaten any of the dead horse that lay nearby; he was exhausted with the effort it took to get his life into the song. Famous Shoes did not know him.

"I was passing and heard your song," Famous Shoes said. "Some of Blue Duck's men were chasing me. I had to kill one of them— that was two days ago."

At mention of Blue Duck the warrior's expression changed from one of indifference to one of contempt.

"I was at the camp of Blue Duck," he said, in his hoarse voice. "He was camped on the Rio Rojo, near the forests. I did not stay. They had a bear there and were mistreating it. The men with Blue Duck are only thieves. I am glad you killed one."

He paused and looked into the fire.

"If I had been there I would have killed the other two," he said. "I did not like the way they abused the bear."

Famous Shoes knew the man was in a state not far from death. It was most uncommon for a Comanche to say he would have fought along with a Kickapoo, since the two peoples were enemies, one of the other.

"What did they do to the bear?" he asked.

"I killed the bear," Idahi said, remembering the expression on the bear's face when he had walked up to shoot it. It had been a sad bear, broken by many beatings.

Though Idahi felt no anger at the Kickapoo who had stopped to talk with him, he did feel a great tiredness when he tried to speak to the man. He had been almost out of life, singing the song of his deeds, but the Kickapoo was not out of life at all. He was a fully living man, still curious about the things that living men did. Idahi found it hard to come back. He had turned inside him, toward the spirit time, and could not easily concern himself with Blue Duck or the things of fleshly life.

Famous Shoes saw that the Comanche was weary and only wanted to get on with his dying. Though he knew it was impolite to detain a person bent on traveling in the spirit time, he could not resist one more question.

"Why are you alone?" he asked.

The Comanche seemed a little annoyed by the question.

"You are alone yourself," he pointed out, with a touch of disdain.

"Yes, but I am merely traveling," Famous Shoes said. "You have killed your horse. I don't think you want to travel any farther."

Idahi thought the Kickapoo was a pesky fellow—that was the problem with Kickapoos. They were all pesky, continually asking questions about things that were none of their business. Probably that was one reason his own people always killed Kickapoos as soon as possible, when they happened on one of them. Idahi decided just to tell this Kickapoo what he wanted to know; maybe then he would leave so Idahi could continue singing his song.

"My people have gone to the place the whites wanted them to go," he said. "I did not want to go to that place, so I left. I went to be with the Antelope Comanche but they have nothing to eat. They live on mice and prairie dogs and roots they pull out of the ground. I am not a good hunter, so they did not want me.

"None of the Comanches have much to eat now," he added.

"But the Comanches have many horses," Famous Shoes reminded him. It had always struck him as a vanity that the Comanches were so reluctant to eat their horses. They were not practical people like the Kickapoo, who would as cheerfully eat a horse as a deer or buffalo.

Idahi didn't answer. Of course the Comanches had horses—even the Antelopes had quite a few horses. But Quanah, the war chief of the Antelopes, still meant to fight the Texans, and fighting men could not afford to eat their mounts while they still contemplated war. Their horses were their power; without horses they would not really be Comanches anymore. He did not want to talk of this to the Kickapoo, so he began to sing again, although in a faint voice.

Famous Shoes knew he had stayed long enough. The Comanche had chosen to go on and die, which was a wise thing. His own people had gone onto the reservation, and the other bands of Comanches did not want him. Probably the warrior was tired of being hungry and alone and had decided to go on to the place that was well peopled by spirits.

"I am going on with my traveling," Famous Shoes told him. "I hope those two renegades who ride with Blue Duck do not bother you—they are very rude."

Idahi did not respond to the remark. He was remembering a feast his people had once had, when they had managed to stampede a herd of buffalo off a cliff into the Palo Duro. There had been meat enough for the whole band to feast for a week—one or two of the neighboring bands had come too.

Famous Shoes did not have much food either; he did not like prairie dog meat, which was the easiest meat to obtain on the dry llano. He would have liked to take a little horsemeat from the Comanche warrior's dead horse, but he knew that it would not be a polite thing to do.

The lone Comanche who had decided to die sang his final song so faintly that before Famous Shoes had taken many steps he could no longer hear him singing.

26.

KICKING WOLF was the last person in the tribe to have a conversation with Buffalo Hump, and the conversation, as usual, had been about horses. Both of Buffalo Hump's wives were now dead; of the two, Heavy Leg had lived the longer, though Lark was much the younger woman. Lark had foolishly let a deer kick her—though the deer was down and dying, it still managed to kick Lark so badly in the ribs that she began to spit blood. Within two days she was dead. Heavy Leg had not been foolish in regard to dying deer, but, in the winter, she had died anyway, leaving Buffalo Hump with no one to tend his lodge.

Of course, Buffalo Hump possessed many horses. He could easily have bought himself another wife, but he didn't. The young women still tittered about the old chief's hump. Some of them wondered what it would be like to couple with such a man, but none of them found out because Buffalo Hump ignored them. Although his lodge soon grew tattered and poorly kept, and he had to prepare his own meals, he did not send for a new wife, or seek one. He spent most of his days sitting on his favorite pinnacle of rock, watching the hawks and eagles soar high above the canyon. He had no visitors. Many of the young people of the tribe had forgotten that he had ever been a chief. Only when there was singing and a few of the old warriors sang about the thousand-warrior raid was Buffalo Hump recalled.

Buffalo Hump himself kept apart from the singing, which, itself, had become a rare thing. Singing was most likely to happen when there was a feast; since there was less and less to feast on, there were fewer and fewer feasts.

Kicking Wolf, of course, was still an active horsethief. He seldom fired a gun at a Texan, and seldom was fired at, preferring, as always, to work at night and depend on stealth.

The reason Kicking Wolf sought out Buffalo Hump was because he wanted his opinion on the horse herd. Peta, the war chief, thought there could never be too many horses, the result being that almost two thousand grazed on the grasslands near the camp.

Kicking Wolf's view was different. He thought there *could* be too many horses. He wanted to divide the horse herd and give some of the horses to the other bands that were still free. He even favored driving some of the horses away altogether, letting them go wild, and he thought his arguments were sound. Having so many horses together made it easier for the bluecoat soldiers to find them. There was not enough grass in the canyon itself to graze so many horses, and their presence kept the buffalo from coming back.

Kicking Wolf was a firm believer in the return of the buffalo. There had been too many buffalo simply to vanish. They had gone north, he believed, because they did not like the smell of the whites, or the smell of their cattle, either. But the buffalo were not gone from the earth; they had merely gone north. Someday they would return to the southern plains—they would, at least, if the People were patient and respectful and did not graze out the plains with too many horses.

When Kicking Wolf found Buffalo Hump he had just climbed down from his rock. It was a hard climb, almost beyond Buffalo Hump's strength. He was sitting in a patch of shade, resting, when Kicking Wolf approached.

"Why do you climb that rock?" Kicking Wolf asked. "Haven't you climbed it enough in your life?"

Buffalo Hump didn't answer—he found the question annoying. It was none of Kicking Wolf's business how many times he climbed the rock. In the last year or two he had not only grown indifferent to company, he had begun to find it irritating. Everyone who came to see him asked questions that were either stupid or impertinent. Better to see no one than to see fools.

For himself, the one sad thing about climbing the rock was that he could no longer really see the hawks and eagles. He knew they were there; sometimes he could almost feel their flight, but he could not see them as he had seen them when he was a younger man. Now his eyes would water when he tried to look hard at a flying bird or even a running deer. Sometimes he would think he saw a jackrabbit, sitting for a moment, but when he came closer the jackrabbit would become a rock or a clump of grass. The plains became a blur now, when he tried to look across them to some distant point. Often his ears were of more use than his eyes—he could tell what animals were near by listening. He could hear an armadillo scratching, hear the slow walk of a possum. Were it not for his skill at snaring small game, he would have had a hard time finding food.

He did not mention his problems to Kicking Wolf—as always, Kicking Wolf had only one thing on his mind, which was horses. He immediately started talking about the horse herd—it was too big, it needed to be divided, it would lead the soldiers to them, it would keep the buffalo from returning. Buffalo Hump had heard it all before. The only part he felt like responding to was the nonsense about the buffalo. It annoyed him that an experienced warrior such as Kicking Wolf, a horse Comanche all his life, could be so foolish as to think that the size of the horse herd had anything to do with the disappearance of the buffalo. What were a thousand horses, or two thousand, to the millions of buffalo that had once roamed the prairies?

"The buffalo won't come back," he said angrily.

Kicking Wolf was startled by the anger in Buffalo Hump's voice—the old chief had seemed half asleep, his eyes staring vacantly across the prairie. But his voice, when he spoke, was the voice of the fighter, the man whose cold eyes had made even brave warriors want to run.

"The buffalo will return," Kicking Wolf said. "They have only gone to the north for a while. The buffalo have always returned."

"You are a fool," Buffalo Hump said. "The buffalo won't return, because they are dead. The whites have killed them. When you go north you will only find their bones."

"The whites have killed many, but not all," Kicking Wolf insisted. "They have only gone to the Missouri River to live. When we have beaten the whites back they will return."

But, as he was speaking, Kicking Wolf suddenly lost heart. He realized that Buffalo Hump was right, and that the words he had just spoken *were* the words of a fool. The Comanches were not beating the whites, and they were not going to beat them. Only their own band and three or four others were still free Comanches. The bands that were free were the bands that could survive on the least, those who would eat small animals and dig roots from the earth. Already the bluecoat soldiers had come back to Texas and begun to fill up the old forts, places they had abandoned while they fought one another. Even if all the free tribes banded together there would not be enough warriors to defeat the bluecoat soldiers. With the buffalo gone so far north, the white soldiers had only to drive them farther and farther into the llano, until they starved or gave up.

"The whites are not foolish," Buffalo Hump said. "They know that it is easier to kill a buffalo than it is to kill one of us. They know that if they kill all the buffalo we will starve—then they won't have to fight us. Those who don't want to starve will have to go where the whites want to put them."

The two men sat in silence for a while. Some young men were racing their horses a little farther down the canyon. Kicking Wolf usually took a keen interest in such contests. He wanted to know which horses were fastest. But today he didn't care. He felt too sad.

"The medicine men are deceiving the young warriors when they tell them the buffalo will return," Buffalo Hump said. "If any buffalo come back they will only be ghost buffalo. Their ghosts might return because they remember these lands. But that will not help us. We cannot eat their ghosts."

Thinking about the buffalo—how many there had once been; not a one remaining on the *comanchería*—Kicking Wolf grew so heavy with sadness that he could not speak. He had never thought that such abundance could pass, yet it had. He thought that it would have been better to have fallen in battle than to have lived to see such greatness pass and go. The sadness was so deep that no more words came out of his throat. He got up and walked away without another word.

Buffalo Hump continued to sit, resting. He could scarcely see the horses racing on the prairie, though he could hear the drum of their hoofbeats. He was glad that Kicking Wolf had left. He did not like it anymore when people took up his time, talking foolishness about the buffalo returning. The medicine men thought that their ranting and praying could make the white buffalo hunters die, but it would surely be the other way around: the white buffalo hunters, with guns so powerful that they could shoot nearly to the horizon, would be making the medicine men die. Worm had already been killed by one of the long-shooting guns; of course old Worm had been crazy at the time. He had smeared himself with a potion made from weasel glands and eagle droppings, convinced that it would stop a bullet—a buffalo hunter with a good aim had proven him wrong.

Later that day Buffalo Hump walked through the horse herd until he located his oldest horse, a thin gelding whose teeth were only stumps. That night he took his bow and arrows, his lance, and a few snares, and left the camp on the old horse. No one heard him go and no one would have cared if they had heard. Buffalo Hump thought the horse might be too old to climb the steep trail out of the canyon, but the horse was eager to go and climbed the trail as quickly as if he were a young colt again, snorting like a wild horse might snort.

When he reached the lip of the canyon Buffalo Hump didn't stop—he rode north and west, all night, only stopping when dawn touched the sky. He wanted to ride to the empty places, the land where he was not likely to meet any of the People, or any whites either. He had left the tribe forever—he wanted to see no more humans. Most of the talk of human beings was silly talk, talk that was of less weight than a man's breath. He had taken leave of all such silliness. He wanted to go where he could only hear the wind, and whatever animals might be moving near him—the little animals, ground squirrels and mice, that lived under the grass.

The thing that Buffalo Hump was most grateful for, as he rode into the emptiness, was the knowledge that in the years of his youth and manhood he had drawn the lifeblood of so many enemies. He had been a great killer; it was his way and the way of his people; no one in his tribe had killed so often and so well. The killings were good to remember, as he rode his old horse deeper into the llano, away from all the places where people came.

27.

"I FEEL LIKE I've been around this ring once too often, Woodrow," Augustus said. "Don't you? The same governor we used to work for wants to send us after the same outlaw we ought to have killed way back when Inish Scull was our boss."

The governor he was referring to was E. M. Pease, one of the few able men willing to take the provisional governorship under the terms of a harsh Reconstruction; the outlaw in question was Blue Duck, whose band of murderers was making travel hazardous from the Sabine to the Big Wichita. The army was busy trying to subdue the few remaining free Comanches; the rangers were depleted in numbers and in spirit, but they were still the only force capable of dealing with general lawlessness of a magnitude likely to be beyond the scope of local sheriffs.

"I agree we ought to have killed him then," Call said. "But we didn't. Now will have to do."

"I dislike it!" Augustus said. His face was red and his neck swelled, as it was likely to do when he was in a temper. Why the temper, Call didn't understand. Governor Pease had been meek as a mouse when he called them in and asked them to go after Blue Duck.

"I can see you're riled but I don't know why," Call said. "Governor Pease was polite—he's always been polite."

"I ain't a policeman, that's why I'm riled," Augustus said. "I don't mind hanging a fat bandit, or a skinny one either, if they're handy, but I've been a free ranger all this time and I don't like being told that all I'm good for is hanging bandits and putting drunks in jail. We ain't to fight Indians now, unless it's to save our hair. We can't chase a bandit across the Rio Grande. I feel handcuffed and I'm ready to quit."

"You've been ready to quit ever since you joined up with Major Chevallie," Call said.

He knew, though, that Gus's complaint was mainly valid. All they had been given to do lately was cool off feuding families, of which there were plenty among the land-grabbing settlers pushing into lands the Comanches were no longer able to contest. The country was changing—it wasn't the Governor's fault.

Call meant to point out that Blue Duck was no modest bandit. He was Buffalo Hump's son, and his gang of ruffians had taken more than forty lives along the military trail that led from Fort Smith to Santa Fe. That trail, blazed by the great Captain Marcy himself, passed through the Cross Timbers and the southern plains.

Before he could present his arguments, though, Augustus marched into a saloon—when in town, he was seldom outside the saloons. Whenever he was annoyed or bored, Augustus drank—and he was all too frequently annoyed or bored. In that, he was no exception, of course; the frontier was laced with whiskey.

What Call could not contest was Gus's fury at the diminished status of the rangers. For years the rangers had provided what protection the frontier families had; it was hard, now, to find themselves treated as no better than local constables. Call, as much as Gus, wanted to be done with it, but he could not feel right about refusing a request from Governor Pease, a kind man who had fought with the legislature many times in his earlier term to get the rangers what they needed in the way of supplies, horses, and weaponry.

He thought that catching or killing Blue Duck was something they ought to do—once they had done it, that would be enough. They could quit their rangering then, though what they would do once they quit he didn't know. Cattle ranching was the new thing—hundreds of thousands of Texas cattle were being driven north every year now. Once, while in San Antonio, he and Gus had ridden out with Captain King to watch one of his herds pass—some four thousand cattle in all. They were being skillfully handled by experienced vaqueros, a sight that interested Call but immediately bored Gus, for the vaqueros were mainly letting the cattle graze along at their own pace.

"Watching weeds turn brown is more interesting than this," Augustus said. "I could have stayed in the saloon and looked out the window at a donkey eating a prickly pear. It would have been just as much fun, and besides, I'd be drunk."

This sally caused Captain King to laugh heartily.

"Use your mind's eye, Captain," he said. "Think of the East, the teeming millions."

"The what?" Gus asked.

"The people, sir," Captain King said. "The millionaires and the beggars. The English, the Irish, the Italians, the Poles—the Swedes and the Jews. People in the finest New York mansions will soon be eating this beef. The cooks in Boston, Baltimore, Philadelphia, and Washington will soon be cooking it."

"Why, what a bother—you'd take cattle all that way so a bunch of foreigners can eat beef? Let them grow their own beef, I say."

"But there's no room, sir—the East is mighty crowded," Captain King explained. "Beef is what will bring Texas back from the war. Cotton won't do it. There's too damn much cotton in the world now. But beef? That's different. All the starving Irish who have never tasted anything except the potato in their entire lives will pay for beef."

"Me, I'd rather have whores," Augustus said.

"Me, sorting dry goods, no thank you," Augustus had said, when Call once mentioned the possibility of their buying a store. He had given a similarly dismissive reply to several other ideas Call had floated. Only the notion of running a livery stable seemed to arouse his interest, if only because—as Gus envisioned the enterprise—there would be Pea Eye and Deets to do the work, whereas he would take the money to the bank and perhaps wet his whistle, against the drought, on the way back.

The thought of owning a livery stable affected Gus much as the thought of the beef-eating millionaires affected Captain King. Every time a livery stable was mentioned, around the bunkhouse, Gus would get a light in his eye and would soon be spinning notions that made the contemplated livery stable unlike any Call, or Pea, or Deets had ever seen.

"Of course, we wouldn't have to just rent horses," he said, one blazing day when the group of them were sitting in the shade of a big mesquite, behind the bunkhouse.

"No, we could rent a mule or two, if we had a couple," Call allowed, only to draw from Augustus the look of scorn he reserved for the hopelessly unimaginative.

"I wasn't talking about mules, Woodrow," he said. "A mule is just a lesser horse, and so is a donkey."

"They may be lesser, but a lot of people would rather rent a mule than a horse, I imagine," Pea Eye said. "A mule won't step in a hole, and a horse will."

"You're out of your depth when it comes to commerce, Pea," Gus said. "You should keep your tongue back there behind your teeth."

Call was puzzled.

"What other kind of animals would you be renting, then?" he asked, though he knew Augustus was probably just launching into one of the elaborate leg pulls he loved so much. He particularly loved them when he had the credulous Deets and Pea to confound and dumbfound.

"Well, we could rent sheep and goats and laying hens," Augustus said, without hesitation.

"Laying hens? Why would anybody pay to rent a hen?" Call asked.

"It could be that a salesman had just come to town for a few days," Gus said. "He might want a nice raw egg with his coffee and of course he'd prefer it to be fresh. We could rent him a hen for a day or two so he'd have his egg."

The answer had a certain logic to it—such a thing *could* happen, though Call knew it never would. That was the devilish thing about arguing with Augustus: he could always come up with answers that made sense about schemes that would never happen.

"How much would I have to pay if I was to rent a hen from you for a day or two, Gus?" Pea Eye asked.

"If it was one of those nice speckled hens I expect I'd require a quarter a day," Augustus said. "If it was just one of those plain brown hens I might let you rent her for fifteen cents."

"All right, but why would anyone want to rent a sheep or a goat?" Dan Connor asked. He was a small, feisty ranger who had joined the troop after Jake left.

"Well, our same salesman might want a sheep around because the odor of sheep repels mosquitoes," Augustus said. "He might want to hitch a sheep at the foot of his bed so the skeeters wouldn't bite him too hard."

That answer, which Augustus delivered with a straight face, stopped conversation for a while, as the various rangers tried to remember if they had slept free of mosquitoes while there was a sheep around. Of course, there *were* no sheep in Austin, and very few anywhere in Texas, so the theory was hard to test.

"What would a goat do, then?" Pea Eye inquired.

"Goats eat up the trash," Deets ventured, unexpectedly. Though he always listened intently to the general conversation, he rarely contributed a remark, especially not if one of the captains was around. Alone with Pea Eye, though, Deets had plenty to say.

"That's it, Deets—that's it," Augustus declared. "Your salesman might have some old ledgers or a few bills of lading he wants to dispose of. We'd rent him a goat for thirty cents a day and the problem would be solved."

"How about pigs, then, Captain?" Dan Connor asked. "A pig has got as good an appetite as a goat. How much would a pig rent for?"

At that Augustus looked stern.

"Oh, we wouldn't be renting no pigs, couldn't afford to, Dan," he said. "It might lead to lawsuits."

"Why would renting a pig lead to lawsuits?" Call asked. He had had enough of the conversation and was about to take a walk, but he thought he would hear how Augustus justified his remark about pigs and lawsuits.

"Now the difficulty with a pig is that it's smarter than most human beings and it has a large appetite," Gus said. "A pig might even eat a customer, if the customer was drunk and not alert. Or it might at least eat one of his legs, if it was in the mood to snack. Or it could eat his coat off, or swallow the nice belt buckle his wife had given him for his birthday, which would get him in trouble at home and cause a passel of bad feelings. Even if it didn't mean a lawsuit it might cause him to tell all his friends not to rent from us, which could mean a sag in the profits."

At that point Call walked off, as Gus was regaling his audience with his wildest scheme yet, which was to locate a zebra somewhere and teach it to pull a wagon, after which they could rent the zebra and the wagon together at a steep price for all manner of festivities.

"It might work for weddings," Augustus allowed. "We could teach it to pull the buggy that the bride and groom ride in."

"As I recall, you walked to your weddings," Call said. "I doubt anyone in this part of the country could afford to rent a zebra, even if we had one, which we don't."

The one point the two of them agreed on was that their future, once they left the rangers, would not be spent in Austin. They had been there too long, seen too much of politics, and had arrested, for one crime or another, a relative of virtually every person in town;

they had also hung, for murder or horsethievery, quite a few men who had been popular in the saloons. They had been the local law too long—it was time to move.

Call walked on to the lots, to begin to get the horses ready for their attempt to catch Blue Duck. The boy Newt was there, as he usually was, practicing his roping on the chickens. Call wondered sometimes about Maggie—since Jake Spoon's departure she had not been seen in the company of a man. Augustus, who gossiped about everyone, had no gossip to dispense about Maggie Tilton. Call remembered the night he had walked all the way down the San Antonio road to the split tree, but he could not bring to mind exactly what his upset had been about. Something had gone wrong between himself and Maggie—he had not been up her steps since she threw the cornmeal at him.

Sometimes he missed Maggie, and would have liked to sit with her for an hour, and enjoy one of her tasty beefsteaks. Still, he knew he was better off than Augustus, who still pined so severely for Clara Allen that the mere sight of her handwriting on an envelope would send him into the saloons for a long bout of drinking. Often Gus would keep one of Clara's letters for a week before he could even work up to opening it. He never said much about the letters, though he did once remark that Clara had lost a boy—a year or two later he remarked that she had lost another boy.

Augustus, when he chose to employ it, had a great gift for politics. He could persuade better than any governor or senator Call had ever met. Gus could easily have been elected a senator, and gone to Washington; he could have been elected governor. And yet, because he had lost the love of the one woman he really wanted, Clara Allen, Augustus had stayed a ranger. Once or twice Gus did consider running for office, but then another letter from Clara would come and he'd drink and put off reading it for a week. It seemed, to Woodrow Call, a strange way to live a life.

28.

LAST HORSE was sitting idly by the fire, sharpening one of his knives on a whetstone, when it gradually dawned on him what the women were saying. The women were always talking some ribaldry or other. Last Horse didn't understand why they talked about coupling so much since most of them, including his two wives, were rarely eager to couple with him—but such was the talk of women, year in and year out. He had only been half listening until one of them mentioned Buffalo Hump. Even though Buffalo Hump was old now some of the women still speculated about coupling with him; but that was not what they were talking about this morning. It was only when he realized that the women were claiming that the old chief had left the camp that Last Horse suddenly realized that something important had happened.

What they said was true: Buffalo Hump's lodge appeared to be empty; there was no sign that he had used it for two or three days. Last Horse started to go inside the lodge and see if Buffalo Hump had left anything behind, but when he got to the entrance he stopped. Buffalo Hump was unpredictable; he might be in his lodge, waiting quietly for some fool to slip in and try to rob him. He might be waiting with his big knife.

Even if he wasn't waiting, even if he was truly gone, entering his lodge was not a step to be taken lightly. After all, he might only have gone on a hunt; he might return and make an issue of the fact that his lodge had been entered without his permission. Last Horse hesitated—he had been afraid of Buffalo Hump all his life. Even if he knew that Buffalo Hump were dead he would have felt the need for caution. Such a chief would have a powerful spirit, one that might come back and work evil on interferers. Alive or dead, Buffalo Hump was a power Last Horse did not want to confront. He immediately got his rifle and set off for the northeast, to look for Blue Duck.

Last Horse had grown up with Blue Duck. Last year, while on a hunt, he had run into Blue Duck and some of his men; he feared trouble, but instead Blue Duck was friendly and even gave him some of his whiskey, a liquid he liked very much, although the sickness that came the next day was not pleasant.

In the morning, to his surprise, Blue Duck had given him two pistols and a watch. Later in the day, while still feeling the unpleasantness that resulted from drinking so much whiskey, Last Horse had a most unfortunate accident while trying to load one of his new pistols. Because he was a little shaky he let the hammer slip while the pistol was pointed at his foot, the result being that he shot off the middle toe on his right foot. Such a foolish accident caused Last Horse great embarrassment, but it amused the ruffians who rode with Blue Duck very much. They began to tease him and call him Lost Toe—their rude behavior annoyed Last Horse greatly. Before he left to go home Blue Duck himself brewed some leaves and made a little poultice to put on his toe.

"How do you know how to make medicine?" Last Horse asked.

"A witch woman taught me," Blue Duck said.

Then he revealed the real reason he had been so generous with Last Horse: he wanted Last Horse to keep an eye on Buffalo Hump and let him know if the old man left the camp to go on a hunt or a journey. Blue Duck made no secret of the fact that he meant to kill Buffalo Hump. All the Comanches, including Buffalo Hump, had known of Blue Duck's intentions for many years, but Buffalo Hump, old as he was, feared no one and didn't let the threat keep him from going where he pleased.

Blue Duck showed Last Horse a fine rifle, with silver on the stock. He promised to give Last Horse the rifle if he would come quickly and let him know if Buffalo Hump left camp.

Once back with the tribe, Last Horse could not get the fine rifle out of his mind, or the whiskey either. That is why the women's news excited him so.

Last Horse asked all the warriors if Buffalo Hump had mentioned where he was going—he even asked Kicking Wolf, a man he was afraid of—but Buffalo Hump had spoken to no one. He had just ridden away. Kicking Wolf seemed a little surprised by the news. He took the trouble to ride out to the horse herd, to see if he could determine how many horses Buffalo Hump had taken with him; when he came back he seemed subdued. He went himself to Buffalo Hump's lodge, to examine the horse tracks—once he had done so he seemed even more subdued.

"He only took that one old horse," Kicking Wolf said. "He has gone to find a place to die."

Last Horse did not wait to question Kicking Wolf further. He set off at once to find Blue Duck. He knew he had to get to Blue Duck as soon as possible; if he delayed, Buffalo Hump might go on and die, in which case Blue Duck would have no reason to give him the rifle.

Last Horse did not feel entirely right about his errand, though. He knew that he was doing a thing that would not be approved of. Buffalo Hump had been a great chief, but Blue Duck was only an outlaw. The People might scorn him for taking Blue Duck such news, but Last Horse kept riding east anyway. He felt sad but he kept riding; his sadness wasn't just from the knowledge that he was doing something that was not too honorable. In the great days of the Comanche people it would not have occurred to him to betray a chief to a brash outlaw who happened to be his son.

The farther Last Horse went from the camp and the tribe, the more he began to doubt that he could ever go back and live among the People again. With the People he was always hungry; everyone in the band was always hungry. The great days of feasting were over. Peta, their leader, had talked to the whites more than once lately; it would not be long before the band would have to move onto the land the whites wanted them to have.

Because of that, Last Horse felt less bad about what he was doing. He pressed his horse until the horse was lathered white with sweat. There was nothing behind him but sickness and starvation; if he rode with Blue Duck there would at least be food, because Blue Duck hunted in the forests where the deer were still thick.

When Blue Duck saw Last Horse coming, his horse pushed

almost to the point of death, he immediately slipped his ammunition belts over his shoulder. If the Comanche had run his horse almost to death it could only be because he had urgent news of Buffalo Hump. Blue Duck went to a little wagon where he kept his whiskey and pulled out a bottle, which he handed to Last Horse as soon as the Comanche stepped off his stumbling mount.

"You have killed your horse, we might as well eat him," Blue Duck said. "I don't know why you were in such a hurry, unless you have a big thirst for whiskey."

Last Horse was almost as tired as his mount. He wanted to deliver his news at once, before he started drinking the whiskey.

"Buffalo Hump left," he said. "He took only one horse and he went northwest. Kicking Wolf says he has gone away to die. Now can I have that pretty gun?"

He saw the rifle he had been promised, propped against a wagon wheel, the sun glinting off the silver on the stock. Blue Duck walked over and picked it up; he looked at it carefully, as if he had never seen it before. Then, instead of giving it to Last Horse, as he had promised, he pointed it at him instead.

"This gun is too good for a thieving Comanche like you," Blue Duck said. "But since you are here I can let you have the bullets."

Blue Duck fired twice; the bullets spun Last Horse around and knocked him to his knees. Several grasshoppers were hopping in the brown grass. Last Horse fell forward. His eyes were still open when one of the yellow grasshoppers hopped onto his face.

Blue Duck took the unopened whiskey bottle out of his hand and put it back in the little wagon. Ermoke, who had been about to snatch it, was disappointed.

29.

AFTER KILLING LAST HORSE, a man so foolish he had shot off his own toe, Blue Duck needed only a few minutes to complete his preparations for his journey in pursuit of Buffalo Hump. He caught four of his fastest horses, because he wanted to travel fast and far. Although he didn't expect much resistance from the old man himself, it was hard to predict what one might encounter on the prairies, so he made sure he was well armed. The week before, his men had come upon two buffalo hunters whose hide wagon had broken down, and had killed them both, mainly in order to get their supply of tobacco, a substance always in short supply around the camp. Blue Duck didn't care about the tobacco himself, but he was always pleased to capture the buffalo hunters' heavy rifles and their ammunition.

Now he strapped one of their big fifty-caliber rifles on one of the horses, an action that aroused the suspicions of Ermoke and Monkey John. They knew that Blue Duck had it in mind to kill his father someday, but they were not aware of the news Last Horse had brought. When they saw Blue Duck making ready to leave, with four horses and a buffalo gun, they assumed he must be going to ambush somebody rich. Blue Duck made no effort to divide treasures when he killed or captured some traveler. He always kept everything for himself, and frequently bullied other members of the robber gang to give him some of their spoils. It was a source of annoyance. When Ermoke complained, which he only did when he was drunk, Blue Duck laughed at him. Two or three men immediately went over and searched the dead Comanche, Last Horse, but he had nothing on him except a knife and one of the pistols Blue Duck had given him earlier—it was the pistol he had used to shoot off his own toe.

When Blue Duck was ready he simply rode away, without saying a word to anyone. As soon as he was out of sight, Ermoke and Monkey John caught their horses and followed him. They caught up with him about three miles from camp. Both men were a little nervous; when Blue Duck acted as if he didn't want company it was well to be cautious. His killing moods were unpredictable. Neither of them had expected him to kill the Comanche who had ridden into camp—earlier he had been quite friendly with the man. Certainly the Comanche had not expected to be killed. He had ridden his horse to death to reach Blue Duck quickly. But now he was dead, and so was his horse. The women were butchering it as Ermoke and Monkey John rode away.

Blue Duck didn't say a word when the two men joined him on his ride to the west. He knew they had followed thinking he was about to kill some traveler with a lot of money. Though it was impertinent for the two to join him when he hadn't asked for their company, he decided to let them come. They didn't know he was only riding off to kill an old Comanche who owned nothing worth stealing. They would make a long ride for nothing, which would serve them right.

Once they found Buffalo Hump, Blue Duck meant to inform the two killers that only he was to kill the old man—he did not want them to interfere. The mission he was on was one he had waited for since he left the tribe. Blue Duck had forgotten none of the insults Buffalo Hump had heaped on him: now he meant to have his revenge.

Blue Duck was convinced, too, that he knew where his father would go to make his death. Long ago, when Blue Duck was a boy of seven or eight, before his father began to insult him, Buffalo Hump had taken him on a long ride to Black Mesa, west of the Beaver River, in country that was so dry Blue Duck thought they might die of thirst. But Buffalo Hump did not intend to die of thirst—he knew of an old lake near Black Mesa, a lake that was then dry. What Buffalo Hump knew was that there was a little seeping spring in the center of the dry lake, hidden under weeds. They had ridden two days without water before they came to the dry lake and found the little seeping spring; Blue Duck had never forgotten the taste of that cool water, and he never told anyone else about the existence of the spring. Buffalo Hump had told him that the People had lived near Black Mesa long before his own time, when they were just becoming a horse people. He had said it was a place of powerful spirits. Blue Duck had a clear memory of the journey and felt sure he could find the dry lake again, and the little spring. He wanted to hurry, though. Last Horse had said that Buffalo Hump had left with only one horse, and an old one at that. If the horse weakened, Buffalo Hump might die before he reached the mesa. Blue Duck rode hard all day, switching horses often so as not to wear out his mounts. Ermoke and Monkey John, foolishly, had not brought extra horses. They had assumed that Blue Duck must be after a victim fairly close to camp, which only showed Blue Duck how stupid they were. They had seen him ride out with four horses—did they think the other three were only to carry loot from his ambush?

Blue Duck showed them no mercy, where speed was concerned. If they rode their horses to death he meant to leave them; if they starved before they could get back to camp it was what they deserved. By the afternoon of the third day Ermoke and Monkey John were far behind. Already they were on a part of the llano they didn't know, and it was very dry. Both men knew Blue Duck would not wait for them, or show them any consideration at all.

Monkey John began to regret that they had come—as usual, Ermoke had been hasty in his judgment. If their horses failed in such country they would probably die.

"Who's he going to rob, out here?" Monkey John asked, several times. "There don't nobody live way out here."

Ermoke didn't answer. He was watching the ground, determined not to lose Blue Duck's track.

"We ought to have brought more horses," Monkey John said, a little later, when he began to feel the force of the desert. They were in a great ring of empty land; the horizons seemed a hundred miles away.

Ermoke was thinking that if Blue Duck didn't slow down he might have to kill Monkey John. That way he would have another horse.

30.

CALL HAD NO TROUBLE persuading Famous Shoes to help them find Blue Duck's camp. Famous Shoes liked to be free to go anywhere at any time, across the plains, into the forests, down to Mexico, over the mountains. The Kickapoo people were widely scattered now— he had to be able to move freely in order to visit his own people. Recently, though, because of Blue Duck and his renegades, he had had to recognize that it was unwise to travel north of the Trinity River, unless he went very far to the west to do it. Famous Shoes did not want to get killed, and he knew that Blue Duck would kill him without hesitation if he found him alone. He well remembered that Blue Duck had once delivered him to Slow Tree, thinking he was delivering him to torture. Slow Tree had let him go, but Blue Duck would not let him go if he caught him now.

So when Captain Call came to him and said that the rangers were going after Blue Duck, Famous Shoes immediately made ready to go with them.

Four days later Captain Call, Captain McCrae, eight rangers, and several sheriffs were hidden in a clump of timber near the south bank of the Red River, waiting for Famous Shoes to find the renegades and let them know how many fighting men they would have to face.

Famous Shoes easily found the renegades' camp, but he soon saw that Blue Duck wasn't there. He knew this news would displease Captain Call and Captain McCrae, and he was right.

"Who *is* there, if he ain't?" Augustus asked impatiently.

"There are twelve men and some women—they are cooking a horse," Famous Shoes said. "Ermoke is not there either. He is a man who rapes whenever he can."

"Where the hell is Blue Duck?" Gus asked. "I hate to waste time on the chiggers he left behind. The sheriffs can handle them."

"Gus, we're here—we might as well help the sheriffs do this job," Call said. "Maybe some of the men know where he went."

"Blue Duck has gone west and he is in a hurry," Famous Shoes said. "He took four horses and two men."

"That's it, let's go get after him," Augustus said.

Call looked at the sheriffs, all local men. They did not look happy at the prospect of being left to fight a dozen renegades. All were poor men—probably they had just agreed to serve as sheriffs because they feared starvation if they tried to continue as farmers or merchants. Money was short and jobs scarce in Texas at the time.

"No, let's help the sheriffs round up these outlaws," Call said. "The sheriffs would be outnumbered if we leave."

In the event, the renegades in Blue Duck's camp didn't fight at all. One man did raise his rifle when the rangers came charging into camp, but he was immediately shot dead. Then ten dirty, half-starved men threw up their hands—the twelfth man managed to wiggle out of the back of a tent into some reeds by the river. He escaped that day but was killed two days later in Shreveport, Louisiana, while trying to rob a hardware store.

Once the renegades were disarmed Deets was given the job of tying them. Jake Spoon, before he left, taught Deets what he knew about knots. Call and Augustus were ready to hand the prisoners over to the sheriffs, but the sheriffs balked.

One of the sheriffs, whose name was Kettler, pointed to a grove of oak trees not far from the river.

"We can't be putting the county to the expense of raising no jury," he said. "It's planting time. The men need to be in their fields. I ain't asking them to take off just to try a bunch of bad 'uns like these men.

"Your nigger there is good with knots," he added. "We'd be obliged if you'd wait long enough for him to tie the hang knots."

Call looked at Augustus, who shrugged.

"I expect they're all horsethieves, at least," Gus said, pointing to the sizable horse herd grazing nearby.

"All right," Call said. "If they're with Blue Duck I've no doubt they need hanging."

None of the doomed men said even a word in their own defense, and none of the slatternly women followed the little procession to the oak grove. The women seemed numbed by the morning's events—they sat in dejection near one of the smoldering oak grove campfires.

"I hope you'll at least take these women with you, Sheriff Kettler," Call said. "I imagine some of them were captives. They'll starve if you leave them."

"We won't leave them," the sheriff promised.

When they got to the oak grove they discovered that there was no one tree with a limb strong enough or low enough to hang all the men from. Deets, who rarely betrayed any sign of nerves no matter how dangerous the conflict, looked uncertain as he searched among the oak trees for a suitable hanging tree. He had never tied a hang knot and was conscious that the eyes of the several hard sheriffs were upon him. He was being asked to hang white men, ten at that. He knew he had to do it, though; besides worrying that he might not get the knots right—the lariat ropes he had to work with were of uneven strength and texture—he had already begun to worry about the fact that he would soon be setting ten ghosts loose, ghosts that might pursue him and work spells against him. None of the ten condemned men had made any effort to plead for their lives. They stood silently among the sheriffs and rangers, looking like whipped dogs.

"Here's one good stout limb," Augustus said. "It ought to hold four of them, at least."

"I'd make that three," Sheriff Kettler said, looking at the limb in question with a practiced eye. "If you hang men too close together they're apt to bump into one another while they're swinging."

"What would it matter, if they're swinging?" Augustus said.

Call found the proceedings an irritant. Time was being wasted. If only the outlaws had put up a fight they could have shot several of them and not had to proceed with such a lengthy hanging. Finally three limbs were selected. The men were put on borrowed horses; Deets carefully tied the hang knots just as he had seen Jake do. Two limbs held three men each and another limb held four. The sheriffs grouped the men carelessly, so that the tallest man ended up hanging from the lowest and weakest limb. His toes, when he bounced on the rope, were less than an inch from the ground.

Deets, despite his conviction that a passel of spells would soon be unleashed against him, did a careful job. None of the knots failed. The heavier men died instantly, while the lighter fellows kicked and swayed for several minutes. Only the tall man occasioned much of a wait. At the end of ten minutes he was still alive. Call, impatient, wanted to shoot him, but knew that would be improper procedure. Finally the man ceased to kick, but, by the time they were ready to ride off, the limb had sagged so much that the tall man's toes rested on the ground.

"I thank you for obliging me," Sheriff Kettler said to Call and Augustus. "This has saved the county a passel of expense."

"Don't forget the women," Call said, as they rode away.

Famous Shoes, too, was impatient—he did not understand the Texans' preference for hanging. If they didn't want to torture the men, why not just shoot them? It would have been much quicker.

As they rode away Call observed that Augustus seemed unusually melancholy.

"What's wrong with you?" he asked.

"It's gloomy work, hanging men in the morning," Augustus said. "Here the sun's up and it's a nice day, but they won't get to live it."

"Besides," he added a little later, "I get to thinking that, but for luck, it could have been me hanging there."

Call was startled by the remark.

"You—why would it have been you?" he asked. "Ornery as you are, I don't think you deserve a hanging."

"No, but for luck I might have," Augustus said, turning in his saddle to take one last look at the grove where the ten bodies hung.

31.

AT NIGHT FAMOUS SHOES ranged far ahead of the rangers, who could not push their mounts any harder without putting them at risk. It was the night of the full moon—the prairies were almost as light as day. The tracks of the men they were chasing had not changed direction all day. Blue Duck and the two men with him were heading northwest, into the deepest part of the llano, a course that puzzled Famous Shoes. They would soon be on the long plain of New Mexico, where there was no water. Even the Antelope Comanche had to be careful when they traveled there; he had heard that sometimes the Antelopes had to cut open a horse in order to drink the liquids in the horse's stomach. That they could do such things was the reason they had not yet been conquered by the whites. So far the bluecoat soldiers lacked the skills that would enable them to attack the Antelopes.

But Blue Duck was not of the Antelope band. He raided in country where there was plenty of water. He would be foolish to think he could continue across the llano and not get in trouble. Besides, there was no one in that country at all—no one, at least, to rob or kill. Of course, there was Quanah and his band, but they were poor, and, anyway, if Blue Duck came near them, they would promptly kill him and his companions.

And yet, the tracks didn't turn. They pointed straight into the longest distance of the llano. Famous Shoes thought that perhaps Blue Duck meant to go to Colorado, to the settlements, where no doubt there were plenty of people to rob. But if he meant to go to Colorado he could have gone along the Arkansas River, where there was plenty of water.

Late in the night Famous Shoes went back to the rangers. Although the tracks of Blue Duck and his men were plain, he had learned that it was not wise to assume that the Texans would see what to him was plain. The Texans—even experienced men such as Captain Call and Captain McCrae—had curious eyes. He could never be confident that he knew what they would see, when following a trail. Often they took incorrect routes which had to be corrected with much loss of time.

In such dry country Famous Shoes did not want to risk having the rangers go astray. When he came, the rangers were just finishing their brief breakfast. Famous Shoes saw to his surprise that Pea Eye Parker had his trousers off—one of his legs was an angry red. Deets was studying the leg carefully, a big needle in his hand.

"Bad luck," Call said, when Famous Shoes approached. "He

knelt on a cactus when he went to hobble his horse. Now his leg's as bad as if he had been snakebit."

When Famous Shoes was shown the cactus in question, he agreed with the captain's assessment. The thorns of the little green cactus were as poisonous as the bite of a rattlesnake.

"The thorn's under the kneecap," Augustus said.

"Get it out," Famous Shoes said. "If you get it out he will soon be well, but if you leave it in his leg he will never walk far again."

"Go to it, Deets—otherwise Pea will have to retire," Gus said.

When Deets finally succeeded in coaxing the tiny tip of the cactus thorn out of Pea Eye's leg, he and all the other men were surprised that such a tiny thorn could produce such a bad inflammation. But Famous Shoes was right. In ten minutes Pea Eye declared himself fit for travel.

Famous Shoes took a little coffee and made a thorough inspection of the rangers' horses. What he found did not please him. Only five or six of the horses looked strong enough to go where Blue Duck was going.

"If you know where he's going, I wish you'd tell us," Call said, although he knew it was probably unwise to put a direct question to the tracker. Famous Shoes had never ceased to madden and frustrate him. Sometimes he would speak as plainly as a white man, but, at other times, no amount of questioning would produce any but the most elliptical replies.

"I don't know where he is going unless it is to Black Mesa," Famous Shoes said. "I don't know why he would want to go there. It is where the Comanches used to go to pray, but I don't know if that is why he is going."

"Doubtful. He don't strike me as being a man of prayer," Augustus said. "I never heard of Black Mesa. How far away is it?"

"It is a mesa where the rocks are black," Famous Shoes said. "I have never been there—there is no water in that country. His men have only one horse apiece. They will die if they try to follow him."

He looked around at the rangers, hoping that Captain Call or Captain McCrae would understand what he meant, which was that they should send most of the men home. He thought either of the captains would be a match for Blue Duck: he saw no reason why they should take eight rangers into the driest part of the llano and try to keep them alive.

Call and Augustus immediately took his point, which was that they too had more men than they could hope to keep alive.

"There's only three outlaws," Call said to Augustus. "I'd say that Pea and Deets are all we need. We better send the rest of these men home while they can find their way."

"*If* they can find their way," Augustus said. "We're way out here in the big empty. They might just ride around in circles until they fall over and drop."

Call knew there was a chance that Gus was right. Few men were truly competent at navigating the deceptive, featureless plains. Even experienced plainsmen sometimes lost confidence in their judgments, or even in their compasses. Some familiar-looking ridge or rise in the ground would tease their memories and tempt them to rethink their course, often with serious or even fatal consequences.

Augustus looked around. It was a beautiful spring day; the sweep of the long horizons was appealing, and yet, except for the arch of the sun, there was nothing in sight that would suggest direction. Some of the men had already become nervous, at the thought of being left with no guide.

"These men hired on to ranger, Woodrow, let 'em ranger on back home," Gus said. A few minutes later, six nervous, apprehensive men, under the nominal leadership of Stove Jones, were trotting away to the southeast, toward the distant rivers and the even more distant settlements. Call, Augustus, Pea Eye, and Deets kept one pack mule. More important, they kept Famous Shoes.

While the men who were being sent home were saddling up and dividing the few supplies, Famous Shoes walked a few hundred yards to the north, to smell the wind. It disturbed him that he could not sense where Blue Duck was going, or what he might do. Why the man would simply plunge into the llano, far from any route where travelers went, puzzled him—and it was while he was walking around in puzzlement that the owl flew out of the ground. A great white owl, with wings as wide as a man's arm spread, suddenly rose right at his feet, in his face. The owl flew from a hole in the ground, near a ridge with a few rocks on it. That the owl flew so near his face frightened Famous Shoes badly—so badly that he stumbled as he tried to run back to camp. His heart began to pound; he had never been so frightened, not even when a brown bear tried to catch him on the Brazos once. The owl that flew in his face went up high and glided over the rangers—it was snow white.

Of course Famous Shoes knew that little brown owls sometimes went into prairie dog holes to catch snakes, or to eat the young prairie dogs—but this was not such an owl. This owl had been snow white, though it was not winter and there was no reason for a white owl to be rising out of a hole on a ridge. Captain Call and Captain McCrae looked up at it, and then it flew so far that Famous Shoes lost it in the white sunlight.

Of course the owl meant death—thus it had always been. But it was not an ordinary owl, so the death it presaged would not be that of an ordinary man. Though Famous Shoes had been very frightened when the owl flew at him, he soon decided that the owl did not want his death. He was only an ordinary man who liked to lie with his wives when he was home and who liked to travel the country when he had got enough, for a time, of lying with his wives. He was a good tracker, too, but not good enough that his death would need to be announced by the appearance of a great white owl.

It was another death, the death of a great man, that the white owl must have come to announce. Famous Shoes thought that one of the captains, who were great men of the Texans, might be about to die. It could mean that Blue Duck's apparent foolishness in journeying into the llano was in fact just a ruse. Maybe somewhere ahead he was plotting an ambush. Maybe he was hiding in a hole somewhere, as the owl had been, waiting to shoot one of the captains.

"Did you see the owl?" Famous Shoes asked, when he reached the captains.

"We seen it, it was right pretty," Captain McCrae said cheerfully. "You don't see too many of them big snow owls low down this way now."

Augustus was happy that the troop had been pared down to the men who were necessary, even though it meant that he would have fewer victims in the event of an evening card game.

Famous Shoes realized then, when he heard Captain McCrae's casual and cheerful tone, that it was as he had always believed, which was that it was no use talking to white men about serious things. The owl of death, the most imposing and important bird he had ever seen, had flown right over the two captains' heads, and they merely thought it was a pretty bird. If he tried to persuade them that the bird had come out of the earth, where the death spirits lived, they would just think he was talking nonsense.

Captain Call was no more bothered by the owl than Captain McCrae, a fact which made Famous Shoes decide not to speak. He turned and led them west again, but this time he proceeded very carefully, expecting that Blue Duck might be laying his ambush somewhere not far ahead, in a hole that one would not notice until it was too late.

32.

As HER STRENGTH began its final ebbing, the thing that tormented Maggie most was the fear in her son's eyes. Newt knew she was dying—everybody knew it. He struggled mightily to relieve her of the household chores. He was an able boy, too: he could cook a little, and clean—if there was a chore to be done that was within his capacity, Maggie seldom had to ask him to do it. He just did it, and did it competently; in that way and many others he reminded her of his father.

Yet it was in thinking of Newt that Maggie found her best peace. She thought she had done a fair job with him. If the rangers or the Stewarts would just take him for a year or two he would be old enough to earn his keep. Maggie hoped it would be the rangers.

"A boy ought to be with his father," she told her friend Pearl Coleman one afternoon. Maggie had managed to get down the steps, meaning to rake a little in her garden, but just getting down the steps exhausted her strength; she was able to do little more than sit amid her bean plants. Newt was particularly fond of green beans and snap peas.

Though Pearl Coleman had suitors aplenty, she had never remarried. Her suitors were mainly men new to the area; most of them didn't know about her rape by the Comanches, didn't know why Long Bill had hung himself. Though Pearl was lonely, she was afraid to remarry. Once the old news came to light her new husband might turn her out, or else do as Long Bill had done.

Because she was lonely and knew that she was never likely to have a child of her own, Pearl offered to take young Newt when Maggie passed.

"He ought to be with his father even if his father won't claim him," Maggie went on.

Pearl had little patience with Woodrow Call, but she didn't want to tire her friend with argument. There would not be many more chances for Maggie Tilton to sit in her garden in the spring sunlight; best not to spoil it.

"Mag, it don't have to be one way or the other," Pearl said. "Newt can stay with me when the menfolks are gone, and bunk with the boys when they're home."

"Well, if you wouldn't mind," Maggie said. It was just a short walk from Pearl's house to the ranger barracks, such as they were. Pearl was such a good cook; it would be a shame for Newt to miss out on her tasty meals.

"I think the Stewarts will be wanting him to work in the store a little, when there's unpacking to do," Maggie said.

Pearl did not particularly like the Stewarts—in her view they were too quick to insist on payment of her bills—but she did not demur. If Newt could earn a quarter now and then, so much the better.

"Everybody in this town likes your boy," Pearl assured her. "He'll be well cared for—you can rest your mind about that."

Maggie knew Pearl was right. There were many kindly folks in Austin who took an interest in Newt—people she had met at church, or served in the store. Hard as times had been, since the war, and poor as most people were, she didn't doubt that people would see that her child was fed and clothed. Knowing that, though, didn't put her mind at rest—how could a mother not worry about her child? She would have liked to have one more good talk with Augustus, about Newt's future; she would have liked, even, to sit at her window and watch Newt practice roping with Deets and Pea Eye—it reassured her to see him with the men who would be his companions once she was gone; it was unfortunate that they had had to leave on patrol just as she felt herself slipping into a deeper weakness.

Newt, in the lots with his rope, would look up every few minutes, to see if he could catch a glimpse of his mother's pale face in her window. He knew his mother was dying; he spent hour after hour with his rope, throwing loops at chickens, or the milk-pen calf, or stumps, or posts, to distract himself a little from this frightening knowledge. He was so proficient with the lariat now that the milk-pen calf and even some of the chickens had taken to stopping submissively when he approached with the rope in his hands.

Sometimes, restless in his apprehension, Newt would walk out of town to the little graveyard. He had been to several funerals now, mostly funerals of people his mother knew from church—and he knew that soon there would have to be a funeral for his mother too. At the graveyard he would sometimes talk to his mother, aimless talk about the rangers, about some superstition Deets had told him, or some belief—such as Deets's belief that Indians lived on the moon, having jumped their horses there at some time long ago when the moon had been only a few feet from the earth. Sometimes Newt would sit and watch the moon rise with Deets, hoping for a glimpse of the Indians; but he could never see them.

Mainly, though, Newt talked at the graveyard so he could get in practice to talk to his mother once she was dead. There were seldom many live people in the graveyard, but there were often one or two, usually an old man or old woman, or a bereaved young husband or wife whose spouse had died unexpectedly. Many times he had heard the old ones muttering over the graves of their loved ones—it seemed to him that talking to the dead must be an accepted practice. Probably the dead continued to want to know about the goings-on of the living; that seemed natural to Newt.

Of course, once his mother died, everything would change. He was hoping that Captain Woodrow and Captain Augustus would allow him to live with the rangers then. Even before his mother got sick he had begun to want to live with the rangers. But even if he had to live with Mrs. Coleman or Mrs. Stewart until he could become a full-fledged ranger himself, it was to be expected that his mother would still want to know what he was doing, how his lessons were going, what had happened at the general store, whether Mrs. Coleman had decided to marry any of the men who wanted to marry her, whether Mrs. Stewart was still hitting Mr. Stewart with the barrel stave when he came in drunk and tardy. Of course, too, she might want to know about Captain Woodrow, or whether there was any news of Jake Spoon, or if Captain Augustus had done anything unusual while drunk. Newt meant to keep a close watch on everything that happened in the community, so that he could come to the graveyard every day or two and give his mother a full report.

When the day was bright, and he was busy with his chores or his lessons, Newt would manage to put out of his mind for a few hours the fact that his mother was dying. He never mentioned his mother's sickness to anyone, not even to Ikey Ripple, who was so old now that he was practically a dead person himself. Ikey and Newt were good friends, though Ikey was so blind now that he had to feel Newt with his hands to make sure he was there. Ikey told Newt terrifying stories about the days when wild Comanche Indians came into town and ripped people's hair right off their heads.

Newt would stop practicing with his rope while Ikey told him stories of the old days, when people often got shot full of arrows, or had their stomachs cut open.

Sometimes, while he talked, Ikey would whittle a stick with his little thin-bladed pocketknife. Although he never looked at the sticks as he whittled them, he never cut himself with the sharp little knife, either. Ikey whittled and whittled, shaving the stick away until it was only a small white sliver of wood, small enough to be used as a toothpick, although, since Ikey only had three or four teeth and didn't really need a toothpick, he would often give the smooth little slivers of wood to Newt, who saved them as treasures.

Scary as Ikey's stories were, nothing frightened Newt as much as laying on his pallet at night listening to his mother's labored breathing. He wished his ma could just sleep peacefully and easily, as she had when he had been younger; he didn't want her to have to draw such hard breaths. Often he would be awake for hours, looking out the window, waiting for his mother's breathing to get easier. He knew, though, that her breathing was growing harder, not easier; when it stopped she wouldn't be well, she would be dead, and would have to be taken to the graveyard and put in the ground.

Then he would have to begin talking to her in a new way: the way the living talked to the dead.

In his fright, in the darkness, Newt would begin to wish more than anything that Captain Woodrow and Captain Augustus would hurry and get back to Austin before his mother died. Every day Newt asked Ikey if he knew when they would be back, and every day Ikey said no, he hadn't heard, they would just be back when they got back.

Of course Captain Woodrow didn't come to see his mother anymore, as he had in earlier years. Though Newt saw him often, in the lots, Captain Woodrow rarely had much to say to him and seldom gave him pennies for sassafras candy now. Still, Newt wanted badly for him to come back. He felt the whole business of his mother's dying would be better taken care of if Captain Woodrow were there, and Captain Gus. They would see that Deets put the grave in a nice spot and see that there was plenty of singing; then, once the funeral was over, maybe they would let him move into the bunkhouse and live until he was big enough to carry a pistol and be a ranger himself.

That was Newt's hope, but he didn't tell it to his mother because she didn't much approve of guns. He didn't intend to mention it while his mother lived; it might make her mad, and when she was mad she coughed up blood, a thing that upset Graciela so that she would start crying and fanning herself and calling out the names of saints, as if it were she, and not his mother, who was dying. Mainly, Newt talked about his dream of having a pistol to Deets and Pea Eye, who saw no reason why he shouldn't have a pistol, and even, now and then, let him hold their own pistols. Sometimes, if they turned their heads, he would even point the pistol at the milk-pen calf, though of course he didn't shoot.

33.

LONG BEFORE Buffalo Hump came to the dry lake where the first people had lain in wait to catch the wild horses that came to refresh themselves at the little seeping spring, he wished he had used better judgment in picking a horse for his own last journey. The problem was that the old horse he had chosen had worn away all his teeth; in the canyon there was tall grass that he could masticate, but on the dry llano, in the vicinity of the Lake of Horses, there was no tall grass. The old horse was reduced to dirtying its nose as it tried to get at the sparse, short grass with its yellow nubs of teeth. Though the horse had frisked along briskly for some twenty miles, its strength soon gave out and it became what it was: an old horse slowly dying for lack of teeth. That was the way of old horses, just as shaky hands and wavery eyesight was the way of old men. Buffalo Hump knew he had made a poor choice. He wanted to reach Black Mesa, to sing his way into death among the black rocks that were the oldest rocks. Some believed that only in the black rocks were the spirits that welcomed one into death.

But, because the old horse had slowed to a walk, Buffalo Hump was still a long way even from the Lake of Horses. He knew, though, that if the little spring was still seeping, the old horse might refresh itself and make it on to Black Mesa.

The old horse was so weak now that he was only stumbling. For a time Buffalo Hump dismounted and led him, a thing he had not had to do in his long life as a horseman. Always, when a horse of his came up lame, he had simply left it, switching to another horse or going on foot if he had no other horse. He had owned many horses in his life and had never let a failing horse slow him down.

But the fact was he had chosen the old black horse to be the horse that would carry him to the place of his death. For him, Buffalo Hump, there would be no more horses; he had to do what he could to get the old horse to take him where he needed to go. It would not do to abandon him, which would leave him afoot in the spirit world; he did not want such a thing to happen. If it did he would be disgraced; all his victories and conquests would be as naught. Where the black horse died, he would die; and he wanted it, if possible, to be where the black rocks were.

For most of a day and all of one night he nursed the old horse along, leading him carefully over the sparse grass, letting him stop to rest when he needed to, watching him nuzzle the sparse brown grass with his stubs of teeth to get a few bites of nourishment. Always, on the llano, Buffalo Hump's eyes had sought the horizon, the distant line drawn by earth and sky. But now, when he looked toward a horizon, there was no line, but a wavering, in which sunlight, sky, and earth were all mixed and indistinct. Once he would have known exactly how far he was from the Lake of Horses and, again, how far from Black Mesa—but he was no longer sure of the distances to either place.

What Buffalo Hump knew was that he must not leave the black horse; their fates were now linked. When the horse stumbled and wanted to stop, Buffalo Hump let him rest. As the horse rested he began to sing again the high songs of the war trail. For a time the old horse did nothing. Then he lifted his head and pricked up his ears, as if hearing again his own hoofbeats from the time of warring.

Buffalo Hump was not singing to the horse—he was singing the memories of his own life—but the horse, once he was rested a little, was able to go a few more miles, though at a slow walk. As the heat of the day grew, though, the horse weakened again, and stopped, though they were not yet to the Lake of Horses.

Now Buffalo Hump began to beat the old horse with his lance. He beat it with all his strength. He twisted the horse's tail and pounded it on the sides with his lance. He was determined, once more, to make a horse go where he wanted it to go, and he succeeded. The black horse, which had been about to sink down and die, quivered while he was being beaten; then he revived and walked on another few miles until Buffalo Hump saw the cracked earth of the dry lake not far ahead. Soon the horse smelled the water from the little spring and became excited. He ran toward the water in a wobbly canter—when Buffalo Hump caught up with him he had pushed aside the thick weeds that hid the spring and was sucking the cold water. The spring was so small that it left only a little film of water around the stems of the weeds.

Nonetheless, it was water—pure water—and it saved both Buffalo Hump and the old black horse. They drank and then drank again. The horse was even able to nibble on the tops of the thick weeds around the spring, nourishment enough to enable him to continue the walk to the north when the cool of the evening came.

Though the horse could eat the tops of the weeds, Buffalo Hump couldn't, and he was out of food. He had his short bow and some snares, but the only animals he saw were some prairie dogs. He could not see well enough to hit one of the prairie dogs with an arrow and did not have the time or the patience to lay an effective snare. He wanted to hurry on to where the black rocks were. In the night, after they left the spring, it was he, rather than the black horse, that faltered. By the middle of the next day he was as unsteady on his feet as a baby just learning to balance himself and stand upright. Buffalo Hump became so weak and unsteady that he mounted the black horse again and made it carry him a few more miles. By the evening, to his joy, he began to see a black rock here and there on the ground, although, strain his eyes as he might, he could see no sign of the mesa land he sought. He began to feel uncertain about the mesa. Perhaps it was only the black rocks that he remembered; perhaps he had imagined the mesa, or dreamed it, or confused it with a mesa in another place. He wasn't sure; but at least he had found the black rocks, the rocks which were said to welcome the dead.

Then, in the heat of the day, the horse fell. It didn't wobble; it simply fell, throwing Buffalo Hump to the ground. Slowly he got up, meaning to beat the horse again and urge him to get up and go on a few more miles, but before he could even find his lance and raise it, the black horse heaved a sigh and died.

For a few minutes Buffalo Hump was upset with himself for having ridden along carelessly, singing battle songs, as if he were a young warrior again, on a spirited warhorse, when in fact he was an old man on a horse that was walking its last steps. If he had dismounted and led the horse again they might have made it a few more miles into the country of the black rocks.

But now it was too late: the horse was dead, and the place where he stood was the place he would die. At least, though, he had reached the place of the black rocks. Buffalo Hump would have preferred to be high on the mesa, looking over the plains where he had spent his life; but that was a thing he had not been granted; he would have to make the best death he could on the spot where his horse had fallen.

Buffalo Hump went to his horse and, with his knife, neatly and quickly took out its eyes and buried them in a small hole. The eyes a horse needed in life were not the eyes it would need when it trod the plains of death. Then he began to gather up as many of the black rocks as he could. He meant to make a ring of rocks in which to sit until he died. He could not find the mesa, which might only be a dream mesa anyway. As he worked, gathering the rocks, he began to remember bits and pieces of his life, scraps of things that had been said to him by various people. Once his memory had been good, but now it was as leaky as a water sack that had been pierced by a thorn. He could not remember very much—just bits and pieces of things said long ago. While memories flowed in and out of his mind, like a river eddying, he worked at gathering the rocks.

As Buffalo Hump was about to finish the ring of black rocks that he meant to sit in until he left his body and became a spirit, he remembered another thing his old grandmother had told him long ago, when he was a boy, too young to ride the war trail. It had been dry in the fall and winter; there were many sandstorms. The sandstorms put his grandmother in a bad mood; she did not like it when the air was dusty. One day when the dogs were turning their tails to the wind that whipped through the camp his grandmother had begun to wail and utter lamentations. Because of her bad mood she began to sing dark prophecies, in which she foresaw the end of the Comanche people. She predicted wars and pestilence; the People would lose their place. The plains would be covered with white people, as numerous as ants; the People would die of their plagues. Then the buffalo would go away and the time of the Comanche would end.

As Buffalo Hump arranged the rocks in a large circle—large because he wanted to show that he was one with the plains, with the great ring of the sky—he realized that his grandmother had prophesied truly. At the time he had thought she was just a bad-tempered old woman who ought to keep her wailing to herself. Now, though, he realized that he had been unjust. The whites *had* swarmed like ants up the rivers, spreading their pestilence, just as his grandmother had predicted. And, as she had predicted, the buffalo had gone.

Evening came. Buffalo Hump seated himself on a fine buffalo robe he had brought with him; he put his bow and his lance and the fine bone shield he had carefully made from the skull of the great buffalo he had killed near to hand. It was a clear day with little wind—the sun sank clearly in the west, free of the yellow haze which blowing sand sometimes produced. Buffalo Hump kept his face turned toward the red light of sunset until the light died and the horizon grew purple. He was sorry to see the sun go. He wanted to keep the sunlight that had bathed him his whole life, but the sun went and the plain darkened; no man could slow the sun.

In the night Buffalo Hump, though weak from lack of food, began to sing a little, though his voice was cracked. Again, he was remembering scraps of things. The wind came up. He was glad he had a good blanket to put over his shoulders. A little dust began to blow, reminding him of his grandmother and her lamentations, her wailings, her prophecies of the end of the Comanche time.

It was then that he remembered his grandmother's prophecy about his own end, a thing he had not thought of in years. She had said that he would only die when his great hump was pierced, and had suggested in her prophecy that this would happen when a dark woman came, riding a white mule and holding aloft a sword. At the time his grandmother made the prophecy Buffalo Hump thought she was just a crazy old woman. Half the old men and old women of the tribe spent their time making strange prophecies. No one paid their mutterings much mind.

But then, a few years later, on a plain west of the Rio Pecos, he *had* seen a dark woman on a white mule, holding aloft a great sword. Buffalo Hump might have tried to kill her, then and there, except that, with her, there had been a naked white woman with a rotting body, singing a high war song and carrying a great snake: a witch, undoubtedly, and a powerful one. All his men had run away at the sight of the naked witch whose body was rotting; even Kicking Wolf had run away. Buffalo Hump had not run, but he did remember his grandmother's prophecy about his hump being pierced. The sight of the witch was so horrible that Buffalo Hump retreated, but he retreated slowly, backing his horse step by step, so that his hump would not be exposed to the dark woman with the sword.

All that had happened so many years before that Buffalo Hump had almost forgotten it. The dark woman with the sword was the servant of a powerful witch—it puzzled him that the witch had made no effort to pierce his hump and kill him.

But then the years began to pass. He fought the Texans and the Mexicans, he stole many captives, he made his first great raid to the sea and then his second; the buffalo were still on the plains and there were hunts to pursue. Buffalo Hump had much to do, trying to drive the white people back so the plains would be free of their smell. The sickness came; it became difficult to find enough good warriors to make war. As the years passed, the memory of the dark woman and the rotting witch faded; his grandmother died and her prophecies were lost, with the many prophecies of the old women of the tribe. He had even forgotten the prophecy about his hump being pierced, but now he remembered it. He remembered how careful he had been not to turn his back on Slow Tree, for fear that Slow Tree would stick him with a lance behind and succeed in killing him.

Though his grandmother had been right about the wars and pestilences, about the whites, and about the departure of the buffalo, it seemed now that she had just been talking nonsense about the dark woman on the white mule. He was dying all right, in a circle of black rocks near the Lake of Horses, but his hump was as it had always been, a thing woven into his muscles, a hunk of gristle that had always been there to slow him when he drew a bow or mounted a horse. He had lived with it and now he would die with it; neither the rotting witch nor Slow Tree would come to pierce it.

Between the setting of the sun and the rising of the moon Buffalo Hump dozed. When he woke he saw a form walking near the ring of black rocks, a white bird which rose when he moved.

The bird was the owl of his dreams, the white owl of death. In flight the owl passed between him and the thin moon and flew away. Though it had annoyed him to see the owl walking around near his circle of rocks, once the owl was gone he relaxed and began to sing his memory songs again. The owl had merely come to tell him to get ready to let his spirit slip away from his body, as the little moths slipped away from caterpillars. Buffalo Hump *was* ready. He was hungry and would not wait too long to slip away.

34.

"FAMOUS SHOES don't like these snow owls—that's four we've seen now," Augustus said. "He thinks it means the world's coming to an end."

"They're just birds," Call said, impatiently. They were in the driest country he had been in since he had been marched as a prisoner across the Jornada del Muerto many years before, a trip that Augustus also had made and survived. This time they were in pursuit of a dangerous man, and had their horses to think of. Finding water for them and their horses was what Famous Shoes ought to be thinking about—water, not the fact that a few snow owls from the north had decided to linger in Texas.

"He ought to be worried about this dry country," Call said. "Not those birds."

Augustus, as usual, found himself having to explain the obvious to Woodrow Call, the obvious being that a white owl meant one thing to a white man and another thing to a Kickapoo tracker.

"He might be right, though, Woodrow," Augustus said. "Maybe the owls mean there ain't no water out here anywhere. If we die of thirst, then the world will have come to an end, don't you see?"

He knew Woodrow Call was a single-minded man who couldn't think about but one problem at a time; but a glance at Pea Eye and Deets, not to mention the agitated Famous Shoes, convinced him that something had to be done to improve company morale, else they would die of worrying before they died of thirst.

Famous Shoes was indeed very upset about the white owls, because they should not be where they were. The white owls were there to bring death. Famous Shoes knew that, and did not care what the whites thought about it. He was very thirsty; so were the other men and so were the horses. That morning, though, he had seen a plover flying north, which meant that there was water somewhere near. Plovers were not birds that flew far. Also, Blue Duck and his two men were still ahead of them, their tracks as plain as rocks. For Famous Shoes, the important thing was that Blue Duck was ahead of them. Where Blue Duck could go, he could go.

Twice Famous Shoes had thought he saw Blue Duck, far ahead, but Captain McCrae, who still had his keen eyesight, insisted that he was wrong—it was only an antelope they saw.

Call and Augustus too could plainly see the tracks bearing to the northwest. The tracks didn't deviate, either, as they would have if Blue Duck and his two companions had been casting about for water. Blue Duck either knew where he was going, or thought he did—he was gambling his life and the lives of the two men with him that water would be where he thought it was.

"Wherever he's going, he's been there before," Call said, when they stopped for the night.

"Yes, he has been there before, and so has the other one," Famous Shoes said.

"Other *one*—I thought you said there were two men riding with Blue Duck," Call said. Augustus protested, confused by the statement.

"There are two men riding with Blue Duck, but there is another one, an old one," Famous Shoes said. "He is the one they are looking for."

"Oh Lord, that's four against us now," Pea Eye said. Although they were five themselves, he feared the Comanche tendency to multiply unexpectedly. If there were four against them today, there might be twenty tomorrow.

"The old one is too old to be dangerous," Famous Shoes said. "He is riding a horse whose feet are split and whose teeth are gone. I think Blue Duck will catch him tomorrow."

"I wish you'd told us about this other one sooner," Call said—like Gus he was confused by the news.

Famous Shoes knew that Captain Call was as smart as any ranger, yet at times he could be stupid as a possum. The tracks of the old man and the old horse were plain to see, right by the other tracks. All of the rangers had missed what was there to see.

"Why would an old man on a poor mount be in a place like this?" Augustus asked. "That's question number one, and question number two is, why would Blue Duck be following him? I doubt he's rich enough to rob."

Famous Shoes had been too preoccupied with the question of the white owls to give much thought to the questions Captain McCrae raised. The white owls had distracted him so much that he had almost forgotten about Blue Duck. But, once he stopped thinking about the owls, it was not hard to know the answers to Captain McCrae's questions.

"The old one is looking for a good place to die," Famous Shoes said.

"Lord, if that's all he wants, he can stop looking," Augustus said. "He's found his place to die."

"Blue Duck is following him because he wants to kill him," Famous Shoes said. "He doesn't want to let him die of thirst. He wants to kill him. The old man is Buffalo Hump. He twists his foot when he steps, because of the hump. I should have remembered this, but I was thinking about the owls."

The name gave all the rangers a start. No one had mentioned Buffalo Hump to them in several years—not since the beginning of the war.

"Buffalo Hump? We thought he was dead," Call replied, startled.

"Blue Duck is his son, I recall," Augustus said. "He ran to his father's camp that day he killed Jimmy Watson."

"It was cold that day," Pea Eye said. He didn't remember the Indians very well, but he did remember the cold. He had supposed he would freeze that night, for want of an adequate coat.

The whites began to speculate about why Blue Duck would want to kill Buffalo Hump, but Famous Shoes didn't listen. The young man wanted to kill the old man for all the reasons that normally drove men to kill one another. In the clear night he had just heard the song of the plover, which meant that water was near.

All night Famous Shoes sat listening. He heard the plover cry several more times, and rejoiced. Men lied often, but the plover only lied when it had eggs to protect; if the plover's nest was near, then water, too, was near. In the morning they could drink.

35.

BLUE DUCK let Ermoke and Monkey John ride his spare horses because of the two Comanches who watched them for a day. Ermoke was the first to see them; it was shortly before his horse gave out. He pulled his rifle and pointed to the west, but Blue Duck, at first, could see nothing that he could clearly identify. Monkey John, so shortsighted that he would sometimes climb on someone else's horse thinking it was his own, could see nothing, but he pulled his rifle just in case.

"What you see is a yucca, or two yuccas," Blue Duck told Ermoke. He was anxious to press on and catch up with Buffalo Hump, whose track was the track of a weak old man—a man who would die within a day or two. Blue Duck did not want his father to die before they found him. He was prepared to ignore everything else in order to catch his father before he died.

It was not until they had limped into the Lake of Horses and were drinking at the little spring that Blue Duck finally saw the two Comanches. He decided that thirst had weakened his vision; sitting well to the west, in plain view, were two Comanche warriors. They were not approaching; they were merely watching, but it made Blue Duck more anxious than ever to hurry on with the chase. Then Monkey John's horse lay down and could not rise, no matter how hard they beat him. Blue Duck knew that the Comanches must belong to the Antelope band—Quanah's band. No other Indians would dare venture that far into the llano. They must know of the little spring—perhaps they were its guardians. If they were there, the rest of the band must not be far.

Blue Duck knew that the Antelope would not consider him a Comanche. If they decided to kill him they would come with enough warriors to kill him, which is why he decided he had better keep Ermoke and Monkey John with him, even if it meant letting them use his spare horses. Both men were reliable shots and three rifles were better than one if it came to a fight with the Antelopes.

They rested for part of a day by the spring in the Lake of Horses; the two Comanches did not approach, but neither did they leave. Blue Duck knew his father could only be a few miles ahead. In an hour or two they could catch him and dispatch him. He wanted the horses to rest and eat. They could fill up on the weeds that grew around the little spring. He did not want to fight the Antelopes unless he had to—it was a fight he would be unlikely to win. He stayed near the spring through the night, until an hour before dawn. He meant to leave before it was light, find his father, kill him, and go north as fast as he could, to strike the Rio Carrizo or the Cimarron. If he moved quickly enough he would soon be back in the tall grass along the Cimarron; he didn't think the Antelopes would follow him there. If necessary he would kill Ermoke and Monkey John and take the horses they rode—better to ride all the horses to death and hope to ambush a traveler on one of the westward trails than to get into a fight with the Antelopes.

In the morning, when it was light enough to scan the whole plain, Ermoke, who was very nervous, made another discovery: the rangers they thought they had outdistanced had not given up. Not only were the two Comanches still in plain sight to the west, but at least four horsemen were pursuing them from the south. Seeing this, Ermoke became bitterly annoyed with himself, for following Blue Duck to such a place. Now there were Comanches on one side and Texas Rangers behind them, in country too dry to live in; and they were there for no better reason than that Blue Duck wanted to settle a grudge with Buffalo Hump.

"We ought to have let him come by himself," he said, to Monkey John. "Them two to the west want our hair and the goddamn rangers want to hang us."

Monkey John was too frightened of the Comanches to worry about the rangers.

"I ain't worried about the hanging," he said. "There's nothing out here they could hang us from. I'd like to keep my hair, though, if I can.

"Besides that, we're out of tobaccy," he added, a little later.

"That's because you chewed it all up, you goddamn hog," Ermoke said. In fact Monkey John, in his opinion, was little more than a human spittoon.

In the back of Monkey John's anxious mind was another worry: Blue Duck. He had not asked them to come on the trip—if the Comanches had not showed up he would probably have left them to starve, and he still might. As they rode north Monkey John found that his worry about Blue Duck overwhelmed his other worries.

"I'm afraid Duck will kill us, once he's done with his pa," he said to Ermoke, who had stopped for a moment to relieve himself.

Ermoke ignored the comment. His own chief worry was Captain Call, whom he knew to be an implacable foe. He knew that Call must be one of the rangers who were following them—no one else in the ranger troop would have been likely to have pressed a pursuit so tenaciously.

Now, to his vexation, he saw that the rangers had found the dry lake and the spring in the center of it. They had all dismounted to drink and water their horses. It made it difficult to count them, but the count in itself was not too important. If Captain Call was one of the rangers it meant that they had plenty to worry about.

"I'm scared of Duck, he's mean," Monkey John said, a comment that amused Ermoke a good deal.

"Mean? Duck? Why, when did you notice?" he said, before he turned back north.

36.

FAMOUS SHOES had heard of the spring in the dry lake from one or two old men whose minds had been cloudy when they talked of it. He had not quite believed that it was a real place, and was grateful to the plover for calling and calling until he was able to find it. It was such a small spring that it took more than an hour for the horses to water—Captain Call forbade the men to drink until the horses had had their fill, an order Captain McCrae agreed with.

"We can drink our piss and make it another day or two, but these nags have to water," Augustus said. Pea Eye and Deets, their tongues thick in their mouths, waited as the two horses drank.

Pea Eye was so thirsty that his head swam. He had begun to see double, too, a thing that had never occurred before in his life.

While the horses were drinking Augustus spotted the two Comanches. Famous Shoes was a few hundred yards to the west, exploring the edges of the old lake; he too saw the Comanches and came running back.

"We should leave here as soon as we can," he said. "Those men may not like it that we have found the spring."

Call could not see the two warriors—eyesight weaker than the norm, or at least weaker than Augustus's, was an old vexation. He did not dispute the opinion, though. The Comanches who lived in the depths of the llano still had all their fight, as many an unfortunate traveler had found out to his doom.

"Blue Duck got here first," Augustus commented. "If they're feeling frisky maybe they'll take after him."

"Maybe—or they might take after us both," Call said.

Famous Shoes thought that the little spring must be holy. The old people who had talked about it said it was near the place where the People had come out of the earth. Now only a few birds and the Antelope Comanche knew where it was. If the spring *was* holy it might not want to give its water to strangers; that might be why it flowed so slowly. He was glad when the horses and the men had finished drinking—he did not want to disturb the spring that might be holy by taking too much from it.

37.

WHEN BUFFALO HUMP AWOKE he reached for his lance, but Blue Duck had already taken it. Buffalo Hump had been deep in a dream—in his dream he had seen millions of buffalo grazing, as they had grazed on the plains in his youth. Because of the buffalo, he did not want to wake up. He wanted to dream his way into the spirit world, where Comanches rode forever. For that reason he had tried to ignore the voices that he had begun to hear in his dream.

The voices were not the voices of Comanches, and they were not ghosts. For that reason he tried to ignore them, to stay in his comfortable sleep, dreaming of buffalo.

But the voices were too loud; soon he felt the prickling in his senses that he always felt when an enemy was near, or when there was some threat from the wild. Once the prickling awakened him when a herd of buffalo were stampeding toward the place where he rested. He had had to mount quickly and ride for his life. Another time the prickling saved him from a great she-bear, angry because a hunter had killed her cub; many times it had alerted him to the approach of human enemies, some of them Indian and some of them white.

Buffalo Hump had come to the place of black rocks to die. He wanted to help his spirit slip away from his body, and, for that reason, he ignored the prickling and the voices. It was when he felt the point of his own lance touch his side that he could ignore the voices no longer.

He opened his eyes and rose to his feet, but he was stiff; he rose slowly, and, anyway, it was too late. Blue Duck had his lance. It was Blue Duck who had poked him in the ribs with his own lance: he thrust with it again, but this time Buffalo Hump blocked the lance with his buffalo skull shield, which he had kept in his lap as he slept.

The lance point hit the shield and, for a moment, stuck in the thick bone of the buffalo's skull. Buffalo Hump held on to his shield, Blue Duck to the lance. The men with Blue Duck, one half-breed and one white, watched the brief moment of pushing and pulling silently. One of them held the short bow that Buffalo Hump had brought with him. It was plain, though, that the man could not shoot the bow. He had merely taken it so Buffalo Hump could not shoot at them with the small arrows that were only good for killing rabbits and other small game. The third man was short and mis-shapen, with eyes like a goat. Buffalo Hump saw that the men were comancheros or renegades of some kind, low men his son had brought with him on his errand of killing.

Finally, with a jerk that almost pulled Buffalo Hump out of the circle of black rocks, Blue Duck freed the end of the lance. He did not speak and neither did Buffalo Hump. It was obvious that Blue Duck had learned of his departure from the camp and had followed him to kill him. It was clear, too, that Blue Duck wanted to kill him badly, for he had gone to a great deal of trouble to follow him to the place of the black rocks. He and his two comancheros might have starved.

Rather than talk, Buffalo Hump took out his knife, the one weapon left to him. A knife was not much use against a lance but was all he had to fight with; and it was a knife that had pierced the vitals of many enemies. Buffalo Hump had taken the knife off the body of a bluecoat soldier near the Rio Concho many years before.

Blue Duck was smiling—he knew it would be easy to kill an old man who had only a knife to fight with. Besides the lance, he and his men had several guns.

"I reckon you took too long a nap, old man," Blue Duck said. He moved just outside the ring of rocks, holding the lance as if he might throw it.

Buffalo Hump saw from the awkward way Blue Duck held the lance that he had not changed. He seemed undecided as to whether to throw the lance or jab with it. Any well-trained Comanche, who knew how to use a lance, could have killed the young fool in only a few seconds. Buffalo Hump felt the scorn he had always felt at Blue Duck's crude disregard of the old weapons. He saw that Blue Duck rode a Mexican saddle and had a buffalo gun strapped to it. But such failings didn't matter now. His son had come to kill him and had even awakened him from his death sleep to do it. All that was left was one fight, and since his son had brought two well-armed helpers, it would not be a long fight. Buffalo Hump crouched a little and waited, hoping Blue Duck would be fool enough to grapple with him. Even though he was weak, Buffalo Hump still trusted his skill with the knife. If Blue Duck were fool enough to come near him, Buffalo Hump meant to slash at his throat. Several times he had opened an enemy's windpipe so cleanly that the enemy would not even know he had been touched until blood blew out with the bubbles of air.

For a minute, there was a circling. Blue Duck shifted the lance from hand to hand; Buffalo Hump held his knife and his shield. Buffalo Hump knew that he could not move well. One of his legs had stiffened when he slept, and it was still stiff. All he could do was wait and hope Blue Duck made some foolish mistake. Buffalo Hump began to sing his war cry as he waited. His voice cracked as he sang, but he wanted his three enemies to know that he was still a Comanche warrior, a man who sang as he went into battle.

The three men looked amused when he began to sing. They thought it was funny that an old man would sing as he was about to be killed. They were men so degraded that they didn't realize it was a warrior's special obligation to sing in battle and to raise a death song if it was clear that the battle was going against him. Other warriors who might be fighting with him would need to hear that their chief was still making war; if it had to be that he must die in the fighting, then, particularly, the spirits needed to be offered a death song, so that they could welcome the warrior into the spirit world once he had fallen.

The *comancheros* didn't know these things. They merely thought he was a silly old man, singing in a weak voice to the men who were about to kill him.

Then Blue Duck disappeared. The other two men pulled knives

and waved them at him, though they didn't come within the circle of rocks. Buffalo Hump, his vision wavery, realized that his son must have slipped behind him; before he could turn to face him, Blue Duck, who was young and nimble, struck full force with the lance. Buffalo Hump had tried to turn but the stiff leg had kept him from being able to pivot as he once had. He had twisted, and then the lance struck his hump. It went in but did not go through, though the force of the blow knocked Buffalo Hump on his face; dust was in his nostrils. He didn't feel the piercing at all, only the force of the blow. Blue Duck tried to push the lance through, or else pull it out, but could do neither. The lance point was stuck more firmly in the big hump than it had been in the buffalo skull shield. Blue Duck, maddened by the failure of his blow, jumped on his father's back and put all his weight on the lance, determined to shove it through.

"Come help!" he yelled at the two renegades—soon Buffalo Hump saw several feet moving around him as the two men and Blue Duck leaned as hard as they could on the lance. Buffalo Hump realized that once again his foolish son had erred. Once he himself had tried to put his lance through the hump of a running buffalo and had nearly lost his life as a result. Before he could push the lance through, the buffalo jerked him off his horse into the path of other buffalo. Now Blue Duck had made the same error by thrusting the lance into his hump rather than his heart. Buffalo Hump lost his war song—the men were stepping on him as they tried to push the lance through; he could not get his breath well enough to sing. He was jerked this way and that as the men struggled with the lance. Once he tried to slash at the feet of the men moving around him, but his fingers had no strength. He lost hold of his knife just as he was losing hold of life itself, his life as a warrior. With a final desperate push Blue Duck shoved the lance through the hump and through Buffalo Hump's body too; its red point went into the earth beneath him, just as his own arrows had once gone through the bodies of his enemies, pinning them to the ground. Buffalo Hump was filled with hatred for his son, for denying him the death of prayer and song that he had hoped for, though he knew, from seeing many men die, most of them at his own hand, that few men were fortunate enough to die as they would have chosen, for death did not belong to the humans or the great creatures either—death came when it would, and now had come to him; he could do no more, and even the last look of hatred which he directed at his son went unnoticed. Blue Duck and the two other renegades were panting behind him somewhere, panting from the effort it had taken to kill him. Even then Buffalo Hump could still move his hands and legs a little, as the lance held him pinned to the earth.

"Look at him!" one of the men said. "He still ain't dead. He's moving like an old turtle."

Buffalo Hump closed his eyes. He remembered that there were old stories—old, old stories, about a great turtle that had let the People ride on its back as he brought them from their home in the earth to the place of light. He remembered the turtle story, an old story he had heard from his grandmother or from someone even older than his grandmother, someone who knew about the beginnings of the People in the time before they knew of the light or the buffalo or the grassy plains. He felt the grass growing beneath him, growing and rising to cover him, growing to hide him from wolf and bear. Then he knew no more.

38.

"HE'S GONE, DUCK," Monkey John said, observing that the old Comanche with the ugly hump had ceased to move his arms and legs.

Blue Duck was still breathing hard from the effort it had taken to kill his father. For a few moments, when the lance stuck in the hump, he had been desperate. His fear was that his father would cheat him again by dying in his own way. His father's last looks, when he had been just a weak old man holding a knife and pretending to be a warrior, had been the same looks of determined hatred that had caused so many men to lose their will and allow Buffalo Hump to kill them. Even when the old man was pinned to the ground by his own lance his look was one of hatred—Blue Duck had been ready to get a hatchet and cut his head off, if it took that to finally kill him; but when he looked again he saw that Monkey John was right. Buffalo Hump was dead. All the same, he started for his horse, meaning to get the hatchet, when Ermoke stopped him.

"Where are you going, Duck?" Ermoke asked him.

"I mean to take his head," Blue Duck said.

"Not today, you ain't got time," Ermoke said, pointing south toward the Lake of Horses.

Blue Duck saw what he meant. On the dry plain the dust thrown up by the four horses of their pursuers hung in the air. It annoyed Blue Duck that the rangers were so persistent, rushing him, denying him the full pleasure of his triumph over his father.

"Goddamn them, what's their hurry?" he said. "I wanted to take his ugly old head home with me—I could use it to scare the boys."

"Let's go, Duck—you can come back and get his head, if you're that set on having it," Ermoke said. "It was hard enough to kill him. That's Call and McCrae after us. I'm for leaving."

Blue Duck wanted to linger, to savor the triumph he had waited for so long; he felt like killing Ermoke for so insistently rushing him off. But he knew the renegade was right. Call and McCrae had followed him where no other rangers and no other whites would have dared to go. Ermoke and Monkey John were no match for them. He himself might be, but only if he could insure himself proper cover, and there was no cover close.

"You kilt the man you came to kill, Duck," Ermoke said. "Let's leave."

"We'll go, but once they're gone I mean to come back for his head," Blue Duck said. He went to his horse, mounted, and rode once more around the still body of his father. He rode close and put his hand on the lance. He wanted to keep it but knew it would take much too long to pull it out.

"He must have liked them black rocks," Monkey John said. "He gathered up a bunch of them before we got here."

Blue Duck had a vague memory of his father saying something to him about the black rocks, long ago on their journey to the Lake of Horses. But he couldn't remember what he had said, and Call and McCrae were getting closer. He left the lance in his father's body and turned to the north.

As they were leaving, Monkey John reached down and picked up Buffalo Hump's big knife.

39.

FAMOUS SHOES had not wanted to go north of the dry lake. He thought the fact that the spring was so small and so well hidden meant that the dry lake was as far as men ought to go—also, he had seen the two Antelope Comanches; it worried him that they were watching. Also, they had no sooner left the lake than he began to notice the black rocks.

The three things taken together were to him powerful evidence that they had followed Blue Duck far enough. All the Kickapoos agreed that black rocks were to be avoided—they were not normal rocks and were only likely to be in places where the spirits were malign.

When they left the lake Famous Shoes said as much to Captain Call, but the captain paid no more attention to his words than he would have paid to a puff of wind. Captain Call didn't care about the black rocks. He *did* care about the Antelope Comanches—he knew they represented danger, but he was not willing to turn back on their account.

"Woodrow wants Blue Duck, and Blue Duck ain't five miles ahead," Augustus pointed out, when the tracker came to him with his worries. "If you think Woodrow Call will turn back with his quarry in sight you've hired on with the wrong company."

Famous Shoes concluded that there was no point in talking to the two captains. He had been patient and intelligent in explaining his reasoning as to why it was unwise to go farther north at that time, yet both men ignored him. They just kept going.

Famous Shoes thought he might as well go home—it was a waste of time to advise men who wouldn't listen. He didn't want to stay with the rangers if they were going to proceed so foolishly. Nonetheless, he went ahead for a few miles, because he wanted to see if there was another lake nearby, or any reason to continue north.

It was while he was trotting ahead of the cautious rangers that he noticed a lance sticking up from the ground a short distance ahead. Since Buffalo Hump was the only man likely to be in that area who carried a lance, Famous Shoes immediately became more cautious, fearing that the old man was plotting some kind of ambush.

While he was studying the land, trying to figure where the old man could be hiding, Famous Shoes saw his body. The lance held it pinned to the earth. The sight startled Famous Shoes so that for a moment his legs felt weak. He had long surmised that Buffalo Hump was making his last journey, seeking a hiding place of some sort, in which to die. But that surmise did not diminish his shock when he saw the body with the lance driven through it.

On weak legs he went forward until he stood on the edge of the circle of black rocks. He was too shocked to wave at the rangers, or do anything but stand and look. Buffalo Hump had been killed with his own lance, and it was undoubtedly Blue Duck and his men who had killed him. The lance went right through the hump; Famous Shoes remembered hearing some prophecy or old story to the effect that Buffalo Hump would only die when his hump was pierced. It might have been Buffalo Hump's own grandmother who told him the story, long ago when he was caring for her as she waited to die.

The old man's great buffalo skull shield lay beside him. It was a shield that many warriors wanted, yet Blue Duck had left it, as if it were a thing without value or power. That too was a shock.

Famous Shoes was squatting just outside the circle of black rock when the rangers rode up.

"Oh my Lord," Augustus said, when he saw that Buffalo Hump was dead. "Oh my Lord."

Call was just as shocked, though he didn't speak. He dismounted and stood by Famous Shoes; the others dismounted too, but, for a time, no one spoke. Deets, who had never seen Buffalo Hump up close, was so scared that he wanted to leave. It was his belief that only a witch would have such a hump, and, though the man appeared to be dead, a lance through his body, it was not clear to Deets that a witch would have to *stay* dead. He thought it would be better to stand a little farther away, in case the witch with the big hump suddenly rose up and did some witchery on them.

Call was curious at last to see Buffalo Hump up close. It had been some years since he had thought much about the man, yet he knew that his career as a ranger had been, in large measure, a pursuit of the Comanche who lay dead at his feet.

Augustus was so startled that all color had drained from his face. "That's a lance like the one he stuck me with, way back then," he said.

Pea Eye, too, wanted to go. He knew that Buffalo Hump had been a mighty, fearsome chief, but now he was dead and it was wasteful just to stand there looking at his body if they hoped to catch the bandits they had been chasing for so long.

Captain Call and Captain McCrae, though, showed no inclination to hurry on, and neither did Famous Shoes. Pea Eye only looked once at the hump; he did not care to examine deformities, for fear it would result in bad dreams.

To Call's eye, Buffalo Hump looked smaller in death than he had looked in life—he was not the giant they had supposed him to be, but only a man of medium height.

"I thought he was bigger," Call added, squatting for a moment by the body.

"I did too, Woodrow," Augustus said. "When he was after me with his lance I thought he was as big as a god."

"He's old," Call said. "He might have shrunk a little in his old age."

"No, we just remember him as bigger than he was because he was so fierce and had that terrible war cry," Augustus said.

To Pea Eye it seemed that the discovery of Buffalo Hump's body had put the two captains into a kind of memory trance.

"He was the first Comanche I ever saw," Call remarked. "I remember when he came racing out of that gully with that dead boy behind him on his horse—I forget the boy's name."

"Josh Com was his name," Augustus said. "He went into the bushes to take a shit and picked the wrong bunch of bushes to go into—it was the end of him."

"This old man was gaunt," Call said. "I doubt he found much to eat, these last few years."

Famous Shoes started to tell the two rangers that they should not be standing within the circle of black rocks as they talked. Buffalo Hump had made a death circle with the rocks, and it should be respected. But he had, himself, another concern which also involved respect. He wanted the great buffalo skull shield. He wanted the shield badly. It was just lying there, ignored by Blue Duck and ignored too by the rangers. Though he wanted it, Famous Shoes knew the shield should remain within the circle of rocks. If he himself took it the Comanches might find out and try to kill him because of what he had done. He knelt down and looked closely at the shield, knowing that it contained great power, but he was afraid to take it.

"We ought to get that lance out of him, if we can," Call said. He pulled, and then he and Augustus pulled together, but they soon saw that the task was hopeless. The lance point came free of the ground, but it did not come free of Buffalo Hump's body. It had gone through his hump, through his ribs, and through his chest.

"It's like a tree grew through him," Gus said.

"He was a great chief—he ought to be laid out proper, but there's now no way to do it with this lance sticking through him," Call said.

"Well, I ain't holding a funeral for him, he's killed too many of my friends," Augustus said. "I expect but for him Long Bill would be alive, and Neely Dickens and several more I could name."

"I didn't mention a funeral," Call said. "I just think any man ought to be laid out proper."

He looked again at the body of Buffalo Hump and then, mindful that their task was not done, turned toward the horses. He didn't feel the relief he had always supposed he would feel, at the death of Buffalo Hump. The man who lay before him was no longer the terror of the plains—he was just an old man, dead. Though they were in pursuit of Blue Duck, Call felt, for a moment, that there was little point in going on. He felt he had used up his energy. When he walked back to his horse he didn't, for a moment, have the strength to mount.

"Those were Comanches watching us at the lake," he told Gus. "I expect they'll find Buffalo Hump and do what's proper."

Famous Shoes knew better. The two Comanches were of the Antelope band, and the Antelopes had always held aloof from the other tribes. Probably the warriors who watched them were too young to have heard of Buffalo Hump—even if they rode over to look at the body, the deformity would scare them away. When they saw the hump they would think witchery was involved. They would want nothing to do with the old dead man with the ugly hump.

He himself wanted nothing to do with the Antelopes. Though their country was poor and harsh, they were not broken men. He didn't know why the two warriors were watching the dry lake, but he was glad there were only two. Maybe the rest of the band were hunting somewhere. If more of them had been there they would probably have attacked.

Captain Call and Captain McCrae lingered by their horses; for some reason they were reluctant to mount and ride on, although their quarry, Blue Duck, was not many miles ahead.

The delay broke down Famous Shoes' resolve in regard to the shield. It was an important thing. None of the whites seemed to realize that; none of them had even picked it up, or looked at it. Famous Shoes, though, couldn't take his eyes off it. Even though he knew he should leave it with Buffalo Hump, so that he could use it in battle in the spirit world, Famous Shoes wanted it too much.

After all, once they left, no one might ever come near the spot where Buffalo Hump lay. They might be the only ones who would ever look on the body of the old chief. But the animals would look. Wolf would come, and Coyote and Badger and Bobcat. Buzzards would come, and beetles, to take what they could of old Buffalo Hump. If he left the shield a wolf or a coyote might drag it away. With all the animals that would soon be coming, the shield of Buffalo Hump might soon be lost, and yet it was a shield made by a great chief from a buffalo skull. With the buffalo now almost gone, it might be that no one would ever make such a shield again.

With such thoughts in his mind Famous Shoes soon convinced himself that he should take the shield, though he did not want to step into the death circle to do it. While the rangers made a careful inspection of their horses' feet—a very wise thing since they had no spare horses—Famous Shoes took a rifle and reached across the black rocks and hooked the shield. He got the rifle barrel inside the rawhide grips that Buffalo Hump had made so that he could hold the shield where he wanted it. Famous Shoes was glad the shield had not been too far inside the circle—he was just able to reach it with the rifle barrel, and in a moment he had it, the shield of Buffalo Hump, an important and powerful tool of war.

He was just about to take the shield to Deets and ask him to carry it in one of his saddlebags when the first shot came.

40.

"WE WERE TOO FAR AWAY—I didn't get no chance to sight this gun," Blue Duck said, in annoyance, when he saw that his first shot from the big buffalo rifle had only hit Captain Call in the foot. At least that was how it appeared. The man held up one leg and hopped behind the horses.

Ermoke was annoyed too. He had wanted to be the one to shoot the big gun. He considered himself a far better shot than Blue Duck, particularly at long distances, and in this case the distance was long. They had made sure to ride well beyond the range of the

Texans' Winchesters before they pulled up and unstrapped the big buffalo gun. There was a little growth of yucca where they stopped, the only cover in sight, but all they needed. With the big gun they could relax and pick off the Texans one by one—only now Blue Duck had spoiled the whole plan by shooting low.

Blue Duck quickly drew a bead on Ranger McCrae but missed again, though the bullet did knock one of the four horses down. He was aware that Ermoke was looking at him critically—Ermoke was vain about his marksmanship, particularly if the distances were long. He had once killed an antelope with a Winchester at a distance of almost a thousand yards, and had never ceased to brag about the exploit.

Even though he had now missed twice, Blue Duck didn't yield the gun. It was his gun, for one thing. He had run the frightened buffalo hunter to earth, and it had been no easy chase. The hunter had three guns and had emptied them all at him during the long pursuit. He might even have escaped had his horse not stepped in a prairie-dog hole. In the fall the buffalo hunter broke his neck. He was paralyzed when Blue Duck walked up and cut his throat. The pursuit had taken all day, and the hunter had no money, only a worthless tin watch and his guns.

Blue Duck had meant to practice a little with the big rifle, but Last Horse had arrived unexpectedly, before he got around to it. He had never shot such a powerful rifle before; now, with the rangers in easy killing distance, he was vexed to find that the weapon shot low. He had missed a clean shot at Call and an even better one at McCrae. Now the rangers were on their bellies in the grass, hard to see. Ermoke clearly wanted a chance to shoot, but Blue Duck didn't give it to him. Instead he shot another of the rangers' horses, even as the black man was trying to hurry them out of range.

"I guess that will stop them," he said. "Two of their horses are down and Call's shot in the leg. They'll starve anyway. Let's go. We won't have to be in such a damn hurry now."

"Monkey's sick—he's shitting white shit," Ermoke observed. He saw that Blue Duck was angry, so he did not ask if he could shoot the buffalo gun. If he asked, Blue Duck might turn the gun on him, as he had on the Comanche who came to tell him about Buffalo Hump.

"What about Monkey?" Ermoke asked, when he saw Blue Duck mount up.

Blue Duck glanced at the stumpy man, who was a few yards away, squatting with his pants down, looking miserable.

"Monkey? He can come or he can stay," Blue Duck said. "I guess our fine waters don't agree with him. You can wait for him, if you like. I doubt I ought to be associating with a man who shits white shit, anyway."

41.

THE FIRST BULLET knocked Call a foot in the air. Immediately, he lost all feeling in his left leg, but he pulled himself around behind his horse; then the second bullet knocked the horse down on top of him, or almost. Pea and Augustus pulled him out from under the horse, which was kicking wildly. A third shot hit Pea's horse and killed it.

"Run with the other horses!" Call yelled to Deets. "If you don't he's going to put us all afoot."

Deets needed no urging. He was already running south, with his brown mule and the other, uninjured, horse. There were four more booms from the big rifle, but Deets was soon out of range and the other men had their faces flat in the dirt. The bullets merely kicked up dirt. The rifleman stopped firing, since he had stopped hitting, but the three rangers kept their heads down, fearing that the rifle-man would soon find the range.

Call glanced at his leg and saw no blood, but he assumed he was probably crippled anyway. The leg was numb from the hip down—his horse, by then, had stopped kicking but lay with its eyes open, panting.

"He's shooting a buffalo gun," Augustus said. "If I'd known he had one I'd have been more careful."

"We ought to have been more careful anyway," Call said. "Anyone can get their hands on a buffalo gun."

Augustus had not yet looked at his friend's wound. In their time as partners it was the first time he could remember seeing Woodrow Call knocked off his feet; the sight made a bad impression on him. If Woodrow was still down it probably meant the wound was mortal. Everyone who worked with Call knew that he had to be killed to be stopped. The thought that Woodrow might die sobered Augustus so much that he put off examining the wound.

"Where'd he hit you, Captain?" Pea Eye asked finally. He too was afraid that the captain was mortally hit, else he would be up fighting.

"In the leg," Call said. He too assumed that his wound was serious, perhaps fatal. He didn't try to rise because he knew his leg wouldn't hold him. Standing up would have been unwise in any case. The man with the buffalo gun had them well marked. He was not a very highly skilled marksman or he would have killed all four of the horses and probably at least two of the men; but he was good enough, and he might improve, once he found the range. Call noticed that his horse had only been hit in the hip, but the minute after he noticed it the horse died.

"Those buffalo guns are powerful," Call said. "That one killed my horse, and the shot wasn't even well placed."

"Don't be getting pessimistic now—so far he ain't killed you," Augustus said. "You're going to have to let us drag you farther away, Woodrow, so we can look at your wound."

"Keep as low as you can," Call said. "I expect it's Blue Duck shooting."

"Yes, that's why we are alive," Famous Shoes said. "Ermoke is a better shot. If he had let Ermoke shoot he would have killed us all."

"I don't know Mr. Ermoke," Augustus said, "but if he's their marksman I'm glad he took the day off. He might have put a bullet in me, and I'm intolerant of bullets."

"Pull me back," Call said. "We better look at this wound."

Augustus and Pea Eye, keeping low, grabbed Call under the armpits and dragged him away, expecting at any moment to hear the boom of the great gun. But no shots came. Deets, looking scared, was waiting with the horse, well out of range of even a buffalo gun.

"You examine him, Deets—you're the best doc we got," Augustus said.

Call noticed that Augustus, always a cool man under fire, looked a little pale.

"What's the matter, are you hit too?" he asked.

"No, but I'm vomity," Augustus said. "It's seeing these horses die. I've never been able to tolerate seeing horses die."

Call felt the same way. For some reason injuries to horses affected him worse than injuries to men. Eating one of his own horses, if it was a case of necessity, didn't trouble him so long as he didn't have to see the animals suffer and die. It was a curious thing.

Augustus crawled off a little distance, to empty his stomach; while he was gone Call surrendered himself to Deets and waited for the black man to tell him he was dying—or, at the very least, crippled or lamed. He felt no pain, just a numbness, which he knew was common enough when a wound was fresh. The pain would come later, and in abundance, usually.

When Deets began to examine the Captain he had the darkest apprehensions. He expected to see a gaping wound, a splintered bone, or both; but he saw immediately, there was no blood on the captain's leg, or on his body anywhere. The horse that had just died bled profusely, but Captain Call wasn't bleeding at all, not that he could see.

"What's the matter?" Call asked, seeing Deets's look of puzzlement.

"You ain't got no blood on you," Deets said. "No blood, Captain."

"I must have, somewhere," Call said. "I can't feel my leg."

But when he looked again himself he saw that Deets was right.

There was no blood on him anywhere. Pea Eye came over to help with the examination, and Augustus, once finished with his vomiting, came too. Deets, Call, and Pea Eye were all dead serious; they were puzzled and almost offended by their inability to spot the blood that would surely issue from such a large wound.

Call took his pants down, fearing that the wound must be higher on his body than he had supposed, but Augustus, after a careful look, smiled and pointed at Call's boot.

"Keep your pants on, Woodrow," he said. "You ain't shot in the leg, you're just shot in the boot heel."

Call looked again at his foot and saw that Augustus was right—the boot heel was entirely missing. He had not been hit at all, and yet the shock of the big bullet hitting his boot heel had thrown him in the air and left his leg as numb as if all its nerves had been removed.

"Well, I swear," he said. "See if you can find the boot heel, Deets. I'd like to tack it back on if I can. Otherwise I've got a long way to hobble."

A diligent search failed to turn up even a trace of the boot heel.

"It's a waste of time looking," Augustus said. "That was a fifty-caliber bullet that hit that boot heel. You won't find it because it's been blown to smithereens."

Call found it hard to adjust to the fact that he was unhurt. His mind had accepted the thought that he was wounded easier than it would accept the fact that he wasn't. Once the notion that he was crippled or dying left his mind it was succeeded by vexation at the thought that the man they had chased so far was undoubtedly getting away. For a moment he was tempted to take one of the surviving horses and go after him, but Augustus would not hear of that plan.

"We're in a bad enough fix as it is, Woodrow," he said. "It's a long way back to where we need to be, and most of it is dry traveling. We've only got one horse and one mule for four men—we'll have to walk a good part of the way and save the horses for when we have to have them. We may have to eat both animals before we get home. We need to think about saving ourselves now. Blue Duck can wait.

"Besides that, there's Quanah and his warriors out there somewhere," he added, pointing to the west, into the empty llano. "I don't know what their mood is and you don't neither. We may have to fight our way back, for all you know."

Call knew he was right. They were a small force, stranded in a desert. They would be easy prey for any strong band of fighters, whether native or outlaw. They would have to stay together to have any chance. But the fact was, he still wanted to go after Blue Duck—he had a hard time mastering himself, and Augustus knew it.

"He's a damn killer—I hate to let him go," Call said.

"You're as bad as Inish Scull," Augustus commented. "He was so determined to catch Kicking Wolf that he walked off on foot."

"Yes, I was with him," Famous Shoes said. "He walked fast, that man. He did not stop until we were in the land of the Black Vaquero."

"I wonder what became of the old Black Vaquero?" Augustus said. "There's been no news of him in years."

"He went back to where Jaguar lives," Famous Shoes said.

Augustus saw that Woodrow Call was still not settled in his mind about Blue Duck. He had never known a man so unwilling to leave a pursuit once he had begun one. It would not be unlike him to go after Blue Duck on foot, even with one boot heel shot off.

"He ain't gone forever, Woodrow," Augustus pointed out. "He'll just go back to the Red River and start raiding again. We can go get him in the fall."

"If they let us," Call said. "They may disband us before the fall."

"All the better if they do," Gus said. "Then we can just go get him for the fun of it—that way we won't have to keep track of the damn expenses."

Famous Shoes was annoyed by the rangers' habit of debating meaningless things while the sun moved and time was lost.

Whether they were to be rangers in the fall did not interest him. There was the llano to cross, and talking would not propel them across it.

"We had better go drink some of that water back at the spring," he said.

His words reminded the rangers of what they faced. They had barely survived the trek out, when they had horses. Now they would have to cover the same distance walking—or, at best, riding double a few hours a day.

"That's right," Augustus said. "It's apt to be a long dry walk."

"I aim to drink all I can hold," Pea Eye said, turning toward the dry lake. "All I can hold and then some. I sure hate to be dry in my mouth."

42.

IN THE NIGHT Newt knew that his mother must have died because he couldn't hear her breathing anymore. The room felt different— it had become a room in which he was alone. But he didn't know what he was supposed to do, so he lay on his pallet doing nothing until the gray light came into the windows by the street. Then he carefully got up, dressed, and put a few things of his into a shoe box—his top, his ball, his book full of pictures of animals, and a deck of cards the rangers had let him keep. Then he put on his hat—Captain Gus had given it to him—looked just once at his mother, dead in her bed, and hurried down the stairs and over to Mrs. Coleman, who began to sob the minute she saw him—Mrs. Coleman continued to cry all day. Newt was sad about the fact that Deets and Pea Eye and the other rangers were gone; he knew they would have wanted to say goodbye to his mother, but now they would have no chance. The grave was dug; that same afternoon they put his mother in it—there was a little singing and then they covered her up.

Mrs. Coleman gave him supper. There was a lot of food, but he wasn't very hungry. Mrs. Coleman had mainly got control of herself by then, though tears still dripped out of her eyes from time to time.

"Newt, I know you'll be wanting to stay with the rangers when they all get back," she told him after supper. "But would you like to just stay here for a night or two? There's nobody much in the bunkhouse."

Newt shook his head. Though he didn't want to hurt Mrs. Coleman's feelings—he knew she had been his mother's best friend—he didn't want to stay with her, either.

"I better just bunk with the boys," he said, although he knew that the only ranger in the bunkhouse at the time was Ikey Ripple, who was far too old to be called a boy. But he wanted badly to stay in the bunkhouse, and Mrs. Coleman didn't argue with him. It was dark by the time the meal was finished, so she went with him the few blocks to where the rangers stayed. Ikey was already asleep, and was snoring loudly.

"I hope you can sleep with that snoring, Newt," Mrs. Coleman said—then, suddenly, she hugged him tight for a moment and left the bunkhouse.

Newt put his shoe box under the bunk where he usually slept when he stayed with the rangers. Then he took his rope and went outside. He could hear Mrs. Coleman sobbing as she walked home, a thing which made him feel a little bad. Mrs. Coleman had no one to live with—he supposed she was lonely. Probably he should have stayed with her a night or two. He climbed up on the fence, holding his rope, and watched the moon for a while. He could hear Ikey snoring, all the way out in the lots. In the morning he planned to go down to the graveyard and tell his mother the news, even though there wasn't much—just that he had decided to move into the bunkhouse right away, so he would be there to help water the horses and do the chores. That way he would be ready to help the boys, when they came home.

43.

WHEN KICKING WOLF HEARD that four rangers were walking across the llano with only one horse and a mule, he didn't know what to make of the news. A lot of strange news had come lately, some of it distressing and some of it merely puzzling. He had not left the camp in two weeks because one of his legs had a bad cramp in it. Of course now and then a man's leg would cramp, but never in his life had he experienced so debilitating a cramp as the one which afflicted his right leg. Sometimes even when he was moving his bowels a cramp would seize him, playing havoc with even *that* simple operation.

Kicking Wolf thought it was his old wife, Broken Foot, who was sending the cramp into his leg. The fact was, Broken Foot had been angry with him for several months—he didn't know why. When he asked her she smiled and denied that she was angry, but Kicking Wolf didn't believe her denials. Even though he was aging, Kicking Wolf was still a good hunter; he owned more horses than anyone in the tribe and supplied Broken Foot with everything she needed. Their lodge was the warmest in the camp. Kicking Wolf knew, though, that having many reasons to be content didn't necessarily mean that a person *was* content, particularly not if the person in question was a woman. Broken Foot, despite her denials, was angry with him—either she had put a bad herb in his food, causing his leg to cramp, or else she had conspired with a medicine man and had had the medicine man work a bad spell. Broken Foot was not much younger than he was, and had grown very fat in her old age. Kicking Wolf gave up trying to get her to stop being angry with him and concentrated on avoiding her. But it was hard to avoid a woman as large as Broken Foot in a tent at night, which was why, as the weather grew warmer, Kicking Wolf started spending more and more nights outside, by himself. It didn't stop the cramps but at least he didn't have Broken Foot there gloating while he tried to get the painful cramps to leave his leg.

It was during the period when Kicking Wolf was sleeping outside

that the strange news began to arrive, most of it brought by Dancing Rabbit, a young warrior who had wanderlust badly and just
plain lust as well. Dancing Rabbit was constantly visiting the various bands of Comanches, hoping to find a woman who would marry
him, but he was poor and also rather ugly. So far no woman had
agreed to be his wife.

It was Dancing Rabbit who dashed up to Kicking Wolf one
morning while Kicking Wolf was sitting by a pile of white cattle
bones, rubbing his leg to lessen the cramp. Dancing Rabbit was very
upset with the news he had, which was that Blue Duck had followed Buffalo Hump to his death place and killed him with his own
lance.

"Ah!" Kicking Wolf said. He had hoped that Buffalo Hump had
been able to make a peaceful death. Certainly he had not led a
peaceful life, but to die at the hands of his own son was not a thing
Buffalo Hump would have expected to happen.

Kicking Wolf didn't immediately believe it, though. Dancing
Rabbit wandered from camp to camp, collecting stories; then,
often, he got them all mixed together before he could get back to
his own camp and tell everyone the news.

"Blue Duck probably just said that—he was always a braggart,"
Kicking Wolf said.

"No, it's true—the Antelopes saw his body with the lance sticking through it," Dancing Rabbit insisted. "The lance went into his
hump and then it went through his body into the ground."

Several of the young men of the tribe had gathered, by this time,
to hear Dancing Rabbit tell his tale about the death of the great
chief Buffalo Hump, the only chief to lead a raid all the way to the
Great Water. Only a few days before, the same young warriors had
scorned Buffalo Hump. To them, while he lived he was just a surly
old man with an ugly hump and a violent temper, an old man who
was weak, who could not hunt, who had to live by snaring small
game. The presence of the young men irritated Kicking Wolf. They
had never seen Buffalo Hump in his days as a raider, and had been
rude to him many times once he was old and couldn't strike at

them; but, now that he was dead, they could not get enough of hearing stories about him. They did not deserve to know about Buffalo Hump, in his view—and, anyway, he himself did not believe half of what Dancing Rabbit was saying.

"How do you know where the lance went in?" he asked, in a tone that was not friendly. "Were you there?"

"No, but the Antelopes saw the body," Dancing Rabbit insisted. "The Texans saw it too. The Texans tried to pull the lance out but they couldn't remove it. Then Blue Duck shot two of their horses—that is why they are walking across the llano. They have little water. We can go and steal their horses if you want to."

Kicking Wolf sat in silence for a long time after hearing this speech. Dancing Rabbit was claiming knowledge he didn't have; also, there were several issues that needed to be studied and assessed before he could make up his mind what to do.

Dancing Rabbit was annoyed that old Kicking Wolf kept silent, even though he had brought him exciting news. The Texans were not far, only thirty miles. They had walked a long way and were tired and low on water. They could easily be killed; or, if Kicking Wolf was not interested in killing them, they could at least steal the Texans' horse and mule. That would be a simple thing, for a master horsethief such as Kicking Wolf.

In fact, Dancing Rabbit was very anxious to go with Kicking Wolf and watch how he went about stealing horses. Dancing Rabbit, at the moment, possessed only two horses, and neither of them was a very good horse. The fact that he was poor and had no horses to offer was one thing that was making it difficult for him to find a wife. He wanted a wife badly, but knew that he would have to get some horses first, if he expected to purchase a wife who had much appeal. That is why he spent so much time with Kicking Wolf, the great horsethief. Dancing Rabbit hoped to get Kicking Wolf interested in stealing horses again; perhaps if they could manage to steal a good many horses Kicking Wolf would allow him to keep a few—enough, at least, to allow him to trade for an acceptable wife. But now Kicking Wolf was sitting by some cattle bones in silence; he showed little interest in the story Dancing Rabbit had ridden all night to tell him.

Kicking Wolf was thinking that most of what Dancing Rabbit told him was probably a lie. For one thing, he claimed that his information came from the Antelope—but the Antelope were an aloof people, so contemptuous of other Indians, even other Comanches, that they routinely made up big lies in order to mislead them.

"If the Antelopes saw these Texans, why didn't they kill them?" Kicking Wolf asked. "You said there were only four Texans. The Antelopes are hard fighters. They could easily kill four Texans."

One of the things Dancing Rabbit liked least about Kicking Wolf was that he was always skeptical. He was never willing just to accept the information that was given him. Now Kicking Wolf was embarrassing him in front of several young warriors by doubting the information he had brought. Now the young warriors, including some of his best friends, were beginning to look skeptical too. Dancing Rabbit was vexed that an old man would put him in such a position.

"They didn't kill the Texans because they don't have very many bullets," he said—in fact he had no idea himself why the Antelope Comanche were letting the Texans get away.

"Gun-in-the-Water was one of the Texans," he added. It was information he had just remembered, and it did cause Kicking Wolf to raise his head and look a little more interested.

"If Gun-in-the-Water was there, Silver Hair McCrae is there too," Kicking Wolf said.

At mention of the two rangers Kicking Wolf lapsed into memory, but it was not the two rangers he was remembering—rather, he was thinking of the young Mexican woman who had been Blue Duck's mother. His memory would not bring back her name, but it did bring back her beauty. He had tried hard to get Buffalo Hump to let him have the girl. He had offered many horses, and fine horses too, but Buffalo Hump had ignored him, insulted him, kept the girl, and then let her run away and freeze in a blizzard, not long after she bore Blue Duck. If Buffalo Hump had only accepted his offer—it had been a handsome offer, too—the woman might be alive and he might not have to suffer the anger of his fat old wife, Broken Foot, every day and every night.

He wouldn't let me have that pretty Mexican girl and now the son she bore him has killed him, Kicking Wolf thought, but he said nothing of what he was remembering to Dancing Rabbit and the other young warriors. Already, several of the young men had concluded that Dancing Rabbit was only telling more lies—they had begun to wander off, making jokes about coupling with women. They were young men, they did not want to waste all day hearing an old man tell stories of the past.

"What is wrong with you?" Dancing Rabbit asked, unable to contain his annoyance with Kicking Wolf any longer. "Are you too old to steal horses from the Texans now?"

"You are just a boy—go away and tell your lies to the women," Kicking Wolf said. "Right now I have to think about some things."

He wanted Dancing Rabbit to calm down and stop pestering him, but, once he had given the matter some thought, he decided to go see if it really was Gun-in-the-Water and McCrae who were crossing the llano. Many Texans came to the plains now, but those two hadn't, not in some years. For all Kicking Wolf knew, they might suppose he was dead. They might think they were rid of the great horsethief Kicking Wolf. It would amuse him to show them that he was still alive, and that he had lost none of his skill where horsethievery was concerned. Also, it might be that if he got far enough away from Broken Foot, the cramps in his leg might subside.

After midday Kicking Wolf began to stir himself. He took several rawhide thongs he used when he was leading horses away. He had acquired a fine rifle in a trade the year before, an excellent Winchester, but, after some thought, he decided to leave the rifle. He only took his bow and a good supply of arrows.

Dancing Rabbit, who had been watching Kicking Wolf closely, saw him making preparations to leave camp and hurried over, eager for the trip to begin.

"Take your rifle—if you don't want to shoot it I will shoot it," Dancing Rabbit said.

Kicking Wolf ignored him. What weapons he took was none of Dancing Rabbit's business. Horses could smell rifles—having a greasy gun along only made them difficult to approach; but that was only one of the reasons that had made Kicking Wolf decide to leave the gun. There were many bad Indians adrift on the plains in these days; comancheros, half-breeds, renegades, and exiles such as Blue Duck, men with no respect for anything. He was an older man—if he ran into some greedy renegades and they saw he had a fine rifle they might kill him for it. It was better to leave the gun at home, where he would be sure of having it the next time he went to hunt antelope.

Of course, Dancing Rabbit came with him when he left the camp. He was so excited by the prospect of stealing horses with Kicking Wolf that he didn't stop talking for many miles.

As Dancing Rabbit chattered on, Kicking Wolf rode west into the llano. It was not until the afternoon of the next day that he finally crossed the track of the Texans—they had been farther away than Dancing Rabbit supposed. By then the young man was so thirsty that he had almost stopped chattering. Kicking Wolf had not gone deep into the llano for several years—he too had forgotten how very dry it was. The Texans still mainly farmed the watered lands—it was not necessary to get thirsty in order to steal their horses.

The good part of the venture they had set out on was that Kicking Wolf's leg did not cramp at all during the night. The next morning he moved his bowels easily, with no twinges from his leg. He mounted his horse with grace. It was so good not to have a tight leg that he felt like kicking or jumping or taking part in a dance. The fact that his leg had immediately stopped cramping once he left Broken Foot convinced him that he had been right all along. His wife was mad at him and had probably fed him bad herbs.

In the dry country the trail of the four Texans was easy to spot. They were traveling slowly and there was something wrong with one of the men's boots. The boots had no heels. The other men left normal footprints. Dancing Rabbit knew nothing about tracking—he even failed to notice that one of the men had no heels on his boots.

Kicking Wolf had not really believed that the Texans would be so far into the llano with only one horse. He had expected to steal several horses and was irritated to find that that part of Dancing Rabbit's story was true. But the tracks were plain: there was only one horse with the Texans.

"They may have had to eat the other horse," Dancing Rabbit conjectured nervously. He saw that Kicking Wolf was irritated that there was only one animal for him to steal. Nonetheless they had come a long way and the old man decided to press on.

They caught up with the Texans sooner than Kicking Wolf had expected to. They had only ridden a little way south when they spotted the four men, dots on the llano far ahead. Immediately Kicking Wolf made a long loop to the west—McCrae had sharp eyes, and so did Famous Shoes. He didn't want to alert the Texans to the fact that they were being followed. He intended to loop well in front of them and wait, in case he decided to steal their one horse. Walking men were sure to be tired—it would be an easy theft if the horse was one he wanted.

During the rest of the day, as the sun fell, Kicking Wolf and Dancing Rabbit made a half circle around the Texans, taking care as they rode to make use of gullies or little ridges to hide themselves so that not even the sharpest eye could detect their presence. Then they came back in front of the Texans to await their passage. Once they had hidden their own horses well, Kicking Wolf told Dancing Rabbit to stay with them, an order that upset the young warrior greatly.

"But I want to see what you do!" Dancing Rabbit protested. "I want to see how the great Kicking Wolf steals a horse."

"You wait!" Kicking Wolf insisted. "I am not going to steal the horse while the sun is up. If I want the horse I will steal it tonight. You can come with me then."

He paused and looked at the sullen young warrior, a young man full of complaint. When he himself had been young he would never have dared protest an order given by an older man. Dancing Rabbit was pouting like a girl when Kicking Wolf left him with their horses.

Kicking Wolf was well ahead of the Texans. He hid behind a low stand of yucca and waited. Long before the Texans passed he saw to his disgust that it was not even a horse they had with them: it was only a brown mule. It was all a waste, his trip. The only use Comanches had for mules was to eat them. Some Comanches thought mule meat tasted better than horsemeat. He himself had mainly avoided stealing mules because they couldn't breed. Why steal a horse that couldn't make colts?

He waited, though, crouched behind the yucca, as the Texans passed, about a half mile away. Famous Shoes had gone ahead, hoping to find water, probably. Gun-in-the-Water was with the Texans, and so was McCrae. Besides them there was a black man and a skinny man, both younger. Gun-in-the-Water limped a little—perhaps it was because he had no heels on his boots.

As he watched the weary men walking toward the big orb of the setting sun, Kicking Wolf suddenly had a sadness fill him. His breast felt so heavy with it that he began to envy Buffalo Hump, who was dead. He knew already that he didn't want to steal the Texans' brown mule, and that was not because he had any liking for Texans or pitied them their long walk. He knew the Texans would kill him, if they saw him, and he in turn would try to kill them if they made themselves easy targets. They had always been hated enemies and were hated enemies still—Kicking Wolf was grateful that he was prosperous enough and free, so that he could still hate Texans as a Comanche should. He was glad that he did not have to pretend to be friends with them to collect a mere pittance to live on.

Yet he felt sad, and, as the Texans stopped to camp, while dusk made the long plain indistinct—shadows here, last streaks of sunlight there—the sadness filled him until he felt he would burst. There, nearby, were Gun-in-the-Water and Silver Hair McCrae, men he had fought most of his life and would gladly fight again if he could. He had stolen many, many horses from them, or from companies of rangers they rode with. Once he and Buffalo Hump had set a prairie fire that had nearly caught the two men and burned them and their company. There had been shots exchanged, arrows shot, lances thrown, and yet the two rangers were still alive; and so was he.

Kicking Wolf remembered, as he watched the black man hobble the brown mule, that once, only a few miles from where they were, he had stolen the Buffalo Horse, right from under Big Horse Scull's very nose. He had stolen him and taken him to Mexico, a venture that had cost Three Birds his life and led to his own derangement, his time of seeing two where there was one.

It had been a great thing, the stealing of the Buffalo Horse, a great horse whose fate had been to be eaten in Mexico by many small dark people. Some of the old men still sang about Big Horse Scull and the Buffalo Horse—he sang about it too, when there were great feasts and dancing, a thing that had not been common since the buffalo went to the north, where they would not have to smell the whites.

Remembering his great feat made Kicking Wolf want to sing— the urge to sing rose in him and mixed in his breast with the sadness that came in him because he realized that the time of good fighting was over. There would be a little more killing, probably; Quanah and the Antelopes might make a little more war, but only a little more. The time of good fighting was ended; what was left for the Comanches was to smile at the white men and pretend they didn't hate them.

Kicking Wolf did not want to smile at the white man. He wanted to die somewhere on the llano, alone, in a spirit place, as Buffalo Hump had tried to do. Not only that, he did not want to steal the puny brown mule, either. Why would a man who had once stolen the Buffalo Horse want to steal a skinny brown mule? It would be an insult to himself, to do such a thing.

So he waited until the moon rose and turned to go back to the gully and the horses, only to discover that Dancing Rabbit, the foolish boy, had disobeyed and followed him.

"What are you doing? I told you to watch the horses," Kicking Wolf said. "If those Texans were not so tired they would steal *our* horses."

"I only came because I wanted to watch you steal the horse," Dancing Rabbit said. "I just want to see how you do it."

"It is not even a horse!" Kicking Wolf said. He grew so angry that he almost forgot to whisper—but then he remembered the Texans and led the foolish boy farther away, to reprimand him.

"It is only a mule," he pointed out, once it was safe to talk. "It was near here that I stole the Buffalo Horse. I am not going to steal a mule.

"You steal it, if you want it so badly," he told the boy.

Dancing Rabbit knew he had not skill enough to steal the mule. Besides, he didn't want the mule—he merely wanted to watch as Kicking Wolf stole it.

"Just show me how you approach it," he pleaded. "Just show me how, in case I see some Texans with a fine horse I could steal."

"I stole the Buffalo Horse," Kicking Wolf said, several more times, but, in the end, he gave in and did what Dancing Rabbit wanted. He sat with the young warrior most of the night, watching the moon arch over the still prairies. He saw Famous Shoes come back and lay down to rest. He watched as the Texans—exhausted, all of them—fell asleep. Even Gun-in-the-Water, whose habit was to stand guard outside of camp, did not stand guard that night.

"When will you do it?" Dancing Rabbit asked him several times. "It will be light soon."

He was worried that Kicking Wolf wouldn't do it; but then he looked again and Kicking Wolf was gone. The old man had been sitting quietly, a few feet away, but now he was gone.

Then, to his astonishment, he saw Kicking Wolf standing by the mule, stroking its neck. The black man who had tethered the mule was sleeping only a few yards away, but the mule was calm and so was Kicking Wolf. The old man stood by the mule for a few minutes, as if talking quietly to it, and then he disappeared again. He had been by the mule, but now he wasn't. Dancing Rabbit had no idea where the old man had gone. Hastily he made his way back to the gully where the horses were, only to find, when he reached it, that Kicking Wolf was there and had already mounted his horse.

"We had better go," Kicking Wolf said. "The Kickapoo will see my track first thing in the morning. I don't think they will follow us, but I don't know. Gun-in-the-Water might chase us on the mule."

"I didn't see you move," Dancing Rabbit said, when they were riding together. "You were with me and then you were with the mule. I didn't see you move."

Kicking Wolf smiled. It had been pleasant to do his old trick again, to walk without making a sound, to go up to a horse, or, in this case, a mule, to touch it and make it his while the owner slept nearby. It was a skill he had that no other Comanche had ever equaled. Though he had had to travel a long way across the llano in dry weather, it was good to know that he still had his old gift. It made up a little for Broken Foot and the cramps in his leg and the sadness of knowing that the old ways were gone.

"I don't move," he said, to the credulous young man who could still not quite believe what he had seen. "When the time is right I am just there, by the horse."

"But I saw you—you were with me and then you were by the horse. I know you moved," Dancing Rabbit said.

"It isn't moving—it is something else," Kicking Wolf said.

Dancing Rabbit pestered him all the way home, wanting to know how Kicking Wolf did what he did when he approached a horse; but Kicking Wolf didn't tell him, because he couldn't. It was a way—his way—and that was all.

44.

When Famous Shoes saw Kicking Wolf standing by the mule his thought at first that it was just another of his dreams. Since seeing the white owl come out of the earth he had had many dreams that were not good. In some of them Comanches were killing his children. In another Ahumado had him, and, in a third, a great flood came while he was on the llano. He tried to outrun the water but the flood swept over him and carried him down to where there was a great fish shaped like a Jaguar.

Compared to those nightmares, seeing Kicking Wolf standing by the brown mule was not so bad. Then, waking , he thought he saw Kicking Wolf walking in the white moonlight—it might have been Kicking Wolf or it might have been his ghost.

In the morning, when he had almost forgotten his dream, Famous Shoes walked over to where the brwon mule grazed and saw at once that no dream had occurred: Kicking Wolf had been there. On the ground, plain to see, was the footprint that he had seen so many times when he and Big Horse Skull had followed the Comanche horsethieves int Mexico. What he had seen in the moonlight was not a ghost but a man. Kicking Wolf had come for the mule and then left it. Famous Shoes found it surprising that the old Comanche would follow them all the way into the llano after one mule, but it was not surprising that he had left the mule once he saw how skinny it was. Kicking Wolf was a man who had always been choosy about horseflesh. He only took the best horses, and Deets's brown mule could not even be said to be a horse.

When Famous Shoes went to the campfire and announced that Kicking Wolf had been there, all the Texans put down their coffee cups and ran over to look at the tracks, bringing their rifles with them, as if they feared attack. They all looked around anxiously, but, of course, the llano was empty in all directions. Captain Call was vexed, but he had been vexed the whole way back because of the trouble with his boot heels. His boots were now so nearly useless that when they were in grass country he often walked barefoot.

On the worst of the walk the rangers had had to drink their own piss, a thing that bothered Captain Call less than the fact that Blue Duck's first shot had ruined his only boots. Fortunately they were only two days from the Brazos now and would not have to drink their own piss again. Far to the south, thunderclouds rumbled—the rain might soon fill the many little declivities that dotted the llano, turning them into temporary water holes.

"Well, I swear," Pea Eye said, looking at the tracks. "A man was here but he didn't take the mule." The sight of the footprints made him nervous, though. A Comanche had come close enough to kill, and no one had heard him. It was a scary thing, just as scary as it had been the first time he journeyed onto the plain.

"Didn't take it and I'm glad," Deets said, for he was very fond of his brown mule, the only animal, after all, to survive the trip—the other horses had either starved or been shot.

Augustus took his hat off and scratched his head, amused by what he saw—even though it was a dark joke. After the walk they had had, any joke seemed better than none, to him.

"Why, he tuned up his nose at our mule, old Kicking Wolf," he said.

Call didn't find it amusing. He would have liked to chase the man—it seemed that half his life had been spent chasing Kicking Wolf—but he had only a tired mule to chase him on. The rain clouds hovering to the south had been dancing away from them for a week; the Brazos River, still a full two days to the south, might have to be their salvation, as it had been for many travelers. Once again he had to carry with him, on a long trip home, a sense of incompletion. They had traveled a long way, hung ten bandits, but missed their leader, Blue Duck, murderer of his own father, and many others besides.

Augustus, though, would not be denied his amusement.

"How's this for a scandal, Woodrow?" he said. "We didn't get our man, and now we've sunk so low that a Comanche won't even steal our mule. I guess that means the fun's over."

"It may be over but it wasn't fun," Call said, looking at the long dry distance that still waited to be crossed.